GRA

By the same author:

Crisis

Coup!

Sky Blue

Hegemon

Holy War

Classified Waste

A Little Empire of Their Own

(as Bruce Farcau)

1

GRANADA

Granada

a novel of Moorish Spain

Alexander M. Grace, Sr.

GRANADA

Published by

Createspace, a DBA of On-Demand Publishing, LLC

Copyright 2015

Bruce W. Farcau

ISBN: 9781522885320

Map Design by Michelle Farcau-Gjonaj

Dedication

This book is dedicated with love to all my ladies: my wife, Maricruz; my daughters Graciela, Alexandra, Michelle, and Sarah; my mother, Ruth, my mother-in-law, Graciela and my grandbabies, Maya, Korra, and Inca. To paraphrase the Bible, I have truly been "blessed among all women."

GRANADA

Table of Contents

Introduction

The Western world is divided largely between two religious cultures. One emphasizes toleration, education, and intellectual and scientific inquiry as well as the recovery and study of the wisdom of past ages. The other is shackled with a violent form of religious fanaticism and superstitious ignorance as well as a burning desire to convert the entire world to its own form of belief.

The time is the late fifteenth century. The culture of toleration is Islam and that of fanatical intolerance is the Christian societies of Europe. Of course, Judaism existed, as it had for centuries and would continue to do for centuries more, as a shadow culture practiced by a people without a home, surviving at the sufferance of their more powerful neighbors. This story is set at the moment when the tides were just about to change. Islam had begun its long decline, both in terms of temporal power and intellectual freedom, while Christianity was in the throes of breaking away from the chains of doctrinal orthodoxy, but neither change would take place overnight or without considerable pain and suffering in the process.

As will be discussed in more detail in the afterword, most of the characters depicted here are historical. While the specific dialogue is largely speculative, this speculation is based on established historical fact as much as possible. It should be noted, however, that one of the joys of historical fiction is the ability of the author to put the reader on the scene of some historical controversy and "show" what "really" happened. Those characters who are fictional creations are also based on historical types whose actions and words as closely follow what a person of that age might say or think as possible.

Times, of course, have changed. It is worth considering, however, that the personages at the time of this tale had every reason to believe that their world represented the natural order of things, just as we do today, and had no inclination that momentous changes were in the offing. Perhaps there is a lesson to be learned there.

GRANADA

Book One

1473

GRANADA

Chapter One

Granada

Muhammad al-Sarif al-Uqayli el Haj leaned back on his stool and let the warmth of the late spring sunshine wash over his face. He closed his eyes to let the sounds and smells of his second favorite place on earth surround him, and he was engulfed by a rewarding sense of comfort and familiarity. As a devout Moslem, Muhammad felt obliged to consider the Grand Mosque of Mecca inevitably to be his favorite place, since it was theoretically the closest to Paradise and to God, but it was only here, seated at a small table at a modest outdoor coffee house in the heart of the *souq*, the bustling marketplace of his hometown of Granada, the soul of the Moorish kingdom of al-Andalus, that he truly felt that he belonged, that he was a part of a greater entity and not just a visitor observing from without. In moments when he was being totally truthful with himself, he had to admit that the harsh, dry winds of the Arabian Desert that scoured the streets of Mecca did not agree with him, and he found the people there just a little insular and even provincial, concerned only with their guardianship of that one portal to the kingdom of God and hardly at all in touch with the world around them. Here, in southern Spain, where it never got too hot or too cold, with rich groves of olives covering the hills with oranges blooming in the valleys and sparkling rivers reflecting snow capped mountains on the horizon, a man could pause to revel in the enjoyment of the paradise that God had created for man on earth, not merely contemplate that which awaited him after death.

As he sat there with his eyes closed, he could hear the rumble of vegetables and fruits or the rush of grain being dumped into long bins in the market stalls, the rattle of the copper and iron pots and pans that hung in clusters in front of the metal workers' stands as they were brushed by passersby. There was the braying of mules and even the ill-tempered growling of camels, complaining about their loads or bemoaning their removal from their desert homelands, the clopping of hooves and the shuffle of hundreds of feet as the crowds wound their way through the narrow aisles between the stalls. He could hear the jabbering, arguing, and wheedling of vendors and buyers in a dozen languages, Spanish, indecipherable Basque, musical Italian of the Genoese and Pisans, delicate French, harsh German and English, and a dozen distinct dialects of Arabic from the sing-song of the Egyptians to the clipped, guttural speech of Berber tribesmen straight out of the Saharan wastes. While most of the Christians, Moors, and Jews native to the Iberian peninsula could switch from Spanish to Arabic with unconscious ease and with no discernible accent in any of the tongues, he could tell them apart without seeing their typical forms of dress and grooming. The Christians appealed constantly to the Saints and to the Mother of God as witnesses to their honesty, the Moors cajoled and pleaded in honeyed tones, and the Jews with their irritatingly irrefutable logic and good sense.

But most of all, in any corner of the *souq*, he could hear the market's truly individual sound, the metallic clink of the lifeblood of the kingdom, the money. In each stall there would be stacks of thick silver coins still bearing the heads of long dead Roman emperors or Visigothic kings, piles of thinner silver *dinars, reales*, and *maravedis*, and shoals of the little copper *dirhanes* that were the only coins the poor would ever see, but, most of all, there was gold. Florins, ducats, bezants, doubloons, *escudos*, and the prized *excelentes de Granada*, sometimes clipped or shaved to reduce their true weight, and he could sometimes even hear the dull thud of leather sacks of gold dust taken straight from the mythical rivers in far off Ifriqiya and shipped by camel caravan across the endless Sahara to the rich Arab ports on the Mediterranean. This was what brought all of these people together, often blood enemies at other times and in other places, but here only to make a little profit and to conduct a little business. As long as the gold continued to flow through the veins of the city, al-Andalus would never die.

And the smells! If he turned one way and sniffed the air, he could smell the apricots, plums, and early apples from the fruit sellers' stalls as well as the ever-present, sweet smell of the orange and lemon blossoms on the trees planted in all of the city's parks and many private homes. Turning another way he could pick up the heavy scent of spices, saffron from Spain itself, but also peppercorns, cinnamon, ginger, and a thousand other precious spices, more valuable than gold, brought from the far off Indies through the continuous empire of Islam which God had seen fit to establish to connect one end of the world to the other. There was the tang of fish and the heady scent of all kinds of meat, both fresh and not so fresh, and the sharp smell of burning charcoal from the little open air eateries and the aroma of broiling lamb and freshly baked bread.

And, underlying it all was a layer of the less pleasant smells of life in a heavily overcrowded city, swollen by the influx of thousands of refugees who had gradually filled up the kingdom of Granada as the Christian barbarians from the north had pushed southward, now hemming the Moors into this small mountainous kingdom in the heel of the Spanish peninsula. There was the tangy smell of human sweat of the porters as they trudged by under their heavy loads, hauling sacks and crates around the market, and that of the host of beasts of burden, camels, mules, horses, even oxen that drew the huge, unwieldy carts that the Christians insisted on using, and the stuffy smell of the dust raised by thousands of shuffling feet. It took no effort to single out the acid smell of urine and other waste matter from the sewers, for, even though Granada was sparklingly clean in comparison to the pig sties where the Christians teemed and bred to the north, there was only so much that even the most efficient sewage systems could accomplish in such a crowded space. Still, this was all a part of him, the land where he had been born, and his father, and his father's father before him, going back for centuries. He might be Arab by blood, but he was a Spaniard in spirit, and the rich valleys, towering mountains, and sunwashed beaches of Spain were his home as the barren deserts of Arabia never could be.

And Granada still carried about it the unmistakable stench of death that brought back to Muhammad the terrifying memory of his own flight from the city six years before, when the plague struck down nearly a third of the city's population. On that one terrible night he could remember hearing the wailing of the dying and the soon-to-be-dying in their houses and of the *mullahs* who prayed endlessly to God to spare the city as he had made his way through the dark streets, knowing that his own wife lay in one of them, not yet dead but soon to follow their daughter to the grave. His wife had begged him to go, to save himself, and there was, of course, nothing that he could have done for her, other than to accompany her in her final hours. But the fact that he had not done that much marked this as the one truly cowardly act of his life.

Turning this craven escape into a *hejira*, a pilgrimage to the Holy Land, from which he had only returned a few weeks before, had given him considerable status in Moorish society, and the right to add the term *el Haj* to his name, but there had been no cleansing of his soul to be found in worshiping in front of the *qabala*, the holiest of Moslem shrines in Mecca. It had rightly been considered an accomplishment of some magnitude given the dangers of the long journey by land and sea, but it provided only a thin veneer of respectability to cover over the tremendous hole at the center of his being which he had never realized had been filled by his wife and daughter until they were gone.

Now, suddenly, another odor rose above all the others and literally pulled his nose to one side. It was the blessed aroma of freshly brewed coffee, made from select Abyssinian and Mochan beans, and Muhammad smiled as he opened his eyes. Before him stood Yusef, the small Hausa slave boy he had bought at the market in Algiers on his way back from his pilgrimage, and he was holding up a tray of polished Moroccan brass on which stood the delicate, long spouted coffee pot, a small glass cup in an intricately worked brass holder, and a plate of cookies covered with chopped almonds with a single, perfect pitted date in the center of each and all glazed with honey.

Before bowing low to his master, Yusef offered a dazzling smile with his impossibly white teeth. His one good eye sparkled with intelligence and mischief, while the other, a milky blue orb, wandered on another pointless errand off to one side. Yusef suffered from a common disease of his people, called "river blindness," which affected the areas around the Senegal River in the far west of Ifriqiya. The affliction had brought Yusef's price down to less than a dozen silver *maravedis*, where an adult male slave would have cost four times as much and even a healthy child of twelve, like Yusef, should have gone for at least twenty. But this had only been to Muhammad's good fortune since he could not have afforded more, and Yusef, probably grateful for being spared a tortured and short life in the salt mines of the Atlas Mountains, had turned out to be an ideal and devoted servant. Even here at the cafe, he refused to allow anyone else to serve his master, and he had quickly developed the varied skills of valet, cook, and retainer worthy of a servant to a powerful lord as well as the uncanny ability to divine Muhammad's needs long before they ever occurred to his master.

Muhammad took a sip of the scalding hot, sweet coffee and replaced the cup on the tray, which Yusef continued to hold for him despite the presence of a perfectly serviceable small round table at his elbow. He then took one of the cookies and paused to look around his domain.

The *souq* would have appeared to be total chaos to the unaccustomed eye, like the scene of a particularly vicious street riot or some natural disaster. The narrow paths between the sellers' stalls twisted and turned with no apparent pattern, encroached upon by bales of cotton, sacks of produce, and cages filled with nervously clucking chickens. Every square inch was jammed with throngs of constantly moving people, rich merchants with their trains of servants and aides, sweating, grumbling porters under their loads, and customers of every description. There were dark skinned, wiry little Berbers in their black burnooses, wicked curved knives at their sides, fat Catalans and Portuguese, pasty-faced, red-haired Bretons, Egyptians with their olive eyes and caramel skin, shifty Cypriots, and arrogant Turks, all babbling away in a dozen tongues, passing goods back and forth and keeping the kingdom alive thereby.

But to Muhammad, this was all a well-oiled machine, as familiar to him as the corner of his house devoted to his little library, for he was the *muhtasib*, the official regulator of the market. It was his duty to make sure the *souq* ran smoothly, protecting both the financial interests of the king and the spiritual interests of Allah, to see that all treated each other fairly and without conflict, at least as far as humanly possible. He was responsible for seeing that the merchants' scales were fair, that the cooks who fried the *buñuelos* pastries did not use substandard oil, that the milk was not watered, nor the wines (a task Muhammad particularly relished performing, as he had never believed that God had meant man to go without a moderate enjoyment of the products of the fruits of the earth), that the sellers of meat, fish, and fruits did not mix the rotten with the fresh, and that the various artisans, weavers, cobblers, blacksmiths, and others, all gave quality service for the price.

His duties went beyond this, however, as the *souq* was like a little kingdom of which he was the lord, and he was also responsible that the enclosed wooden balconies which jutted out from the upper stories of the houses bordering the marketplace, often almost touching their neighbors across the narrow street and blocking out what little sunlight made its way into the cramped, crooked passageways between them, extended only so far and no farther. He could chastise women who shamelessly strayed too far from the door of their own homes to gossip and even flirt with passing men, or who failed to properly conceal their charms with hood and veil, although some of these prohibitions from the Koran were becoming impossible to enforce with the lower classes, intermixed as they often were with Christians and Jews whom God had not seen fit to instruct in proper behavior. Muhammad could not prevent the swarms of beggars from invading the rich hunting grounds of the *souq*, nor could he even interfere with the frauds committed by the false blind men, lepers, and cripples, since, if a passerby felt moved to contribute to them as the Prophet had urged and Islamic law encouraged, it was the soul of the giver who still benefited in the eyes of God, so no real harm was done. He did keep a sharp eye out for thieves and cut purses, but given the radical discipline of Islamic law, which called for immediate amputation of the offending hand, the only regular criminals were Christians passing through, their Moslem colleagues having usually long since joined the ranks of the beggars with their callused stumps as their calling cards. Muhammad could also not entirely prohibit gaming, which flourished in the alleyways just off the *souq*, but he was merciless in exposing and driving out the conductors of fixed games of cards or dice. Lastly, the *muhtasib* was responsible for seeing that no business was conducted, even by infidels, after the call to prayer on Fridays, that the faithful complied with the five decreed daily calls to prayer wherever the wailing of the *muezzin* happened to find them, that they held to the ordained fasting periods, and contributed a true tithe as their *zakat* as ordered by the Koran, and that the mosques in his district were properly maintained and kept clean, out of respect for God.

In many ways one might say, and a number of Muhammad's older friends and relatives had done so, that the position of *muhtasib* was rather beneath him. After all, Muhammad's family itself was of distinguished lineage, tracing back to a veteran of the Battle of Badr, one of the Prophet's first victories over the unbelievers of Meccan society over seven centuries before. This almost gave one the status in the Moslem world of being a co-founder of Islam, with everyone else, Arab, Persian, Egyptian, Berber, to say nothing of Europeans, who now professed the faith, to be nothing more than recent converts. He could also trace his heritage in Spain back to the court of 'Abd al-Rahman, a survivor of the Umayyad dynasty from Syria who had established himself in a hew caliphate in Cordoba back in the 8th century of the Christian era, shortly after the conquest of Spain by the Moors.

Even in his youth, Muhammad, an inveterate reader and student, had earned the title of *hafiz*, one who has memorized the entire Koran, which marked him early for the life of academic study. He had even been granted an *ijazah* by his teacher (and not from some long dead author in a dream, the way some supposed scholars had done), a certificate qualifying him to teach certain books of the Koran to others, by the age of fourteen. And he had seriously considered a career of devotion to God, but there was something about his studies that seemed altogether too personal to him for him to turn to the study of the Koran as a profession, as if that would somehow cheapen his relationship with the creator. Besides that, there had always been something about the throbbing, pulsing life of the *souq* that had called to him, something that flew in the face of the life of conscious negation of the commercial and the material that the life of a religious scholar implied. He had met and married his wife, and he had taken the unorthodox step of consulting with her about what sort of career he ultimately should pursue, something most Moslem men, or Christians either for that matter, would never have considered, and she had, demurely of course, hinted that, while she would be immensely proud to watch him, from afar, as he sat surrounded by eager students, she thought that he would be happier doing something in his beloved *souq,* leaving the mosque strictly for his days of worship. And she had been right, as she usually was.

Then, during the years of his absence from al-Andalus, after the deaths of his wife and daughter, he had studied further at the great Mosque of Az'har in Cairo, one of the most prominent centers of the study of *Shar'ia*, Islamic law, in the world. He had gone on to become a disciple in Tunisia of the school of Ibn-Khaldun, the great philosopher of an old Spanish Moorish émigré family. Following in the footsteps of Ibn-Khaldun, who had been an advisor to the king of Granada in the previous century, Muhammad had already written and published a number of treatises, in the rhythmic *adab* style of rhyming prose, on the possibility of developing a true "science" of politics based on the "hard" sciences such as mathematics, physics, and astronomy. His theme had been that the primary goal of academic study should be the production of a philosopher king along the lines suggested by Plato, whom Muhammad had also studied, along with Aristotle, Ptolemy, Euclid, Tacitus, and other Western writers, having mastered Greek, Latin, and Hebrew along with his native Arabic and Spanish. He had further extended his scientific studies to include medicine and had developed a certain skill at identifying plants with medicinal properties for producing powders to induce sleep, ease pain, aid digestion, and salves to cure burns and wounds as used by learned men throughout Asia and North Africa. He was dissuaded from pursuing a career as a physician, however, by the disdain which his personal speculation that cleanliness had something to do with avoiding diseases in general and the putrefaction of wounds in particular had engendered among the most learned doctors he had encountered.

Certainly, Muhammad's relatives had frequently and insistently pointed out, a man of these accomplishments, valued in Islam as they were, should have found employment of a more exalted nature than that of a mere custodian of a squalid market, but Muhammad did not agree. It had always been his belief that the market served the kingdom as the heart served the body, and the man who controlled the market (or failed to do so) held the fate of society in his hands. In any event, economic times were hard for Granada, with the Castilians compressing the kingdom into an ever smaller corner of the peninsula while Aragonese and Portuguese privateers prowled the seas, making the vital ties between Granada and the rest of the Islamic world tenuous at best, and wealthy patrons of academia were hard to come by. Until such time as a rich and influential magnate chose to recognize Muhammad's unquestioned talents, therefore, he was more than content to rule in his little domain among the fishmongers and moneychangers. Perhaps this was his way of recreating the happy little world he had occupied when his wife and daughter had been alive.

Muhammad's one cherished goal now remained to find the time to write a definitive history of the Nasrid dynasty of Granada in the kind of poetic style that would make it a work that would be studied and memorized by scholars for generations to come, along the lines of the revered Abu-l-Hassan Ali al-Masudi, the tenth century encyclopedist who had produced the massive thirty-two-volume study of the geography, biology, history, religion, and philosophy of Islam entitled *Meadows of Gold and Mines of Precious Stones.* However, it seemed highly unlikely that such would be possible for a humble and busy *muhtasib* when his workday often lasted from just before dawn until well after dark, and candles were a luxury not to be wasted on mere study.

Muhammad was just reaching for a second cookie, when a set of voices seemed to rise above the general hum of the market place, and he turned in their direction. He observed a tall, middle-aged man, dressed in black robe, turban, and pantaloons with a short vest elegantly brocaded in silver, holding aloft a burlap bag for all to see, while a short, stocky Greek, a seller of spices, who was new to the *souq*, whitened his eyes and turned up his palms in the universal sign of total innocence. The only thing which distinguished the buyer as a Jew, and not a Moor of high birth, was the corner of a discreet yellow shawl which was just visible under the folds of the train of his turban which hung down and was wrapped around his neck in the North African fashion, implying that he was the *mayordomo* of some great Moorish family, probably one of the large landowners out in the rich Vega plain not far from the city. The Greek, meanwhile, wore a simple red cloth tied carelessly about his own neck as a sign of his Christianity, and Muhammad wondered whether these dress codes to identify unbelievers were truly necessary, as if good Moslems would ever act this shamelessly.

While he could not make out their words, it was apparent that there was some discrepancy over the Jew's purchase. Muhammad hoped that it would work itself out, as these things usually did, the initial confrontation being merely part of the traditional melodrama that accompanied all civilized business negotiations. However, when he saw the two Sudanese servants of the Jew step forward, fingering the knives at their belts and the helpers of the Greek picking up stout poles such as held up the awnings over the sellers' stalls, he sighed, replaced the cookie on the tray, and slowly stood up.

Muhammad cut an imposing figure as he strode forward, and the growing crowd of gawkers quickly made way for him. He stood nearly six feet tall, large for a Moor, with his height enhanced by the thick felt boots and turban he wore. He was dressed in an elegant burnoose of simple cotton, but of a fine weave, and of a startling whiteness that only Yusef's personal efforts could have achieved, which set off his neatly trimmed black beard and his mahogany skin, which had the look of polished leather from long exposure to the sun and wind on his travels. He wore no badge of office, and only a small, curved dagger dangled at his belt, but his bearing left no doubt that he was the *muhtasib.*

As soon as they saw him, both parties to the dispute turned toward him and began wailing their misfortune. The Jew spoke the louder, and in perfect, classical Arabic, which the Greek apparently did not understand.

"My lord," he began with a bow. "We call upon you to witness the perfidy of this lowly seller of unclean goods. This bag of ginger, for which we have paid, should weigh an honest pound, and the one we first inspected did so, but he has switched it for one that seems filled with feathers instead of spices." The Jew tossed the bag once in the air to demonstrate its near ability to float, and then handed it deferentially to Muhammad.

The Greek was glancing suspiciously from Muhammad to the Jew, but he undoubtedly knew the nature of the claim, for he began to protest in broken Spanish.

"Honorable official," he growled. "This man has taken most shameless advantage of myself. He knew that I am almost finished selling my wares and refused to pay more than half of what these fine spices, brought from the far ends of the earth at great peril, should be worth, and now he goes back on our agreement to drive down the price even farther, as he knows that I must be on the road no later than midday."

Muhammad tossed the sack once himself, and it did seem rather light. Then, without a word, he held out his other hand, and Yusef placed in it the small case of varnished cedar wood in which he carried his official set of weights. The Greek still had his one-pound weights set on the rusty scales which sat on the crate he used as a counter, and Muhammad took one of the polished metal weights from the case and gently set it on the opposite plate of the scale. He glared into the eyes of the Greek all the while, and, from the trapped look in his face, did not have to turn to watch the official weight plunge with a clank.

Muhammad shook his head. The man was definitely new to the trade, since the placing of a few pebbles in the sack of ginger would have accomplished the same purpose of making up the false weight and would most likely not have been discovered until long after the buyer reached home, at which time the purchaser could never be certain whether the merchant was guilty or his own servants, skimming a little of the valuable spice to sell on their own.

The Jew threw up his hands to heaven, praising the justice of God and the wisdom of His local representative, the *muhtasib*, and calling for all the punishments of the Lord of Hosts on the perpetrator. The other merchants, who had clustered defensively about their colleague, began to drift silently away, not wanting to be associated anymore with such a brigand, while the Greek sputtered out some unintelligible excuse for his behavior. But Muhammad just held up his hand for quiet.

A pair of gold florins lay on the crate, the purchase price for the spices, and Muhammad picked one of them up carefully. The sudden silence from the Jew spoke volumes, and Muhammad flicked his dagger from its sheath and deftly pared away a sliver from the edge of the coin, revealing a thin wafer of copper in its center.

It was now the turn of the Jew to jabber something about having been duped twice in one day, first by the thief who had given him this coin in change, and now by this spice seller for the short weight, while the Greek laughed heartily at the Jew's discomfort while discreetly signaling to his men to begin to pack up their belongings for a possible quick getaway.

"Both of you get your carcasses out of my *souq*," Muhammad snarled. "The dishonesty of each cancels out that of the other, but I will not have either of you taking advantage of my people." He turned to the Jew. "Tell your master to send someone else to do his buying from now on," knowing that this would be the ultimate insult to a self-important servant, and one that would certainly become instant gossip in the kitchens of the household, thanks to the Sudanese guards, even if the Jewish *mayordomo* thought to conceal the fact from his master.

Then Muhammad wheeled on the Greek, who needed no further encouragement, enjoying the immediate disappearance of the smile from the man's face. "And don't bother coming back to Granada, you..."

Muhammad was interrupted as he searched for an animal metaphor of suitable intensity by Yusef tugging firmly at his sleeve, and he turned impatiently, but the boy had a concerned expression which killed his impulse to scold him. Yusef gestured with his chin toward a corner of the *souq*, a nook formed by the corners of two buildings and a pile of grain sacks in which three muscular Moors crouched, peeking around the corner of a building toward one of the entrances to the market. They wore the coarse dark blue robes typical of a strict fundamentalist religious order from Morocco, adherents of which manned a number of *ribats* along the border with Castillian lands, those monastery-like little fortresses in which Moslem zealots spent their lives guarding the frontiers of Islam in exchange for the chance to plunder the Christian lands beyond. The men had the aspect of thieves, but it was broad daylight, in the center of the busiest market in the kingdom, and the soldier-monks were not, in any case, given to stealing from their co-religionaries.

Then he saw it. Down one of the crowded passageways through the *souq* came a small, glittering little company of oiled and perfumed young men. They were laughing, giggling really, clowning about, putting copper pots on their heads or cucumbers between their legs as they snatched items from the stalls as they walked past. They all wore silk tunics in bright colors and vests embroidered in gold thread, impossibly baggy trousers, and delicate golden slippers. Muhammad thought that the whole group together could not have produced enough facial hair for a single respectable beard.

He recognized the leader of the little pack immediately, the prince Abu 'Abd Allah Muhammad, son of the king Abu l-Hasan' Ali and his *umm walad*, his first wife Fatima, first wife in terms of status, that is, not necessarily in chronology, as the old king had had many too many wives for anyone to keep track of. At the age of twelve, prince Abu was the heir apparent, but there were no firm rules about succession in al-Andalus anymore, and there was a powerful faction which supported the claims of the king's brother, Muhammad b. Sa'd, also known as al-Zagal, a renowned warrior of the faith and the favorite of the fanatics of the ribats. The succession was further muddied by the claims of the king's chief concubine the former Christian captive lady Isabel de Solis, who had converted to Islam and taken the name Aixa, and who was now pressuring the king to recognize one of her own children as heir to the crown despite his technical illegitimacy.

Once, centuries before, al-Andalus had been a powerful state, a caliphate, united under the rule of the Omayyad dynasty begun by Abd alRahman who had fled Syria when the Abassids had seized control of the heartland of Islam. Abd al-Rahman's empire had dominated the peninsula, demanding tribute from the tiny Christian enclaves which clung to the northern coasts of Spain and even from the Franks beyond the Pyrennes, as well as from most of the Moslem states along the coast of North Africa. But that was long ago. Al-Andalus had shattered into a mosaic of warring principalities, as often making alliances with the Christians against their fellow Moslems as uniting to fight against the infidels. The Christians had taken advantage of the weakness of these *taifa* kings, the "party" kings, a term that originally referred to factionalism but also accurately implied a certain lack of seriousness that was all too accurate. Now only this little corner of Spain remained in Moslem hands, and even here factions had grown up, further weakening the kingdom and turning the tables to the point that it was now the Moors who paid tribute to the kings of Castile and Aragon in exchange for being left at peace in their rugged mountains. But, even when relative peace reigned between Christians and Moors, the factions within Granada often came to bloody confrontations in the very streets of the capital, as gangs of young toughs supporting one side or another roamed the streets looking for rivals to vanquish and took the opportunity to extort money from merchants and other city residents in exchange for their "protection" from the opposing side.

It was this fact that now concerned Muhammad. Prince Abu should rightly have been accompanied by a dozen bodyguards, preferably the trustworthy Christian men-at-arms, who, although mercenaries, had been hired by his father precisely because of their lack of interest in the political factionalism within the kingdom. At the very least there should have been some sturdy men of the Abencerrajes clan to which Fatima belonged, but Muhammad could see no escort of any kind. Perhaps the young fool felt constrained by having constant chaperones, or perhaps he was out in search of some prohibited pleasure and did not want the news to get back to his parents, but, as Muhammad watched the three dark men slowly draw their short, broad-bladed knives, he realized that that could prove to have been a fatal mistake.

Muhammad held out his hand, and immediately closed his fingers around the shaft of his staff, which Yusef had silently fetched from its resting place just inside the doorway of the cafe. It was a sturdy piece of oak, as thick as his wrist and five feet long, artistically carved with twining vines and berries and shod at the base with a cap of iron and the top with a thick ring of bronze studded with short pyramidal spikes. Despite Yusef's maniacal efforts to keep the metal polished, the iron foot was gouged and scuffed from hundreds of miles of use as a walking stick during Muhammad's travels. It had also proved a formidable weapon on more than one occasion, as Muhammad found that it provided a certain air of authority and thinly veiled threat without the blatantly challenging nature of a blade. He now carried it with an easy confidence, spinning it casually as he strode quietly and swiftly toward the site of the ambush.

As the prince and his noisy party rounded the corner of the nearest house, the tallest of the assailants leaped into their path and drew back his arm to make a sweeping slash with his curved knife at the level of the prince's throat. But Muhammad arrived first, the head of his staff came crashing down on the man's wrist, the sound of cracking bone mingling with the his wail of pain as the blade clattered to the cobblestones. The prince and his courtiers stood transfixed, their mouths open and their eyes wide with horror, transformed instantly from a supposed gang of young toughs into a cluster of frightened little boys.

Without turning, Muhammad jabbed backward with the foot of his staff, catching the second assassin in the chest and thrusting him backward and over a barrel of dried apples. Muhammad spun now to face the remaining enemy, his staff twirling in front of him like the blades of the windmills that dotted this hills of Spain, and the assassin bobbed and danced looking for an opening for his knife. Muhammad suddenly changed the axis of spin of the staff from perpendicular to horizontal, whacking the man on the side of the head with a stunning blow which sent him staggering to his right, and then back again to his left as Muhammad caught him with the backstroke across the mouth, sending a shower of blood and teeth onto the paving stones.

Muhammad heard the second assailant cursing as he stumbled over the spilled apples, trying to gain his feet, and he lunged forward, trying to finish off the third man before he could be attacked from two directions, but there was a dull thud behind him and the cursing stopped. Muhammad stole a quick glance and found Yusef straddling the inert form of the attacker, holding aloft the stool upon which Muhammad had been seated earlier and preparing to club the unconscious man well into the next world, a vast, satisfied grin spreading across the young slave's face.

Muhammad smiled as well, but the distraction had given his other opponent time to recover and he now caught the staff firmly in the crook of his arm and sneered cruelly as he drew back his knife for a fatal thrust. Muhammad, however, merely released his grip on the staff, causing the man to lose his balance momentarily, and used his two free hands to clap him sharply over both ears, rupturing his eardrums. The man howled in agony and dropped his weapon as Muhammad grabbed his tangle of long, matted hair with both hands and drove his head down onto his knee, smashing his nose. With that the man went limp, and Muhammad tossed him to one side, pausing only to pick up his staff again.

Muhammad turned to check on the young prince and found him sitting on the chest of the first man, giggling once more, as the prince playfully slashed the curved blade of his little jeweled knife across the man's throat, sending a thick stream of blood across his chest. The prince and his followers moved to the second man and repeated the procedure, making sure to rouse him before the courtiers pinned his arms and legs and the prince moved in to commit the murder, and then doing the same with the third. Muhammad felt a chill run down his spine as he stood there, unmoving.

"I guess *that* is a mistake that they won't make again," the prince announced gaily, wiping the blade of his dagger on the robe of his last victim. "Imagine planning an assassination in broad daylight, right here in the *souq*. Al Zagal must truly be slavering for the throne to have gone to such extremes."

Muhammad remained silent, willing his face to hide any look of disdain. Although Prince Abu was not king yet, he was immeasurably higher on the social scale than a simple *muhtasib*, and it would not be Muhammad's place to criticize him. To do so would have been a violation of the principle of *taqlid*, respect for authority, which was one of the cornerstones of Moslem society. Then the prince stepped forward and took Muhammad's hand in both of his own as his friends gathered round. Muhammad bowed deeply.

"Although I think we could have handled the matter ourselves easily enough," he said with an arrogant waggle of his head, his friends sniggering in agreement, "you, good man, did the right and noble thing, throwing yourself in the path of danger to protect your lord, and I thank you."

"It was but my duty, lord," Muhammad mumbled. "This is *my* marketplace, and I do not allow criminals to use it as a playground."

"Quite right," the prince said uncertainly. "What is your name, *muhtasib*?"

"Muhammad al-Sarif al-Uqayli el Haj, my lord."

"Ah, yes," the prince said, brightening. "I have read one of your treatises on government."

Muhammad's eyes widened and his head cocked to one side. There is no quicker way to disarm even the most skeptical scholar than to show a familiarity with his work, the more obscure the better, and Muhammad was no exception. His disapproval of the prince's recent action flew directly out of his head like a dove released from his cage and was replaced by a newfound respect for the young man's taste and judgment. This was the first time he had ever stood face-to-face with any of the nobility, and the young prince was a beautiful boy with smooth olive skin and large, grey eyes. He stood no higher than Muhammad's shoulder, forcing the older man to stoop a little to prevent him from having to look up to his inferior. His head was uncovered, and his hair was oiled and perfumed, hanging in ringlets to his narrow shoulders. Muhammad had to forcibly expel the thought from his head that the boy could have made a comfortable living in the little rooming houses off the back of the *souq* where the pleasure people plied their trade.

"I am honored, lord, that my humble scribbling should have come to your attention."

"Well, I can't say that I truly understood all of it," and the prince made a silly grin and crossed his eyes, sending his companions into gales of new laughter at his wit, "but perhaps you will explain it to me. I am in grave need of a tutor, a private secretary, now that I am come of age, and how could I do better than a man of scholarly achievements whose loyalty to me has been proven by our fighting side-by-side?"

Muhammad could not recall the young prince actually participating in any of the fighting, but he bowed deeply.

"You honor me again, lord."

"You will come then to the Alhambra tomorrow morning? I am certain that my mother and the king, my father, will want to hear of our exploits and to welcome you to court."

"I could wish for nothing better, lord," he replied, bowing yet again.

"Done, then," the prince squeaked, his voice cracking slightly, and he and his followers swirled about, flowing back up the street whence they had come, pausing only to spit on the inert corpse of one of the attackers, their laughter like the chirping of a flock of birds, and then they were gone.

Muhammad stood there for a long while, staring blankly up the street after them. Yusef eventually approached and took him by the sleeve, leading him through the narrow streets toward his home in the Albaicin quarter as if he were a blind man. It was time for lunch, and Yusef did not suffer his schedule to be disrupted for anything so minor as the fact that Muhammad's life had suddenly changed completely. They had to pause along the way as the *muezzin's* shrill call for the midday prayer carried out over the city. Yusef snapped out Muhammad's prayer rug, which he kept tightly rolled under his arm, automatically orienting it toward Mecca, and they both knelt, as did everyone else on the narrow street. As Muhammad went through the motions of bowing and rising and symbolically rubbing his face, he knew that he was committing a sin as his thoughts were not on God at all.

It was entirely possible, of course, that the guards at the palace gate would bluntly turn him away tomorrow, the young prince having forgotten the detail of informing them and possibly having also forgotten that Muhammad had saved his life the day before. And that might actually be for the best, as life could then return to its comfortable, familiar routine, the events of the morning safely relegated to memory. But, for the moment, Muhammad had suddenly risen from *muhtasib* to the rank of *katib*, personal secretary to the young man who would one day likely be king of Granada. In itself that hardly sounded much more exalted than the ruler of the *souq*, but he would be at court, meeting and conversing with the nobility and the most illustrious scholars in the country and of the rest of the Moslem world. And it was not unheard of that a *katib* of exceptional prowess might become the *wazir*, the man who truly ran the kingdom while the monarch was off hunting or attending to his many wives. Muhammad's head was swimming. This might be his opportunity to create the very philosopher king of whom he had dreamed for so long, to put Plato's concept into practice.

Yusef silently sat him down in his favorite cushion in one corner of the tiny patio of his modest home. This was placed on the low, foot-wide ledge or *diwan* that ran around the edge of the patio, a device Moorish architects used in place of the cumbersome European chairs. While Muhammad loved the bustle of the *souq* and its inexhaustible source of entertainment and interest, with the street door of his home closed, and seated in the patio surrounded by potted bougainvillea that climbed the columns in the four corners up toward the roofs, he felt transported to a world that was much like what he imagined Paradise to be. The patio was barely six paces across, and the two-story house which surrounded it cut off all sunlight except at precisely this hour of the day. A small stone fountain sat in the center, and the splashing of the water cooled the place and helped to mask the rude noises which filtered in from the street and the clanking of Yusef's pots on the kitchen, while a man-high lemon tree in a tub in one corner filled the air with the scent of its blossoms, canceling out the less welcome odors of the city. A minute patch of grass around the base of the fountain, literally only inches wide, which Muhammad laughingly referred to as his "lawn" was kept a deep emerald green through Yusef's attentions and made a nice contrast to the red brick of the house and the bright magenta of the bougainvillea. It was here that Muhammad did most of his writing, a lacquered box filled with paper, pens, and ink always handy at the side of his seat, but he had no mind for writing today, too filled was his head with dreams of greatness. The only thing that gave him pause was that his wife and daughter were not there to share the moment with him. He turned his head at the creaking of a floorboard somewhere upstairs and smiled. They knew, he nodded.

The next morning Muhammad, dressed in his finest white silk tunic, in fact his only one, his best pair of felt boots and wool trousers, belted with a broad green sash and a turban that Yusef had scrubbed to blinding whiteness, and carrying his staff importantly in his hand, made his way slowly up the winding streets toward the red brick eminence of the Alhambra which was perched on the top of a steep hill overlooking the city and the narrow valley of the Darro River on one side and of the Genil on the other. It would be a long walk, since the lower class Albaicin district was on the north side of the river, and the switchback road that led up to the entrance to the palace complex was on the south side of the Alhambra's hill, obliging him to wend his way through most of the city to get there.

The Roman idea of a grid network of streets and plazas had never really caught on in Spain, and what order there might have been to city planning had deteriorated during the nearly eight centuries of Moorish domination. Houses sprang up wherever the owners chose to build them, causing streets to bend and twist or simply stop all together with great suddenness. To a stranger, any Moorish city presented an impenetrable maze of alleyways and avenues, bordered by very similar two or three story buildings with largely unadorned, whitewashed walls and often with overhanging balconies from which the women could discreetly watch the people passing in the street through wooden louvers without violating the laws of propriety. This was not just a product of chaotic building and lack of regulation, but an inheritance from the Moors' desert ancestors, since a pedestrian would never find himself too long exposed to the sun before an angle of the street provided him with some welcome shade. Any decoration on the houses would be concentrated around the central interior patio, since Moors logically saw no reason to attempt to impress the casual passerby, reserving whatever beauty the owners could afford to the enjoyment of his own family or those persons specifically invited to enter the inner sanctum.

At this early hour, just after the morning prayer, the streets were already crowded, but mostly with servants running errands before the masters arose. Muhammad pushed his way past heavily veiled women carrying trays of bread dough covered with cloths against the dust of the streets as they took them to the communal ovens for baking, each round dough marked with the sign of the house to which it belonged, as all cooks took greatest pride in their ability to make good bread. There were farmers from the Vega with their donkeys laden with fruit and grain for the *souq*, and Muhammad sighed at the sudden realization that, if things went as planned that morning, the *souq* would no longer be a part of his life, as Yusef would do the shopping, since it would simply not do for a man of his new rank to be seen haggling over figs or fish like a housewife. He passed through the different neighborhoods, often grouped by the occupation of the residents, metal workers, cobblers, weavers, dyers, and by their nationalities as Jews and Christians were obliged to live separate from true believers. He wondered if in all the world there was another city as full of vibrant life as this.

The square red towers of the Alhambra rose above him as he began to climb steadily up the steep path, leaving the cramped residential quarters behind him. There were some large houses on the slopes of the hill, residences of the lesser nobility and ministers to the court, and these grew larger and more opulent as Muhammad approached the crenellated walls surrounding the palace complex itself, since the inhabitants had to be able to pay for the view which improved with each foot of elevation. But the last hundred yards or so of the hillside were barren except for thickets of shoulder high, buff colored chaparral and scattered clumps of stunted cypresses and pines. This isolation gave the Alhambra the semblance of a huge ship run aground atop a mountain, its prow pointed westward toward the heart of the city below.

Muhammad had visited the Alhambra on a number of occasions when the mosque and some other parts of the public buildings were thrown open to the common folk, but he now expected to be closely interrogated before being allowed entry and half supposed that he would be turned away at the gate. Most of the daily traffic of the city-within-a-city which was the Alhambra used the Gate of Arms, but Muhammad had chosen the Gate of Justice, that being closer to the Comares Palace where the king and his court had their living quarters and audience halls, and he strode the final few yards up to the gate alone, trying as hard as possible to look as if he belonged there. A squad of about a dozen black-skinned Sudanese guards in steel breastplates over their white robes and black hooded capes, armed with long lances and crossbows lounged in small knots about the tall doorway. While they paused in their conversations and watched Muhammad pass, they did not challenge him and quickly returned to their own affairs.

Muhammad passed through the series of right angle turns in the entrance way, designed to slow down an attacker and subject him to punishing fire from the arrow slits built high up in the walls and ceiling of the tower which loomed over the gate, and emerged into an open avenue beyond. There he stopped. He knew that the Comares Palace would be directly ahead, the lower inner city for residents of the palace and the Alcazabal off to his left with the upper city and the gardens to his right, but he now realized that he had no idea of just where in this complex, which stretched more than half a mile from end to end and a quarter mile across, he was to report, and he let out a helpless sigh.

Just then he felt someone grab his wrist, and he assumed that the guards had suddenly realized that an interloper had penetrated their fortress and were about to eject him forcibly. Although Muhammad held his staff in his other hand, he was not about to take on the entire garrison who were merely performing their proper duties. Muhammad turned and found himself facing one of the grinning young minions of the prince whom he recognized from the *souq* the day before. He was slender, with skin the color of cinnamon and dark eyes and hair and a very sparse beard and moustache, no wider than a finger, that traced a delicate line around his chin and up over his upper lip. He was dressed in a flowing robe of peach-colored silk with a tall turban to match and a belt made of a chain of gold coins.

"I am Hafez al Murabi al Aziz," the young man giggled, dipping his hips in something like a curtsey. "Abu sent me to come fetch you." He had an effortlessly superior tone about him, and Muhammad had a sense of how dogs or horses must feel when people spoke to them, even pleasantly.

Muhammad bowed slightly as the young man's name implied very exalted lineage. "I am most grateful." He was about to explain his embarrassment at not knowing what his destination was to have been, but Hafez simply tugged at his wrist and led him quickly through the grounds that were elaborately decorated with lawns, low hedges, and fountains toward the palace itself without further comment, weaving through other pedestrians who marched back and forth, singly or in small groups on what must certainly have been very important business of state.

As with most Moorish buildings, the palace itself was not overly impressive from the outside, just another red-brown brick structure with a tile roof, although larger than any other building in the city, but in a moment they had passed through an archway, and Muhammad found himself in the *Golden Room*, a small antechamber which was the entrance to the palace. The room itself was nothing spectacular at first glance, just a clean marble floor with a small, flat fountain in the center, leading to three steps up, but this was designed to not distract the viewer from the glorious wall that they now faced.

There were two rectangular doors, the one on the right leading to the king's private quarters, and the one on the left opening to a series of passages that led to the mosque. Each was surrounded by a border of mosaic tiles of blue and white set in complex geometric patterns. Above each door, near the top of the wall, was a small window, each divided by a pillar into two lobed arches with a third arched window in the center of the wall. The entire facade was covered with an array of carved panels in wood and stucco with an infinity of delicate floral and geometric patterns and verses from the Koran, all in a warm yellow-beige which gave the room its name. Muhammad could have stood there for days studying the symmetry and endless detail of the carvings, but Hafez tugged impatiently at his wrist once more, as a nurse might lead a recalcitrant child, and hustled him through the right hand door. Muhammad was appalled at first, but then he thought that even the Prophet must become jaded to the gates of Paradise through which he passes every morning on his way to work.

Muhammad found himself in a small room whose only adornment was a panel of mosaic tiles with blue and white sunbursts which extended about three feet up from the marble floor and ran around all four walls. Light streamed into the room through a series of double arched windows in one wall, and the place was filled with the scent of expensive perfumes and oils. Prince Abu was there, dressed in a long silk gown of pale green, as were his young friends from the previous day, each vying with the others in the elegance of their dress and accessories, and a bevy of servants in white livery, standing at attention, waiting to be asked for something. Muhammad had more than half expected to be presented to the king, or sultan as he sometimes styled himself, Abul Hassan Ali, and his ministers, but the only other figure of note was a woman, younger than Muhammad, but with a regal bearing that left him in no doubt that this was the *umm walad,* Fatima, the first wife of the king. She was tall, taller than most Moorish women, and her fair skin and gray eyes, like those of her son, showed a possible Circassian ancestry no uncommon among Arab royalty deriving originally from Syria. She wore no veil, which made Muhammad feel uncomfortable, although her hair at least was discreetly covered with a silk shawl, and he averted his eyes from her face, as he bowed, first to the prince, then to her.

Her laughter was like the tinkling of little silver bells, and the prince and his friends quickly joined in, as Muhammad expected they were wont to do whether they understood the source of merriment or not. Fatima did not even have the discretion to cover her mouth when she laughed, and he caught a glimpse of dazzling white teeth that caused him to duck his head yet again. He could see from the glint in her sparkling eyes that his discomfiture was something she was used to and reveled in.

"You needn't worry, *muhtasib*," she scolded. "My son has told us all about your valor and his plans to make you his *katib*. If that is to be the case, you will be virtually a member of the family, and even the strictest interpreters of the *shariah* do not require women to be veiled in front of their own families. You will soon find that the entire palace is like one big family, even if we do have a tendency to try to kill each other off from time to time."

Muhammad looked up into her face, not rising to his full height as a sign of respect. She was quite beautiful in a pallid sort of way, although not to Muhammad's own taste which usually tended more toward dusky women, when he gave such things any thought at all. But he could see why the king had been taken with her, as much for the liveliness of her spirit as her physical attractions.

"I merely did my duty in keeping order in the king's *souq*, mistress," he stammered. "If I was able to be of service to my lord in so doing, that was the will of God."

"Everything's the will of God," the prince simpered in a sing-song voice.

His mother smiled impassively. "Do you have any idea who the men were who tried to rob my son?"

"No, mistress, other than that their clothing indicated that they belonged to a *ribat*." He paused for a moment. "But, at that hour of the day, in the center of the *souq*, an ordinary robbery would have been a very unorthodox endeavor. I have to assume that they had even more sinister motives in mind."

"Of course," she replied, tilting her head to one side condescendingly. "My husband, the king, prefers not to believe that we are in the midst of a civil war right here, inside the city walls, so you must learn to use euphemisms for such events. But the men were not known to you?"

"No, mistress, and. . ."

"And my son's valiant action in dispatching all of them prevented us from questioning them further."

Muhammad cleared his throat nervously, but Fatima let out a sigh and shook her head.

"You can see that my son is in dire need of a tutor, a mentor, someone who has some maturity and who has shown his devotion by making the holy pilgrimage to Mecca. Obviously, to find someone who has proven his loyalty and courage, placing the safety of my son above his own life is a blessing indeed. Someday my son *will* be king, like his father before him, and he must be worthy of that burden. He thus needs the help of others in preparing him to shoulder it."

There was something about her emphasis on the word "will" that made Muhammad suspect that the issue of the succession was even more in doubt than the gossip of the idlers in the *souq* implied.

"If there is any small contribution I could make toward that end, mistress, it would be a great honor."

Fatima arched one delicate eyebrow high up on her forehead. "You may regret those words in time, *katib*," she said with a sly smile, changing his title with no more effort than that, and Muhammad's life from that point on. "Bring your things to the palace," she went on. "We will expect you to take up your new duties in the morning."

"But I have a perfectly good house in Albaicin," he objected feebly. "There is no need to trouble yourselves about lodging for me here."

"You obviously have a limited understanding of the role of the *katib*," she replied. "You will be more than a mere tutor or secretary, and you must be available to the prince day or night to help him puzzle through the thornier problems of state. You have spent your life studying the art of government, from what we are told. Now it is time for you to learn what its practice is like. You can hardly do a creditable job of that if you must spend several hours every day simply trudging from the lower quarters up to the palace and back."

Muhammad opened his mouth again, but Fatima had turned her back and headed toward a passageway where two of her more demurely veiled ladies in waiting met her. The Prince simply gave Muhammad another inane smile and shrugged his shoulders as he and his sniggering cohorts turned to follow his mother, but, before they had gone more than a few steps, another group entered the room. Before Muhammad could identify the new arrivals, he saw Fatima stiffen and the young prince flinch as if someone had struck him an invisible blow.

The group was led by a pair of short, dark-skinned swordsmen in bright steel breastplates and helmets with blood red cloaks on their shoulders, Yemenis, Muhammad guessed from the blue tribal tattoos on their cheeks. They came through the doorway, paused for a moment, surveying the scene, then parted, taking up positions on either side, keeping their hands on the pommels of their swords. They had made way for a tall man, nearly as tall as Muhammad, but broader in the shoulders and thicker in the waist, and he was dressed in the finest silk robes, with a silk turban on his head set with a large gem. His dark beard was carefully barbered, and Muhammad could smell the scent of sandalwood and fragrant oils about him, but there was nothing in his manner like that of the pampered young prince. His skin was leathery from long exposure to the sun and wind, and a jagged scar ran from one corner of his eye down to the edge of his jaw.

The servants were the first to bow, dropping to their knees as if felled by an axe, as did the other courtiers, but Fatima and the prince only followed suit reluctantly, just bending at the waist, and Muhammad noticed that Abu kept a wary and nervous eye on the man even as he paid homage. Muhammad immediately realized that this was the king, and he too bowed, but more deeply, and with a courtly sweep of his arm, reverently lowering his eyes.

"So, is this the hero of the marketplace?" the king asked airily. "Is this the man who saved your *son*?"

Muhammad thought he detected something like a sneer in the king's voice when he pronounced this last word, a suggestion that a man should not need saving. He also noticed that the king did not apparently like to acknowledge his paternity, although that could have just been a figure of speech. Muhammad suspected that his introduction to court might have made him a little over-sensitive to possible hidden meanings in everything that the great and powerful chose to say when it was entirely plausible that they were no more careful in the choice of their words than the common folk of the *souq*.

"Yes, my lord," Fatima replied coolly. "Muhammad al-Sharif al-Uqayli el Haj. I have just asked him to join us here in the palace to serve as our son's tutor."

The king tilted his head back as if looking down his nose at Muhammad gave him a better perspective. "Ah, yes," he said. "I believe I knew your father."

"I am honored as is his memory, your highness," Muhammad answered.

"A wise and good man he was," the king went on. "It would be unfair of me to say any less."

"And how very reassuring it will be to have your strong arm poised over the little prince's neck," a sugary, delicate voice added as a lithe young woman appeared from behind the king.

Even though she had only taken a step, it seemed as if she had been dancing, and Muhammad imagined that he had never seen anything done quite so gracefully in his life. She was small, but beautifully proportioned. Her golden hair cascaded freely to her shoulders, which were nearly bare as she wore a velvet gown of Christian fashion that must have set the teeth of the palace mullahs grinding in its shamelessness. Her skin was creamy and her features perfectly formed, but there was something about her mouth, a full, sensual mouth to be sure, but with a subtle tightness at the corners that spoke of bitterness and hatred carefully suppressed. Muhammad made a discreet effort to avert his eyes, as was only proper, but he found that he could not, and, after a moment, he also realized that his mouth had been hanging open.

This would be Aixa, the king's favored concubine, and as Muhammad glanced at Fatima as the two women eyed each other, he imagined that, if he had held up a bunch of straw between them, it would have burst into flame of its own accord, such was the animosity that virtually crackled through the air from one to the other.

The king merely nodded languidly, took one more look at Muhammad from head to foot, then turned and left. Aixa smiled openly at Muhammad over her shoulder as she walked away, just as one might smile at a small child who was desperately trying to accomplish a clearly impossible task. Then, suddenly, in a flurry of robes and skirts, Muhammad was alone in the room, but a cold tension filled the air long after the various parties had gone.

When Muhammad returned to his home, he found half a dozen porters lounging at the doorway, and he could see the eyes of the neighbor women pressed hard against the slats of their balcony windows as they tried to gather the maximum amount of information about his fate. Yusef was bustling about inventorying and stacking his possessions, ready for transfer to the palace, bossing other porters about with great relish and fussing over the packing of Muhammad's precious books and papers. Since Moorish homes did not have closets, or even much in the way of furniture, with kitchenware, clothing, linens, and most everything else normally being stored in trunks and boxes of sweet-smelling cedar wood, the preparation for the move was already nearly completed, as a messenger from the palace had apparently advised Yusef during the course of Muhammad's brief interview. Muhammad, therefore, simply sat meekly on the lip of the fountain as his world was disassembled, stowed, and strapped onto the backs of the waiting porters for the trek up the hill.

Yusef stood in the doorway for a moment, looking back anxiously at his master, but Muhammad absently waved him on and looked around his little patio one last time. He had only just tasted the wonders of the gardens of the Alhambra and knew that it would take him months, if not years, to explore the architectural and artistic wonders of the palace complex, but he doubted whether he would ever again have the peace of mind he had enjoyed in his own little corner of paradise. He dipped his fingers in the fountain and wiped the cool water over his forehead as he had done a thousand times at the end of a hot, trying day. He visually traced the pattern of the twining bougainvillea up the stone columns, and marveled again at the lush color of the flowers, just the shade of purple that he liked, not too much red or orange.

When Muhammad had returned from his travels, he had at first feared reentering this house, feared that the spirits of his wife and daughter would be there to haunt him, to reproach him for fleeing that terrible killer that had lurked in the water, in the ground, in the very air they breathed. He had crossed that same threshold with trepidation, expecting a cold, clammy draft to enter him and the hum of the city to be transformed into undecipherable, accusing whispers in the corners of the house that would finally drive him mad. And he had been half right. The spirits had been there, and he had felt their presence, but they had suffused the house with a warmth of welcome, of love, and of forgiveness. Instead of terrifying him, the sense that his wife had just disappeared around a corner or that his daughter was watching him over his shoulder as he wrote there in the patio, as she had done since she had been old enough to stand, had at least partially filled that empty space in his soul that their deaths had left. Tears still came to his eyes when he unconsciously reached out for them and grasped only thin air, but that was the penance he would always have to pay for the sin of having survived. His wife had even come to him in a dream, and, after they had made love, she had told him that her one wish was that he do something important. He had asked her to explain, but she had merely smiled and faded into the shadows.

Muhammad finally sighed and arose, scuffing his feet along the cobblestones as he passed through the street door and paused to caress the heavy oak frame that had sheltered him from the outside world. The hem of his robe caught for an instant on the corner of the door, and he smiled and waggled his finger at the air. His daughter, his little Miriam, had always been playful. He would not rent out this house to others but would come back here whenever he needed to rest, and to visit. He was far from a rich man, and probably never would be one, but this was one luxury that he would afford himself. Then he turned and walked wordlessly past his curious neighbors toward his new destiny.

Chapter Two

Cordoba

The procession was making its slow way down the narrow street. Hundreds of men dressed in long robes, first a group in black, then another in white, then another in red, each wearing a tall conical cap with a hood that covered their faces, leaving only two small holes for the eyes, and large crosses embroidered on their chests and backs, led the tall statue of the Virgin, carried on the shoulders of still more men. They swayed rhythmically from side to side as they walked with tiny steps, and the drone of their chanted prayers sounded like a night wind just before a storm. The incessant clanging of the bell carried by the leader of the procession was like a death knell, while the clouds of incense that floated upward from the column could not hide the odor of unwashed bodies or the distinct smell of fear.

Raquel stood at her window on the second floor of her father's house and crossed herself repeatedly as the statue of the Virgin approached, her lips moving in silent prayer. But her prayers were not the Latin verses she had memorized during nearly every waking moment of the thirteen years of her life. They were in Hebrew, for Raquel Blanco de Ecija, daughter of Ruben Blanco Herrero and his wife Miriam, was Jewish.

Outwardly, the Blanco family was *converso*, one of the thousands of Spanish Jewish families that had been obliged to convert to Christianity less than a century before. In 1391 there had been bloody anti-Jewish riots in Sevilla, Toledo, Burgos, throughout Castille and Aragon, and right here in Cordoba, and thousands of Jews had chosen the option of conversion rather than violent death, while hundreds who refused had been butchered in the streets. The Blanco family, which had then born the name ben Abraham, had held firm, sheltered by some local Christian nobles who had fought to protect the Jews against the looting and murdering of the lower class mobs. Then, however, twenty years later, a new threat had emerged, and the Jews throughout Spain had been shut up in their *aljamas* or ghettos, not allowed to live alongside Christians, to speak with them, or to trade with them, nor were they allowed to *leave*. Facing the prospect of slow starvation, Raquel's great grandfather had finally surrendered to save his family and undergone baptism, along with many other Jews. However, while many of the converts had truly accepted the Catholic faith, apparently believing that their own religion had failed them, Raquel's family, which had changed its name to the more Christian-sounding Blanco, chose to maintain their ancestral faith, although in hiding. It was hoped that the wave of persecution which had swept through Spain, a country where Jews had traditionally prospered, unlike France, Germany, or even England where they had been massacred and expelled, would eventually pass, and it would be possible to return to their religion, maybe by moving to a different city with a new identity. At least they would be alive to try.

That had been some sixty years ago, and during that time the Blancos, their children, and their grandchildren had gone to Mass, had observed the normal Christian feast days and fasts, and had duly contributed their tithe to the Church. Meanwhile, they had quietly kept the Sabbath, had avoided pork and other prohibited foods, made anonymous gifts of oil and other goods to the synagogue, which still had a precarious existence, and had studied the Torah that they kept hidden in a secret compartment underneath an armoire in the bedroom of Raquel's father.

At times Raquel's head throbbed and her heart felt as if it were about to burst, and she was convinced that there was no room in the human soul for two Gods. Her father had patiently explained to his little daughter when she went to him in tears that there was only one God, worshipped by Jews and Christians alike. It was only that the Christians, who were not God's chosen people, needed crutches to help them in their faith, the panoply of saints and martyrs, the Virgin Mary, and Jesus Christ, lesser beings that they could relate to more directly until God saw fit to give them the understanding to appreciate His own divine nature. He pointed out that Mary, who had been a young Jewish girl just like Raquel, had had to flee persecution in her time, and their family was doing the same, fleeing inwardly rather than across a border.

While her father's words always comforted her, Raquel could not help feeling a sense of hostility and evil emanating from the crowd of worshipers as they paraded below her window. The growling that came from the crowd lining the street did not indicate religious fervor, but rather hatred, for the division between Christian and Jew, it seemed, could not be erased by something so simple as baptism or even by several generations of living as Christians. The former Jews were known as *conversos*, or even more politely as New Christians, but more commonly as *marranos*, a word derived from a term for "pig".

At least part of the animosity felt by the majority of Spaniards for the Jews had always been the prominent role played by the Jews in the economic life of the country. Where Christians were prohibited by Church law from lending money at interest, that did nothing to eliminate the need for credit, and the Jews had filled the role of money lender, sometimes at the point of a sword wielded by a Christian lord. Occasional forays by the monarchs over the centuries against the Jews, forcing them to forgive large parts of the loans outstanding on the assumption that even carefully written contracts, freely entered into, hid usurious interest, had done little to placate the borrowers, particularly the lower class artisans and workers who needed ready cash to pay their obligations to the nobility and the Church. The Jews had also had an unfortunately notable role in the profession of tax farming, in which an entrepreneur would give the king or local noble or clergy a fixed amount in advance against the revenues of a region (another form of hidden loan) and then collect the taxes due himself, allowing a certain percentage as payment for this service. Naturally, many tax farmers, both Christian and Jew, had become obscenely wealthy through this practice, and both the commoners who owed them money and the nobles who coveted these rich positions were eager to attack this element of society, the distinction being that they had a built-in pretext for attacking the Jews.

No one knew precisely how many Jews had been living in Spain at the end of the 14th century, but it had probably been in the hundreds of thousands as the Jews had been driven with fire and sword from much of the rest of Western Europe since the start of the Crusades. There had been persecutions of the Jews in Spain as well, on both sides of the Moorish border, but nothing like the slaughter in Germany or England, and the Jews had prospered. Besides tax farming and money lending, the Jews also used their ties throughout the Mediterranean Basin to form the links of trade with the Middle East and Europe, and other Jews had become skilled craftsmen, scholars, and physicians to both Christian and Moorish royalty, although these achievements only provided more cause for jealousy and envy on the part of the largely illiterate Christian masses. With the bigotry born of ignorance, rumors occasionally arose implying that Jewish physicians were poisoning popular leaders and that Jewish scholars were somehow communing with the devil himself. When the pogroms began in the 1390s, it was estimated that more than half of the Jewish population had been forced to convert, apart from those who had been murdered outright or forced to flee abroad.

But many of the new converts had simply settled into their old patterns of activity. As Christians they could no longer lend money at interest openly, but there were ways of getting around this, by purchasing crops before their harvest or goods before their delivery to market for example, and the concept of pawning valuables, of one person "buying" jewels or silver plate from another and then selling them back to the original owner at a previously arranged, higher price at a given time, had been well-developed by this time, and the economy could not function without it. The *conversos* also took advantage of their connections within the nobility, their generally superior education and social position, and their new status as Christians to occupy formally positions at court and within the Church itself and to marry into Christian families of noble lineage as they could never have aspired to do before as Jews. Needless to say, the same people, both commoners and nobles, who had resented the influence and wealth of the Jews before, resented that of the *conversos* just as much now.

So, the concept of *limpieza de sangre*, purity of blood, had been born. It was argued by some religious fanatics, usually when preaching to the volatile Castillian masses, that a simple act of baptism could hardly turn a Jew into a Christian and that the taint of the race that had been responsible for the murder of Jesus Christ could never be fully expunged, thus disqualifying the *conversos* from high government office or any position in the Church. The *conversos* among whom appeared a number of prominent Christian theologians, priests, and even bishops, pointed out simply that Jesus, Mary, Joseph, and most of the disciples, as well as virtually all early Christians, had been Jews, so there was nothing in the Jewish blood which might prevent them from accepting the true faith. The kings of Castille and Aragon, who valued the learning and business acumen of the *conversos* may or may not have been convinced by this argument, but they largely ignored the ranting of the anti-*converso* faction all the same.

And in most instances, the charge was simply untrue. The majority of converts to Christianity had accepted their new religion faithfully and raised their children in it over several generations. Some had sensed that Christianity had truly triumphed and was the wave of the future, others converted so as not to lose their wealth and social position, but most had never thought to attempt to hide their true feelings. Raquel's family was thus in a small minority within the *converso* community, and they operated on the decision made by her great grandfather that, God would forgive an outward display of conversion as long as they held true to their faith in their hearts and that it would only be for a limited time in any event.

In desperation those forces opposed to the *conversos* then took up a new tack. They began to spread stories that the *conversos*, all *conversos*, had only pretended to become Christians while continuing to observe Jewish rites and traditions in secret. Since this would hardly have inspired anyone to take serious action, the stories went on that the Jews had converted, not to escape death and torture, but as a means of penetrating the Church to destroy it from within. There were fantastic tales of false *conversos* using the mystical powers of the Host to perform all sorts of occult ceremonies to bring sickness and madness down on the Old Christian communities and of joining their Jewish brethren in clandestine satanic rites involving the sacrifice of Christian children. In a world of mystery and fable, where demonic explanations of such things as the plague, droughts, civil war, and famine were more plentiful than scientific ones, it was stories like these that served to arouse the rage of the Christian populace, thus filling the needs of those who sought to seize the wealth the *conversos* had amassed and to occupy the positions they had achieved in society.

This was the purpose of the procession that was now passing beneath Raquel's window. Processions of this sort were certainly not uncommon, taking place on major feast days throughout the year like this one of Corpus Christi, but this crowd was composed of ruffians from the artisan quarters on the other side of Cordoba who had intentionally planned their route to pass through this formerly Jewish, now *converso,* neighborhood in search of trouble. They had brought their own "spectators" with them, more men with brawny arms, many of them still carrying their tools, the heavier ones that would be of most use in a street battle or in breaking into a house, and the growling of the crowd did not speak of devotion to the Virgin Mary but of a thirst for blood. So the residents of this quarter remained behind closed doors, only venturing to peek out of their upper windows, as Raquel and her family were doing, ostensibly to pay homage to the passing Virgin in order not to give the marchers the pretext for violence that their total absence might have done.

Raquel looked up from the procession and found herself looking at the smiling face of her friend, Marisol, another *converso* girl who lived across the street and was, like Raquel watching from her window. People had often said that Raquel and Marisol looked like sisters, even twins, both tall and slim, with the same fair skin and long auburn hair and blue eyes. But, where Raquel was a very serious girl, always studying and following her father around, asking him penetrating questions about his work casting metal bells and guns for the Spanish nobility, Marisol was far more concerned with curling her hair and finding the prettiest clothes, brooches, and pins and with gossiping about the boys in the neighborhood. When there would be a tournament of competing knights in the city, Raquel would only have an interest in the new designs of armor worn by the participants, while Marisol would be in a virtual swoon over the handsome young men who were competing, dreaming of the day when one of them would ask to carry some token of hers into the grand melee and return it to her after, covered with blood and glory. Raquel could hardly imagine what Marisol would look like without a smile or what her voice would sound like without her infectious laugh.

Now Marisol was making funny faces at Raquel, crossing her eyes and sticking out her tongue, making Raquel giggle in spite of the gnawing fear in her stomach of the crowd below. Then, with a mischievous glance downward, Marisol began to mimic the crowd, waddling from one side of the window to the other, rocking back and forth like the men carrying the heavy platform on which the statue of the Virgin stood. When Raquel, horrified, made frantic gestures for her to stop, Marisol merely arched and eyebrow, accepting the challenge, grabbed a tall candle from her dresser, threw a dust rag over her head, aping the hoods of the marchers, and continued the pantomime.

Unlike Raquel's family, who smuggled their uncle Ysaque into the house on holy days to serve as rabbi, Marisol's had truly accepted the Christian faith, and her older brother was a priest of the Hieronymite order. But Marisol simply could not take anything seriously, and the more pompous the people who performed any ritual, the more likely she was to make fun of them. Raquel's look of terror had sent Marisol into paroxysms of laughter, and Raquel knew that Marisol would have to seek ever higher levels of playfulness until she had finally exhausted herself. As if in response to Raquel's fears, Marisol discarded her dust rag and looked about her room excitedly for some other prop for her clowning.

As Raquel watched, the events of the following seconds seemed to stretch out into hours. She saw Marisol snatch up a small pitcher, waggle it menacingly, and then rear back and toss its contents in Raquel's direction. The street was only about ten yards wide, and the overhanging balconies of both houses cut this distance even further, but it was still farther than the water could travel in the light breeze which swept over the city. The jarful of water separated almost immediately into a shower of tiny droplets which arched gracefully downward instead of continuing across the gap between the houses, and Raquel even saw a brief, mocking rainbow as the droplets fell and pattered against the heads of the marchers and robes draping the statue of the Virgin below. The pitcher crashed to the floor, and Marisol's hands flapped helplessly like the wings of a little trapped bird as she sought somehow to erase the disaster.

Simultaneously, the heads of twenty marchers snapped upward and to their right, looking for the source of the water, and a dozen fingers jabbed toward Marisol's window, as the dull grumble of the crowd rose in volume as isolated shouts and screams pierced the air. At the head of the procession, a few yards beyond the girls' homes, the leader turned and snatched the black hood from his head. Raquel recognized the grizzled head of Pablo Ortiz, an itinerant black smith who had occasionally worked, very badly, for her father and who was known as a rabble-rouser, a propagator of hatred for Jews and *conversos* alike. His shaggy black beard stuck out in all directions, and his beady eyes flamed red as he extended a hairy arm toward Marisol's window along with the others.

"Filth!" he screamed. "You see what the secret Jewish scum throw on our Virgin? Filth!" And the crowd shrieked its agreement.

Any pedestrian in a Spanish city knew that he or she took a certain risk by walking down a residential street. Servants had a habit of emptying out chamber pots without warning, aiming indifferently in the direction of the gutter which ran down the center of most streets, and, although most people took some pains to avoid passersby, not everyone bothered. Of course, while to perform such house cleaning chores over the heads of a religious procession would naturally have been forbidden, it was also traditional practice to show disdain for any passing person or group by "saving up" ammunition for just this purpose, and this was the interpretation the crowd was putting on Marisol's innocent action.

"They desecrate the Virgin!" someone shouted.

"Death to the *marrones*! Death to the false Christians!"

The response seemed all too quick for this to have been a spontaneous reaction, Raquel thought. The platform on which the Virgin stood was roughly set down, and the marchers threw off their hoods and cassocks, revealing that most of them were armed with clubs and swords which they drew with a hiss of metal. The workers who had been on the sidelines now took their tools to the heavy oak doors of Marisol's house, pounding it with heavy mattocks and hammers, chopping at the wood with axes and picks, and prying away the hinges with cold chisels.

Raquel could hear screams coming from the other women in her own house, her mother and the servants, and her father shouting to close the shutters on the windows, but Raquel could not move from the spot, nor could Marisol, and the two girls stared at each other in horror as the crowd surged like an angry sea beneath them and paving stones began to rattle off the walls and windows.

With a groan, the doors of Marisol's house were torn from their frames and hurled aside. The crowd, men, women, and even children, roared in victory and poured into the building while others went to work on the doors and windows of other houses up and down the street. Raquel could hear more screaming and the crash of broken glass and smashed furniture, and a twisting curl of smoke began to rise from one of the downstairs windows. Raquel saw the door to Marisol's room burst open behind her, and Marisol's father was there, a big, stocky man, an accomplished pharmacist with a thick black beard, and a look of grim desperation on his face. He tried to brace himself against the door, but hands had already appeared around its edges, and with a sudden heave the door was thrust open and into the room poured half a dozen men brandishing swords and wooden staves. Marisol's father snatched up the tall brass candlestick that Marisol had been using and smashed one man on the neck with it, sending him staggering to one side, but another stepped forward with a two-handed sword and lopped the father's right arm off at the elbow as easily as if he had been slicing bread, and a spout of blood spewed from the ragged stump. Another brought a stave down hard on the father's head and a small circle of men formed around him, their arms rising and falling rhythmically as they pounded him with whatever heavy objects came to hand.

Then one of the men turned and noticed Marisol for the first time and a strange, crooked smile came over his face as he stepped slowly toward her, tossing a bloody axe to one side. Marisol screamed and turned back toward the window, stretching her arms out toward Raquel, who did the same, leaning far out the window, but their fingers remained far apart. The man grabbed Marisol about the waist and dragged her back into the room. She clutched desperately at the window frame until another man came up and pulled her hands free and the two of them carried her toward her bed. The last image Raquel had of her friend was her fear-filled eyes staring pleadingly at her over the shoulder of the first man who was laughing as he nuzzled her neck.

The second man paused a moment and leered, pointing a bloody finger at Raquel.

"You're next," he shouted over Marisol's shrieks.

Just then Raquel's father rushed up from behind her and slammed the window shutters closed.

"We have to get out of here," he said in an eerily calm voice.

"But Marisol!" Raquel protested.

"There's nothing we can do," her father said, gently steering her toward the stairs. "We have to hurry."

With the din from the street somewhat reduced behind the doors and windows, Raquel could now hear the confused sound of hurried packing and occasional sobs coming from one of the servants. Her father led her across their interior courtyard and through the kitchens and servants' quarters at the back of the house, followed by her mother, the houseboy and Maria, a stout young *converso* woman who had served as the family cook since before Raquel was born, and two maids, each carrying an expensive silk oriental rug thrown over their shoulders like a bag, filled with the family silver, her mother's few jewels, and a few other valuables. One of her father's apprentices had battered a small hole in the back wall of the house with a sledge hammer, and now her father helped him enlarge it, kicking away the loose bricks with his heavy boot. Meanwhile, hands appeared from the other side of the wall, helping to pull the rubble away from the hole, and Raquel saw the bearded face of their neighbor, Jacobo Tobias, a *converso* tax farmer, suddenly appear in the opening. His profession made Tobias highly unpopular, but, it made him extremely rich as well.

"This way, hurry," Jacobo whispered, as if the sound of the hammering at the wall would not have attracted any attention. "The rioters seem to be working the other side of your street first, so we must move to the south."

Raquel's father nodded, and he shoved his wife toward the hole. She held back for a moment, looking around the house, the one in which Raquel had been born, tears streaking her cheeks as she reached up to caress the side of a large porcelain water jug there in the pantry, but her husband gently took her by the arm and firmly pushed her toward the hole in the wall, forcing her to bend at the waist to pass through. It was then that Raquel noticed for the first time that her father was wearing a sword. Although his career was the manufacture of weapons of all kinds, cannon, arquebuses, swords, daggers, and crossbows, she could not recall ever having seen him go armed himself. The two male servants, one a converted Jew and the other a converted Moslem, also had blades tucked into their belts. A chill ran down Raquel's spine.

There were over a dozen men, women, and children now clustered in a tight group near the front door of Jacobo's house which opened out onto a street south of the one where the riot was taking place. Jacobo and Raquel's father were peeking out into the street, and they could hear the sound of breaking furniture, angry shouts, and terrified screams coming closer.

"Where can we go?" Jacobo asked, and he swallowed hard.

Raquel's father's voice was still calm and deep, as if he were reading her a bedtime story. "To the *judería*. It's the only place."

Jacobo turned to him with a shocked look on his face. "That would be like jumping out of the frying pan into the fire, wouldn't it?"

"Not now. It's the *conversos* they're after this time, not the Jews themselves. And the *judería* has walls and men to defend them. It's our best hope."

"No," Jacobo argued, "we should try to find Alonso de Aguilar. He's a nobleman and he's promised to protect us."

"I trust de Aguilar well enough," Ruben agreed, "but he may not be able to stop the looting. When word gets out that it's open season on rich *conversos*, greedy peasants from miles around will pour into the city, and de Aguilar only has a handful of soldiers, if he can trust all of them. No, the *converso* neighborhoods are too scattered to defend, even with his help. Our only hope is to hide out in the Jewish quarter and hope that the mob's blood lust doesn't get totally out of control."

With that, Ruben pushed open the heavy oak doors and led the way out into the street. This narrow avenue was deserted, and the two families followed quickly, with Jacobo bringing up the rear, carrying a battle mace in one hand and a long bladed knife in the other. At the first intersection, Ruben held up his hand for them to halt, and they all pressed themselves up against the wall of the nearest house while he peered around the corner. To the left, about a hundred yards away, the street was clogged with rioters who were busy carrying furniture and other goods out of a burning house past several crumpled bodies that littered the pavement.

Just then, from the opposite direction, came the heavy clattering of horses' hooves on the cobblestones and the rattle of metal on metal and the creaking of leather as a troop of cavalry cantered past in the direction of the mob. The men wore no particular uniform and only scattered bits of armor, a breastplate here, a few helmets, a coat of chain mail thrown on over street clothes, implying a hasty preparation, but they were all armed with long swords and lances, tear drop-shaped shields strapped to their left arms.

"It's Alonso de Aguilar!" Jacobo shouted gleefully, pointing to the portly, aristocratic looking man who led the column. "I told you so. He'll soon put things to right."

Ruben did not reply, but they all edged farther out beyond the corner of the building to watch the confrontation. The horsemen, about twenty in number, fanned out from their column of twos to block the entire street, which dipped down here, allowing Raquel and her family to see over the heads of the riders. There was too much noise still coming from the rioting in the neighboring streets for them to hear the exchange, but the men and women closest to Aguilar had stopped their looting and drawn back a little.

Aguilar was shouting something, gesticulating with his sword, and Raquel saw the dark shape of the blacksmith Ortiz emerge from the crowd and approach the nobleman, no sign of deference in his posture or his expression. Meanwhile, the crowd behind the blacksmith continued to grow as more and more shabbily dressed people drifted in from the side streets. More disconcerting, Ruben pointed upward to the rows of heads which could now be seen peering at the scene from the rooftops of the houses on both sides, far too many to have been those of the original residents. The horses seemed to sense being shut in, and they capered nervously from side to side, trying to pull back, forcing their riders to use both hands to control them.

Both Aguilar and the blacksmith were shouting now, and Raquel saw the blacksmith make some violent gesture at the nobleman, she couldn't see what, but his upturned face exuded defiance. Aguilar's sword rose and fell in a long sweep, and the blacksmith crumpled to the ground. A roar went up from the crowd and a shower of paving stones and roof tiles filled the air. The soldiers tried to protect themselves with their shields, but a couple of them toppled over, blood streaming from head wounds, and others were thrown by their plunging mounts.

Another shout and the crowd surged forward at a run. Aguilar wheeled his horse and he and his men galloped back up the street, sparks flying from their horses' hooves, as bottles and stones continued to crash around them. Clusters of rioters surrounded the fallen men with squeals of delight, and they went to work with clubs, knives, or any other object that came to hand. Even a fully armored knight was helpless when pinned to the ground by men with time to find the joints between the protective plates. These soldiers never had a chance.

Ruben did not wait to see any more.

"They'll run for the citadel and hole up there," he shouted, catching Raquel by the hand and running back up the street in the direction they had come.

"We should try to follow them. We'll be safe in the citadel. This rabble could never take it," Jacobo objected.

"We'd never make it. It's too far, and I don't think your wife is up to a long run uphill."

He pointed to the large woman, whom Jacobo was already half carrying, her plump face beet red and her breath coming in tortured gasps.

Ruben led the way down another street and quickly turned several corners, pressing up alleyways sometimes so narrow that they had to move in single file, even turning sideways between the jumble of buildings. They finally came to a small, arched doorway in a long wall, about thirty feet high and without any windows. Ruben banged on the door with the hilt of his sword.

"Who's there?" a voice asked from beyond the door.

"Let us in. We seek shelter," Ruben replied.

"Go away," the voice answered. "If you belonged here, you'd already be on this side of the wall."

"I am Ruben Blanco Herrero," he continued, but this time in Hebrew. "I am the brother-in-law of Ysaque Perdoniel. Find him. He will vouch for us."

There was a pause, which seemed to last for hours. Muffled voices could be heard through the door, and the padding of feet, but Raquel and the others were more attuned to the steady increase in the sounds of the riot, the roaring of the mob, the shattering of glass, the screams of terror and rage, and the distinct smell of smoke, which filtered down into the alley where they were all crammed, making their eyes burn. Jacobo's wife fell into a fit of coughing, interspersed with sobs and moans, as Raquel's mother tried to comfort her although without much effect.

Finally, there was the sound of rasping wood and the thud of bolts being drawn and the thick little door opened inward enough to allow the barrel of an arquebus to emerge, pointed at Ruben's chest, the match glowing brightly in the gloom of the alley.

"That's him," she heard a thin, quavering voice call, and she could just make out the cadaverous head of her Uncle Ysaque bobbing excitedly behind the shoulder of the man with the gun.

The door opened farther, and Ruben began to push everyone through the opening, pausing to look up and down the alley himself before stepping into the *juderia*. Half a dozen men crowded around the door, all wearing the distinctive yellow cowl required of all Jews, and all of them armed with pikes, crossbows, and arquebuses. Raquel noted a clear look of disdain on their faces as they examined this pitiful band of *conversos*, who had only been able to find refuge among the people they had shunned in their conversion to Christianity.

But Ysaque embraced Ruben, his wife, and Raquel in turn, leading them down the street as the Jewish militiamen disgustedly bolted the door again and laid a heavy crossbar into its brackets set in the wall. Ysaque then led the group through a series of twisting streets that were even more narrow and cluttered than those on the Christian side of the wall until they finally entered a worn green door which opened on his own modest home. Raquel and her parents, Ruben and his wife, and Ysaque remained in the single large, sparsely furnished room which served as living and dining room and as a school where Ysaque taught Hebrew, as well as Arabic and Latin, while the servants of both families bustled off to the kitchen to help prepare a meal for the entire entourage.

Raquel had visited the Jewish quarter only rarely while she was growing up. Her father had often smuggled Ysaque into their own house to serve as rabbi on various holy days as well as to teach Raquel her Hebrew, and they had occasionally visited him here over the years, but her father had always considered it important to their charade of Christianity to maintain a marked distance from practicing Jews in public, even of their own family. She looked about now and she shuddered in fear at the sight of a menorah and a copy of the Torah, carefully wrapped in richly embroidered velvet, openly displayed on an oaken trunk near the window, things which her own family kept hidden in a secret compartment under some loose bricks in the floor of their bedroom, behind a heavy armoire. She envied her uncle Ysaque's freedom to declare himself to be what he was and not to have to hide as she did. She understood the reasons for her father's and his father's decision and had certainly heard stories of the massacres of Jews at the end of the last century, but today's events began to call into question in her mind whether they had achieved any real measure of security, and at what price?

"We heard about the procession early this morning," Ysaque was saying as a servant appeared with a tray of glasses and began distributing wine to the new arrivals. "It sounded like it could turn ugly, although we here imagined that we would be the target, which is why we sealed off the *judería*."

"It was horrible," moaned Jacobo's wife, seated heavily in an armchair, rocking back and forth while she gulped her wine between words. "The murderers were using the very Holy Virgin herself as a shield to rob and slit the throats of good Christians."

Jacobo's wife was from an Old Christian family, Raquel knew, and Jacobo himself, a third generation *converso*, had never made any pretense of maintaining ties to his ancestral religion. If anything, he had been rather ostentatious in his celebration of the new religion, donating heavily to the Church and participating enthusiastically in all religious feast days. Jacobo was aware that Ruben and his family secretly honored the Jewish faith, as Jacobo's father had done the same during his lifetime, but Jacobo kept this knowledge strictly secret, primarily in order to avoid bringing suspicion on himself and all other *conversos*, although he clearly disapproved of the risk they were running, just has he had disdained his own father. He was a businessman, pure and simple, and didn't really care much for any form of worship, only appearing in church because he had to in order to avoid hostile gossip and to make useful contacts with other church-goers. Raquel could see that he was nervous about being in the Jewish quarter, and he remained standing in the center of the room, as if fearful of being contaminated by the furnishings.

"We should have gone to he citadel," Jacobo mumbled. "We would have been safe there."

"We couldn't have gotten there in time," Ruben explained patiently. "Even assuming that they would have let us in."

"You saw don Alonso fighting for us yourself," Jacobo protested. He had a habit of always being deferential to those in authority, even in their absence.

"I saw him run away too. It's not a question of lack of desire to help us, just lack of ability. There are too many of the rabble, too hungry for loot, and how many Christians are going to give their lives to maintain order in the city if the only victims are going to be the *marranos*."

"Actually," Ysaque joined in, "we have heard that there is fighting going on between Old Christians and the rioters, and some of the more defensible *converso* neighborhoods have been able to hold off the attackers on their own."

Jacobo ignored him and walked over to the window, pressing against the bars to try to look up and down the street.

"There, you see? This is the last place we should have come. Those bastards are accusing all *conversos* of being secret Judaizers. If they were to find us here, that would only prove their point." He turned and faced Ruben. "I don't begrudge you your right to make your own decision about how you worship. Every man to his own, I always say, but don't you see that you're exactly what puts the rest of us at risk? It just isn't fair."

Ruben drew himself up to his full height, half a head taller than Jacobo and powerfully built, whereas the businessman had a prominent paunch which he now thrust out defiantly, his thick legs braced wide as if to accept a blow.

"My family accepted public conversion to save their lives years ago, literally on the way to the stake. We have never been proud of not having the courage of Ysaque to openly profess our faith, but we believe that God understands." He paused and took a step closer to Jacobo, his voice rising in both volume and pitch. "Your family, on the other hand, was always protected from the worst of the persecution and violence by your wealth and your connections at court. They were tax farmers to the king, the nobles, and the high clergy when they were Jews, and when the anti-Semitic zealots in the Church got laws passed prohibiting Jews from holding government office or tax farming, your people converted, not to save their lives, but to maintain their social status."

"It doesn't matter why they converted," Jacobo was shouting now. "I am a Catholic, not a Jew. I've never even set foot inside a synagogue. My father was a Catholic all his life, even if he did keep some of the old traditions in secret, and, if my grandfather was born a Jew and later became a Christian, well, so did Jesus! I don't know why my family and I should have to pay for what others do."

"Why didn't you stay around and explain that to the mob, then?"

"Because they *know* there are people, just like you, who pretend to be Christian but continue to practice the old faith behind their backs, not just avoiding pork but in the way that they actually think about God, and the rioters didn't look to be in the mood to bother to sort us out. You know as well as I do that people have gotten used to taking the law into their own hands during these years of civil war, or nearly civil war between King Enrique and the Infanta Isabel and her husband Fernando of Aragon."

"It's because they hate you for your wealth and position, just as they hated your Jewish ancestors. The fact that you have Jewish blood, that your blood is *unclean*, is just a pretext that they're using, the rabble, to loot your house, and the Old Christian nobles to remove you from your positions of influence with the government."

"It's you who've put us all in danger by insisting on hanging on to this out-dated religion, one that's been proven not to have the support of God. If you were the chosen people, why are Christianity and Islam spreading all over the world and the handful of Jews that are left are lucky to cling to existence in any corner they can hide in?"

"No, it's you that put us at danger with your greed and ambition! I'm a master metal worker, a maker of weapons for the king to use against the Moors. No one hates us for that."

"It would seem," Ysaque said in a quiet but firm voice, stepping between the two men and pushing them apart with a gentle shove, "that neither of you have found the protection you sought by becoming Christians, either completely," he nodded toward Tobias, "or superficially," he nodded to Ruben. "One is tempted to think that God was not impressed with either of your actions. We Jews, those of us who may not be happy about having to wear this yellow cowl, but are not ashamed to belong to the people who are forced to do so, may be subject to violence on occasion, and we have few protectors, but when we speak to God, we do not have to begin with excuses."

Ruben and Jacobo glared at Ysaque and then at each other, but no one spoke for a long moment. Finally, Jacobo turned around and strode to the window, waving his arms.

"All of this is getting us nowhere. Here we are, hiding in a Jew's house while our own homes are being burned and our neighbors murdered. How are we going to get out of here with our skins?"

"These things usually die down in a few days," Ysaque said in a soothing tone. "King Enrique cannot afford to have mongrels roaming the streets, destroying property and disrupting the peace. If the local nobles can't control things, royal troops will eventually arrive and restore order, although you may be disappointed if you expect those guilty for the looting and killing to be brought to justice. They generally have their own protectors at court who find it useful to have gangs of thugs on tap when needed, and even your most powerful *conversos*, assuming they have escaped the violence themselves, are usually satisfied with trying to put things back the way they were. You and your families are more than welcome to remain here under my roof for as long as you like." He made a graceful sweeping gesture, taking in the cramped room in which they stood. Jacobo looked around uncertainly and with more than a little distaste showing on his face.

"I'll see that you're well rewarded for your hospitality," Jacobo grumbled, and Ysaque winced.

"If I should ask you for payment, I expect that you will provide it promptly and completely, but, until I do, I trust you will not dishonor me by mentioning that again."

Jacobo just cleared his throat and hid his face by downing the last of his wine.

"I agree that we're as safe here as anywhere and that the worst of the danger's probably past," Ruben said, "and we deeply appreciate the refuge you have provided us, Ysaque," he added, bowing to the little man with the long grey beard and the fiery eyes. "Our problem is a longer term one. If the rioters get off unpunished, as I suspect that they will, this will only encourage more violence against all *conversos*, both here and throughout Castile. Since there's nothing we can do to change the fact of our Jewish heritage, the only way we can assure our safety is to put ourselves in such a position that *we* will have the more powerful protectors the next time something like this occurs. Protectors that are not only interested in the common good, like de Aguilar, but who see our survival as being closely tied to their own."

"I thought that's what you were criticizing me for doing," Jacobo interjected. "I would humbly suggest that my work for the bishop and for King Enrique himself, collecting the funds they so desperately need, and in a very efficient way I might add, should have made me indispensable for them, but they don't seem to have been on hand to stand up for us today. In fact, it was just that indispensability that made the Old Christians all the more jealous, at least according to your thinking."

"Exactly. By doing that particular work, you've earned too many enemies elsewhere," Ruben countered. "I should remind you that the money you give the crown is ultimately not yours but is drawn from the working classes, who naturally resent it. And your efficiency has provided you with a very comfortable lifestyle that others envy, and they would like nothing better than to replace you in that position. No, I was thinking of providing some service that others were not willing to do, something that benefited the crown directly."

"Like what?" Jacobo asked skeptically.

"I'm the craftsman, you're the businessman. If you could guarantee me a regular source of high quality iron, bronze, and steel, something which is always in short supply, I could turn that into weapons the like of which no one has yet seen. In doing that, we could not easily be replaced, and the king would know that, so he would protect us. Moreover, the other factions at court would be competing for our favor, hoping to obtain the same armaments for their own forces. No one could afford to alienate us."

Jacobo began stroking his wiry beard pensively, and a grim smile began to play across his face. Raquel, who was observing this from a window seat, trying to comfort Jacobo's infant son, since the boy's mother had chosen to swoon after drinking all of the wine ready at hand, could practically hear the beads of an abacus clicking back and forth as his mind worked the figures.

"The idea has some merit, I'll admit. Of course, besides protection, that kind of product would be the kind that would command just about any price one chose to put on it. But why would you do this grand favor for me, brother?" Jacobo asked.

"Anyone who can handle a job as difficult as tax farming as well as you do can certainly manage the administration of a mining and smelting operation with a minimum of waste, and I do need that metal. It also has to be done efficiently to keep costs down. Besides, I have another favor that you can do me in return."

"I thought you might." He smiled and seemed to recover something of his self-control, now that he was on more familiar ground, cutting a deal.

"I know that you have good connections at the court. I want you to find a place for my daughter, Raquel, in the household of the Infanta Isabel."

Raquel gasped when she heard this, and her mother rushed over and took her hand in hers. Although she had always known that at her age she could expect to leave her parents' home at any time, either to be married or, like this, sent to attend in a noble's household, the normal road to social advancement for someone of her class, she had always assumed that this would be a topic of discussion between her and her father, a man who had never abused his paternal authority over her before. She knew very well that most fathers simply made the decision on their own, perhaps with the agreement of the mother, but rarely bothering to consider the preferences of the daughter. That was the way of the world. Sons were to inherit the family lands, titles, or business and trade. Daughters were for wedding, and everyone knew that a young girl could hardly have the maturity and wisdom to make the proper choice in such a matter. But her father had always been different. Most girls didn't get educated either, many of them not ever learning to read or write, but Raquel's father had not only tolerated her somewhat "unnatural" interest in his work, but had actually seemed to encourage it, just as he had approved of her study of languages and other scholarly pursuits with Ysaque.

"That's a daring move," Jacobo said, chuckling into his beard. "Despite the Treaty of Toros de Guisando, there's no guarantee now that Enrique will honor his pledge to pass the crown on to Isabel, who is only his half sister. He's given strong enough hints that he might renege on the pledge already. Even if he does keep his word, only his death will make the crown available, and if that happens, there are plenty of nobles who would take the field against her, claiming the recognition of Enrique's daughter, Juana, *la Beltraneja*, who would also be supported by Portugal if it came to a fight. I don't have to tell you that Isabel's fortunes, at least in Castile, won't be worth a copper *dirhan* if Juana becomes queen. Oh, Isabel will eventually become queen of Aragon and the Two Sicilies when Fernando's father dies, but she won't have any title in her own right."

"There are no guarantees in life, Jacobo. I'm not worried about making my daughter handmaiden to the empress of the world, just putting her in a position of safety. Here in Castile, in Aragon, or wherever. From what I hear about Isabel, a young *converso* girl will be better protected with her than with anyone else we could find. Besides, from what I hear, one city after another has been declaring for Isabel, so she may be able to come out of this conflict with her crown intact after all."

"True enough. Well," Jacobo went on, stroking his beard vigorously, "I do happen to have a contact that might serve in this matter. Have you ever heard of Andres de Cabrera?"

"The *mayordomo* of Segovia?"

"More than that," Jacobo explained. "He controls the citadel of Segovia, which would be important enough, especially since Enrique's treasury is guarded in the citadel, but there's more. He recently married Beatriz de Bobadilla, Isabel's favorite lady-in-waiting, and he played a key role in producing the Treaty of Toros de Guisando between Enrique and Isabel, which formally recognized Isabel as heir to the throne, which indicates that he's trusted and valued in both camps."

"And why would he help us?"

"Partly because he is a *converso* himself, which not many people know. He's taken some pains to muddy the waters about his family background. But he has also been a client of mine for years, and I've helped him amass a sizeable personal fortune that has given him the ability to finance his political career. If *I* ask him for this small favor, he won't be likely to turn me down."

"Excellent," Ruben said. "Now the only question that remains is whether you will make that request."

Jacobo's smile broadened and he let the question hang in the air for some time. He had obviously often been at this point in negotiations, when he knew that he held the necessary cards, relishing the other party's nervousness. He walked over to the window again and looked up and down the street. Raquel knew that the decision had already been made. He was just drawing out the waiting time for her father, relishing in the power it gave him after having spent a terrified morning confronted by his own impotence. Finally, he turned slowly to Ruben and spoke.

"Of course we'll need to work out the details of this arms manufactory proposal of yours, but as grateful as I am to have survived today, I'm prepared to be generous. Yes, I will send a letter to don Andres at the first opportunity."

Ruben simply nodded and walked over to Raquel. She turned her face up to his, tears brimming in her eyes, and he rested his large hand on her shoulder tenderly.

"But, Papa. . . ," she began, but he placed his finger against her lips.

"If I had my own way, my little bird would never have to leave the nest, but you must trust me, child, that this is for the best, not just for you, but maybe for all of us."

Raquel winced. For that instant she hated her father. He had touched on the one area that he knew that she could not argue. If she did earn herself a place at court, maybe even become a friend of a high noble lady, or the queen herself, she might be in a position someday to help protect her father and mother. She knew that they would give their lives gladly for her. Could she do any less for them?

Ysaque had taken a seat in a large wooden armchair against one of the walls, and he spoke, not to anyone in particular, but up toward the ceiling.

"One cannot help but notice that the solutions you have come up with for your problems have focused exclusively on your personal situations, not with trying to prevent future attacks on either Jews or *conversos*."

"But what could we have done?" Jacobo sputtered. "Do we have it in our power to eliminate the evil forces that constantly try to destroy both your people and mine? At times like these every man must look out for himself." Ruben nodded his agreement.

"Oh, I don't pretend to know what else might have been done," Ysaque admitted. "It just occurred to me that perhaps part of the reason our people continue to suffer these persecutions, and I mean all Jews, overt, covert, and those who are simply marked with the 'taint' of Jewish blood, is because we never seek to strike at the source of our problems. We just focus on getting through this day, this year, saving this family, or finding a new town to settle in."

"Maybe that's also why we have survived as a people at all," Ruben suggested. "History is full of stories of peoples who simply resisted openly and were erased from the face of the earth."

"Perhaps," Ysaque said, and he sighed deeply. "Sometimes I dream of the day when there will be a place where Jews can survive on their own terms, and not at the sufferance of anyone else, no matter how benign. We Jews had a golden age here in Spain for several hundred years, developing our own culture and sharing it with our Christian and Moslem neighbors. We had power and influence, or so it seemed, but we were always 'the king's Jews', his property to do with as he pleased. We were protected, just like his horses or his cattle, when he saw it in his interest, but we were just as quickly sacrificed when he felt it was necessary, or when he decided he wanted a steak or a new pair of shoes."

"It's a nice dream," Ruben agreed.

"But not in this world," Jacobo added. "The Jews have been condemned never to have a land of their own, to survive at the whim of others for the crime of having murdered Christ. God decided that they would not have the sweet release of death, even to suffer eternal punishment in Hell, but would also suffer for all eternity here on earth."

Ysaque did not respond immediately but stared at Jacobo for a long moment with a look of infinite pain and patience. "You don't really believe that, do you, Jacobo?"

The tax farmer snorted and turned back toward the window. "It doesn't matter whether I do or not. The Christians do, and God seems to agree, since that's the way things are."

As predicted, the riots died down within a few days, and Raquel and her family were relieved to find that, while their home had been looted from floor to ceiling, the block of houses in which it stood had not been burned. They were further relieved to find that the hiding place of their Torah and other Jewish artifacts had apparently not been discovered. Life returned to something like normality, with an uneasy truce existing between *conversos* and the Old Christians, while patrols of well-armed soldiers provided by the king made regular rounds of the city to keep the peace.

Raquel had half expected that the plan to send her away to court, the traveling circus of royalty, nobles, courtiers, and hordes of servants which moved from city to city throughout the kingdom, there being no properly established capital, had been forgotten when the crisis had passed. Weeks went by, and her father made no mention of the proposal. Then, as the chill winds and rain that marked the beginning of autumn began to enclose the city, a messenger arrived from the house of Tobias that Raquel had been invited to join the entourage of her highness, Isabel, Infanta of Castille. It said that Isabel would be in Segovia by early December and that Raquel should meet her there. Raquel's mother had wept uncontrollably, but Raquel had sat quietly on her bed, watching the servants pack her few possessions into some small leather trunks, and she had passively allowed the tailor to measure her for the new clothes her father had ordered so that she would be properly dressed for mingling with the uppermost levels of Spanish society.

On the night before her departure, Raquel was sitting at her window, contemplating the charred, broken walls of Marisol's house across the way, shattered beams sticking up at crazy angles and covered with a light coating of frost. Having lost her best friend had been bad enough, but the thought of now losing her entire family was almost more than she could bear. Her father entered her room silently and sat down heavily beside her on the window seat, putting his thickly muscled arm around her shoulders.

"Please don't make me leave, Papa," she whispered, leaning her smooth cheek against his raspy, bearded one. She could feel the cool tracks of his tears against her skin. "I'll stay in the house. I'll be safe here."

"None of us are safe here, little one," he replied. "I cannot tell you how my heart breaks at the thought of not finding you at the table at breakfast and dinner and during the Sabbath, not having you with me, bothering me with your thousand questions about my work, but if I kept you with me it would be out of selfishness." He jerked his chin at the ruins of Marisol's house. "I cannot protect you. I could only do what Marisol's father did, die for you, and that is simply not enough."

"But that can happen anywhere, Papa," she argued. "And, if I'm with the court, you won't be nearby at all."

"Well, that isn't entirely true, I'm happy to say," he said, lifting her chin with his callused finger. "We have heard from don Fernando about our plans for new artillery for his army, and he wishes to talk to me in person. He will be returning from Aragon, where he has been helping his father in his wars against the French, and he will be joining Isabel at Segovia as well, so we will be able to travel together. With a little luck, my work will bring me to court very often. But even without that I would have to send you to the princess. No mobs will attack the royal court, and the attitude of both Enrique and Isabel is generally favorable to *conversos*, if not so much to Jews themselves, ourselves," he corrected himself. "As long as you make every effort to present yourself as a serious Christian girl, there will be no reason for you to fear in their company.

"I am also planning to send Maria with you," he went on. "Actually, it was your mother who suggested the idea and Maria who insisted that, whether we sent her or not, she was going on her own in order to see that you were properly looked after at court. Faced with that kind of determination, there would have been nothing I could have done, although it did help put my mind at rest knowing that you wouldn't be totally alone."

Raquel hugged her father fiercely. At least the separation would be postponed by some weeks, perhaps even months, and that was the best she could hope for now. Raquel was the youngest of the Blanco children. The eldest son, some fifteen years older than Raquel, had run off to sea and was reportedly living in Genoa. Two other children, a boy and a girl, had both died in infancy, before Raquel had even been born, so she had been raised as an only child. Her mother had always been very self-sufficient, closely tied in with her group of *converso* ladies, sometimes, it seemed to Raquel, reluctant to become too close to her daughter for fear that she too would leave home or perish like the others. Her father, on the other hand, had clung to his one remaining child desperately, and she had sometimes awakened in the middle of the night to find her father sitting be her bedside, holding her little hand in his big, meaty paw. She had returned this devotion in full measure and had spent every possible moment at his side, taking interest in everything he did, far more than was considered proper for a young woman of any of the cultures of Spain in those years. Now her mother's premonition was coming true, and Raquel would be leaving home, and her mother became even more distant as a result while her father drew even closer to her.

The trip to Segovia would take several weeks. Raquel and her father, along with Maria and her father's two apprentices, one a Moorish and one a Jewish convert to Christianity, although the latter practiced the Jewish faith in secret along with the Blanco family, all joined a wagon train of merchants carrying casks of olive oil north for sale in the markets of the Basque country. The Blancos had hired a small two-mule cart that was wedged in between the heavy oxcarts of the merchants, and the apprentices took turns at the reins while Raquel and her father rode on horseback alongside. The cart carried their clothes and other belongings and boxes filled with her father's drawings and calculations about the design of new weapons, the casting of cannon, and the employment of artillery in siege warfare that he would show to Prince Fernando in Segovia.

Although winter was fast approaching, the weather in the south was still relatively mild, but, as the column of wagons wound its way up onto the *meseta*, the central plateau, a cold, bitter wind tore over the brown stubble of grass and grains and cut straight through even the heavy woolen robe Raquel wrapped tight around herself. They were following the trail of the *mesta* the annual migration of tens of thousands of sheep from their northern, summer pastures, to the southern ones used in the winter. Although the sheep had long since passed in the opposite direction, they had stripped the ground bare in a wide swath, as far as they could see on either side of the road. There was no snow yet, and they would not encounter any until they crossed the passes through the Sierra de Guadarrama north of the town of Madrid, but the puddles remaining in the roadway from the recent rains had frozen over and cracked and crunched as they oxen trampled them.

Despite the hardships, this was still the first real journey of any length Raquel had undertaken, and it was filled with wonders for her. She watched the vegetation change from the greens of the south to the browns and grays of the north, olive and orange groves giving way to bare pasture and dark pine forests in the mountains, and the thrill of seeing people on the roads who were total strangers, not the same faces of neighbors with whom she had grown up in the tight-knit society of Cordoba. The fact that her father was with her banished all thought of fear and permitted her to enjoy the spectacle to the fullest. For the time being she could put out of her head the looming thought that this was not a pleasure outing, but an embarkation on a new phase of her life, with no turning back.

The merchants and teamsters were all heavily armed. Those that could afford it rode powerful horses and wore coats of mail, helmets, and metal plates protecting their bodies and limbs, carrying swords and short javelins. The retainers riding the wagons carried crossbows at the ready, and they all eyed every outcrop of rocks or clump of trees as a potential ambush site. Hundreds of men who had fought in the civil wars which had ravaged the countryside for years had drifted away from the various armies, whose control over their troops had never been very stringent, and now preyed upon any passing traveler or group of travelers they thought they could overpower. Since these marauding bands had swollen with the hard economic times to small armies in their own right, virtually no one was safe on the roads. To make matters worse, the party was obliged to avoid most cities along their route as local lords had taken to demanding tribute for the right of way, and the merchants pulled their wagons into defensible circles at dusk out in the countryside instead of taking advantage of the shelter of city walls. But apart from false alarms sounded by nervous camp guards in the night, the trip was uneventful, and they finally crested the last ridges of the sierra and came within sight of Segovia, perched atop a rugged hill.

The train of merchants branched off here, continuing their journey northward, and Raquel and her father waved them off into the distance before moving on. They passed beneath the majestic Roman aqueduct, over a thousand years old Raquel's father told her, which still carried water to the city, and wound their way up the switchbacks to the city itself. Word of the arrival of Isabel, Fernando, and Enrique with their entourages had apparently gotten out, and the approaches to the city gates were clogged with crowds of vendors of all sorts, traveling mountebanks, fortune tellers, ladies of questionable reputation, and dozens of lesser nobility, all dressed in their most colorful and luxurious clothing, and all hoping to make a profit from the sudden influx of people of means, either through plying their respective trades or seeking personal favors at court, or simply picking their pockets out in the street. They found indifferent lodgings at an inn near the church of San Esteban, deposited their things under the care of the two apprentices, and then made their way to their interview with Andres de Cabrera in the Alcazar whose ochre-colored walls and tall blue spires loomed above the rushing waters of the Duero River hundreds of feet below.

Although only Isabel, of the royal personages, had yet arrived in the city, security at the castle was very strict, with guards in royal livery checking Ruben's papers carefully before allowing them to pass. There had been too many attempts by members of the various political factions to solve their problems through the assassination or kidnapping of members of the royal household for the guards to take for granted the allegedly peaceful nature of the planned meeting between Enrique and Isabel that was the ultimate purpose of their visit to Segovia. Either side could have concocted the meeting as a pretext for an ambush, and anyone could prove to be an assassin in disguise.

After waiting for several hours in a drafty antechamber while other petitioners were shown through the large double doors leading into Cabrera's apartments, an indifferent steward finally called out Ruben's name and held the door open for them just as the servants were coming around to light the hundreds of candles that gave a ghostly illumination to the rooms. Cabrera was a gaunt, yellow-skinned man whose elegant silk robes only added to the impression of his being a cadaver laid out for an expensive funeral. He was hunched over a large oak desk littered with piles of papers, and he was grimly scratching notes in the margins of one of them with a quill pen. He continued to write for several minutes as Ruben and Raquel stood there. Her father cleared his throat several times without effect, but Cabrera finally set aside the paper he had been working on and looked up at them from under bushy white eyebrows.

"Tobias has spoken to me of you, sir," Cabrera said in a croaking voice without rising or offering his hand. "I'm certain that King Enrique will want to speak with you about your armaments project as well as the young Fernando."

"Naturally, I am at the service of the royal family, don Andres," Ruben replied.

"Aren't we all?" he chuckled, the laugh turning into a dry cough. "Aren't we all? A very wise policy. You and I will have an audience with the king," he turned toward Raquel with a puzzled look, "once your family is settled."

"I believe don Jacobo also mentioned to you the possibility of finding a place for my daughter as well, among the ladies attending to the Infanta Isabel."

Cabrera paused for a moment, cocking his head like a curious crow, his dark eyes taking on the same opaque sheen of a bird's. "Oh, yes. Well that is hardly worth bothering about. She'll find Isabel down along that corridor. In fact, she can run along now and get acquainted while we chat about business."

Ruben and Raquel looked at each other, and Raquel grabbed his hand nervously. This was hardly the way she had envisioned the rest of her life being dismissed, as a minor inconvenience.

"But, certainly you will want to make a proper introduction, sir," Ruben protested.

"Nonsense," he coughed again with a wave of his hand. "It's the second door on the right. She should just knock, I imagine she knows how to do that, and say that I sent her. We really needn't waste our time on something like this."

"But. . ."

"I'm sure you noticed in the outer room that I have other business at hand," Cabrera snapped. "Perhaps you'd like to come back another day when you've had time to think."

"No, no, sir," Ruben submitted, and he had to use his right hand to free his left from Raquel's grasp. "It will be all right, child," he whispered to her. "Just go along and introduce yourself, politely now, and come look for me here when you've done."

She shook her head in terrified little jerks and tried to brace her feet against the floor, but her father steered her toward the door Cabrera had indicated and gently pushed her through.

She found herself in a dimly lit, narrow corridor between the outside wall of the castle and the inner rooms, the ceiling arching inward many feet above her head in the darkness. She inched along, barely able to make out the form of the doorways, blacker shadows amid the gloom and knocked timidly on the second one. If someone had had an ear pressed firmly against the door on the other side, he or she might have discerned the knock, but this was not the case, and Raquel took a deep breath and knocked harder. She tried again, with force this time, and finally a thin voice came back.

"Enter."

Raquel had imagined a grand hall, lit with torches and filled with courtiers dripping in gold brocade, but she found herself in just another dark bedchamber, lit only by a cluster of candles in the far corner where a young woman was doing embroidery, all alone. She stood in the doorway a long moment, unsure of what to do. If this were Isabel herself, the future queen of Castile, it certainly wouldn't be proper for Raquel to address her directly, and, if it were not, then Raquel was clearly in the wrong room. The woman, who was probably taller than Raquel and in her early twenties had a fine, fair complexion and long, chestnut hair, the shade considered the most desirable for a woman among the Spanish. She had a long face, but not unattractive, and she was dressed in an elegantly embroidered satin gown of deep red with a necklace of pearls and gold rings on her fingers, but Raquel supposed that most everyone connected with the court dressed that way. She knew that her father had had to dig deep into his savings to afford the silk dress she was wearing and which she was sure would be considered very drab by court standards.

"Please either come in or go away," the woman said without looking up from her embroidery frame. "This old castle is drafty enough without intentionally abetting the chill wind."

"Excuse me, mistress," Raquel stammered, making a clumsy curtsey without moving from the doorway. "I was looking for the Infanta Isabel. Don Andres sent me."

"Cabrera?" the woman sniffed. "Well, he might not be very trustworthy, but at least he is competent enough at giving directions. I am Isabel."

Raquel gasped and curtseyed more deeply, nearly banging her forehead on the stone floor. "Oh, I beg your pardon, your highness." Her heart sank. Where they had sought out Cabrera as a source of influence with Isabel, it certainly sounded as though there was no love lost between them.

"I obviously do not cut a very imposing figure, sitting here stitching away like a village housewife," she said, and Raquel noticed a mischievous smile playing around the corners of her mouth. "Nevertheless, I assure you that I am Isabel, daughter of Juan II of the house of Trastamara, and wife of Prince Fernando, son of Juan II of Aragon. Now what is it that you seek?"

It was a moment before Raquel could force the words from her throat, which felt as though she hadn't had a drink of water for weeks.

"I, that is we, my father and I, were told that don Andres had spoken to you about the possibility of my joining your household in some humble capacity, your highness, but perhaps we were misinformed. I beg your pardon, and I won't bother you any further."

"Oh, do stop groveling and shut the door," Isabel said, shaking her head. She finally put her sewing aside and sat up straight in her chair. "Now, let's have a look at you. Come here, girl."

Raquel took a few tentative steps across the room.

"Please hurry up," Isabel snapped. "I may still be young, but it won't last forever at this rate. There are many people in this castle you might have reason to fear, but I'm not one of them."

Raquel tried a shy smile and came up to the circle of light cast by the candles.

"That's better. Tell me something of your family, child."

"My father is Ruben Blanco Herrero of Cordoba."

"The gunsmith?"

"Your majesty has heard of him? He will be most honored."

"Whom do you think it was that set up the interview for your father with my husband? The only value Cabrera sees in cannon is as a means of taking a commission for himself on their purchase."

Raquel was so dumbfounded that she momentarily forgot her nervousness. "But we understood that Cabrera was a great friend of the whole royal family, that he had arranged for you to be reconciled with the king, your brother, and that he was presently attempting to do the same again, for the good of Castile."

The smile disappeared from Isabel's face, and Raquel saw a cold light in her eyes that reawakened her fear. She only hoped that the icy anger contained within would never be directed at her. What in the name of heaven was she doing raising questions about high politics with the future queen of Castile? Raquel wondered just how bad the dungeons would be.

"It is, of course, not common knowledge that, as payment for this valuable service to his country, Cabrera is demanding control over the royal treasury here in Segovia as well as the right to hold my only child, my daughter Juana, as a hostage for my good faith."

Raquel's mouth dropped open. "But, surely, that cannot be allowed." Raquel tried to bite back the words, but she found that they had already slipped out of her mouth. Perhaps she would be granted a mercifully quick death.

Isabel smiled again, but there was nothing mischievous about it this time. "People outside the court have an image of us, the royal family, as possessing great power and wealth. In reality, much of our wealth depends on the good wishes of others, all of whom have their own interests at heart. I have already had to send the treasured family jewels to Valencia as surety for loans from the merchants there more than once. And as for power! As long as most of our troops are raised by the nobles themselves, and each one has control of one or more castles, the smallest of which can require months of costly siege operations to overcome, we are little more than first among equals, often not even first, and the nobles are able to use our concern for the good of our people and the security of the crown as a weapon against us, threatening both with subversion and foreign alliances in order to get whatever they demand. And now I am asked to give up my daughter, the one thing in this world which is truly mine, to these vultures." She hung her head.

"Well," Raquel stammered, but finding herself gaining strength. If this was going to be her one conversation with Isabel, she might as well say what she felt. "Don't do it, your highness. You may be a princess and will be our queen one day, but you are also a mother. The people would understand and support you."

Isabel looked up with a puzzled look on her face. "Come here, child." She reached out and took Raquel's hand in both of hers. "You say that you want a place in my little court?"

"My father has said so, and I am his daughter," she replied, tears filling her eyes.

"I like you, what was your name?"

"Raquel, daughter of Ruben Blanco Herrero, your highness."

"Well, Raquel, even if you were recommended by Cabrera, you shall have your wish, or your father shall have his. It would please me to have your company on my lonely journey. Hopefully, you will come to be happy with the result."

Raquel went down on her knees and kissed Isabel's hand. "I will serve you faithfully, your highness, and my father will also, I swear it." Then she looked up after a moment, blinking back her tears. "You say that you have an interest in my father's work?"

"I have seen the drawings he sent to Fernando and Cabrera. I have also seen enough of warfare in my life to appreciate your father's vision. I may be a frail woman, but I am of warrior stock, and I fear that it is the fate of Castile always to be at war, with itself if not with others. So, it is my duty to take an interest in these things."

In the days that followed, Raquel would have been hard pressed to believe that there had ever been any bad blood between Isabel and her half-brother, King Enrique, when he arrived in the city with his own court. There were endless rounds of dinners, tournaments, and entertainments, with the entire combined assembly, now that Fernando had also arrived from Aragon, resplendent in silks and satins, brocades and furs, and everyone dripping silver, gold, and jewels. The gloomy halls of the alcazar were awash with light from a thousand torches, candles, and lamps, and the castle throbbed with the sound of music and the beat of hundreds of dancing feet. And there was the constant buzz of conversation in the elegant Castilian Spanish of the court that had already developed into something different from the more slurred speech Raquel was used to in the south. Raquel was too young and too obviously not from an influential family to attract much attention, and she spent most of her time haunting the corners of the halls, watching the spectacle, and then joining Isabel in her private chambers for long talks that lasted often well into the night. The men were often away throughout the day, hunting in the hills to the south of the castle with swarms of hounds or with hawks perched arrogantly on their arms, or closeted away in endless, boring meetings from which the women were largely excluded, giving Raquel even more time to spend with Isabel alone.

She had been presented to Fernando and was taken with his powerful bearing, a born military man. He was larger than the average Spaniard, with a strong chin and carefully coifed hair, but there was something about his eyes that reflected a certain dullness which was in marked contrast to Isabel's vivacity and wit. He was a soldier, born and bred, and, while he had already gained something of a reputation both on the battlefield and of being a machiavellian plotter at court, it was clear to Raquel that it was Isabel who would be the brains of this family and of the dynasty they hoped to found.

Their marriage had been one of the most brilliant strokes of matrimonial diplomacy in European history, and it was all Isabel's doing. She had explained to Raquel the terms of the famous Treaty of the Toros de Guisando, which Cabrera had helped engineer between her and Enrique. It obliged Enrique to recognize Isabel's claim to the crown of Castile in exchange for her agreement that she would enter into no marriage without his concurrence. This implied that Enrique, as sovereign, would be free to arrange a political marriage for Isabel that would enhance both his present position and the future greatness of Castile. There had been plenty of suitors for Isabel's hand, including the current elderly king of Portugal, Joao, and Isabel had been considered one of the most valuable diplomatic assets on the continent, since Enrique himself was apparently unable to produce an heir to the throne. But Enrique had eventually produced such an heir with his second wife, Juana of Portugal, a daughter who was also named Juana, showing a remarkable lack of imagination among the nobility when it came to christening their progeny to Raquel's way of thinking. However the widespread rumors of Enrique's impotence and even possible homosexuality and the barely concealed flirtatiousness of the queen, supported the supposition that Princess Juana's father was actually Juan de Beltran, Enrique's political advisor and a long-time confident of the queen.

Enrique began to waver on his commitment to Isabel's right to succession, prompted by the energetic lobbying of his wife for the rights of her own daughter. So Isabel had seen her only chance as establishing a power base among the many nobles who opposed Enrique, and the only way to do that was to make a powerful marriage alliance for herself. She knew that any marriage arranged by Enrique, who was acting as Isabel's guardian, would be designed for his benefit alone, so she would have to take charge of the matter on her own account. She did this by negotiating the match with her cousin Fernando, even going to the trouble of obtaining papal dispensation for a marriage within this close bond of consanguinity. Fernando had already been recognized as King of Naples and Sicily, and he would also inherit the crown of Aragon from his father Juan one day. Castile and Aragon were bound by ties of language and culture, where there could be no hope of a permanent union between Castile and Portugal, and this fact was not lost on the Castillian nobility. With deft planning, Isabel had managed to celebrate the marriage and consummate it some five years ago, before Enrique was ever aware, presenting him with a *fait accompli* which he could do nothing about without risking immediate war with Aragon. Now, any thought on Enrique's part to going back on his promise for Isabel's succession also carried with it the threat of war, as Juan of Aragon would not accept such a development placidly.

Besides all of the hard-headed reasons for the marriage, it soon became apparent to Raquel that Isabel was deeply in love with Fernando. They made a fine team too, where Fernando was blunt and direct, Isabel was sly and devious. Fernando had the military skills and the daring to put Isabel's long term planning into practice, and she could work out the logistical and political backstopping for his adventures where he gave such details little thought. Most importantly, he could command the respect of the male-oriented Castillian society in a way no woman, no matter how intelligent, ever could hope to do. They spent hours talking of their plans for the united Spain they intended to create together, but, when this talk was done, Raquel sensed real moments of tenderness between them and a feeling of emptiness in Isabel during the inevitable long separations from her husband who often had to ride off to Aragon, as a loyal son, to prosecute his father's endless wars against France.

Raquel could not help but overhear gossip at the court, most of it dealing with sexual liaisons which occurred nightly amid much giggling and whispering in the back corridors of the castle, but also with shifting political alliances between the powerful members of the nobility, the clergy, the wealthy merchant class in the increasingly influential cities, and the envoys of the various foreign powers, Portugal, Burgundy, France, Genoa, and the Pope himself, who haunted the court looking for advantage.

Because of her age and generally unimpressive appearance, Raquel found that the magnates of Castile did not bother even to lower their voices when she walked by any more than they would worry about talking in front of a dog or a horse, and Isabel came to appreciate Raquel's value as a conduit of confidential information, which she faithfully passed on to her mistress.

Although Raquel was quickly learning to discount ninety per cent of what she heard in her wanderings through the castle and the town, late one night, while slipping down to the kitchens to sneak a gift into the shoes of one of the maids as part of the mid-January celebration of the arrival of the "three kings," she saw two shadowy figures huddled in a dark doorway in one of the inner passageways. Even that late on an ordinary night, the castle was never quite asleep. Friars and nuns would be shuffling back and forth to the chapel in the wee hours for *matins*, and the cooks would be up and selecting vegetables and meats and preparing bread for the daily fare well before dawn, so it was not surprising to find other people up and about. But there was something deathly serious in the subdued tones in which this pair spoke, and Raquel flattened herself against a column to listen. She did not recognize their voices, but one of the men interspersed his conversation with bits of Latin, implying that he was a priest, while she could see from the silhouette of the other that he wore armor and spoke in the gruff language of a soldier. She waited until they were finished and had gone their separate ways, the soldier passing within inches of her but too preoccupied with his plans to notice her slim form wedged into the corner. She stood in that spot, afraid to breathe, for a long while after they had gone, then sprinted silently back up the corridor to the chambers of the princess.

"Your highness!" she gasped. "You must fly from here!"

She stopped suddenly when she realized that Fernando, who had been out hunting boar and was not expected back until morning, had returned early and the pair were snuggling on a window seat in one corner of the room. Isabel gave Raquel an impatient look but checked herself when she saw the pallor of the girl's face.

"What is it?" Isabel asked, untangling herself from Fernando's arms.

"Two men, just now," she panted. "They are talking of attacking your quarters and capturing both of you and your daughter as well."

Fernando was on his feet in an instant, reaching for the sword, which lay on a nearby table.

"Who were they? I have enough troops here in the castle to take care of this myself."

"I didn't recognize their voices, and it was too dark to see their faces. A priest and a soldier, I think."

"Pacheco's people, in all likelihood," Isabel said.

"Pacheco?" Raquel asked.

"Juan Pacheco," she spat out the name. "He has been a close advisor to Enrique for years and gathered considerable wealth and power in the process, even though he's from the lower classes himself. This is something that has plagued Castile for ages, like with Alfredo de Luna who played the same role in the court of my father and who started Pacheco on his career. Pacheco fears losing his power if I ever come to the throne, and he's not wrong in that. He hopes that, by getting control of us, he'll be able to dictate terms, get us to guarantee his title to lands and offices throughout the country and those of his followers. That's the same game that Cabrera is playing, although on a smaller scale, by demanding that I leave Juana here with him as a hostage."

"With his head mounted on a pike, we'll have far less to worry about from him," Fernando growled, heading for the door. "I'm tired of all this sneaking and whispering."

Isabel rushed after him and pulled him back gently. "Now is not the time. Pacheco is too strong, and you'd never be able get to him. He controls a dozen castles that would take your army years to capture, even if Enrique stood back and let you do it, and he is the Master of the military Order of Santiago which gives him access to at least as many troops as you could raise, even if your father could spare forces from the war with France. There's a better way to deal with this threat."

"And what might that be?" Fernando snapped.

"You must leave, me, my dear," Isabel said calmly to Fernando.

"What? Leave you at the mercy of that baseborn brigand?" he roared. "Never!"

"Yes," she went on, "you will. Instead of putting us in danger, your departure will ensure our safety. It is only by getting us all together that Pacheco can achieve his aim. If you are still at large, under the protection of your own troops, it would serve him nothing to seize Juana and myself, since you could then make war on his supporters."

"I cannot do that, my love," Fernando argued, but Raquel could detect a tone of pleading in his voice, not the bellow of command that he used to shout orders to hundreds of fighting men over the din of battle. "We can make a fight of it here, once and for all."

"How many men do you have with you, here in the castle?" she asked.

"Well, perhaps twenty, all picked men, with another two hundred in quarters around the town."

"Pacheco could gather ten times that number, especially if Cabrera is in league with him, which he might well be, and their men control the walls and the gates. Either your men couldn't fight their way in, or they would be unable to fight their way out, to say nothing of the fact that there would be no guarantee that Juana and I might not be killed in the battle," she added, raising one delicate eyebrow.

Fernando hung his head and sighed. There was no arguing with Isabel once she had made up her mind. Fernando's lower lip protruded in the pout of a disappointed little boy. Isabel embraced him, reaching up to kiss him on the cheek, and turned him gently toward the door. A few moments after he had departed, Raquel heard the clink of metal and found that Fernando had left half of dozen of his men, fully armored, to guard Isabel's quarters. Then, as the two women listened, they could hear the sudden clatter of hooves on the cobblestones of the courtyard, followed by shouts of alarm as the clatter turned to drumming as Fernando and his escort raced across the drawbridge and off into the night.

Just as their hoofbeats faded, dozens of heavily armed soldiers started pouring out of the barracks near the gate while Isabel and Raquel looked down from their window high in the castle.

"Unusual for so many men to be awake and armored at this hour of the night," Isabel commented dryly.

The soldiers milled about in the courtyard for some time, some of them struggling to get horses saddled, until a thick-bodied man in full armor stalked out of the castle and gave a series of harsh orders, waving angrily in the air. The men paused to listen, then dejectedly began to unsaddle their mounts and return to the barracks.

"Well, that's that!" Isabel whispered, smiling smugly, as she pulled the drapes closed and turned toward her bed.

The subsequent months passed slowly. With Fernando gone, Isabel took no interest in any of the normal festivities of the castle, relying more than ever on Raquel to bring her news of what was going on at court. Winter gave way to spring, then summer, then fall, when, finally, word came in October that Juan Pacheco had died, mysteriously of a "catch in the throat." When Raquel brought this news to Isabel, it struck her that the princess was not nearly as surprised as she might have been, just smiling slightly, and adding this announcement to a letter that she was writing to Fernando, then campaigning in Aragon.

"We must obtain a papal bull to get the Mastership of Santiago into the power of the crown," she told Raquel as she wrote. "It involves considerable military power and patronage which will be of value to us when we come to the throne."

It struck Raquel as odd that Isabel had recently begun to us the royal "we". It began to make more sense less than two months later when word came that, weakened by a life of drinking and reveling, Enrique had died in Madrid. While there would be those who insisted that Enrique's own daughter Juana should assume the throne, most of the Castilian nobility stood by the Treaty of Toros de Guisando and Isabel's right to the crown. Raquel noticed that Isabel had engineered her marriage contract in such a way that, while she had gained full recognition to her own rights in both Naples and ultimately in Aragon, Fernando's only claim in Castile came through his status as Isabel's husband, as royal consort, and her name always came first when referring to the royal couple in Castile. This did much to mollify the touchy Castilian nobility, but Raquel suspected that, after a life of uncertainty in the hands of unscrupulous and more powerful men, Isabel did not want to ever take a subordinate position again, even for love.

The morning after the messenger had arrived with word of Enrique's death, on the 12th of December, Isabel, Raquel, and the other ladies of the court, dressed in white serge, the traditional mourning garb, attended a Mass for Enrique at the cathedral, which was draped in black bunting, and with Enrique's standards lowered to signal the passing of the monarch. The mood during he ceremony had been solemn and dignified, but hardly distraught, as Enrique had never had many fans among the members of Isabel's court.

That same afternoon, however, dressed in an elaborate green gown, glistening with gold thread and encrusted with gems, and with a heavy gold necklace with an immense ruby at her throat, Isabel reappeared in public mounted on a magnificent white gelding for a hastily organized procession through the city. Cabrera rode ahead of her carrying an unsheathed sword high over his bald head as a symbol of the power of the Castilian monarchy, the first time the gesture had been made for a woman. A troop of armored knights and a number of local nobles decked out in their finest silks, satins and furs, completed the entourage which proceeded through the winding cobblestone streets to the beat of a brass drum. The sound and the spectacle caught the attention of clusters of townspeople along the route who gave ragged shouts of support, although they did not yet know for what. Other people began to gather in the plaza, knowing that, if anything were afoot, it would be staged there sooner or later. There were household servants, still carrying their brooms and dust rags, fishermen with their catch slung over their shoulders en route to the market, and housewives herding along clusters of rowdy children, all hoping for the sight of something edifying and entertaining, like an execution or a public flogging. But they were rewarded with the sight of Isabel mounting a hastily constructed platform with skirtings of cloth bearing the Castilian coat of arms to hide the shoddiness of the construction, set up on the *Plaza*

Mayor where she would officially accept the crown of Castile.

Only a few *grandees* were present in the city at the time. Cabrera sat at one end of the platform with the other notables, clearly uncomfortable and displeased with situation, but powerless to prevent this impromptu coronation. He had argued for a delay, at least until Fernando could arrive from Aragon, but Isabel would have none of it. She argued that the supporters of Juana la Beltraneja would not hesitate to crown their candidate at the earliest opportunity, and being the first to wear the crown, especially the historical crown taken from the treasury in Segovia's *alcazar* and with the ceremony conducted at the traditional site of Segovia, would give Isabel a strong claim to legitimacy that a meeting of the *Cortes* would be likely to confirm in the near future. Waiting for even a few days could prove fatal to her cause.

On the platform, a public notary read out a proclamation to the modest crowd of spectators, both minor nobles and curious townspeople, even some peasants who had been rushed in from the countryside to attend the ceremony with the promise of free food and drink. He announced that the king was dead and that Isabel had been recognized as his heir in the treaty of 1468, sworn to by all the nobles of the land and the *Cortes*. Isabel's four-year-old daughter Juanita was also held up for the acclamation of the crowd, which had now grown to a respectable size and had warmed to the occasion now that they realized its importance.

"Castile! Castile! Castile!" a herald shouted. "For the very high and powerful princess and mistress, our lady doña, Queen Isabel, and for the very high and powerful prince and king, our lord King Fernando, her legitimate husband!" The crowd took up the shout and cheered to the echo.

The officials of the town ceremonially turned over their staffs of office to Cabrera as a symbol of their subordination to the crown, and he graciously returned them. Cabrera then bowed deeply turned over the keys of the *alcazar* to Isabel, although Raquel noticed that it was only with effort that he forced his fingers to release their grip on the heavy iron keys. But Isabel dipped her head and promptly returned them, confirming Cabrera in his position as her *alcalde* in Segovia, keeper of the royal treasury, and Cabrera breathed a visible sigh of relief.

Isabel looked over the top of Cabrera's balding pate to where Raquel stood at the edge of the crowd, and clearly, unmistakably, winked. A wink from a queen, Raquel thought, on her coronation day. If such a thing could be held and packaged, it would be worth more than a bag of gold.

GRANADA

.

Chapter Three

Trujillo

Juan Ortega de Prado sat his horse at the crest of a low ridge, looking back toward his family home, a small, fortified manor house near the town of Trujillo in Estremadura. He was a physically imposing young man, tall, and with a neck thicker than his head, with long arms with muscles like twisted ropes. He rode *al jinete*, with shortened stirrups set farther back, causing the rider to lean forward as if in a constant position to launch himself at the foe. This style of riding had been adopted from the versatile Berber light cavalry from North Africa and was quite in fashion on both sides of the borderlands since the rugged mountain terrain in which most of the fighting took place in recent years made the more traditional heavily armored knight in a stiff, high-backed saddle with a long lance and heavy shield, largely ineffectual.

The horse, a tall, powerful black, was well-groomed but was several years past his prime, and the leather and metal work of the saddle and bridle showed the wear and tear of long usage. Juan's sword was of the finest Toledo steel, and his armor carefully oiled, but both bore dents from battles long before Juan's birth. In a society that often judged status not by achievement but by external trappings, Juan longed for just a bit of gold, some clasps for his cloak perhaps, which was also ragged about the edges, so that he would be taken more seriously by the older men. But he knew that there was no money in the whole family for such luxuries.

It was nearly dusk, and a cold wind swept across the plain, barren except for the stubble of brown grass and an occasional gnarled oak. At one time, over two centuries before, when this land had recently been reconquered from the Moors with the help of the swords of Juan's ancestors who had fought alongside King Alfonso at the Battle of Navas de Tolosa and crushed the power of the mighty Almohads, the Ortegas had been given lordship over vast tracts of rich farmland along with hundreds of Moorish peasants to work the land. Unfortunately, it was the Spanish practice to divide the estate of the father among all the healthy sons, and the Ortegas had been blessed, or cursed, with particularly large families. Thus, the patrimony of his father now consisted of the poorly maintained house, a few head of livestock, and perhaps four hundred acres of farmland on which the system of irrigation installed by the Moors had long since been allowed to fall into disrepair. To make matters worse, Juan was the youngest of three sons, and his father had decided early on that to divide the land any further would leave each of his offspring in a position little better than that of free peasants, too poor to support even a few servants and forced to work the land themselves, something any Spanish nobleman would rather die than accept. He had consequently decided to leave the entire estate to the eldest son, Francisco, who was nearly a decade older than Juan. Juan could not argue with this logical decision, but he only wished that Francisco had not been such an insufferable ass, so full of himself that he projected the impression that the land was his by right, regardless of his order of birth, even though he had neither a head for business nor the stomach for a fight, and he lost no opportunity to humiliate Juan and to remind him of the imminence of his coming into the property at which time Juan would be obliged to move along.

This left young men like Juan and his brothers with few options in life. While there was always the chance of marrying into a propertied family and receiving an adequate estate as part of the dowry, this was just one more factor of life where the rich got richer and the poor, poorer. Even though the Ortega name still merited respect in the annals of heraldry, the family's financial straits were also well known in local high society, and it would be extremely unlikely that any member of the upper nobility would allow a daughter to dip down so far on the social ladder. Even widows and orphaned girls with property always came with powerful protectors who would prevent such a mismatch. It was one more cause Juan had for resenting the *grandees* who had consolidated Castile's lands into larger and larger conglomerates, easing out the minor nobility and hogging all positions of authority in the government, and the lucrative jobs they commanded, for themselves and their lackeys.

Of course, there were the daughters of the increasingly numerous and wealthy merchant class, and merchants were always on the lookout for ways of ennobling their lines through marriage into the title-rich but land-poor aristocracy. One of Juan's brother's, the second eldest, had tried this route, but the merchants were shrewd men, having been obliged to go out and make their fortunes instead of inheriting them like honorable men. They always built in clauses and conditions into the contracts granting money or land to their new sons-in-law that managed to keep the young man beholden to the father-in-law for every *maravedi*, a constant reminder of who it was that held the purse strings and a humiliation that Juan could never accept. He was sure that, in a similar situation, he would be unable to resist hacking the low-born shopkeeper to bits and shoving his damned money down his bloody throat.

That left only two alternatives, and Juan's other brother, Albaro, had taken one of them, joining the clergy. While there was a certain measure of respect involved in devoting one's life to God, and a good living to be made from it in most cases, here too one needed money and connections to get started. Most of the more prestigious orders required substantial donations in cash or land before accepting young men and women into their ranks. In such orders life could be good, with palatial housing, the same recreations of hunting and feasting as enjoyed by the best nobles, and the political power needed to gain more of the same. Even the strictures regarding celibacy were largely winked at, and, while children born in such conditions could not be formally recognized and the family line continued, still bishops and archbishops often did well by their illegitimate offspring. But the financial conditions of the Ortega family could not support such aspirations, and Juan's brother had become a simple, tonsured monk of the Dominican order, living a life little better than that of a peasant, with the added burden of constant prayer, self-negation, and penance which held few attractions to Juan.

There remained, therefore, one road for Juan Ortega de Prado, the career of a soldier. Now *that* was a purely honorable profession, and one for which most members of the Spanish nobility prepared themselves from boyhood. Juan was a master with the sword and rode like a centaur, and had done almost since before he could walk. Even at the tender age of twenty he had already participated in half a dozen *cabalgadas*, raids of hundreds or even thousands of knights and men-at-arms, into the lands of the Moors to capture livestock, slaves, and noble-born prisoners for ransom. He had also established himself as a master *escalador*, a specialist in the storming of castles, the end game of all siege warfare. He could virtually run up a wobbling assault ladder without using his hands, which were needed for his weapons, and hold open a breach or a section of parapet indefinitely against any number of opponents until reinforcements could arrive.

But the policy of the weak King Enrique had robbed Juan of even this chance for recognition and advancement. Enrique, about whom Juan was more than ready to believe the rumors of a lack of manliness, pursued a course of compromise with the Moors. He engaged in raids from time to time, just to keep his nobles from directly accusing him of treason to the Christian cause, but he did not seek to capture new territory, the only way a young noble could hope to gain new lands for himself. Returning home from a raid with half a dozen sheep or a new Moorish serf in tow might help Juan keep the wolf away from the family door for a brief while, but it would not make his fortune. Even in the constant civil strife which had been tearing Castile apart for decades, Enrique seemed to prefer compromise and forgiveness for his enemies, terms which sounded good in a sermon but gave his followers no confiscated lands to distribute as reward for their services.

Juan could only hope that the new sovereigns, Isabel and Fernando, who had already taken to calling themselves the Catholic Kings, would have a different approach. Juan was ready to believe this as Fernando already had a strong reputation as a warrior from his campaigns in Italy and Aragon, and rumor had it that, as tough as Fernando was, it was Isabel who had the real balls in the family. What was more, the young monarchs had little cause to be grateful to the old, powerful noble families of Castile, who had consistently supported Enrique against them. Juan had heard that Isabel and Fernando planned to crush the power of the nobles and concentrate that power in the crown, a policy that his father opposed just on principle, still thinking of himself as a member of the nobility, no matter how impoverished, but in which Juan saw a glimmer of hope for his own situation. If the crown were going to take on the upper nobility, they could not do it alone. They would need support, military support. The common merchant class and the Jews were too busy making money to be bothered with risking their lives on the battlefield, so this support could only come from the ranks of the poverty-stricken lower nobility that the *grandees* had been looting and suppressing for decades.

For this reason, Juan had jumped at the chance to join the newly-formed *Santa Hermandad*, the Holy Brotherhood, a kind of national police force originally designed to curb the rampant crime and brigandage on the country's highways, but which promised to become much, much more. For centuries, every town and region had had a local *hermandad*, a kind of voluntary militia controlled either by the local noble or clergyman or by a town council, whose duty it was to patrol the nearby roads and to serve as a basis for providing trained manpower to the feudal armies that might be raised from time to time. But these militias were still armed and paid by and under the direct control of whatever lord happened to hold sway in the region where they were raised, or increasingly under the control of the mixed noble/merchant councils that ruled the towns. The new *Santa Hermandad* would have their first loyalty to the crown itself and would be the first troops on which the crown could count other than those raised on the lands belonging to the monarchs themselves. The crown would be appointing the officers and seeing to their promotion and reward, and the new Catholic Kings would certainly be on the lookout for promising young soldiers, of good family to be sure, but who could rise quickly if they proved to be of use to the monarchy. Juan was certain that he could.

As Juan brooded about his fate in life, he heard the muffled pounding of hooves coming across the stubble field from behind him. A single horse, his years of experience told him, but riding hard, and he slipped the dagger from his belt and concealed it in the folds of his sleeve. In case of need, he could hurl the dagger with devastating accuracy nearly twenty yards. When the rider was close enough, Juan wheeled his horse and immediately recognized the flushed face of the Basque.

His real name was Alvestegui, but his background was so murky that everyone simply referred to him as the Basque. He was about thirty years of age, short and solid, with comically short, almost dwarfish legs and long, muscular arms. He had appeared from the north of Spain a decade before, looking for service in the wars against the Moors and was now the closest thing the Ortegas had to a retainer, their single vassal, since he had attached himself to Juan's father and showed no signs of going back home, even though the limp-wristed King Enrique had never shown any sign of carrying the war to the Moors.

It took a moment for the Basque to catch his breath, as if he had been carrying the horse instead of the other way around. His build gave him a poor seat when mounted, but his tremendous strength and absolute disregard of danger made Juan glad that he was second-in-command of Juan's little *hermandad* unit.

"A traveler just reached the village," the Basque puffed heavily. "A Jew. Part of a little party of traders. They were attacked by bandits not two hours ago. He's the only one who survived as far as he knows. Rolled off his horse and into an irrigation ditch and crawled away while they were massacring his friends."

"Bravely done!" Juan laughed, although, if this proved to be the band that Juan and his men had been chasing for the past several months, another fat trader more or less would hardly have changed the outcome of the struggle. "Did he see which way they headed?"

"That's the good news," a smile spread across the Basque's florid features. "The traders were carrying new wine, and the man heard them smashing open casks and guzzling away before he even got out of earshot. I sent out word, and the men should be ready by the time we get back to the village."

Juan needed no further explanation and dug his huge spurs into the flanks of his horse, tearing down the hill at a furious gallop toward the manor house. As he hauled back on the reins in the courtyard of the house, he tossed his cloak to a servant and leapt from the saddle. Two of the house stewards, not real fighting men but members of the *hermandad* just the same, were already armed and sitting astride their bony plow horses as Juan raced into the storeroom they used as an armory. A boy was there, ready to help strap on his breast plate while Juan jammed his helmet down over his long black hair, a simple helmet, without any visor that might obstruct his vision but which protected his head and the back of his neck. He then attached a small round target to his left forearm. He wouldn't have time for anything more elaborate. Then he drew his long, basket-handled sword and slashed the air with it, twisting it about in his hand to form complex arcs on both sides of his body.

Juan's father clapped loudly and slowly in the doorway. He was a large man, grown extremely fat, even as his family's fortunes had dwindled, as if he had eaten them up all by himself. His pink cheeks puffed out above a bristling white moustache and beard, reducing his eyes to dark slits beneath the snowy fringe of a single eyebrow that ran the width of his face. Just behind him stood the pudgy, pale figure of Francisco in the pose Juan always associated with him, a sly smirk on his face, but hiding behind his father's bulk, since Juan had been able to trounce him with little effort for half a dozen years now and had done so joyfully, even with the beatings from his father that such adventures always earned.

The only friendly face in the room belonged to Juan's hulking mastiff, Asco, a trained war dog who now looked more like an immense puppy, an insipid smile on his wrinkled face and a long train of drool dangling down to the floor as his bushy tail alternately slapped against the thighs of the two other men.

"Off to fight for God and country, eh?" his father chortled, and Francisco blew his nose loudly into his hand, flinging a glistening glob of snot into the dirt at Juan's feet.

"If that queer king of yours could have found me a war, and I'd be off fighting Moors for you now, but anything is better than nothing," Juan snapped.

His father took a threatening step closer, but Juan merely cocked his head and deftly flipped his sword back into its scabbard. Juan was certain that his father's attitude toward him was largely a reflection of the resentment that Juan felt toward the father, as much as he might try to conceal it. Juan knew that it was not necessarily his father's fault that his forebears had frittered away their lands, nor did he disagree with the logic of giving what remained of those lands to Francisco without further fragmenting them. It was not even his father's fault that there had been little or no chance to gain more lands in battle in his lifetime, yet he was so frustrated by his limited prospects that it was all he could do sometimes to keep from spitting out the truth of the man's failure to accomplish the one significant goal of a Spanish *hidalgo*, to provide his sons with a worthwhile inheritance. Actually, the predicament of the Ortega family had become so widespread that the very term *hidalgo*, had changed meaning from being the son of *a somebody* to that of being the son of *someone or other*, whose name was of no importance.

"A little respect for your late sovereign," the father snorted, and Francisco bobbed his head vigorously but in silence.

"I have little enough," and Juan strode back out to where the grooms had prepared his horse, tying on a long quiver with three six-foot javelins on one side and a light cross bow in a sheath on the other.

"Well, we'll see how these young puppies do in his place," the father growled as Juan launched himself into the saddle in one bound and caught up the reins.

"I imagine we will," he replied, then turned to Francisco. "Should we wait for you to put on your armor, brother?"

Francisco's face turned a deep shade of pink, and it took him a moment to produce a mechanical, nervous laugh. "I'll leave the sweeping up to the garbage men," he blurted out in a voice that was a little too loud. He clapped his father on the back to encourage him to join in the joke, but Juan could see his father wince and avert his eyes without further comment just as Juan jerked his horse's head around and trotted out the gate.

Juan and his small party thundered through the little village and were joined my more riders as they went, finally forming a squadron of about twenty men, plus Asco, who galloped along beside Juan's horse, his thick black neck now encased with a formidable spiked collar, and a look of grim determination in his brown eyes. They all now wore the newly issued cloaks of the *Santa Hermandad*, black with red lining, and in the fading sunlight he imagined that they looked like nothing less than the flames of Hell as they swept up the road and into the hills, and Juan knew that this was what he had been born to do. It didn't matter whether he lived another day or another fifty years. As long as he was able to ride hard in pursuit of an enemy, his body encased in armor with good steel at his side, he was alive. The day that he could no longer do this, he would just as soon slash his own throat and be done with it. He would never linger on as his father had, a useless old baggage, of no use to anyone, just sucking up air, and wine, and food to no purpose. That wouldn't be living at all.

They found the site of the attack easily enough. Half a dozen bodies were scattered about on the road or nearby, the feathered shafts of arrows protruding from the corpses. The dead had all been disemboweled by the bandits, probably on the assumption that Jews had a habit of swallowing gold coins to hide them from assailants, and greasy trails of intestines criss-crossed the ground. Juan had to call Asco back to keep him from gorging himself on all this fresh meat. From the agonized expressions on the faces of the victims, it appeared that some of them were still alive when the bandits began the searching process. Bits of clothing tumbled along the ground in the freshening breeze, and another man, hanging by a rope from the limb of a tree, rocked back and forth slowly. The Basque slipped from his horse and studied the ground.

"This way," he pointed after a moment.

Juan signaled his men to spread out into a skirmish line, and they proceeded at a walk toward a wooded knoll about a mile distant as a pale half moon lit their way. In a moment, Juan could hear screaming coming from the wood, and loud singing in a deep baritone voice. Juan led his men into a small gully where they dismounted and tied their horses, taking with them their crossbows and holding onto their swords to prevent any clanking that might disclose their approach.

A large bonfire was burning in a clearing in the wood. Juan held out his arm and his men halted and knelt down, watching and listening for the sentinels that they expected to be posted. But there was no sentinel. Juan could see the forms of at least twenty men sprawled around the clearing, obviously in a drunken stupor. Another dozen were standing in a cluster near the fire, some leaning against each other or swaying woozily while they watched as one of their number brutally mounted a naked woman and another sat next to them singing a bawdy ballad, stroking the woman's long hair and pouring a stream of wine into her mouth from a large wineskin every time she opened it to scream. Nearby lay the body of another naked woman, older and fatter than the one at the center of the circle and who had apparently been unable to withstand the attentions of the bandits.

Juan scanned his line of men who now formed a semicircle around the clearing, no farther so that they would not fire into each other. He paused until he could see that all were watching him, then he raised his own crossbow. The quarrel slashed through the smoke of the fire and lodged in the throat of the singer, catching him in mid-note and sending him toppling over backwards. A couple of the other men glanced up as the singing stopped, but shrugged and turned back to the main entertainment with rough laughter. Then the strings of a score of other crossbows twanged and the bolts thudded home in the backs of half the men standing, sending them staggering and crumpling to the ground, some of them clutching vainly at the stub ends of the arrows and howling in pain.

A few of the standing brigands turned uncertainly, drawing swords and reaching for axes or hunting spears, but Juan had already cast his crossbow aside and was in among them with his longsword in one hand and a short, broad-bladed dagger in the other, the Basque taking up his usual protective position to Juan's right and a little behind him, swinging a double-bladed battle axe over his head and bellowing like a wounded bull. One bandit with a matted black beard and flaming eyes lunged at Juan with a short spear, but Juan deflected the point with his dagger and, with the same smooth motion, slashed his throat with the tip of his sword, sending a jet of dark blood down the front of the man's filthy grey tunic. The Basque neatly lopped the legs off the next man at the knees, while the other militiamen pressed forward their attack on either side, and Asco chased down one of the bandits who attempted to flee, first tripping him up and tearing out his throat with his great fangs while the man vainly flailed with his arms and legs until he lay still. The man who had been raping the woman was struggling to his feet when Juan ran him through from behind, and he fell heavily back on her, starting her screaming at an even higher pitch as she struggled to free herself from the corpse.

Juan could feel his heart beating faster. In fact, it was times like these that were the only ones when he was certain that his heart was beating at all. He could smell the trees, the dust in the air, the smoke from the fire, and, above all, the unmistakable scent of fear all around him as he could not have done moments before. He could *see* everything about him and he knew just what every man there would do. He knew when a brigand would raise a shield, thrust with a spear, turn to run moments before the man did it. And he knew what his own men would do, apart from his shouted commands, he led them through the force of his own spirit, willing them into the right position at the right time, moving them up on the flanks, standing fast in the center, and they responded like his own arms and legs. He knew when one of his men might falter and could spur him on with a word or a look. God, he thought, thank you for this night, for this battle, for this life!

In a moment it was all over. More than half of the thirty-odd bandits were dead and the remainder, who were too drunk to realize what had happened, had been rounded up and each tied to an individual trees around the glade. The woman had finally disentangled herself from the dead thief and pulled some tatters of her clothes about her as she dragged herself over to the body of the other woman, perhaps her mother, moaning softly. The Basque was turning over the corpses one by one, looking hard into the dead faces.

"I recognize a couple of them," the Basque grunted. "Soldiers from Pacheco's army, I'd say."

"Did any get away?" Juan asked.

"I don't think so."

"Good, let's finish up here and get back home, it's getting cold."

Juan bent down and picked up a small wooden chest with a broken lid. He shook it and found half a dozen gold *dirhanes* which he slipped into his pouch, tossing the chest aside. He would need money to buy new armor and horses if the rumors were true that the new monarchs had pledged to carry on a war of final destruction against the Moors at Granada, and Juan had sworn that he would be a part of any such campaign. Besides, this was just due payment for his services, and the victims were Jews after all, so God alone knew whom *they* had stolen this money from to begin with.

Several men were forming a line about forty yards from where one of the prisoners was tied to his tree. First one, then another took turns firing their crossbows at the howling bandit. The first arrow hit him in the shoulder, the next in the groin, to the immense enjoyment of the militiamen.

"A fine of thirty *maravedis* for any man who misses completely," Juan shouted over the din.

He picked up his own crossbow, and grasped the iron lever under the stock and, with his huge strength, drew the string to its catch in one smooth pull. He placed a quarrel in the groove and took careful aim, sending the bolt directly into the man's heart, causing the other men to groan with disappointment as they moved off to the next target. The Basque, meanwhile, was busy hacking the finger off one of the corpses to get at a large silver ring, and he smiled at Juan as he walked past, winking playfully.

There were half a dozen horses and a couple of mules, which were also part of the legitimate booty, and the weapons of the bandits themselves, although they did not appear to be worth much, and Juan arbitrarily snatched the bridle of the healthiest looking horse as his share. At least it would be of some help on the farm. He kicked through the debris of the camp while the rest of the prisoners were being dealt with but found nothing else of value. The ignorant bandits had already guzzled most of the wine they had stolen and smashed the other casks, staining the ground red all around the fire, leaving hardly a sip. At least this was one band that wouldn't be preying on travelers in his district anymore, Juan thought grimly, and word the of little battle would spread through the taverns and inns hereabout, probably growing in the telling, and adding to Juan's reputation, which was all to the good.

He started walking back toward the horses along with most of his men and noticed two of them stooping over the woman, who was doubled over next to the dead woman, still sobbing. He thought for a moment that they were being unusually sensitive for hardened fighters until he saw one man grab her hands while the other threw up her skirts and prepared to mount her from behind as she began to shriek anew. Juan chuckled and shook his head. He knew that, when a man had his blood up from a fight, even a short one like this, there was no denying his appetites. Besides, the woman owed them a little something for saving her from certain death, to say nothing of the attentions of a lot more than two men. And, she *was* just a Jewess, after all.

There were still lights burning in the storehouse when Juan, the Basque and the two stewards wearily led their horses into the courtyard of the manor, just as the first streaks of dawn marbled the sky over the hills to the east. Juan left the horses for the groom to unsaddle and trudged through the door, unstrapping his armor as he went.

"The warrior returns!" bellowed his father, who was seated alone at a crude trestle table on which a wine jug and wooden cup stood. From the slurring of his words and the dark burgundy stain running down the front of the old man's chin and into the white of his beard, it looked as though he had kept himself well entertained during his wait. "And what have you brought us, the head of a Moorish prince on your lance?"

Juan tossed the leather purse onto the table. He had taken the liberty of hiding two of the gold *dirhanes* in a pocket of his tunic, for he would be needing the money himself if he ever did get to go on a proper campaign, and he could not bring himself to go to his father and beg for it later. "There's a good horse in the paddock, but they were only poor bandits."

"About forty of them," the Basque added brusquely from the doorway where he leaned casually. Although his status in the family was unclear, the Basque obviously considered himself more on the level of a distant relative than that of a servant. "You should have seen your son, sir. You would have been proud of the way he waded through that mob, hacking them left and right. No, there's no doubt of his parentage, none at all."

The old man swallowed hard, and Juan thought for a moment that he could see the glimmer of a tear in the corner of his red-rimmed eye. But then again, what with the wine and drool dribbling out of his mouth and the snot caking his moustache, the discharge of a little fluid, more or less, could not be seen as overly significant. The father sat there, wordlessly, for some time, then picked up the purse and hefted it.

"It's a shame I didn't train you as a carpenter, boy," he snarled. "At least you could have earned a living wage."

With that the old man rose unsteadily from the three-legged stool on which he had been seated and walked, very slowly and carefully, out of the room and up toward the main house.

Juan bit down hard on the finger of his glove, the veins at his temple bulging and his vision clouding over.

"That old goat," he hissed. "Whatever I do, it'll never be good enough for him. And him such a failure himself."

"But he did sit up waiting for you," the Basque offered, hanging his own breastplate from a hook on the wall. "You noticed that, didn't you?"

"He was just too drunk to get up out of the chair."

The Basque shook his head and sighed. "Speaking of which, there is nothing to cap off an evening of adventure like a little recreation." He grabbed Juan roughly by the arm and virtually dragged him back outside where they were just in time to prevent the stewards from unsaddling two of the horses.

It was nearly dawn by the time the riders reached the gates of Trujillo, whose sand-colored walls rose smoothly from the barren hill on which the town was perched. The gates were closed for the night, but a few copper coins were sufficient for the Basque to convince the guards to open a postern door and allow them into the town where they quickly disappeared down the dark, winding streets leading into the poorer quarter of town.

Juan had been extremely reluctant to make this foray with the Basque, and he had been making mumbled excuses about having a sore head, or a bruise from the fight, or how he had heard a rumor that there had been two cases of the plague in town in the past week, but the Basque ignored him and continued pulling him through the alleyways as one would lead a skittish horse. They finally came to the low door of a shabby house whose roof leaned drunkenly at an angle, and the Basque kicked at it until a raspy voice from within, which might have belonged to man or woman, growled at him to respect the sleep of honest folk.

"If there are any honest folk in there," the Basque replied brusquely, "then I'm clearly in the wrong place."

There was a harsh laugh, and the door finally scraped open, and a short, stocky woman of indeterminate age thrust her face out into the chill air, nostrils flaring, and eyes burning in the red glow of the fireplace within. Her hair was scattered in every direction, and her nightshirt had slipped off one shoulder, exposing nearly every inch of her immense, sagging breasts, but her snarl turned into a broad smile when she recognized the Basque, who held out his arms to her as a child to its mother.

"My king!" the woman bellowed in a muleteer's voice. "Why have you come so late? All the best wine has been drunk, the best stories told, and the best girls taken hours ago."

"How can you tell such lies, my sweet," the Basque purred, "when you stand here yourself before me?" and the two collapsed into each other's arms in helpless laughter as she pushed the door open wide for them to enter.

Juan had to duck his head to pass into the room, and even inside he could not quite stand erect amid the sooty beams that barely held up the sagging roof. There was a collection of roughhewn tables and chairs scattered about, all vacant now, but some still with pewter mugs and wine bottles on them. The place smelled of smoke, urine, vomit, sour wine, and sweat in more or less equal proportions, typical of a lower class tavern, and the only light came from the still-glowing embers in the hearth at the far end.

Despite the odor, Juan breathed a sigh of relief at the absence of the tavern's usual compliment of whores. It was not that Juan had any moral objection to sporting with any available female, but he had noticed that he was having a *problem* of late, the kind that he was far too young to have to worry about yet. Naturally, as befitted a young man of noble birth, even of the lower end of the nobility, Juan had made free on his father's hacienda with slave girls and maidservants, willing or not, ever since he was twelve years old. It was not until relatively recently, however, that he had had the money, or the inclination, to join his friends in sampling some of the loose women who plied their trade in town or in the traveling market. Even though his severely limited means had precluded his visiting the elegantly dressed, heavily perfumed women who catered to the officers of the garrison and successful merchants, the idea of being with a real *professional* had, at first, appealed to him, even as a sort of educational exercise, part of his coming of age. Besides that, his family could no longer afford many servants, and the only women now among them were older than his father and hardly more attractive.

Disastrously, however, Juan had experienced, on more than one occasion, a sudden loss of ardor and stamina when he found himself alone with one of these confident, even aggressive women, some of whom seemed even more eager than he for the coupling once they had had a look at his thickly muscled arms and broad shoulders. If the truth were told, a couple of them had even suggested that he would be welcome to visit them whether he had the price of their favors or not. Although he would enter into the encounter with the best will in the world, he often found himself either exploding uncontrollably far too early on or literally going numb and limp, *down there* at the most inopportune time. He knew that he had never had this trouble before, when he would drag some cowering serving girl into the pantry for a quick romp after dinner or catch a Moorish slave girl alone in the fields where he would throw her down on the newly turned earth for a little plowing of his own, as he liked to call it when laughing about it later with his friends.

Consequently, he had tried to make the most of his domestic opportunities to relieve his stress and to assure himself of his virility while avoiding possible embarrassment with the prostitutes, at least until he could figure out the cause of his dilemma and, perhaps seek out an apothecary who could suggest a potion that might resolve it, and when his family could no longer afford the servant girls, he had just preferred to do without. What terrified Juan the most was that, while the women with whom he had *failed* thus far had been fairly discreet, he had noted a look of mixed disdain and amusement in their eyes. He knew that these women gossiped endlessly, not just amongst themselves, but with their other customers as well, and there was nothing quite so humiliating to a Spanish male as the questioning of his masculinity. Why such rumors had nearly been enough to bring down King Enrique from the throne itself, hadn't they? And with Juan planning on a career as a soldier, he needed the respect and trust of his men, and everyone knew that no man would follow a virtual eunuch into battle!

So, Juan felt relieved to be able to growl that he would require at least a cup of wine before the Basque and their hostess wrestled each other into one of the back rooms, confident that he would not be called upon to *perform* that night. However, the woman leered openly at Juan, a thin string of drool dangling out of one corner of her largely toothless mouth, and she turned to shout down a narrow hallway that led back into the depths of the house.

"Carmen! Carmen, wake up! Look what a tasty morsel we have for your breakfast!" she cackled, nodding approvingly at Juan as if to take credit for reading his mind.

A small, slender, sleepy-eyed girl staggered into the room, running her fingers through her thick tangle of dark hair and pouting at the woman in annoyance. Her eyes opened wide at the sight of Juan, and her stagger turned miraculously into a hip-swaying saunter as she strolled right up to Juan and hooked her fingers inside his belt.

"I'll take this over eggs and bread any day," she cooed, running a long pink tongue over her full lips and pulling Juan to her. "Maybe a nice sausage," she added, as the Basque and the woman dissolved in gales of laughter as they disappeared down the hallway, bouncing roughly off the walls as they pulled frantically at each other's clothing.

The girl was none too clean, but then Juan was used to that, and she was pretty, with big brown eyes and pert breasts that strained at her night shirt. At least there wasn't a mob of drunken, bellowing soldiers or other local patrons crowding the inn, Juan thought, and he began to relax as the girl tugged at his sword belt, then at the laces of his breeches, backing toward another low doorway, pulling him along with her as her tongue provocatively wetted her lips.

Juan found himself in a gloomy room with a ceiling even lower than that of the main hall of the tavern, and the only illumination was the moonlight, which streamed in through a gaping hole in the roof. The only piece of furniture in the room was a bed, or really a large burlap sack filled with straw and piled with ragged blankets. Juan could hear the rats scuttling along the roof beams and could see the silhouette of one peering in at the edge of the hole in the roof, but he was far beyond worrying about such minor inconveniences now.

The girl giggled as she launched herself backward onto the bed, still grasping Juan's belt firmly, which pulled him down on top of her, her legs wrapped around his waist. With one hand, she now grabbed his hair and forced his face down between her breasts as she arched her shoulders forward and together to maximize her cleavage. With her other hand, she let go of his belt and began kneading his buttocks vigorously, all the while cooing to him and calling him her "brave knight."

Juan began kissing and licking as best he could, but she was holding his head so firmly that he could hardly move it, in fact, he could barely breathe. The tangle of bedding had now trapped his arms, preventing him from getting his balance, and he began to get an uneasy feeling in his stomach. Suddenly, the girl twisted to one side and effortlessly flipped his body off hers, allowing her to get at his belt, which she undid with practiced rapidity, pulling down his breeches to his knees in one smooth motion. She they reached up under his long shirt and grabbed him painfully with her muscular hand, and Juan involuntarily jerked back.

There was a pause, that probably did not last more than a second, but it seemed to Juan as if time were standing still. The girl had stopped her giggling as she took hold of his flaccid member, giving it a couple of half-hearted strokes. The she slowly lifted her head, looking into his face with her large, dark eyes before she exploded with laughter.

"What's this?" she chortled. "I know you can lead a cow with either a prod or a rope, but there's only one kind of tool that's of any use for this kind of work, and you seem to have brought the wrong one."

She jokingly waggled the limp organ from side to side as if trying to wake it up, then bounded off the bed and took a step toward the door shouting, "Maribel! Come and have a look at this!"

Juan spun the girl around by the shoulder and caught her full in the face with his open hand. She staggered under the force of the blow, but Juan hit her with the backstroke and then once more forehanded with the same snake-like speed he used when sword fighting. A mist of blood and saliva sprayed out of her mouth, along with two of her teeth, and Juan snatched up a handful of the girl's hair to keep her from falling.

The knife blade glinted in the moonlight, almost too fast to see, but Juan had known that these girls always carried a dagger, and he caught her wrist with his free hand, snapping the bones with a sharp twist, causing the girl to gasp in pain, too stunned to scream. She looked up at him now, but there was no longer any amusement in her eyes, not even the brief flash of anger he had seen, just sheer terror, and Juan could suddenly feel himself rising, rising uncontrollably, and he smiled.

He threw the girl back onto the bed, and she whimpered, trying to hold her injured arm out of his way, a slender white sliver of bone clearly visible protruding from the skin. He flung her skirts up and plunged into her, but something was missing. With one powerful hand, he encompassed her throat, squeezing slowly but inexorably, watching her eyes roll back in her head and her breath come in shallow croaks in time with his frenzied pumping.

When he was finished, the girl lay motionless where he left her, legs splayed and head cocked at an unnatural angle. There was the sound of arguing and scuffling coming from beyond the door, but Juan just sat on the edge of the bed, his head thrown back as he breathed deeply and savored this feeling of total satisfaction. Finally, the door burst open, and the older woman shoved her way in, thrusting the half-naked Basque to one side, as she rushed to the girl. She lifted the girl's head gently and then recoiled at the touch, crossing herself repeatedly and mumbling prayers under her breath.

"Murderer!" she hissed, turning her dark eyes on Juan, who looked at her as if she had accused him of taking an extra slice of bread.

"What happened?" the Basque was asking, and Juan could see that the tousled heads of a couple of other curious tenants were peering around the doorframe.

"The little bitch pulled a knife on me," he responded calmly. "You know how these gypsy thieves are." He nodded toward the slender blade lying on the floor near the wall.

The woman was wailing, rubbing her hands, bobbing up and down at the waist, and the Basque was casting nervous glances in her direction and at the onlookers in the hallway.

"Do you have any gold?" he asked in a whisper, and Juan casually dug out one of the gold pieces he had taken from the bandits.

The Basque rushed over and pressed the coin into the woman's hand. "If we hear any more of this affair, it'll be steel that you'll be earning, not gold," he growled.

But the woman had amazingly overcome her grief when she felt the weight of the coin and had had a chance to test it with her few good teeth. She now busied herself with tidying up the bed and with flapping her skirts to shoo away the other tenants while the Basque grabbed Juan firmly by the arm and led him out into the night, their sword belts thrown over their shoulders as they both hitched up their pants as they walked.

As they hurried up the street, Juan turned to gaze back at the tavern and with a sigh said, "Thank you, my friend."

"I could not have done less, sir," the Basque said, still whispering. "It might not have gone well with either of us if the town authorities had shown up to look into the matter. A death, even that of a whore, can sometimes prove troublesome if you're not a person of influence, so I had to get you out of there in a hurry, and we'd better not show our faces in this place for some time."

"No," Juan said absently, "not for getting me out. Thank you for bringing me." He sighed and a contented smile spread across his face.

The Basque did not reply, but just looked long and hard at Juan with one shaggy eyebrow raised halfway up his forehead.

GRANADA

Book Two

1482

GRANADA

Chapter One

Segovia

Raquel had long since gotten over her awe of being at court. The more she learned of the pettiness, the personal weaknesses, of even the wealthiest and most powerful nobles, with lineages reaching back to the days of the Visigothic kings, the less they had appeared to her to have been selected by God to rule other men than the least of her father's laborers. She had grown up to be a beautiful woman, if the attentions paid to her by the male courtiers was anything to go by, and her apparent lack of interest in them had only made her all the more attractive a prize in the eyes of the bored young men whose only regular source of entertainment was their continual competition for *conquests* among the ladies of the court.

She could not say that she had been unhappy in her years at court. Although the only person in whose company she felt completely at ease was that of her maid Maria,

Raquel had even made some actual friends, notably Hernando de Talavera, a middle-aged priest of the Hieronymite Order who had recently taken over from the grim Tomás de Torquemada as Isabel's holy confessor. He was a kind and gentle man, not at all given to diatribes against either the Jews or the *conversos* as his predecessor had been, although the rumor was that this was because he himself was of *converso* stock. There was also a credible rumor that Torquemada also had Jewish blood back on his father's side, but that fact had hardly stopped him from launching the most vicious attacks conceivable against the Jews or their descendants or from promoting laws concerning *limpieza de sangre*, purity of blood, that would exclude *conversos* from many key government and Church posts.

Raquel generally attempted to avoid the company of Isaac Abravanel and Abraham Seneor, Isabel's Jewish political and financial advisors, although both had spent considerable time with her father working on his plans for capitalizing an armaments industry for the crown. She did like to listen in on their conversations on any topic, when she could do so unobtrusively, as she considered their thoughts to be so much more, enlightening than the mundane gossip of most of the courtiers. However, given the suspicions of Torquemada and others like him about the existence of a network of secret Judaizers in the kingdom, Raquel thought it most prudent not to have herself associated with them openly. And she felt ashamed of that fact.

Isabel continued to confide in her, perhaps less so now that the civil wars were over and the throne appeared to be more secure, especially since the death of Juan of Aragon, Fernando's father, the previous year, had given the couple undisputed title to the crowns of both Castile and Aragon, as well as that of Naples and Sicily, arguably making the most powerful political unit in all of Europe. The queen appeared to value Raquel's straightforward manner and her commonsense approach to all sorts of problems with none of the selfish angling for favors that was so common among the nobles at court, and she often used Raquel as a sounding board for her ideas on everything from the color scheme on a kerchief the queen was embroidering to how best to distribute the tax burden in the provinces. Long familiarity with the royal household had made the royal family all appear a little less god-like to Raquel than they had at first, but it still gave Raquel something of a thrill to be in a position to speak frankly with her sovereign, and she took some pleasure at the ill-disguised jealousy of some of the courtiers to her unlimited access to the royal presence, and their dismay at her unwillingness to trade on that access in exchange for personal favors, or even money. Hardly a day went by that she was not offered some fine piece of jewelry by some old man or, more crudely, the thinly veiled promise of unlimited sexual satisfaction by some young one, if only she could manage to place this or that document in the hands of the queen or arrange a personal interview for some supplicant with an obviously just case to plead, but she shunned them all with an impartiality that was all the more infuriating to them.

What Raquel missed most was her father. While he did spend some time at court, consulting with Fernando and others of his closest military advisors about his innovations for the royal artillery, he spent far too long, sometimes weeks on end, supervising the casting of guns, the smelting of metal, and the production of gunpowder. Raquel, on the other hand, was obliged to travel with the court from one end of the kingdom to the other, staying a few days to a few months in each of the major cities only to move on when local supplies of food for the vast host of people and animals began to run low or rumors of an onset of the plague sent the court flying to healthier surroundings. Raquel was no longer a child, of course, and her father did spend all of his free time with her, when he did happen to be in the same city as the court, sometimes just talking about family matters or sharing with her his new ideas for his craft, but she still felt disconnected in a fundamental way. What she truly cherished when her father was around was observing the Sabbath with him, or other Jewish holidays. Raquel knew that there were other clandestine Jews at court, and even knew or strongly suspected who some of them were, but she trusted none of them enough to reveal herself to them and preferred to console herself with saying her Hebrew prayers at night in the privacy of her own quarters. It was only now that she realized just how wise a policy that strict secrecy had been.

There had been talk of the establishment of an Inquisition for years, but this in itself was nothing new. Inquisitions had traditionally been nothing more than investigations, either under royal or papal auspices, usually related to obscure matters of theological practice or land title. The new Inquisition was, however, specifically intended to root out individuals who claimed to be part of the Catholic faith while actually practicing Judaism, or, more dangerously, attempting to woo others away from the True Faith of Christianity or otherwise undermine the power of the Church. Even though this certainly struck close to home for Raquel and her father, the fact that the Papal Bull authorizing the Inquisition had been signed in 1478 and that nothing had yet been done about formally establishing it had given Raquel's father the confidence that it was no more than an empty gesture meant to satisfy Torquemada and the crowds of lower class fanatics that were periodically stirred up by itinerant preachers to violence against Jews and *conversos* alike.

Raquel had never been so sure of that. It seemed to her that the delay in enacting the bull had more to do with an effort by Torquemada, who was clearly the favored candidate for the post of Inquisitor General, and Isabel, his mentor, to ensure that the Inquisition would be under royal, not papal, authority, that the Catholic Kings would be able to appoint and dismiss inquisitorial officials at will and influence both the nature of cases studied and the outcome of those cases. The Pope had not surrendered this perquisite lightly, but Isabel had recently won out on this point, and now the wheels of the process had finally been put into motion. Raquel recognized that the Inquisition would be used, less as a means of seeking spiritual purity for the Christian community in Castile than as a means of enhancing the power of the monarchy. The danger of that was that Torquemada was apparently using the same tactics as Raquel and her father, to make himself indispensable to the power of the crown of Castile as a means of getting their blessing to pursue his agenda of religious fanaticism.

Raquel had not been impressed with the alleged reason behind the imposition of the new Inquisition. Several years before, in 1478, a young Christian gentleman who was allegedly having an affair with a Jewish girl in Seville, claimed to have stumbled on a collection of *conversos* performing mysterious rites which only later were explained to him were ceremonies of the Jewish faith. There had been a strong implication that these rites were not merely holy sacraments of another faith, but were somehow connected to black magic and ultimately designed to destroy both Christianity in general and the people of Spain in particular. This had been the justification for the Papal Bull authorizing the Inquisition which arrived within a matter of months, but it took nearly two more years before the first tribunal was set up, suggesting that the indignation felt by the Spanish sovereigns which caused them to use their influence to get such quick action from the Pope, was more feigned than real.

Even then, the effects of the Inquisition seemed to be minimal. It was not until the beginning of 1481 when a supposed conspiracy by *converso* leaders had been discovered in Seville, the only city originally affected, that the trials got underway in earnest. The conspirators allegedly had planned, in order to hide their clandestine worship and practice of black magic, to massacre the inquisitors themselves and stage an armed rebellion against the crown, but their scheme was exposed at the last moment by the loose lips of the daughter of one of them who was having an affair with a young man of an Old Christian family (and the inclusion of this romantic angle in this story as well, of which Spanish poets were so fond, gave Raquel all the more cause to suspect creative writing rather than fact). Still, the local authorities had acted, arrested the suspects, and forced them to confess under torture, revealing the names of other conspirators and caches of arms and money to be used in the rebellion.

By the end of the year, nearly three hundred men and women had been burned at the stake and another hundred condemned to perpetual imprisonment, their family property confiscated for the crown and the Church. The fact that a political act, that of rebellion, had been required to get the process moving gave Raquel the impression that this was all a political maneuver and had little, if anything to do with religion, her mind having become very attuned to the nuances of the competition for power over the past eight years. It might well have been that the crown was using the Inquisition to uncover and destroy common political opponents, of which there never was a lack. The only problem was that, if the *converso* community was somehow becoming identified with opposition to the crown, that could have negative ramifications for Raquel and her family as well.

This feeling was reinforced by the crown's other actions against the nobility. Since Seville was one of the leading *converso* centers of Castile, many *conversos* on seeing the frightening possibilities for the Inquisition, sought to avoid the attention of the inquisitors, whether charges had actually been brought against them or not, by fleeing the city and taking refuge with powerful nobles in other parts of the country with whom they had influence. In ordinary times, being under the protection of a nobleman like the Marquis of Cadiz, who was known to be a friend of the *conversos* and who wielded tremendous military power in Andalusia, would have been enough to protect anyone from anything, including direct charges of treason. But, in this case, the crown had immediately issued a decree that anyone, literally *anyone*, found to be harboring fugitives from the Inquisition would be investigated by that august body themselves and have their lands and property confiscated (supposedly to be returned in the unlikely event that the investigation, making liberal use of torture, turned up no negative findings.) Where previous summonses calling for the surrender of a noble's protégés to royal authority would have earned nothing more than a scornful snort from a man like the Marquis, there was something inherently sinister and pervasive about the Inquisition that terrified everyone. The Marquis alone sent back eight thousand men and women who had sought refuge on his lands, to face the Inquisition in Seville.

While legal proceedings of one sort or another had long been used to intimidate political opponents of the crown, there was something different about the Inquisition. For one thing, although the normal proceedings of the judicial system in Spain were hardly above reproach, under the Inquisition, the vaguest hearsay evidence was fully acceptable, and the accused had no opportunity of even learning the identity of hostile witnesses and thus being able to point out to the tribunal that a particular individual might have a personal motive for making false testimony. The best that the court would allow was for the accused to make up a list of all people he or she knew who *might* have a grudge against them, leaving it to the inquisitors to sort through this list to determine whether testimony might be false. Needless to say, many victims of the system chose to name virtually everyone they had ever met and to concoct the wildest possible stories of misdeeds by all of them to discredit any testimony they might have made. These proceedings themselves became gold mines of information for further investigations by the Inquisitors, since the most telling accusation one could make of a potential hostile witness was that that person was actually a secret Judaizers him or herself.

Another daunting aspect of the Inquisition was that confessions obtained under torture were perfectly admissible. In fact, since the supposed main purpose of the Inquisition was the saving of the soul of persons who were accused of having fallen away from the True Faith, the Inquisitors considered it their duty to get the victim to cleanse his or her conscience by making a full confession, not only of their own wrong-doings but those of everyone else the victim might know. In fact, a simple confession given early in the process was generally not considered sufficient, and it was common for the subject to be given a healthy dose of physical encouragement to allow the Inquisitors' minds to rest easy that he or she had actually revealed all the relevant information. Since the Church officially frowned on confessions obtained through torture, however, the accused would be allowed to rest for a few days after breaking and then be required to repeat the confession of "his own free will". If the accused should happen to gain new strength during this period and recant the confession, the torture would begin all over again until his "free will" coincided with what the Inquisitors had in mind.

This form of jurisprudence might not have appeared so harsh in a society in which, until relatively recently, held trials based on armed combat or the holding of red hot irons to determine the truth of testimony. What made this new form of Inquisition most terrifying, however, and different from anything that had gone before, was the extent to which literally everyone in society was made a party to it. Children were forced to implicate their parents, wives their husbands, servants their masters, merchants their customers, and anyone later found to have been *likely* to have known about a person's anti-Christian practices would also fall under suspicion, enough to earn them a trip to the torture chambers in their own right. This turned all of Castile, and later Aragon and Portugal, into one vast network of spies or potential spies in the service of the Holy Office.

There was normally a period of grace allowed, usually about thirty days, after the arrival of the Inquisition to a region, during which the residents were encouraged through sermons given at Mass, to search their consciences and determine for themselves whether they, or anyone they might know, were guilty of a violation of the laws of the Church. Those who came forward during this period and who made a convincing case to the Inquisitors of their sincerity before charges were levied were guaranteed to be spared the worst of the institution's arsenal of persuasions, virtually regardless of the nature of their transgression, generally receiving no more than a modest fine and some form of public penitence, such as wearing a hair shirt and parading about the town with a sign hung round their necks proclaiming their failings. However these periods of grace might have been originally intended, they turned out to be a very powerful psychological weapon, forcing people to agonize over what *might* have been or might yet be reported against them under torture and calculating whether it might not be best to preemptively confess in order to avoid the necessity of facing torture and then proving their absolute innocence to the Inquisition itself.

Interestingly, the one group that was almost entirely exempted from the horrors of the Inquisition was the Jews themselves. Since the Inquisition was designed to cleanse the Christian community of false converts, those who openly practiced the Jewish faith, by definition did not fall within its jurisdiction. However, even the Jews were occasionally dragged in, albeit indirectly, in that rabbis were strongly admonished to reveal to the investigators the names of those people who, while ostensibly having converted to Christianity, continued to worship in the Jewish fashion, visiting the synagogues, sending traditional gifts of oil, or calling on the rabbis to perform weddings or burials. Failure to report such activities would amount to something very close to treason, and the reluctant rabbi might find himself being tortured and imprisoned, perhaps by the civil authorities instead of the Inquisition, but the difference would be largely academic. Occasionally, a rabbi would succumb to the pressure, mainly in the form of threats against the overt Jewish community, and would testify before the Inquisition, but even this was usually limited to cases where the Inquisitors were already convinced of the person's guilt, and the rabbi was merely providing confirmation for the record.

As with most other tragedies that befall the human race, there was also money to be made in the Inquisition. Whether the convicted party was ultimately burned at the stake or merely forced to perform some sort of humiliating penance, marching about town in a tall conical hat for example, the penalty almost always imposed by the court was the confiscation of all or most of the person's property for the benefit of both the Holy Inquisition itself and for the crown. Since the confiscations normally took place immediately upon the opening of the case, there was thus a strong incentive for the court to find the defendant guilty. To prevent the holy fathers who formed the investigative panel itself from having to intervene in such mundane secular manners as the seizure of land or livestock, the special post of *regidor* of the Inquisition was created, occupied by a layman, who would take charge of the assessment of the accused person's goods, their seizure, and their sale, with the proceeds to be deposited in the royal treasury, less a certain percentage as commission for the *regidor* himself. Since it was the *regidor* who determined the total value of the property, there was ample room for him to make huge profits by grossly undervaluing the goods seized. It came as no real surprise to Raquel that Tobias, the *converso* tax farmer from Cordoba and her father's partner in the arms manufactory, had eagerly taken on the additional job of *regidor* for that city.

Many *conversos* chose to flee the country to more amenable surroundings such as in Genoa or the Low Countries, but hundreds were spotted along the roads or in the ports which swarmed with members of the *Santa Hermandad* on the prowl and brought back in chains. Since it was known than such escapees would likely be carrying as much of their portable wealth as possible with them, they were also prime targets for bandits of which new bands were constantly springing up, and these often worked in concert with local lords, townspeople, and innkeepers who kept them informed of the passage of promising groups through their areas.

"I don't think I can stand this," Raquel had whispered to her father during one of his visits. "Every day we see or hear of people we know who have been arrested and interrogated. Some of them I know are innocent, and a few only get some disgusting penance, but too many have been sentenced to burn."

"That will not happen to us," her father assured her with a curt tone that implied that he did not want further discussion of the topic.

"How can you say that when you know that we are *guilty*!" she countered, her voice rising in spite of her fear.

"We are guilty of nothing but living by God's law as best we can, child," he responded with a harshness in his voice that shocked Raquel like a slap across the face, but he softened almost immediately. "Come and look at this."

He pulled from his travel pack a metal plate on which was embossed a round shield with the symbols of Castile,

Leon, and Aragon arranged in a triangular pattern, with a lance and a long cannon barrel crossed behind it.

"This is the mark that I am putting on all of the cannon that I am casting, the mark of our house," he explained.

She shrugged.

"Do you see these little points here around the edge of the shield?"

There were six small triangular protrusions, evenly spaced around the circle. She nodded. He took a piece of charred wood from the fireplace and sketched lines connecting the edges of the points across the face of the shield, forming a Star of David.

"You see, the crown protects us. We are still Jews, just living under protection, under their shield."

Raquel shuddered and put her hands to her face. "I feel like I'm about to explode, at war with myself. I don't think I could stand up to torture."

"You must not," her father said coldly, pulling down her hands and staring into her face. "You must not, do you hear me? If they arrest you, confess. Confess it all, at once. I am your father. I made you a Jew and kept you from being a Christian. Tell them you're ready to convert sincerely now, and they will spare you."

"And you? And mother?"

"There's nothing you can do about that, so there's no point in worrying about it. If you, or any of us are arrested, we will all be suspected in any case. In fact, we would probably all be arrested at the same time. The only thing is to avoid the torture they will undoubtedly use just to get you to say what they already know. Say it first, and save yourself."

He said this as an order, not a plea, a statement of something that had to be.

Maria suddenly appeared in the doorway to Raquel's room, and Raquel gasped at what she might have heard, and she had to ask herself what Maria would do, even after her long years of service, almost as a member of the family, if she had heard something. Raquel had considered more than once the possibility of confiding in Maria, who had done more to raise her than Raquel's own mother, but she could not bring herself to impose that kind of burden on an innocent person, to force her to choose between the dictates of her faith and her loyalty to her adopted family, and Raquel had kept her silence unbroken. But now the stocky woman was out of breath from having just run up the stairs, and their was nothing in her florid face to hint that she had overheard anything..

"Her majesty is looking for you, mistress. And it appears to be a matter of some official nature, although it's certainly beyond my place to make such judgements. All I can say is that everyone else seems to be taking this matter very seriously, so, if I were you, I'd make my best speed down to her chambers before we're all in deep trouble."

Raquel had to smile at Maria's way of squeezing a five-second message into ten minutes of conversation. Her father took a kerchief from the pocket of his waistcoat and daubed at the corners of her eyes.

"It won't happen," he whispered. "War is coming. War against the Moors and war against the nobles if they try to resist the power of the throne. The crown needs my cannon to consolidate their power. No one else can deliver what I can, and they all know it. Let them have their Inquisition. There will be plenty of other victims around to slake the thirst for blood of any monster, and there are fatter sheep for them to fleece and slaughter. Now, off with you and make yourself just as indispensable as I am. It's our best defense."

Raquel gathered up her skirts and hurried from the room, following in Maria's broad wake, down a narrow spiral staircase built into the wall of the castle and out into the courtyard where Isabel already sat mounted with several other ladies of the court and her confessor, Hernando de Talavera, the only one who smiled briefly at Raquel's arrival. Everyone else in the party wore expressions of solemnity and concentration. Isabel herself was deep in hushed conversation with a secretary of the court who stood next to her mount.

"There is a ceremony we must attend," one of the women said curtly to Raquel as a groom helped her up into her side-saddle, and the little entourage rode out the gate in a column of twos, with a squadron of lancers leading the way and another behind.

They rode for half an hour to a large Dominican monastery, a massive red brick structure, north of the city and left their horses at the stable. The grounds of the monastery were almost deserted, but the church at the center of the complex was crammed with people, monks, government officials, even peasants from the countryside, and the walls were lined with soldiers of the *Santa Hermandad* in their sinister black and red capes. At the center of the nave the pews had been cleared away and a large dais raised there on which sat a panel of three Dominican friars in their black robes, one of whom Raquel recognized as Torquemada himself. She could tell that he was taller than the others, and gaunt, with a close-cropped black beard, sunken cheeks, and dark rings under his eyes. Where bishops and even common priests often wore thick rings of gold and fine robes, he wore nothing more than the coarse homespun brown robe of his order in an ostentatious display of self-denial. Even while the entourage was at the back of the crowded church, with all of the occupants hurrying to rise as the queen entered, it seemed to Raquel as if Torquemada's burning dark eyes sought her out alone, and a shaft of burning yellow light angled down from one of the tall side windows, illuminating Torquemada like the image of a saint in a religious portrait, probably not by accident, Raquel surmised. Several benches upholstered in red velvet had been set against one wall near the dais for Isabel and her group. Raquel's blood ran cold. This was an *auto de fe*, a trial of the Inquisition.

In a cleared area in front of the dais was a low wooden bench on which sat a man, hunched over in a yellow smock with red lettering on front and back and a tall conical yellow cap. He was a large man with long grey hair dangling down from under the cap, and he stared at the floor blankly. Raquel moved slightly to one side as someone brushed up against her, and she turned to see Hernando de Talavera alongside her, leaning close but not taking his eyes from the proceedings.

"That's Diego Henriquez, the treasurer of the cathedral of Cordoba, and a *converso*," he whispered. "He is an important man, which is probably why he's being tried alone and not in a big group like they did in Sevilla."

Next to Henriquez stood a slender young man dressed in a tight fitting black velvet suit with gold piping and a stiff white lace collar about his neck and soft doeskin slippers on his feet, very much in fashion, too rich to be a priest. His skin was smoother and more fair than Raquel's own, so he was not a soldier either as he had obviously not spent much time out in the sun and wind. He must be a lawyer, she thought.

"That would be the *Promotor Fiscal*," Hernando continued, "the prosecutor who is supposedly the advisor to the clerical tribunal, but that is just keeping up the fiction that the Inquisition is a Church, and not a governmental organ."

Gesturing with his chin at the robed figures on the platform, he went on. "There are two inquisitors, a jurist and a theologian. Torquemada would be the theologian. Then there's the assessor who valued the property of the accused, and a constable who is in charge of the *familiars*," he nodded toward a pair of thick-waisted older men standing off to one side and then to another cluster of alert young gentlemen at the foot of the platform, all of whom wore swords and daggers at their belts. "They are to protect the inquisitors from assassins." They were not wearing mail or armor, but rather fine court dress like the *Promotor*, and their weapons were more of an ornamental than of a martial variety, so Raquel suspected that the threat to the security of the tribunal was really not considered to be all that great, and their presence was more to give the impression that the Holy Office was actually involved in a war with an evil power than to stand in the way of any perceived danger.

Hernando had a weariness in his voice, and Raquel glanced at him out of the corner of her eye. She knew that the friar was over fifty years of age, making him almost elderly in comparison to most of the members of the court, but now his jowls had begun to sag, and there was a grayness to his complexion that made him appear even older. He was a large bear of a man, his brown robes making him look all the more like an forest animal that had been dragged prematurely from his winter hibernation, and the shaggy hair that ringed his monkish tonsure was heavily flecked with gray.

Hernando continued with his commentary. "The prosecutor is just finishing the reading of his official 'complaint,' and the witnesses, if there were any, must have already been heard. It is now the turn of the accused to make his answer, or his confession," he added with some irony in his voice.

"Has he confessed already then?" Raquel asked, since this was her first actual attendance at an *auto de fe.*

"I'm sure he has, or the wouldn't have been brought here. The tribunal doesn't like surprises," Hernando sighed. "It breaks my heart that there are people about in the world who might do so much to try to undermine the Church and to do harm to true believers. The Church has a right, even a duty, to defend itself and its people. I'm only sorry that this right is being perverted and used as a means of gaining earthly power. Whenever there is money involved, it brings out the worst in human nature, I'm afraid." He was now leaning very close to Raquel, barely whispering in her ear.

"But the Pope has blessed the Holy Office, has he not?" she asked, trying to keep the sarcasm out of her voice.

"Not this, nothing like this. The Pope fought against these excesses as best he could." Hernando made a helpless sweep of his hands. "Of course the Church is right to rid itself of heretics, even, if necessary, by killing them, although every effort should be made to show a person the error of his ways and to bring him back into the fold. *That* is what our Lord would have done. He talked of rejoicing more of the one stray lamb recovered than of the ninety-and-nine who did not wander, but the machinery of the Inquisition is just too efficient a way of gathering wealth and power, for the crown and the Church both, and using the process for that purpose has been a fatal misstep, I believe. As with most little sins against the will of God, it has opened the door to even greater ones, when men like Torquemada can use the institution to attack people just for being what they are."

"Are you talking about Jews?"

"*Conversos*, yes. Even though almost no family in Spain nowadays is completely free of Jewish blood, not mine, not yours, not even those of the King and Queen or Torquemada himself, I sense a desire to burn out what

Torquemada sees as a taint on himself by literally burning it out of society as a whole. It's all very sad."

Raquel was suddenly terrified that this priest was confiding in her in this way. She had known him for some time, in a superficial way, ever since he had become the Queen's confessor, and she could not help liking and respecting him. But what he was saying was virtual treason. Isabel and Fernando had badgered the Pope for years for a Bull authorizing the Inquisition and then had fought over the right for the crown to name its officials. There had been repeated complaints from Rome about the brutality of the torture used in the interrogations and accusations that the entire enterprise was primarily a means of raising funds for the crown, but these had largely been ignored despite the ever-present threat of excommunication that such an action posed. And this was not a threat that could be taken lightly, even beyond the immediate risk of one's dying suddenly without the benefit of last rites, at a time when insidious plagues were always stalking the land, and spending eternity in perdition. There was also a political aspect for a sovereign in that excommunication essentially freed the sovereign's vassals from any duty and, in fact, demanded them to cease their support for the crown as long as the ban was in force. In fact, the faithful were not supposed to have any dealings with someone under ban of excommunication, even to speak with them in the street, or they themselves would suffer excommunication and not be allowed to hear Mass or take communion or anything. But Popes had been excommunicating kings for centuries for one reason or another, and the absence of sudden bolts of lightning striking the crowned heads had done something over the years to lessen the impact of the threat.

"But what about the Jews being responsible for the plague and doing black magic to try to wipe out the Christians?" she asked teasingly. "I've heard those stories often enough, and from the pulpit too. Why should a man of the Church be worried about what happens to the Jews, or people of Jewish blood, for that matter if even half of what we are told is true?"

Hernando shook his head sadly. "Only the basest of the common rabble believe that the Jews or *conversos* could have anything to do with the plague. Those of us who have studied the matter of disease seriously know that suffering on such a scale could only be the work of God, a great punishment for a whole people for a great sin. It's foolish, and even a little barbaric, to believe that there is anything that man could do to *cause* something like that. I'm really shocked that you would say such a thing, Raquel. I understood you to be something of a woman of science and learning." He turned toward her with his eyebrows raised.

She just shrugged. "It's just all the hatred about these days. One doesn't know what to believe anymore."

"What makes it all the worse," Hernando went on, "is that this unfortunate purging of the body of Christianity is being done in such a good cause. You may not be old enough to really remember the terror of the civil wars, with every little duke or baron virtually running his own little kingdom and warring with everyone else, but the strength of this royal house has put an end to that, so what could be holier than a measure designed to strengthen that house and ensure the peace it has provided to the people? Men can travel now between cities without the protection of a whole army, trade has resumed, farmers can sell their produce and merchants their wares, and everyone is better off. And if their majesties are looking to gather funds, it is only for a just war against the Moor, and what could be a more noble goal than to free the last of Spanish soil from the domination of the infidel and to free the thousands of Christian souls held captive there? And if a few have to suffer in the process, perhaps that's not too high a price to pay." He shook his head heavily as if unconvinced by his own words. "I can only thank the Lord that I do not have to make those kinds of decisions."

Hernando stopped talking suddenly and looked with apprehension at Raquel. She could see in his eyes a questioning expression, and it occurred to her that only now did he realize just how freely he had been talking. She reached over and squeezed his arm reassuringly. Perhaps even priests need a confessor now and again, she thought. But a worrisome thought crossed her own mind then. Why had he chosen her? Was there something about her that told him that she shared his doubts and would not betray him? It was true, but if it was that obvious to him, might it not be obvious to someone else? That would be most dangerous. She turned again to face the dais and found Torquemada still apparently glaring directly at her, and she felt a shiver of fear ripple over her body.

One of the officials nudged the prisoner now, and he began to speak without raising his head, like a student reciting a memorized lesson. His voice was a dull croak, barely audible over the shuffling of feet and soft muttering of the crowd in the nave. Torquemada swept the room with a harsh gaze, and all speaking instantly ceased.

"I took a communion wafer from the cathedral and hid it in my shoe."

"And why did you do that?" the prosecutor asked looking out over the heads of the crowd and not at the accused, a smug smile playing across his face, confident of the justice of his work. It was clear that the answer would not be a surprise to him.

"To perform unholy rites and to use the power of the Host to conjure up demons," he murmured in reply. "But the wafer began to bleed and my foot was dyed red, which led to the discovery of my crime because I could not wash it off.

My wife saw the blood and asked me about it. I found that I could not speak to answer her. My mouth moved but no words would come, and she duly reported me to the Holy Office."

"The power of the Lord," the prosecutor said with a little bow.

"Let the tribunal see the foot," Torquemada intoned from the dais.

"Unfortunately, Father," the prosecutor paused to clear his throat and said, again to the open air, "the procedures in putting the question to the accused, who was initially reluctant to cooperate," and he paused to cast a scolding glance at the prisoner, "included the use of 'the boot'."

Raquel craned her neck and could now see that both of the prisoner's legs were wrapped in blood-soaked rags, and she shuddered. She had heard of "the boot," a heavy wooden or metal mold-like device which was fitted over the victim's foot. Then either metal wedges would be driven in between the skin and the boot, shredding flesh and eventually crushing bone, or the boot would be filled with boiling oil or molten lead, until the victim chose to confess. The fact that both of the victim's feet had been worked on implied that he had held out a long time under interrogation, an occurrence that was generally viewed by the inquisitors as a sign of demonic interference rather than a suggestion of innocence and usually inspired them to ever more aggressive means of interrogation.

"I have been observing Jewish religious practices in secret," the man went on without waiting for further prompting. "I have made scornful comments about Our Savior. I have avoided eating the wholesome meat of pigs or rabbits. I have changed my linen on the Sabbath for no good reason, and I instructed my family that I wanted to be buried in the Jewish fashion when I should die. And I planned to convert my wife, my children, and even my servants into the Jewish faith as soon as I might be able to do so. But their faith was too strong for me," he added desperately, emotion appearing in his voice for the first time. "I failed in my plan. I did!"

The prosecutor ignored this minor outburst and scanned the crowd, as if daring anyone to suggest that the completeness of this confession could possibly be questioned.

"Do you freely confess these crimes of your own will?" Torquemada asked in a bored voice from the dais without looking at the accused.

"Yes, Father."

Hernando snorted softly and shook his head.

"Look around the room," he hissed to Raquel. "You don't see anyone that looks like a concerned friend or relative, do you? My bet is that the wife was tired of the man or had already found a lover and is using this procedure as a convenient means of making herself into a widow. I suspect that you'll find that a fair share of the poor fool's money will find its way into her purse as a reward for her *unshakable faith*."

"But the man made a point of protecting her, and his family," Raquel whispered back.

Hernando gave her a sidelong glance. "Perhaps he doesn't know. Perhaps he is concerned about his children. In any case, it makes one think that perhaps the wrong person is sitting on that bench if our purpose here is to root out evil."

"Then it is the decision of this court that you be relaxed on this day for your sins, and may God have mercy on your soul." Torquemada concluded lazily. "Do you wish to have the final rites of the True Church?"

"Yes, Father," the man answered almost indifferently.

Hernando sighed again. "Since the Church cannot legally sentence anyone to death, we have to use a code to indicate what kind of sentence we want the secular authorities to carry out. I assure you that there is nothing relaxing about what they have in mind for the prisoner."

Torquemada and the other members of the panel, whom Raquel noticed had not been consulted before the announcement of either the verdict or the sentence, rose and slipped out a side door of the church, while the prisoner was led into a small side chapel. Isabel and her group were then led out the main door of the church and outside the monastery walls to a large clearing in a field nearby. Hernando stopped just outside the door of the church and watched solemnly as the royal entourage moved away, then turned, his shoulders slumping and reentered the building. Raquel shuddered. She knew that members of the clergy were not allowed to attend the final act of an *auto de fe*.

Out in the field, four large, crude plaster statues of the four prophets from the Old Testament, Abraham, Moses, Isaiah, and Ezekiel, mute witnesses to the event, had been set up marking out a rough square. Raquel could see piles of ashes that had been swept off to one side, implying that this was not the first *auto de fe* held here recently. Benches had been set out for the queen and her party, with a clear view of the proceedings. Raquel walked slowly, hanging back in the group, focusing all of her strength on not vomiting from a mixture of fear and repulsion. From her vantage point, she watched the Queen, whose face was set in a solemn mask, and Raquel realized that this was apparently the first *auto de fe* that Isabel had attended in person as well. Other members of the royal party tried to make light conversation, but their efforts seemed more than a little strained.

After a brief wait, the crowd from the church came out in a body, surrounding the prisoner who was dragged between two burly *familiars* and hurled into an ox cart that stood near the door of the church. He was now wearing a new San Benito, the yellow smock decorated with a black St. Andrew's cross and the figures of dancing devils embroidered in red as a sign of his condemnation. The cart was apparently used in normal times to transport manure, and no effort had been made to clean it out for today's ceremony.

Beside the filth, the cart carried other cargo. Along with living victims, the Inquisition was perfectly happy to exhume corpses for trial, sentencing, and public burning, along with effigies of those who had escaped. Since a major goal of the court was to seize the property of the accused, the conviction of a corpse still entitled the Inquisition to appropriate estates, money, and furniture regardless of the innocence of the heirs, while corpses tended to make wonderfully complacent defendants. As a final indignity, the living prisoner would now ride to the *quemadero*, the place of burning, accompanied a corrupted, skeletal corpse, the mocking, lipless smile unaffected by this new punishment, and two paper maché figures, effigies representing victims of the Inquisition who had fled abroad to escape justice, each wearing a San Benito similar to that worn by the living victim with crudely lettered signs describing their sins.

The jubilant crowd sang hymns to the music of flutes and tambourines, and some danced ahead of the throng as if escorting performers at a fair. The prisoner slumped in the back of the tumbrel, wringing his hands and sobbing silently while two files of soldiers marched along flanking the cart to keep the crowd at a distance. It appeared that many of the spectators had taken the precaution of bringing along a supply of rotten fruit, stones, and even excrement, with which they pelted the prisoner as they screamed insults at him. Raquel watched one soldier smash a man to the ground with the butt of his spear when a clod of dung meant for the prisoner miscarried and splattered against the soldier's helmet. The other participants found this wildly amusing.

When the cart had finally covered the few hundred yards from the church to the place of execution, the cadaver and the effigies were tossed onto piles of kindling to one side where they would be disposed of separately. The living prisoner was taken to a tall stake that had been sunk at the center of the square and was tied firmly to it with lengths of chain. The *familiars* had to hold the man up until the chains could be wound under his arms to support his weight, and he moaned pitifully whenever one of his mangled feet touched the ground. Workmen quickly brought out bundles of dried sticks and began to pile them around the stake, and the man began to twitch and wail as if he could already feel the flames lapping at his skin, which delighted the crowd no end.

The prosecutor strode out to face the crowd and announced, "The initial reluctance of the prisoner to make his confession has inclined the tribunal to consider him *vehemente* and not to offer him the mercy of the garrote." He made a little derisive snort indicating the inevitability of this decision and walked to one side, making a casual gesture with his hand. Since the Church could not be associated with the shedding of blood, even indirectly, all of the penalties for apostasy and judaizing connected with the Inquisition had been calculated to inflict death without resorting to the more traditional (and arguably more merciful) beheading.

The city executioner in his black hood strode forward with a burning torch in his hand. Custody of the case had now been formally passed over completely to the civil authorities to carry out the sentence, explaining the lack of any clergy at the *quemadero*. Raquel found this abandonment of responsibility particularly distasteful and wished that Torquemada and his followers could be made to view their handiwork, although she doubted that the sight of this pathetic wreck of a man would have much impact on them after all.

"This is what you do, this is what you get!" bellowed the executioner in a rich baritone turning as he spoke so that his words would reach every corner of the audience. He took a long look around the crowd, bowed low to the queen, then faced the prosecutor, who nodded gravely. The executioner then plunged his flaming torch into the base of the pile of kindling.

The wood must have been treated with oil or tar, for the flames raced all the way around the ring of sticks and straw in an instant. The man watched the flames, as if fascinated, for an instant and then let out a high-pitched howling noise and began twisting violently one way and the other, in vain, against the chains that held him. The crowd cheered and laughed at his antics and began to toss little bundles of sticks onto the fire to help it along. Several of the court ladies turned their heads or shielded their faces with their fans as the man's smock caught fire, but Raquel dared not. Might it not be taken as a sign of sympathy for the prisoner? She glanced over at Isabel, who watched with cold detachment. At least she was not displaying any sign of enjoyment at the spectacle, Raquel thought.

The wood was very dry and gave off little smoke, and Raquel could see quite clearly through the wavering currents of hot air how the man's skin rose up in blisters over his face and arms. The blisters then burst and new ones arose, like the bubbling of the surface of a pot of soup. The man was making a kind of animal noise now, not screaming, just a hooting sound that he repeated over and over, and he managed to get one arm free from his chains as he jerked hard to one side, but the arm just flapped up and down, vainly beating at the flames, and then, finally, it was still. The crowd found this hilarious, and one young wag stepped out into the open area and mimicked the dying man to howls of delight. The condemned man was held upright to the post by the chains, now glowing red hot and sunk deep into his charred flesh. His head lolled back, his mouth wide open, as the flesh melted off his bones like the tallow off a candle and the flames leapt higher and higher around him.

As the royal party rode back to the city, Raquel made her face a mask of stone, not sad, not grim, just disinterested. She thought for a moment that, amid the roar of the crowd and the crackle of the flames, the last coherent thing she had heard the man shout was, "Say *kaddish* for me." The more she thought about it, the more she was convinced that this had been her imagination, but, that night, after everyone else had gone to sleep. She stood by her window and said the prayer for the dead in Hebrew. She said it out loud, if softly, and she wondered if it would help.

GRANADA

Chapter Two

Alhama

The column of men picked their way in the pitch darkness along the narrow banks of the rushing river, sometimes forced to wade waist deep in the frigid waters as the cliffs and piles of boulders on both sides of the gorge that the stream had carved crowded them into the river. Chain mail and body armor were very comforting to have during a battle, but they also conducted the cold terribly well, and the men could feel their limbs turning numb and their lips quivering as they kept moving, more to keep warm than out of a dedication to the task at hand. There had been some grumbling among the men when they learned of the planned stealthy and roundabout approach to the citadel of the town of Alhama by a small force of hand-picked troops. They had complained especially when Juan had told them that they would have the leave their horses behind with the main force, although he explained to them that a horse could wicker or snort at the wrong moment and get them all killed. But it soon had become clear to them that this was the only chance, however slim that might be, of quickly capturing the fortress before an effective resistance could be mounted by the

Moors. If they failed, the defenders of the town could take shelter behind their high walls and hold off a sizeable army for days, weeks, or even months, inflicting heavy casualties on the attackers, and very likely beating off their assaults completely, even if help were not to arrive.

A quick capture of any town was always desirable. A lengthy siege tied up valuable troops that might be better employed elsewhere, required continued supplies of food and munitions, and there was always the risk of disease, which increased exponentially with every day a large body of unwashed men gathered in the same spot with only the most primitive of sanitary arrangements, to say nothing of the chance that a larger enemy army could turn up at any moment and drive off the attackers, making the entire effort a waste.

What made it imperative at this time was the fact that the small Christian army of which Juan Ortega de Prado's detachment was the spearhead was already three days march deep within the borders of the kingdom of Granada, unsupported by any other force and, thus far, undetected by the Moors. For three consecutive nights the army, comprised of about twenty-five hundred horse and three thousand foot, had wound its way through the most desolate passes of the sierra, hiding in caves and groves by day to avoid notice, eating cold rations of stale bread and cheese and salt beef and pork as all camp fires were prohibited, and taking extensive detours around every small hamlet or *ribat* along the route of march. They had left their heavy baggage and artillery behind at the River Yeguas to speed their advance, and now, a mere eight leagues from the frowning walls of the city of Granada itself, Juan's small advance party of just two hundred veteran assault troops, planned to seize the citadel within the town of Alhama in the pre-dawn hours, allowing the rest of the army to sweep in and take this rich prize from right under the noses of the Moors in their capital, hopefully against little or no resistance.

As risky as this undertaking might be, Juan personally had no doubts about its ultimate success. In his years fighting for the Aragonese against the French, and later during the civil war in Castile, fighting for Isabel and Fernando against the forces supporting Juana *La Beltraneja*, which had recently ended, he had earned for himself something of a reputation as an *escalador*, a specialist in scaling the walls of towns and castles, and he had proven this ability time and again, developing his own unique tactics in the assault of fortified positions. With even a few moments of time, with covering fire provided by artillery, musketeers, or archers below, he could find a sheltered bend in a wall, and unguarded corner, and use it to penetrate the mightiest stronghold, opening the way for the rest of the army. He had gathered together a tight little company of hardened mercenaries, headed of course by the Basque, but now including the Castro brothers, a pair of tall, red-haired Galicians from northwestern Spain, Gamal, a lanky, dark-skinned Algerian who had decided to sell his sword to the Christians, Diego Escudero, a Minorcan expert with the crossbow, and half a dozen other swarthy, unruly, fighters from Juan's native province of Estremadura in the south. They followed Juan because their services were worth more as a unit than individually, and the renown Juan had won in his campaigns had earned him the ear of many powerful warrior nobles. His sword commanded a good price in a seller's market, and his war record was an unbroken string of successes, which told his men that they would have rich booty (being among the first to enter an enemy city) and would most likely live to enjoy it, a key consideration for mercenaries who rarely saw the profit in dying for a cause.

His reputation had served Juan well when he proposed the idea of an assault on Alhama to the powerful lords whose armies guarded the southern marches of Spanish Christendom, which was another reason why he was so convinced of success. On the surface, it seemed like a desperate, almost suicidal enterprise. As the Christian kings had pushed the Moors farther and farther south over the preceding years, thousands of Moslem refugees had crowded into the remaining mountainous enclave of Granada, making it the most heavily populated part of the peninsula. And, because of the frequent raids across the border by Christian war parties in search of cattle and slaves, it was also the most heavily fortified, with each little hamlet surrounded by stout walls and literally hundreds of sturdy *ribats*, fortified, monastery-like outposts manned by ten, fifty, or a hundred fanatical Moslem warriors, the *ghazi,* mostly North Africans, who had come to help defend the land of the faithful against the infidel barbarians of the north. Alhama itself was perched atop a towering ridge and flanked by a fast-flowing river, guarded by its own citadel and garrison and the city walls, and lying barely a day's march from Granada itself, deep in the heart of Moorish territory, hardly a ripe piece of fruit just waiting to drop into one's hands.

What had prompted Juan to come up with this scheme was the sudden shock at court over a similar exploit by the Moors in which a Moorish army had surprised and seized the Christian town of Zahara late the previous year, sweeping off the entire population to the slave markets of Granada and North Africa. After years of relatively docile relations with the Moors, who had traditionally paid tribute to the kings of Castile, the king of Granada Abu el-Hassan, had taken advantage of the preoccupation of Isabel and Fernando with the internal quarrels of Castile over the succession to the crown to cease payment of his tribute, and this surprise offensive was merely another step in that direction. But it was one that infuriated Fernando, who took it as a personal insult since his own grandfather had been the one who had originally delivered Zahara from the Moors years before.

The town had been considered safely distant from the border and also enjoyed a strong position atop a mountain, which led the garrison's commander into a fatal laxness, and the long-time dominance of the border area by Christian raiders heading into Moslem territory had lessened the alertness of the residents of the area to a possible counterstroke from Granada.

Consequently, Juan had found fertile ground for his idea among the bellicose nobles whose lands lay along the frontier. As the civil wars had wound down, Juan had taken time to conduct a number of personal reconnaissance journeys deep into Moorish territory, a daring step in itself, and he was convinced that the citizens of Alhama were depending on the daunting geographic position of their town, high atop its rocky hill, and their distance from the border, for their security, just as the people of Zahara had done. Posing as a merchant, and accompanied on his trip by the Basque, the Castro brothers, Gamal, and Diego, Juan had stealthily approached Alhama alone one night and walked silently beneath the walls, listening to the sentries pacing the ramparts, talking to each other. He noted the hour of the changing of the guard and their numbers, but it was not until he reached the citadel itself that he noticed that these walls, even higher on a rocky outcrop towering above the town itself, were largely deserted. What's more, he was able to plot out an approach route that would bring a small party up to the outer wall of the citadel without exposing itself to view from the town. He had then rejoined his party, camped out in the Vega plain, and they had then made their way back to Christian territory with this vital information.

What made Alhama particularly attractive was that, if the place could be taken by a *coup de main*, without a lengthy siege, its strong defenses would enable a determined force to hold out there almost indefinitely. Of even more importance was the fact that Alhama was used by the Moors as a collection point of tax revenue for the whole of the rich Vega agricultural region, taxes that would have just recently been gathered, both in coin and in produce, offering substantial booty to the successful assailants as well as ample supplies should they have to withstand a siege themselves. Since a small army of Christian raiders could not hope to conduct a siege without being attacked by superior Moorish forces from all over the kingdom, and since a larger Spanish army could not reach the town without first defeating the main Moorish armies in open battle, the *only* way the town could be taken was by the daring stroke that Juan had conceived.

Juan had first approached Diego de Merlo, the royal assistant of Sevilla, with his project, who enthusiastically endorsed it and introduced Juan to the powerful Don Rodrigo Ponce de Leon, Marquis of Cadiz, a renowned crusader in his own right, whose forces constantly harassed the Moors by land and sea. The Marquis, who had long been a supporter of the late King Enrique, had been looking for a way to win his way into the good graces of the new sovereigns, and the raid seemed like a promising means to that end. If the new Catholic sovereigns were serious in their talk of driving the Moors out of Spain once and for all, a bold move like this would gain their immediate attention as well as earn their gratitude for shaming other Spanish lords of the center and the north into raising their own levies and marching to the sound of the guns. It was thus at his own expense, albeit with contributions of men, munitions, and supplies from other booty-hungry nobles along the border, that the Marquis had raised his banner and gathered and equipped the army that now trailed along in the wake of Juan's vanguard.

During the approach march, Juan's scouts had probed far ahead of the main column, leaving camp hours earlier each day, searching for stray shepherds or travelers on the roads, although these were rare as few people dared to be outside of city walls after dark. When they found the odd straggler, Juan's crossbowmen would eliminate him silently. They had also wiped out the inhabitants of a few isolated cottages they encountered on their route of march, men, women and children, and, to the best of Juan's knowledge, no word could have gotten back to the Moors of their approach. The bodies had been hidden, and, even if they had been discovered, would probably have been attributed to the work of brigands as Juan's men scrupulously robbed the corpses of anything of value.

Juan now looked up the steep slope and could just make out the silhouette of the slender minaret of Alhama's mosque against the deep blue of the night sky over the crenellated walls of the city. Here and there a few pinpoints of light glowing warmly from the windows of the taller houses also told him that his small force now huddled against the cliff was directly below the town, at the point he had judged best for attempting the ascent. The men had smeared their armor with mud to reduce the glint of moonlight on metal, and wrapped as much of their gear as possible with rags to limit the clanking noise of their passage, and they all wore black cloaks and hoods to make them appear just another bunch of shadows moving along on a dark night. Most importantly at this point, there was no indication of any heightened state of alert in the town, no patrols roaming about outside the walls, no watch fires lit, no sounds of men in armor clattering along the ramparts. He let out a low whistle, barely audible above the rushing of the river, that was repeated down the line of troops, and the men in their dark cloaks all crouched down where they were and began to prepare for the climb.

Juan pulled from his belt a pair of climbing picks he had designed himself. The head had a long, narrow steel point, and a broad horizontal blade on the opposite end with a two-foot wooden shaft. With one in each hand he could claw his way up an almost vertical cliff, as he had done before in similar assaults in the Pyrennes, and the axes also made deadly weapons if needed when he reached the top, just as capable of penetrating chain mail and helm as a rocky cliff face. The Basque and the Castro brothers, all born mountain men, were similarly equipped, and each carried a thick coil of hempen rope draped across their shoulders to lower to the remaining troops once they had reached the top. There was an inevitable clatter of armor and gear, but the monotonous rushing of the water in the river and the moaning of the chill wind in the narrow valley helped to mask the noise as Juan took a deep breath and jerked his chin upward as a signal to the others to begin the ascent.

The cliff here was not quite vertical and was a mixture of soil and rock, enough to allow easy purchase for Juan's picks, so the climb went quickly. He moved like some great, lanky four-legged beast, right pick, left foot, heave upward, then left pick, right foot, faster and faster as he got into his rhythm, soon leaving the others behind. Halfway up the slope his shoulders began to burn, and each stroke took greater and greater effort. He paused and hooked an arm around the woody stem of a prickly shrub that had wormed its way through a crack in a large boulder, hanging there a moment to catch his breath, gazing down at the foaming river a hundred feet below and the pale, upturned faces of his men as they watched his progress. He then swung out to his left and clawed his way onward, emerging at the top of the crest alone and panting for air, listening to the muffled grunting of the Basque moving up on his flank. When the four climbers had at last arrived at the top, they tied each pair of ropes together, making two longer ones, which they lowered and then hauled up two much heavier rope ladders which they securely tied off on tree stumps to allow the rest of the force to climb up in relative safety.

As the first pink rays of sunlight turned the eastern sky into an angry bruise, the bulk of the assaulting force was finally huddled against the base of the wall of the citadel itself along the narrow ledge, pressing close into the shadow of the wall. If a sentry saw them now, they would all die, but, at this point, a man would have to lean well out between the merlons in order to see them as the designers of the citadel had failed to build a tower here that would have allowed a view along the base of the wall. Below them and to the right lay the town of Alhama itself, occupying the crest of the lower part of the ridge on which the citadel sat and spilling down the sides with houses built precariously onto the edge of the very cliff face.

Juan busied himself with assembling the sections of a wooden assault ladder that had been painstakingly hauled up the face of the cliff, long enough to span the forty feet of sheer stone wall that towered above them. They could not risk the sound of hammers, so the sections were lashed together with leather strips. This made for a very flimsy construction which wobbled frighteningly in the stiff wind as the men eased it upward to lean it against the wall, easing it forward the last few inches to keep it from banging against the stone.

"Take the first three companies to the gate," Juan whispered to the Basque, pointing down the ledge to where a small oaken postern door could be seen about fifty yards farther along the wall," and be ready to move in as soon as we open it. And don't let anyone drift down into the town in search of loot. There will be time enough for that when the main body arrives, but until then we'll have to hold out on our own in the citadel and will need everyone to man the walls."

The Basque just nodded the dented helmet he wore, smiling in the leering way he had on the eve of a battle as if they were sharing some private, ribald joke. Then he gestured to several of the senior men-at-arms and led them and most of the men in single file along the base of the wall. They had to turn, backs against the wall, holding their spears, shields, and crossbows in front of them, trying to keep metal from hitting against metal, as they edged along the ledge that was often no wider than the length of a man's forearm.

Juan took a step back from the ladder, as much as the ledge would allow, here barely a yard wide, drew his thick-bladed dagger, tightened the straps on the small round oak and leather target fixed to his left arm, and lunged upward. The ladder sagged dangerously under his weight and the weight of his armor, and the legs slid a terrifying inch closer to the drop off, despite the efforts of two other soldiers to brace them with their boots, but he kept moving, controlling even his breathing for fear that a sentry might be just a few feet away along the rampart who might still give the alarm when his men were in their most vulnerable position. Trapped above the cliff and unable to retreat but still not controlling any part of the citadel wall, they could be cut down by archers or arquebusiers firing at their leisure from above with no hope of protection or escape. The defenders could pour arrows and stones down on their heads at will, and the adventure would end right here either in death or capture and slavery.

He reached the parapet and cautiously peeked through the opening between two merlons, feeling the ladder shudder as another man began the climb behind him. There, in a corner of the wall next to a small tower, he could see the shape of a man leaning, half-sitting, against the wall, braced upright with a long spear about which he wrapped his arms, the sound of muffled snoring reaching him on the breeze, and Juan smiled grimly. He levered himself through the opening and leapt gracefully onto the rampart walkway without a sound and moved smoothly to where the sentry slept. He clapped his gloved hand over the man's mouth at the same time that he buried his blade into his throat, allowing a thick spout of dark blood to gush down the front of the man's hauberk. He heard a dull thud as Gamal landed on the rampart, quickly turning to fasten a rope which he tossed down to the waiting troops before he moved along the wall in the opposite direction. The little tower at the end of the walkway was vacant, and Juan looked down through one of the arrow slits, taking in the view a defender would have had of his men, clearly visible in the growing light as they struggled up the ladder or hauled themselves up ropes one at a time. He swallowed hard. He had calculated that one couldn't see that section of the wall from here. If that sentry had not been asleep. . .

With a section of wall and its flanking towers now firmly in his hands, Juan breathed a little easier and left the Castros in charge here as he led Gamal, Diego, and a dozen other men along the inside base of the wall to the main gatehouse. The citadel itself was a small square stone castle, not more than two hundred feet on a side with a tower in each corner and a few low stone structures built up against the insides of the walls, storehouses or barracks and a single gate with its own tower that opened out onto the town below. It was meant as a last refuge for the defenders if an attacking force came over the walls of the town, where the garrison could hold out until a relief force arrived, and it was never expected that it would be the attackers that would hold the citadel *first* and come at the town from that direction. Juan's men pressed themselves against the stones of the wall as the guttural sounds of Arabic came to them, and the light of a pair of torches in the arched gateway threw golden images onto the ground.

"Now!" Juan growled, and he suddenly rushed forward, sword in his right hand, dagger in the other with his small target strapped to his forearm, his men fanning out on either side. Like his men, he wore only light armor, a long shirt of chain mail covered by a leather jerkin and breast plate with guards on their forearms and shins and with a steel helmet that also protected the nape of the neck but with no face guards. This ensemble would probably turn an arrow or a glancing sword blow but would not interfere with the man's movement or limit his vision, unlike the full suits of armor worn by mounted knights or men-at-arms defending a breach with their heavy oaken shields, undercoats of chain mail, and every possible inch of skin covered with steel and roundels fixed over the vulnerable joints at shoulder, elbow, and knee. There were four Moors lounging about in the entrance to the gate tower, all armed with spear, sword, and shield, but none alert. Juan ran one through from behind before he was even noticed, and Gamal threw himself on another, pinning him to the ground as he slit his throat. A crossbow shaft took a third, but the last man darted to one side, narrowly avoiding a quarrel that glanced off the stone wall, and disappeared into the tower stairway, screaming unintelligibly at the top of his lungs.

But it was too late for the defenders. Juan then raced to his right to the small postern gate in the outer wall. It was unguarded, and in a moment he had smashed the rusty lock with his climbing axe. He slammed his shoulder into the door, and it creaked open reluctantly. The Basque and his men poured through the opening, hustling along as fast as they could, each man listening intently for the sound of alarm in the town. As soon as they were inside, they spread out through the little citadel in search of the garrison, while Juan, Gamal and a handful of men raced out across the drawbridge, hugging the shadows of the city wall, down the slope of the ridge to a sally port that opened out onto flatter ground near the river. This door too was unguarded, and Juan battered at this lock, every stroke of his hammer sounding like the slamming of a door in hell. This lock was in better shape than the other and took a dozen blows before it shattered. He and Gamal shoved it open, and then they waited, their breath coming in great gasps.

Back at the citadel, the Basque had sent one man to the highest point in the gate tower with a large torch, specially treated with chemicals to make it burn with a bright green flame. It was still dark enough for the flame to be easily seen, and the man waved the torch frantically as a signal to the Marquis of Cadiz, who by now would have marched up along the river with several hundred more men. Juan peered out into the darkness for several anxious moments before the shadows finally took shape, and the Marquis and his men rushed through the sally port two abreast and followed Juan at a run across the open slope to the gate of the citadel. Asco came bounding up with them, covering Juan's outstretched hands with a coating of slobber and nearly knocking him off his feet as they ran. As soon as they were all inside, Juan had the bridge raised and the portcullis lowered again, sealing them off from attack from the town, where random shouts and the slamming of doors told them that the alarm had been belatedly raised there as well.

The green torchlight also was a signal for the main army under the joint command of Don Pedro Henriquez, *adelantado* of Sevilla, Sancho de Avila, mayor of Carmona, and Diego de Merlo, which would only now be approaching the gates of the town below. A second man stood beside the torch bearer, and he now blew a long curved brass war horn for all he was worth to make certain that the signal was noticed. They would know that the defenders were caught between two hostile forces and doomed to defeat.

The Marquis was covered from head to foot in beautifully crafted armor, with silvery plates shaped like fish scales on chest and back over a fine coat of mail, polished greaves on his arms and legs with roundels in the form of seashells protecting his shoulder, elbow and knee joints, and a full helm with visor topped with lime green plumes. He embraced Juan roughly at the gate in his powerful arms. He was perhaps ten years older than Juan, in his early forties, but the ravages of small pox and undoubtedly heavy drinking had left his face a network of broken blood vessels and caverns above his grizzled red beard and made him look much older. He was shorter than Juan and stocky, the rigors of his frequent campaigns apparently being no match for the generosity of his table and the depth of his wine cellar.

"Well done!" the Marquis shouted as his men filed quickly past him into the fortress. "That's the first step done."

"But we have to take the rest of the town before reinforcements arrive for the Moors or we'll be trapped here. Most of your army is still out in the open, and us up here without much in the way of food stores or ammunition and no artillery. We must have the whole town if we are to have any chance at all."

"Well, let's get on with it then," the Marquis laughed.

Juan nodded and, leaving Gamal in charge of a small force to hold the gate, Juan raced through the buildings tightly packed within the compass of the citadel walls, flanked by the Basque, but they found only blood trails and dismembered Moorish bodies as their men had preceded them, hacking away indiscriminately at the bleary-eyed defenders as they staggered out of their beds. There had only been a handful of men in the garrison, the others apparently preferring to sleep more comfortably in quarters in the town, relying on their lofty perch and their distance from any known enemy as their best defense, exactly as Juan had hoped they would. There was not even an officer present whose life might have been worth sparing in hopes of a hefty ransom from family members in Granada and as a possible source of information about the rest of the town's defenses. The surprise had been almost too complete.

With the citadel secured, Juan now organized its defense. Fifty of his men were posted around the walls, stripping the Moorish armory of its best weapons, steel crossbows, arquebuses, and even a pair of small brass swivel cannon which he mounted on the walls flanking the main gate, putting the Basque in charge of it all. He then took his remaining men, and joined those of the Marquis to prepare for a thrust down into the city to the main gate, perhaps four hundred and fifty, all afoot, but well-armed and all experienced veteran fighters. It was growing daylight now, and the Castilians could see Moors scuttling back and forth between the houses below, building hurried breastworks of timbers, wagons, and furniture to block the narrow streets.

A tight phalanx of the Marquis's men, now tricked out in additional armor, with large round shields taken from the Moors, formed up at the gate of the citadel. Juan gave the signal that sent the drawbridge crashing down and, with a roar, they charged down the slope toward the nearest houses. But they were met with a deafening crash as a volley of arquebus fire from the windows and rooftops tore into them, accompanied by a hail of arrows and crossbow bolts. Dozens of men were cut down in the first seconds, and the others raced back to the protection of the gate tower, leaving the open ground littered with dead and wounded. The Moors took pleasure in practicing their marksmanship in picking off the wounded one at a time as they tried to crawl back to the citadel while Juan's men opened a scattered fire from the walls to try to keep the Moors' heads down, although this was largely ineffectual.

"I thought this town was full of nothing but fat merchants and bakers," the Basque growled in Juan's ear.

"Even a cur will fight in its own yard," Juan replied. "They know about what the Moors did at Zahara, and they can't expect any better treatment from us than they gave our people there. They're fighting to protect their own lives, their homes and wives and children. With our army outside the walls, and us up here, they don't have anywhere to go.

Besides, they're probably expecting a relieving army from Granada to arrive at any moment, so all they have to do is hold us off for a little while. That's what's giving them courage."

The Marquis was trying to rally his men, promising them the run of the town when it was taken, all the wine they could drink, all the booty they could carry, all the women they could handle, but another rush from the gate met a similar reception to the first and was driven back after advancing only a few yards. The scattered dead now began to become an obstacle in their own right as the attackers had to vault over them as they tried to cover the open ground, and the only thing the sortie was able to accomplish was to drag some of the wounded back to the citadel as they retreated under the cover of their shields that were now studded with arrows.

"What to do?" the Marquis shouted to Juan over the clatter of musketry. "Is there a sally port we could use to avoid that killing ground?"

They could hear the shouts and trumpets of the main army in the distance as it also battered away at the city walls below, but, without heavy artillery, they would be limited to trying to storm the walls, which were now fully defended. Even if they happened to be successful, which appeared unlikely, they might well lose so many men in the attempt that the combined force would prove too weak to hold off the forces from Granada that would be sure to be marching to Alhama in a matter of hours.

"No, my lord, there's none but this," Juan replied. "If they're covering this gate, we'll just have to make our own. If you can just keep your men busy here, firing on the Moors and threatening an advance to keep their attention, my lord, I'll do the rest." The Marquis nodded grimly.

Juan turned and led the Basque and his own men along the wall away from the gate. He paused after following a bend in the wall and rubbed his gloved hand over its surface. The city walls were made of stone, but here they appeared to be mud-dried brick, and the mortar between them was old and crumbling. He grabbed a pick from where a Moorish work party had apparently been repairing the street the day before and began pounding away at the bricks of the wall.

"Right here," he said to the Basque. "The Moors know this town and will have concentrated their fire to cover the gate, but they won't expect this. And we should be out of sight here from their barricades."

His men soon got the idea, grabbing up other workmen's tools as well as their own battle axes and spears and battering the wall and prying away loose bricks until a small breach had been made, large enough for a single man to push through at a time. As usual, Juan led the way. He now carried a large round Moorish shield, boiled leather studded with bronze and iron on a framework of hard wood, and he had to slide it through the opening sideways. The sun was up now, but blocked by low clouds and a mist was rising off the river, but he still felt terribly exposed as he moved to one side to make room for his men. He could just make out the shapes of houses across the open ground and could see the occasional flash of an arquebus or small gun off to the right where the Moors were still skirmishing with the Marquis' men around the gate, but there was no sign that anyone had noticed his action. He crouched low along the base of the wall, his shield in front of him as his men quickly filed out through the hole and took their positions around him.

Juan formed his hundred-odd men into a "turtle", a close rectangular formation with interlocked shields on the outside and others held overhead as a kind of roof, and they moved off at a practiced trot into the town down a narrow street that the Moors had not barricaded. They could hear the roar of battle just a hundred yards away, but out of sight because of the intervening houses. They could also hear more clearly shouting and wailing coming from terrified residents within the shuttered homes closer at hand, but the streets themselves here were deserted and open, and only an occasional arrow clattered against the shields from some stray Moor who had jumped to the right conclusion, that these were not his countrymen, even if they carried Moorish shields. The column swung around toward the back of the barricades in front of the citadel gate, Juan and his men casting nervous glances through the narrow gaps in their shield fortress at the rooftops of the houses that crowded in on either side of them. Then they turned a final corner and found themselves behind the Moorish barricade.

Juan roared out a command and charged forward, and the "turtle" disintegrated as the men spread out into a fighting line. One of the men raised a banner high overhead and waved it frantically as a signal to the Marquis to attack on his side, and Juan was followed by the Basque and most of his men while the Castros each took a contingent and stormed the houses on either flank of the barricade. The Moors turned in terror to find the Castilians behind them and fought desperately. Only a few of the Moors were fully armored and appeared to be regular soldiers. The others fought with whatever came to hand, hammers and farm implements, while the women who gathered in a mob in the open street, hurled stones and insults at the Christians and screamed encouragement to their men before turning and rushing away in total panic.

Juan knocked aside the spear of one defender with his shield and then slashed downward with his sword, cleaving the man from shoulder to navel, his quilted leather vest providing no more protection than a silk robe. With his backstroke, he knocked aside the barrel of an arquebus that was being aimed at the Basque just as it fired, and another Moor took the ball in the back of his head, and Juan spitted the arquebusier cleanly through the belly. He glanced up and saw one of the Castro brothers hurling a Moor from the roof of a house, while Castilian crossbowmen now fired down from the windows into the backs of the Moors still trying to hold their positions.

But the contest was a one-sided one now. Assailed from two directions, the Moors broke and fled. Juan slashed and hacked blindly, cutting down half a dozen men before cresting the barricade and waving the cheering troops of the Marquis forward, despite the risk of making himself a target for their arrows and bullets as well as those of the Moors. The Castilians then swept down through the streets of the town and along the walls toward the main gate, bowling over everything in their path. They finally reached the gate tower, and Juan and his men used an iron bench to batter their way through an inward-facing door, ignoring the arrows and stones that rained down on them from windows above. They finally forced their way through and rushed into the tower, slaughtering the last few guards in the sentry room and on the stairs leading upward before lowering the outer drawbridge and throwing the gates open to the cheering troops on the outside who poured through led by Diego de Merlo and the other nobles, and the city was as good as taken.

A handful of Moors had chosen not to surrender but had taken refuge in a large mosque near the city wall and briefly held up the attackers there with the concentrated fire of their remaining arquebuses and crossbows. Juan watched as a squad of Castilians from de Merlo's forces rushed the door of the mosque, pushing a wagon laden with bales of cotton in front of them as cover. They then rammed the wagon against the tall double doors and set fire to it, escaping under cover of the billowing black smoke. Screams of women and children came from within the building as the doors caught and the fire spread to the dry wooden rafters. Several Moors forced their way through the flames, trying to push the wagon away, but they were cut down, one after the other, by murderous crossbow fire from the neighboring houses. The fire spread, and soon the entire structure was engulfed. The screams rose to a high pitch and then gradually died out, and Juan had to turn away from the intense heat, even at the distance of over a hundred yards. The Castilian troops cheered to the echo as the roof of the mosque collapsed, sending a geyser of sparks and smoke skyward.

Juan's shoulders and legs ached, and he was bathed in sweat. He had taken a spear thrust along his ribs that had been deflected by his armor, but he knew there would be a nasty purple bruise there if not a broken rib or two. His mouth and nose were clogged with dust and smoke, and tears streamed from his red-rimmed eyes, but he felt truly alive, and the pain only emphasized this. He wiped the blood from the blade of his sword on a strip of curtain that dangled from the window of a looted house (as dried blood could cause the blade to stick, and that could prove fatal) and finally sheathed it. He turned and trudged back with the Basque and the Castros toward the small plaza fronting on the main gate of the city where he found a small delegation of richly, if hurriedly dressed Moors, all unarmed, waiting for their conquerors in a nervous cluster.

"We throw ourselves on the renowned mercy of the valiant warriors of Castile," an elderly Moor announced in a shrill voice which cracked with emotion. His thin, wispy grey beard hung down to the middle of his chest, but it did not conceal the long wattles of wrinkled skin that hung down from under his chin and trembled as he spoke. "You have taken our citadel and the town walls, my lords. We realize that resistance is useless and yield." He stepped forward and laid an elegant curved scimitar with a jewel-encrusted haft on the ground at Juan's feet. It was a clearly a ceremonial sword, the kind that had gone out of fashion with soldiers decades before. Juan broke into a grin as he scooped up the sword and slipped it into his belt without a word, patting the hilt and winking at the Basque.

A cheer rose up from the troops who filled the plaza, and they surged forward through the streets of the town, their weapons drawn, but obviously more interested in loot than in the prospect of further combat. Juan glanced over his shoulder and saw that his own men had already melted away, wanting to be the first to ransack the richest houses. Juan was unconcerned with such minor pickings now. As the conqueror of a town, his reward would come straight from the Marquis, or even from the monarchs themselves, in land and slaves, perhaps even his own title. Now, *that* would have to impress his old wreck of a father. There would be no more rummaging about in prisoners' pockets for him.

Then the Marquis marched up, now accompanied by Diego de Merlo and the other noble captains, and the Marquis held both arms over his head in victory to the cheers of the troops who still crowded the plaza. He still carried his sword, a huge two-handed one, which was encrusted with blood down to the hilt. Juan proudly took the Marquis by the arm and led him over to the little knot of Moorish officials who were huddling closer together as soldiers hovered about them like hungry wolves, and the crowd parted for them like the Red Sea for Moses. The old Moor knelt before the Marquis and again mumbled something about trusting to the mercy of his Christian lord, bowing to touch his head repeatedly on the flagstones, and his colleagues from the town did the same. The eldest Moor went, alternately praying and mumbling in Spanish about the compassion expected by God of the great toward the humble, but the Marquis waved him silent.

"We have taken this town by storm, and it and all it contains are ours by right. True," he went on, "we did not offer the option of surrender, but neither did the townsmen put out white flags and offer a parlay at any point, even when they saw that the citadel was in our hands. They continued to resist and must pay the price. This would be true even if the Moors had not already dealt us foul at Zahara. I have promised my men the plunder of the town and the ransom of all prisoners, and I must keep that promise."

The Marquis paused, as if to ponder the question, although the crash of broken doors and the occasional scream of women told Juan that the discussion was becoming largely academic in any event. Every soldier knew his rights, perhaps more exactly than any scribe or court official, and they were happily helping themselves to their due.

"Mercy, oh lord," the Moor whined, echoed by his colleagues, who were bobbing their heads like a flock of cranes in a wading pool. "We are helpless before you. It will be a measure of your greatness how compassionate you are to us in our hour of tragedy. It was not we who made war on the Christians. We must only do what our king commands us, but we are not a warlike people. We have always only sought to live in peace with our neighbors, to grow our crops, conduct our honest trade, and raise our families. Please do not visit your wrath upon us for the crimes of other men, my lord."

"For many years the kings of Granada were wise and paid the kings of Castile and Leon a just tribute," the Marquis declared, raising his voice so that all could hear in the plaza, "for the privilege of living on land that was rightfully ours. Two thousands doubloons and freedom for sixteen hundred Christian prisoners every year from among those captured in wars with other Christian powers. They would make the pilgrimage to Cordoba to bow before the Christian kings and pay their tribute, and they were always treated honorably.

But then, four years ago, your king Abu el Hassan proudly told our monarchs Isabel and Fernando that he would no longer pay the tribute. He said that the Moorish kings who had paid tribute to Christians were dead and that the workshops of Granada had turned to making swords and spears to receive anyone who questioned this. Then, in a cowardly attack, he took our town of Zahara last year, killing or enslaving all the people, and we are here now to make him pay for his insolence. The Moors could have lived peacefully here in Spain for many generations yet to come as they have lived for generations in the past, if they had only acknowledged the justice and power of our Catholic Kings, but they would not. This is not just the taking of a single town. It is the first step on a long road of conquest that will finally end in the return of all Spanish land to the realm of Christ, our Savior." The soldiers cheered lustily.

The Moors looked at each other nervously. At least the eldest one spoke fluent Spanish, and the lack of mumbled translations between them during the monologue implied that the others did as well. They were probably asking themselves, were they all to be sold into slavery? Would they be able to buy off these Christian warriors with some tribute or ransom collected from surrounding villages? The Marquis paused for effect, and Juan shifted anxiously from one foot to the other, also awaiting the answer.

Just then, the mob of soldiers who were clustered in the little plaza parted and a small group of wraith-like figures appeared, staggering down from the direction of the citadel, being herded along like sheep by the Basque. They were all men, but of undetermined age, all with long, tangled beards, sunken eyes, tattered clothing, and gaunt frames. Some held their hands up to shield their eyes even from the pale morning light, and all had scabby patches on their wrists and ankles, the kind made by long acquaintance with iron shackles.

"We found these in the dungeons of the citadel, my captain," the Basque proudly announced.

"Where were you taken, my man?" the Marquis asked gently, taking what appeared to be the eldest of the group by the shoulders as the man looked distractedly about him.

"Near Antequera, ten years ago, I think," he mumbled in reply. "Some of the others came from Zahara. Others from other places." He began to sob silently, and the Marquis patted him lightly on the back with his mailed arm, which caused the old man's slender frame to shake, and the Moors sunk lower, obviously wishing above all things to be able to melt into the ground.

There were Christian prisoners in virtually every Moorish city and town. While the women and children and most productive-looking men who were captured on raids usually found themselves in the open slave market, and the wealthy few would be ransomed by their relatives back home for cash, holding living prisoners was an important status symbol for any town. On a more practical level, the presence of these prisoners was what prevented the Spanish Christians from treating the thousands of Moslems living on their side of the border with the same disrespect and harshness that they treated the Jews. There was always the clear threat that the Moors here, or the Turks in the Holy Land, could reciprocate any cruel treatment of their co-religionists on the heads of the Christians under their control. The prisoners also served as ready currency for trade against any Moslems from each town who might fall into Christian hands in the course of a raid or battle. The Moorish elders trembled at the surly looks they received from the Christian soldiers at the sight of these walking ghosts, and loud grumbling could be heard spreading through the ranks as they pressed closer, their bloody weapons still in their hands.

The Marquis cleared his throat, and addressed the Moslems, although he raised his voice again for the soldiers to hear as well. "I think that this has supplied us with an answer. The Moors showed no mercy when they took Zahara, just sold the whole population into slavery, and now the people of this town and all Granada will have to pay for their king's folly. I want no unnecessary violence done to the people of this town," he went on. "They are our property, yours, mine, and the king's. Let them be locked up in the mosques for the time being, but I want no massacre here."

The Moors saw the inevitability of their situation, and began to bow their thanks for this small favor as they were led away by some soldiers. But thick columns of smoke were beginning to rise from a number of points in the city, and Juan could see soldiers smashing up expensive furniture in the street with their swords, just for the sheer joy of wanton destruction. Many of the troops were men who would never be rich enough to own a real piece of furniture in their lives, and the fact that infidels lived in such opulence was more than they could bear.

"My lord," he said confidentially in the Marquis' ear. "We must get our men in hand. I fear that they expect us to raze the town and escape to our own lands. If you plan to hold this place, we cannot let them destroy any of the supplies we might need for our own survival once the Granadans arrive in force."

Just as he spoke, Juan glanced out through the open gate and saw a thick column of Moorish cavalry emerging at a gallop from the hills just a few miles away. On they came, but then they must have seen the Christian banners floating over the battlements, and the column twisted like a speared snake and came to a halt on the plain. There were only a few hundred riders in the force, enough to have possibly made the difference while the fighting had gone on for the city, but worthless now that the Christians held the walls. A regiment of Castillian cavalry, still outside the city, was forming up to challenge them, but the Moors turned and headed back in the direction from which they had come at full speed.

"You're quite right," the Marquis finally answered, and he gestured for the other nobles and for Juan to take some men and patrol the city and to try to restore order. "Let the men have their fun, but don't let it get out of hand," he shouted after them.

"Then there is no hope of our just getting away?" Juan asked as the others moved off. "We will have to hold the town then?"

"It was obvious from the beginning that we would have to hold here. If we try to cross the Sierra again, half of our men wouldn't make it," the Marquis replied. "The Moors would be alerted and would cut us down in the passes, and to try to march around the mountains we would have to make a flank march across the enemy's front at Granada. Suicidal, to say nothing of unprofitable. We would not be able to carry much in the way of booty or prisoners with us, to say nothing of our own wounded, so the entire enterprise would have been for nothing."

"So what do you intend to do, my lord?"

"We have no choice but to hole up here and withstand a siege, probably a long one. I have already sent off riders to advise Fernando of our success, but it will take him time to raise an army and fight his way through to us. I have also written to other lords in Andalusia to request their aid, but even that may take time."

"And if we can hold out here, Isabel and Fernando will be under a tremendous pressure to come to our aid," Juan concluded for him.

"Which, I assume was part of your plan from the start," the Marquis suggested, raising one bushy eyebrow and smiling slightly, but Juan merely cleared his throat. Juan had not actually given much thought to the possibility of having to hold out here, just a few short miles from the walls of Granada, at least not for more than a few days. He had assumed that a large army under Fernando would have been on the march right behind them, and the taking of Alhama would merely have served as bait to lure the bulk of the Moorish forces into the open where they could be dealt with more easily than behind the stout walls of their fortresses. In fact, he had had the vague idea that this might lead to one glorious battle that would destroy Moorish power in Spain once and for all and that he would be hailed throughout the land as its architect. He had never given much thought to the possibility that the monarchs would not even consider beginning to raise and dispatch an army until *after* Alhama had been taken. But, apparently, while Juan had done a fine job of convincing the local nobility of the borderlands of the viability of his plan, they had not done a similar job with their sovereigns.

The Marquis clapped Juan once more on the back, hard enough to make him stagger forward a step, laughing loudly, and strode off to try to organize the defense of the walls of the city and a raid into the countryside to round up any livestock or grain that might be available to help the Castilians survive the coming siege, as well as to deny supplies to the Moorish army that would soon be encamped outside the gates.

Juan had been left in command of the citadel itself and walked back through the streets of the town in search of his own men. He could see that the doors of many of the houses had been smashed open, and the streets were littered with broken furniture and heaps of clothing that had been tossed from the upper windows by the rioting troops. A bloody corpse hung from the protruding beam of one of the taller houses, a Christian renegade who had been in the service of the Moors as a guide for their raids into Andalusia, and Juan hawked and spat in its direction as he strode past. Juan was pleased by the fact that, this being a Moslem town, there would be little if any wine to be found, so the only intoxicant that would be driving the troops this night would be that of power and blood lust. The screams of women came from most of the houses, as the men took their soldierly due from the conquered population, but there would be little random killing, probably just the odd husband who could not stand by as his wife or daughter was ravished, but the men well knew that prisoners meant money, even if the Marquis might not allow them to simply sell the whole population into slavery. After a couple of turnings, the Basque fell in with Juan and took him by the elbow, steering him into a side street. "Of course, we have not forgotten our great captain," the Basque said playfully. "We have saved something special for you."

The Basque led him through the arched doorway of a large and well-built house, probably that of a wealthy merchant or landowner. There was a spacious patio in the center with a tall marble fountain. Half a dozen of Juan's men sat about in the patio, gorging themselves on roasted chickens which trembling servants were shuttling out from the kitchen. Juan smiled. The men had had to go without hot food throughout of their passage of the mountains, surviving on stale bread and sausages, and not much of that, and they waved drumsticks at him in happy salute as he passed.

They entered a long room, probably used for dining, where a mountain of goods had been piled onto a trestle table. There were gold and silver goblets and plates, several bolts of fine silk cloth as well as a small chest with gold and silver coins and even some pearls. The Basque proudly grabbed a handful of coins and let them rain back down into the chest.

"Better than scavenging dead bandits," he grunted, winking, and Juan nodded in approval. "We'll share this out among the men, after taking out the royal fifth and what's due to the Marquis, of course," he added quickly. "With your portion of this alone, you'd be able to double the size of your family estate back home, if you chose."

"I'll not *buy* land like a damned store keeper," Juan sneered. "I'm due lands for my service, and those will come from the hand of my lord, the only honorable way any *hidalgo* should receive his property."

"Well said, sir," the Basque laughed. Then he moved toward a narrow stairway and beckoned, winking to Juan again.

Upstairs were some cramped bedrooms, outside of one of which stood a small cluster of soldiers, peering in at the doorway from which issued a rhythmic moaning sound. As he passed by he could see the heaving bare buttocks of another soldier on the bed and the slender arms and legs of a woman splayed in all directions beneath him. In one corner of the room a Moorish man with a thick black beard was tied in a kneeling position. His dark eyes burned with rage and the glistening tracks of his tears were visible on his tanned cheeks. A small boy of perhaps six years was tied up next to him, burying his head behind the father's shoulder, his own slender frame shaking with weeping. Juan snorted. They had little right to be upset. This was better than immediate death, which would have been the likely outcome had there really been a struggle for the town, fighting street to street. There might be a lifetime of slavery in store for them, the family broken up forever. But in a few hours this would all be over and they would be alive, a little the worse for wear, and a little poorer, but at least alive and perhaps even free, if a relative somewhere could pay their ransom. In the coming war there would be many families who would gladly trade fates with them.

The Basque pushed open the door of a corner bedroom and steered Juan into it, closing the door part way behind him with a bawdy chuckle and leering look. Juan found himself in a dark room, lit only by a single candle set on an upturned trunk in one corner. Against one wall was a low bed on which huddled, amid the jumble of blankets and embroidered pillows, a girl of about fifteen years of age. She jerked her arms more tightly around her body as he entered the room, and of her face he could only see two immense brown eyes staring at him in terror over the edge of a red-gold caftan.

Juan turned and gave the Basque a lewd smile and pushed the door shut against the Basque's joking resistance, then leaned his forehead against the door and sighed. It would not do for Juan's men to know of his *problem*, and it had been horribly difficult to keep it from them over the years. Juan's bravery in battle, his total disregard for his own safety, his willingness to continue to fight with blood streaming from a dozen cuts and slashes, his ability to march under a heavy load when men ten years his junior were collapsing by the roadside, and his uncanny sense for a battle, where the enemy would counterattack, when they would break and run, had earned him the trust and respect of his men. But soldiers, even the most bloodthirsty ones, only spent a small fraction of their time in battle, and a commander's reputation rested almost as much on his exploits off the field as on.

Juan could certainly hold his liquor, which was one important measure of manhood in any army, although he didn't get the same satisfaction out of drinking as the Basque and even the Marquis evidently did. He could guzzle impressive quantities of wine when the need arose, and vomiting it back up immediately thereafter did not detract from the performance as long as one took it in good part and could joke about it afterward. But the other area of endeavor at which a man-at-arms was supposed to excel completely eluded Juan, and this was the one in which no failure to perform could be tolerated among the men of Castile.

Poor King Enrique had been haunted by tails of his impotence and alleged preference for nubile young men throughout his reign and these stories had ruined his daughter Juana's chances for the succession, since it was assumed that her father must be someone else. More than anything else, his feeble policy toward his political enemies, his policy of appeasement toward the Moors which some could have considered simple generosity, his inability to get the economy of the country on an even footing, it was this lack of manhood that had undermined Enrique's regime, for no self-respecting Spanish man could long follow a cuckold or a known sodomite or a man who just couldn't get the job done in the bedroom. This was why Juan had gone to tremendous lengths to conceal his own *problem.*

Juan wasn't sure when this might have started, but ever since that night with the prostitute in Trujillo, he recognized that the only thing that really aroused him was the smell of fear and the power he had over a woman, much more than the idea of sex itself. That incident had been hushed up with his gold and the threats the Basque had returned to the inn the next day to deliver, but that had not been the end of Juan's suffering. Juan had convinced himself that his desire was not totally unnatural, that it was man's God-given role to dominate, and he merely took that role to its logical extreme. Sometimes, if he were drunk and aggressive enough, he would inadvertently inject enough fear into the situation with a woman to satisfy the unhealthy desire he knew lurked within him, but he found that it took increasing levels of violence on his part to achieve satisfaction, and failure in this resulted in his failure to be able to perform at all. This kind of behavior caused most prostitutes to reject his return business, and it had also occurred to him that the women with whom he had failed had a long tradition of constantly gossiping both with co-workers and with other clients about humorous experiences on the job, and someone might begin to analyze this pattern and spread stories about him. Fortunately an almost constant employment at war had offered him ample opportunity to have women in whom the fear was a very real thing, and not something he had to manufacture. The trouble was that, as enjoyable as this might be as entertainment, it would hardly do as the basis for marriage, and even the traditional right of a husband to judiciously beat his wife fell far short of the kind of "play" to which Juan had become accustomed.

That was why, at nearly thirty years of age, he was still unmarried. He found himself absolutely paralyzed with anxiety on the rare occasions when he was obliged to attend the court of some aristocrat, like the Marquis, and the young ladies would flock about him, begging for stories of blood and gore, tales of some battle in a far-off land, or tantalizingly tracing the line of the scar on his neck with a delicate fingernail and asking how it had been received and where it led once it disappeared down the collar of his shirt. Of course, a good Spanish husband could rightfully beat his wife, if she deserved it in his eyes, and could justly force her into the conjugal bed, but Juan knew in his heart that the feeling would not be the same, and an unguarded look of reproach, amusement, or worse yet, pity, would send him into the same crimson rage that had led to the death of the gypsy slut years before. If the woman were the daughter of a man of means, which is the only kind of marriage that would be suitable for a young man of ambition like himself, there would be no escaping the consequences, so Juan was obliged to shun the company of women, giving the impression that he had sworn off marriage until the Moor was driven from his homeland. Perhaps he would have been best advised to follow a career in the Church after all.

Juan now began to cross the room with slow steps, unstrapping and discarding his swordbelt and pieces of armor as he went. He feared for a moment that the girl might give herself up, trying to please him in the hope of his sparing her life, and he would therefore have to dispose of her. But, as he placed one knee on the bed, his fears fled as she lashed out at him suddenly with her nails, shrieking defiance. She gouged a pair of narrow, bloody furrows across his cheek, and he caught both of her arms with one of his massive hands, pinning them behind her with one vicious twist, and she whimpered as he forced her back onto the bed. He tore the caftan from her slender body with one yank, revealing a pair of small, firm breasts and a flat stomach that quivered with fear. No, tonight would be just fine after all. He smiled.

Juan stood atop the tower over the main gate of the town next to the Marquis and his lieutenants, and together they watched the Moorish army flow down from the north, crossing the now-barren fields of the Vega which would be ready for plowing in time for the spring planting in a few weeks, if anyone remained alive to do the plowing. There were only about three thousand horse, barely more than the cavalry the Marquis had with him. It also appeared that, in their haste to assemble, the Moors had not brought up any heavy artillery or siege engines either, and there was no timber nearby with which to construct any. However, the clouds of infantry tipped the balance irrevocably in the Moors' favor, perhaps fifty thousand of them, by the end of the day, heavily armored retainers from the king's household troops, dark-skinned Berber infantry with long pikes or throwing javelins, and hordes of ragged militia from the surrounding villages, some armed with only farm implements and wearing only quilted cotton vests as their armor, but there were just so many of them and, in a siege, it was infantry that counted. Juan could identify some of the banners of the major noble houses in the Moorish army, but most of them were strange to him. It was the sheer number of them that was frightening.

The most worrisome contingents were the solid phalanxes of crossbowmen and arquebusiers. The Granadans had a reputation of being the most skillful men with the crossbow in the world, taking pride in inter-village competitions during times of peace, and their abilities with the arquebus were not far behind. Juan had an inherent distaste for crossbows in particular, as effective a weapon as they might be, for with a minimum of training and equipment, any peasant could conceivably murder a knight, the product of years of hard physical training and generations of breeding, wearing armor worth more than the total income of a small town for a month. It was positively indecent, and the Pope had done well to attempt to ban the use of the disgusting weapon, at least among Christians, although the infidel nations would obviously never comply, so it was incumbent upon all countries to make use of them. Actually, older bows, like the English longbow or the double-curved bows used by the North Africans, had a higher rate of fire and almost the penetrating power of the crossbow, but these too required long training of arm and eye, where anyone with a trigger finger could send a quarrel to the target.

The only thing that gave the Christians a decided edge over the Moslems in warfare on the peninsula in recent years was that the fleets of Castile, operating out of Sevilla, and those of Aragon, operating out of Barcelona and Valencia, had swept the Western Mediterranean largely clean of Moslem vessels. The kings of Granada could no longer count on regular reinforcements of the steady Berber infantry or their terrifyingly swift cavalry to come to their aid when the Christian armies pressed too close as they had done for centuries. Moreover, with the burden of heavy tribute to the Castilian crown and the severe restrictions on Moorish trade over the past years, the economy of Granada could not afford to keep up with the Christians in the development and manufacture of modern weapons, particularly heavy artillery. Even their crossbows were lighter, with flimsy wooden stocks, and much less stopping power than the new steel versions being imported from France or developed in Northern Spain, which used a series of pulleys to give the bolt tremendous force, more than the simple lever-powered weapons used by the Moors, and capable of penetrating virtually any suit of armor.

But that was thinking on the strategic level. The quarrel of an inferior crossbow would still kill you satisfactorily dead if it hit you in the right spot, and there appeared to be plenty of those on hand for the job. Juan watched, entranced, as the Moorish columns peeled off the main road, sweeping around to the right and left to form a complete circle around the town. The last squadrons of Castilian cavalry danced away from the advancing Moors, driving in a few more head of cattle, and finally taking refuge within the walls as the drawbridge was raised, the iron-studded portcullis lowered and the massive gates were swung shut and barred from within. Then teams of masons, conscripted from among the Moorish prisoners, began to wall up all but a couple of the smaller gate openings with stones taken from buildings they had demolished outside the walls to give the defenders a clear field of fire.

A few richly caparisoned Moorish knights rode forward individually to within an arrow shot of the walls and pranced back and forth on fabulous steeds, showing off their horsemanship and waving spear or sword defiantly at the watching defenders. Juan instinctively turned to the Marquis, as did a number of the younger knights, but the Marquis solemnly shook his head. Single combat for honor was still practiced often enough along the frontier, and knights of both sides often traveled to opposing cities under a *laissez passer* to compete in tournaments, which sometimes were almost as bloody as regular battles. But the Catholic Kings had decreed that this was to stop. War was not a sport. It was a holy undertaking, and risking a valuable fighting man for vanity was a disservice to the crown, however much this angered the youth of the nobility. Juan believed that the monarchs failed to realize that one of the things that made the nobility better than commoners was precisely this overweening pride, a feeling that should be nurtured instead of discouraged. So, the Moors jeered at the Christians, and rode off laughing as the common foot soldiers began the work of setting up their camps and digging the first encircling trench which would signal the beginning of the siege.

But before settling down to a siege, Abu el Hassan, the King of Granada whose pavilion could be clearly seen from the walls, surrounded by the banners of the various contingents of his army, had apparently decided to push for a quick resolution, and two strong columns of infantry could be seen forming up at opposite ends of the city wall where the relatively flat plain allowed an easy approach. At least two thirds of the circumference of the walls was guarded by a long loop of the river and the same high cliffs Juan and his men had scaled, but the remainder opened out onto the Vega and was protected only by a modest dry moat and the city walls themselves, perhaps forty feet high and twenty feet thick, studded with square towers every hundred yards, which jutted out and allowed the defenders to shoot down at attackers who might reach the base of the wall itself without exposing themselves to return fire. The Christians had made use of the brief time since the capture of the town to reinforce some weak spots and shore up the wall where it had fallen into disrepair, but the defenders' main hope of salvation came from the dozen separate messengers the Marquis had sent galloping northward with word for Fernando and the other lords of Castile of the capture of Alhama and pleas for relief.

Juan had been pleasantly surprised and honored that the Marquis had changed his mind at the last moment and given another officer command of the citadel and sent Juan's detachment to defend one of the points of the wall that was now threatened with attack. The risk would be greater, of course, but so would the chance for further recognition and reward, which was the point of the whole exercise, as far as Juan was concerned. From their study of the terrain, this was a logical point of assault, as a dip in the ground beyond the dry moat gave the enemy a relatively protected approach to within two hundred yards of the walls. There would be pressure all along the line, but both Juan and the Marquis agreed that this was where they would launch their main effort if they were in the role of attackers, and they expected the Moors to act no differently. The Marquis raised his arm and a trumpeter sounded the call to arms. Juan saluted and raced along the parapet to his post, while the Marquis himself took command of the another threatened sector where a rocky outcrop near the walls would also provide the enemy some cover in their approach. Getting this assignment was a signal honor for a man of Juan's age, with so many more senior commanders in the army, and he had no intention of letting this chance for advancement slip.

Juan's sector of the wall was probably the weakest on the perimeter, both for the dead ground that gave the enemy an good approach and because, as the ground dropped away toward the river to his right, the wall here was relatively lower and flatter than anywhere else, so enemy scaling ladders would work better here, a point that would not be lost on the Moorish commanders. He now stood with the Basque at his side in the tower that flanked his sector, the one he estimated would be at the center of the Moorish attack, watching as a thick column of infantry turned and disappeared into the depression, like a snake slithering into its hole, the sounds of kettle drums and trumpets and of the lilting singing of what Juan supposed to be Moorish hymns making their way to them on the breeze while sunlight glinted off the steel of their spear points.

His men were spaced out along the wall, taking cover behind the merlons or peeking through the crenels for a sight of the enemy, stacks of crossbow bolts taken from the Moorish armories by their sides. The arquebusiers had extra horns of gunpowder and bags of shot, and there were even piles of paving stones pulled up from the street below to hurl down on the heads of the assault troops when they got close enough, primitive but still effectively deadly for all that. There were also sheaves of javelins for throwing, and each man had his own weapon of choice, sword, mace, or battleaxe, should the enemy reach the top of the wall, and long bill hooks for pushing away scaling ladders. As long as the Moors did not bring up artillery or siege engines, there was little chance of their making a breach in the wall, and mining underneath the walls would take time, so any fighting now would be done here along the ramparts.

Juan's sector was also equipped with some light artillery, but he had never had much use for these clumsy and inaccurate pieces of equipment. To make matters worse, the pieces left by the Moors were particularly old-fashioned. Other than a few wall-guns, just heavier versions of the arquebus set in a swivel atop the wall for support, there were three larger falconets, one in each of the towers in Juan's section of wall. These were long narrow iron or bronze tubes set in a wooden frame with a removable back end into which the powder charge and different forms of shot would be crammed. The rear piece would then be fitted into the larger tube and held in place with iron wedges hammered into the frame, a lengthy and dangerous process for each shot. The problem was that gunpowder was of highly uneven quality and could either burn too slowly, giving the projectile little force, or too quickly, risking an explosion of the tube and the dismemberment of the gunners and anyone else nearby. But

Juan had seen to the collection of a stack of case shot rounds, balls composed of metal scraps held together with cement which would disintegrate upon firing, spraying the attacking troops with shrapnel. He might not trust the weapons, besides considering them promiscuous and dishonorable compared to a stand-up fight between two men with swords, but he would use everything he had, and the flying metal would tear horrible gaps in the enemy lines if the guns worked at all. At least the thunder of their firing would tend to give heart to the defenders and to frighten the Moors.

Juan could now see spear points and the glint of metal just over a roll in a slight rise in the bald terrain to his front, and he knew that the Moors would be forming up for their assault. Suddenly a high-pitched voice rose above the crunch of marching feet outside and the buzz of voices along the wall, chanting something in Arabic, probably a summons of Allah to witness their struggle. This was answered by a deep roar from a thousand throats, a sound that gave even an experienced soldier like Juan a brief moment where his own breath stopped, and the first wave of enemy infantry poured over the crest and raced toward the dry moat brandishing swords and spears, with large round shields held up over their heads for protection.

Juan could see that some of the men carried bundles of branches, fascines which would be thrown into the ditch to construct a temporary causeway, and others carried shovels and picks for carving out protective holes for the archers who would provide covering fire for the attackers. Teams of men awkwardly hefted long ladders over their heads as they trotted forward, and all were urged on by a handful of noblemen, more richly dressed than the others, mounted on fine horses. They wore almost as much armor as was common among the Christians, while the common foot soldiers generally only had a coat of mail and a helmet, perhaps with a vest of quilted cotton or boiled leather for added protection against arrows. The Moors had always preferred quickness and ease of movement while the Christians tried to cover every exposed part of the body with metal plates, if the wearer could afford it. Juan himself had now put on a full suit of armor, just dull and dented iron, not beautifully worked and ornamented metal like that of the Marquis, and most of his men had scrounged additional coats of mail or bits of plate armor from their looting of the town, anything that would turn an arrowhead or spear point was worth trying, no matter how heavy or cumbersome, as each defender on the walls would probably not have to move more than a few paces in any direction during the course of the battle.

"Shoot!" Juan screamed, and his command was echoed by a dozen sergeants up and down the wall.

The simultaneous twang of the crossbows and the rattle of the arquebuses were lost as the three falconets were touched off. Juan winced, but none of the guns seemed to have exploded, and he breathed a little easier for the moment. The iron bolts and lead balls, even at the extreme range of one hundred and fifty yards, could hardly fail to find targets among the tightly packed Moors, and dozens of men pitched forward, leaving gaps in the formation, but these were quickly filled by those pressing on from behind, their speed only increasing as the attackers envisioned the defenders frantically reloading for another volley.

The front rank of Moors reached the ditch and held up their shields like a wall while those behind them heaved the fascines over them and into the moat, gradually building up a considerable pile. The shields stopped or deflected most of the arrows, but an occasional one would punch straight through, as would the arquebus balls and the solid shot from the wall guns, or find a small space between the shields, killing the shield bearer, who would crumple, opening a wider gap, into which the defenders would pour a deadly fire until another Moor was able to get a shield up. Meanwhile, those crossbow bolts that overshot the shield wall would almost invariably find a target among the rear ranks of the enemy.

But now the Moors were close enough to return fire as well. Arquebus balls began to spatter against the crenellated parapets, chipping away stone and whining off into the distance, or occasionally thudding into the head of an incautious defender, sending him toppling over backward off the wall. There were also clouds of Moorish archers, using the same composite bows their grandfathers had used. These had far less range and force than steel crossbows, but the archers could loose three or four arrows to every crossbow quarrel, and they were trained to fire indirectly, sending showers of arrows cascading down almost vertically on the heads of the defenders who were forced to cluster close to the wall as their only protection. Other Moors had taken up position on a rocky hill which rose higher than the walls of the city at one point off to the left end of the wall and also rained arrows down on the defenders from that direction at long range, forcing the Marquis to order the doors taken from the houses in that quarter and used to make an extension to the parapet on that part of the wall for a little extra protection.

The tower where Juan stood was a key to the defense of the wall. It constituted a little castle in its own right. In order to pass from one section of the wall to another, it was necessary to gain access to the towers that blocked the rampart and rose twenty feet above them, giving the occupiers a clear field of fire down onto the wall and along its base on both sides. The stairs within the tower were also the only easy way down to the ground from the wall, short of simply jumping nearly forty feet. To enhance the defensive value of the tower, there was a gap of about three feet between the doorway to the tower and the walkway along the wall. Normally, this would be covered with planks, allowing easy access to the tower for the defenders, but these planks could be removed by the tower garrison, leaving any attackers who did manage to get a foothold on the wall with no way of gaining access either to the tower or to the town below, unless, of course, the attackers were quick enough to seize control of the planks and the tower door before they could be secured.

The Moors had by now heaved enough fascines and baskets filled with earth into the dry moat to form a narrow, sagging causeway across to the town walls, and they surged forward, screaming, some of them carrying scaling ladders which they now planted in the ground and leaned against the wall. The defenders were firing every weapon as fast as it could be loaded, and the bodies of dozens of Moors helped to fill in the moat along with the fascines. Juan raced down the tower stairs, Gamal now at his back, to the wall level and grabbed a bill hook from a rack with which he shoved a scaling ladder away from the wall, toppling two Moorish soldiers into the ditch. They screamed as they fell. Although it was only twenty or thirty feet, not enough to kill a man unless he happened to land on the point of an upturned spear, even a broken leg could prove a fatal wound here as the man would be unlikely to be able to drag himself out of range before an arrow or lead ball found his back. The man next to him caught an arrow in the eye and fell to his knees, clawing at the shaft with both hands, howling plaintively, but Juan was too occupied to notice.

"They're enraged at what we did to their dead," Gamal shouted in Juan's ear.

"What?"

"I can hear their mullahs screaming at them from behind the shield wall. The dead from the fighting in the town. We just dumped them out in the fields where the crows and wild dogs got at them, and the mullahs take it as a sign that we just massacred the whole population and desecrated their bodies."

"What did they expect us to do, leave them in the town to fester and raise the plague?"

"I don't know, but that's what they're yelling at us. I don't expect, sir, that they plan to take many prisoners."

Juan just grunted and lunged with a short spear at the chest of a Moor who was just trying to clamber up over the lip of the wall. There seemed to be no end of Moors, but almost as suddenly as the assault had begun, it started to wane. Juan could now see a company of Spanish knights come charging out a sally port in the wall to his left, catching the Moors in the flank on the ground below and carving a swath through the more lightly armored Moslems, who began to give way. The men on the wall cheered and loosed another volley of arrows and bullets into the tightly packed ranks of the enemy.

Then the Moors broke. Those at the front turned to run but were blocked by hundreds more still trying to press across the narrow bridge over the ditch. Some just dropped into the moat and were trapped there, unable to climb the steep slope on the far side, until they were cut down by archers on the walls. The knights, led by Juan de Vera, the man who had carried Fernando's demand for renewed tribute to Abu el Hassan in Granada not long before the attack on Zahara the year before, hacked their way through the fleeing enemy like reapers at harvest time, seemingly invulnerable, some with three or four arrow shafts sticking in their armor but carried on by their blood lust, the fury of battle upon them.

When the last of the Moors on the near side of the moat had either been killed or had crossed over, it was the turn of the knights to run for shelter as a steady shower of arrows now pelted all around them. Juan let out a sigh and collapsed on the walkway, his back against the parapet. He had not slept in over forty-eight hours and had conducted a long forced march, scaled a mountain, and fought two separate battles during that time. And his all of men had done the same. He could see the look of fatigue on their faces as they flopped down all around him, their weariness even taking over from their sense of victory or their relief at having survived. Juan was ready to fall asleep right where he sat, but just then a shout went up from the streets below.

"Captain Ortega!" a sergeant was calling up to him. "The Marquis needs you at the water gate immediately."

Juan looked over at Gamal, who just shrugged and groaned as he pulled himself to his feet, extending an arm to help Juan up as well.

"The Moors are trying to divert the river," the Marquis said a few minutes later when Juan arrived, having paused only long enough to dunk his head in a horse trough to try to wash the dust and smoke from his eyes. The Marquis was dabbing at a bloody gash at his temple with a dirty rag as he leaned on his sword.

Juan stood with him along with de Vera and de Merlo and several other leaders, all stoop-shouldered and bathed in sweat mixed with blood, their own or that of their enemies. Even the most elegant armor now dented and gashed, their brightly colored surcoats now hanging in tatters from their shoulders.

"This is their town, and they know very well that there are no wells or springs within the city walls. Since their initial assault has failed, their best means of forcing our surrender is by driving us mad with thirst. A man can go weeks without eating, but only a couple of days without water. They've got men just upstream from the town driving pilings into the river to steer the river out across the Vega and away from the walls. We've got to stop them or we'll be done for in less than a week."

Nearly a thousand Spaniards poured out of the small gate near the river. Normally, inhabitants of the town could make their way down to the very edge of the stream by a covered way to draw their water. but Juan could see as he descended the narrow stairway and emerged through the heavy oak door that there was now nearly fifty yards of open ground, slippery, muddy open ground that water bearers would have to cross and that hundreds of Moorish archers had stationed themselves among the rocks along the opposite bank and were keeping up a steady fire on this killing field where a dozen bodies already lay, beginning to attract crows. About half of the Christian forces turned left and rushed upstream, the men shifting their shields to their right arms to cover themselves as best they could from the Moorish archers. The remainder dragged heavy mantlets, panels of wood and straw, to form a makeshift wall behind which a relay of men could hustle jars, barrels, and buckets down to the river, filling as many as possible under the galling fire and dragging them back up into the town.

Juan and his men were with the storming party, and they moved at a weary trot, every step an agony to their strained muscles, but they knew that every second they were exposed increased their chances of death before accomplishing anything. Juan could see that a strong body of Berber infantry, several thousand of them, arrayed in ranks ten deep, were formed in a blocking position about one hundred yards to the front, and behind them hundreds more were frantically hauling rocks and logs along the near bank and had built a mole nearly twenty yards out into the stream, forcing at least part of the river's flow over the opposite bank into what had been a dry gully leading away from the town where the muddy water now gushed, as if celebrating its liberation from the restrictions of the river banks.

The Christian knights and men-at-arms formed the front rank, allowing the crossbowmen and arquebusiers to take shelter behind them and loose a hurried volley which opened a few gaps in the Moorish line, but not enough. The dark-skinned North Africans stolidly stepped forward over their own dead, bracing their long spears to meet the Spanish charge.

"Santiago and at them!" shrieked Diego de Merlo, and the Christians advanced at a run, a large banner of the Holy Virgin well to the front.

The Spanish line collided with the Moorish phalanx with a loud crash. Juan knocked the point of a spear to one side with the edge of his shield and hacked downward at the Moor behind it, then reversing his blow to take out the man to his right. Gamal had ducked under the row of Moorish shields and thrust upward with his long, curved blade, and the Basque was hewing a path for himself on Juan's right with a double-bladed battle axe, sending chunks of wood and leather from the shields he destroyed flying about him in every direction. The Castros formed the wings of the wedge, with Juan at its apex, and the Minorcan stood in the center cocking and firing his crossbow feverishly to the right and left, picking out targets through gaps in the shields wall to prevent the Moors from closing them back up.

The Moors gave ground grudgingly under the weight of the heavily armored Spaniards, but reinforcements pressed forward, and their line held, forcing the Spanish to fight for every foot. What was worse, since the Moors outnumbered the Castilians by four or five-to-one, while the right of the Christian line was anchored on the riverbank, the Moorish lines extended well beyond the Christian left, and the Moors pressed around this flank more and more with every step the Spaniards advanced. This threatened Juan and his compatriots with being cut off and destroyed beyond supporting distance of the town walls, pinned up against the river.

Then there was a bugle call from the direction of the town, and Juan turned to see another company of knights, these mounted on richly caparisoned horses, charging along the wall to come up on the Christian left and drive the Moors back. He could see the Marquis, riding a large gray, at the forefront of the attack, scattering the Moorish infantry before him with his greatsword hacking to left and right as he rode. But this could only be a brief respite as even the finest knights could only make so much of an impression on the enemy when they were only forty or fifty against thousands. More Moors were marching up to the sound of battle, and the Spanish had already suffered heavy losses, nearly all of their men being wounded to some degree, and Diego de Merlo took advantage of the disorder caused in the enemy ranks by the cavalry sortie to call a retreat.

The Castilians backed toward the river gate, keeping their shields up and stepping over the dead and wounded. They dragged as many of their own wounded with them as they could and paused only to dispatch any Moors in their path who might still be living. The Moors pressed after them now for the first fifty or so yards, keeping up their shower of arrows and bullets, happily falling on any stragglers too weak to keep up with the main body. They had been hoping for the Spaniards to break, as an army is at its most vulnerable when in flight, but when the Spaniards held together, the equally weary Moors decided to let them go. Then, once the column had fallen back to within range of the town walls, the arquebuses and cannon served to keep enemy at a respectful distance, and both sides were content to call an end to the day's fighting, the Christians in possession of the town, but the Moors free to continue their work of diverting much of the water flow of the river.

Juan staggered back through the sally port of the river wall, tripping over the legs of other men who had only had enough strength to get this far before collapsing. Water casks were stacked everywhere, but he noticed that not all of them were full. The Marquis had just dismounted in the courtyard inside the walls and was hanging on the saddlebow of his mount. The wound on his temple had dried, but he now had a deep gash on his forearm where the blow of an ax had cut through his steel greave, and his squire was gingerly removing his mail gauntlet as the Marquis winced.

"This doesn't look good, my lord," Juan sighed.

"It's worse than you know," the Marquis said. "We just got word that Don Alonso de Aguilar from Cordoba had raised a small force to come to our aid and was bringing our baggage trains from the Yegua River with him. Unfortunately, he was still in the mountains when the Moorish army arrived here. If he had continued on his way, the Moors would have crushed him out in the open before he could have reached us, and we could not have helped him. So, he turned back. At least he was able to save our baggage and artillery for the time when a larger force can be collected, but it means that we cannot hope for relief for days at the very least, probably more on the order of weeks."

"It would have been well to have our artillery and supplies," Juan commented.

"I would have been satisfied with the men he had with him. It was the baggage that slowed him down. An extra thousand men would have been very useful. We have barely enough troops to man the walls when the Moors are active, and those will tire out very quickly."

Juan nodded sadly and was about to sit down on a crate when renewed shouting and trumpeting from the walls told him that a new enemy assault was in progress, in his sector. He jerked his chin at the Basque and the others, who groggily dragged themselves to their feet and followed him along the street leading toward his tower.

While the intensity of the Moorish attacks dropped off in the coming days, there was never a period of more than a few hours without some kind of alarm at one point or another around the perimeter of the town. Even when Juan's sector was not directly targeted, this usually involved the men being called to arms, and although the Marquis had given Juan a fine two-story house for his personal use, he and his men spent most nights sleeping in their battered armor and torn chain mail, propped against the battlements as best they could. The Moors, with their great superiority in numbers, which were augmented by the arrival of new contingents almost every day, could afford to rotate units in direct contact with the Christians and to replace their losses, and they were gradually wearing the defenders down by attrition. Juan and his men were like walking corpses just looking for a place to lie down, and they all responded to the trumpet calls which signaled a new enemy attack by slogging forward at a walk instead of their usual steady run.

As bad as the combat fatigue was, however, far worse was the constant thirst. In their random sacking of the town after its surrender, the soldiers, most of whom assumed that they would be burning the whole place to the ground and making a quick getaway, had carelessly destroyed a good deal of the provisions that had been available within the walls, but there was still enough food to last for some time. The town had a reserve of grain that had only recently been gathered, and every house had a small stock of fruits and vegetables on hand while most of the town's residents had either died or fled. But, with every trip to the much-diminished river involving a full-scale sally by nearly half the garrison in the face of frantic Moorish harassing fire from the heights on the far bank, what water was obtained had to be carefully rationed, little more than a cup a day per man.

Since Juan and most Christians tended to equate bathing with Jews and Moslems, they hardly missed the opportunity to wash themselves, although the stench of the sweat and blood soaked bodies was becoming a bit much even for their jaded noses. It was only spring, so the worst of the oppressive heat of the summer was not a problem, but the exertions of the men in the constant fighting and labor parties to repair sections of the wall that the enemy destroyed drained them, and Juan's tongue felt swollen to the size of his foot and his lips were cracked and peeling. Even the discovery of a large half-filled cistern hidden within the walls only served to prolong the agony instead of to relieve it.

For there was no indication for several weeks of when relief would come. Then, finally, a messenger, a converted Moslem soldier, had managed to slip through the Moorish lines from the north with news that the Count of Medina Sidonia was marching at the head of some five thousand horse and nearly fifty thousand foot to the relief of Alhama. This normally welcome news caused the Marquis to fall into a fit of rage, since his family and that of Medina Sidonia had been engaged in a blood feud for years, and the Marquis said more than once that he would just as soon die on the walls as owe his life to a man to whom he attributed more than a natural fondness for farm animals. But there was no questioning that Medina Sidonia had as well-earned a reputation as a field commander as did the Marquis, and the spirits of the entire army were raised, each man finding time to climb to the highest tower to scan the horizon for signs of the dust cloud which would presage the arrival of the relieving force.

But word of Medina Sidonia's march had reached Abu el Hassan even more quickly. Since the new Christian army was at least as large as his own, the Moorish king could not afford to be caught in the open between the tough garrison of Alhama and this second force, so he had to make one final effort to take the town or abandon the siege all together. His plan was to repeat the performance of Juan Ortega himself, sending a small force of picked fighters to scale the most inaccessible part of the walls, first clawing their way up the cliffs on the river side of the fortress, where the Christians would be least vigilant in the early hours of the morning, and when they would have the smallest force on the walls.

Juan's shrunken contingent, which included his small band of regular followers, the Basque, the Castros, Gamal, and Diego Escudero, the Minorcan, plus about one hundred men-at-arms, all that remained of the two hundred men who had scaled the walls of the citadel with him, had been given charge of the tower protecting the main gate of the town. Most of these were stationed within and on top of the tower itself, to fire down on the dry moat beyond the walls, which had largely been filled in by the Moors, as this was one of their favorite points of attack. Juan and about twenty men occupied the street-level guardhouse just inside the gate, protecting the windlasses that controlled the portcullis and the heavy wooden drawbridge as well as the inner doors of the entrance to the town. He and the Basque were sprawled on a rough wooden bench, fitfully sleeping, when a soldier stumbled into the doorway, blood streaming from a gash over his eye.

"The Moors! They're inside the walls!" he gasped, and Juan was already on his feet, his sword in his hand.

"Where?" Juan grunted.

"Over by the river side. They climbed the wall and killed the sentries before they were discovered. My master, Diego de Merlo has retaken the walls, but we think a company of Moors slipped away from the fighting and is probably headed this way to try to force open the gates to their army."

"They've got no other way out now," the Basque said, slipping a shield onto his arm and hefting his axe. "So they'll be highly motivated gentlemen."

Juan stepped out of the guardhouse while the Basque ran through the rooms rousting out the other men. He could hear the faint sound of fighting from two directions, the dull thud of cannon and rattle of arquebuses from the north, but that had been going on for some time, probably a Moorish diversion for this main attack. But now there was something far closer, the clash of steel and a trumpet call from just around the corner of one of the streets leading into the little plaza facing the gate. And just then there appeared a pair of Christian pikemen, running hard for the gate, but one of them stumbled and fell, an arrow protruding from the back of his neck. Behind them emerged the head of a tight column of bearded Moors, trotting easily and chanting something unintelligible in time with their pounding steps.

Most of the Moors were heavily armored, much like Christian knights, and these surrounded with their bodies and shields a core of lighter troops carrying crossbows and arquebuses, the slow matches of which Juan could see glowing red in the early morning shadows which suffused the town with a faint blue light. Juan recognized them as *ghazi*, the fanatical, even suicidal, holy warriors who dedicated their whole lives, which did not tend to be very long, to the battle against the enemies of Islam. They always sought out the hottest part of the fight, and they *never* surrendered.

The plaza was about fifty yards across, and Juan and his men were forming up in front of the gate entrance. There weren't enough of them to form a solid front, so Juan spaced them out, about a full pace apart, at least turning necessity into a virtue by giving them more room to use their weapons. He turned and saw Diego, the Minorcan, waving his crossbow from atop the gate tower, flanked by half a dozen other archers and musketeers. Unfortunately, most of the firing ports in the tower faced outward, not in toward the city, so they would be only of limited help in the coming battle, and the Moors outside the walls would certainly be coming to try to storm the gate at the same time, preventing Juan from weakening his forces on the walls. There would be more Christian reinforcements coming any moment, he hoped, but until they arrived, Juan and his men were all that stood between these Moors and the gate, and thus with mastery of the town's defenses. He would only be on his own for ten or fifteen minutes, but he expected that that would seem like a very long time indeed.

Diego's men loosed a volley of missiles from above as soon as the Moors came within range, but only a couple of attackers went down, the others protecting themselves ably with their bronze embossed shields. The Moors shrieked and broke into a dead run, splitting up to hit each of Juan's men with an advantage of two or three to one.

Juan side-stepped the charge of the leading Moor, a huge man wielding a two-handed sword, and shoved him aside with his shield to throw him off balance for a moment. He then stepped up to attack at the two men following the leader, who had apparently assumed that their chief would take out this opponent. One was armed with a short thrusting spear and a sword, the other carried a large shield and a spiked ball on a chain, what the Christians called a "holy water sprinkler." Juan hacked downward at the shield man, neatly lopping off his right leg at the knee, then spun to deliver a wild blow at the other, hoping to get lucky. The spearman parried the attack, but the shield man was down on the ground, an astonished look on his face as he tried to staunch the spurting blood from the stump of his leg with his hands.

Now the big man had recovered his footing, and Juan was forced backward, totally defensive as he blocked slashes and thrusts with his sword and shield frantically. Juan kept skipping to one side, trying to keep himself between the attackers and the gate and also maneuvering to try to put one attacker in the other's path so that he would only have to deal with one at any given moment. Suddenly, Juan felt something whistle past his ear, and the smaller man jerked backward, dropping his weapons, the tail of a quarrel sprouting from one of his eye sockets. He heard Diego grunt just behind his shoulder as he levered the string of his crossbow back into firing position.

"We couldn't pick targets from up above with you all mixed together down here," Diego wheezed as Juan knocked aside another blow from the big Moor and thrust at him with his own sword.

"Just in time," Juan replied.

Not all of Juan's men had been as lucky, and nearly half of them were down, the others pressed back into an increasingly tight ring in front of the gate, harried by at least fifty Moors to their fifteen to twenty. Even Asco had joined the battle, a proven veteran, who would pick his moment and dash forward latching onto the exposed ankle or wrist of an attacker precisely when it gave one of the Spaniards a chance to slip in a killing blow, and then darting back to the protection of the men and their armor. Juan was about to call a retreat into the tower, abandoning the gate and hoping to keep the Moors from opening it by shooting at them through the "murder holes", arrow slits built into the walls and roof of the passageway through the gate tower, when another trumpet call sounded, and he saw a mob of Christians, four or five knights leading an assortment of foot soldiers, teamsters, and servants, armed with whatever had come to hand, charging out from a side street with a cry of "Santiago and at them!"

Some ten of the Moors turned about to face this new threat, while the remainder pressed on against Juan's men all the harder, but the Christians could feel that the tide was turning. Houses pressed close on either side of the gate here, constricting the approach, and allowing Juan to form a solid, if thin, line, while not all of the Moors were able to bring their weapons to bear. Juan slashed wildly, right and left, no longer trying to score blows against his opponents, just hoping to use his blade to create a barrier for long enough for more garrison troops to show up to crush the enemy from behind. Off on one flank the Castros were fighting back to back, as the Moors tried to turn around and get behind them. Gamal was on his left, screaming obscenities in Arabic that Juan, with his sketchy grasp of the language, could barely understand, something about the Shia way being the only true road to God, while Sunnis were destined to perform oral sex with dogs and pigs in Hell for all eternity. This had something to do with a factional problem within Islam that Juan had never really comprehended. The Basque was on his right, as usual, making graceful, powerful arcs with his axe, and Diego would poke his crossbow over Juan's shoulder from time to time, firing a bolt into the face of an opponent and slipping back to reload.

It was the Moors who were tiring now. They had probably been marching and climbing all night and fighting since before dawn, while more and more Christian troops came rushing up behind them and others took up positions on the rooftops of the houses bordering the plaza, pouring a galling fire down on their heads. There was even a steady trickle of reinforcements that was reaching Juan from the stairway within the tower after having made their way to the scene along the walls. There were less than thirty Moors left, many of them already wounded, but fighting on in puddles of their own blood, with no hope of escape or even quarter. They fell, one by one. A small Moorish cannon could be heard thumping away at the outer wall, but, unless the assault party could open the gates, they stood no more chance of battering their way through now than at any other time during the siege.

The big Moor was still on his feet, an arrow lodged in one shoulder, with one hand grasping the banner of the company, the other fending off Juan and two other Christians. He backed up against the wall of a house for his last stand, weaving a cage of steel around himself that blocked every blow that Juan threw at him, but Diego finally lunged forward, hooking his sword arm with the cross piece of his bow and holding it aside for one crucial second as Juan rammed his sword point home with all his weight behind it, just under the man's breast plate. The Moor's eyes bugged out, and he coughed up a spurt of blood, went down on one knee, and collapsed, wrenching Juan's sword out of his hand, but by now he was the last of the attackers, and Juan crumpled to the ground next to him, completely spent as well. Too tired to cheer with the others, he leaned against the bloody corpse while some of the newly arrived troops hacked off the heads of the fallen Moors and rushed off howling like madmen to hurl them over the ramparts into the ranks of the attackers outside.

Two days later, during which time the Moors had done little more than probe the defenses in a half-hearted manner, the lookouts on the walls awoke the garrison at dawn with the welcome news that the enemy trenches were empty, their tents struck, and the tail of their army was only just visible in the dawn light as it made its way across the plain toward Granada. They had left their campfires burning during the night to give the impression of occupation, but these had now burned down to smoking ashes, and the Moorish army was gone. At the same time, the brightly colored banners of Medina Sidonia's army were just picking out the first rays of sunlight coming from the west, and the faint rattle of drums and the brassy din of trumpets could now be heard if the wind were just right. The men swarmed to the battlements, screaming and pounding their swords against their shields, while the Marquis and a small band of his captains mounted up to ride out to meet their saviors.

Juan, being one of the lowest ranking men among them, rode in the rear of the little party, and his thoughts were troubled. Knowing the bad blood that existed between the Marquis and their rescuer, he would not be surprised if these late comers demanded a share in the spoils of the capture of Alhama, which would certainly be no more popular with the haggard defenders than it would be to Juan himself. On the one hand, he could not deny that the little garrison could not have held out forever against the Moors and would have had to been relieved in order for the gold, silks, and slaves they had taken to have any real value. On the other hand, it was Juan and the others who had marched and fought for weeks against tremendous odds, facing death every day, while Medina Sidonia's men had hardly even drawn their swords or gone without a meal since crossing the border in their leisurely approach march.

The Marquis led his small group of riders out past the old Moorish camp onto a small rise to await Medina Sidonia. With the two armies contending so nearby, the peasants had not bothered to plant these fields, but the soil was so rich that the odd grains from last harvest that had fallen here were already sprouting tender green shoots between the horses' hooves, a reminder that the true wealth of this territory was not in gold but in the land itself. Close at hand, Juan could see a cluster of stumps where a grove of mulberry trees, used in Granada's famous silk industry, had been chopped down for the construction of mantlets and abatis for the Moors' siege works, now abandoned about the city. Just beyond the grove of stumps, Juan could make out row after row of freshly turned mounds of earth, where the Moors had buried their dead, the only thing in the scene that gave him a sense of accomplishment.

Medina Sidonia led a column of some fifty horsemen at a smart canter out ahead of the main army. They stood in marked contrast to the Marquis' men. The former wore shining armor and colorful cloaks and surcoats, carrying beautifully embroidered silk banners and pennants on the lance heads. The latter looked as if they had been dressed from the cast off from a scrap metal yard, their armor dented and creased, their mail hanging in tatters, and rust-colored bandages taking the place of fine undergarments. The horses of the new arrivals capered and pranced as their riders used their skill to hold them in one place, while the mounts of the defenders of Alhama, stood with drooping heads, tentatively searching with their lips for any stray bit of grass amid the pebbles on the hilltop, their ribs and hip bones sticking out at all angles, and their hides bearing as many scars as those of their riders.

The two aristocrats rode toward each other unsmiling, and Juan would not have been surprised if they had drawn their weapons, but, instead, Medina Sidonia reached up and removed his helmet and bowed, deftly getting his own tall charger to bend its forelegs at the same time.

"Hail to the conqueror of Alhama!" he shouted for all to hear, and his men took up the cheer, raising their lances on high.

The Marquis was obviously taken aback and took a moment to collect himself. "We welcome our most noble guest and protector," he replied at length.

"All Christendom has heard of your deeds, and we only hope that you will allow us to provide you with fresh troops to garrison this fortress and allow your men to return home with their justly earned spoils. Let them rest for the day when we can ride together against the infidel from this powerful enclave you have carved out in the heart of the Moorish lands. We have taken the field for God and our royal sovereigns. There will be plenty of other Moorish cities to plunder, so I wish your valiant men joy of the booty that they have taken from the clutches of the enemy."

And that was it. Juan felt himself suddenly release the breath he had not realized that he had been holding. The two men grasped forearms and talked for some time as the Marquis led them all back to the city, but there was no longer anything to fear. Juan's booty would not be stolen, and now they would be free to return to Andalusia and possibly to an audience with the king, where his real fortune would be made.

There was no more trouble from the Moors, and the remnants of the original expedition rode north few days later, leading pack horses laden with the loot of Alhama and long columns of prisoners, those whose relatives in Granada had not managed to provide a suitable ransom. Juan sent the Basque off with a pair of fine horses, eight strong Moorish slaves, and a small fortune of nearly one hundred gold ducats to deliver to his father back at Trujillo, more to snub the man and Juan's brother than to help the estate recover, while Juan himself accompanied the Marquis to Antequerra where the Catholic kings, Fernando and Isabel were awaiting a detailed account of the campaign. The Moorish girl he had enjoyed for several nights during the siege, in his rare free time, had finally managed to get a sharp bit of glass and slash her wrists, but Juan was just grateful that she had not chosen to try to cut his own throat in his sleep. She had long since ceased to excite him, having become all together too resigned to her fate and to the punishment he inflicted on her, although he resented being deprived of that one last look of desperate terror that a girl gets in her eyes when she realizes that her final moments on earth had come. Still, there was nothing to do about it now, and there would be other girls.

The town of Antequera was perched on top of a steep hill for defensive purposes, as were most of the towns in this part of the peninsula, the cream colored walls of the town and its houses seeming to grow out of the top of the dun hillside. Juan had not expected to be included in the talks of the noble commanders of the army with the sovereigns, and he wasn't, although the Marquis did take the trouble to introduce him briefly to Fernando and to give the king a fulsome account of Juan's deeds in the conquest of Alhama and its subsequent defense. The King had taken Juan's hand in his firm grip and stared deep into his eyes.

"I see from your cloak that you are of the *Santa Hermandad*," Fernando said without releasing Juan from his handclasp.

"That is my honor, sire," Juan replied.

"Good. We need men like you. With the permission of the Marquis, I would like you to join my military household."

Juan glanced toward the Marquis who snorted theatrically, then just winked at him and nodded.

"I can think of no greater joy than to serve my lord."

"It's settled then," the King went on, and, breaking off his discussion with the Marquis, he personally took Juan by the arm and led him through the passageways of the small manor of the governor of the town to the hall where the rest of the court was gathered.

Juan had never been to court before. His contacts with the upper nobility had always been on campaign, in the field, and the dinners and entertainments to which he had been invited in the past had always been those given by the local gentry. He could immediately see the difference between real quality people and the country bumpkins with whom he was used to associate. As an economy measure, Juan's household, that of his father back home in Trujillo that is, had always been accustomed to retire at nightfall to save on the cost of candles just like common peasants, but here the hall was ablaze with hundreds of candles, torches, and oil lamps, and the lights were reflected by and glistened on the acres of cloth of gold worn by the crowd of elegant ladies, by their necklaces of silver and gold set with all sorts of jewels, their bracelets, diadems, and the polished ceremonial armor and only slightly less evident jewelry of the gentlemen. Although he had had a chance to change into fresh clothing, the best he had, and even to bathe before meeting the King, Juan had an inescapable feeling of inferiority, both in dress and intellectual preparation for this encounter with the ruling class of Spain.

The King escorted Juan through the crowd, which parted effortlessly for him, conversation ceasing, the men bowing and the women performing curtseys to the King, but all eyes were on Juan, the new boy in town to whom the King was showing such attention, wondering who he was and where he was from. The crudely embroidered coat of arms of his house that he wore on his left breast would not be any more familiar to them than his face. This in itself was a new thrill for Juan, and he met the jealous, hostile glances of the male courtiers with arrogant defiance, and he replied to the coquettish smiles of the ladies by dipping one eyebrow in what he imagined was a sensual look, although his stomach churned at the thought that any of them might think to take him up on the offer.

They finally came to a cluster of ladies who did not move aside for the King, although they too curtseyed prettily. One bowed less deeply than the others and then reached out to take the King's free hand.

"My dear," the King began. "This is the young cavalier of whom *everyone* is speaking, the one who took Alhama almost single-handed." Juan could feel the color rise in his cheeks. *Of whom everyone is speaking?* And this from the king's own lips.

The Queen was cool and aristocratic and gave him a distant smile. She extended her hand, and Juan went down on one knee and brushed her knuckles with his lips.

"Your Majesty. Juan Ortega de Prado, your humble servant."

Isabel pulled gently at his hand as a signal for him to rise.

"All Christendom owes you a debt, sir. You have bearded the Moorish lion in his den and shown that, while he may be a valiant fighter, he is not to be feared by soldiers under the protection of our Lord, the True Church, and the Holy Virgin."

"I only played a small part, Your Majesty," Juan mumbled, but even as he spoke to the Queen, his gaze drifted past her shoulder to the face of a young woman standing just behind her. She was tall and had chestnut colored hair and hypnotic deep blue eyes. She was not as finely dressed as the Queen or some of the other ladies, but she clearly was a regular member of the court from her comfortable attitude, not a jumped up provincial like himself. The woman smiled politely, but only just, and then turned to hide her face behind her fan, and Juan realized that his mouth was hanging open. He had never seen a woman as striking, someone who simply robbed him of his self-possession so completely. The King cleared his throat, and Juan felt his face go deep red once again.

"I thought it might be appropriate to take this opportunity to show our gratitude, sir," and he pulled his sword from its sheath.

Juan stood there for a moment, dumbly staring at the jeweled hilt of the sword and the highly polished blade, suddenly feeling ashamed of the battered and chipped blade of his own sword at his side. Then he realized what was happening and knelt. Fernando tapped him lightly on each shoulder with the blade of his sword.

"Arise, Don Juan Ortega de Prado, Knight, and show yourself to my court." Fernando turned slightly and snapped his fingers at a young page dressed in red velvet marked out with the yoke and arrows symbol in gold. The page appeared to understand the gesture and handed the king something wrapped in a red velvet cloth similar to his livery. The king flipped aside the corners of the cloth, revealing a slender pair of gold spurs.

"As a symbol of your entering on your knighthood, sir," he announced in a deep baritone, holding the spurs up high for all to see. "You will also find that we have selected for you a fine gelding, properly equipped with saddle, armor, and bardings in the colors of your family crest as well as a decent suit of armor, which it is our wish that you will wear into battle the next time you choose to beard the Moorish lion in his den."

There was a general murmur of approval from the crowd and scattered applause, but the king held up his free hand for silence.

"And, lastly," he went on, "in recognition of your valor and the contribution you have made to the reconquest, one that the troubadors are no doubt already at work putting into verse to immortalize you, we have chosen to name you *señor* of the town of, of...." The king half turned toward the page again.

"San Juan de la Roca," the page whispered discreetly.

"Yes, of course, San Juan de la Roca," the king boomed out. "A good name, since your name is Juan, and you are like a rock. It's not much of a town, of course, more of a village actually, somewhere near Lucena. It also lies perilously close to the Moorish border, so it will take some looking after, but one doesn't expect that that will cause a warrior like yourself much concern. It does have a stout stone tower and about fifty peasants whose produce will offer you a modest income, once the tithes for the Church and the king's taxes have been paid, naturally."

The king let out a hearty laugh that was immediately echoed by everyone in the hall, except for Juan. Juan took the spurs dumbly and just stood there, turning his body slowly, his shoulders hunched with embarrassment, but his eyes seeking out the young woman, glowing with the thought that she had witnessed this, the proudest moment of his life. The other courtiers smiled and nodded, and some clapped limply, but she was gone.

Chapter Three

Granada

Muhammad was proud to acknowledge that he had been the principal trainer of the young prince in the use of arms. The youth had grown into a lithe but powerful young man, skilled with sword, lance, and crossbow and a graceful and enthusiastic horseman. It was true that he had not had occasion to put these skills into practice on the field of battle, his life being too valuable to risk unnecessarily, only in the stylized tournaments held at festivals, but it was clear that he would perform well against a real enemy when the situation demanded, as it inevitably would of any king of Granada.

Muhammad was less proud to admit that he had also been the prince's tutor in things intellectual and political, in the intricate maneuvers that were involved in governing a fragmented kingdom and in dealing with the jealous and powerful nobles that dominated it as well as with the intricacies of international diplomacy in a dangerous world. Although the prince was certainly intelligent enough, he had a tendency to be ruled more by his emotions than by his reason, and Muhammad had the grim feeling that the prince's emotions were not stable, nor were they geared toward the common good of the kingdom. While it might be true that the kingdom belonged to the sovereign by the grace of God, it was Muhammad's belief that the ruler must put the welfare of the people first in order to be respected, obeyed, and even beloved, yet the young prince saw everything in life only in terms of how it made *him* feel, and those things that did not make him feel good, immediately, simply did not get done.

Ever since the king had returned from his disastrous campaign against Alhama, his once proud and powerful army reduced by battle and disease to a ragged column that looked more like refugees than veteran soldiers, he had been openly jeered in the streets of Granada by widows wailing over the pointless deaths of their menfolk, and talk within the halls of the Alhambra criticized the king as the leader who had allowed the Christians to establish a powerful enclave in the very heart of what remained of Moorish Spain. The soldiers in his defeated army had been greeted warmly enough by their own relatives as they rode through the city, but the entourage of the king and his notables had been showered with rotten fruit, the contents of chamber pots, and even the pots themselves, as they hurriedly made their way through the narrow streets and up to the sanctuary of the Alhambra. The population of Granada had always been notoriously fickle, and their attitude hardly surprised Muhammad. News of a victory over the Christians in a minor skirmish would have them throwing flowers instead of rotten eggs tomorrow. What worried Muhammad was the young prince's attitude.

"Now is the time, I tell you," the prince would chant to anyone who could be forced to listen. "There is a prophecy that I will become king, and the old man's defeat has opened that door to me. There is no point in waiting until he is dead, when perhaps it might be too late and there will be no kingdom at all left for me to inherit. Now is the time to make the prophecy come true."

"I do not hold with prophecies that do not appear in the Koran, my lord," Muhammad would patiently explain to him. "'Astrology is the silly step daughter of astronomy,' as Aristotle once said, and it has no basis in fact. But, if you insist on believing in such things, I should remind you that the prophecy also mentions that your reign will mark the downfall of Moorish Spain, so why should you be so eager to bring those things to pass?"

"That is the part of the prophecy that we can change, *muhtasib*," the prince had replied, slapping his tutor on the back genially. Whenever he disagreed with Muhammad, which was happening more and more often these days, the prince liked to remind him of the rather humble origins from which the prince had raised him.

Unfortunately, there were plenty of courtiers in the little flock of perfumed young men who clustered about the prince who were more than willing to reinforce his own notions of grandeur. They were men who would never rise to power through their own merits and only hoped to do so by pleasing the prince, saying what he wanted to hear and then riding to greatness by clutching at the hem of his robes. Some of them were simple adventurers, some sons of noble families in their own right, like the syrupy Hafez who belonged to the powerful Abencerrajes clan, but Muhammad would have sooner trusted his fate to the common sense of a flock of sheep than to their combined analytical capabilities.

What concerned Muhammad most, however, was the attitude of Prince Abu's mother, Fatima. She was obsessed with the idea that her son would become king, and engaged in a constant guerrilla warfare within the palace with King Abu l-Hassan's other wives, notably the sensuous Aixa, and their progeny. Unlike the prince's foppish hangers on, there

227

was no doubting Fatima's political acuity in most matters. It was only on the issue of Abu's ascending to the throne, and sooner rather than later, that she was so single-minded that all normal reason went directly out the window, and Muhammad had come upon her more than once, droning into her son's ear that it was his destiny to become king and that no one and nothing must stand in his way, while the prince would just smile and nod blankly. Muhammad suspected that she had been doing this since he was an infant, her version of the traditional nursery rhyme, to compensate for the years of terror through which she must have suffered, never being certain when the old king would shunt them aside or some palace rival would see to their more permanent elimination in the deadly game of chess that was the passion of the court. Muhammad knew that she and her son had even been imprisoned on more than one occasion, with every likelihood of a sudden and painful death as a result of palace intrigues, either by official execution or the more subtle poisoning that was most fashionable in court circles. She had come to the conclusion that the only way to ultimately guarantee their security was for her and her son to seize power for themselves, oblivious to the fact that her search for total power was itself a threat to those around her who would necessarily work all the harder, and more unscrupulously, against her. It was also clear to Muhammad that it was Fatima who planned to be the power behind the throne. Under Moslem law, she could not hope to take the crown for herself, unlike her counterpart Isabel in Castile, and it was only through Abu that she would be able to rule. The fact that she would likely make a much better sovereign than many men who had held the position in recent years did nothing to alter Muhammad's concern that Fatima would not hesitate to run any risk of destroying the kingdom in order to secure the throne for her son.

Finally, when what Muhammad had feared would happen did happen, it all happened too quickly. The residents of Granada had fully expected the king's bedraggled troops to be followed in short order by hordes of Christian knights, encrusted with armor and bristling with weapons, thundering at the gates of the city, and there had been hurried efforts to reinforce the walls and lay in stores of food to withstand a siege. But the Christians seemed content to thank their God for their successes, to replace the garrison at Alhama with fresh troops and to withdraw the bulk of their army across the frontier without further ado. Life in the capital, therefore, eventually returned to what passed for normalcy, the merchants crowding the *souq*, although never as many as before the fall of Alhama, workers hustling from one job to another across the city, and bands of armed men roaming the streets looking for trouble, purporting to be in the service of the prince, the king, or the king's brother, the doughty warrior Muhammad ben Sa'd, known as el Zagal, who also was known to have his eyes on the throne.

This false sense of calm had apparently convinced the king that it was safe to return to his usual pattern of activities, and, soon thereafter, Muhammad watched as a small party of elegant nobles, dressed in flowing robes of silk and accompanied by an escort of lancers and by mounted musicians playing tambourines, flutes, and drums, rode their fine stallions out the gate of the Alhambra for a royal visit to the bath houses in the nearby town of Alixares. Muhammad, in his role as semi-professional physician, was a great believer in the healthfulness of frequent bathing, unlike the Christians who associated contact with water with disease and death. He often went to the baths of the Colmenares Palace within the Alhambra, passing from the *frigidarium*, the refreshingly cool pool built on the Roman model, to the other bathing rooms with warm water, and then the steam room and back again. The water was heated by fires constantly stoked beneath the baths, with the pipes for the warm water running under the tile floor, giving the entire building a pleasantly humid tropical aspect. As far as

Muhammad knew, the rooms had actually been in regular use since Roman times, which explained the retention of Latin names. The king, however, was going to the natural thermal baths outside the walls, which were also enjoyable and reportedly very therapeutic, but Muhammad had to question the wisdom of the display of pomp and leisure at a time when the city was effectively in a state of mourning and when the population was seething at the insult to Moorish pride inflicted on them by the Christians and longing for revenge and a ruler who would give it to them.

Perhaps the king felt that he needed to demonstrate his presence to the population, to reinforce their awe of the crown with a show of wealth and power, to give them confidence in their own safety by his own ostentatious attention to leisure activity. In any event, this was not how the outing was taken by the people, many of whom were still wearing the traditional white mourning garb for lost friends or relatives killed at Alhama. From the walls of the palace complex, Muhammad could see people blatantly turning their backs on the little procession, shopkeepers pulling their shutters to until the horsemen had passed, and he could hear anonymous catcalls emanating from shadowy side streets, voices calling on Allah to witness the lack of respect shown by the king for those who had died in his service.

As Muhammad watched this, he felt a hand rest lightly on his shoulder.

"You see," the prince's honey-sweet voice whispered in his ear. "The king has lost the sympathy of the people. There only remains one thing for us to do."

"And what is that, my lord?"

"Just watch this."

The prince simply turned Muhammad around by the shoulders and led him to the interior side of the walls. Below them a column of about fifty of the prince's Sudanese guards were marching toward the Gate of Justice, resplendent in their brilliantly white robes and turbans, their round black shields, their long lances, and their ebony skin in sharp contrast. The gate was guarded by a squad of the king's own Christian bodyguard, stocky men-at-arms dressed in chain mail and iron breastplates and greaves whose long blonde or red hair protruded from under their helmets and covered their shoulders like furry capes. Muhammad expected the gate guards to challenge the Sudanese at any moment and start a free-for-all for control of the passageway, and he was about to beg the prince to call his men off to avoid provoking an open civil war within the palace itself.

But, just then, the captain of the Sudanese raised his hand in greeting to the commander of the Christians, who responded in kind. The Sudanese troops then moved into the gatehouse while a few of them helped the Christians to swing the massive gates shut and to bar them.

The prince turned to Muhammad with a vacant smile of victory.

"It seems that my mother has been saving money secretly for some time from her household expenses and paid the captain of my father's bodyguard over a thousand gold dirhanes, plus title to a small village out on the Vega in return for his, uh, recognition of my title as king. This same little drama is being played out at the Gate of Arms and all of the other gates of the Alhambra. When the king returns from his bath, he will find himself with nowhere to sleep, no troops, and with a hostile city at his back. In short, he will find that he has been well and truly cleansed," the prince giggled a little behind his hand.

"And if he raises troops and storms the palace? Or if he goes off to Malaga or one of the other cities that still owe allegiance to him and returns with a real army? There are many powerful nobles who would support him over you, if only out of fear that they might lose their titles at your hands, and the king is a powerful warlord. He may have lost at Alhama, but he has won many other battles while we have no generals to compare to him or el Zagal."

"Then we will fight him and beat him once and for all. Did I ever tell you about the months I spent imprisoned in the dungeons under the Captive's Tower? He killed off a number of his other sons to please that Christian whore he sleeps with now, and ceremonially too with me watching as just a little boy." The prince held out his hand at about waist level. "It was right at the Fountain of the Lions, so I had plenty to occupy my mind in those days and long nights, wondering when they would come to get me and my mother and do the same to us with those wicked long knives. Rumor had it that he wanted to get rid of me to preempt that prophesy that I would be king but that I would preside over the fall of Granada. Obviously, if I were dead, that could never come to pass, but his astrologers told him that this sort of thing had to be done delicately, when the stars were in accord, and that was the only thing that saved my life, his superstitious belief in the words of some court charlatans, not any affection of a father toward his son. I think the king would benefit from some time outside the palace to contemplate his life and the decisions he has made. My mother and I only managed to escape when she bribed some of the servants to get us out of our cell and then to lower us by rope in a basket over the walls. I was only four or five at the time, but I remember that night very well indeed."

Muhammad watched as the prince chewed nervously at the hem of his robe and nodded his head vigorously as if in support of his own comments. It was clear to Muhammad that there was no point in trying to argue the question now. What bothered him most was that, even if the prince's ploy worked to perfection, the best that could be expected was that the kingdom would be irrevocably divided and plunged into civil war, opening the way for new Christian conquests. And if it didn't work out quite so well, they had an example of the king's mercy when, only recently, he had invited nearly fifty of the leading members of Queen Fatima's Abencerrajes clan to a lavish dinner of reconciliation right there in the Alhambra. At some point during the meal, the waiters, one of whom stood behind each guest, suddenly produced long curved knives and simultaneously slashed the throats of each of them. Their bodies were beheaded and then dumped unceremoniously outside the palace walls within view of the windows of the queen's apartments where she could watch the crows, stray dogs, and pigs rooting among her uncles' and cousins' entrails for several days. The paving stones of the courtyard where the dinner had taken place were still stained a rusty pink with their blood. Considering that the king had taken this action merely in response to vague rumors of unrest among the Abencerrajes, Muhammad had little doubt what his reaction would be to an outright act of rebellion. And he had no doubt that the anger of the king would be broad enough to embrace a royal tutor or two.

He returned to his own quarters to consider the matter and found a distraught Yusef pacing back and forth in the main room, wringing his hands and wailing prayers to Allah for the preparation of a place in paradise for a young believer who was undoubtedly about to depart his earthly existence.

"She refuses to leave, my lord," Yusef groaned in a thick whisper, clasping both sides of his head in his hands as soon as Muhammad entered the sparsely furnished room that served as a small reception area for his apartments.

"Who refuses to leave?"

"The king's lady Aixa," he responded as if it could be no other.

Muhammad took a moment to catch his breath, then stalked past Yusef and into the bedchamber. He immediately noticed that the blanket along the far edge of the bed was bulged outward and was quivering in a most unusual fashion. He walked quietly around the bed, actually just a thick pad stuffed with fresh straw and covered with several blankets, and lifted the cover with the toe of his boot. There, cowering on her knees, with her infant son in her arms was Aixa. There was no sign of the haughtiness or hostility that he had come to expect of her, just two huge, beautiful, terrified eyes staring out of a tear-streaked face.

"Oh, please, I beg of you," she whispered. "Please do not give us away. They will kill us and feed us to the dogs."

"Who will kill you?" and what dogs might be persuaded to eat you? Muhammad added to himself. He had seen enough of the young concubine's poisonous nature in dealing with anyone who displeased her, from the lowliest servants to the most powerful nobles, to suspect that her flesh would prove fatal to even the least discriminating carrion crow.

Aixa snorted with derision. "Your precious student, of course. He has ousted the king, or hadn't you heard? And certainly the first thing that he will do will be to eliminate all other claimants to the throne," she hissed and clutched her baby even more tightly, causing it to whine pitifully.

It certainly had not taken long for word of the coup to get around the palace, Muhammad thought, for Aixa to have heard of the coup and then had time to get to his apartments before his own arrival. It occurred to him that she might have had advanced warning, in which case Abu was supremely lucky that his father had not learned of it even an hour before, in which case the young prince could very well be right back in the cell in the Captives' Tower that still haunted his nightmares. At first, Muhammad had the impression that Aixa was merely projecting what would likely be her own behavior, if she had had the power, onto Prince Abu, but then Muhammad had to remind himself of the young prince's actions that day years before in the *souq*, and he had to admit that murder was certainly within the spoiled young man's repertoire.

Before Muhammad could reply, however, there was banging on the apartment door, and Aixa let out a muffled shriek and ducked back under the coverlet, no better concealed than she had been the first time. Muhammad hurried back out into the entry area, nodding to a very worried looking Yusef to open the door and casually picking up his staff from its resting place in the corner.

As soon as Yusef had lifted the latch, the door was unceremoniously pushed open, and Hafez strolled into the room like a new owner taking possession. He was accompanied by two swarthy Berber guards armed with short swords, which were still sheathed, but they kept their hands curled threateningly about the pommels as they glared around the room. Hafez smiled sweetly and looked about him like a buyer in the market hunting for bargains.

"Good day to you," Muhammad finally said after a moment when Hafez failed to speak. "Can I be of some service?"

"I certainly hope so," Hafez sighed. Muhammad could smell the young noble's perfume, in fact it made his eyes water. He was wearing a light silk tunic of a brilliant blue that shimmered as he swiveled his body, swinging his arms from side to side like a child contemplating some mischief. His dark hair was in long, glossy ringlets, and his scant beard was long and woven into a ridiculous braid that dangled down to his chest. "The new king, your master," he went on after a moment, "has sent me on a mission to help secure the palace against traitors and rebels, so I have been checking room by room to make certain that there is no one lurking here who might pose a threat to his life." He sighed again. "I never realized that the palace had quite so many rooms," and he fanned himself theatrically.

"There is no one here who threatens our master's life," Muhammad said flatly.

Hafez sneered. "You surely don't mind if we take a quick look, for your own protection, of course," and he jerked his chin at the two soldiers who took a half step forward.

Muhammad flipped his staff up, spun it once, and held it horizontally in both hands, blocking the doorway behind him. "There are few people that I would suffer to question my word and to get away undamaged," he growled, "and you, my lord, are not one of them."

The soldiers paused and looked to Hafez, who swallowed hard, perhaps thinking back to that day in the *souq*.

"But I act on the authority of the king," Hafez stammered.

"So you said, but you will have to forgive me if I insist on hearing this from his own lips as you are not officially an officer of the crown, or perhaps you could come back when you have some more soldiers," Muhammad added helpfully.

"Perhaps I will," Hafez giggled nervously as he turned toward the door, but there was a burning look of hatred in his eyes. "Someone with your knowledge of politics must appreciate what his fate would be if it were to be discovered that he had played the new king false. The king's gratitude is like a fine garment, it cannot be expected to last forever, especially if it is taken out and worn too often, and that little scuffle in the *souq* was so very long ago."

"My lord's best interests have always been my utmost concern, and they will always be the guide of my actions."

Hafez swept out of the room like a strong breeze, the two Berbers following him, smirking slyly at each other.

Muhammad closed and locked the door and rushed back into the bedroom, but the telltale bulge under the coverlet was gone. Instead he noticed a pile of books and papers stacked in one corner of the room while Yusef lounged on a large leather trunk, smiling.

"Well done," Muhammad said. "Get some men to carry this down to my house in the city, and use the servants' stairs. She'll be able to get to her own people from there."

Yusef nodded and trotted quickly from the room. Muhammad lifted the trunk's lid and removed a jumble of clothes to reveal the trembling Aixa and her child.

"Bless you," she whispered. "This will not go unrewarded, I promise you."

"I want no reward," Muhammad replied. "And don't make the mistake of confusing compassion with disloyalty. I'm doing this only because having your blood on his hands would not be in my master's best interests, and what he might do in a moment of excitement now he would regret at his leisure later."

She frowned and pouted petulantly but then ducked back down into the trunk at the sound of the door opening again. Muhammad hurriedly replaced the clothes and fastened the trunk lid securely.

Muhammad spent the rest of the day nervously pacing the walls of the Alhambra, looking for a response from the king, while the prince went off to celebrate with his friends. At one point, just before dusk, he thought he saw a dust cloud appear on the horizon in the direction of Alixares, as if from a body of horsemen riding at full tilt. The cloud reached the outer wall of the lower city, but stopped there for a long moment before receding again into the distance. By now, of course, the city gates, not just those of the palace had been secured by the prince's followers, but Muhammad was a little surprised that it had taken this long for word of the coup to have reached the old king. He could hear the beating of drums and the clang of symbols coming from the Albaicin district, his old neighborhood and one that was most outspokenly in favor of the young prince and opposed to his father. Muhammad felt more than a little embarrassed that his protégé had concocted this scheme without his approval or advice and even without his knowledge, despite the network of spies that Muhammad had carefully established throughout the palace among the servants. What was more, it appeared to have worked, and thankfully without any bloodshed in the city, although Muhammad knew that the true test of strength was yet to come and that old Abu l-Hassan' Ali would not surrender his kingdom quite so easily.

The test came a few nights later when Muhammad was awakened by screams and the clash of metal on metal. He leapt from his bed and rushed to his window. Below him he could see in the pale light of the moon, confused groups of shadows struggling on the walls of the Alhambra itself. He thought he recognized the massive figure of the commander of the garrison, Aben Cimixer, laying about him with a two-handed sword, flanked by several of the Christian bodyguards, as they retreated slowly toward the Tower of the Two Princesses under attack by twice as many assailants. Other small groups of men in dark robes were fighting with the guards at a small postern gate, and lights were beginning to appear in the residential quarters of the city below, and Muhammad knew what he had to do.

Yusef, again demonstrating his disconcerting way of reading Muhammad's mind even before the thoughts were born, was standing by his bed, holding up a dark grey burnoose for him to slip into, and Muhammad dressed quickly. He looked around for an instant for his sword, but Yusef was holding up his staff, his well-known badge of office from the *souq*, and Muhammad smiled at his slave's wisdom. He did slip a dagger into his belt, however, and Yusef followed him as he rushed down the corridor, strapping on a short sword himself. Yusef had not grown as tall as many of his race, but he was solidly built and very quick, having served as the young prince's sparing partner during long training sessions in the use of arms, and Muhammad knew instinctively that Yusef had consistently let Abu win only out of deference to his rank, even though the young prince had proven quite skilled at arms himself.

The hallways were clogged now with wailing women, clutching veils to their faces, and trembling courtiers looking for a means of escape. The old king's thirst vengeance was almost legendary as the memory of his treatment of the Abencerrajes clan was still fresh, and he would certainly have no mercy for anyone he suspected of even passively supporting his son's coup. But Muhammad pushed past them all, ignoring pleas for help or whining claims that he or she had always told the prince that it was madness, even sinful, to consider deposing his own father and that Muhammad must stand witness to that fact.

Muhammad made his way to a small sally port in the north wall of the palace compound, and the nervous guard let them through without question. They raced, half sliding, down the steep path, stumbling over the brush and rocks until they found a man with a small boat who agreed to take them across the river to the Albaicin for the price of ten copper *maravedis*, about twice the normal rate.

It was nearly dawn, and the streets had begun to fill with the usual traffic of farmers and tradespeople making their way toward the market in the blue half-light, although there was lacking something of their usual hustle, as men on the street looked over their shoulders and women leaned far out over their balconies, craning to peer up at the Alhambra, straining to hear the sounds of the battle they all knew was taking place, trying to guess which side had the upper hand and whether it would have any impact on the day's business.

Muhammad stormed into the already bustling *souq* and leapt upon on a barrel, holding his staff over his head with both hands.

"Listen to me, brothers!" he shouted. "You all know me. I am Muhammad al-Uqayli el Haj."

"Yes, *Muhtasib*, we know you," a man called back. "What's the matter? Did the royal family question the quality of the peaches?"

"Shut up, you fool," growled another. "He's the advisor to the new king now." There were mumbled comments of agreement through the crowd as it gathered around him, and as the light grew, Muhammad could begin to recognize the faces of some familiar tradesmen, artisans, and a scattering of pickpockets.

"You have all experienced the harsh rule and heavy taxes of the old king Abu l-Hassan," Muhammad continued, "and you all lost sons and brothers at Alhama. They may have gone on to Paradise, but the Christians are still there, only a few leagues from this very spot, laughing at us. We know that Allah the Merciful is on the side of the faithful, as he has always been. The only explanation for the defeat of our glorious army is that its leader, the old king, has lost the *baraka*, the favor of God. Nothing a ruler does can prosper when that happens."

"Do you pretend to speak for God?" another shouted from the back of the crowd.

"My master is an *ulama*, a scholar who knows the Koran inside and out, you peasant," Yusef roared.

"I may be a peasant, but at least I'm not a slave."

"Silence, let the man speak," a woman screeched from her window overlooking the market. A couple of men looked angrily up at her, since it was not a woman's place to enter into such discussions, even the relatively liberated women of the marketplace, but she had spoken the thoughts of the majority, and the noise died down.

"You may think that this is a matter better left to the nobles and their soldiers to sort out for themselves, but that has not been the way of Granada," Muhammad went on, gaining momentum as he spoke. "Here it is, and always has been the people who decide their own fate, free men under the will of God. I am asking you to come with me now, to bring whatever weapons come to hand, but at least to come and show the old king that he is no longer wanted here. Instead of having a bloodbath in our streets, if we can show him that the people have chosen a new king, he will withdraw of his own volition without further fighting."

"It is the will of Allah!" Yusef shouted helpfully, jabbing the man next to him in the ribs to encourage him. And soon the entire market was roaring, men waving cargo hooks, butcher's knives, and smith's hammers over their heads.

"Follow me!" Muhammad called, jumping off the barrel and starting off at a trot for the palace. He did not dare to look to see how many followed him, but the thunder of feet on the cobblestones told him that he certainly was not alone.

The mob, for they were obviously no more than that, filled the street and poured along like water through a pipe, with more and more men joining at every intersection and square. Men in the group called to their friends to bring weapons and horses, and the women in the balconies urged them on with the piercing, ululating cry of the Arabs, holding their veils discreetly over their mouths as they shrieked.

Muhammad intentionally kept the pace down so as not to lose too many adherents from simple fatigue as they climbed the winding road up to the Alhambra, but, as they neared the Gate of Justice, he turned and saw that what seemed like half the city was with him. They lacked armor, except for a handful of soldiers swept along by the movement, but many of them had crossbows, lances, or swords, although more only had simple clubs or rocks they had picked up along the way, and they all had the grim look of common working men finally roused from their labors by a higher calling. The prince had always had the greatest support in the working class district of the Albaicin while the king could claim the loyalty of the majority of the nobles. This was largely because the taxes imposed by the government fell most heavily on the workers, where the nobles were largely exempted, and the prince had frequently offered generous feasts on holy days for the workers with ample, if unsophisticated, food and drink, all at Muhammad's urging, of course. These common men did not stop to think that the taxes would continue no matter who sat on the throne. They had simply reached the point familiar to many men down through the years that they felt that any change was bound to be for the better.

Muhammad was relieved that he could still hear the ring of steel on steel as the thick column surged toward the gates, which still stood open before them. The mob emerged into the open area on the inside the walls and found bodies strewn all about. Off to one side a small knot of men, Christian and Sudanese mercenaries, was making a stand in front of the gatehouse, beset by twice as many well-appointed Moors, one of whom carried the king's banner. Muhammad did not hesitate.

"For the prince and God's will!" he shouted as he charged forward.

At the moment he wished he had taken along something a little more lethal than his staff, but, freed from the confining walls of the gate passageway, the men behind him spread out to either side and some of the younger ones quickly outdistanced him, their goal finally in sight. Some of the king's men turned to face this new threat, but a cloud of arrows and stones from the mob cut down several of them, and the others immediately realized the futility of trying to resist such numbers. Their swords and lances clattered to the pavement, and they raised their hands in surrender, calling to Muhammad as the obvious leader of this army for mercy.

"Take them prisoner and lock them in the guardhouse," Muhammad shouted to the mercenaries before the enthusiastic mob could tear the prisoners to pieces in their excitement. And so sudden was their deliverance and so forceful Muhammad's voice, that the soldiers obeyed unquestioningly, herding the king's men efficiently inside to safety while Muhammad and the crowd swept on toward the palace itself.

A few of the king's men had escaped from the gate area and word of the mass onslaught had spread quickly. The streets of the Alhambra were now deserted, empty of all except the scattered bodies from earlier fighting. It was full daylight now, and Muhammad turned a corner just in time to see a large group of horsemen galloping off toward the Gate of Arms to the cheers of men on the roof of the palace who hurried them on their way with another volley from their arquebuses.

The tall doors of the palace, now scorched black where the attackers had tried to set them on fire with a hay cart that had been pushed up against them and torched, scraped open, and the prince emerged, dressed in a gleaming breastplate and helmet and with a blood-stained sword in his hand, surrounded by a tight phalanx of his bodyguard who eyed Muhammad's followers uncertainly.

"Is it time for my lessons already, tutor?" the prince called cheerfully. "I see you've brought more assistants than normal, but I'm glad to see them all the same."

"It was your father, the king, who was teaching you a lesson, my lord, and you know how jealous we academics are of our tenure."

"The former king, you mean," Hafez, corrected him, stepping out from behind the prince. Muhammad could see that Hafez's eyes were still wide with terror and that the elegant curved blade he now flourished gracefully over his head was not stained with blood or even dented by battle.

"Of course, sire," Muhammad said, ignoring Hafez and speaking directly to Abu.

"Yes, the matter has been settled once and for all, as I said it would be," the prince said, standing next to Muhammad and acknowledging the cheers of the crowd.

"I doubt that, your majesty," Muhammad argued. "The king, I mean your father, will join el Zagal in the south, and now the kingdom will be divided in the face of the Christian armies that are gathering to attack us."

"But the main Christian army withdrew once Alhama was secured."

"They'll be back. Don't forget, they won the battle, and victory has never done much to dissuade an aggressor. Now that you are our king, it will be your responsibility to face those new armies when they arrive, and you will have to do so with half the resources your father had at his disposal when he was defeated. And if you do fail, all of these enthusiastic men you see dancing about you now will be screaming for your head just as enthusiastically."

"You're such an old woman sometimes, *katib*," the prince pouted as they headed back into the palace. "You can always find a way to spoil even the happiest of occasions."

"There would have been an old woman as midwife to your birth, sire, and this old woman just saved you from an early grave, so don't underestimate us. Now, you'd better order your stewards to distribute food and drink to my 'troops' while they're still in a good mood, or your reign might be the shortest one on record."

But over the coming days the prince, who had adopted the new name of Muhammad XII as his official title, proved to have little interest in the details of actually running the kingdom now that he had the crown. His father, the former king, and his uncle, el Zagal still controlled the vital port of Malaga and much of the coastal land. This meant military control as well as the collection of the lucrative taxes derived from the still-substantial trade in and out of the region by sea. Instead, the new king spent his time enjoying the luxuries of the Alhambra itself, the royal city-within-a-city in which his father had once imprisoned him and in which he had always, even in the best of times, been just another potential heir to the throne.

At least there was no more open warfare between the rival Moslem factions within the kingdom, but the news of the two rival kings, with el Zagal a possible third force, had not been lost on the Christians, and a new expedition was mounted by Fernando the following spring. Muhammad frowned over the intelligence reports that reached him about the campaign. Instead of returning to Alhama and the Vega in the neighborhood of Granada itself, Fernando and his army drove on the town of Loja, winding their way through obscure mountain passes with a minimum of baggage with an apparent view to catching the defenders off guard as they had done at Alhama. The lumbering army of knights and infantry had, however, been spotted soon after crossing the frontier, and the city of Loja was well-prepared with the garrison under the command of el Zagal himself.

Muhammad had urged the new king, whom he still thought of by his given name of Abu, to put aside his rivalry with his uncle and send forces to the aid of their co-religionists at Loja. Scouts had reported that the Christians had sited their camp outside the city walls very poorly, so the chances were excellent that a sudden attack might result in a resounding victory, but even the act of showing up to defend the faith would do much to enhance Abu's prestige throughout the kingdom. He must be seen as putting the good of the realm above any partisan strife with his uncle and his father to be seen as a rightful king. Abu, however, refused to commit his army and instead marched it about the northwest of the Moorish lands coercing the towns there that still gave allegiance to his father to submit to his own rule, knowing that no help would be coming to them with el Zagal tied up with Fernando's invasion. Muhammad had argued that this would give the impression that Abu was actually in league with the infidels against his own people, and it certainly would not have been the first time such a thing had happened in the history of al-Andalus, making it that much easier to believe. Muhammad had even heard whispers within the palace about messengers traveling secretly between Granada and Cordoba carrying terms of just such an arrangement, although Abu had adamantly denied such allegations to Muhammad.

The wisdom of Muhammad's words became brilliantly clear, at least to himself, when word arrived that el Zagal had led his army in a daring sortie from Loja and delivered a sound defeat to the much larger Christian force, nearly capturing Fernando himself and driving his army back over the border in near rout. Muhammad spent the days following the arrival of a courier with this news strolling unobtrusively through the markets and squares of the city in the simple garb of the *muhtasib*, and the talk he overheard was almost constant of how the new king had disgraced himself, both as a king and as a man for not taking part in the campaign which had ended so gloriously. The soldiers felt robbed of the booty of the lavish Christian camp and the ransom of the many noble prisoners, since the victory now seemed to have been preordained by Allah, and the common citizens simply reflected the shame of their new king not having raised a hand against the invader.

But, grumbling in the marketplace did not translate itself immediately into action. One of the major reasons for this was the renowned ability of the old king, Abu l-Hassan, to bear a grudge, and it was widely feared that, should he ever come back into possession of the city of Granada, he would devote considerable time and energy to rooting out all those who had any hand in ousting him or in supporting his son in the meanwhile. So life again drifted back into its time-worn channels. The summer waned and it was time to harvest peaches and nuts out on the Vega and to plant asparagus and lima beans. In September the olives were hanging black and ripe on the trees and the countryside was permeated with their heady odor while that of the towns was full of the spicy aroma from the cooking of *membrillo* and apples for preserves. The winter rains came, and Muhammad actually welcomed the gloomy, chill weather as he sat before his cozy fire in his apartments reading and writing while Yusef played his flute indifferently in another room.

There were no further alarums from either the Christians or from el Zagal, since the roads were turned into quagmires by the rain and the rivers and streams were swollen and impassable in most places. Muhammad kept up his tutoring sessions of the young king, still hoping to convince him to reach some sort of accord with his father by carefully selecting parables of the wisdom of compromise from history, but to no avail. Whenever he seemed to have made some progress, Abu would visit his mother who would throw cold water on the entire notion, claiming that her son would not survive five minutes in company with the old king, that he would be butchered or poisoned or simply thrust back into prison, and her nagging carried far greater weight than the simple logic that Muhammad was able to employ.

As spring approached, so did the campaigning season, and there was loose talk in the palace about mounting a major raid into the Christian lands to exact vengeance for the incursions of the previous year, but no firm plans were made. Then came still more unwelcome news from the south. A strong Christian force led by the Master of the Order of Santiago had made what was apparently meant to be another lightning invasion through the mountains, apparently with the hope of storming the key city of Malaga with its bulging warehouses and lucrative trade. But the shepherds and farmers on the hard scrabble plots in the hills had reported the passage of troops promptly, and the entire force had been caught in the narrow passes and massacred, almost to a man. The terrible Marquis of Cadiz, conqueror of Alhama, had barely escaped with his life, leaving several of his brothers and cousins dead on the field, and the flower of Andalusian chivalry were either feeding the kites and vultures that now hopped clumsily about in the valleys, too bloated to fly, or were chained to the walls of the dungeons of Malaga, praying for ransom. Ordinarily, Muhammad reflected, this would have been wonderful news, but there was a cloud of gloom in the Alhambra because, once more, the victory belonged to el Zagal and the old king, and the young Muhammad XII and his army had not taken part.

Abu did not wait this time for unkind gossip to spur him to action but called a council of war almost immediately.

Muhammad was there, along with Abu's father-in-law, Ali Atar who, even at nearly seventy years of age was a doughty warrior, several other generals of the king's forces, and the usual band of courtiers, and, of course, Abu's mother Fatima. The group sat on cushions in the rough circle in the Hall of Ambassadors in the Comares Tower with the harsh light of a cold winter's day streaming in through the tall arched windows set high in the walls. As the conversation droned on without results, Muhammad lolled his head back and studied the intricate ceiling, made up of thousands of wooden panels showing an infinity of stars laid out in seven receding levels to represent the seven heavens of Islam, and he vaguely wished that he could just float upward through that ceiling and join his wife and daughter up there in Paradise, leaving his earthly worries below forever.

"The military power of the Christians has been broken," Abu announced, although not as happily as Muhammad might have expected from a faithful Moslem. "Their best men are dead or captured, their garrisons all along the border stripped of troops who won't be coming home now. For too long the tide of the Christian advance has moved in only one direction. Now is the time for us to reverse the flow and to take back some of the lands that they have conquered."

"My spies among Arab merchants traveling into Christian territory have reported that the town of Lucena is almost undefended, and it might be an appropriate first step," Ali Atar declared confidently, stroking his long white beard and nodding in agreement with his own comments. "The walls are in disrepair, and there are almost no reserves of gun powder or other munitions. We could drive across the border with a fast-moving force, as fast as any messenger, and hit them while they are demoralized and disorganized. Rather than try to sneak an army through the mountains as the Christians did at Alhama and failed to do at Loja, we would use speed as our concealment. Lucena is the central point of a rich cattle-raising region, and, at the very least, we can steal hundreds of head of cattle and horses to replace what the Christians have looted from our lands. And the odds are that we won't even have to fight for it."

"More importantly," Fatima interrupted, disregarding the scandalized stares of some of the old soldiers present at the thought of a woman speaking out among men, even if she were the queen mother, "my son will be seen as the bearer of the standard of Islam into the lands of the infidel. What battles el Zagal has won were defensive. He fought because he had to, while we will be the new conquering wave of the faith into heathen lands, and you will see men and towns who have been wavering in their loyalty come running back into our arms, begging to be included on the next campaign, maybe even the kings of North Africa might join in if the prospect of loot were bright enough for them to risk the crossing of the sea. If there will be any kind of accord with the old king," she paused and nodded markedly in Muhammad's direction, "it will be on our terms. In the meanwhile, my son must purchase the security of his throne by placing himself at risk on the field of battle. We cannot have it be said that the old king fights the infidel while his son spends his time enjoying the pleasures of the Alhambra in safety."

Muhammad had to admit that he tended to agree with the logic of her argument, but there was something about the idea that made the hairs on the back of his neck rise. He was not a pacifist by any means and had longed for years for some brave warrior king who could successfully lead the legions of Islam back to the north. To reconquer sublime cities of Moorish splendor like Cordoba or Sevilla could mark the dawn of a new golden age for al Andalus, and he would gladly give his life just to be part of it. Still, there was a serious doubt in his mind that the grinning boy he had trained was the man for the job. A great general must be audacious, to be sure, but that audacity needed to be born of sound judgment, something of which Abu had habitually been short. At least Ali Atar had considerable experience in actual warfare, even if he was terribly old for a battlefield commander, and Muhammad trusted to his knowledge and his influence over the young king to help them to avoid any major blunders in the field. There was also something about the burning glow in Fatima's eyes that still frightened Muhammad more than a little. She still possessed the same stunning beauty he had first seen when he had come to the palace years ago, but there were now little lines about her mouth and at the bridge of her nose that made her look greedy and obsessive in a way that made him very uneasy about any projects that she put forth.

The army was mustered in early April, but it was not an overly impressive host. There were only nine thousand foot and barely seven hundred horse, although the cavalry included the sons of Granada's best families, all elaborately decked out in fine silks and brocades, their armor glistening in the morning sunshine, and their spirited horses prancing and tossing their heads, their bardings designed to match the livery of the rider and his house. Muhammad had envisioned a smaller force of pure cavalry, to take advantage of speed and surprise, but it seemed that most of the nobles with money enough to afford to arm themselves as mounted knights had gone over to the old king's faction in Malaga.

Muhammad was not one to give much thought to omens, but, as the young king led the column of mounted men and infantry through the Gate of Elvira, his lance with its green banner held aloft to the cheers of the crowds assembled there, the point of the lance caught in the crosspiece of the portcullis and, when he attempted to jerk it free, snapped off short. The cheering suddenly died out, and even the prince stared in silence for a long moment at his broken weapon, then shrugged and tossed it aside and continued on his way. The army followed, but the cheering was replaced by a dull murmur in the ranks and among the spectators.

To make matters worse, as the army filed out of the city onto the Vega plain, a fox suddenly broke from a clump of brush by the side of the road and scampered the entire length of the army, dodging this way and that as soldiers showered it with spears, arrows, and stones. After about five minutes of this game, the fox flitted off up a gully, completely unscathed. Abu turned to look at Muhammad, his eyes wide with concern, and Muhammad put on his best stone face to mask his own worries. The troops lacked this consideration for their monarch, and the buzz of heated conversation became such that sergeants could be heard growling at their men to shut up as the march continued, but the question remained hanging in the air, "How could an army that could not kill a small fox possibly storm a fortress and defeat an armed enemy?".

The early stages of the campaign, however, did not bear out these bad omens. The Moors crossed into Christian territory unchallenged and the army was broken up into flying columns which swept the rich fields around the towns of Lucena and Aguilar, bringing in hundreds of head of sheep, cattle, and horses as well as a number of merchants' wagon trains stuffed with goods. They also had the pickings of a few smaller, poorly protected villages along the way. The army then settled down to the siege of Lucena itself, since surprise had not been total and the town was in a state of defense. Unfortunately, in the interests of speed, Abu and Ali Atar had again decided not to bring along any artillery with which to batter down the town's feeble walls, and it would be necessary for the army to dig trenches and to build makeshift mantlets of wood and hide in order for the troops to work their way closer to a point from which storming parties could fill in the moat, raise ladders, and bring battering rams into play against the gates, a process that would take valuable time. Still, it was hoped that the weakened Christian forces along the border would not for some time be in any condition to raise a relieving army so soon after their recent defeats at the hand of el Zagal.

Life in camp in the meanwhile was pleasant enough. The livestock and grain the foragers had brought in meant that food was plentiful, and it would be some weeks before this relatively small army could turn the camp into the sort of fetid pit that bred disease. As much as Muhammad missed his books and papers, and his room in the palace with its view of the city, it was good to be out in the open, sleeping in a comfortable tent near the king's and taking an occasional turn around the lines with the commanders. But Muhammad was nervous. The same lookouts who had warned Lucena of the Moors' approach would have also ridden farther afield to raise troops to lift the siege. It might be that the Christian forces in the south may have been depleted by the fiascoes at Loja and Malaga, but Fernando could draw on troops from all the way up to the French border and from Aragon too and even from Sicily, now that he was king of those lands as well, to say nothing of the crowds of adventuring knights from all over Europe who liked to take in a little military tourism whenever a war against the Moors was in the offing in Spain. It would take time to gather such a force, but Lucena had withstood several half-hearted assaults, and a well-stocked town, perched on its hilltop, the cream-colored walls rising smoothly from the living rock, could often hold out for weeks or even months unless the defenders were suitably weakened by the effects of thirst, hunger, or plague.

Muhammad had raised these issues with Abu more than once, but to no avail.

"*You* might be willing to face my mother if we come back with our tails between our legs, dragging along a handful of ragged sheep, but I'm not. Trust me that a swarm of Christian knights and bowmen does not begin to compare in terror to my lady mother when she is angry," Abu had said, only half joking, as they sat before the campfire drinking steaming cups of coffee on a chilly and foggy morning. "I'll take my chances on the field of battle against the whole Castilian army, thank you very much."

"But at least send back for more troops and artillery to batter down those walls. Time is our greatest enemy here."

"And what if el Zagal takes advantage of our being far from Granada, with our defenses weakened, and captures our capital. Where would we return to then?"

Muhammad almost said something about the young king taking care not to project his own lack of scruples onto others, since el Zagal had never shown any sign of taking an action that would work to the Christians' benefit for his personal gain, but a sudden flurry of trumpet calls came to his rescue. The horns were not within the camp, nor were they from the walls of the town, but seemed to come from all around the Moorish encampment. Men leapt to their feet, snatching up weapons and trying to throw saddles on horses that sidestepped as far as their tethers would allow them, causing their owners to scream curses that only frightened the poor animals even more.

"What's going on?" the bearded old Ali Atar roared, as he burst from his own tent, buckling on his sword.

A rider came pounding up and sawed his reins right in front of the king. "The Christians! Mounted knights caught one of our foraging parties in the hills and cut them to pieces, and now they're not two minutes behind me."

"How many, you fool?" Ali Atar asked, half pulling the rider from his horse.

"We couldn't tell. The fog is too thick. Hundreds, maybe thousands. But enough that they're not afraid to attack our whole army head on."

Yusef had brought up both the king's and Muhammad's horses, saddled and ready, and Muhammad was pleased that Abu at least did not hesitate to vault into the saddle and grab a shield and lance from a nearby rack.

"Let's go have a look," Abu yelled, and he galloped off into the fog pursued by a dozen of his Christian bodyguard on their heavier steeds while Ali Atar bellowed orders to his lieutenants to form their troops for battle.

"Master, half of the men are busy herding the livestock back toward the border and securing their own loot," Yusef whispered hoarsely in Muhammad's ear as he mounted. "They're not interested in fighting here at all."

Muhammad just grunted and swung into the saddle. He had a long, straight sword at his side, a *jinete espada*, which gave him excellent reach when mounted, although a little unwieldy when on foot, as well as a quiver of several throwing javelins at his knee, and Yusef handed him up a large, round shield of wood and leather with bronze studs to fix to his left forearm. There was no time for regular armor, but Muhammad had taken the habit of always wearing a shirt of light mail under his cloak while out in the field for just such an occasion. He also wore silk undergarments, not for fashion's sake, but because the Arabs had learned from the terrible Mongols that silk would wrap itself around a penetrating arrowhead and make it easier to extract from the body. Thus equipped, he spurred his horse off into the mists in the direction the king had ridden.

The fog was starting to break up like an old rag, clinging in patches in the valleys, and drifting this way and that in a light breeze. Muhammad crested a low hill in time to see a line of about a hundred heavy Castilian knights riding abreast, thundering down a slope less than a mile away at a confused gaggle of Moorish infantrymen that an officer was trying to form into a tight phalanx. The heavy dew had made the arquebusiers' guns useless, but a few crossbow bolts zipped out and a couple of the horsemen fell, but the others drove into the ragged line of infantry with a resounding crash of horses and steel. Each rider speared an opponent with his lance, and continued straight through the body of Moors, slashing left and right with his sword, then wheeling in the open ground behind them, turned and cut a fresh path back the way he had come. The surviving Moorish foot soldiers simply dropped their weapons and ran for the dubious shelter of the Genil River to their rear. At least, Muhammad noted, there were not *thousands* of knights, not even hundreds, but the danger was real enough if this small force managed to stampede the Moors and open the way for the garrison of the town to sally and join in the attack. Once an army broke, it tended to break hard, and there would be no forming the Moors this side of the walls of Granada. The men would be burdened with their booty and unable to organize the disciplined ranks that would be their only defense against the Christian cavalry, and they would be cut down as they ran.

Just then a cloud of Moorish cavalry swooped out of the mist in pursuit of the Christians, and Muhammad recognized Abu, riding his pure white charger at their head. He spurred his own horse to join them and caught up to the king just as the Moors reached a tangle of rocks on a steep incline. Christian infantrymen were hidden there and unleashed a deadly hail of arrows and bullets that cut down many of the lightly armored Moors, while the survivors vainly sought to get at the Christians through the protecting boulders. A faint trumpet call from the rear drew Muhammad's attention, and he saw a thick column of horsemen pouring down the slope from the gates of Lucena, bulling through the haphazard Moorish lines and into the deserted camp, just as he had feared that they might do.

Abu fought on, and Muhammad took up a position at his side, hacking away at the infantrymen who kept trying to work their way around to the left rear of each Moorish rider, the point at which he is most vulnerable, and firing crossbow bolts point blank into the bodies of the horses, toppling animal and rider while other men would pounce on them and cut them to pieces with knives and axes on the ground. Ali Atar, his face streaming blood that now streaked his beard, slid from his saddle, and Muhammad could see that there was no point in even trying to reach him through the mob of Castilians who swarmed over him, burying their pikes in his body.

"To the river!" Abu shouted at last, and the few remaining horsemen wheeled to follow him, the last of his Christian bodyguards, falling as they vainly tried to stem the pursuit, knowing that the enemy would not bother to take them prisoner, being considered renegades against their faith for serving a Moslem lord.

The fog had largely burned off, and Muhammad could see that the river bank was crowded with refugees from the Moorish camp, no longer soldiers with any organization, but men simply trying to escape with as much booty as possible. A sand spit downstream was already piled with the bodies of those who had tried to swim the river, their pockets weighed down with gold, and a cluster of Christian crossbowmen stood on a bluff picking off those who tried to swim their horses across.

"Our horses are both blown, *katib*," Abu said breathlessly as he pulled up next to Muhammad. "Even if they could swim the river, they won't carry us a mile farther."

"Our only chance is to hide in the reeds down by the bank and wait until dark," Muhammad replied. "If we can catch a piece of driftwood and float downstream a few miles, we can cross over and make our way to the nearest friendly village on foot."

Abu nodded, but Muhammad could see that, along with a thin line of blood from a slight wound over one eyebrow, the young king's face was streaked with tears. They dismounted and slapped their horses' rumps to drive them off, the animals needing no further encouragement to escape the chaos of the battlefield. Abu threw off his scarlet robe and tore away any badges of rank on his clothing while putting his rings and other valuables in a small purse as they would come in handy if they had a chance to bribe some lone soldier into letting them escape. Then they both crawled into a particularly thick clump of reeds, wading out until the water was up to their chests and pulling more reeds around them like a curtain.

All about them they could hear the screams of the dying and the pounding of horses' hooves moving up and down the bank. There were voices calling out in Spanish from both sides of the river now, and it was clear that the enemy was busy rounding up prisoners, finishing off the wounded, and looting the dead. Time went by slowly and clouds of tiny insects flew in their faces, attacking their eyes and crawling into their noses and mouths, but they dared not swat them away, or move at all. While the day had been warm, the water was icy cold, fed by the snow runoff from the mountains, and Muhammad's teeth chattered uncontrollably. He stuffed a corner of his robe into his mouth for fear that the enemy soldiers milling about could actually hear the rattling.

Then there came a scream from not more than a yard away, and a tall Sudanese fell, crashing through the reeds directly in front of Muhammad, a javelin protruding from his chest.

"That's it, we've got to run," he whispered. "Head back to the camp, and perhaps we can catch a horse or two. Then ride for all you're worth. Don't worry about me."

Abu nodded again, and they began to slosh through the water, their armor and wet clothing heavy and dragging them down, while their limbs were numb with the cold and the hours of standing still. The enemy soldiers were making so much noise of their own that they were not discovered immediately, and they reached the edge of the reeds, flopping down on the gravelly soil. And there was a horse, standing placidly barely twenty yards away, apparently unhurt, although there was a thick red stain on its saddle. It turned to look at them, cocking its ears curiously, and snorted, shaking its head as if to warn them off. But Abu was already on his feet and sprinting toward the animal.

"There goes one!" a man shouted in Spanish, and Muhammad could hear men crashing through the reeds.

Muhammad leapt up and drew his sword, placing himself between the king and his pursuers. There were four of them, one with a pike, two with swords, and the fourth with a crossbow that he was in the process of aiming at the king's back. Muhammad snatched the dagger from his belt and flipped it underhand, catching the man in the stomach. He dropped his bow and clutched at the haft with both hands, moaning as he fell, but the others came on.

These were not green militia, but experienced soldiers, Muhammad could tell at a glance. The pikeman kept his distance, lunging at Muhammad's face with his twelve-foot weapon, while the other two worked around either side. Muhammad kept retreating, knocking the pike aside and parrying the tentative thrusts of the swordsmen, but now there were Spanish voices behind him as well, and he stole a look over his shoulder and saw Abu tossing his own sword at the feet of a tall knight who was flanked by four other Castilians. Muhammad's own opponents stepped back, smiling, and Muhammad let his shoulders sag and dropped his own sword to the ground.

The rooms allotted to Abu and Muhammad, along with a few other Moors of noble birth, in the castle of Vaena were really quite elegant. Abu had attempted to hide his identity at first, but the gasps of the other Moorish prisoners and their indiscreet bowing when he was brought into Lucena, had given the game up. Abu had insisted on having a small entourage accompany him in his captivity, and the Castilians seemed to be so overjoyed at their success that they practically tripped over themselves in their efforts to please him, as if he were an honored guest rather than a prisoner. Muhammad had even been able to find Yusef among the common prisoners, since he had refused to flee without his master, and the young Senegalese joined the royal party. Unfortunately, it seemed to Muhammad that this treatment, if not calculated for its effect on the young king, could not have been better devised to undermine his will power.

Messages had quickly arrived from Fernando and Isabel, apologizing for the inconvenience of Abu's captivity and full of the pain they felt for having to make war on such a worthy sovereign. But Abu outdid them in courtesy, going so far as to reply that he had long planned to submit himself to their rule as a vassal, now that he was king in his own right and free from the evil influence of his father. Muhammad had attempted to caution him that, while the Catholic Kings could afford gentle words in the moment of their victory, anything along those lines that Abu said were likely to be taken very seriously by the Castilians and used against him in any future negotiations. But Abu was so unaccustomed to dealing with fellow monarchs that their words of respect completely turned his head, and Muhammad's advice was once more ignored.

Muhammad had wasted no time in handing out some gold coins he had hidden in his clothing to some of the servants and petty officials who abounded in the castle in exchange for information. Although Abu and his party were treated with the utmost courtesy, well-fed and comfortably quartered, even being given back much of their personal property which was recovered from the looted camp, they were restricted to a small apartment in a high tower in the castle. From the windows they could see that the walls and courtyards of the citadel swarmed with men-at-arms in the expectation that the Moors might launch a new raid to rescue their king. Thus it was doubly vital for Muhammad to learn the state of play outside the walls.

This proved not to be hard to come by as this small town was abuzz with all of the details of the only important event to occur there in centuries. It seemed that both Abu's mother, who had taken over as regent in his absence, albeit of little more than the city of Granada itself, had sent envoys to Fernando offering a huge ransom, future tribute, and the release of hundreds of Christian captives in exchange for her son. She clearly realized that Abu's claim to the throne was tenuous enough, and that his defeat and captivity would quickly spell the end of his reign if he were not delivered promptly. But there were also envoys arriving from Abu's father, offering money and the exchange of the many prisoners taken at Loja and Malaga, if the young pretender were delivered into his hands. There was little doubt that the father was not concerned for the welfare of the son, and it could well be imagined what fate would await Abu if he were to be turned over to the old king.

The debate apparently raged through the Castilian court. Those with relatives among the captives taken the previous year by el Zagal naturally wanted to deal with that faction. The Marquis of Cadiz and others, however, pointed out that freeing Abu, or Muhammad XII as he called himself, would perpetuate the split in the Moorish ranks and facilitate the ultimate conquest of the entire kingdom. While Fernando was undecided as to what course of action to take, limiting himself to sending enthusiastic expeditions into Moorish lands to take advantage of the dissention there for raiding and burning villages, Isabel, who had remained with her court in the north, sent word that releasing Abu, or Boabdil as the Castilians managed to butcher his name, was the only means of ensuring the success of their policy toward Granada. Muhammad thought it significant that, no sooner had the queen declared her views than they were adopted by Fernando. It sounded as though Fatima had her equivalent in the Christian court.

The terms of the peace treaty were about as humiliating for Abu as could be conceived by the Castilians. A two-year truce was to be granted to all towns in Granada owing allegiance to Abu, which meant that the Castilians would be free to fight against only half of Granada at a time. Four hundred Christian captives were to be released immediately and seventy more each year for five years, even if they had to be ransomed by Abu from his father or some other Moorish ruler. Twelve thousand *doblas* of gold were to be paid directly to the Castilian treasury, and Abu was to ensure supplies to any Castilian troops passing through his lands, which they would be free to do for the period of the truce. Furthermore, Abu agreed to surrender his own young son as a hostage to Fernando, along with children of a dozen other prominent Moorish noble houses, something that Muhammad could see troubled him more than the other clauses of the treaty, for, whatever his faults, Abu was a devoted and loving father. It was hardly likely that any harm would come to the boy, who would be treated in accord to his royal station, and he would be accompanied by his own Moorish servants and tutors, but the ultimate purpose of a hostage was to exchange a life in the event that Abu should break the truce. Lastly, the treaty stated that Abu would rule

Granada purely at the pleasure of the Castilian royal house, as their vassal, implying that, when it suited Fernando and Isabel, they could demand that Abu hand over all of his cities, and even his crown, to the Christians.

"You cannot possibly agree to these terms," Muhammad told the king crisply. "If word of this arrangement gets back to your people, your life will be worth nothing, and it will only be a contest of whose assassins will reach you first."

"The Castilians have promised to keep the terms secret," Abu sniffed, staring out the window of his room toward the distant, snow-capped mountains which marked the border with Granada. "But what choice do I have? If I stay here, I am not king, or would not be for long in any case. At least, once I've been freed, I will be back in the Alhambra and will be able to demonstrate to the people the wisdom of my rule."

Muhammad had his doubts about that. "And if you accept these conditions you will cease to be king in spirit, whether here or in Granada. You will be sacrificing, not just the throne of your ancestors, but the kingdom itself, in exchange for your own position, and that for just a short while. I beg you to reconsider."

"And I beg you to give me an alternative," Abu snapped, his face reddening. "If I do not accede to the Castilian terms, they will be perfectly happy to sell me to my father, and you can well imagine how long I'd last at his hands. The Castilians won't just sit around waiting for me to come to my senses. There's a strong faction here pushing for just that sort of a deal."

"But, my lord, perhaps we could still reach our own agreement with your father. We could offer to have you give up the throne now in exchange for a promise that he will make you his heir irrevocably. He is old and ill and will probably not last more than a year or two. We could reunite the kingdom in the face of the infidel threat. He could reign over a united Granada for what little time is left to him and then you would reign in his place over a single kingdom without having to make these onerous promises to the Christians. And the people would honor you for putting the good of the realm ahead of your own ambition. Most of the people don't claim to know much about the workings of the government, but they'd recognize that much and love you for it all the more."

"Surely, in your years in the palace, with your little network of spies, you must have learned something of the nature of my father. He would rather die than come to an agreement with me, so long as he could have the pleasure of seeing my die in agony before him. And the rest of the kingdom be damned!"

Muhammad hung his head. He had to admit that there was no acceptable solution to their predicament, and pointing out the fact that it was Abu's own headstrong insistence on this raid that brought them here would accomplish nothing other than to further alienate him from his monarch at a time when Muhammad needed all of the influence he could get if there would ever be any hope of salvaging the situation, not just for Abu, but for Moorish Spain as a whole.

If the Castilians had been accommodating and polite before, now that they had this disastrous compact with Abu in their hands, they fairly fawned on the young king. He was escorted in state to where the royal court was now sitting in Cordoba. More nobles of Abu's faction had been smuggled across the border to make up a proper retinue, and Muhammad was obliged to abase himself to receive a weekly stipend in cash from the Christians on behalf of the king from which largess Abu could play the benevolent monarch, giving out rich gifts to the governor of Vaena castle when his party departed, and hosting sumptuous feasts at the various towns the entourage stopped at along the way to Cordoba.

For one brief moment, the sight of the ancient city of Cordoba, centuries before the fabled capital of Omayid Spain, as they crossed over the old Roman bridge across the Guadalquivir, almost seemed to make the entire drama worth it. Technically speaking, Abu and his party were no longer prisoners now that the treaty had been signed, and, within limits, they were allowed the freedom of the city, and Muhammad excused himself as soon as they had passed through the gates for a visit to the Grand Mosque.

Muhammad approached the east porch of the Mosque and dismounted, handing the reins of his horse, along with a copper *maravedi,* to a street urchin while he simply stood there admiring the elaborate carving of the lobed archway over the bronze-plated door for a long time before pausing at a fountain to wash his feet and entering. Over the years his teachers had described this, sometimes called the "Blue Mosque" to him a thousand times, and, as he passed into the dimly lit interior, he hardly needed to see to be able to find his way although he had never set foot here before. It was like a forest of pillars, two tiers high, each supporting a network of multiple-lobed arches, all exquisitely carved in floral and geometric patterns. The pillars were of marble or other stone, as the building had been augmented and redesigned over the centuries by different Moorish monarchs. He imagined that this motif would have reminded the original builders, five or six centuries before, men who had ridden right out of the desert, of a grove of date palms in a fantastic oasis. He quickly found the main aisle leading to the *mihrab,* the holiest corner of the mosque, the focus of the spirit of the mosque. It was an otherwise small room, set off by elaborate, shimmering gold mosaics, with phrases from the Koran marching in steady rows above the lintel. It was past the time for the midday prayer, but he felt obliged to kneel and meditate for a few moments in any case. He took the rolled prayer rug from under his arm and spread it on the floor, kneeling, and symbolically washing his face as he bowed again and again, reciting verses from the Koran in his head and feeling the fatigue of the road and of the burdens of his office lift from his shoulders as the spirit of God filled him with peace.

He had dreamt briefly of returning this mosque to the worship of its rightful God, riding at the right hand of a wise and powerful Moorish king who would drive out the barbarian invaders, and he had failed. The Christians had converted the building into a church, but they had done little damage to the actual structure, yet. They had gutted the central part of the vast building and constructed a choir and an altar and they had converted the minaret into a bell tower, but most of the structure had remained untouched. Muhammad rubbed his face vigorously and swept his hands back up over his forehead and through his hair, again symbolically cleansing himself and begging forgiveness of Allah for his unworthiness.

When he rejoined Abu's party at the citadel where the Castilian court was then sitting, he was struck with just how barbaric these Christians could be. Muhammad had had only fleeting contact with them during his life, mainly international traders and the odd mercenary who drifted into Granada, and these had often been largely Islamicized in their habits. Even the lord and his attendants of the castle at Vaena, although they had mingled little with the prisoners, living hard by the border in recently conquered lands, had acted and dressed, well, in an almost civilized fashion. But the court of the Catholic Kings, even here in Cordoba, the heart of Andalusia, was largely composed of northerners, and there had been little progressive Arab influence in their circles that Muhammad could see.

Muhammad was first struck by the overwhelming odor of the reception hall, a smell so intense it was like being hit in the face with a club, causing him literally to stagger for an instant. The northern Europeans, he knew, were convinced that bathing was a dangerous and unprofitable exercise, best gotten out of the way at birth, since it tended to bring on all sorts of mysterious diseases and was a practice associated with Jews and Moslems. The closest most of them ever got to water was in an occasional river crossing, but as more and more bridges were built, even this became increasingly rare. He imagined that some of them might display more attention to cleanliness than others, but the combined effect of more than a hundred bodies milling about a poorly ventilated hall created a community of odors that was impossible to segregate. And to make matters worse, they seemed determined to compensate for their own unique scents by layering over them an endless variety of perfumes and fragrant oils that did little to disguise the original problem but merely served to crowd more of the breathable oxygen out of the air.

Once Muhammad's eyes had cleared somewhat, after the initial shock of the miasma of the hall, the next thing that appalled him was the attire of the women. Or rather lack of attire. He had seen relatively few Christian women in his life, and those who lived in Moorish lands prudently adopted a decent form of dress, more or less like Moslem women, concealing their legs, arms, shoulders, and their hair, or they risked getting their legs switched by any passing *muhtasib* or *qadi* for their brazenness, to say nothing of the lewd remarks and gestures from any passing workman, about which they would not be in any position to complain, having provoked them by their dress. But here the women were not only not kept locked away, as was only right, Abu's mother being a remarkable exception to this rule in Granada, but they were practically naked. They may have had dresses which reached the floor and dagged sleeves that came down to their fingers, which was well enough, but their necks, shoulders, and breasts were completely exposed, these last pushed up somehow from underneath, with only a pretense at decency by having the actual nipples barely concealed. Muhammad attempted to avert his eyes, but since the shameless creatures swarmed throughout the room, not even bothering to huddle in one corner in silence as was proper, Muhammad had to force himself to push his jaw closed and focus only on foreheads, since none of the harlots deigned to wear a veil either, of course.

The hall itself was tastefully designed, probably the work of *mudejar* craftsmen, Moorish artisans living and working under the Christians, but it was gloomy, even in the daylight that filtered in through the tall, narrow windows and fitfully helped by some greasy torches hung along the walls. There were colorful banners hung from the rafters, and the floor was covered with fresh rushes that might have been intended to help combat the stench of the occupants. Muhammad then noticed that rows of banners were Moorish standards taken in battle, and he suspected that the humiliating effect the guests was not all together unplanned.

Muhammad swallowed hard and was attempting to regain his composure from the dual assaults of odor and the vision of female shoulders and breasts when he saw Abu at the center of a large circle of people, both Christians and Moslems, men and women, and the young king was gaily waving him over. As soon as he had managed to weave his way through the crowd, trying to breathe as little as possible, Abu took him by the arm and whispered in his ear.

"I have just had my audience with Fernando and Isabel, and they were most gracious," he gushed. "Fernando refused to allow me to kiss his hand, as would have been only right as I have surrendered to him. He treated me as an equal."

Abu puffed out his chest and cocked his head as if to challenge Muhammad to find fault with such an occurrence.

"And did they offer to change any of the terms of your release, sire?" Muhammad asked in a flat tone, hoping to avoid a confrontation in front of the enemy.

Abu's eyes flared. "Well, no, of course not. That has all been agreed. This is just a protocol visit, but I am certain that, once we demonstrate how useful we can be to them, the Catholic Kings will restore us to our full rights, help us to eliminate the old king and el Zagal, and allow us to rule as their vassals, very much like the kings of Granada did for years up until the time of Juan II." Abu seemed proud of himself to have been able to throw a little history lesson back in his teacher's face, but Muhammad just sighed and shook his head wearily. He did not choose to point out that, while the kings of Granada had been forced to pay a modest tribute in the past, they had never conceded that they held their own crowns at the sufferance of the Christian kings.

Abu snorted. "We'll only be here a few days. Why don't you make use of your world famous language skills and circulate among these people." He leaned closer conspiratorially. "I suspect that they have divisions in their ranks just as deep as those in ours, and perhaps a little knowledge might prove to be of use to us later, eh?" Abu nudged him sharply in the ribs and turned on his heel, the skirts of his gold embroidered coat, paid for with Castilian money, flaring out about him like the tail of a peacock.

Muhammad wandered aimlessly for awhile, allowing the Castilians to ogle up and down, him although none of them had the courage or the courtesy to actually speak to him, feeling like an animal on display in a traveling menagerie, and he had a crazy desire to caper about and make ridiculous faces, to at least give them a proper show for their money. Then he felt a touch on his shoulder, as light as the brush of a butterfly's wing, and he turned to find himself facing a stunningly attractive young woman with deep dark blue eyes, a shade he had never seen before, who was smiling in amusement. Muhammad allowed his eyes to drift downward for an instant to the sight of her décolletage as her firm, round breasts rose and fell with her breathing, but he quickly snapped to and focused on her forehead. Perhaps he had become inured to the odors in the room, but it seemed to him that she at least was not a source of anything but a delicate scent of violet water.

"I understand that you are a scholar, sir," she began in passable classical Arabic.

Muhammad cleared his throat modestly. "I have spent more time reading books than doing more constructive work. That is true, madam."

"I ask because I was wondering if you happened to know a man named Ysaque Perdoniel," she said, lowering her voice. "I believe he left Cordoba for Granada last year. I would not presume, just because you were in the same city, that you would know him, but he was also a man of letters, and I thought your paths might have crossed."

Muhammad thought for a moment. "Yes, I believe so. An older man, a linguist, is that not so?"

"Exactly."

"Yes, he has been working as an interpreter at the palace. I do not know him well, but we have met, and I believe I have read some of his analysis of the philosopher Maimonides, very astute."

"That would be the man."

"But he is a Jew, is that not the case?" Muhammad had noticed at least one man dressed in the obligatory subdued garb of the Jews amid the glittering elite, but he had always understood that there was little overt contact between the two religions here in Castilian lands beyond a handful of moneylenders and tax farmers, and he had never considered the possibility of any kind of blood relationship across the religious divide.

"Yes, but he is a relative, a distant relative," the woman said, but she immediately stiffened, and Muhammad sensed someone approaching from behind him.

"So, this is one of the dreaded Moors," a gruff voice said as a large, muscular man stepped closer and intentionally brushed against the woman. Muhammad saw her stiffen and recoil at the touch. He had the look and bearing of a soldier and appeared to be ill-at-ease in his satin doublet and hose and probably would have been much more comfortable carving his way through a crowd with a battle axe than making small talk.

The man wore a black and red cloak that Muhammad understood to belong to some sort of Christian military order, the *Santa Hermandad*, and he had a large and obviously well-used sword at his side.

"I must say, it's interesting to see one up close," the man went on. "I only had a chance to see their backs at Alhama." His face was flushed with wine, and his eyed were slightly glazed over. He had the thickest neck that Muhammad thought he had ever seen, with muscles bulging on his shoulders to make a small pyramid, but he moved with a smooth grace that implied that he would be a dangerous man to face with a blade, not just brute force, but speed and art as well.

Muhammad let a smile cross his lips. "And we can all thank God that you were spared the tragedy of Malaga, or you might have had occasion to get to know us much better, as have so many of your less fortunate friends."

The man's nostrils flared and a vein began to bulge near his temple, but he composed himself and merely snorted while Muhammad quickly bowed graciously. He noticed that the uncomfortable expression that had appeared on the woman's face at the man's approach had been replaced by a subtle grin.

"But we have not been formally introduced. I am Muhammad al-Sarif al-Uqayli el Haj, personal secretary to his majesty, King Muhammad XII."

"And I am Raquel Blanco de Ecija, lady-in-waiting to her highness, Queen Isabel," the woman said nervously and curtseyed. Muhammad noticed how the man eyed her hungrily as she bent at the waist before him.

"Captain Don Juan Ortega de Prado," he grunted, and the conversation seemed to freeze in the air.

Muhammad cleared his throat. "If you would be so good as to excuse me, I must see to my lord's needs." He bowed again and left the two standing awkwardly. There was definitely something going on between these two, but he had little interest in pursuing the matter. The personal affairs of barbarians were of no importance to him any more than he cared which of the dogs that roamed about the fringes of the hall was mating with which bitch out in the yard later in the evening.

"You will talk to a Moor, but whenever I try to speak to you, you turn away," Muhammad could hear the man growling as he nodded his way into another conversational group nearby.

"You've had too much to drink, sir," the woman replied and tried to leave, but the man grabbed her arm roughly.

"Look at this," he whispered harshly, pointing at a jagged scar on his neck that stood out a pale pink against his sunburned skin. "I got this in battle against the enemies of God and this realm, and I think I've earned the right to a little respect from the 'ladies' of the court, don't you?"

Muhammad spun around and offered Raquel his arm, which she quickly took.

"Excuse me, but your mistress the Queen has apparently been asking about for help in translating an Arabic phrase into Spanish, and it occurred to me that, between us, we might be of some service to her."

The woman looked at him with silent gratitude, but the man just glared and did not release her arm immediately.

"Perhaps the gentleman would care to accompany us, but, in my country, it does not do to keep a monarch waiting."

Muhammad saw the woman wince slightly as the man gave her arm a final squeeze before turning on his heel and stomping off in the direction a large wine cask where servants were filling a constant stream of cups.

"Thank you, sir," she whispered as he led her out onto the broad veranda which ran alongside the hall. "I take it there was no summons from the Queen."

Muhammad paused at a potted flowering plant and delicately fingered the petals.

"Did you know that the seeds of this flower, if ground up and mixed with the right proportion of water and a little milk, produces a potion that can put a person to sleep and make him impervious to pain. I have used it when treating wounded men. It is so much better than simply having someone hold them down as you set a leg or remove an arrow. The milk taken from the bole of a certain kind of poppy works even better, almost too well, in fact, as a patient can become dependent upon it."

"So, you are a physician as well. That must be what makes you sensitive to the suffering of others."

She looked into his eyes and smiled. Muhammad had offered his arm originally as he knew this to be the Christian custom, and now he discreetly moved his elbow away from his body as soon as they had left the hall, as a signal that she was free to release his arm, but she had hung onto him. He was unused to such close contact with women, at least since the death of his wife and certainly not in public, even with her, but now he could not help but to begin to feel a strange sense of exhilaration at her touch.

"It is good to know that boors are not the exclusive property of Granada," he replied. "I was a little surprised that you did not address the situation yourself. Even at our brief acquaintance, you strike me as a woman who has the full use of a female's arsenal, and I have seen women use words with far greater effect than any warrior uses his sword on the battlefield, to cut a man so skillfully that he doesn't even realize that he's bleeding until after he gets home."

Raquel shuddered and shook her head. "He is of the *Santa Hermandad*, not just a common soldier. They are the strong arm of the monarchy, a kind of police force, but a secret, sinister kind. I don't know if you are aware of the Inquisition, but this is not a good time to make enemies unnecessarily. Too many people have found themselves under interrogation because of accusations made in secret for personal grudges, and a word from a commander of the *Hermandad* would carry a great deal of weight."

It was reassuring to hear that the Christians were clawing at each other's vitals just as the Moors were in Granada, but Muhammad could not help but feel a certain pity for this young woman, and he patted her hand reassuringly.

"Then let us talk of science," he said, and they did. And when a great bell was rung in the hall, she led him in and arranged to sit next to him at one of the long trestle tables that had miraculously appeared, now groaning with food as course after course was served. She explained to him all the unfamiliar dishes and warned him of those that contained pork or rabbit or other prohibited foods. The guests were all seated along the outside of each of the two rows of tables, leaving the servants free to work in the center of the room. Muhammad was impressed to see that the meal was being served on pewter dishes, as he had heard that most Christians uses slabs of day-old bread, or trenchers, as edible dinnerware, and the tables had been laid with long linen tablecloths that hung to the ground on the guests' side of the table, also serving as a communal napkin for those inclined to wipe their mouths. He was appalled, however, that the Christians made constant use of their left hands, which civilized people reserved for cleaning their private regions in the garderobe, not for eating, but here they were, intentionally holding bread in the left hand and breaking off pieces with the right, instead of just holding it in the right and biting off pieces as God intended. The first two offerings, a stew or brewet, of capon and a soup of leeks, were not objectionable, but several of the vegetable dishes had been cooked with ham, and this was followed by grilled rabbit, so Muhammad, who was quite full enough anyway, merely waited for the fruit and cheese.

Muhammad spotted the soldier sitting at the other table across the hall, an empty seat at his side, and the man's burning eyes never left them throughout the meal. Muhammad had the distinct impression that, when the man mutilated a slab of beef with his knife, he was imagining that it was Muhammad's flesh that he was cutting, and it made the hair on the back of his neck bristle.

The next few days passed quickly. Since Abu had largely excluded Muhammad from his council for the moment, where Hafez, who had unfortunately survived the battle as well, now held sway, Muhammad had plenty of time to sit and talk with Raquel about medicine, literature, and philosophy. They would take walks to various points of interest in the city, and Muhammad enjoyed pointing out the historical significance of different building, almost as if she were the visitor and he the one who had been born in Cordoba, but his stories were always of glories long dead, of an age long gone. He often suspected that she knew as much or more about the city than he did, but she was far too gracious to spoil his lectures. He had rarely found anyone with such an interest in all of the passions of his life, certainly not among the crowd at the *souq* and rarely in the Alhambra, but never, ever in a woman. He did not see the irate soldier again and assumed that he was off happily killing people in the countryside, since Fernando was celebrating his new treaty with Abu by sending raiding parties into the territory of the old king.

At times, when they would stroll through the city, Muhammad especially enjoying the fresh air and scent of the blossoms on the orange trees that abounded in the many small plazas, Raquel would become suddenly pensive and silent, as if she were searching for the words to say something. Muhammad let these silences stretch out, giving her time, but each time she would find some minor point of interest to distract them, or a passing individual to comment upon, a little too brightly, he thought. Then, one morning, she surprised him.

"I'm a Jew, you know," she said in a low voice after looking about the plaza through which they were walking, to make certain that no one was near.

"Of Jewish descent, yes, that I surmised if Perdoniel was your relative. I understand that is quite common in Christian Spain."

"No, I mean that I am a Jew in my heart."

Muhammad raised his eyebrows and turned to her. "But you do not wear the garb of a Jew. Even in Granada, where our rules are far less strict, both Christians and Jews must wear distinctive clothing."

"My family pretended to convert in order to save their lives years ago, and now I must practice my faith in secret while attending Mass and seeming to be a Christian."

There was a quaver in her voice, and when Muhammad touched her shoulder he could feel that she was trembling.

"Certainly that cannot be too unusual in a kingdom where people of your religion are persecuted. There was an Arab writer, a poet, who said, 'I lift my voice to utter lies absurd,. . .'"

"But speaking truth my hushed tones scarce are heard," she finished for him with a sigh.

"You know al-Ma'arri?" he asked, raising his fingers to his lips in surprise.

"Is it shocking that a heretic in one world would find a kindred spirit in a heretic in another? My uncle used a copy of his *Luzumiy y at* to teach me Arabic, and many of the verses have stayed with me over the years."

"'I perceive that men are naturally unjust to one another," he began.

"But there is no doubt of the justice of Him who created injustice," she continued. "That is one of his statements about which I have my doubts, but he speaks to me nonetheless."

"And I have always thought that his obsession with death as a sweet release of the pressures and pains of life was a message sent down directly to me through the centuries," Muhammad replied, lowering his gaze. Raquel brushed her fingers along his cheek.

"Your wife and daughter?" she aksed.

He nodded and then quickly tried to change the subject. It had only just occurred to him that he had mentioned the death of his family and how lonely that made him feel, but he now realized what a pathetic figure he must have made of himself for Raquel to have taken note of it.

"In Islam we have a practice known as *taqiyya* in which it is perfectly acceptable to pretend to leave the faith to save one's life, although, in honesty, it is mostly meant for a Moslem to pretend to be a Christian, for example. I suspect that it would not be considered so laudable by the imams for a Moslem heretic to pretend to orthodoxy."

"That is a very enlightened policy, but there is no such practice for Jews, at least not here in Spain. I am a traitor to my faith, both of my faiths. But that is not the real problem."

"If not that, then what?" he asked.

"It's the Inquisition. *I'm* the person that they're looking for."

"You individually?"

"Yes, well, almost. It's not directed against Jews, just me. Many former Jews really did convert, some of them generations ago. Some don't even know what being a Jew is like, but now they're all at risk because of me."

"Then declare your faith and end the charade. I suppose you would lose your position at court, but what is more important?"

"I cannot do that either. Then I would be a heretic, a betrayer of the Catholic Church and would be punished for that, besides being tortured to find out who 'converted' me to Judaism again. They would go after my father and mother, everyone I know and love."

"Then leave. Come to live in Granada." He surprised himself by saying it and brought himself up short when she stopped walking and turned to look into his face.

She smiled sadly and shook her head. "Thank you, but, no. My life is here. My father is here."

"Then give up your old faith and become a real Christian," he said, turning and pulling her along with him as they walked, unable to stand her direct gaze any longer. "It is my personal belief that God looks to the heart of people and cares little about the form of rituals they perform during their time on earth."

"I cannot do that. It is not for fear of punishment by either the Christian or Jewish God. I just cannot. I am Jewish and cannot deny that to myself, whatever I may have to deny to my queen, to the world, and in the confessional."

"Then you truly have a dilemma, lady," he sighed. After a pause, he went on. "And why did you tell me this, especially if I cannot help you, as much as I would like to do."

"Because I had to tell someone or I would just burst, and I believe you're the only person I know who would not, could not, reveal this to the Inquisition. At least I feel better for that. I hope that I have not imposed too much on our very recent acquaintance, but I consider you a friend, one of the few that I have."

"I am glad to have been of some little service," he mumbled. "And I am honored to be numbered among your friends," he bowed deeply.

Then, suddenly, a change came over her face, from deep seriousness to blithe gaiety. She pointed out a bustling, overweight court official scuttling through the street and happily told him an anecdote about how the man had been caught selling cat meat to the army instead of beef and had been flogged through the camp for it but then had managed to buy back a position providing food for the court, which always made her uneasy at mealtimes. Muhammad looked at her for a long moment, then let the matter drop.

On his final day in Cordoba, Muhammad was obliged to stand by in abject humiliation with a knot of Moorish and Spanish officials just outside the gates of the city as Isabel and Fernando bid farewell to their Moorish "guests." Hundreds of Spaniards crowded the battlements of the city walls above them while more thronged the fields on either side of the road to listen to the gracious speeches by both the Spanish and Moorish monarchs. Abu hugged his young son to his chest, sobbing openly and running his fingers through the boy's dark curly hair. There was no doubt that the boy, along with the other hostages, would be well cared for by the Castilian court, nor was there any likelihood that the boy would come to any harm, even if the accord between Abu and the Christians should break down. However, it was just as certain that the boy, Abu's only son, would be lost to him forever, raised and indoctrinated by the enemy, even if he were allowed a veneer of Moslem religious instruction. In fact, the only possible circumstance which might allow the boy to return to his parents would be the fall of Granada to the Christians, the final destruction of Moorish power in Spain, which would make it a matter of indifference to Isabel and Fernando whatever Abu might choose to do in the future. And Muhammad could not help but feel in his heart that it was only a question of time before such events should come to pass, not whether they would do so. The other scenario, in which a massive Moorish victory would allow Abu to dictate his own terms to the Christians now seemed too remote for contemplation.

Muhammad stood to one side to watch as Abu's son was delivered through the gates leading into Cordoba by an escort of Berber lancers. Abu rushed to the elaborately caparisoned pony of the boy, who was only about six years old, and lifted him to the ground once more, smothering him in an intense bear hug and kissing him repeatedly on one cheek and then the other while murmuring soft words to him. Muhammad noticed that the boy was as stiff in his father's embrace as a piece of cordwood, his own large eyes quite dry, and seemed to stare off into the distance over Abu's shoulder while he cooed to the boy. Abu stroked the boy's cheek gently with the backs of his knuckles and spoke to him for a long while, but the boy did not respond, and Muhammad could finally see pools of tears welling up in his dark eyes, although none touched his cheek. Surely, Muhammad thought, even a boy of this tender age could not have grown up in the political cesspool that was the Alhambra palace without some notion of how his life would figure as a pawn in a vast game the rules which he could never hope to fathom. Even the threat of sudden and violent death would never have been far from his thoughts, with very plausible hooded assassins infesting his nightmares while other children dreamt of fantastic monsters that disappeared with the morning's light. Still, it was clear that the boy realized that Abu was purchasing his own freedom with that of his son, a reversal of the traditional parental role, and it was also clear that a chasm had opened between father and son that no amount of caressing would ever close. Finally, Abu turned the boy over to a clutch of Castilian ladies who fussed and gushed over him as he was led off, but the boy turned, just as he was being escorted through the city gates and turned a cold look of disdain on his father that caused Abu to wince visibly. Then he was gone.

When the Moorish party finally prepared to depart, loaded down with gifts from the Castilian monarchs that Muhammad saw as just one more evidence of their shame, he strode over to where the members of Isabel's court stood by the roadside in all their finery and pressed into Raquel's hand a small gold ring he had picked up in the market in Cairo on his journeys years before. It had barely fit on his own little finger, but he knew that it would be too large even for her thumb, so he had hung it from a gold chain for her to wear around her neck.

"The engraving is a phrase from the Koran invoking God to protect travelers," he mumbled, finding himself oddly nervous. "It's a very banal thing that tradesmen sell to visitors."

"Then won't you be needing it?" she asked.

"I may be riding away, but I feel that you are on a journey of your own, my lady. A journey of a different sort and one in which you might be able to use the protection of Allah."

She smiled sadly and nodded. "I suppose having one more window to God won't hurt anything."

He was not sure what she meant, but the column of richly dressed Moors, escorted by a strong body of Christian knights to protect them from other Moors, had finally begun to ride out through the city gates and to head down the road leading to the east and Granada, toward *home*, and Muhammad only had time to wave to her as he swung into his own saddle and then cantered up to ride alongside his king.

Book Three

1484

GRANADA

Chapter One

Toledo

Raquel held her long chestnut braids back with one hand as she carefully measured scoops of the different powders into a cloth bag held open by one of her father's apprentices. She then stirred the contents methodically with a wooden spoon and nodded for him to tie the bag off with a length of string.

"Ram it home," she said, and he placed the bag in the mouth of the long, narrow cannon while the other apprentice pushed it all the way to the back of the barrel with his ramrod. The men had long since learned not to bother to look to Raquel's father before complying with any of her orders, and they had often remarked, when they were absolutely certain she could not overhear that, while some women's tongues were sources of pleasure, Raquel's certainly was not if anyone should have the nerve to question her authority. She had heard them, of course, and she had no problem with their way of thinking.

Raquel's father stood with his arms crossed, shaking his head. This was most unseemly for a young lady, even knowing about the secrets of explosives and metallurgy, much less putting that knowledge into practice, and he had told her so many times. It wouldn't have been so bad if he had been a tailor, a baker, a fuller, or even a jeweler. It was not unheard of for wives or daughters of men in those trades to help with the work and even develop a certain skill, but war and the tools of war were inherently masculine things that no woman should understand, much less excel in. Still, the pride glowed brightly in his dark eyes.

"Some men's daughters are busy stuffing chickens and capons for the oven, mine is stuffing a falconet," he laughed.

Raquel did not smile. "I think we've been going in the wrong direction, father," she said in the hurried, clipped tone he'd noticed that she'd adopted in recent months, as if she were either impatient with him, or with the whole world in general. "Everyone's trying to create bigger and bigger cannon, capable of throwing larger stone balls, but that isn't what's going to knock down castle walls faster."

"If bigger balls don't do it, what will?" he asked, and the two apprentices hid behind their hands as they giggled, knowing that there was a rumor going around the court that Raquel had bigger balls than most of the male courtiers, what with her obsession with the unfeminine arts of warfare and military technology.

"*Harder* balls, thrown harder," she replied. "Bigger cannon have weaker barrels. We just can't make them thick enough or strong enough to withstand the larger charge you need to throw balls of two or three hundred pounds over any distance. But, if we can increase the speed at which the ball leaves the muzzle by making a longer, narrower barrel, the destructive force should be greater, and if we can use a ball that will withstand the impact, one that is harder than the stone we're trying to break, well, that's the key."

"But, stone against stone, the balls will just shatter unless they're heavier," her father objected. "Some kinds of stone are more brittle than others, of course, but the facings of castle walls are usually built of the toughest stone available already."

"That's why we need to use iron balls, something that's harder than the stone we're trying to knock down." She looked up at him as if to ask if he were finished wasting her time, and casually brushed a stray wisp of her long, auburn hair out of her face.

"Won't that be prohibitively expensive?" he asked warily. "Casting balls is tricky work, and the metal is expensive as everyone is using iron to forge new weapons of every type. It will be hard to convince the king to buy more iron just to throw it at the enemy."

"How much does it cost to keep an army of five thousand men in the field for one day?" she responded. He knew that, while the question was meant rhetorically, she probably had the exact figure at her fingertips in terms of food for the men, fodder for the livestock, salaries, and even a daily average for the depreciation on the equipment. Isabel had become the unofficial quartermaster general of the army, and Raquel was her chief accountant in tabulating the funds raised and expended in support of Fernando's armies. "If you can end a siege even a little sooner using better technology, the investment will quickly repay itself. And that's not even counting the wastage of men and animals through disease in a siege camp or the risk of the enemy turning up with a relieving army if you give them enough time to do it."

Her father just shrugged and looked off toward the wall of the ruined abbey they were using for practice, some two hundred yards away. Raquel handed an iron ball about six inches in diameter to the loader who rammed it down the barrel of the gun with a piece of rag for wadding. She then sighted along the barrel and judged the elevation, gesturing to the gunner to hammer another wooden wedge under the rear of the piece to lower to angle slightly and to pour a little fine powder into the touch hole. She turned to her father, who gave her a nod, and she picked up the burning match and laid it across the touch hole.

The gun barked and lurched backward, sending a tongue of flame and a plume of bluish white smoke down range. Raquel ran ahead past the smoke to view the fall of shot, and her father scurried along behind her.

They found the ball, undamaged, lying at the base of the abbey wall, just below a huge gouge in what had been a smooth stretch of masonry just over a foot in diameter and several inches deep. Raquel smiled at her father and raised one curved eyebrow. To either side of this test shot were the shattered remnants of what had been half a dozen larger stone balls which had been fired at other sections of the wall, which had barely been dented.

"I suspect that you were fairly sure of your success," her father grumbled, kicking at the iron ball gingerly, since it was still too hot to pick up.

Raquel shrugged and gestured to him to hold one end of a measuring string that she carefully stretched across the hole in the wall at its widest point, fastening each end to the wall with a wad of soft wax that she had been chewing for the purpose.

"And that would explain why you asked to have seven more of the new guns set up here, with a supply of iron balls and the new fine grain powder we've been working on."

She shrugged again, and her father could see that Raquel was struggling to suppress a mischievous smile.

"I thought that we should put on a proper show for the queen," she said softly as she inserted a marked stick into the hole, perpendicular to the string. "Nearly six inches of penetration," she announced. With the structural integrity of the wall decreasing with each blow, we could blast through three feet of solid stone in an hour with a single battery."

"Wait a minute," her father said, letting the string drop. "What was that bit about the queen?"

"She's due to be out here this afternoon to observe the new artillery in action," she said. "Now, some castle walls are twenty or even thirty feet thick, but only the outsides are faced with stone with the gap filled with rubble and mortar, which will fall away almost by itself once the outer wall is shattered, and we could alternate using stone balls to knock that part out at a reduced cost. With a battery like this, well sited, and served round the clock, you could have a viable breach in a day or two at most in any wall, in any castle in Spain."

But her father was no longer listening. He was stalking about with long strides, flapping his arms like a snared eagle.

"How could you do this? We're not ready for a demonstration for the queen. What if powder gets wet, or a barrel bursts? All of our careful work at setting up the arms factory could be jeopardized, our funding cut off, and then where would we be?"

Raquel looked casually at the burning blue sky. "No sign of rain, so I don't know how the powder could get wet, and Pablo and Ismael will be doing all of the loading themselves, not some half-trained conscripts. They've been your apprentices for years and have learned a thing or two about guns. I'd load myself, but I don't think that the court would think it very ladylike."

"And they'd be only that much more likely to ridicule us," her father agreed, wringing his hands nervously. "Maybe we should pick a stretch of wall that's, well, a little weaker, just for effect, or maybe move the guns a bit closer."

"But that won't prove anything, and there are men at court who don't believe in artillery and will be looking for just that sort of trick to discredit us. They think that the only way to take a castle is by storming the walls or starving the defenders into submission. I've talked to the queen, and she understands that the first costs too many lives and the second takes too long *and* costs too many lives, especially if plague or cholera breaks out in the siege camp. She's behind us precisely because she grew up when any minor baron could sit in a castle with fifty armed men and bite his thumb at the crown for months, and the issue would only be resolved by whether the plague hit the defenders or the attackers first. No one but the crown can afford large quantities of artillery or the trained men to operate the guns, so the power of the nobles will finally be broken. That means that the constant cycle of civil wars will come to an end, the peasants will have peace to grow their crops and raise their herds, and merchants will be free to conduct trade in some security, so the whole country will prosper."

Her father just groaned and waved his arms in the air some more, then went to fuss over the row of long, black cannons, peering down the barrels, instructing the gunners in their alignment, and closely examining the pyramid of iron balls next to each piece. Raquel just chuckled as she sat on a keg of gunpowder and accepted a wooden plateful of coarse rye bread and fresh local cheese from a servant.

The royal party was late, as Raquel had expected, since important personages consider it obligatory to keep subordinates waiting, the longer the wait, the more the difference in rank was emphasized, and the queen was notoriously conscious of her rank. This was just another source of anxiety for her father. He shaded his eyes every five minutes and nervously checked the level of the sun as it dipped toward the low hills to the west and then peered down the road toward Toledo, where the court of the queen was currently in residence on its perpetual migration from one part of the country to another, there being no formal capital in Castile as there was in England or France. The tips of the lances of the escorting cavalry finally emerged from behind a rocky outcrop, colored pennants snapping in the breeze, and the little group swung into view. There were only half a dozen mounted men-at-arms as a guard, but Raquel noticed that the queen was also accompanied by the Marquis of Cadiz and several officers of the *Santa Hermandad* along with those ladies of her usual entourage who rode well and also Father Hernando de Talavera, his thick body bouncing uncomfortably in the saddle.

Raquel rose as they approached, and she recognized the bothersome, intense stare of Juan Ortega who rode just behind the queen, a stare that set the hair on the back of her neck to prickling. She noticed that he was apparently better off financially now than when she had first seen him, the day he was knighted. His *Hermandad* cloak of red and black was now made of velvet instead of coarse wool, and was fastened in front with an ostentatious gold clasp in the form of a clenched fist. He rode a tall gray stallion of obvious spirit, possibly the one Fernando had given him, not a hastily conscripted plow horse like many of the poorer men-at-arms. He had thick rings on his fingers and gold buttons on his surcoat, but there was a certain roughness about him that brought to mind all-night drinking bouts and unexcused belching in a rural manor while pigs and dogs scavenged for scraps under the tables. But what was most irksome was the way he never took his eyes off her, even when he was talking with someone else, and people had started to notice and whisper and titter whenever he was around. Since Raquel could hardly stand his presence, it had begun to worry her that people might start to take notice and to consider them a couple, as much as she usually disdained the normal flow of court gossip, in that common etiquette dictated that such looks could only be bestowed by a gentleman on a lady with whom he has some sort of discreet agreement.

And it had to be admitted that Raquel was way beyond the normal age of marriage for a young lady, virtually to the level of spinsterhood in her mid-twenties when most young women were well married at fifteen or even as young as twelve, which gave rise to rumors either that she would fall at the feet of the first man who gave her a second glance or that she was already the secret mistress of some high-born noble, if not of Fernando himself, who was a notorious, if discreet, womanizer. This last point had caused Raquel some discomfort as Isabel was just as notorious for her jealousy, and it was only her own intimate relationship with Raquel that seemed to put Raquel beyond suspicion.

In fact, it was just that Raquel could never bring herself to trust any man enough, whether he be Old Christian or *converso*, with the awful secret of her true faith, and, if she could not confide that, how could she possibly marry? There had been young men over the years at court who had certainly tugged at her heart strings, but the more deeply she felt about them, the less could she consider the danger she would be putting them in by tying them to her when the Inquisition could come banging on her door in the small hours of any night. She could not marry a Jew and ask him to abandon his faith, nor could she convert herself, as the Church saw conversion as a very one-way street to Christianity, and not the other way. If she chose a Christian, how long could she keep up her secret worship without being discovered, and, in any case, if she loved a man enough to marry him, how could she put his life in danger by exposing him to the risk of being accused along with her by the Inquisition some day. The only possibility would have been for her to find a mate among the secret practitioners of Judaism among the *converso* community, but that was a very small pool of candidates indeed, and, if she could discover a man's hidden faith, how much easier would it be for the Inquisition to do the same? No, Raquel had decided, the best thing was to just lead her life alone and balance the isolation against the security it gave her.

The queen was dressed in a fine satin gown of deep blue, the most fashionable color that season, and at her neck she wore several long strings of pearls. She might have been a person of simple tastes herself, but the queen always reminded Raquel that the *people* needed to see their monarchs elegantly attired if they were to have any respect for them, and Raquel had never doubted the queen's wisdom in political matters. Even the mule she rode, since mules were more sure-footed than horses, and it would not do for the queen of the Spaniards to take a fall, was draped in folds of blue satin with the yoke and arrows symbol of Isabel and Fernando's house embroidered in silver thread throughout. Her mount's bardings alone cost enough to feed and house a common artisan's family for several years.

Raquel's father bowed low while the grooms rushed to carry a set of wooden steps over to the queen's horse to help her dismount, and Raquel curtseyed in a respectful but casual way. She placed her hand over her breast as she did so and cursed herself for having chosen the revealing dress she wore, since nothing was more disturbing than the way this Ortega fellow insisted on craning his neck and gawking at her cleavage.

Isabel distractedly allowed Raquel's father to take her hand and kiss his own thumb, if not the royal skin itself, as she strolled over to the gun line and fondly caressed the barrel of one of the cannons.

"So these are the devils that will finally deliver Granada to us from the Moors after over seven hundred years," she said gaily. "Or perhaps I should call them angels," she added, and the courtiers burst out in gales of laughter until the queen's subtle frown warned them that she did not think the jest worthy of such hilarity.

"No damned iron tube is a substitute for a strong sword arm," Juan grumbled from the rear of the group, but it was immediately clear from the look of shock on his face when all heads turned toward him that he had not intended to say this aloud.

Isabel smiled as Juan turned a deep shade of pink. "We were rather hoping that this iron tube would save some of our strong sword arms for other tasks, since we have already lost so many in the reconquest," she said to no one in particular, and she gestured with her chin for Raquel's father to get on with the demonstration.

"Sword arms were not enough at Ajarquia," Raquel mumbled under her breath, but the words carried very well, and she glanced up to see the faces of both Ortega and the Marquis redden suddenly at the reminder of the recent disaster to Spanish arms at the hands of the Moors, and she began to tremble.

Several months before, the Marquis had led a force of several thousand Andalusian knights and footsoldiers on a raid deep into Moorish territory, primarily with a view to booty taking advantage of expected Moorish demoralization in the wake of their defeat at Lucena, but with vague hopes of possibly being able to storm right into the key Moorish port of Malaga by *coup de main*, if all went well. As it turned out, it was the Christians who had been ambushed in the rugged passes of the Sierra Nevada by hordes of alert and apparently very undemoralized Moors and cut to pieces. Hundreds of Spaniards were killed and hundreds more marched off as prisoners either to await ransom or for sale as slaves. The Marquis himself had lost three of his brothers cut down before his eyes, and he and Ortega were among the handful of survivors who made their way back to friendly towns by way of back trails in twos and threes over the following days. Raquel thanked God that she had not blurted out something about the almost equally disastrous attack on the town of Loja just prior to that in which an over-confident Fernando had almost lost his own life. She knew the queen well enough to understand that any implied criticism of the king's strategic judgement would not have been well-received, no matter how well justified.

"Our swords were good enough to take Alhama," Ortega roared, shaking a huge fist in Raquel's direction, totally forgetting the presence of the queen who stood between them. "I climbed the walls just as I did at a dozen other fortress towns, with the Marquis at my side," he added quickly, "and we took the place back from the damned blackamoors without so much as a whiff of gunpowder!"

In his heart Juan knew that the recapture of the town whose fall had precipitated the current war was no more than a propaganda victory. The entire Christian population had long ago been herded off into slavery and only a small garrison left to hold the place for Granada, but the quick victory had been trumpeted across Spain and had secured Juan's place as a legendary *escalador*, but it was his knowledge that such victories would be few and far between without recourse to the new technology of which he had little understanding and which devalued his greatest talents that fueled his anger now. The fact that this threat to his position was being posed by a *woman*, and a woman about whom he had become increasingly obsessed since he had first met her after the fight at Alhama, only made matters worse.

"I think that there is no denying that our destruction of the enemies of Christ and the True Faith will always call for the employment of good Toledo steel," the queen interjected in an amused tone, reaching out to touch both Raquel and Juan gently on the forearm as they had moved closer together and now stood glaring at each other. "Still, we cannot hope to surprise the garrison of every Moorish stronghold the way you so brilliantly did at Alhama, and it behooves us to consider any means that the Lord puts within our grasp both to shorten the duration of the war and to enhance our likelihood of emerging victorious." The two contenders both lowered their eyes and sullenly accepted her intercession.

Ruben, alternately glaring at his daughter and glancing nervously from the queen to the Marquis to Ortega, cleared his throat loudly in an attempt to break the tension. Isabel gave him a nod, and he hurriedly waved the cluster of ladies and other noble guests back to a safe distance as the women tittered behind their fans. Since even these new bronze guns could burst upon discharge, Ruben did not want to have to explain to the king how bits of jagged metal got lodged in the queen's body.

"This wall is only about three feet thick," Raquel explained to Isabel in a voice loud enough for the others to hear, "but it's solid stone and well made. What these small guns can do here in an hour, some slightly heavier pieces can do to any castle in the land in a few days."

"Instead of months," Isabel nodded. "That would certainly be an improvement." Juan snorted loudly and folded his thick arms across his chest.

Ruben raised his burning taper to show that he was ready.

"Cover your ears, ladies and gentlemen, and take a good look at the wall so that you can judge the effect," he announced and placed the glowing tip to the touch hole of the first gun.

There was a crash and a billow of smoke, and the gun leaped backwards, but Ruben had moved on to the next gun before the echo returned from the hills, and the guns roared one after another until all eight had been fired. The pall of thick white smoke hung like a curtain in front of the cannons, but the gunners were already swabbing out the barrels, removing smoldering embers of wadding before the apprentices carefully stuffed fresh charges down the tubes.

When the light breeze had finally dispersed the smoke, Isabel and her followers took a few steps forward for a better look. The wall had been smooth white stone, and it was now gouged and scarred all across its face, and a small pile of rubble had formed at the base.

"It's still standing," one of the ladies whispered in disappointment.

"Of course it is, you goose," Isabel snapped over her shoulder. "One volley isn't going to bring it down. Now be quiet and let Master Ruben do his work."

The gunners worked their pieces quickly, and another volley soon followed, then another and another, and the echoes mingled with the reports of new rounds fired. The smoke hardly cleared at all now, and the men began stripping off their jackets as they warmed to their task, which brought some lewd comments and continued giggling from the ladies, evaluating the muscle tone of the gunners and the obvious symbolism of the rammer and gun tube. The women kept their hands over their ears, but neither the Marquis nor Juan bothered, and Raquel had long been accustomed to the roar of the guns, although she had taken the precaution of stuffing small tufts of cotton in each ear before the shooting began. In between the explosions, she could pick out the muffled sound of crumbling masonry, and she was confident that the test was going well.

When the bells of the churches of Toledo began to sound for vespers, Raquel made a discreet gesture to her father to cease firing, and the guns one by one fell silent. When the smoke finally cleared in the light breeze, a gasp went up from the spectators. The wall had been nearly ten feet high and forty feet long in this stretch, and it now comprised a pile of shattered stone of less than half that height in the middle of the wall with only a rare pinnacle of ravaged masonry left standing here and there where the fire of the guns had not overlapped.

"Very impressive," the marquis was the first to acknowledge. "I could see our old bombards hammering away at that thing for a week to no appreciable effect."

"Exactly, your grace," Ruben explained enthusiastically. "With enough guns, served constantly, you can make a breach in any castle wall in very short order."

"And how do you propose getting those guns *to* the castle you propose to destroy?" Juan asked, evidently finding new courage when discussing tactics among men and not directly contradicting the queen herself. "Almost all of Granada is covered with mountains the like of which you've never seen, and very few roads. Those things are not made of feathers, and you can hardly stick them in your pocket and skip over the ridges."

"No, sir, we cannot," Ruben admitted. "Where the situation required, you would have to widen or even build new roads and bridges."

"Which would also serve for supply wagons for the troops," Raquel interjected impetuously when she saw Juan rolling his eyes.

"And who is going to pay for this new artillery park and these roads?" Juan asked of Ruben, ignoring Raquel. "Just one of these guns costs more to produce than the arming of a whole regiment of infantry, and cutting roads through mountains takes hundreds of men and animals."

"And who pays for the upkeep of a whole army in the field?" Isabel joined in, smiling again, as Juan hunched his shoulders as if he had just received a blow. "If a siege can be cut short by as little as a month, freeing an army of, say, ten thousand men, a whole grand battery of guns would have more than paid for itself. Besides that, now that Master Ruben has established his manufactory at Ecija, producing the guns in quantity, they are costing less per capita."

"What's more, your highness," Raquel added, now taking her turn to ignore Juan, "once one or two towns have been taken in this way, the word will spread that there is no effective defense, and I'd be willing to wager that many others will simply surrender without a shot being fired."

"But is there no defense against these new weapons?" the Marquis asked. "I would hate to think of all of our own cities becoming suddenly as defenseless as those of the Moor seem to have become this afternoon if this little experiment can really be reproduced in the field. If we can produce artillery of this sort, surely they can as well, or the Turks, or the Berbers in North Africa."

"To say nothing of the French or Portuguese," Juan added.

"For one thing," Raquel continued, "the Moors can't build cannon the way we can. They don't have the access to iron mines or the expertise in construction or the money. The Turks might be able to, but they're on the other side of the Mediterranean and have shown no interest thus far in helping their brothers in Granada. We can draw on gunsmiths from France, Italy, all of Europe, and the Moors are lucky to get a ship through the blockade of Catalan and Castilian ships to or from North Africa these days. And there is a defense. When all you had to worry about was storming parties, the ideal castle had tall, straight walls that would be hard to climb." She illustrated by holding one delicate forearm and hand vertical and the other horizontal, making an "L." "And you have a broad base to discourage mining. Now, you will build lower, broader walls sloped inward to deflect the cannon balls and made more of earth than stone, to absorb the shock of the attacker's fire, and you will rely on firepower, not stone, to defend the city from assault. Muskets and cannon mounted on the walls will sweep the approaches, and you can install heavier cannon in a fort, cannon that need never move and would have a height advantage over the attacker for better range, than you can reasonably construct and haul to the point of attack."

"No army worth its bread will be turned away by bullets and arrows alone. You need high walls to stop them," Juan insisted.

"But if your walls are piles of rubble after a few days of bombardment, they won't answer either," the marquis joined in. "And you yourself have demonstrated time and again that high walls are hardly a perfect defense, my young friend," and Juan noticeably blushed at the compliment. "But we don't have the money to rebuild every castle in Spain."

"That's just it," Raquel went on. "The Moors certainly don't have time or the money now to rebuild their castles, which will all become obsolete, as you have pointed out, and when the Moors have been conquered, what use will we have of our own castles, except perhaps along the frontiers with Portugal and France?"

The marquis started to say something, because a noble like himself could think of a very plausible use for his castles. They were the basis of his own resistance to the power of the crown, should the need arise, as it had often enough in the preceding decades, but he merely cleared his throat and wandered over to examine the guns. Isabel nodded wisely at Raquel and began to lead the group back to where their mounts were tethered, talking quietly to Ruben as she went.

"And will we have enough guns ready for the campaigning season once the winter rains have stopped?" the queen asked.

"A general never feels he has *enough* of anything before a battle, but, for a limited campaign, yes, Your Majesty. They will be ready."

"Good, because the army will be marching on Alora in June, and this time we intend to take it."

Raquel overheard the conversation and held her breath. Alora was only twenty-five miles northwest of Malaga, near the site of the most stinging of the Castilians' recent defeats, and the entire prestige of the crown would be riding on this campaign. The "strong sword arms" of Juan Ortega and his ilk had notably failed to defeat the Moors in the field at tremendous cost in treasure and blood. If a signal victory could now be achieved by her father's artillery, their case would be made, and her family would finally be safe, the unquestioned protectors of the crown and the source of its power against all enemies, both foreign and domestic.

In the days that followed, as the first buds began to appear on the trees, the army began to gather. The flower of Castilian nobility was present, with the aging Cardinal Mendoza as the overall commander while Fernando was occupied trying to cajole money for the campaign out of the Aragonese Cortes to the north. Conscripts, feudal levies, the military households of the nobility, foreign mercenaries, and the growing number of royal troops from the *Santa Hermandad* marched into Cordoba or set up their tent cities in the outskirts of the town. Soon, they had stripped the countryside bare of supplies, and Mendoza took a force of 12,000 cavalry and 6,000 foot off to ravage the rich V*ega* plain of central Granada north of Malaga and sweeping back through Antequera, both to obtain new supplies at the expense of the enemy and to give the land of Andalusia a much-need rest from the pestilential presence of the army. Although no major cities were taken, the success of the raid boded well for a more serious campaign of conquest later that year.

Fernando arrived in Cordoba a week later and by 10 June, with a combined army of over 30,000 men, he mustered the forces present for the advance to the border of Granada. For a full day and most of the next night the town and the surrounding military camp had been filled with hustling men, the creaking of wagons, and the shouts of teamsters trying to prepare the massive column for the march.

There was no formal, standing Spanish army, no standard units like regiments or battalions into which they could be mustered. The forces arrayed in the plains surrounding Cordoba comprised little more than individual gangs attached to the persons of the more powerful nobles. Generally speaking, the army was organized, if that term could be used, into "battles" which might contain anywhere from a few hundred to several thousand men, both foot and horse. Alonso de Aguilar commanded the first "battle" or wing, the Marquis of Cadiz the second, and the Duke of Medina Sidonia the third. Each "battle" would be commanded by the noble who raised and paid most of the troops included with no regard for the military capability or experience of the lord in question. The masters of the military orders of Santiago and Calatrava and other lesser groups were the most prominent of these, and there was constant competition and wrangling between the nobles for positions of "honor" in the battle line based on such considerations as length of genealogical standing or relationship to the king instead of the composition of the forces under their command. It was virtually impossible for anyone to tell the size or composition of the entire army at any given time, as nobles wandered off with their followers on private business or drifted into camp unannounced at their whim.

Fernando had been experimenting with a new structure based on his own royal guard and the *Santa Hermandad*. These troops would be organized into squadrons of five hundred men. These would be either horsemen or infantry, with each infantry unit composed either of a combination of arquebusiers or crossbowmen for missile fire and soldiers armed with sword or pike for defense and shock action. Each squadron would be led by a captain appointed by the king by virtue of military experience. Although the captains would necessarily also be noblemen, these were sometimes of rather modest rank, and it was entirely possible for a particularly capable officer to distinguish himself and come to the notice of the sovereign, thus earning further promotion. It was a small but significant step toward the establishment of a professional army and would be put to its first test as the army began to stream southward along the dusty roads.

Raquel's father had gone with the army, shepherding his precious guns over the uneven roads heading south, even supervising the construction of wooden bridges and retaining walls where needed to augment the scant road system over the jagged ridges and rain swollen streams that crisscrossed their route of march. But Raquel was too busy to really notice his absence. While Fernando had some undoubted skills as a commander of troops in the field, he would have been the first to admit that he did not have the brain or the patience for the million small details that went into the proper organization of a logistical network that would be required to adequately support an army of over thirty thousand men on an extended campaign. Fortunately, Isabel did have such a brain, and it was she, in close coordination with Raquel serving as her secretary, accountant, and counselor, who collected the contributions of townships throughout Spain, either in men, arms, foodstuffs, or money, and saw to their efficient transportation to the army. It had been Raquel's suggestion that the levies in all of these categories be divided into two tranches, half now, and half three months hence, in order to prevent grain and meat from spoiling before they could be used and unnecessary hordes of men from either dying plague in overcrowded camps or deserting in droves before they could effectively be put to use. Since this provision also eased the immediate burden on the townships, it was eagerly seized upon and adopted by the queen.

Isabel and Raquel also saw to the establishment of regular hospitals, both mobile ones to accompany the army, and permanent ones in cities throughout Andalusia to receive and care for the sick and wounded from the coming battles. Heretofore, it had been standard practice for all armies to leave their wounded on the field, except of course for those of noble birth, to be cared for by their comrades or to die as might be, since this was seen as the will of God. This practice encouraged many soldiers' wives to accompany the army on its march, adding hundreds of useless mouths to feed and often fueling competition between the men for the attentions of a limited number of women, some of whose dedication to their marital vows was less than adamant, but it at least guaranteed to the married soldier that someone would come looking for him among the shattered bodies on the field if he did not return. The soldiers considered Isabel's attention to their welfare as proof of her saintliness, but both the queen and Raquel saw it as simple good business, trying to return trained fighting men to the lines instead of letting them bleed to death from superficial wounds. Not that the medical care was particularly sophisticated, but in many cases merely a quick washing of a wound and a relatively clean bandage could spell the difference between a slow and painful death and a quick recovery. Even something as simple as providing food, water, and shelter to the wounded was a long step in the right direction.

As busy as the queen was, she was never one to deny herself a certain amount of healthy recreation. In keeping with her image as the *mujer varonile*, the "manly woman" and taking advantage of one of the rare periods of her adult life when she was not pregnant, Isabel had developed a marked interest in the hunt, everything from the relatively passive use of falcons to the rough and tumble of the mounted pursuit of boars or even bears. Alone among Isabel's ladies in waiting, Raquel often accompanied her on these outings, along with the inevitable horde of grooms, stewards, bodyguards, huntsmen, and male courtiers. On a crisp spring morning after the departure of Fernando's army, Isabel rousted Raquel out of bed early to join her on one such hunting expedition.

The queen was, as usual, mounted on a spirited gray gelding, rather than the mule that Spanish custom required for women of breeding, and Raquel had chosen her favorite bay mare. They both wore sensible long wool dresses and felt boots, both against the chill air and to protect them against the briars and brambles of the woods, their hair bound up in turbans, and sturdy leather gauntlets on their hands. They rode sidesaddle, of course, since not even Isabel could dare anything so scandalous as to ride astraddle a horse, although Raquel longed for the ability to simply don a pair of breeches and sit a horse as men did rather than perch precariously, one knee hooked on a protruding saddle horn, and badly off balance, especially when it came to throwing a javelin. Both women were, however, fine equestrians, and led the chase over rolling hills, just now coming alive with sprinklings of wildflowers, toward the dense woods to the northwest of Cordoba.

Lines of beaters had been deployed in a rough box covering several square miles with the end toward the hunting party left open. Hundreds of peasants and castle servants crashed through the underbrush, banging drums and blowing flutes, startling the game down toward the approaching hunters. A groom ran alongside Isabel's and Raquel's horses, armed only with a hunting knife. Their primary function was to rewind the mechanism of the women's crossbows and to retrieve their hunting spears once thrown. There were several noblemen in the party, although most had accompanied the army to the south, but Raquel was distressed to notice that Juan Ortega was among the party as he had stayed behind to escort a new contingent of *Hermandad* cavalry to the front which had been late in arriving at the rendezvous. She was grateful that the men discreetly kept apart, hovering in packs on either side of the women, ready to swoop down to their rescue should they be confronted by some slavering beast, but otherwise respecting Isabel's oft-repeated wish to conduct her own hunt. Still, Raquel could feel the man's eyes on her every moment. She dared not look to confirm her belief, however, lest he take this as a sign of acceptance, so she stuck close by Isabel's side and concentrated on the game.

"Tell me about your mother," Isabel suddenly said as they crested a low hill and stopped to examine a thick clump of woods in a small valley before them.

"My mother, your highness?" Raquel asked dumbly.

"Yes, your mother. You've talked for hours about your father, occasionally about your brother, the one who left home long ago, but almost never about your mother. She is still alive, is she not?"

It took Raquel a moment to reply. While she had spent countless hours talking with Isabel over more than a decade now, sometimes with both of them in tears about the most intimate aspects of their lives, she suddenly realized that neither had really discussed either of their mothers. While Raquel had never had a problem with her mother, they had never been particularly close either. Raquel intentionally expounded on her father's skills and attributes for obvious reasons, since this reinforced Raquel's and his own position with the queen, but she had rarely discussed her mother simply because there was not much of interest in the life of a middle aged housewife that she could see. For a moment Raquel wondered if Isabel had some private and horrible news about mother, but this would have been an odd way for the queen to bring it up. Unless it had something to do with the Inquisition, Raquel thought in a moment of horror, but she must not reveal her suspicions, so she fought to keep the banter light.

"Yes, your highness. I had a note from her just last month."

Isabel nodded sadly. "It has been a long while since my mother could write a note. You should be thankful."

Raquel could hear the beaters hooting and clanging away in the forest, and the sound was approaching. They really should have been paying more attention to the game as rabbits could already be seen scurrying through the brush, and flocks of birds clattered through the trees to safety in other woods. The other parties of hunters looked anxiously at the queen, waiting to take their lead from her, but Isabel sat her horse coolly, her hands resting on her knee, oblivious as only a queen could be of the concerns of others.

"I was about the same age as you were when I was sent to court, taken away from my mother," Isabel went on in a distant tone. "As in your case, the decision was not mine, but at least it was your own father who took you, who wanted to put you in a position of safety." The queen smiled when Raquel started at this. "Oh, I realized early that the request to place you at court came very close upon the anti-*converso* riots in Cordoba, and it was natural enough for your father to feel that you would be better protected at court. A very prudent move indeed. In my case, however, my own brother, Enrique, my half-brother I should say, took me to court, not to protect or educate me, but to have me handy if it ever became convenient for him to do away with me. I might have only been twelve years old, but I soon realized that, although my mother had cared for me and educated me herself, it was *she* who depended on me."

Isabel's chin was quivering now, and Raquel knew that she was not meant to respond, only to listen.

"I received messages from faithful servants over the following months about my mother's decline. I could see that she was unraveling from her letters, and I did what I could, little twelve-year-old Isabel, to reassure her, to convince her that I was well and safe and that we would be together again soon, but it was no use. Alone and isolated in a remote convent, her demons fed on her unmolested, and they devoured her mind, turning a brave, strong, healthy woman into a shell, a ghost who still breathed, tortured by fears of death for herself, my brother, or me, and fears that were not totally insane either. It would have been far more merciful of them to have simply killed her outright." Isabel turned to Raquel. "Would your mother have given her life for you?"

"I'm certain that she would, your majesty," Raquel answered firmly.

Isabel nodded. "My mother sacrificed even more for me, for a vision she had of Castile with me as queen. She gave up her very soul."

Raquel opened her mouth but had no words to reply. She took another breath as if to try again, when there was suddenly a wild crashing through the underbrush just in front of the queen's horse, and a massive boar rushed into the open snorting and gouging furrows in the earth with its great hooves, slashing at the dry grass with its dirty yellow tusks.

Isabel's horse shied, and the queen sawed her reins trying to control the animal. A shout went up from the huntsmen and the mounted nobles on the next crest, but they were several hundred yards away now, too far to do any good. Even their grooms had allowed the queen to pull well ahead, although they would have been able to do little against a boar who weighed more than all of them put together. Raquel's mount also reared, but she was in no danger of being thrown. Instead, she grasped a javelin out of its sheath and intentionally slipped from the saddle, planting herself on the ground between the boar and the queen.

The beast paused for a moment, regarding the frail creature before it. The whites of its eyes shown, rimmed with red, and its foul breath came in gusts and kicked up thick clouds of dust from the dry ground that hung in the still air. It tossed its ugly head once in defiance and charged. Raquel knew that she did not have the strength to throw the javelin with enough force to kill the animal, so she braced the butt against the ground, positioning herself squarely in the boar's path and gritted her teeth to await the impact. Her only thought was that, in the time it would take the animal to kill her, the queen could escape, or help might arrive. The animal emitted a terrifying sound, something between a squeal and a roar, a cry of rage, and it lowered its head in preparation for a vicious upward slash with its curved, sharp tusks. Raquel could hear nothing but its grunting and the scrabbling of its hooves on the loose gravel of the slope, and she closed her eyes, awaiting her death.

Suddenly, there was another squeal and a tremendous thud that Raquel could feel in the ground itself, and she opened her eyes to find the boar on its back, its legs thrashing wildly, just inches in front of the point of her weapon with a hunting spear passing completely through its neck and pinning it to the ground to one side. Juan Ortega was already off his horse, another spear in his hands, rushing past Raquel to dispatch the beast with a swift thrust to the base of the animal's skull, leaning on the shaft with his full weight and twisting the point savagely.

Raquel let the javelin fall from her trembling hands and collapsed to her knees. It was only after another moment that she let out a gasp and found that she had not been breathing for, God knew how long. She felt Isabel's arms around her, and she buried her face on the queen's shoulder.

"With brave vassals like these," Isabel was saying in a loud voice as the other members of the party galloped up, her own voice quavering with emotion, "who can hope to stand against the crown of Castile?"

Raquel looked up and saw the burly figure of Ortega standing over them, his legs braced and his thumbs hooked into his belt, with a smug grin on his face, and she suddenly wondered if she would not have preferred to deal with the boar.

"I had moved forward to have a better look at the woods, your majesty," Ortega explained while the huntsmen and nobles congregated to examine and admire the fallen boar, "and I caught a glimpse of the boar just as it was coming out of the thicket. I took the liberty of riding up unbidden in the hope that I might be of assistance."

Isabel helped Raquel to her feet, and Ortega reached out a hand to steady her. Raquel drew back for an instant, but then laid her hand on his muscular forearm. Why should she feel such an aversion to this man? He had done her no harm. In fact, he had just saved her life. He might be a typical boorish Castilian petty nobleman, more concerned with bashing heads and grasping all the land, wealth, and privilege within his reach and then ostentatiously displaying that wealth and privilege than with even making a pretense at developing his mind, but perhaps she was setting an artificially high standard. Ortega certainly had not invented this style of living or this attitude toward society. He was merely a product of his upbringing, just as Raquel was of her own.

She looked again at Ortega, cocking her head like a curious bird. He was not bad looking, in a rough sort of way, and she thought she detected a certain clumsy nervousness in him, like a farm boy suddenly thrust into high society and unsure of how to comport himself, which he probably was. In that light, he no longer seemed to be so threatening and offensive to her. He may have displayed some signs of violence and virulent jealousy, even though he had no right to be jealous over her, but he was a man in a violent profession, and they lived in violent times, so such behavior was hardly unique, even if it was distasteful. Of course, she was terrified that he might find out about her true religious beliefs, being an officer of the *Santa Hermandad,* but that was hardly less true with anyone else at court, and there was certainly no chance that this bumpkin could ever outwit her, if the queen could not. She found herself smiling timidly.

"Thank you, sir," she said softly.

"I'm sure you had the situation well in hand, my lady," he stammered, scuffing at the ground with the toe of his felt boot, "but I was concerned that you'd get blood all over that charming dress, the boar's blood, that is," he added hastily.

Raquel found herself giggling like a young maid, although it was probably from the emotional relief of her narrow escape from the boar. They were surrounded now by a horde of servants, huntsmen, courtiers, and soldiers, all jabbering at once, recounting their own versions of the incident, prodding at the still-quivering hulk of the boar with

311

their spears, and crooning soothingly to the queen who brushed aside their solicitude impatiently.

There was no point in continuing the hunt, and the entire party mounted for the ride back to the city. Raquel found herself riding alongside Ortega. He was talking nervously about nothing whatever, about the weather, about gossip from the court, about his lands, his own lands, not those of his father, he was careful to point out, and an endless account of his role in the battle for Alhama. Raquel hardly responded, since a lady was not required to, just making an occasional genteel noise or nodding her head in apparent interest.

Her mind drifted back to the year before and the tall, dark Moorish scholar she had met at court. Now there was a man with a mind, a man with whom she could discuss the affairs of the world and the thoughts of the great philosophers. She could hardly imagine any member of Isabel's court fitting that role, but, she sighed inwardly, there was no point pining for something that she could never have. She had assumed that she never would marry, being already well past the age when young ladies normally wed. She had resisted advances for more than a dozen men at court, both old and young, both honorable and not so honorable, over the past ten years, and the offers had gradually stopped coming in as the eligible bachelors either sought out women with substantial dowries, which she certainly never would have, or nubile young maidens to satisfy other desires. She had begun to view herself as the elderly aunt, never married, taking care of other people's children, as she had often taken care of the queen's four offspring. Her arms had ached at the sight of babies being suckled at the breasts of red-faced peasant women tending their market stalls or wet nurses in the gardens of the palaces visited by the court, but she had accepted the fact that she would never know the feeling of giving life and sustenance to a little creature from her own body. Perhaps, she had been surrendering too soon. But Ortega? That muscle-bound lout?

Raquel gradually reawaked to reality. The longer they rode, the louder Ortega talked and the more he gesticulated with his hands, laughing boisterously at his own comments to which she just smiled pleasantly. By the time they approached the city gates, Raquel had the distinct feeling that most of the rest of the party had stopped their own conversations to listen in on that of Ortega and Raquel, or that of Ortega at least, and even Isabel turned in her saddle to glance back at them, crooking a delicate eyebrow well up her forehead. Raquel bridled at this and as soon as they reached the courtyard, she quickly dismounted and excused herself, rushing back to her room and closing the door firmly. It was as if they could all read her mind, thoughts she had only tentatively allowed herself to indulge in, and they were practically laughing out loud at her.

It was Friday and late in the afternoon. No one would mark her absence from dinner after the day's excitement, and she felt a deep need to observe the Sabbath in the privacy of her room. She missed her father deeply at times like this, the droning, relaxing tone of his voice as he recited the traditional prayers, always in a whisper lest they be overheard, and she longed to visit a synagogue, to be surrounded by fellow believers, without having to worry about being discovered. Could there never be a place where her people could worship freely? Where they would not have to fear the whispers of their neighbors? Where they would not feel like strangers, unwelcome visitors in a foreign land, even one where they and their forebears had lived for centuries?

She opened a cedar chest and rummaged under the clothes and books for the menorah her father had made, but the silence of the room was suddenly broken by the shrieking of a young girl. She quickly closed the chest and rushed through the connecting door into the next bedchamber. Four-year-old Juana, Isabel's third child stood in the center of the room screaming at the top of her lungs at Raquel, jabbering something about Raquel's having abandoned her all day. A flustered nanny was vainly tugging at the little girl's arm, gently of course as this was a princess of the blood, but Juana was a stocky child, and it was unlikely that the young woman would have had much luck moving her if she had seriously tried.

Raquel had not seen much of Isabelita, the eldest daughter who was now twelve and had been living for two years in Moura, Portugal, with an aunt, being schooled in the fine arts of maidenly poise and bearing in preparation for making a valuable marriage of alliance for the crown. Juan, Prince of Asturias, and heir apparent, was constantly cloistered with his male tutors, both scholarly and religious, as well as masters at arms who, even at his tender age of five were coaching him in games designed to make of him a powerful knight like his father. Little Maria, only one year old, was still with the wet nurse, which left Juana as the only one of the children currently under the direct care of the ladies of the court, which meant Raquel more often than not, as Isabel was constantly occupied with governmental business, and the other ladies were far too busy gossiping about or participating in amorous liaisons with the gentlemen of the court to be bothered spending much time meeting the needs of a small child who was starved for attention and affection in the bustle of royal affairs. Raquel had even been present at her birth, holding Isabel's hand while she sat in the special birthing chair, a low slung wooden affair with a hole in the bottom for the baby to pass through with the help of gravity as was traditional.

Raquel had welcomed the chance to mother little Juana. She was a beautiful, chubby little girl, who loved to cuddle and would spend hours in Raquel's arms listening to stories or napping quietly. But she was demanding as well. In fact, she could hardly stand to be alone, even for a moment. She was terrified of the dark and insisted that bad people were whispering in the corners and in the shadows when no one was with her. It was far more than simple childhood insecurity, and Raquel feared that these might be early signs of the kind of obsessive behavior and unreasoning fears that plagued Isabel's mother's troubled mind. Raquel did not know if such maladies were hereditary, but there were ample rumors around the court that this was indeed the case. The queen certainly did not appear to suffer from them, but then Raquel understood that character traits sometimes skipped a generation, like different colored fur in rabbits, and there were those who believed that the same might be true among humans.

It would not normally have been difficult to comply with Juana's demands not to be left alone. There were certainly plenty of servants about the household, but not just anyone would do. Raquel suspected that Juana would have much preferred to have been catered to by her own mother, but even the little child knew that this was not possible. So, she had settled on Raquel as an acceptable substitute, not constantly, just when her special demons chose to torture her, and tonight was one of those nights. According to the maid, Juana had been having a tantrum of moderate intensity all afternoon, but when she had heard the excited chattering of the castle staff about the queen's, and Raquel's, narrow escape from the boar, which had been carried back to the city by swift-running messengers long before the arrival of the royal party, she had been driven into a frenzy of fear and worry. Now, she insisted that only Raquel could put her to sleep, and, as tired and drained as she was, Raquel took the child in her arms and laid her on the silk sheets of her small but elaborately carved bed with its embroidered bed curtains. Raquel knelt by the side of the bed and rested her head gently on the pillow as Juana encompassed her neck with her short, dimpled arms, and she told stories of gentle animals, wise and good, and of saints living lives of sacrifice and dedication, but none of those involving bloody persecution, until the arms went limp and the breathing came in slow, measured rhythm. Slowly, carefully, she disentangled herself and nodded to the maid who nestled on a pile of blankets in the corner of the room and only then returned to her own quarters.

The door to her room stood open, but that was hardly unusual as servants were constantly hovering about, looking for things to put away or lay out, but she now shut it behind her and turned the heavy iron key in the lock. It only just now hit her that she had failed to lock her door earlier when she had been about to bring out her hoarded religious articles. Juana, of course, would not have known what they were, but any of the servants could have done so, and there was plenty of bitterness of her privileged position at court to say nothing of the chance for simple blackmail. A chill went down her spine as she thought of how close her carelessness had brought her, and her whole family, to disaster.

It was long past sundown now, but she took out her menorah and went through the complicated series of twisting, bending, and snapping motions required to turn it from a simple triple candlestick into the symbol of her faith, the feet of the original now miraculously converted into separate candleholders along with the three, as part of her father's ingeniously deceptive design. She fingered it lovingly, seeing her father's rough hands as they had fashioned every intricate bend of the metal of which it was made and the faith that had guided his hands as they had done it. From the false bottom of the chest she also drew forth her copy of the Torah, printed in book form, the well-worn leather cover proclaiming it to be the *Santa Biblia*. Since most servants could not read Spanish, much less the Latin in which Bibles were produced, it was unlikely that anyone finding the book would thumb through the pages and recognize the Hebrew letters for what they were. At least that was what Raquel told herself.

She knelt again by the window and, in the light of the candles of the menorah, arranged a shawl over her head, and began to read the prayers which she hardly needed the written page to help her memory. She read aloud, in a low but confident voice, with the same rhythmic, soothing style that her uncle Ysaque had used on the evenings when they had spent the holy days together with her family. She found herself rocking back and forth, and the glory and power of the Lord enveloped her, draining the aches from her neck and back and the needles of fear and anger from her mind.

GRANADA

Chapter Two

Toledo

Juan had not meant to hide in the room. A man of his stature, an officer of the Royal Guard, of the *Santa Hermandad,* after all, was not normally one to conceal himself behind curtains in a lady's bedchamber. But he had come looking for her, found the door open, and the sound of slippered feet hurrying along the corridor had suddenly filled him with trepidation about being found there unbidden and unannounced, and, without thinking, he had ducked behind a tapestry in one poorly lit corner of the small room.

He had to admit that he had become obsessed with Raquel since he had first seen her. The fact that she had not paid him the least attention, even with the adulation he had received at court after the capture of Alhama, had only served to enhance his fascination with her. True, she was rather older than the usual maiden, but that concerned him not at all. Juan had always assumed that he would never marry, because

319

of his, condition, regarding women, but there was something about this woman that made him put those thoughts aside. Perhaps the mere fact of her age and lack of fortune might make her all the more amenable to a match with a rising young officer, and there was always the chance that, with the right woman, someone he truly loved, his problems would simply all go away. In fact, the thought that love might take the place that coercion had always done in stimulating him had reinforced his conviction that Raquel was precisely the woman who would prove his salvation, both in this world and in the next.

Juan knew that he had not handled his encounters with Raquel well over the preceding months. At first he had assumed that his new status as part of the royal household would speak for him and that Raquel, as well as the other ladies at court would swarm around him like bees around honey, and many of them had, but not Raquel. This reticence on her part, or what he chose to interpret as coquettishness, caused him to seek her out at every opportunity, attending functions he would normally have avoided, such as the daily Mass attended by the queen and her entourage, since Juan had never been an overly religious person. He would find a spot over to one side of the nave, slightly in front of wherever Raquel stood, where she would have a clear view of him and from which he could casually glance in her direction when he knelt or rose in the course of the ceremony, and he had convinced himself that he had caught her ogling him on more than one occasion. And he had to admit that he had nothing to worry about regarding his appearance, with his muscular form showing to particularly good advantage in the new silks and velvets, especially in comparison with the pasty, flabby men that normally clustered at the court.

This conviction gave him the courage to approach her directly at some of the entertainments offered by the queen. But his sallies, he realized himself in retrospect, were consistently clumsy, boring, or even rude and had received the indifferent reaction they deserved. He thus became all the more nervous in Raquel's presence, causing him to stammer, which infuriated him, making him aggressive and frustrated, and he had heard the giggling, not from Raquel, of course, she was far too serious a woman for that, but from the loose-tongued ladies of the court, which infuriated him, making him all the more nervous. He could imagine the picture Raquel now had of him, a florid-faced baboon, virtually drooling and babbling inanities. He had made every conceivable misstep in front of her except perhaps stumbling over his own sword, but he was confident that he would achieve that soon enough.

And today, he had actually saved the woman's life, stood between her and certain death and delivered her, not to mention the queen. Raquel had been magnificent, of course, bracing herself there with her ridiculous little spear, although the boar would have done little more than pick his teeth with the thing when he had done with both of them. And Juan had been magnificent too, swooping in just at the right moment and flawlessly finishing the beast. It could not have been better had he planned it, scripted it out, hurling his javelin with unerring aim and vaulting from his horse with the grace of a dancer. But had she fallen into his arms, covering him with kisses? No! Although there had been those half-hidden smiles, a discreet batting of the eyelashes, and that long, glorious conversation on the way back from the hunt, that had been it. He had never talked to a woman so much in his life, and she was such a superb listener. But then he had to admit that he certainly had some fascinating stories to tell, if anyone would take the time to listen.

That was what had given him the courage to jabber on with her all the way back to town. He had not been tongue-tied then. Perhaps he had been a little too voluble, his veins still throbbing with the excitement of the moment and certain that she felt the same way. But then she had simply disappeared from the courtyard without a word, virtually snubbing him in front of the entire court. People had actually come up to him and asked him where she might be, as if they already considered them to be a couple, just as he had dreamed, but he had looked the fool for not having been able to answer them, because, of course, he had no idea where she might have gone, which immediately destroyed the image. Now he had come here to have it out with her once and for all. To demand that she pay him the respect due to him for his rank and for his actions, or, if not that, at least to ask her what she wanted of him, why she ignored him. To force her to put it into words, if she could. And now he found himself in a worse position than he had ever been in with no way out, a filthy burglar hiding behind the curtains. He had not found her in the room, and when he heard her footsteps returning, he had panicked, and ducked into the first hiding place that came to mind, afraid of what she might say to find him standing, uninvited, in her own bedroom. And now it would be even worse if he were to be discovered. There was some kind of curse on him, Juan was certain of it, at least when it came to women. Maybe that gypsy girl back in Trujillo was having her revenge after all.

Juan stood in the shadows of the tapestry without moving for a moment when she entered. For an instant he was about to step out and announce his presence, but then he realized how ridiculous that would look. She would either scream in terror or break out in humiliating laughter, and he knew that he could not account for himself in the face of either reaction. So he hesitated. Then he realized that every second that he remained hidden there only worsened the situation. As she went about the room, busying herself with what he assumed were her preparations for bed, Juan realized that he was not just trespassing but was violating a lady's most private moments, not the surest way to win her affection, but probably the surest way to destroy all that he had built up to date, and he began seriously to contemplate simply standing there, motionless for an hour, two, three, or as long as it took, until Raquel should be sound asleep, or even until morning if necessary, and he could slip out of the room unseen. He noticed that she had taken the precaution of carefully locking the door, which almost made him groan out loud in anxiety.

He shifted his weight slightly from one foot to the other, flexing his knees, and prayed fervently that he would not doze off and come crashing to the floor. But then, taking advantage of his predicament, he began to take an interest in Raquel's activities, peeking out around the edge of the wall hanging. She was not undressing, but was kneeling by a chest near the window, removing a variety of items, a book, a candlestick, and he assumed that she had her own evening session of worship, as many pious women did. But there was something unusual about this. Juan might not have been the most religious of men, but he had sat through enough Church ceremonies and watched his own mother at prayer often enough when he was a lad to know instinctively that Raquel was not performing any ritual that he had ever seen, and he might not speak Latin himself, but he would certainly have recognized the words of the rosary or the *pater nostrum*, and Raquel was intoning completely different words. She was not speaking in Spanish. Of that he was certain, and she had not crossed herself even once.

Then it dawned on him. She was a *Jew*! She was a Judaizer, practicing her black arts right here, not one hundred paces from the chapel where she placidly sat through Mass every day, taking the Host, just like a Christian, possibly secreting it to perform her satanic rituals in private. He half expected her to sprout horns and a tail and begin capering about, her eyes glowing red, with clouds of sulfurous smoke coiling up around her, and he actually began to be afraid. Facing death on the battlefield was one thing, and he never really had much fear or respect for your average old priest, but there might be powers at work here straight out of the most terrifying nightmares he had ever had as a child. But she just remained on her knees, rocking slightly and saying what were apparently Hebrew prayers in a slow, rhythmic pace.

Juan's hand moved to the hilt of his sword, and his mouth opened as he prepared to scream his disgust at this abomination, but no sound emerged, and his arm dropped listlessly to his side. He had to think. Then, slowly, an idea began to dawn on him. This situation presented him with a unique opportunity. Without considering further, he stepped out from behind the tapestry and strode casually across the room, whistling tunelessly. The look of sheer terror on Raquel's face when she spun around was the most exciting vision he had ever beheld.

She staggered to her feet, and Juan grabbed her roughly by the shoulders and pulled her to him. She put up her hands, weakly pushing on his chest, but he wrapped his arms about her, letting his hands roam over her smooth back and down to knead her buttocks through the clinging fabric of her silk chemise. She was trembling and breathing heavily, her breasts heaving upward as Juan prolonged the moment, drinking in every inch of her creamy flesh, the sparkle of her eyes as they darted back and forth like those of a rabbit caught in a snare, and the delectable taste of her fear. He grasped the nape of her neck with one hand and kissed her, hard, and she whimpered softly as she now tried desperately, and vainly to free herself. He let his mouth slide from hers, along her cheek to her ear, then down her neck and down to her cleavage.

"No, please," she finally whispered, but Juan only chuckled and began to tear her chemise from her shoulders and to turn her slowly and push her backwards toward the bed.

"You little Jewish whore," Juan hissed close into her ear. "The Queen herself has taken you to her bosom, given you a position of trust and honor. You accompany her to Holy Mass, and I have seen you there often enough, taking Holy Communion, and all the while you were looking up at the wounds of our Lord on his cross and thinking of them as your own handiwork. Proud of them too, I'll wager."

She did not answer him, just turning her head as far as possible and gritting her teeth as her breast rose and fell violently under him, her eyes shut tight as if to deny the reality of what was happening.

This was better than Juan could ever have imagined. He now had the woman he wanted, and there would no longer be any question of having to win her affection. She would accept him or burn at the stake, as she obviously understood, since she was not calling for help, and her gaze shifted between Juan's sneering face and the cursed Hebrew candlestick that now lay on the floor by the window. And the terror in her eyes satisfied his deepest desires and fantasies. Perhaps, he thought, as he loosened his belt and began to undo the buttons of his tunic with one hand, using the other to pin her squirming body to the bed, she would learn to love and respect him as her husband, as he loved her, but that hardly mattered now. There would be no more of her haughty behavior, no more public snubs or curt answers. She would submit to his will, as she was meant to do.

For an instant, a nagging little voice spoke to Juan. If he took this secret Jewess to wife, would he not be just as much her prisoner as she his? If he were to denounce her now, of course, even after enjoying her, no suspicion would fall on him as having known of, or possibly even having condoned and participated in her damnable pagan rites, but later, years from now, a husband would be assumed to have known about all his wife's activities. He'd seen that argument raised more than once at the Inquisitions that he had attended. But, almost as quickly as it had arisen, the worry departed. He would likely be on campaign with the army for months at a time, and it would be more than possible for a devious little minx to disguise her beliefs during her poor, benighted husband's rare visits, returning to them with fervor while he was off defending the frontiers of Christendom, just as she had hidden them from the queen herself for years. And wouldn't it be just like a clandestine Judaizer to attempt to snare a rising young soldier, a man of growing wealth and ambitions for high office? Of course, he would be in a perfect position to expose the little wench whenever it suited him, now, a week from now, or ten years hence. He could even make a sincere effort to win her over to the True Faith, but that could wait for the time being. And, meanwhile, he would never have to worry about his *performance*. Her fear of him would let him do to her all that he had ever done to the whores and captives he had taken in the past, only this was so much better.

"Perhaps you've been hoping to be discovered, you bitch," he growled. "Maybe you're the kind that likes a little pain, that dreams of those long nights tied to a rough wooden table with those love-starved freaks in their brown robes crowded around, poking this delectable body with hot irons and ripping off nice bits with sharp pincers. And don't think that they don't dip their shriveled little wicks from time to time as well, one after another with a queue running out the door."

Raquel was biting her hand now, to keep herself from screaming as tears coursed down her cheeks. Juan knelt on the bed, pulling her loins up to his and thrusting viciously as she arched her back. He was pleased to note that she was, indeed, a virgin, which only made the experience all the sweeter. She gasped in pain and humiliation as he continued heaving, now panting himself with the exertion. When he had finally spent himself, he flopped down on the bed at her side. She twisted away from him, facing toward the wall, her shoulders hunched and her knees drawn up to her chest.

"My sweet wife," he growled, rubbing her flank familiarly, and she winced at his touch as if his hand were made of ice.

"Oh, God, no!" she groaned in a husky voice.

"Oh, yes, my dear. I won't ever let the Inquisitors get you. I'll be your shield and buckler, your lord and protector for all time. We'll be making the announcement tomorrow, and we'll be wed as soon as I come back in triumph from Alora."

"But why?" she asked, half turning to him over her shoulder. "I am a Jew. You saw that. Why in God's name do you want to marry me? You've raped me. You've had your way. What more could you want?"

"Why, you, darling," he responded, snuggling closer and sliding his arm around her waist. Raquel cringed but remained still in his embrace, and he nuzzled his bristly face down between her breasts. "I love you and have done for some time. Surely you knew that, even as you flirted and then cruelly repulsed my advances, time and again, sure of your advantage."

"But I'm a *Jew*!" she insisted. "Are you insane?"

"Not in the slightest. I will be your husband. That is all there is to it."

"But, my father," she pleaded desperately.

"Will consent happily enough, knowing that that alternative is an earful of molten lead or having the skin flayed from his back. With that in the bargain, I would expect that he'd find me an estimable match for his little girl, don't you? Even without considering my property or my standing in the army of the king, to say nothing of my bearing one of the more honorable names in Castile. And what's he? Just a jumped up artisan. The only gossip around would be why I dipped so low on the social ladder for a wife. I assure you that he will be most delighted with his new son-in-law. You may want to write him a letter, which I will be pleased to deliver to him in the field."

Raquel shuddered and buried her face into her already sopping wet pillow.

Juan stood proudly next to Raquel at Mass the next morning in the cathedral. Isabel and the other ladies of the court frowned and gave amused and querulous looks, but Raquel stared fixedly at the floor in front of her while Juan smiled broadly and winked playfully at them. As the queen and her entourage exited the cathedral, Juan grabbed Raquel's arm in his firm grip, pushed to the front of the crowd and spun her about on the steps to face them on the steps.

"Your highness," he called out in a loud voice, shading his eyes against the bright sunlight that now shone in his face, "ladies and gentlemen, I have an announcement to make of the most glorious kind! I have, just this past night, asked for the hand of the Lady Raquel in marriage."

Isabel came to a halt, raising one eyebrow suspiciously, as Raquel stood there passively, but turned solemnly to one side.

"With your highness' gracious permission, of course," he added hurriedly. As a member of the queen's court, Raquel was something of a ward of the crown, even though she was well past the age of consent. "In the absence of her parents, I believe it is up to the crown to decide to grant me this boon."

Raquel looked up hopefully to the queen, but then turned aside once more, making her face a complete blank.

"Well," Isabel murmured. "If this is Raquel's wish. . ." Isabel paused, cocking her head, trying to catch Raquel's eye, but Raquel only nodded silently. "In that case, I suppose there could be no objection to the union of two houses that have so distinguished themselves in service to the crown," she concluded without much conviction.

"Then the match is made!" Juan crowed, raising the plumed hat and waving it triumphantly over his head. A thin cheer went up from the throats of a couple of pampered young wags while the ladies clapped their gloved hands almost soundlessly or simply tittered behind their fans. "We will publish the banns this very afternoon and be wed when I return from the campaign."

Early the next day a column of Navarese levies, a mixed force of crossbowmen and halberdiers, arrived from the north, and Juan was designated to lead the column on to Alora along with his *Hermandad* cavalry. With Fernando's column slowed by the heavy supply wagons and artillery carriages, Juan would have no trouble catching them up with his light force, probably before they even reached the target city, but there was no time to lose. The Navarese were given only a few hours to eat and were then quickly formed up for the march.

A small knot of courtiers had gathered at the city gates to bid Juan farewell, primarily because Isabel was there, and Isabel had only come because Raquel had done so, and Raquel had only come because Juan had demanded that she do so. Juan was resplendent in a glistening cuirass, meant for show, not for combat, and a suit of golden velvet and a red and black cape of the *Hermandad*. The troops stood, leaning on their arms in the dusty roadway, clearly none too pleased with not having been allowed to enjoy the pleasures of the city even overnight, but the Navarese had a well-earned reputation for brutality and rowdy behavior toward friend and foe alike, on the battlefield and off, and it was just as well to get them on their way. Juan gathered Raquel into his arms and kissed her passionately, while she limply surrendered to him. A loud hooting went up from the column of soldiers, and Isabel said a few words of encouragement or praise to the soldiers which were muffled by the mists that drifted up off the river and hung motionless in the air of the afternoon. Juan swung gallantly into the saddle of his richly caparisoned horse and led the column off at a brisk pace, guiding his steed to dance sideways under the portcullis as he turned to wave a silk scarf at his intended, a favor she had presented him with at their parting. He then cantered across the bridge over the river, the other horsemen trotting along behind followed by the column of infantry. Raquel stared blankly after him with no show of emotion whatsoever.

The march to Alora was uneventful. Juan's column crossed into Moorish territory and passed through empty fields, blackened stubble where the grain should have stood nearly knee-high by this time of year, but Fernando's army had scoured the plains to deny the enemy food for the coming winter. The only other traffic along the roads was herds of cattle and sheep being driven north by grinning Castilian infantrymen, taking home the first of the booty of the campaign. They found the army just beginning to set up camp in a rough circle around the base of the hill atop which sat the walled town of Alora. Juan quickly turned his charges over to a Navarese captain, and galloped off to find the Basque and his own company and then to report to the king.

Fernando's tent, a massive four-sided affair set on a knoll southwest of the town, was already being surrounded by the tents of the senior commanders, their servants racing about, arguing, and even coming to blows with each other as they competed for the choicest spots, not too rocky, not so low that they might flood in a sudden rain, but, most importantly, as close as possible to the tent of the king.

Access to the crown was power, and power was everything. Juan smiled at the Basque as they strode from Juan's tent the twenty or so yards to that of the king.

"You didn't actually kill anyone to get this spot, did you?" Juan asked out of the corner of his mouth.

The Basque's grin exposed a gap where one of his front teeth had once been knocked out by a blow from a mace. "Most lords send mere servants to see to things such as the pitching of their tents. The Duke of Medina Sidonia's men were not much competition for a company of soldiers, sir. After just a moment of discussion, they decided to seek other quarters."

Juan chuckled, but the laughter died in his throat as they rounded the corner of the king's tent. Alonso de Aguilar, the Marquis of Cadiz, Medina Sidonia, the Count of Medinacelli, and several other senior nobles stood in a tight, sullen cluster at some distance, while Fernando bent over a map which had been spread out on a wooden chest, in company with Cardinal Mendoza and another man, this one dressed in a simple black smock and leather apron in sharp contrast to the gold brocade and silks of the nobles. The Marquis spotted Juan and beckoned him over.

"My lords," Juan said, bowing slightly.

"I'm afraid the king will have little time to talk with the likes of you or with us, Ortega," the Marquis growled. "He is busy consulting with his *military* advisors."

Juan could only spread his arms and splutter in confusion, but the Marquis held up his hand.

"Of course you are befuddled, captain," the Marquis went on with bitter amusement. "You can be excused for thinking that *we* might have been considered to be the king's military advisors, but that no longer seems to be the case. It would appear that his highness prefers the council of a gunsmith to that of his generals, noblemen and soldiers who have fought in literally hundreds of battles. He has decided to make an experiment of the siege of Alora, a *scientific* experiment. We are to take the place through the use of artillery alone, no storming parties, no mines, no blockade, just artillery."

"But that has never been done before," Juan objected.

"And it will hardly be done now, but his majesty is desirous of trying."

"But we're less than a dozen leagues from Malaga," Juan insisted. "We have no time to waste in such nonsense. A relief army could be on its way at this very moment to attack us from the rear. By the time the guns have been positioned, a determined assault could already have taken the walls."

"Oh, but not to worry," the Marquis laughed humorlessly. "There will be no time-consuming traverses dug and embrasures constructed. The guns are to be run forward under no more protection than simple mantlets. The army will stand by to prevent sorties from the town, at least reserving us that much of a role. They will rely on a superiority of firepower both to silence the fire of the defenders and to bring down the walls. One would imagine that we will also form a key part of the victory parade after the town's inevitable surrender, so we should not complain too loudly."

"I have it on good authority," the Count of Medinacelli, chimed in, a tall, spare man with a long aquiline nose and dark, piercing eyes, "that we will also be allowed to help gather up the spent cannon balls after the battle." The other nobles snorted.

Juan just shook his head in disbelief. He glanced over his shoulder to where the man he now recognized as

Raquel's father, Ruben, was marking off distances on his map while Fernando nodded enthusiastically.

It would have been normal for a besieging army to take several weeks to complete a set of entrenchments surrounding the town, slowly advancing its positions under cover of either trenches or covered ways protected by walls made of large baskets filled with earth and rubble and roofed with hide-covered pallets. Artillery and missile weapons would be used to keep the defenders from concentrating their fire until the attackers had time to undermine the walls or were able to make a breach and storm the town. The process could be delayed if the defenders sallied from the walls during a moment of carelessness by the attackers and destroyed the works, spiked the guns, or dug a countermine. The entire effort could take three, four, six months, easily for a well-sited town with stout walls and an adequate supply of food and water, as Alora had. Of course, an outbreak of the plague within the walls might speed things up, and it was common practice to hurl pestiferous carcasses over the walls with a trebuchet in the hope of encouraging such a development. But it was just as likely that sickness would break out in the besiegers' camp, all the more likely the longer the siege went on.

It came as something of a surprise to Juan and the other commanders when Ruben rushed his guns into position within twenty-four hours, dozens of them, from small falconets to sweep the parapets to the older massive bombards throwing stone balls weighing hundreds of pounds. He and his crews, including dozens of Frenchmen, Germans, and Italians worked round the clock with a veritable Babel of languages shouted back and forth along the line. Reinforced firing positions were thrown up and the barrels of the guns carefully aligned on the sectors of the wall identified by Ruben for demolition. Pits were dug to store gunpowder, and pyramids of stone or iron balls were erected next to each battery, all under a galling fire of musket balls and arrows from the desperate defenders on the walls who could see their doom rapidly approaching but had been taken aback by the suddenness of the development as had the Spanish commander. And then the bombardment started.

The roar of the guns grew in volume to a continuous roar that went on day and night, with each gun having two crews that worked in shifts around the clock. Ruben concentrated his fire at the main gate and the two towers flanking it, and the town was soon blanketed with a cloud of smoke and dust. The main firepower was provided by several batteries of twelve-foot lombards, guns too large to cast which were constructed of a ring of iron bars, each two inches in diameter, and held together by bands and rivets of iron. A separate battery of smaller falconets and a company of arquebusiers had been had been concealed opposite a small postern gate that had been identified on the flank of the town, and when the anticipated Moorish raiding force sallied from the gate, they were cut down by a storm of fire, and no further attacks were attempted. Only once a day, when the afternoon breeze was at its stiffest, would the firing stop, allowing the smoke to blow away and Ruben and the king to assess the effect of the bombardment fire, realign the guns, and bring up new supplies of powder and shot.

So frenzied were Ruben's activities during the first days of the siege, Juan did not have an opportunity to see him alone. Ruben would spend hours on end digging in and sighting the guns, and more hours in closed consultations with the King, finally falling into a dead sleep among his gunners and loaders in the pits themselves, oblivious to the roar of the cannon and the bustle all around him. Finally, however, after several days of bombardment, Juan spied Ruben staggering back to his own modest tent to steal a few hours sleep late in a dusty afternoon, and he strode boldly into the tent behind the artillerist without bothering to announce himself or ask permission. Ruben had already thrown himself down on a pallet made of coarse blankets, and he growled unintelligibly at the sound of the chinking of Juan's spurs.

"I have a letter for you from your daughter, master gunner," Juan announced, kicking Ruben's foot. "I regret that I haven't had the opportunity to pay court to you before, what with you being busy running the war and all."

Ruben opened one bleary eye without even making a pretense of rising. "Ah, yes, Captain," he mumbled. "I thank you for your consideration. If you'll just be kind enough to leave it there on that chest, I'll read it as soon as I'm in a condition to appreciate it more. You must understand. . ."

"Get on your feet when you're in the presence of a Castilian nobleman, gunsmith!" Juan snarled, kicking Ruben again, this time firmly in the ribs, half lifting him off the pallet. "Read the cursed letter now!" he enunciated through clenched teeth.

Ruben rolled over, holding his side and glaring up at the knight in anger and confusion and quietly took the single sheet of folded vellum, breaking the red wax seal and opening it without taking his eyes off the intruder.

Juan smiled as Ruben's face went pale despite the deep tan born of endless hours under the Spanish sun, and his eyes grew wide. He waited patiently as the armorer read through the letter over and over. Juan didn't know precisely what it said, having been far too confident to have felt that necessary, but it was obvious that Raquel had touched on all the salient points of their situation. Ruben hung his head and fed the letter into a small brazier where it quickly was consumed by the flames. He sat with his thick arms dangling loosely on his knees, his bushy head hanging forward limply.

"And what do you propose to do, my lord?" Ruben asked without raising his eyes. "You clearly have us in your power."

"First of all, I'll see you on your feet when speaking to a Christian, Jew!" Juan said in a deceptively quiet voice, and Ruben slowly rose, his large, callused hands balled into fists the size of small hams. He was shorter than Juan, but his shoulders were even broader, and Juan half hoped that the fool would be mad enough to attack him, calculating how long it would take to draw his dagger and plunge it in Ruben's throat, about half the time it would take one of those paws to swing and strike, he estimated.

"I, *father*, imagine that your charming daughter has informed you of our impending wedding. Your enthusiastic endorsement of the union will be more than sufficient, for the moment," he added significantly, and, without waiting for a response, Juan turned on his heel and strode from the tent.

Juan had watched the bombardment every day in company with the other commanders, half hoping to see little damage to the walls, but the towers looked as though they had been mauled and gnawed at by a titanic bear. There were piles of rubble reaching halfway up the front face of the walls and partially filling the dry moat in front of them, and one of the towers had been reduced to barely three quarters of its original height. One of the two massive oak gates had been splintered and hung precariously from its hinges, revealing a makeshift barricade of timbers and stones that the Moors had erected behind it in expectation of the final collapse of the doors. And that had been after only a few days. As the siege progressed, it occurred to Juan that the daily respite in the bombardment might be even harder on the battered defenders than the deafening thunder itself, knowing that it would resume any moment, bringing death and destruction and drawing ever closer the inevitable capture of the town, the silence tearing at their nerves as much as the thunder of the guns.

And then, in less than one week, it was over. During the halt in the firing on the 20th of June, which revealed that a viable breach of several meters in width had been created next to one of the towers, which had been pounded down to the height of the surrounding walls. Columns of Castilian infantry had begun moving forward for a possible night attack. But white banners had been unfurled all along the tops of the walls, and a small delegation of mounted Moorish officials appeared, picking their way through the debris and across the practically filled moat.

The victory, although Juan had trouble actually considering it a valid victory, left the army at something of a loss as to what to do next. Normally, a siege of this nature would have taken the whole of the summer campaign season and well into the fall, and that only if all had gone well, but now Fernando was obliged to find a new task for this huge force. He subsequently marched his army, less a small detachment left at Alora to garrison the place and supervise the repair of the walls by teams of Moorish prisoners, back up the Guadalhorce River on which Alora was located, back toward the border in a wide loop to make the maximum use of the roads they had constructed for the passage of the artillery on the approach march. The river forked near the border, and the Castilians then followed the western branch past the town of Cuevas and dipped back into Moorish territory to the castle of Setenil, a rugged fortress that guarded the northern approaches of the key Moorish town of Ronda, gateway in turn to the port of Malaga down on the coast.

With the time it had taken to get the army on the move from Alora and then in the construction of more roads up to the rocky hill upon which the Setenil fortress stood, it was early September by the time the artillery was in a position to fire. Juan was secretly hoping that the rains would set in early this year, ruining the stocks of powder that had been so painfully and expensively collected and thereby forcing Fernando to consider a more traditional assault on the castle walls in lieu of simply calling off the siege and leading an ignominious retreat to friendly territory and winter quarters. However, Ruben had drilled his gun crews to a fine level of perfection, and they now pumped out between one hundred and one hundred and fifty rounds per day against the walls, when only a few years before a third that rate of fire would have been considered prodigious. The Moors simply had no weapons with the range to reach the big guns, even given their advantage of being able to fire down from their hilltop position, and their desperate forays with infantry and cavalry had been easily turned back by Fernando's huge army. Juan had had his share of action in these battles and had comported himself with his usual valor, but he bitterly resented a rebuke he had received from the king himself for attempting to lead a party of knights to storm the castle's postern gate on the heels of the retreat of one of the Moorish raiding parties. Instead of being rewarded for his initiative and daring, as had been the case in the past, it was now somehow no longer his place to attempt to take the battle to the enemy. And in less than a week, this castle too surrendered.

The return march to Sevilla was a gloomy one for Juan and many of the military commanders. They could hardly express their opinions openly, since the campaign had reaped far greater conquests than anyone had expected, and the cost in Spanish lives had been virtually nil. Even the astronomical cost of procuring and supplying the artillery train had been largely offset with the spoils from the raids on the *Vega* and the captured towns, including several other small towns that had sent unsolicited delegations of surrender to Fernando just in case he intended to drive further into Moorish territory. Hordes of refugees from the borderlands had swarmed all over Moorish Granada spreading stories of the invincibility of the new Spanish army, its implacable progress, and the inevitability of defeat when faced with its terrible cannon. The terror spread by these stories was hardly any less than the resentment felt by Juan and the Castilian nobility that their army had been reduced to the role of babysitter for the precious guns, as this news spelled the end of their power and influence in Spain, perhaps not immediately, but soon. Although Juan normally would have welcomed any downturn in the fortunes of the upper nobility who hogged the privileges and posts of honor in the kingdom, he had always dreamed of becoming one of them, not participating in their extinction. Even reports that Rodrigo Ponce de Leon, the Duke of Cadiz, had recaptured the town of Zahara by direct assault, whose fall had prompted the renewal of the wars against the Moors, had done little to lift the mood of many in the column that wound its way back to meet Isabel's court at Sevilla.

Most of the army had been disbanded soon after crossing the border and after the initial division of the booty, to allow the men to take part in the fall harvest, and it was only a relatively small body of men, Fernando and his personal entourage, a handful of powerful nobles who had not gone off to see to their own vast estates, and a detachment of *Hermandad* cavalry led by Juan, that finally swung into sight of the Guadalquivir River and the salmon pink walls and towers of Sevilla rising out of the morning haze. Juan's spirits were somewhat brighter on this crisp autumn morning. The artillery had been diverted to Cordoba to be left there in readiness for the coming year's campaign, and with it had gone that insufferable Judaizer, Ruben, who had virtually monopolized the king's time for months as they endlessly poured over maps and diagrams of angles of fire and designs for new guns. Even more importantly, Juan knew that Raquel would be here in Sevilla, accompanying the queen, and there would be no pretext for her to postpone their wedding.

Sevilla had never suited Juan very much. It was just a little too cosmopolitan, too sophisticated, too effeminate, too *Moorish* for his taste. To Juan's way of thinking, the delicate stonework and mosaics that adorned the public buildings of what had once been the capital of the Almohad kingdom in Spain should have been replaced with good, solid, austere brick as in Trujillo, not perpetuated through the employment of *mudejar* craftsmen who decorated the buildings as if the reconquest had never taken place.

Sevilla was also a bustling, modern city, its riverside docks always crammed with shipping from all points around the Mediterranean, from the North Atlantic ports, and even from the new territories in the Canary Islands and along the coast of Africa. Walking its streets, one could hear a babble of nearly every tongue known to man, besides the howling and squawking of caged monkeys and parrots, and smell a vast array of tropical fruits, the arctic fish in large leather water vats, and oriental spices. And the people there, mostly fat merchants who would no more think of raising a sword in defense of their homeland or the True Faith than they would of lowering their prices half a *maravedi*, had an air of superiority about them that he found absolutely insufferable. They had a way of sizing one up in an instant and determining whether or not there was any money to be made from being courteous, and, if not, a sneer would grow over their faces as if they had just stepped in a steaming pile of cow dung. Needless to say, there was no money to be made from the likes of Juan, but it did his heart good to see the merchants tremble, *conversos* all of them, probably, at the sight of his *Hermandad* cloak.

Juan was beside himself with joy as the day of the wedding approached. Things could not possibly have worked out better. Of course, there had been night after night of unrestrained access to the bride-to-be, as that sort of thing was largely winked at among members of the court, especially since neither bride nor groom were exactly children, and her silent suffering had only heightened the pleasure for Juan, while the wags at court merely tittered about their obviously passionate love for each other. The churlish Ruben remained in Cordoba preparing the artillery for the next campaign against the Moors, and Raquel had made no effort to bring her mother in to attend the ceremony, which made Juan all the more comfortable at not having to deal with them, not that he had anything to fear.

However, in the absence of the bride's parents, and with Fernando having impetuously taken off with another hastily organized expedition to attempt to storm the town of Loja, taking advantage of the disorder in Moorish ranks and the factor of surprise that would accompany a winter attack, Isabel herself had set aside precedent and had chosen to stand in herself in the role of Raquel's guardian. Even though she was a woman, she successfully argued with Hernando de Talavera that her role as *pater familias* of the nation entitled her to command armies, levy taxes, and receive foreign ambassadors, normally very manly pursuits, and this implied that she could assume the place of a young woman's father symbolically in a wedding ceremony and give the bride away. This caused no small amount of gabbling and gossiping in court circles, not only about the boldness of the queen's move, but also about the immense prestige that this showed the young couple to have, and Juan had noticed how the Marquis of Cadiz and other senior members of the nobility had made an effort to draw Juan into their conversations more often about weighty matters of state and military affairs at the endless rounds of dinners and entertainments during the weeks leading up to the wedding.

The ceremony itself was hardly opulent by court standards, although far beyond anything that Juan or

Raquel's family could have ever afforded on their own, even with the steady income from his new lands and his share of the booty of the recent campaigns, but Isabel insisted on footing the bill for virtually all of the eating and drinking. A small but elegant procession decked out in silks and satins in robin's egg blue, the most fashionable color that season, formed up in the courtyard of the palace built by Pedro the Cruel from what had remained of the old Almohad palace, for the short walk across the plaza to the cathedral. Juan had been obliged to deliver several sharp, surreptitious pinches to the underside of Raquel's arm to get her to lift her eyes up from the floor as they proceeded the last few steps down the aisle together, but he had to admit that she did a creditable job of playing the role of the shy but enchanted bride, both in her actions and in conversations he had overheard with various members of the court. Still, Juan could not help but notice some intensely concerned looks directed by the priest, Hernando de Talavera, who performed the ceremony, and the queen herself at Raquel when they thought he wasn't watching, looks virtually begging her to speak up and stop the wedding. But she did not speak up. She knew better than to try.

Father Hernando asked the obligatory questions of the couple, whether they were of age, whether they were within the prohibited limits of consanguinity, and whether they were true Christians. Juan's answers had been delivered in a booming battlefield voice, and Raquel's mere whispers, but they had served. Then Juan had taken the thick gold band from under his belt and slipped it on and off three of Raquel's fingers, starting with the index fingers, for the "Father, Son, and Holy Ghost," before leaving it on the third one and planting a firm kiss on her lips. The shudder that went through her body made him harder than he could ever remember having been. When the Mass was ended, and the congregation surged back out into the plaza to form a gauntlet through which Juan and Raquel had to pass under a blizzard of flower petals. There was nothing unusual about a bride crying at her wedding, many of the ladies of the court were also dabbing at their eyes at such a romantic sight.

The celebration which followed was somewhat muted, but this was generally attributed to the shadow of continuing war that hung over the land, especially since word had just come in that morning that Fernando's forces had been repulsed before the walls of Loja with heavy losses, although the king himself had not been injured, and the army was now in sullen retreat back to Christian territory. It was also true that the Christmas holidays had only just passed, and most people were already sated with celebrating and would have much rather spent the afternoon napping in front of a cozy fire. There was music, of course, with a small group of jongleurs playing lively tunes on flute, drum, and mandolin in one corner of the great hall of the palace of Pedro the Cruel, and tables lined the walls, groaning under the weight of platters of food and large earthen jugs of spiced wine. A few couples pranced about in the center of the hall, more or less in time to the music, but many of the guests had already slipped away on the way back from the church, and most of those who remained clustered in small groups, talking in hushed voices, once the last course of the feast had been served. Raquel had hardly eaten a bite, but that was also to be expected.

Of the greatest satisfaction to Juan was the presence in the hall of his father and brother, both decked out in the finest attire the substantial sums he had sent home from the war could provide, and still looking like a pair of country bumpkins just climbed down from the manure cart after their first ride into the city. Juan took great pride in introducing his father, and especially his brother to the Marquis and other nobles and in watching their rolling eyes as one famous *grandee* after another sang his praises as one of the greatest warriors ever to have been sprung from the bosom of Spain.

He relished watching his florid, porcine brother squirm in the presence of the great and powerful of Spanish society, people who were Juan's real family now.

The only sour note came when Juan introduced his father to Raquel. The gruff old man who had never had a gentle word to say to Juan in his whole life, took Raquel's hands in both his own and kissed them, then looked into her face with his rheumy old eyes and said, "May God bless you, my child."

Raquel had merely smiled her ironical, sad smile and given him a little bow. Then, when his father had turned to leave the hall, his brother already having positioned himself near the door in eager anticipation of departure, the old man turned to him and said, "You won't hurt her, will you?"

"Whom I hurt, and whom I don't is none of your concern, father," Juan had snapped. "I am a man of power and connections now. I will do as I please, just as you would have done had you had my skill and my luck. Now, get back to herding your pigs!" Juan gave the old man a discreet shove toward the door, but he saw him turn to look back over his shoulder with pity and fear as Raquel talked quietly to other guests. He knows, Juan thought. He knows what I am and that I must have something over her, but it doesn't matter. In fact, it's all the better than he does know. It will be almost as good as having him sitting there as an audience while I have my fun.

After making a circuit of the room, receiving the blessings of one and all, as well as a steady clinking of gold and silver coins that were dropped into a silk purse the bride carried tied to her wrist, the newly weds parted company to mingle with the guests on their own, although Juan leaned close to Raquel's ear, not to give her a loving kiss, but to warn her not to stray from his sight. She nodded passively in reply.

Juan strolled up to one group centered around the Marquis of Cadiz, Alonso de Aguilar, and a number of other prominent Andalusian warlords who graciously made room for him. The Marquis had on a sleek velvet suit of vertical blue and yellow stripes that unfortunately accented his sagging belly, and he wore only an ornamental dagger at the gold-encrusted belt that looped below his paunch. His beard was, for once, neatly combed and tied into several points with small yellow ribbons, by far the least martial ensemble that Juan had ever seen the old warrior wear. He even smelled of jasmine and lilac water, layered on over an ineradicable base of sweat, since, even at court, there was obviously no reason to put one's life in jeopardy by unnecessary bathing.

Juan had made a discreet circle of the group first in order that he would end up facing toward Raquel, who was approaching the queen on the far side of the hall beneath the tall windows. The lords made courteous nods in his direction, which caused Juan's chest to swell with pride, since, a few years before, none of them would have slowed his the pace of his horse to avoid trampling this young nobody in the street. There was a brief lull in the conversation, during which the men glanced at one another before the Marquis cleared his throat and spoke up.

"Well, my young buck," he began, "it's not in any doubt that your lady is a charming creature, and we can well appreciate that you are more than a little eager to get this business over with and get on to more important matters." He paused during a chorus of gruff laughter and theatrical clearing of throats. Juan noticed that, even though the Marquis had dropped his voice to what would have been, for him, a whisper, although it would still have carried well across a medium-sized battlefield, the buzz of conversation around them had died out, and he could see more than one courtier inching closer to their group to hear. Most interesting, Juan thought. For the first time in his life, his doings were the talk of the high and mighty of Spain.

"What has us puzzled, though, and the question must be asked," he went on, taking in his colleagues with an open-armed gesture, " is why a promising nobleman like yourself, a proven battle leader with a respectable name, some property to his credit, and a future that will only bring much more wealth and glory, wouldn't have shopped around a bit more before diving into matrimony. I mean," he added hastily, "Doña Raquel is a fine girl, and all, but she has no *family* to speak of. A *converso*, after all, and the daughter of, well, practically a blacksmith. I say this only with the greatest respect, Juanito, but you should know that you're of a level where marriage should be part of a carefully engineered plan, looking to political alliances, to say nothing of a dowry. What could this girl have brought to the table, a couple of cannon balls?"

There was more rough laughter, but Juan just shook his head and smiled broadly. He didn't doubt that the Marquis had meant this to be a discreet discussion, not a public announcement, yet half the court must have heard.

"No, lord, I believe that *I* already have all the balls that this marriage will ever need."

The Marquis nearly choked on his wine as he doubled over in laughter, turning red in the face and leaning on Juan's arm for support while Aguilar pounded him gleefully on the back.

"Well said," he finally gasped, wiping a tear from his eye, " but you know what I mean."

"Of course," Juan went on, "and don't think it didn't cross my mind. You'll notice that my own father is not present at the feast, so it's obviously crossed his mind as well. He is uncommonly proud of our family's tradition." A tear very nearly came to his Juan's eye when he thought about how perfectly his life was working out. Everyone in that hall must have known that his family name had been virtually worthless, a precious but empty relic of the past, but, through his own actions, through the strength of his sword arm, Juan had clearly given it some value once more, and in the eyes of some of the greatest men in the nation. "But," he continued, "that's all very well for the head to consider. Yet it all means nothing when the heart dictates otherwise."

There was another chorus of deep-throated, manly growls of understanding and the bobbing of heads by the ladies nearby.

"As you gentlemen know," Juan added, "I have dedicated my life to the profession of arms and gave little thought to the idea of starting a family. I had always thought that, since I'm still young, I could always start later, if I lived. And, if I didn't, which seemed more than likely on several occasions . . ."

"Like that time at Alhama," the Marquis chimed in," when we all went out to fetch water." And they all laughed again knowingly.

"For example. Or if I just got too much wine inside me one night and fell off my horse and cracked my skull open. It's a rough world, so why worry about these long-term commitments, I always said. But then I set eyes on my lady, my wife I can now call her, and all that calculation went right out the window."

Aguilar nodded. "Not to disagree, but I can't quite see this young knight falling off his horse even if someone picked the beast up by its legs, turned it upside down, and shook it. There isn't that much wine in Spain."

They all laughed again, and Juan casually brushed a tear from the corner of his eye with one thick finger. For a moment, he wished his father could be back here to listen to this, praise from the lords of the realm for his unwanted, wastrel son, but the old man or Juan's brother might have found a way to ruin the moment after all.

Raquel moved through the hall in a daze, walking gracefully as she had been trained at the gentle hand of Isabel, a look of calm contentment on her face, but largely oblivious to the curious glances she received and hearing the words of the crowd only as the droning of bees on a hot summer afternoon in the garden. She nodded pleasantly at each group of guests that she passed, not registering who they might be, all the while aware of the glare of Juan's eyes on her back like two burning brands. Isabel was silhouetted against the tall windows of the hall, standing next to Beatriz de Bobadilla, both women dressed in green silk gowns with long tapered sleeves and with their hair done up in matching green turbans in the Moorish style which was fashionable just now. Both women had pearls sewn into their gowns and wore pearl necklaces on their bare necks, but in every aspect, Beatriz's attire was just one degree less elegant and expensive than that of the queen, a studied effect since Isabel never allowed anyone to outshine her in her own court. Raquel fastened her gaze on Isabel's face and guided toward her like a ship aiming for a lighthouse, sailing on the edge of a storm.

"Considering the effort that went into making this day memorable," Isabel began, as if speaking only to Beatriz, "it would not seem that the lady of the hour is enjoying the spectacle as much as one might have expected. Did you know that we brought in dozens of *mudejar* gardeners from Valencia specifically to brighten up the grounds of the *alcazar*. They even brought their own orange and lilac trees with them."

"Perhaps the bride is too busy thinking of a tree of her own," Beatriz giggled, being reputed to be the most flirtatious of the ladies of the court, " or at least its trunk," and she made a motion with her hands as if encircling a thick rod.

Isabel gave Beatriz a scolding look, but this changed to one of some concern when their comments had no apparent effect on Raquel, who stared vacantly past them out the window. Isabel leaned closer to Raquel and took her gently by the arm.

"Is something the matter, my dear?" she whispered.

"No, your highness," Raquel sighed, shaking her head slightly. "It's just been a very trying day."

The queen frowned. "I might have expected as much had this been an arranged marriage. The Blessed Virgin knows that I had to fend off more than one of those myself, but I understood that don Juan was your personal choice, that your parents were only informed after the two of you had made your own pact. I know you to be a very decisive and thoughtful young lady, not unlike myself, "she smiled and poked Raquel in the ribs, without effect, and went on in a serious tone, "so don't tell me that you're having second thoughts now, so late and so soon."

"No, no, your majesty," Raquel shook herself again, as if trying to wake up from a deep sleep. "I am quite content with the match. It's just," she paused, searching for words, "that I do wish my father could have been here."

"I see," the queen frowned more deeply in disbelief and glanced over Raquel's shoulder in the direction of Juan.

Raquel's eyes grew wide and she whispered anxiously, "Please, your majesty, don't look at him, or he'll think that we're talking about him behind his back."

"I believe that's just what we're doing," Isabel replied. "And what of it? Whose back is a woman to talk behind if not her own husband's?" she added, but there was no humor in her face as she turned back to Raquel. "You are mistress of your own fortune, my dear, but I must tell you that I would be most vexed if I were to learn that there was some sort of problem about which you felt that you could not confide in me. I'm sure that you know that there is nothing in this kingdom for you to fear as long as I live."

The scowl that crossed Raquel's angelic face caused both Beatriz and the queen to pull back for an instant, but it was gone as quickly as it had come. "Oh, no, your majesty," Raquel recovered herself. "I swear to you that my only problem is the nervousness of any maiden on her wedding day. I beg you to forgive me."

"Of course, child," Isabel said in a cool voice, letting go of her arm. "Of course."

Just then Juan appeared at Raquel's side, taking her elbow firmly in his huge hand and bowing to Isabel.

"If your majesty will excuse us, there is a duty we have to perform in accordance with the wishes of the Church as dictated by Holy Scripture." His voice was slurred, implying that he had not been shy about helping himself to the wine, and his comment brought a chorus of half-concealed sniggering from a troop of young gentlemen and ladies who followed close behind him.

Isabel cocked her head in his direction and gave him what might have been described as a smile, but it was the tightest, coldest smile Raquel had ever seen. She was certain that Isabel assumed that Juan had done something to force this marriage, and it was somewhat comforting that the queen would react in this way, especially when young women were bound in matrimony every day to men they hardly knew or even heartily detested, with no one batting an eye. But Raquel was just as certain that Isabel must be speculating that Juan's power had to do with something mundane, like money, a bad debt of her father's perhaps, and that if this, most Catholic of sovereigns were to guess the true hold he had over her, Raquel would not merit even this chilling look. Isabel reached up and touched Raquel's cheek, and it was all Raquel could do not to scream.

Bowing repeatedly, and staggering slightly, Juan led Raquel away and across the hall to the merry hoots and ribald comments of the crowd. They made their way into the corridor and up a narrow staircase to a bedroom that had been reserved for their use on one of the upper levels of the palace. Juan bolted the door, and the throng of revelers pounded on it energetically, both men and women, all well-lubricated with wine, calling out for a chance at the "leftovers." Others gathered in the patio below the window and began a raucous serenade of bawdy songs and a barrage of flowers, tied to small stones for better aerodynamic qualities, that rattled against the louvered shutters.

Raquel stood trembling before the bed and awkwardly began to undo the lacing of her bodice, but he lunged toward her, his face flushed deep red, and his breath coming in short gasps.

"No, not so easy," he hissed, too softly for anyone outside the door to hear. "That's the way a good Christian wife would get it, not my little Judaizing whore!"

He grasped the edge of the gown with both hands and tore it from neck to hem in a single tug. He grabbed her by the waist and lifted her easily from the floor, burying his face between her breasts and biting her savagely. She squealed, despite herself, and Juan laughed gruffly, which sound sent the crowd in the hall into paroxysms of enjoyment, assuming the romantic young couple to be exploring Venus' bower for the first time, at least for Raquel. Juan tossed her onto the bed effortlessly, spinning her so that she faced the headboard. He took her hands in his and clamped them firmly onto the carved oak of the bedstead.

"Brace yourself," he growled. "This is how the pigs do it, so it will suit a *marrana* well enough."

As terrified, as humiliated, and as angry as Raquel was, her mind kept working. On the one occasion when her mother had ventured, years before, to talk with her about wifely duties other than those of supervising the kitchen and household staff, her mother had left her with the distinct impression that intercourse was not meant to be enjoyable for the woman, and it was the role of the faithful wife to determine what her husband wanted and to give it to him as quickly and painlessly as possible. While her mother had never been the most astute of women, Raquel had gotten the impression even from her that men were relatively easy to manipulate when they were letting the "smaller of their two heads" do the thinking, as the ladies at court often said in their endless hours of gossiping and fantasizing about romantic adventures. From the ladies of the court, Raquel had learned that the act could indeed be made quite pleasurable for the woman, but that it was mathematically improbable that the man chosen for her husband by her parents or guardian would also be the one able to "do it" for her, thus making it the woman's responsibility to find ecstasy at her own leisure. Raquel had noticed that Juan did not respond to her attempts to feign passion, which actually only infuriated him, while her trembling with fear or gasping with pain were what drove him to climax. So it would be, she reasoned, even as he grunted and thrust behind her, that she would have to lead this bull by the nose, and her moans and sobs became ever more theatrical with a corresponding increase in the beast's own frenzy until he had, at last, spent himself.

He shoved her unceremoniously from the bed and pulled the white sheet onto the floor. He stood there, naked from the waist down, not having bothered to remove his jerkin, tunic, or belt, and he leered at Raquel, cowering against the wall, her sweat-streaked hair hanging in her face, and pulled a small vial from a pouch at the belt. He pulled the cork with his teeth and carefully poured the contents into a red puddle in the middle of the sheet, then roughly rubbing the material to spread the stain wider.

"Pig's blood," he giggled as he whispered. "In your honor, my lady."

He took the sheet to the door, pulled back the latch, and tossed the bundle out into the hall.

"There!" he shouted. "Lap that up, you dogs!"

The partygoers roared with laughter and finally the sound of their chatter diminished as they retreated, satisfied with having done their duty. Juan locked the door again and strode back across the room, pulling off his remaining clothing.

Shortly before dawn, Juan pulled a nightshirt on over his head, smoothed his hair back as best he could with his fingers, and stumbled down the hall toward the palace kitchen. The previous night's wine had left a sour, dry taste in his mouth, and he wanted a piece of fruit to munch on before the servants would be bringing up the breakfast tray later in the day. Raquel was huddled at the foot of the bed, where he had left her when he had finally felt exhausted and flopped across the width of the bed to sleep some hours before. Ordinarily, he would have simply kicked her awake and ordered her to find him some refreshment, as was no more than a wife's duty. However, he had given her a couple of open-handed swats across the face during the course of the evening, just out of enthusiasm, even though she had done everything he had demanded and more, and the bright pink marks of his fingers were still quite visible on her fair skin. Of course, it was well within a husband's right, if not his God-given duty, to beat a recalcitrant wife on occasion, a practice that knew no limits as to social class, so Juan was hardly fearful of any damage to his reputation from such evidence, but, given Raquel's standing with the queen, there was always the possibility that any sign of violence toward her protégé might discreetly sour the queen's, and therefore the king's, attitude toward him, and that was a price that Juan was not willing to pay. No, better just to make his own way to the pantry and find himself a little something.

The stone paving of the corridor was icy cold, and even his campaign-hardened bare feet flinched with every step. The only light was the stub of a candle that Juan had brought with him, the flame of which guttered dangerously in the multitude of drafts and cross-currents, forcing Juan to cup his free hand around it, blocking most of that poor illumination. He stubbed his toe more than once, always the same one too, on uneven bits of flagging, a step, or the corner of an unseen wall, and he cursed under his breath continuously as he shuffled forward. Finally, he rounded a corner and could see the reddish glow at the end of the hall that must come from the kitchen's ovens, already fired up for the palace's daily ration of bread, and he advanced more quickly.

The fires were burning brightly under the ovens and in the man-sized hearth where a large black kettle of something was bubbling as it hung over the flames, and the warmth made this probably the only truly comfortable room in the palace on an early winter's morning. But there were no cooks bustling about as Juan had hoped. Instead, a loaf of steaming bread lay on a large work table, along with a small round of cheese, and portions of each were spaced around the table as if several people had been in the process of having their breakfast and had suddenly been called away. And a small arched doorway leading out into the gardens stood half-open, letting in an unwelcome gust of cold air. Juan scratched his head and picked up a hunk of bread and cheese and began to munch on it as he explored the kitchen, but then he heard the crying.

It was very soft and seemed to be coming from the back of the kitchen where a long work table had been built into the wall at waist level. Juan moved cautiously in that direction, not entirely sure why he should suddenly be afraid of what he might find. After all, he was a nobleman, a guest of the royal family, and had every right to be there, besides which there was not a man in the castle whom he could not trounce, even hung over and in his nightshirt. But he moved very slowly just the same, peering into the shadows and thrusting his little candle as far out ahead of him as he could.

There, under the table, in the farthest corner of the kitchen, he finally saw a pair of small feet poking out from the shadows, but at the same instant, he was struck with a powerful stench that had previously been masked by the smell of the fresh bread and the smoky fire. He wrinkled his nose and inched closer, just as a body rolled out into the full light of the fire, and Juan jerked back with a gasp.

It was a young scullery maid, judging by her clothes and long chestnut braids tied with bright bits of ribbon, but the face was that of a horrible old hag. The skin was drawn tight across the skull, the eyes sunken deep in their sockets, and the skin itself was turned black and blue as if from a horrible beating, or as if the still-living girl had been rotting in her grave for months. The chest of the girl's smock was stained black with vomit, and a new wave suddenly erupted out of her mouth, spewing across the floor as Juan shrieked in pure terror and leaped backward.

"Plague!" he screamed as he ran from the kitchen, and he did not worry that this voice of a veteran of many campaigns was several octaves higher than usual. He had heard of this kind of plague before, although soldiers who had fought the Turks in the eastern Mediterranean said that it was far more common out there. It was not what they called the Black Death that had wiped out a third of Europe's population in the previous century and made occasional reappearances in different countries. That one you could recognize by the huge pustules that covered the body during the short period between contracting the disease and the almost inevitable death. This one was different and seemed to drain the fluids right out of a healthy body, sometimes within a matter of hours, causing the victim to appear to shrivel up and age right before one's eyes. What made this particular plague all the more terrifying was that it seemed to ignore the quarantines that at least helped to limit the spread of the Black Death. Walling up a victim's house, with all the family inside, and burning it down was standard practice for the Black Death, but this new one would pop up again at scattered locations, and no one knew why, although some radical deacons preached that it was the work of the Jews. Juan could believe that readily enough.

Juan ran down the hall, screaming as he went, his arms out before him to fend off the invisible walls in the darkness. He had lost his candle, but he now realized that he still carried the bread and cheese with him from the kitchen, and he hurled it away with another shriek, spitting out what was still in his mouth and trying to wipe his tongue clean on the sleeve of his shirt as he plunged on.

Juan burst into the bedroom, and Raquel jerked herself into a protective ball before peeking between her fingers to see, not the lust-crazed animal of the night before, but a terrified child with a tear-streaked face and pleading eyes standing before her, looking ridiculous in his skimpy nightshirt, his arms flailing wildly about him. She almost laughed, but thought better of it. He had a large bump on his forehead, apparently from having collided with something, but what could have happened to frighten him so badly? And he obviously had something to convey to her, something of tremendous importance for which he could not seem to find any words. What could have happened? If the entire Moorish army were scrambling over the walls at this very moment, his only thought would be to get his sword and ensure his share of the slaughter, but Juan was clearly now frightened right out of his mind.

And how would she reply to him, whatever he might have to say? Surely, he would not be coming in, in this harried state, just to mention some mundane bit of news from the marketplace or court gossip, but what if he were? Raquel had already come to terms with the idea of putting on a façade of normalcy when in the company of others, she had long practice at doing just that, albeit for different reasons. But what about when they were alone together? When he was not actually brutalizing her, was she supposed to play the role of the complacent wife, to mend his socks, and make small talk while he drank his wine in front of the fire of an evening? She frankly had no concept of how to act, so she just stared at him dumbly and waited while he gasped for air and jerked his head from side to side as if on the alert for some unseen assailant.

"Pack!" he finally croaked. "We have to pack, right now! There's plague in the palace! We have to get out of here this very minute!"

Now plague was something that Raquel knew something about, as did most everyone more than a few years old. There were always stories of outbreaks of some disease or other, all generally referred to as "the plague" if more than just a couple of people became ill and if the symptoms were sufficiently serious, even though there were certainly a wide variety of sicknesses involved. Although she was far too young to have experienced the passage of the true Black Death more than a century before, tales of this time of suffering were still used to scare small children, and she herself had seen victims of various epidemics during the course of her life and had fled along with the rest of the court from more than one threatened city in circumstances not unlike this. Given the limited skill of most doctors, flight was the only remotely effective measure when confronted with a spreading disease, although she suspected that this merely spread the sickness farther and faster.

But what had always affected her most about these outbreaks of sickness was that, if the losses were severe enough, or if the pestilence did not dissipate rapidly, someone inevitably found a means of blaming the Jews, and by extension the *conversos*, for the tragedy and sought to expunge their grief in a torrent of blood. To make matters worse, Torquemada was now in Sevilla and had been widely rumored to have encouraged a group of lay deacons to stir up the populace with a series of vitriolic homilies against both Jews and *conversos* at the Masses attended by the working class parishioners over the preceding days, so there would be fertile ground for even the wildest accusations now that the plague had made its appearance.

Then Raquel suddenly felt a chill wave of calm wash over her. For all the agony through which she was now going with her new *husband*, at the very least she and her family now had a more powerful protector than they had ever expected to have. As useful as Ruben had become to Fernando and the army in its campaigns, he was still but one, humble artisan and there was nothing he could do that another reasonably competent artillerist could not accomplish, and there was a flood of such men now pouring into Spain from France, Italy, and the Low Countries. No, it would hardly cripple the royal family's plans for the reconquest if they were to have to shed themselves of a man of suspect *Judaizing* leanings. However, Juan de Ortega was a nobleman and a leading figure in Fernando's military council, and his voice would be listened to. Moreover, no matter how much he might pretend ignorance of Raquel's religious practices, should she stand accused by the Inquisition, every day that passed would make that story sound thinner and thinner. A man with Juan's obvious obsession with social standing and official recognition could hardly tolerate such a shadow falling on his good name, even if he avoided the stake, therefore it would be in his own interest to keep Raquel's secret, if only to protect himself.

Thus from the depths of her darkest despair, Raquel instantly saw a ray of hope. Certainly she would have to bide her time and learn to placate this animal in any way she had to for the foreseeable future, but it would ultimately be Raquel who would have the upper hand in this battle of wits, she was certain of it. And she chose this moment to begin to position herself for just such an eventuality.

She sat up suddenly and turned a firm gaze on Juan. "Does the queen know?" she barked in her most officious tone, the voice she used when shouting orders to her father's gunners over the roar of their cannon.

Juan's head snapped in her direction, his eyes still unfocused, but his mind clearly struggling to shake free of its shackles of terror in order to respond to a command, just as it must have done a hundred times in battle.

"No," he stammered, "I don't think so. I don't know."

"Well, which is it?" she insisted. "She has to be told at once, and the first person to warn her will automatically rise in her esteem."

"I, I was alone in the kitchen," he babbled on, although his breathing was starting to come a little more regularly. "I think the other servants saw the woman but ran off. There were sounds in the halls, but I don't know if the queen has heard."

"Right then," Raquel growled like the master gunner she truly was, as she pulled a simple smock over her head and shook her hair free. "I'll go speak to the queen while you gather up some clothes and whatever else we might need for the next few days. There are a couple of traveling bags over there by that chest and organize horses for us and at least one pack animal. We probably won't be going very far, but you should count on having to camp out for at least a couple of nights, so make sure you bring blankets and bedding." That word stuck in her throat but she forced herself to continue. "Above all you must not give the impression of panic to anyone, not the servants or the other members of the court. Be businesslike and don't waste any time, but don't raise your voice or get nervous over any delays. Do you understand?"

To her immense delight, he nodded dumbly. She had to remind herself that he was trapped in an unreasoning terror that would not come along every day, but she had to make the most of the opportunity while it offered itself.

"But the plague?" he whined feebly as she headed toward the door.

"I've seen this kind before in Cordoba," she said over her shoulder. "It's not the kind that seems to pass from one person to another. It hits everywhere at once, usually worst in the poorest sections of the city, which makes me believe that it doesn't have to do with touching a sick person or breathing the air in the same room. It probably has something to do with the food, or the water, or some kind of bad air that settles on a whole area at once. So, if you don't have it already, you probably won't catch it."

Out of the corner of her eye, she saw him stumbling around the room like a drunkard, and she suppressed a small smile.

When Raquel reached the queen's quarters it was apparent that word of the outbreak had already reached there. Pale-faced servants were rushing in and out of the room with bundles of clothes and other items, sometimes only to rush back in carrying the same things, but Isabel sat in a window seat, taking advantage of the early morning light to work on some embroidery with a studied air of disinterest, a picture of a mythical bird in metallic blue thread rising out of a brilliant orange and yellow fire. Her eldest daughter, Juana, knelt at her side, resting her head on the queen's thigh and with a vague, vacant stare in her eyes that so many member of the court found disconcerting. She did not turn toward Raquel as she approached but merely wiggled her fingers in welcome, as if she were busy watching a play in some parallel universe invisible to all but herself.

"I just heard, your majesty," Raquel began at once. "I assume that the court will be moving now."

"Yes," Isabel replied coolly. "Officers of the Santa Hermandad discovered several bodies, obviously victims of the plague, floating in the river late yesterday, but we had hoped that they had been washed downstream from some other town. That was clearly not the case. We now know that there have been dozens of deaths in the poor quarters down by the river, but the people were hiding the dead in their houses, burying them under the basement floors and such, for several days, fearing that they would be quarantined or that their homes would even be burned down about their ears if word of the contagion got out."

"Which is what is normally done in these cases," Raquel noted.

"Of course," Isabel added dryly. "Actually, this comes at a convenient time, if such things can ever be considered convenient," Isabel sighed. "It was high time we moved on to Cordoba to help with the preparations for the coming campaign against the Moors. At least now we won't have to sit through endless rounds of mewling complaints from our Sevillano hosts begging us to stay just a little longer, as if any city would want to have this swarm of locusts camped on their doorstep a moment longer than absolutely necessary."

"Surely your majesty does not plan to leave before the *auto de fe*," a high-pitched voice broke in, and Raquel caught her breath as the tall, slender figure of Torquemada strode into the room, his face like an ominous thunder cloud.

He was followed by Isabel's confessor, Hernando de Talavera, and there could not have been a more distinct contrast between two men of the cloth. While Hernando was tall and broad, his round face speaking of the forgiveness and charity which were, or should have been, the hallmark of the Christian religion, Torquemada had the haunted look of an Old Testament prophet, the kind that called down divine retribution on wrongdoers with fire and wind and plagues. While both wore the simple robes of their monastic orders, Hieronymite for Hernando and Dominican for Torquemada, the former's girth indicated a weakness for the good food and wine available to members of the court, while Torquemada's gaunt frame and tense features hinted at no weaknesses whatsoever and no sympathy for any human frailty in others.

"I was not aware of any planned trials," the queen responded, and Raquel involuntarily shrank back to the queen's side for protection.

"My office has been conducting intensive investigations these past months, your majesty," the priest insisted, "and we have a list of hundreds of bona fide suspects. We believe that word of our triumph has gotten out, which may have more than a little to do with this sudden outbreak of plague in the city. A clever ploy the Judaizers have used more than once, if not to annihilate the population of true believers, at least to distract us from our holy calling."

"Surely you don't believe that, father," Raquel found herself saying, very much against her better judgment. "Every time there is a sickness, or a drought, or an earthquake, there is a frantic effort to find someone who is *guilty* of causing it. Can't these things just happen of their own accord."

"Nothing happens on this earth that is not by the will of God, child," Torquemada snapped. "But there is evidence enough to suspect foul play among the sworn enemies of the True Faith. *Qui bono,* girl, look at who benefits, and you will invariably find the culprit."

"But don't all the people suffer the same, Jews, Old Believers, and *conversos*? I could see it if all the victims were of one class or one part of society, but they never are."

"They're much too clever for that, too clever by half!" he retorted. "But not as clever as they think they are! Just look here."

He stepped over to the window and pointed out across the ranks of red tile roofs stretching off toward the river.

"It is the dead of winter and even this far south there is ice in the gutters at this time of the morning," he stated. "Now look at the chimneys and tell me what you see."

"Smoke?" Raquel ventured, and the queen raised a quizzical eyebrow in her direction.

"Exactly," Torquemada continued. "Smoke from nearly every chimney pot, even from those hovels down by the docks, but now look over here." He turned and pointed a bony finger toward where the sun was just clearing the skyline in the east. "Now, what do you see?"

Raquel and the queen shaded their eyes against the glare. The rooftops were clearly visible, with their tall chimneys, some of them sporting the broad nests of storks, but, unlike the previous view, where there was a solid layer of bluish haze hovering just above the houses, here only one chimney here and there had a thin column of smoke rising from it.

"Well?" the queen asked, but Raquel already knew the answer.

"It is Saturday morning, your majesty," Torquemada sneered. "And *that* is the old Jewish quarter, the part of the city where the *conversos* live now. You may not be aware, but it is part of the Hebrew tradition to extinguish all fires on Friday evening until the Sabbath has passed. You see, try as they might, they just cannot hide themselves from the vigilant eye of the Lord. But that is only one hint of Judaizing. You will see them at banquets, discreetly passing by the dishes containing pork or rabbit. They will change their linen far more often than is absolutely necessary, or even desirable by normal Christian standards. I have even seen cases where they give themselves away in death! A Jew will always turn his face to the wall when about to expire in the Jewish fashion, and we can then begin our investigation of the entire surviving family."

Raquel turned to Hernando, who just shrugged his shoulders helplessly. "But you can't condemn someone just because they happened to run out of kindling or because the throes of death left them facing to the left rather than to the right in their bed!"

"Condemn, no," Torquemada conceded, bobbing his head to one side, "but such signs give justification for further investigation."

"Through torture!" Raquel insisted, her stomach churning with terror, her mind screaming at her to shut up to no avail.

"In some cases, yes," Torquemada replied coolly, "but not all. We have already had many confessions, heart-rending ones, during the period of grace. Sometimes, of course, it is necessary to ensure that the accused has thoroughly cleansed his, *or her*, soul," he added with emphasis. "Then it behooves us to use drastic measures. You must remember that we are not struggling against simple men and women, but against the power of the devil himself. But I can assure you that 'putting the question' is merely a technique. I know that no amount of torture would oblige *me* to renounce my faith or to bear false witness, and I see no reason to presume that other members of our society have any less backbone than I."

Raquel glared at the priest and dearly wished that she would be given the opportunity to put that boast to the test someday.

"I see," the queen said quietly. "It does cause us pain that there seems to exist so much deception within the bosom of the True Faith, but there is no denying that it is there. But that is why the Holy Office exists in the first place."

"Precisely, your majesty," Torquemada concluded, bowing low. He reached under his robe and withdrew sheaf of folded papers that he passed to the queen. "These are a list of the goods and monies that have been seized from the persons currently under interrogation by the Holy Office, your majesty."

Raquel kept a close watch on Isabel's face. Her eyes had been narrow slits, indicating her boredom with the debate about the validity of the Inquisition, but now they popped wide open, her eyebrows shooting up her smooth forehead and virtually disappearing under the silk turban she wore.

She bent closer to the page, her finger running down one list of figures after another, her lips moving slightly as she read. Raquel glanced sideways and saw a sly smile creep across Torquemada's face.

"But this must come to millions of maravedis!" the queen exclaimed, reaching the end of the document and turning to start anew.

"Roughly twelve million by my calculations, your majesty," Torquemada chirped.

"But these goods are merely being held in trust, your highness," Hernando interjected, "until the guilt or innocence of the accused can be proven."

"There are over a million maravedis listed there in fines that have been collected from those who have already fully confessed their guilt," Torquemada countered. "And by the regulations of the Holy Office, all goods immediately become the property of the crown until such time as *innocence* has been proven beyond a doubt."

"At which time the full value will, of course, be returned to the rightful owner," Isabel concluded. "There is no doubt of that, but what wonderful use we will be able to make of these funds right now!"

"But your majesty," Hernando argued, but Isabel cut him off.

"In the meanwhile," Isabel went on, silencing him with a look, "the crown is faced with the choice of taking out loans from the Genoese or Valencian merchants at horrendous rates of interest, or simply making use of these funds, which our legally ours. We only just sent off five thousand mules loaded with provisions for the garrison at Alhama. Do you have any idea what that cost? And that was nothing! We are now preparing the grand muster at Cordoba for a campaign against Ronda. We have been very lucky of late in taking isolated towns very quickly with our new artillery, but Ronda is a proper fortress, and there is no guarantee that the campaign there might not go on for weeks or even months. And every blessed day tens of thousands of men, horses, and mules need to be fed and supplied and paid. Every day!"

"But might not using this money for the prosecution of the war, as holy an undertaking as it obviously is," Hernando insisted although with less conviction now, holding his arms wide, "be seen as giving the crown and the Holy Office a definite incentive *not* to find any of the accused innocent? After all, if they are found guilty, the money does not have to be returned at all."

"I challenge anyone to point to a single case tried by the Inquisition and to prove that the judgment was determined on the basis of something as immoral as monetary gain," Torquemada hissed.

"The Pope has made just such a charge more than once," Hernando growled, turning to face the other man.

"But nothing has been *proven*," Torquemada sneered. "I thought that this was the whole point of those who whine about the virtue of the *conversos*. If they are innocent until proven guilty, then should not the Holy Office not enjoy at least the same privilege?"

"It doesn't matter," Isabel cut in. "By the time the trials are all completed, the campaign will almost certainly be over, and I am confident that we will receive more than enough in captured goods, the sale of captives, and from ransoms for the high born to replace any funds we find it necessary to appropriate at the present time. Then there will be much less reason to suspect the judgment of the Holy Office, and the wheels of justice may roll smoothly wherever they will."

She looked up at Hernando and cocked her head, and the set of her jaw told them all that the discussion was at an end.

Raquel returned to her quarters to find several maidservants frantically packing clothing, bedding, and anything else that was not moving fast enough into an assortment of trunks, boxes, and cloth bags. She noticed that they kept looking nervously at the doorway as if they expected the plague to come marching down the hall to claim them at any moment.

"Where is Don Juan?" she asked, sitting on the lid of a trunk to help the maid to get it closed.

The maid did a quick bob to Raquel. "He left just a few moments ago, my lady," she stammered. Even though Raquel was not really of the nobility, this girl was a local servant of the palace and would not know that. Then again, Raquel suddenly reminded herself, by virtue of her marriage, she *was* now a member of the nobility, although the distinction did little to ameliorate her situation. "He said that his duty bid him to join the king's army in the field and that he would write to your grace as soon as he had a moment."

Raquel turned her head to hide a smile. It seemed that the slavering beast was as frightened of those things he could not see as any peasant. He probably steered clear of woods and bridges when traveling alone after dark, for fear that an evil spirit would pounce upon him from hiding and turn him into a stone. At least now she would not have to summon the courage to face him in the broad daylight and could devote all her thoughts to supporting the queen in her organizing of the supply effort for the war, the job she did best. She would also now have some time to ponder a plan of action, the seeds of which had only just begun to germinate in her mind.

The court departed later that day with as much dignity as their headlong flight could allow. The baggage train, which stretched for several miles, besides the carriages and litters of the members of the nobility and the columns of mounted men-at-arms of their escort, made slow progress, and it took more than two weeks for the procession to cover the ninety miles to Cordoba, moving sedately up the Guadalquivir River valley. Messengers had no trouble catching up with the column with news from Sevilla, and Hernando kept the queen, and thus Raquel, posted on the progress of the Inquisition, which ended up trying over 500 persons, most of whom pled guilty to some degree in exchange for fines and public penance, and he was relieved to note that *only* some 19 unrepentant Judaizers had ended up being burned at the stake. Meanwhile, Torquemada wrote that he had received an endless stream of advisories from other cities in Castile and also in Aragon, warning of the presence of dangerous bands of heretics and apostates that it would be the duty of the Holy Office to eradicate. Raquel noticed that, whenever the name of a suspect was included in one of Torquemada's reports, an estimate of the individual's net worth generally accompanied the account of his alleged crimes, and it was to this page that Isabel always turned first, often not bothering to read the rest of the report.

GRANADA

Chapter Three

Almeria

Muhammad was obliged to admit that, if one were required to live in exile, there were many worse places in the world in which to do it than Almeria. He stood on the walls of the citadel that was perched on a sharp ridge at the western end of the small port city. The whitewashed buildings and red tile roofs of the town spread out around the half-moon bay, sheltered by imposing gray walls on the landward side, and providing a nice contrast to the glowing turquoise of the sea. Dozens of ships clustered in the harbor, sleek galleys with colorful lateen sails from North Africa and Egypt, fat Genoese caravels and galleases, and even bulky, lumbering merchantmen from as far away as the Hanseatic ports on the North Sea. The docks were crowded with stevedores, busily loading and unloading goods, silks, olives, and woolens from the hinterland outbound, and spices, fish, and Berber metalwork coming in. There were no Castilian or Aragonese warships patrolling on the horizon to block the commerce

371

since Abu's treaty with Fernando and Isabel, and everything about the city seemed to speak of peace and prosperity. And yet there was a mood of unrest in the air that Muhammad could neither dispel nor ignore.

Upon Abu's return to Granada after his captivity, his court had hoped to resume its activities as if the disastrous campaign against Lucena had never occurred. Abu's mother, Fatima, besides raising the huge ransom paid to the Spaniards for her son's release, had also spent lavishly on free food and needed public works in the poorer neighborhoods of Granada in the hope of endearing her son to the population, but there was no disguising the disgust in which Abu was held for having succumbed to the enemy in such a humiliating fashion, and this feeling was encouraged by agents of the old king who circulated among the population and spread further dissention. The people ate the food and enjoyed the public fountains and improved streets, but they complained bitterly nonetheless about Abu having essentially surrendered his independence, and that of his people, merely to save his own skin. The fact of having to pay some kind of tribute was not new, although it was certainly unwelcome, but detailed accounts of Abu's obsequiousness to the Spanish monarchs had turned even his most ardent supporters away in shame. And no Moorish king in living memory had ever had to give up his own son as hostage to the hated Christians.

It was thus that the old king, backed by the veteran troops of his brother, el Zagal, had been able to steal into the city unnoticed and seize control of the Alcazar, forcing Abu and his followers to take refuge in Muhammad's old neighborhood of the Albaicin, for a time. For weeks, armed bands of followers of both parties roamed the streets of the capital, attacking each other with stones, clubs, even swords and firearms, and dozens of good men died with neither side gaining a decisive advantage. Even when Abu's father, disheartened when Fernando and Isabel had rejected his own offer to resume the payment of annual tribute to Castile in exchange for an end to the war, had suffered an incapacitating stroke which left him nearly blind, virtually unable to speak intelligibly, and only able to hobble about the palace supported by two strong slaves, Abu's support within the city rested primarily with his mother's own Abencerrajes clan and with those mercenaries purchased with her gold and jewels, of which there remained very little.

It came as no surprise then that el Zagal had himself designated the new king of Granada by a council of nobles loyal to his cause, taking the title of Muhammad XIII (since Abu had already claimed Muhammad XII), whether with or without the knowledge and consent of the old king, no one could say with any certainty. The old king had been "retired" to the tiny port city of Almunecar under a guard of el Zagal's soldiers and was now effectively out of the game. In any event, this emergence of a third contender for an increasingly small throne did nothing to ameliorate the situation in the city, with artillery emplaced on the heights of the Alhambra regularly firing down into the Albaicin quarter so that the capital was crowned with a turban of smoke to add to the overall gloom. Finally, Abu felt obliged, against the shrill remonstrations of his mother, to flee for his life with his small army, now no more than a few thousand horse and foot, along with their respective families, and to take up residence elsewhere.

Unfortunately for the young monarch, whose traditional sobriquet of "the unfortunate" was appearing to be more and more prophetic, there were very few towns of any size willing to take him in. Malaga, the kingdom's major port, was firmly held by adherents of el Zagal, as were Guadix and Baza and most of the other towns to the northeast of the capital. Only in Almeria was the constable an Abencerraje with a garrison that had been prudently paid on time by Fatima, while most other Moorish troops went without their salaries. There only could Abu and his entourage find refuge, and now the court had been set up with all of its expected glitter and gaiety, regardless of the depths to which its patron had now fallen.

Muhammad's network of local informants, working largely through Yusef, advised him that the vast majority of the population of Almeria did not share the views of the town constable. In the public view, it was the forces of el Zagal who continually took the field against the Christians at Alora and Setenil and sent columns of cavalry to harass the Castilian raiding forces that now ravaged the *vega* right up to the walls of Granada, while Abu reserved his own troops to do battle with fellow Moslems for control of the crown. What was more, when el Zagal fought the Christians, he won. By the terms of the treaty by which Abu had regained his freedom, the towns loyal to him were not only prohibited from obstructing the passage of the Castilian forces entering the kingdom to do battle with the armies of el Zagal, but were even obliged to provide them with food, water, and fresh animals upon request. The fact that this was hardly the first time that a Moorish lord had sought out allies on the Christian side of the border in their internal disputes, even without the added justification of acting under duress while a prisoner of the Spaniards, did little to raise Abu in the estimation of his people. El Zagal was seen as the true defender of the faith now throughout the kingdom, and the *mullahs* chanted his praise and denounced Abu as an apostate and a traitor in their endless sermons on a daily basis. Since virtually the only way that the common people received their news and guidance in society was through the mosque, the animosity of the clergy was devastating to Abu's position, and there was absolutely nothing his supporters could do to muzzle the holy men without making their charges of an abandonment of the faith appear even more true.

Thus, even though the wealthy merchants of the port city and the petty nobles of the surrounding countryside still frequented the court and pandered to Abu's weakness for flattery and superficial loyalty, Muhammad could sense a growing hostility among the common working classes in the town, the very people among whom Muhammad had spent so much of his life. When Abu and his courtiers rode through the city on the brightly caparisoned horses, their silk robes flowing and their jewels glinting in the sunlight, Muhammad saw the streets empty ahead of them as passersby ducked down side streets or into shops, or merely turned their backs. Ordinarily, such was the fascination of the common folk with royalty, and Muhammad knew this to be just as true of Christian societies as Moslem ones, even unpopular monarchs could enjoy a certain measure of public adulation just by taking the effort to allowing the working men and women the chance to gaze upon the richness that their labors had provided to the nobility. It was a proven form of entertainment that was precisely why royalty consciously put itself on display as much as it did. The fact that the people of Almeria were proving immune to this kind of hero worship Muhammad found most disturbing, but there was nothing that he could say to Abu to convince him of this fact as the young king preferred to live on an optimistic world of fantasy.

Others of Abu's advisors, notably the ubiquitous Hafez, insisted on pouring honey in the young king's ear, assuring him that the people truly loved him for being the only one willing to take on the task of bringing a disastrous war to an end, to allow them to carry on their lives in peace. They whispered that el Zagal whipped his troops into battle and swelled their ranks with thousands of North African *gomeres*, mercenary tribesmen who only lived for battle and booty and who served to keep opposition to his bellicose policies suppressed. There was just enough truth to their statements to make them believable, since merchants, like those who dominated society in Almeria, were often willing to have peace at any price, so long as they could carry on their trade, and there was a certain sense of despair among the common people over the relentless advance of the Christians with their seemingly unstoppable arsenal of heavy artillery.

Even as he watched from the battlements, he could make out the figure of a *mullah* haranguing a small crowd in a dusty square near one of the city gates. The man wore the tattered robes and long, tangled beard so popular among ascetics since the earliest days in the Holy Land, and he waved his arms about him wildly, speaking, or rather shouting, with his face upturned to the heavens as more and more tradesmen, housewives, and street vendors gathered around him. He was much too far away for Muhammad to hear his words, but the way men in the crowd occasionally turned to glare up at the citadel and shake their fists, he assumed that the holy man was not offering up prayers for the safekeeping of their lord and king. What concerned Muhammad most was that several soldiers from the gate guard had now drifted into the crowd and, far from attempting to muzzle the speaker and his probably seditious talk, they seemed to be paying rapt attention and even nodding their heads in agreement. That was an unmistakably bad sign.

Of course, Muhammad had no need to hear the *mullah's* words. After having been turned back by the defenders of Loja, through the efforts of el Zagal and his supporters, Fernando's army had gone on a rampage, ravaging the rich *vega* for miles in every direction. Although the inhabitants would generally be able, through the system of watchtowers that dotted the landscape, to have enough advance warning to reach the shelter of the nearest fortified town or *ribat*, their homes would be burned, most of their cattle and sheep herded off to the north, and their precious olive, fruit, and mulberry trees, the product of decades of labor, would be chopped down and burned. It was winter, so there were no crops in the field to be lost, but the systematic poisoning of wells would make much of the land unproductive for some time, and the peasants would face a hard year, if not outright famine. And they blamed poor Abu for this. He had made his own peace with the infidel, and the towns owing allegiance to him were generally spared, but there was the persistent argument that, if he had not divided the power of the kingdom in his pursuit of the throne, first with the father, and now with his uncle, the Christians would not be able to run roughshod over the defenses that had withstood their onslaughts for centuries. Also, even if towns supporting Abu were not attacked, most of the residents had relatives and friends in towns owing their allegiance to el Zagal, and they resented the Christian onslaught almost as much as if they were the victims themselves.

While Muhammad had to admit that there was some substance to this position, it was also increasingly clear to him that the Castilians now possessed a power that the Moors would be unable to match, at least not unless they could generate some support for their cause in the courts of Fez, Egypt, or among the Turks, and it could equally be argued that, since this support had not been forthcoming to date, Abu was actually making the most sagacious accommodation possible with forces entirely beyond his control. However, Muhammad also well knew that the faithful and patriotic people of what remained of the Moorish kingdom in Spain would not be likely to make that kind of cold calculation. All they could see for certain was the rape of their land by an invader and this young king's apparent unwillingness or inability to take the field to contest it.

Suddenly, Muhammad felt a presence behind him which caused him to ease his hand toward the hilt of the dagger in his belt, but then came the welcome aroma of

Yusef's coffee, and Muhammad reached out his hand for the cup without bothering to turn.

"I have found a place for us, master," Yusef said as he joined Muhammad in observing the *mullah* below.

It bothered Muhammad just a little the way Yusef would often begin conversations with him in the middle, much the way old married couples do, and it bothered him all the more because he understood perfectly well what Yusef meant most of the time. But what bothered him the most, or rather, just made him sad, was the fact that he longed to have such conversations with his dear, departed wife.

"Will it be that bad, do you think?" he asked.

"Yes, master," Yusef replied. "This time there will be no negotiations, no polite exile. El Zagal is coming and he is after blood."

Muhammad only grunted in reply. Down below the crowd around the holy man had swollen to well over a hundred people, but now the squat figure of the commander of the garrison had arrived and stood facing the *mullah,* fists firmly planted on his broad hips. He was flanked by a pair of spearmen as he apparently chastised the cleric for his interference in temporal affairs, but the soldiers were nervously looking about them at the swarming, hostile crowd and, almost imperceptibly, inching away from their commander as he spoke. The officer then turned on the crowd making sweeping motions with his arms and probably threatening them with all the horrors of the apocalypse, and they finally began to disperse, including those soldiers who had formed part of the crowd, although these notably turned their backs on their superior and swaggered off while he still bellowed after them. Not a good sign at all.

"Maybe you'd better show me this place," Muhammad mumbled, and he followed Yusef down from the walls and through a maze of little alleyways that wound between the barracks and storerooms that were clustered within the walls of the citadel. They entered one of the storehouses by a back door and climbed a rotting set of wooden stairs to a loft that ran along the front wall of the building, high above the piles of sacks of grain and bales of hay with which the bay was filled. A small doorway led to a single, dark room in which old furniture and rolled rugs were stored, and Yusef climbed over a pile of these to what appeared to be an exposed vertical beam in the wall that would have faced out onto the small courtyard of the citadel.

Using a thin-bladed knife, Yusef ran it along the inside edge of the beam and a section of the wall suddenly swung free, opening inward like a door. Yusef gestured, and Muhammad wedged himself closer to look into what was a narrow space, no wider than a man's shoulders, between this false wall and the outer wall of the storehouse. Pale evening light filtered into the space through a grate at about eye level.

"This would be perfect," Muhammad admitted, leaning into the room to peer through the grate out onto the courtyard below, "but what makes you think that we won't find a dozen people already crammed in here in the event of a crisis, or that everyone in town doesn't know about this place and that it would be the first place they would look for refugees? It would be bad enough to be caught by a mob and torn limb from limb, but I refuse to be laughed at first."

Yusef gave a sly smile, his one good eye glinting mischievously. "I learned about this little nook from the female slave of the merchant who owns this warehouse. She was from my own homeland, and she was nostalgic for many things." He grinned and hitched up his rope belt. "Her master has taken his family with him on a buying trip to Tripoli, so they would not be using this place, and she assured me that the caretakers don't know about it."

Muhammad cocked his head and shrugged. "Excellent. Let's just hope that we won't have any use of it either."

That evening, however, Muhammad arrived after prayers for dinner in the large hall of the citadel that Abu used as his reception room and as the dining area for his small court, being wary of venturing down into the town, especially after dark. He found the room ablaze with lamps and torches and crowded with elegantly dressed courtiers, all laughing and talking loudly while a small orchestra valiantly competed with them from one corner with their drums, strings, and flutes. Before Muhammad had a chance to ask anyone the cause for the celebration, such a marked departure from the recent depressed state of morale, Abu himself came rushing up and grasped the taller man firmly by the shoulders.

"This is truly a great day, *muhtasib!*" Abu gushed as Hafez sidled up beside him and attempted to press a cup of wine on Muhammad, rolling his eyes and clucking his tongue when Muhammad politely refused.

"I was unaware of any cause for celebration, your majesty," Muhammad sighed, pulling a roll of parchment from under his arm. "On the contrary, I have just received a reply to a message I sent to ruler of Fez in search of military support. It seems that he had struck a separate peace agreement with the Castilian crown and will not only refrain from sending us any of his own troops, but has promised to discourage recruitment of *gomeres* mercenaries within his territory. He graciously offers to continue to trade with us, on a cash basis, but we can no longer count on any reinforcements from across the straits, and that has always been a great reservoir of strength for our kingdom in the fight against the Christians."

"And I always thought that you were so well informed, councilor," Hafez simpered, "with your network of spies and tattletales."

Abu raised his hand, the smile only broadening on his face. "For one thing, we are not at war with the Christians, if you recall," he insisted. "We have a peace treaty and have no need of those uncontrollable Berbers. Good riddance, I say."

He paused to take a deep draught from his own golden cup of wine, some of the red liquid dribbling down his chin as one of the capering courtiers jostled his arm, but he only laughed and good-naturedly shoved the man aside.

"No, what we are celebrating has nothing to do with Africa, but something much closer to home. A rider just came in not an hour ago with the news that my father has died! At last we are rid of that shadow of evil."

"Well, your majesty," Muhammad replied, "that does eliminate one pretender to the throne, but not the most potent one."

"Oh, don't be silly," Hafez scoffed. "El Zagal was only tolerated by the people of Granada because he was seen as acting for the old king. He has no real claim to the throne when the king's son is alive and well. Besides that, we understand that there is popular grumbling that el Zagal refused to have the king burned in a state funeral, as tradition demands, giving some weight to the rumors that he had a hand on the old man's death. He's taken that bitch Aixa up to Granada, along with her two whelps and has them all imprisoned in the Comares tower, and there's a lot of ugly talk about *that* too!"

"Now there's justice for you," Abu went on. "I've spent my time in the tower, and I only wish that I could be there to watch that viper and her offspring suffering there. Still, one can't have everything."

"But el Zagal has been seen as the commander of the forces fighting the Spaniards for some time," Muhammad argued. "He does have some claim on the throne in the popular mind at least."

"Yes," Abu agreed, "but you know just how fickle the mob in Granada is these days, or always has been really. He's a hero when he wins, but when he loses, and he will lose eventually, the people will only see him as the cause of their suffering. Let the people of the city go through a lean winter with no produce from the *vega* coming in, and they'll be screaming for his head before the first flowers bloom in the spring."

Hafez put an end to the conversation by dragging Abu off to join a circle of dancing men, arms entwined over each other's shoulders, and Muhammad was left to roll up his papers and head wearily back to his apartments. But, just as he was picking his way through the outer ring of servants toward the tall double doors of the hall, a slender waiter carrying a tray of dates was suddenly hurled to one side, his tray flipping end over end in the air, showering sticky fruit on the irate guests, and there stood the short, stocky figure of the constable, his broad chest heaving under his coat of mail, his mouth moving soundlessly, like that of a fish recently pulled into the boat.

Finally, he caught his breath. "El Zagal is at the gates!" he roared, and the buzz of conversation stopped abruptly throughout the hall, although the wailing music continued for a moment as the orchestra enjoyed its brief reign.

"Are you sure?" Hafez asked, his voice cracking slightly.

"I saw his banner at the head of a column of horse approaching the town," the constable replied. "I ordered the gates closed, but there's a mad *mullah* out there preaching to the soldiers to let him in, and I can't answer for what they might do."

"You *will* answer!" Abu shrieked desperately, but he caught himself, placing his hand on his forehead. "No, of course, I have to think. How many men did el Zagal have with him?"

"I would guess a thousand, but that might be only an advance guard," the constable went on. "But that isn't the problem. Even if he has his whole army, this town is capable of resisting for months. We have good stores of food and water, and el Zagal has no way of blockading us from the sea. The question is whether our soldiers will fight at all. I trust my guards up here at the citadel well enough. They're my own men, but the town militia has been heavily influenced by the holy men, and, at the very least, their hearts won't be in any fight we have with fellow Moslems."

Just as the constable said this, a soldier shoved his way into the hall behind him. He bowed quickly and then hesitated a moment, wondering whether to address himself to the king or to his commander. Then he just shouted out to the room at large, "They've taken the city gates. A mob from the city overpowered the guard and opened to el Zagal and his men."

Abu did not bother to respond. He bolted from the hall with Hafez and a dozen other courtiers on his heels. Out in the courtyard a groom was holding a horse, probably the constable's, and Abu shoved him aside, grabbing the reins and swinging gracefully into the saddle, then wheeling and pounding out a side gate of the citadel in the direction of the docks with Hafez and the others sprinting along behind him.

Muhammad did not follow them but slipped along the wall of the citadel to the alleyway leading to the warehouse. He found Yusef waiting for him at the top of the stairs and together they wedged their way into the hidden room. He was pleased to notice that Yusef had taken the precaution of stashing a skin full of water, some food, Muhammad's armor and sword, and even his venerable staff, in a corner of the space. This left the two of them barely enough room to stand, but the gear would undoubtedly come in handy if they had to sit out a prolonged search.

Muhammad peered out through the grating and could see the constable issuing orders to a small phalanx of soldiers, but things did not appear to be going very well for the officer. He pointed to one man and told him to take half a dozen men to the walls, but no one moved. The constable paused and then told another man to put the cross bar in place on the citadel gate, but, again, no one moved. The men just milled about, shuffling their feet and looking over their shoulders at the open gates of the citadel. Muhammad could see, even in the flickering light of the torches in their sconces around the courtyard, that the constable's face was turning brick red. He let out a string of curses on the heads of his troops, their mothers, their livestock, and their children down through the tenth generation, and the men finally began to trundle off, but not to take up their positions, they moved off to both sides and gradually formed an arc around the constable. The officer immediately noticed this as well and stepped back, drawing his sword as he did so, but, even before the tip was clear of the scabbard, a javelin shot out from the back of the crowd of soldiers and pierced the constable's thigh just above his iron greaves. He let out a roar, and another soldier lowered his spear and charged, but now the constable parried with his sword, holding onto the shaft of the javelin with his free hand, and whipped his blade around in a neat spiral, catching the soldier on the side of the neck and sending a gout of blood splashing over the paving stones. Muhammad saw a grim look of contentment in the constable's face as half a dozen crossbow bolts sprang out and embedded themselves in his body. The soldiers then rushed forward and encircled him, slashing viciously at his fallen form long after he must have been quite dead.

The gates to the citadel were quickly opened, and in marched the tall, swarthy figure of el Zagal surrounded by a cordon of heavily armored infantrymen and a mob of cheering townspeople. Muhammad recognized Abu's latest rival from various court receptions in Granada, and he had to admit that the man looked the part of a king rather more than Abu did, but Muhammad wrote this feeling off to the fact that he knew all of Abu's foibles only too well, while all he knew of el Zagal was his undoubtedly inflated reputation as a defender of the faith. El Zagal stood in the courtyard with his fists planted on his hips, surveying the scene, while his soldiers rushed into the various buildings of the citadel.

Muhammad and Yusef held their breath as the sound of a heavy boot kicking in the door of the warehouse could be heard downstairs. There were muffled words in Berber-accented Arabic and the sound of boxes and sacks being shoved about on the ground floor. Then they could hear someone moving cautiously up the creaking stairs, and the smell of burning pitch told them that the searchers had a torch. The footsteps came up close to the false wall, but they did not pause, and soon they could hear the man descending the stairs and an increase in the volume of the voices out in the alley as the door of the warehouse was opened and then closed once more. Muhammad smiled at Yusef. The grain stored in the warehouse was not valuable enough to attract looters, but too useful to el Zagal and his army for anyone to consider burning the place. Yusef had chosen very well.

Out in the courtyard, soldiers were dragging a number of men and women out of the barracks and other buildings and throwing them to the ground at el Zagal's feet. Muhammad recognized several of Abu's courtiers, all members of the Abencerrajes clan, a number of simple servants, about twenty in all, and finally, a young boy, Abu's brother Ben Ahagete, barely thirteen years of age. The prisoners cowered together on the ground, all except the boy, who stood erect, his beardless chin jutting out at his uncle, who glared at him in return. Then, without a word, el Zagal made a slashing gesture in the air with his open hand, turned on his heel and marched back out through the gate to where the crowd received him with loud cheers, whistles, and the shrill ululation of the women. The noise almost drowned out the screams as the soldiers, both el Zagal's men and those who had only recently formed the citadel's garrison, closed in on the prisoners, hacking away with their swords like reapers moving through a field of wheat. Muhammad saw the young prince's legs wobble for an instant before he recovered and braced himself for the thrust of a spear that passed straight through his slender body, raising his feet up off the ground as his legs twitched in the air and blood flowed from his open mouth. Then Muhammad closed his eyes and covered his face with his hands, offering up a prayer for the souls of the dead.

Muhammad and Yusef spent the next two nights hidden in the little room. Throughout that first night the city echoed to the sound alternately of screams as supporters, or suspected supporters of Abu's regime were rooted out and dispatched and frantic singing and cheering by el Zagal's adherents. They found that they could move about in the warehouse safely enough, as no one had bothered to return to conduct a more thorough search, but by the second day their food and water had run out, and Muhammad determined that it was time to go.

They waited until just after dawn, when the streets were beginning to fill with fishermen bringing in their catch and bakers' boys rushing about with fresh bread. The gates of the city were always kept closed during the night, but now they stood wide open to allow villagers to enter the city with their produce. Muhammad took only his staff, while Yusef followed behind carrying a pack filled with his armor and what other possessions they had managed to salvage, and marched purposefully out of the citadel and down through the city. His years as a *muhtasib* had given him an unmistakable air of authority, of belonging wherever he chose to be, and none of the guards dared to question his passage. They timed their arrival at the city gates, where there might well be a watch out for survivors of the massacre, to coincide with the morning call to prayer, and when the *muezzin* began his wailing lament from the top of the nearest minaret and the gate guards bowed down facing toward Mecca, that is in toward the city, Muhammad and Yusef were positioned behind them and slipped across the drawbridge and out along the coast road without being seen. Of course, Muhammad stopped as soon as they were out of sight of the city walls, and he and Yusef paused to pray themselves, not wanting to run the risk of angering Allah at a time like this.

The traveling was relatively easy once they were on their way, as Yusef had thought to bring along the substantial gold purse that Muhammad had stashed in his apartment. They bought horses at the first town and moved north in easy stages, stopping at the most appealing inns along the way. They learned from a group of traveling merchants that Abu had made good his escape, having kept a galley crewed and ready in the port for just such an occasion, one of the few bits of Muhammad's advice that he had bothered to heed, and had arrived in Christian Murcia without incident. He now held his much reduced court in the town of Velez el Blanco, heavily protected by Castilian troops and enjoying the patronage of the Catholic monarchs who saw that he was well-supplied with all of the amenities necessary for a royal existence, all, that is except a kingdom. Muhammad saw no pressing reason to hurry to join his sovereign, if such he could still be called, and planned out a route that would take him back through Cordoba, where he hoped he might be able to take time once again to examine and appreciate the ancient

Moorish capital and its Blue Mosque before resuming his duties at court in exile.

Even with war afoot, there was little problem in a couple of Moors crossing into Christian territory. Literally hundreds of thousands of *mudejares*, Moors who had chosen or been obliged to remain in the territory that had been overrun by the advancing Christians during the course of the centuries-long reconquest of Spain, and many of these had both family and business connections within the kingdom of Granada. While a party of fifty, or even a dozen, Arab horsemen might constitute a raiding party, a pair of dusty travelers attracted little attention, and Muhammad and Yusef passed through the border checkpoints like a single grain of sand through a sieve.

A few days later, Muhammad felt spiritually revitalized after having prayed at the great mosque and spending most of the morning closely examining the intricate gilt mosaic on a deep blue or burgundy background that adorned the façade of the *mihrab*, the focal point of the mosque. He read over the verses of the Koran that were carved there and lovingly traced with his finger the delicate floral patterns that surrounded the lobed archway of the *mihrab's* doorway. How could a people who could produce such a masterpiece, he asked himself, in homage to the one God, be conquered by a mass of hairy, evil-smelling barbarians? He did have to admit that the Christians had evolved to a certain extent, both culturally and scientifically from the illiterate hordes that the Moors had overrun some seven centuries before, but this was largely due, he believed, to their exposure to elevating Islamic influences. It had been Arab scholars who had reintroduced the knowledge of the ancient Greeks, of Archimedes, Aristotle, and Pythagoras, to Western Europe where it had been lost since the collapse of Rome and the onset of the Dark Ages. Arabs had taught techniques in architecture, medicine, and metallurgy that the increasingly numerous Christians now, unfortunately, used to terrible effect in supporting their southward expansion against the more enlightened but weakening Moors.

But even as he asked the question, Muhammad knew the answer. The Moors had defeated themselves. Ever since the explosive spread of Islam, which in a few decades had extended from Arabia across North Africa and into Spain and southern France in the West, throughout the Balkans and into Central Asia in the north, and across Persia and India to the east and beyond, the Moslem peoples had spent far more time fighting each other than in any other activity. The Turks fought the Egyptians and the Persians. The Tatars fought the Turks and the Persians. The Egyptians fought the Turks, the Arabs, and the Algerians. And within Spain there had always been any number of petty kings more than willing either to make alliances with Christian princes or to call on swarms of semi-barbaric North African tribesmen to pour across the straits and support their efforts to claim dominance in Moorish al-Andalus. So, even though the Christians had been almost as badly divided among themselves, they had gradually gained the upper hand to the point that, Muhammad had to admit, Moorish Spain was fast reaching the end of its existence. There would be no sudden resurgence to drive the invaders back and recapture what was lost, and the dark monks who held Mass just a few feet away in the center of this great mosque that had been converted into a Christian church would remain, while true believers like Muhammad would, in the future, only come here in the role of tourists or eventually disappear all together.

Having refreshed his soul in the mosque, Muhammad headed out into the brilliant sunlight to seek out the other point in any city at which he felt at home, the *souq*. It was true that, as a Christian city, the marketplace of Cordoba was not precisely a *souq*, being a little dirtier, a little more noisome, and a little less organized, but the essence was still the same. Muhammad could stride through the crowded aisles between the sellers' stalls, swinging his long staff, and imagine himself back in the only position that he had ever really felt competent to hold, that of *muhtasib*. No one bowed to his authority here, of course, vendors did not scurry to switch their false weights for good ones, and squabbling competitors did not bother to lower their voices at his approach, but he could still smell the fresh produce, the not-so-fresh meat, the livestock, and the human sweat as these hundreds of people milled around him going about their business. The only thing that was missing was that sweet Moccan coffee from the little shop at the corner of the *souq* and those little cookies with dates and almonds to go with it. Muhammad stood at the center of the bustling market, ignoring the shoving porters as they bulled past him, and sighed, smiling wistfully.

"Sir," a delicate female voice called out to him, rising above the bellowing of the cattle and the clink of coins, "I did not expect to see you here. What a pleasant surprise!"

He recognized the voice immediately and could not resist smoothing his tunic and straightening his shoulders as he turned to face her. Even though he had kept the image of her in his mind for the nearly two years since their parting, he was still stunned when he saw her. She looked no older, certainly. Her skin was smooth and glowed with a delicate warmth he remembered perfectly, her deep blue eyes were just as hypnotizing as before, and her figure just as trim, encased in a silk gown of pale blue with silver embroidery across the front and puffed sleeves framing her daringly bare shoulders, bosom, and neck. Her hair was pulled back and gathered in a silk hair net decorated with tiny pearls, its chestnut color glowing in the sunlight. Still, it seemed that she had aged in some other way. She had a smile that still caused his heart to lift at the immodest thought that he had been the author of that smile, and yet there was a shadow somewhere deep within her eyes that suggested that all he could see was a mask, a façade put on from onlookers but hiding something painful within. It made him want to take her in his arms and force her to reveal this burden to him so that he could remove it. He shook his head slightly to clear away the cobwebs and returned her smile.

"My lady," Muhammad stammered. "I only just arrived this very morning and heard that the court was here in the city. I had planned to send my respects to your mistress, the queen, at the very first opportunity and had hoped that I might have the good luck to enjoy your company again." He bowed deeply, touching his fingers to his breast, lips, and forehead, and Raquel performed a graceful curtsey.

"And you thought to do some grocery shopping first?"

"Ah, no," Muhammad replied, grinning. "You may recall that I told you of my former career supervising the marketplace of Granada. I was simply taking a moment to relive that happier time when my greatest concern was which foodseller's stall to choose for my midday meal."

"I can understand that feeling," she said, wistfully, and again Muhammad got an overpowering desire to put his arm about her shoulders and comfort her, although he did not know why. "However," she went on, "while princes may be born into positions that they are reluctant to fill, it has been my observation during my years at court that no one rises to a position of influence in any administration without actively seeking it, whether the seeker realizes it or not. There is just too much competition for power and the attention of the monarch for that."

Muhammad smiled shyly, like a boy caught with crumbs on his chin after denying that he had stolen any cookies from the kitchen. "That may be true, my lady. While the job I hold did largely fall into my hands without any planning on my part, I must admit that I was originally very enthusiastic and did everything in my power to exert what I believed was a healthy influence on my sovereign. I had a vision of making a mark in history, and I was not above fighting behind the scenes with other counselors in an effort to enhance my own position. However, I have since learned that such games are often not worth the candle. I would still like to make my mark, of course, to do something worthwhile with my life, but, if I had my choice, it would be something much more modest now, something probably of more value."

"And what would that be, sir?" she asked kindly.

"I think I would like best of all to be a *qadi*, a judge, in some small village, using what wisdom I possess to try to help people sort out their troubles. Perhaps then I would also find the leisure to write something meaningful, something that would last beyond my time. I have a vision of some student, years from now, reading through some treatise I have written, smacking his forehead and exclaiming, 'That's it! Why didn't I see it earlier.' I'm afraid that that is the only kind of immortality that I can reasonably hope for now, now that my family is gone."

She paused for a moment and then said, softly, "I think you would make a very good judge, the kind anyone could trust to sort through their problems."

Raquel unconsciously reached up to caress Muhammad's cheek as she saw a wave of sad memories pour over his face, but she caught herself and turned the movement into a casual gesture to brush away a rebellious strand of hair that had escaped and blown across her smooth forehead, and it was then that he noticed the thick gold band on her third finger.

"I see that congratulations are in order, my lady," he said, more coldly than he had intended, and he could not help sighing to himself.

At first, Raquel gave a quizzical look and then noticed the band herself, as if for the first time.

"Oh, yes, that. I was married only recently."

"I wish you and your fortunate husband every blessing," Muhammad said, bowing slightly. "I take comfort from the fact that you will no longer have to worry about some of the more boorish male members of the court, like that overbearing fellow with the thick neck."

Raquel cleared her throat and looked away. "Actually, it is Don Juan Ortega de Prado who is my husband."

Muhammad raised his eyebrows and cocked his head. He could see from Raquel's reaction that this was hardly the gushing happiness one often associated with newlyweds, himself included those many years ago. Still, arranged marriages were more or less the norm in both their societies, and who was he to have any views on the matter at all? He had never even met his wife until the day of their wedding, and that had not stopped true love from growing. Yet, from Raquel's frequent, fond references to her father, it did not seem likely that he would have forced her into a match not of her liking, but Raquel was, after all, not only an adult but could quite justly be described as having been long overdue for marriage at her age. Perhaps it was a question of simply loneliness or fear of spinsterhood, although Muhammad also had trouble convincing himself that a woman of such beauty, intelligence, and charm would have had any shortage of suitors from whom to pick. At last, he had to ask himself why he should even be pondering the marriage choice of this Christian-Jewish woman with whom he had had only the most limited of acquaintances, and the answer was so obvious to him that he blushed beneath the dark tan of his face.

"I most sincerely apologize if I have offended, my lady," he finally mumbled.

Raquel waved his statement away with a flick of her wrist. "You had no way of knowing, sir." She started to say something about possibly not having seen her husband in the best possible light, but she did not think she could do so without her voice breaking, so she changed the subject completely in self-defense.

"In any case, it is extremely fortunate that I have come across you here, " she said, much too fast. "I have been combing the market for that flower you showed me when you and your lord were at court, the one that relieves pain, and I haven't been able to find any."

Muhammad was just as relieved to have another matter to occupy his mind. "I remember very well. I trust that you are not ill?"

"Oh, me, no," she said breezily. "Her majesty the queen has been having trouble sleeping on some nights, and she also has developed a painful bruise on one of her toes from striking it against the stone hearth one morning."

"Ah, of course. That flower would do quite well for both problems. If you grind the seeds into a powder and mix it with wine, it is an excellent sleeping draught, while soaking the leaves and stems in water and then mixing the liquid with olive oil creates a salve that relieves pain and even stops bleeding if there is an open wound. But you won't find that in the marketplace, I'm afraid," he added. "Its properties are not well enough known to create much of a demand among the public."

"Oh," Raquel sighed.

Muhammad found himself desperate to think of some way to be of service, feeling like an adolescent lost in an infatuation, although he knew that this could not be the case.

"But I believe I know where some could be found," he stammered. "In a small gully just off the road that brought me into the city, just beyond the bridge. I could have my servant bring some in a moment if you would like."

Her radiant smile more than compensated Muhammad for his discomfort. "Wonderful! But if it's just across the bridge, and if you have no other pressing engagements, perhaps you could take me there yourself. That way I might learn to recognize the plant in its natural environment."

Muhammad's mind was racing. Of course there was no precedent for such a proposal from a lady, married or not, to a man in Moslem society, but it seemed that such an outing might cross the boundary of propriety for Christian mores as well. The very idea of a man and woman talking like this in public was daring enough, even though it was truly a chance encounter, but to go strolling together through the city, that was almost scandalous. Still, Muhammad could not even imagine himself turning down the request.

"I am at my lady's service," he said, bowing low once more, "but might your husband not think it unseemly for you to be seen walking about with a Moor?"

Raquel just laughed and shook her head, the bob of her hair swaying gently with the movement. "My husband is off to the war," and she paused to judge whether she might have touched upon a sensitive subject, since her husband was likely off killing this man's co-religionists, albeit the enemies of his own master. But Muhammad did not blink at the thought, and she went on. "And I doubt whether anyone could find fault with a simple botanical expedition in broad daylight, especially since we were presented at court. That would make this virtually a diplomatic mission on my part."

Muhammad bowed his head and made a sweeping gesture with his arm in the direction of the city gate behind him. As they turned to proceed, a thrill went through Muhammad's body when Raquel, apparently unconsciously, placed her hand at the crook of his elbow as they walked. He then began to sweat profusely, despite the cool temperature of the day, as he began to question himself over whether the plants he had seen were the ones they needed or whether they had been in some other gully, across some other bridge at some point in his travels. He did not think that he could deal with the shame if he turned out to have been mistaken.

It took less than an hour to pass out through the city gates and cross the bridge, attracting no attention from the occasional passing merchant or peasant with a small flock of sheep, find the correct plants, and Muhammad sighed with relief, and head back into the city with a large bunch of them tucked into a net bag Raquel had brought with her. Muhammad found himself talking at breakneck speed about all his adventures since their last meeting, the fighting within Granada, and the escape from Almeria, and Raquel would express concern, joy, or any other appropriate emotion at the correct time, although Muhammad was certain that he was making a tremendous ass of himself.

"Have you secured lodging here in the city?" she asked casually as they passed back through the gate.

"Well, I'd just sent my servant off in search of some when we met," he mumbled, praying fervently for what might come next.

"I know that her majesty would never forgive me if I did not offer you the hospitality of the palace during your stay. You made a very favorable impression upon her during your last visit with your talks of your travels and your expertise in medicine. I should mention that we've put some of your suggestions into practice regarding trying to keep wounds clean and in airing out the tents in the queen's hospital that accompanies our army."

"I would be most honored, my lady," he replied with another bow. Ordinarily he would have been humiliated at the thought of having to accept housing from the monarchs who were hell bent on destroying his country, and he had bitterly criticized his own sovereign for doing much the same, but now all thoughts of chauvinism fled from his mind as a warm glow of contentment spread throughout his being at the idea of spending more time in Raquel's company. "I trust that you recalled that one should not overdo the cleaning. Maggots may appear disgusting, but they only eat rotten flesh, so they actually serve to purify a wound and should not be removed prematurely." Even as he said this, the thought did strike him that he was providing advice on how best to treat enemy soldiers and possibly enable them to return to the field of battle against his people, but again, he had simply ceased to care as long as he had something about which to talk intelligently with this woman.

The evening meal in the great hall of the palace was a rather reduced affair, with so many of the noblemen away campaigning with Fernando, and barely fifty diners were seated along the long trestle tables set up in the hall, with approximately double that number of servants to attend them and several dozen musicians, dancers, jugglers and tumblers for entertainment. Muhammad was seated in the place of honor at the right hand of Isabel as the eminent representative of her "good and faithful vassal" Abu, or Muhammad XII as he was formally referred to by the queen, and Raquel sat on his right. It was only now that Muhammad learned with certainty that Abu had indeed reached Murcia where he had established his pathetic little court in the town of Velez el Blanco near the border with Granada and under Castilian protection.

Out of protocol, Muhammad spent the entire meal speaking to the queen, never daring to turn his back to her as much as he wanted to devote his time to Raquel, but he spoke in a loud enough voice, exuding charm from every pore, reciting Spanish poetry and Arabic poetry he translated into Spanish on the spot, to be sure that Raquel could hear every word. He managed to avoid the pork dishes that were offered, but he did drink his share of wine, a heavy, tart red from northern Leon, spiced with cloves, cinnamon and oranges, and this made his words flow all the more easily. By the end of the evening, he became certain that the slight pressure on his right knee was from Raquel's leg and not from one of the large dogs that habitually passed in and out of the hall at will, and his ears burned so much that he felt obliged to touch them to see if they were actually in flame.

After the last of the plates were cleared away, and the diners had begun to retire to their rooms for the night, Muhammad was disappointed to see that Raquel was also leaving, accompanying the queen through one door while a servant was being quite insistent that Muhammad should follow him through another. He had been constructing a fantasy in his mind for at least the last hour in which it would be Raquel who would show him to his room, actually lead him inside, and then, who could tell what might happen? Instead, after bowing deeply to Isabel as she left the table, Muhammad found himself trailing along behind a decidedly unattractive boy of about seventeen, tall and gangly, badly pock-marked on his cheeks and chin, and with an unmistakable odor of fish about him. He was told that Yusef had been given a bed with the other servants down by the kitchens and would be up at dawn to help Muhammad attend to his toilet. Muhammad pressed a copper coin into the boy's hand and slumped down on the huge bed which dominated a large room, flagged in stone, and with a pleasant view of the moonlit gardens below. He found his pack already in the room, and his nightshirt laid out on the bed, and he sat there for a long moment, gazing at the guttering flame of the candle on the bedside table.

He must have dozed off, because the creaking of the door brought him suddenly fully awake. He slipped the dagger out from under his tunic, and it occurred to him that it was surprising that the Christians had not bothered at least to ask him for his weapons before allowing him, a Moor, to sit next to their beloved sovereign, but he was glad for it now. He had spent too many years in the Nasrid court to discount the possibility of violence at any place or any time, but a gentle shushing sound from the doorway put him at ease immediately.

She was in his arms as soon as he rose from the bed, and they fell back down upon it heavily. He was about to speak, although he did not know what he should say, when she placed her fingers over his lips and then kissed them. They passed the night together without a word being spoken, and she slipped away just as quietly before first light. Yusef appeared at the door with a steaming cup of coffee within moments, and his cool expression and vaguely self-satisfied air gave Muhammad the distinct impression that he had been waiting in the hall and had seen the mysterious guest depart, but he was far too discreet to mention the matter to Muhammad.

The next day Muhammad was in what he imagined heaven to be like. He and Raquel spent several hours in the morning in the gardens, talking about science, or philosophy, or their respective lives. Then she had to attend to the queen, obviously planning the logistics of the campaign that would eventually crush Moorish Spain out of existence, but he did not resent this goal so much as the demands the campaign placed on Raquel's time. Muhammad then retired to the great mosque, and it was here that it occurred to him that he had dreamt of heaven only as the place where he would finally be reunited with his wife and daughter. Now the concept took on new meaning, a paradise here on earth, and he was torn by feelings of guilt and betrayal. For years now he had hardly allowed the thought of a woman to cross his mind, his penance for having survived the plague that had so brutally crushed his little family, but now he was bounding about like a randy old ram with a female with whom he could never hope to have any kind of a future. Even if she were not already married, what kind of a life could they have together being of different faiths? And that was not even taking into consideration that they were on opposite sides of a war, perhaps not at the moment with Abu's treaty with Fernando, but Muhammad had no illusions about the long term plans of the Spanish monarchs. They would not rest until the Moors were swept from the peninsula like rats from a storehouse.

That evening at dinner, Muhammad again spoke graciously to the queen but, this time, did not mentally direct all of his comments over his shoulder to Raquel. He wondered if she could have noticed the difference.

He was standing by the door of his room when he heard the delicate footfalls in the corridor, and he opened the door before she could reach for the latch. She raised her arms wordlessly to embrace him, but he held her at a distance.

"I have to apologize to you most sincerely, my lady," he whispered.

"What on earth for?" she asked, still trying to pull him to her.

"For allowing you, no for allowing myself the pleasures of last night. It was wrong. You are married, although I suspect that love has little to do with your union, but beyond that, it is wrong to give ourselves hope for something that cannot ever be."

"Hope is a commodity in which I have never dealt," she said with amazing bitterness in her voice. "I came to you for the same reason you accepted me. The loneliness was more than I could bear, and you helped to keep me alive. If I have been mistaken, then it is I who must apologize, and I will trouble you no more. But, if not, then let us take shelter here for one more night. Tomorrow the queen and her court will be moving on, and you must return to your king. I promise that I will do no more than hold the memory of these nights in my heart, but please do not deny me that little comfort."

Muhammad swallowed hard. He had never thought of it in that light, and it suddenly seemed to him the height of selfishness to deny this glorious woman whatever comfort he could provide her. The fact that she, too, was raising his heart from a deep pit of despair no longer seemed like a cause for shame, but all the more reason for them to be together.

They talked no more, and in the morning when Muhammad awoke, Raquel was already gone. The court did begin packing for another change of venue, and try as he might, Muhammad could find no trace of Raquel anywhere. In desperation, he sent Yusef out among the servants with strict instructions not to return without word of Raquel, giving up any pretense of secrecy to the grinning young man who winked and smiled broadly before scampering off through the back corridors of the palace. Within the hour he had returned with the news that Raquel had already departed, escorting the *Infanta* Juana and others of the royal progeny to visit the town of Toledo, far to the north. Yusef raised his eyebrows, his one good eye shining with mischief as he asked which gate of the city they would be using for their own departure.

"The east gate, you worthless mongrel," Muhammad growled, and the smile disappeared instantly from Yusef's face. "We have a duty to our lord and must rejoin his court. Perhaps he will be more willing to listen to my council now, and perhaps it is not yet too late to avoid the complete destruction of al-Andalus."

GRANADA

Book Four

1486

GRANADA

Chapter One
Granada

Muhammad shivered slightly as the chill wind whipped across his face, and he drew his thick woolen cloak more tightly around him. His horse shifted nervously beneath him and shook its head vigorously as if in complete disagreement with their presence on this barren hillside overlooking the small town of Pinos Puente and its ancient bridge over the River Genil. Behind them was the fortress of Moclin, still secure in its mountains against the Christian invaders but garrisoned by troops loyal to el Zagal. Before them lay the rich valley of the Genil, the fields now just brown plots covered with frost and short wheat stubble between the low stone walls, the orchards mostly stripped of leaves, and the vineyards just tangles of gnarled branches that clung perilously to the wooden frames, swaying in the wind. Beyond that rose another range of mountains, and atop one of the rises Muhammad could make out the sepia-colored walls of Granada itself, the spires of its minarets silhouetted against the rising sun. They were deep within el Zagal's territory, Muhammad, Abu, and a handful of Abencerraje noblemen and attendants, and if the meeting they awaited did not go as

Muhammad had planned, there would be no chance of escape back into Christian territory. Muhammad began to wonder whether his horse might not be right after all.

And Muhammad had to admit that the presence of the royal party in this precarious position was entirely his own doing. For months he had endured their exile in Velez Blanco on the border with Christian-controlled Murcia, watching more and more of Abu's adherents slipping away back into Granadan territory as stories reached them of new Christian conquests. Abu's thinly concealed pleasure at each report of a defeat for the forces of el Zagal sat very ill with virtually all of his soldiers, indeed with everyone except Hafez and Abu's bitter, venomous mother, who unfortunately had Abu's ear. They had convinced him that a Christian victory was the only way that he would ever regain any part of the old kingdom, albeit as a vassal of the Castilian crown, but Muhammad could see the smoldering resentment in the eyes of even his most faithful warriors when Hafez would sing sarcastic little ditties that he composed, poking fun at el Zagal's fast-shrinking realm, particularly since Abu, their ostensible king, seemed to find them so amusing.

So, Muhammad had taken Abu aside and argued with him for hours about the need to come to some kind of reconciliation with el Zagal, even at the cost of recognizing him as the legitimate king of Granada, perhaps in exchange for being named his heir. Abu's uncle was at least twenty years his senior, and his constant warring made it highly likely that he would not live to a ripe old age. In the meanwhile, Abu could attempt to remove the stain of capitulation to the Christians, and even the appearance of even being something of a lap dog to them, by fighting along side his fellow Moslems in defense of what remained of their lands. Even if it were inevitable that the Christians would ultimately triumph, the Moors would likely be able to wring better terms from the Castilians if they presented a united front than by allowing Isabel and Fernando to play one

Moorish faction off against the other. And, if Abu should happen to die in battle, well, at least it would be an honorable death, one that would bring his descendants no shame.

Much to Muhammad's surprise, Abu had agreed with him, and, even more surprising, Hafez was not able to turn his head with syrupy arguments about just waiting out the war in safety and earning the gratitude of the Christian monarchs by helping them to keep their new Moslem subjects pacified and productive. Of course, what had ultimately decided the issue was that Abu's mother, Fatima, had finally chosen to side with Muhammad, although her motivation was that she understood that Abu would have no power at all if all of his fighting men deserted him for el Zagal and that Abu might stand a chance of mounting another coup to oust his uncle from the throne, but this would only be possible if he were already established within the borders of the Moorish kingdom with an army under his command.

And now they sat their horses, squinting into the sharp wind as another body of horsemen, a much larger and better-armed party, appeared around a bend in the road coming from the direction of Granada. At the head of the column rode el Zagal himself, dressed in a full suit of armor and with his green banner smartly snapping in the wind just behind him. With him rode Hamet el Zagri, the commander of the powerful garrison of Malaga, and half a dozen other prominent commanders that Muhammad recognized from his days at court. Their escort was provided by more than a score of dark-skinned North Africa *gomeres*, nearly naked despite the cold, with their round bronze shields and long, slender lances. El Zagal's party stopped on the far shore of the Genil, waiting for Abu to make the first move, to show his subservience by crossing the river to present himself. Muhammad paused a moment, then nudged his own horse forward, and Abu and the others gradually followed behind him.

It was up to Muhammad to make the flowery, obsequious greetings that were part of the protocol of such an encounter, sparing Abu the humiliation of doing so himself, although, by this point, Abu's morale had fallen to such a point that he probably would have done anything to be granted even a morsel of power and respect. When Muhammad had finally talked himself out, Abu moved his horse forward and cast a sidelong glance in Muhammad's direction as if to ask if he should dismount to greet his uncle, but he gave Abu a discreet shake of the head. There was no point in groveling. At least in the eyes of a number of his countrymen, it was Abu who had the more legitimate claim to the throne, even if the existing balance of power was in el Zagal's favor.

El Zagal had listened to Muhammad's discourse with smug satisfaction, leaning back in his saddle, his lips pursed amid his tangle of grizzled beard, occasionally turning to Hamet and smiling wordlessly. After a long moment, he cleared his throat noisily and spoke.

"I am more than a little surprised that my nephew would venture so far into *Moorish* territory without an escort of Christian soldiers."

Muhammad gritted his teeth, but he had to admit to himself that the bulk of the garrison at the town of Velez Blanco where Abu had taken refuge was actually composed of Aragonese men-at-arms, not renegades as often were found fighting on the side of the Moors in search of plunder or to escape the law at home, but regular troops donated by Fernando to protect Abu from his own people. Muhammad glanced nervously at Abu, half expecting him to draw his sword at this insult and condemn them all to a swift death in an unequal battle, because, for all his foppish ways, Abu did have more than his share of his father's violent temper, but Abu only sighed deeply and dipped his head to his uncle.

"I cannot argue with my uncle's anger," he began in a level tone. "For too long have I been made a dupe by the

Christians, a tool in their hands with which to weaken the strong walls of our beloved Granada, but no more! Everyone knows that I had no choice but to treat with them when I was their prisoner, and I admit that I have made common cause with them in my struggle for the throne of my father as many Moorish princes have done in the past. But I now realize that the people of al-Andalus do not have the luxury of cooperation with the infidels any longer. There is no more ebb and flow of the border between our lands and those of the Christians. They continually move forward, and once a castle or a town is taken by them, it is lost forever. They raid deep within our territory, and the trees and vines and livestock they destroy can no longer be replaced, while our raids into their territory are no more than mere pinpricks. When we fight them, no matter how brave our warriors, those that die have no more brothers or sons to take their places in the line, and the kingdoms of Africa can no longer send us troops as they have done for centuries to fight the *jihad* against the non-believers, while Christian knights and mercenaries come in their thousands from France, Italy, Germany and England to join the ranks of the Castilians and Aragonese, who breed like flies on a stinking corpse."

Muhammad had never heard Abu speak so eloquently and so fluently. He had always left that to others, preferring to express his ideas within the small, comfortable cluster of his courtiers and friends, and not even that if his mother were present to dominate the discussion. He had been a plotter, not a politician. Muhammad now noted that, without changing his haughty, aggressive expression, el Zagal was at least listening, and listening very carefully to his nephew. That was a better reaction than Muhammad had dared hope for from the old man.

"I do not know if the combined might of what remains of our homeland will be sufficient to defeat the Christians, or even to hold them at bay for much longer, "he went on. "But I do know that, as long as we are divided, even to the point of fighting against each other, we have no hope whatsoever. As long as Moslem is slaying Moslem, even Allah will turn his face from us as defeat and subjugation will be no more than we deserve."

Muhammad was hardly surprised by Abu's words, since they were the very thoughts that he had hammered into the young monarch for weeks. What surprised him was that they had registered at all with Abu when Muhammad had been relatively certain that they had been lost in the cacophony of conflicting advice that he was getting constantly from his mother, his courtiers, and his tight little circle of friends. What also surprised Muhammad was el Zagal's attentive reception where he had half expected a torrent of scorn and abuse, if not outright murder at the hands of his *gomeres* on the spot, although this was still a distinct possibility.

El Zagal remained silent for a long moment after Abu finished speaking, a very long moment to Muhammad's way of thinking, staring vacantly off down the valley in the direction of the walls of Granada and stroking long dark beard. Then he turned to his nephew.

"That's all very well, and nothing that we haven't known for a long time. It's good that Allah has seen fit to finally enlighten you with His hard truth, but what do you propose to do about it?"

"I propose," Abu stated, in a voice loud enough for all present to hear, despite the whistling of the wind, "to relinquish my claim to the throne of Granada and to support you as king in your lifetime. In exchange, I ask only that I be named your heir, that my followers be left in possession of their property and titles without harassment, and that I be given the opportunity of proving my dedication to our cause by being placed in the forefront of the next battle against the infidels."

Muhammad could just see el Zagal pursing his lips amid the thick bristles of his beard as he thought over the offer. Muhammad had long ago crafted the proposal with a view to restoring something of Abu's standing with the Moorish people, to attempt to erase the image of him as a puppet of the Castilians and an active participant in the dismantlement of the Moorish kingdom. He did not have any illusions about the validity or permanence of Abu being named el Zagal's heir. It was more than likely that Abu would end up having to fight either el Zagal or some other Moorish lord for the throne sooner or later, but the important thing now was to establish a power base of his own in preparation for that day. The only question now was whether el Zagal would take Abu's declaration at face value and welcome him as a vassal, or whether he would see through the ploy but would be desperate enough for support against the Christians that he would accept the end of the civil war in the short run as the only way to avoid defeat in detail by the invaders. It was entirely possible, of course, that el Zagal would discern Muhammad's ultimate objective and would simply choose to eliminate the only real contender for the throne right here and now and unify the kingdom in that way, with a quick stroke of the sword, but Muhammad had nothing else to bargain with but their lives.

El Zagal backed his horse a few steps and leaned closer to Hamet and several of his other military commanders, and they conferred in low tones for what seemed to be a very long time. Muhammad was pleased that Abu sat his horse without moving, without changing his expression, gazing only at the towers of Granada in the distance, without displaying any of the anguish he knew the young man must be feeling. Hafez, of course, did his best to ruin the image of tranquil waiting by looking back and forth anxiously between Abu and Muhammad and talking in stage whispers with his attendants the whole time.

Eventually, el Zagal again rode forward from the knot of riders, but not close enough to Abu to imply any warming of their relationship.

"We have decided to accept your offer," he announced flatly. "The civil war within our kingdom is hereby ended, and we welcome you back into the ranks of the faithful in the battle against the infidels."

"I rejoice in your decision, uncle," Abu said, but with a general lack of enthusiasm matching el Zagal's. "Now, where would you have me enter the fight?"

"Loja," el Zagal replied. "Your followers will continue to hold the territories they have in the north, Velez Blanco, Huescar, and the port of Mojacar, but you will also be given command of the garrison of Loja, the point at which we expect the next Castilian attack to fall, and we will see what you can do then."

Muhammad knew that this information was correct. From his time in Cordoba the previous year, he had gleaned details of the coming campaign by Fernando and had even seen documents that pointed to the Christians planning to raise an army of no less than 12,000 horse and 40,000 infantry, besides a strong siege train of artillery including professional gunners from as far away as Germany, Italy, and the Low Countries. Naturally, Muhammad would not have taken advantage of his relationship with Raquel to obtain such information, even though she was in a perfect position to have provided it, but Yusef's stealthy work among the unnoticed servants who haunted the back corridors of the palace had paid impressive dividends.

It was highly unlikely that the Moorish defenders would be able to hold out against such a host, so it was logical that el Zagal would welcome the opportunity to have his nephew take the blame for the inevitable defeat and possibly manage to get himself killed into the bargain. Still, the Christians had been beaten off from Loja more than once before, and any battle was always a throw of the dice to some extent. Heavy rains could keep the Christian artillery from arriving, sickness could decimate their camp, and a lucky sortie could rout them as it had done just a few years before when Fernando had been fortunate just to have escaped with his life. It could happen again for Abu, and, if it did, Abu's standing in the Moorish community would be immeasurably enhanced.

"And to help you with this task," el Zagal continued, speaking over the buzz of conversation among Abu's followers, "I am sending my lieutenant, Hamet el Zagri, to join you in the defense." The powerfully built Hamet grinned menacingly from under his bushy eyebrows.

It was clear that Hamet was being sent along to keep an eye on the untrustworthy Abu, and Muhammad could hardly fault el Zagal for taking this precaution, but he could see anger smoldering in Abu's eyes, and he prayed that he would again swallow his pride and accept the terms. Finally, Abu let out a long breath and bowed his head, however slightly, and the deal was done.

Just before the two parties turned to go their separate ways, however, another figure pushed its way through el Zagal's troop. It was a holy man, dressed in a ragged, dirty robe, his hair and beard long and unkempt, laying in tendrils across his back and chest, and he steered his mangy donkey past el Zagal's elegantly caparisoned charger and up close to Abu, peering at him like an old man who had nearly lost his sight, as might well have been the case. Abu's horse shied, and it was with difficulty that he was able to control the animal and keep it in place.

"I warn you, lord," the old man croaked in a hoarse voice that was barely audible above the wind, "to be true to your faith. You have a choice to be a sovereign or a slave. Be careful which you pick."

"It will be as Allah wills," Abu responded uncertainly, and the old man snorted, turned his donkey, and trotted off down the valley on his own.

Unlike most towns in Spain, either in Moorish or Christian territory, Loja was not built atop a rocky crag dominating the surrounding plain. Instead, the thick walls of Loja rose up from the fertile soil of the Genil River valley and were surrounded by sprawling suburbs, themselves protected by a less imposing outer wall, and by a network of interlocking irrigation canals that watered acres of orchards and fields. The damage done by the invading Castilian forces in 1482 had largely been made good by this time, and the fields of early summer were green with thick grain while the air was heavy with the strong smell of ripening olives. To the west of the town, the bare topped hill of Albohacen loomed, surrounded by a belt of woods like the hair on the head of a tonsured monk, but the hill was too far from the city walls to be of use in the placement of artillery.

Muhammad rode just behind and to the side of Abu in the long column of armored lancers, but he carefully turned his head to avoid meeting his sovereign's eyes whenever Abu happened to glance his way, and the pale moonlight and the long shadows it cast helped to hide Muhammad's features. He could not hope to conceal his disdain and disappointment for Abu indefinitely and, for the first time since he had entered into his service, Muhammad seriously considered abandoning him, fleeing the country if need be, but he did not know how he could continue on this way.

Muhammad still felt that he could be excused for feeling a little self-satisfied after the reconciliation between Abu and el Zagal some weeks before. He had, after all, almost single-handedly put an end to a bloody civil war that had opened the kingdom up to invasion by the Christians, and he had given his lord at least a fighting chance of repairing the damage that ill luck on the battlefield and his own bad judgement had caused to his reputation and his standing in the Moslem community. He did not excuse, however, the degree to which he had been taken in by Abu's performance at Pinos Puente, his absolute conviction that the young king had been won over by his reasoned arguments to the need to come to an agreement with his uncle and to unite in a common war against the infidels. But Muhammad could not now ignore the evidence that Abu's acceptance of a truce with el Zagal and of the responsibility for defending this town had been merely a sham.

Muhammad had this evidence from no less a source that Abu's formidable mother, Fatima, who, while often at loggerheads with Muhammad on the details of national strategy, had nonetheless never wavered in her patriotism or her opposition to any more concessions to the Christians than were absolutely necessary, if only because she saw those causes serving her ultimate goal of ensuring the throne of Granada for her son. Just the night before, long after the rest of the court had retired to bed, Muhammad had been summoned to the queen's quarters by a young serving girl, in itself an amazing breach of protocol. There, alone with Fatima, who sat on her bed, her long dark hair streaming down past her waist and her still-exquisite body barely concealed by a silk sleeping gown that forced Muhammad to avert his eyes to keep his concentration, she had told him of her son's perfidy.

It seemed that, no sooner had Abu been given authority over Loja's defenses than he had written secretly to Fernando and Isabel, without, of course, consulting with Muhammad, or with Fatima either, for that matter. It seemed that Fatima had her own network of spies and informers throughout the court, one that easily surpassed that of Yusef and his talkative servant friends. Abu had offered to deliver up Loja to the Christians at the king's demand and to allow the Castilian army unhindered passage through the rough country around Loja to permit a surprise attack on the key Moorish port of Malaga, one of the principal cities that owed its allegiance exclusively to el Zagal. Presumably, in exchange for this treachery, Abu hoped to be placed on some kind of titular throne in Granada after el Zagal's final defeat, which the fall of Malaga would virtually assure, and live out his days in luxury and security as the vassal of the Castilian crown.

Much to Abu's surprise, however, Fernando had summarily rejected the offer. He considered Abu's reconciliation with el Zagal, not as part of an intricate plot that Abu had constructed to further his own advancement as well as the aims of his Christian overlords, but as a betrayal of the treaty he had entered into in order to obtain his freedom after the battle of Lucena. In his reply Fernando boldly announced the size of his advancing army and promised that he would have Loja without Abu's cooperation soon enough in any event.

Knowing the devious workings of Fatima's mind, Muhammad had been reluctant to believe this story, even after she had shown him the very letter Fernando had sent, but Yusef's competent network of informants had substantiated key parts of her account, the comings and goings of discreet messengers, at least one of which was quietly put to death on Abu's orders to conceal his knowledge, and Muhammad had ultimately been obliged to accept it as the truth. Since the damage of the deed was already done, it was never clear to Muhammad just what Fatima had hoped to achieve by revealing the duplicity of her son to his senior counselor, but Muhammad strongly suspected that she would come in search of payment for this favor sometime in the future. It was also entirely possible that the woman was mostly enraged that her son, whom she had risked all to place on the throne more than once, would take such a momentous and dangerous step without seeking her guidance, and that she sought some sort of revenge even against him, although there was little that Muhammad could have done about any of it by that time.

Muhammad had stood for a long moment in front of her, there in her bedroom, and it occurred to him briefly, that perhaps this passionate and almost intoxicatingly attractive woman might have wanted some kind of physical compensation, right then and there. There had been a look of warmth and openness in her large, shining eyes for an instant, or at least Muhammad had flattered himself that there had been, and Muhammad had cleared his throat nervously. For some strange reason Muhammad had the impression that, even though they were both widowed, he would have been cheating in some intangible way, cheating on the married Christian woman he had left, or who had left him, months ago in Cordoba. But the longing look disappeared from Fatima's face as quickly as the light from a snuffed candle, and she had snapped at him, "That will be all, *katib*," before turning her back and walking slowly to the balcony of her room. Had she seen the reluctance in his face and taken offense? She did not appear to be the kind of woman who was very accustomed to rejection.

And now Abu was leading a daring attack on the approaching Castilians, partly to help conceal his efforts at betrayal, which he must surely expect to leak out sooner or later in the porous world of his tiny court, and partly as an act of desperation in the hope of actually defeating the Christians. This would put Abu in a position either to make another claim on the throne at Granada, riding on a wave of popular adulation that would naturally follow such a victory, or to bargain more effectively with Fernando, having proven that he would make a valuable ally for the Christians or a very dangerous foe, whichever they chose.

Word had come in from scouts posted in the hills north of Loja of the approach of the Castilian army. As expected, the Castilians had detailed thousands of men to carving new roads through the mountains over which could travel their heavy artillery and their baggage trains. But, also as expected, it was impossible to rein in the vigor of some of the Spanish commanders, and the feared Marquis of Cadiz had ridden ahead of the main body of the army with a force of no more than 2,000 lightly armed horsemen, probably with a view to reconnoitering the Moorish positions and scooping up any livestock and other foodstuffs that the Moors had not yet been able to gather and take into the protective walls of the town. Consequently, in the early hours of this morning, Abu had called up 500 of his best horsemen and a force of 4,000 infantry, about as large a force as he could spare from manning the city walls, well-armed with crossbows and arquebuses, to march into the mountains and fall on the Spanish advance party and annihilate them before the main body could come up to their assistance. Although the force under Cadiz only represented a small fraction of the total force at Fernando's disposal, Abu knew that an early and sharp defeat would undermine the morale of the whole enemy army and make it unlikely to be able to hold together for a lengthy siege. Some of the independent-minded nobles might well remember pressing business back home and take their local levies with them, and some of the foreign adventurers might find the whole project more adventurous than they had had intended and return home as well. Also, a contingent of mounted knights might well contain a high percentage of nobles whose death or capture might dishearten their men with Fernando's army, and noble prisoners could be released on a promise of taking their troops home, further weakening the Christian forces. At any event, Muhammad had to agree that it was a risk worth taking at this point.

The Moorish column moved quickly out of the open river valley farmland, having departed the city well after dark in case the Castilians already had scouts posted on the surrounding hills, and headed north into the forested hill country. In the thin blue light just before dawn, Abu led the cavalry into a sheltered gully off to the west of the road, just past a narrow saddle where the road was hemmed in on both sides by rock-strewn hills. The infantry split into two bodies, each moving off the road and into the hills on either side and carefully concealing themselves amid the boulders and gnarled trees and bushes. Muhammad found a deep cut in the side of the mountain, heavily overgrown with brambles, where he tied his horse and Yusef's mule, preferring to join the infantry for the battle and thus keeping away from Abu. He then took his shield from Yusef, who was armed with a crossbow and a thick bundle of quarrels under one arm and several throwing javelins under the other, and moved up onto the hillside to take command of a small contingent of archers and arquebusiers.

As he crouched behind a large rock, his chain mail coat and steel helmet clammy in the early morning chill wherever they touched his skin, Muhammad looked around him. The men who sighted down their gun barrels and along the shafts of their arrows at the road below were not professional soldiers. Although most of the men had fought against the Christians more than once, there was a scattering of young boys among them as well whose wide eyes and nervous fidgeting implied that this would be their first time in combat. Like Muhammad, these were common citizens who had been called up to repel the invader, and there was only a look of grim determination in their faces, no lust for battle and killing, only the knowledge that, if they failed in their duty, even once, if not today, then tomorrow or a week from now, the barbarians would be over the walls of their town and in among their women and children. Most of them had seen what the Christians could do during the pillaging of a town, or they had heard exaggerated stories from refugees from other towns that had fallen to the infidels, so these men would not run. In fact, they might not run soon enough, Muhammad feared, to get back to the city if this skirmish failed in its purpose.

The sun rose, bringing color to the view from Muhammad's perch, replacing the monochromatic, ghostly scene with the bright greens of early summer. Muhammad found it mildly amusing that, amid the waving patches of yellow and lavender wildflowers, he could just make out the menacing helmets of the hidden attackers waiting on the other side of the road, strange new blossoms to be sure. He watched as a group of men readied a large cart loaded with straw behind an outcrop of rock near where the two hills nearly touched, separated only the width of the narrow dirt road and others piled round boulders behind a makeshift barrier of tree limbs high up on the steepest part of the slope. Then a long, low whistle was carried to them by the breeze, and they could see the flashing of a mirror from a hilltop to the north. Now, all work ceased, and the men hunched lower behind whatever cover they could find. The lookouts had sighted the approaching Spaniards.

It took nearly half an hour for the sound of horses' hooves, the tinkle of armor, and the creak of leather to reach Muhammad at the back end of the ambush. He peered between the leaves of a stunted bush and could see a yellow cloud of dust rising up from around a bend in the road, just before the wooded canyon where Abu and his cavalry waited, less than a mile away. Then a handful of riders came trotting into view, Moors by the look of them, either renegades or converts, lightly armed with small round shields, padded cotton armor, and long lances, the advance party of scouts. But even before the scouts had come up to Muhammad's position, a double column of heavier cavalry rounded the bend, Spanish knights in heavy plate armor and mounted on tall horses with the white and blue banner of the Marquis of Cadiz at their head and wearing capes in the same colors. They were overconfident, Muhammad could see. They were still at least ten miles from Loja and thought they were moving faster than word of their approach could have arrived, and now the entire force would be in the canyon by the time the scouts reached the end of it. Muhammad shook his head. What point was there in sending scouts ahead if they could not have time to give the main body time to deploy in reaction to whatever they discovered?

Just then the scouts passed around a rock outcrop just below Muhammad's position, and he made a slashing motion in the air with his sword. A dozen crossbow strings sang, and the scouts were all tumbled from their saddles, each with several arrows sprouting from head, neck, or chest. Dark men scuttled out from the underbrush and dragged the bodies away, quieting the horses and leading them off the road, still just out of sight of the Spaniards.

The knights came on, talking loudly among themselves, some of them laughing, and someone down the column with a fine, light tenor singing a hymn. They were all sturdy men, bigger and thicker than the Moors. The nobles among them had elegantly tooled armor and wore tall plumes on their helmets, their visors up, revealing their florid faces. The men-at-arms, the majority of the force, wore the typical Spanish coal scuttle helmet with its long tail in back covering the nape of the neck, breast and back plates, and a chain mail tunic that ran from neck to wrists with a skirt that reached to the knees and with metal or boiled leather greaves on forearms and shins. In addition to their lances and pointed shields, each man also carried a sheath with two or three throwing javelins tied to his saddle bow and a longsword or battle axe on his belt. They wold be a formidable force out in the open, able to run down opposing infantry and break up defensive formations with their javelins or crush the lighter Moorish cavalry with a charge with couched lances, but in the restricted terrain of the mountains, it was the archers and men with light firearms and infantry that could move easily through the cover of the rocks and trees that would have the advantage.

Just then a shout went up from the head of the Spanish column, and a plume of fire appeared as the Moors put a torch to the straw-filled cart and shoved it downhill to block the roadway with a blazing barrier. At the same time, the wooden props were knocked out from under the piled boulders, and these came roaring down a bare stretch of hillside to crash into the center of the column, snapping horses' legs like match sticks and sending their riders into a panic. Now the hidden Moorish militia rose up all around and poured a deadly volley of arrows and lead balls into the milling Spanish horsemen before ducking back down under cover to reload. Many saddles were emptied, and more of the horses were killed, but most of the trapped men managed to dismount, some with three or four arrows lodged in their shields, and they formed a double line in the road and began to work their way up both slopes to clear away the attackers with the sword.

Meanwhile, at the rear of the column the ground was more open, and some of the Castilian commanders had rallied some hundreds of their men to charge along the sides of both slopes parallel to the road to take the ambush in the flank and relieve some of the pressure on the trapped vanguard. With a roar of "Santiago and at them!" the Spaniards surged forward, but just as they began to spur their horses up the rise, a high-pitched howl came echoing out of the canyon as Abu, with Hamet at his side, led his cavalry in a wild charge that hit the Spanish rear ranks with an audible crash.

The Castilians were now beset on three sides with a flaming barricade and a tangle of boulders and twisted bodies blocking any movement to the front. The surviving members of the front half of the column who had managed to work their way up into the rocks were relatively safe from the fire being directed down on them from above, although they were frequently picked off by Moors firing into their backs from across the road, and they could not advance any further without exposing themselves. The mounted men at the rear of the column had turned to fend off Abu's attack, but they too were now wedged into the narrow defile, while the Moorish horse could maneuver more freely and send clouds of javelins arching down on their heads. To make matters worse, Moors from nearby villages, attracted by the sounds of battle, were coming in, first singly, and then in bands of a dozen or more, armed with farm implements, bows, daggers, whatever weapons happened to be at hand, and the ring around the Spaniards was drawn ever tighter.

Muhammad had moved down closer to the road to help beat off a desperate attack by some Spanish men-at-arms who had nearly broken through the Moorish line on this side and threatened to gain control of the crest of the hill, but he spent most of his time under cover of a boulder, letting the crossbow and arquebus men do most of the work from the relative safety of their positions on the upper slope. Through the drifting smoke of the wagon fire, he could just make out the swirling mass of horsemen at the rear of the column and, at the top of a small knoll, there sat Abu atop his white charger, slashing about him with his sword and surrounded by half a dozen Moorish riders who were helping to fend off attacks by twice their number of Spaniards. Muhammad sighed. Whatever his faults as a king, there was no claiming that Abu lacked physical courage, just the moral kind.

Suddenly, a javelin arched up from the fray, passed just over the edge of Abu's shield, and pierced his shoulder, knocking him back onto his horse's rump and almost unseating him, although he was quickly supported by riders on both sides. An anguished moan went up from the Moorish ranks as a blow to the commander was always demoralizing to any army, and a simultaneous cheer was raised by the Spaniards who redoubled the fury of their attacks.

A bugler down in the midst of the Spaniards trapped by the road had been tooting and blatting for all he was worth since the battle began, but now a thin, faint echo could be heard coming from somewhere in the north. At first Muhammad had imagined that it was just that, an echo from the surrounding hills, but this echo now played a different call, and he could see Castilian soldiers below pointing with their swords to a dark smudge on the northern horizon, another dust cloud that could only be Fernando with the main body of his army coming to the rescue. Muhammad watched as the local villagers shaded their eyes to examine the dust cloud and then quickly sprinted up the slope on their mountaineers' legs to disappear over the crest. The Moorish cavalry also now broke off their attack and swept around the eastern hill to head back to Loja through a parallel valley in that direction, leaving Muhammad and the poor, bloody infantry to find their own way home. He had lost sight of Abu, but it had appeared that he was being carried off the field as well, although there was no way of telling whether he was alive or dead at the time.

Fortunately, although the fall of Abu and the imminent arrival of reinforcements had put new heart into the Spaniards, they had been marching all night and then fighting desperately under the blazing sun for several hours, and the idea of clawing their way up the rock-strewn slopes to face a foe of uncertain size did not appeal irresistibly to all of them, and the infantrymen who had been locked in hand-to-hand battle with the Christians were able to pull back slowly under covering fire of the archers and arquebusiers farther up on the crest of the ridge. Muhammad moved back with them and, once he had nearly reached the summit, he turned to judge his men's progress.

He saw that only a small wedge of Spanish men-at-arms was advancing with any vigor, the reinforcements not having come up yet, but this group was moving quickly, pausing only to dispatch the occasional wounded Moor and to cut down the slow of foot that they encountered. They were still far enough behind that Muhammad was about to turn and make for his horse, when he suddenly recognized the burly figure of the man leading the charge, none other than Juan Ortega de Prado. Even though he wore a full suit of armor and a helmet with a nose guard that partially obscured his face, there was something about the bulk of the man, the thickness of his neck, and his ruddy complexion when the sun, that was now behind Muhammad, shone full in his eyes that made him certain that this was the brute who had married Raquel. Well, she would not have to worry about this particular animal anymore he swore to himself!

With a rage that he did not consciously understand, Muhammad spun about and snatched the crossbow from Yusef's hands. He stepped on the foot brace and jerked the bowstring back to its latch. He quickly inserted the iron quarrel that Yusef provided and took careful aim just to the right of the nose guard as Juan paused to pull his sword from the body of an unlucky Moor, and Muhammad allowed himself a moment to relish just how well the man would look with an inch or two of the feathered shaft just protruding from his eye socket. The arrow shot forward, but, just at that instant, another Christian man-at-arms happened to leap onto a large rock just in front of Juan and caught the bolt in his neck, the force of the impact bowling him over leaving a crimson arch of foaming blood in the air.

Muhammad cursed under his breath and bent down to cock the weapon again, but Yusef tugged urgently at his sleeve, pointing down the hill to the north. Muhammad could see a ragged line of Spanish light cavalry spreading out up the slope from the north, sweeping along it in their direction with considerable speed. He also noticed that he and Yusef now appeared to be the last Moors left on this side of the ridge, at least alive, with Juan's men climbing steadily up from the road, and these new arrivals moving along parallel to it. With another snarl, therefore, he tossed the crossbow back to Yusef and the two of them dashed along the paths between the largest boulders that led back to where they had hidden their mounts. As they came down to the mouth of the gully, however, they found nothing there but brambles and the prints of many feet, men as well as animals. Muhammad roared at the heavens, but he could not claim to have been very surprised as the rights of ownership to any means out of a deadly situation were hardly inviolable.

The two men were already panting, sweating, and covered with dust, and the bugles of the Spaniards could be clearly heard getting ever closer. Instead of heading back to the road for the quickest route down to the river valley and Loja, Muhammad led Yusef off to the northeast at the ground-eating pace he had developed on his travels, something short of a run, but not much. They would stick to the hill country, as the remnants of the Moorish force would undoubtedly follow the road back to the city, and, with any luck, the Spaniards would follow them. The two escapees could then drop down to the valley somewhere closer to the city and, hopefully, still arrive there well ahead of their pursuers.

It took them most of the rest of the day to come within sight of the town of Loja in the valley below them. For the first several hours of their journey, the sound of hoofbeats and trumpets had been quite clear, and they had stuck to the most heavily wooded parts of the hills, the steepest slopes, and the rockiest gorges, but as the sun had begun to set, all was silence. The Moorish peasants who worked the vineyards and orchards on the flanks of the hills had long since escaped to the shelter of either the town or the nearest fortified outpost, along with their sheep and cattle. Only the occasional scrawny dog could still be seen lurking about an abandoned farmer's hut, watching their approach tentatively and then slinking away into the shadows.

The town was clearly visible on the valley floor amid the lengthening shadows of the long days of late spring and a string of smoke columns with bright flames at their bases leapt up from what had been a series of villages along the valley heading from west to east, toward the city's outlying suburbs. Apparently the Spaniards had pressed on very quickly indeed, and the Moors had not been able to organize a meaningful defense in time to stop them before they had poured forth from the narrow mountain passes into the open valley floor, possibly even confusing the advance guard of the invaders with the returning survivors of Abu's small army. But now Muhammad saw his duty clearly, and he led

Yusef in a headlong dash from the hills in the direction of Loja's nearest outer gate. They half slid, half ran, down the rocky slopes, covering themselves with dust, sweat, and an assortment of scrapes and scratches from the rocks and bushes, but they covered the distance in less than an hour.

They arrived amid a scene of total confusion and panic at the gate of the outer wall. Clusters of infantrymen who had fought in the mountains, many of them wounded and all of them exhausted, were straggling up the road from the valley, pushing and shoving for primacy with mobs of terrified peasants herding their small flocks of sheep and children into the relative safety of the city and with overladen oxcarts of merchants who had been caught out on the road. They all kept throwing nervous glances over their shoulders as the bugles and drums of the advancing enemy cavalry could now be clearly heard in the near distance. Only a pair of decidedly anxious spearmen in padded cotton armor stood guard at the gate, and they could provide no intelligible answer to Muhammad's repeated questions regarding the whereabouts of their commander or the captain of the guard or whether the king and his cavalry had made it back to the city yet. These queries were shouted over the hubbub of voices raised in arguments, women's screams and wailing, and the curses of the teamsters, but, if the dull-looking guards could make out the words at all, they either had no information or simply could not focus enough to understand the questions.

Sending Yusef on into the city to attempt to find an officer responsible for the defense of the walls, Muhammad placed himself at the gate, forcibly hauling able-bodied soldiers from the flow of refugees and placing them in the guardhouse, although a steady trickle of deserters from this collection prevented its number from rising above more than a score or so of willing defenders. Finally, a column of horsemen galloped up to the gate, scattering the pedestrian traffic like leaves before a strong wind. Muhammad scanned the dirty, sweaty faces as they moved past until he finally recognized that of Hafez and jumped into the road to grab his bridle. Hafez reached for his sword, the whites of his red-rimmed eyes showing his fear, but Muhammad used his free hand to pull the young nobleman from his saddle and to hold him propped up against the heaving flank of his horse.

"We need men here to hold the Christians at bay," Muhammad shouted into Hafez's drawn face. "With some cavalry and light infantry we can cut them to pieces among the irrigation ditches and garden walls here outside the gates. We know the ground and they don't, and their heavy cavalry can't be of much use. If we can cause them enough losses among their nobles, they might still call off the attack on the city as they've done before. At the very least we can dissuade them from trying to storm the walls today, because, if they try, they will succeed. We need time to get our defense organized. But we have to have some men to fight with right now!"

Hafez shook his head disconsolately. "It's no use! The king was badly wounded and so was Hamet."

"I saw Abu go down, but will he live?"

"How should I know?" Hafez shrilled. "There was blood everywhere. He's already been taken into the citadel, and he was still breathing and talking when last I saw him, but the men have no fight left in them. We were lucky to get away at all, riding through that maze of canyons with the Spaniards right on our heels. They're coming now, not two miles behind us, so you couldn't organize an effective counterattack, even if you had the men to do it. Now let me go!"

Hafez's voice had risen to a pitiful squeal, and he pulled away violently and ran on through the gate, leaving his lathered horse to Muhammad, who gave up on Hafez and quickly swung up into the saddle. He could feel the horse stagger slightly under his weight and saw a long gash on the animal's flank that left his ribs and one front leg bathed in blood, now caked with dust, but he dug his heels into the horse's sides and urged him back out into the roadway to the chorus of a new stream of curses from the press of humanity trying to force their way into the city.

Just then a troop of mounted North African *gomeres* trotted up the road. The men slumped in their saddles, and their horses' necks and muzzles were caked with dust and dried sweat and blood, but they all still carried their lances and shields, unlike many of the soldiers and riders mixed in with the civilian refugees who had long since discarded their weapons to facilitate their flight. Muhammad pulled his horse up in front of the apparent leader of the group, raising his hand.

"I know that your men are tired, but we need some cavalry to try to hold up the infidels and give the city defenses time to get organized," he stated in a matter-of-fact tone. "Can you help us?"

The dark-skinned officer frowned for a moment, evaluating Muhammad. It was apparent from Muhammad's own dusty clothes and a cut along his cheek that had spilled a disproportionate amount of blood down onto his tunic that he was no idle courtier but had also taken part in the morning's battle. It was also possible that the man was unused to being *asked* for help instead of being given direct orders, so he was momentarily at a loss for words, and he merely shrugged.

"That is what we've been doing all day," the officer said, jerking his head back over his shoulder to the road behind him which was now almost deserted. "I expect that the next people whom you'll see coming this way will be calling on the Blessed Virgin, not Allah, for protection in battle." He sighed heavily, then went on. "I don't see why we can't keep on a little longer."

Muhammad smiled broadly and grasped the man's hand just as Yusef tugged at his trouser leg.

"Master," Yusef puffed, the sweat glistening on his black forehead, "all of the officers seem to be holed up in the citadel, attending to the king, or hiding from the battle," he added under his breath. "The only people I could find were the militia leaders who have been busy putting men on the walls all around the city."

Yusef nodded to an elderly, stooped man with a long gray beard and with a crossbow balanced on his shoulder who was standing close behind him.

"I am Ahmed ben Rashid," the old man said, bowing deeply, "a merchant in silks and tapestries. We were informed by the constable that the soldiers would not try to defend the suburbs, only the city itself, so we who have our homes and places of business outside the city walls have armed ourselves to fight at least for the outer wall. We hardly have enough men for that, but if, as your servant has explained to me, you plan to make a fight outside the walls, I have come with one hundred men to support you. We are not many, but we are all equipped with arquebuses and crossbows, commodities in which I also trade on occasion."

"And I am Muhammad al-Sarif al-Uqayli el Haj," Muhammad began to identify himself, straightening his back and attempting to use his most officious marketplace voice, although the dust in his throat turned his words into a barely intelligible croak.

"Yes, I know," the old man cut in, "*wazir* to the king."

"Not *wazir*," Muhammad corrected him, "merely his *katib*, an exalted sort of secretary, but I do act on his authority."

"But I have known you these many years, sir," the old man insisted. "As I said, I am a merchant and often did trade with Granada in the time when you were *muhtasib* there. And any man who can master a marketplace would find the conduct of a simple battle so much child's play, in my humble opinion. We are at your orders, sir."

"Good," Muhammad declared. "Then I will leave you with twenty of your men in command of the gates here along with the soldiers I have collected. It will be your job to hold the gates open for us until the last possible moment, but do not hesitate to close them if the Spaniards show up in force before we do. The rest of the your men will join me and the captain's troop to harass the enemy as much as we can and for as long as we can among the gardens down below." The old man bowed and spoke rapidly to his men who were crowding in close behind him, then quickly lead a score of them off toward the gatehouse. They ranged in age from mere boys of perhaps twelve or thirteen to wizened graybeards who used their spears and crossbows like walking sticks. None of them had proper armor, but some had hauberks and helmets of boiled leather, and all had the determined, fatalistic look of fathers, husbands, and brothers who were resigned to fight to the death to protect their families. Muhammad was well satisfied.

A broad swath of land surrounding the city walls of Loja was taken up with an extensive network of gardens, vineyards, and orchards, mostly owned by wealthier city residents, with plots demarcated by waist-high stone walls, with small shacks for caretakers and for the storage of tools, and criss-crossed by a series of irrigation canals that covered the entire area like a grid. While some of the canals were less than a yard wide and only a few inches deep, no hindrance to the movement of troops, several of them were deeper than a man's height, with perpendicular banks, and too wide for man or horse to jump, thus limiting passage to a handful of narrow stone or wooden bridges. There was no time or manpower available to attempt to demolish the bridges, so Muhammad placed his infantry in hidden positions amid the fruit orchards and behind the walls to cover the bridge approaches. He, meanwhile, took station with the cavalry in a central position near the main road up to the town.

They did not have to wait long as a squadron of over one hundred Spanish light cavalry soon came pounding up the road with a tall blue silk banner at the head of their column. The Moorish infantry let the first few pairs of horsemen cross over one of the bridges and then loosed a sudden volley of gunfire and arrows at the cluster of riders waiting to cross. At the same moment, Muhammad raised his sword and let out a roar, leading his own cavalry into a sudden charge into the disordered ranks of the Spanish advance guard. Some of the trapped Christians countercharged, but they were now outnumbered and were quickly routed, leaving several wounded men in Muhammad's hands as prisoners, while others attempted to recross the bridge, only to be cut down by the arquebuses and crossbows of the militia. The rest of the Spanish force rapidly reformed and raced back down the road to be lost to sight among the trees.

As the Spaniards disappeared from sight, many of the militiamen rushed out to scavenge among the dead for money, jewelry, and expensive items of armor with which many of the nobility often rode into battle. Muhammad steered his horse among them, scolding them hoarsely and even swatting at their backs with his quirt, but to no avail. He knew only too well that this first unit was nothing more than an advance party scouting out the ground for the main enemy force, but no amount of shouting or reasoning would divert the looters from their task.

Then, suddenly, one of the militiamen rooting among the bodies at the far end of the bridge, jerked upright for an instant, then toppled silently over the low wall into the canal, a javelin protruding from his lower back. The others watched in horror and then turned to race back to their positions, many of them tossing aside their spoils, but it was already too late. Another column of Spanish light cavalry charged out of the very dust cloud raised by their predecessors, spearing any Moor they could catch and rushing toward the bridge. At the same time, a line of Spanish arquebusiers laid their pieces along the top of another garden wall and fired a well-ordered volley across the canal into the *gomeres* horsemen who were still milling about trying to rally after their own charge. Muhammad's men returned the fire as best they could, but their own troops were now between them and the Spaniards who were steadily working forward toward the bridge, moving from wall to wall under cover.

"Fall back to the gate!" Muhammad shouted over the rattle of gunfire, but his men needed little urging in that direction. The surviving cavalry formed up once more to hit the flank of the advancing Spaniards, but were easily beaten off with heavy losses, while many of the militiamen simply dropped their weapons in panic and raced up the road, screaming to their colleagues on the walls not to fire on them.

Muhammad also turned for the gate, but his horse finally buckled under him, tossing him unceremoniously onto his face in the dust. He scrambled to his feet and joined the general retreat, finally pausing for breath after passing through a ragged line of Moors armed with pikes, pitchforks, and a handful of crossbows.

"This is no good," he yelled to the old merchant, who saluted him stolidly. "We've done as much as we can out here. Get back inside and close the gates."

Some of the men turned and simply ran into the town and disappeared among the narrow lanes and houses, never to be seen again, while the few soldiers among them steadfastly backed their way in, maintaining a thin wall of spear points in the direction of the enemy as the last of the militia and *gomeres* also came in, including the captain, whose left arm, now a bloody stump, hung limply at his side as he swayed drunkenly in his saddle.

With a roar, a dozen Spanish mounted men-at-arms charged up the slight rise toward the gate just as Muhammad and his men put their shoulders against it, trying to swing the two halves of the gate closed and bolt them from within. The wall here was just an afterthought, not a major fortification with a defensive moat, massive towers, and drawbridge to protect the gates, just a curtain wall thrown up around the sprawling suburbs of the city. It would be an obstacle to a raiding party, but it was never planned to withstand a determined assault by a large force. But it was just an obstacle that Muhammad needed now, if only he could get the gates closed.

One armored horseman shot through the narrowing opening, slashing to his right and left with a great broadsword, while several others braced themselves against the heavy oaken doors and others tried to force their way through the shrinking gap. Muhammad snatched at javelin from a rack on the wall and hurled the missile deftly into the back of the Spanish horseman, toppling him from his mount. He then pulled his sword and chopped through the rope holding up the portcullis, which came rattling and crashing down about ten feet behind the gate itself, cutting off the enemy advance, but also trapping several of his own men who were still holding the outer gate and vainly trying to push it shut against the press of onrushing Spaniards, but there was nothing he could do for them now.

Muhammad backed away from the portcullis, a grid of heavy oak beams, studded with iron bolts, which gave him a clear view of the trapped Moors. One of them was the captain of the *gomeres* who was trying to push on the gate with his one good arm. He turned in shock when he heard the slam of the portcullis behind him, but his look turned to resignation as he nodded to Muhammad and drew his dagger to slash at the arm of a Spaniard who was pushing the gate from the other side. Inch by inch, the gates swung open and more Spaniards spilled past them, cutting down the Moors one by one, the captain dying last, pinned to the portcullis by the thrust of a spear.

By now a group of Moorish crossbowmen had moved up to fire through the openings in the portcullis at the attackers who crowded into the narrow passageway to their front, and half a dozen attackers fell in a matter of moments, but Muhammad saw that it was no use. While the attack on the gate was taking place, other bodies of Spanish infantry, carrying torches in the gathering gloom of evening, had brought up scaling ladders and climbed the walls at several points and were already chasing the scattered defenders before them. Muhammad felt a tug at his sleeve and turned to find Yusef standing next to him, his muscular chest heaving, a thin trickle of blood running from the corner of his mouth, and Muhammad could see that at least two of his huge white teeth were missing.

"The Christians have built a bridge of boats across the river below the city, and they brought some of their infantry up in horse carts or riding double with the cavalry," he panted. "They've already overrun two towers in the outer wall south of here, so there will be no holding them outside the curtain walls."

Muhammad nodded and shouted to those close enough to hear him. "Fall back to the city wall. We can't hold the suburbs now."

He turned and, with Yusef half pulling him along, they made their way up the cobblestone street toward the main gate of the city itself. He only now realized just how exhausted he was, his legs feeling like lead and his breath coming in painful gasps, while his left arm ached terribly, and he feared he might have broken his wrist when he was thrown from his horse, but there was not time to stop now.

The few soldiers and *gomeres* who were still alive joined them in their withdrawal, but Muhammad saw that old Ahmed and the other militia were fighting where they stood, while the swarms of Spaniards were already torching one house after another as they spread along the walls and up through the dwellings toward the city walls. These were their homes, and he suspected that many of the family members were still in them, there not being enough room for the whole population, plus thousands of refugees from the countryside, inside the old city walls. Muhammad felt a pang of guilt for leaving them to fend for themselves, but he had to admit that they would not be the first or last to die in a hopeless cause, and perhaps their sacrifice would at least buy the remaining defenders a little more time and take a few more of the attackers with them, maybe enough to stem this initial onslaught.

At least the defenses of the city were a little better organized than those of the suburbs had been. The survivors of the battles on the outskirts of town were being shuttled through a small postern gate in the massive stone wall, the main gates having already been firmly closed, with teams of masons hurriedly building a solid stone wall behind these as a further line of defense. There were soldiers here, not just militia, and Muhammad was quickly recognized and allowed to pass through the mob to make his way up to the citadel where Abu's command had made its headquarters. He was reassured to note that nearly every plaza and open lot he passed had been fenced off and was crowded with sheep and cattle, while piles of grain sacks made small mountains outside of the already full warehouses. Clearly, the city was in about as good a condition as possible to withstand a siege.

Muhammad found Abu stretched out on a couch, his face an ashen yellow, and his eyes sunken and red-rimmed. He was surrounded by a cluster of courtiers, several elderly-looking medical men, and his mother, who hovered over him protectively. He was propped up on a pile of pillows and was shouting orders to all and sundry over heads of his attendants in a cracked and shrill voice. Apart from a clean white bandage which covered his shoulder, chest, and upper left arm, he did not appear to be too much the worse for wear, considering the circumstance, although Hafez stood to one side wringing his hands, and Fatima's face had a drawn, exhausted look about it. When Abu saw Muhammad approaching, he waved both his arms in the air, the left one causing him to wince, with an expression of true relief on his face.

"Thanks be to Allah," Abu called out. "I thought for certain that you had been taken."

Muhammad bowed perfunctorily. "I have been fighting down by the outer wall, your majesty," he said without a proper greeting. Muhammad was far too tired and dispirited to worry about his own role as courtier. "I'm sorry to inform you that the suburbs have been lost."

"I knew that," Abu said, shaking his head. "I never thought they could be held once we got routed in the hills. No time to organize the defenses."

"They were supposed to have been organized already, sire," Muhammad went on. "That was why we took so few men with us in the advance. The rest were to have been readying the city, but it seems that they only devoted their time to the inner defenses. If the Spaniards could have been stopped at the outer wall, they would have had to mount a prepared assault there, with artillery and siege engines, and that would have taken them days, if not weeks, and every day we can prolong the siege, the more likely it is that sickness would appear in their ranks or a relieving army arrive to force them to retire. Now they are here at the gates, and their artillery will be able to hit any part of the city as soon as they are able to bring it up."

Abu simply shrugged his shoulders. "What's done is done. And it will still take them weeks to bring up any artillery through the mountains. The important work has been done well. We have ample supplies within the city walls, and we are not stuck trying to defend the entire circuit of the outer walls with an inadequate garrison. Now we can concentrate our men more effectively."

Muhammad found Abu's attitude somewhat disturbing. Despite having suffered a serious defeat in battle, and having almost simultaneously lost half of the city he was bound to defend, all on the very first day of the campaign, Abu gave the impression of one who saw everything unfolding exactly as planned. He obviously did not consider the deaths of so many of his soldiers, to say nothing of the residents of the suburbs of the town, as a serious setback. Muhammad looked to Fatima, who would normally have been taking the lead in discussions of politics or even of military planning, but she remained silent and avoided Muhammad's gaze. He finally decided that it was time for some sort of reconciliation with his king.

"I am delighted to see that your majesty's wound does not appear to be as bad as I had feared. I saw you hit out on the road and only recently learned that you had survived at all."

"Oh, it hurts like the devil," Abu said absently, flexing his shoulder and grimacing, "but I'm a lot better off than old Hamet. I would be surprised if he were to live through the night," he added with a half smile in the direction of Hafez, who turned away nervously.

"It was a very strange wound," a deep voice spoke up from the back of the room, and all turned to see a tall, lank officer with a hawk nose and sunburned features. He was one of the contingent of troops that el Zagal had sent along with Abu to help defend Loja, or, more precisely, to keep an eye on Abu. "He seems to have been struck in the back with a crossbow bolt."

"But the fighting was so confused," Hafez suddenly chimed in with his shrill voice. "The Spaniards were coming at us from all sides. There is certainly no shame in being hit from behind if the enemy is all around."

"Hamet el Zagri never turned his back on the enemy, and any man who suggests it had better be ready to defend his words with his life!" the officer snarled, and Hafez scuttled behind Abu's couch for protection. "At least he never turned his back on the enemy *knowingly*," he added with emphasis, looking hard at Hafez.

"In any event," Abu went on, sweeping aside the interruption with a languid wave of his good hand, "we are in excellent shape to hold out here indefinitely. Now, I suggest, *katib*, that you get yourself cleaned, fed, and rested now while you can. The Spaniards will take some time to get organized for an assault, but it will not take them forever, and once they get going, who knows when we shall rest again?"

Yes, Muhammad thought, and it will take them time to kill, and loot, and rape their way through the outer city, but he said no more and simply bowed his way out of the room, making a detour to visit the apartments of Hamet el Zagri to check on his condition. But he found the doors heavily guarded by dozens of fierce North African troops who were obviously more concerned that a fellow Moslem might have it in mind to do their commander harm than that a pack of Spanish raiders might suddenly materialize inside the walls of the citadel. Muhammad could not honestly say that they were being unwise. He had seen Hafez's reaction just now, and he remembered that the young courtier had ridden off into battle with a large crossbow hanging from his saddlehorn.

In his own room he found that Yusef, who had not bothered to wash the blood and grime from his own body, had prepared a hot bath for him in a large olive oil vat that he had had trundled into the apartment. With a pang of guilt, Muhammad surrendered himself to the soothing warm water and allowed Yusef to stitch up his cheek with delicate hands that would have done any surgeon proud. He finally chased Yusef off to take care of his own comfort while he picked briefly at a plate of fruit that had been laid out for him and then simply collapsed on his bed and into a deep, dreamless sleep.

The sun was well up in the sky, the light streaming in through the lobe-arched window of his room, when Muhammad blinked awake to the smell of Yusef's coffee brewing over the little brazier in the corner. At first he thought that the drumming he felt more than heard was in his own head, a by-product of the pounding his body had received the day before, but he soon realized that it was coming from outside.

"Alarm drums, master," Yusef commented, without being asked, as he brought the coffee. "The Spaniards were able to move right up near the walls during the night through the houses in the suburbs. It seems that no one thought to pull any of them down to clear a margin of open ground away from the city walls. There were already two attempted assaults against the walls just before dawn, but they were beaten off. Still, the Spaniards have men with guns and crossbows stationed all around, keeping up a steady fire on the walls, and I hear that we have already been taking substantial losses."

Muhammad took his cup over to the window and squinted into the bright sunlight. The citadel was positioned on the highest point in the city, and his room gave him an unobstructed view that looked out over the walls where a pall of smoke still hung over the parts of the outer city that had been burned down before the Spanish commanders had gotten their own men in hand the night before. Now he could hear the rattle of musketry, like the sound of pebbles dropping into an empty barrel, rising above the call of trumpets, drums, and cymbals. He could also hear an occasional ominous thudding, deeper than the gunfire, that sent small tremors through the wall as he leaned one hand on the window frame.

"The Spaniards can't have brought up artillery already," he mumbled, half to himself. "Those must be our guns on the walls firing."

"I believe they have done so, sir," Yusef contradicted him as he straightened out the bedding. "I was told by a scout who just returned a couple of hours ago that they have already positioned some small cannon in the houses facing the main gate, not big enough to knock down the walls, but enough to knock of chunks from the battlements, depriving our men of cover, and dismounting some of the wall guns as well. They have also worked all night bridging the canals and the river and widening the road down from the mountains. They had thousands of men working on it besides all the peasants who didn't manage to escape them. They're like ants building up their hills just before a rain shower."

As they spoke, Muhammad watched as a small black dot arched into the sky from beyond the walls. It grew quickly larger and left a trail of smoke and sparks as it sailed over the wall and came crashing down on the roof of a house, spewing flaming material in all directions. It had not rained for weeks, and the dry wood of the overhanging balcony on the house quickly caught fire, but soon teams of dark figures had scrambled up onto the roof and were pouring buckets and jars of water onto the flames while others ran about on the street below, beating at stray sparks with wet brooms and empty grain sacks. But even before this conflagration was completely under control, another burning mass flew over the walls, landing in a market stall the awning of which quickly ignited, then another and another struck at different points around the city, and thin columns of smoke began to rise as the number of blazes began to be too much for the fire brigades to handle in a timely fashion. Cannon balls, apparently made red hot in ovens before firing, were also lobbed into the houses, crashing directly through the roof tiles to set new fires in the attics.

"Incendiaries," Muhammad commented. "They must be using trebuchets to launch those fireballs. Old fashioned, but they still work."

"I was about to mention," Yusef added, "that they had brought with them wooden siege engines broken down into pieces that they put together during the night."

Muhammad just shook his head. The Spaniards were becoming more and more organized, methodical, in their approach to war, a process that showed no sign of being matched on the Moorish side. He noticed that, even though the barrage had only been going on for a short while, the fire brigades were already being overwhelmed. At least a dozen fires were now raging that he could see, and some had begun to spread from house to house as a stiff breeze fanned the flames and scattered sparks across the city. Although new groups of workers appeared wherever an incendiary round landed, none of the fires had been completely extinguished, and some men now had to rush from fighting existing blazes to deal with another one close at hand.

The servants who scurried through the halls of the citadel were already dabbing at red-rimmed eyes with their sleeves as smoke from the fires in the city wafted upward and filtered in through the windows. Muhammad quickly made his way to the constable's apartments where Abu had set up his court, but an officious page sniffed at him and told him that his majesty had left on a tour of the walls. Muhammad had to approve of such a step, showing himself to the troops and evaluating the tactical situation at first hand, and he and Yusef hurried through the winding streets of the town and mounted the battlements themselves.

Making use of the cover provided by the houses of the suburbs that were built right up to the city walls in many places, the Christians now had firing positions placed all around the city for arquebusiers, crossbow men, and light falconets with which they peppered the defenders, forcing them to keep their heads down. Muhammad placed his palm against the wall and could feel a dull throbbing, implying that Christian sappers were busy mining underneath the walls as well. Since they would not have to start far away from the walls and tunnel up to them, as would be the case in a normal siege where the defenders had a clear field of fire for some distance out from the walls, this old fashioned method might well prove even faster than artillery, if the Spaniards chose not to wait for their heavy guns to be brought forward. They would tunnel under the walls, then expand their hole, propping up the roof with timbers. Finally, they would cram the tunnel with straw and other combustibles and set fire to the whole thing, with the tunnel collapsing when the timbers burned through, and the wall above collapsing with it to create a breach. The Moors were now paying for the assumption that a city this far within the borders of the kingdom was virtually immune to attack and allowing residents to crowd their dwellings right up against the walls, but there had been no time to do anything about this in the short time since Abu had arrived, and there was certainly nothing they could do about it now.

Muhammad and Yusef kept moving, eventually making a complete circuit of the walls, often having to dash across open spaces where Spanish guns had already blown away the parapets, dodging the fire of Spanish sharpshooters who targeted the gaps. Although Muhammad continually asked the commanders of the companies he encountered whether they had been visited by the king, none of them had seen or heard from Abu all that day, and, as he made his way back up to the citadel, Muhammad began to become more and more worried.

He found Abu, once more on his couch, surrounded by courtiers, but this time without the presence of either his mother or any of the officers that had accompanied the detachment of Hamet el Zagri. Muhammad was pleased to see that Abu was looking substantially better today, although he still winced every time he moved his injured shoulder, but there was something troubling in Abu's eyes that made Muhammad a little uneasy.

"I've been looking for you," Abu said absently as he glanced over some correspondence from a stack held by a servant kneeling at his side. "Where have you been?"

"Out on the walls, your majesty," Muhammad replied, bowing. "I was told that I might find you there."

Abu gave him a sharp look, as if attempting to determine whether this was meant as a slight or not, but he simply waggled his hand in the air to dismiss the thought.

"I had planned to go, but some other business came up," he said, nodding at the jumble of parchment. "Have to establish some sort of inventory over the supplies present inside the city, have to get the people to cough up what they may have hoarded in their private stocks. No telling just how long this siege will last."

"Might I suggest, your majesty," Muhammad interrupted, causing a nervous snort from Hafez at his impudence, "that a tour of the defenses would be well worth your time, if you are up to it. There are plenty of clerks who can conduct an inventory, or I would be glad to compile it myself. And the situation on the walls . . ."

"We're surrounded, unless I am badly misinformed," Abu snorted. "And by a great many Spaniards who are most eager to get in here. Does that about sum it up, *muhtasib?*"

"Yes, your majesty," Muhammad answered, making a supreme effort to control his own rising rage. "But I think you'd recognize, if you were to look over the defenses personally, that there are several points at which the Christians could put up scaling ladders right now and, with covering fire from the houses, storm the walls before sunset. I also believe that the enemy is mining the walls from at least one direction. Plans need to be made for the deployment of mobile forces to counterattack any such offensive, and the local officers don't have the authority to do it. With Hamet out of the battle, you are the only one in command over the whole garrison."

"I've been in a battle or two myself, you know," Abu snapped, "and I don't really think that . . ."

Just then the citadel shuddered, causing a gentle fall of dust to float down from the rafters, followed by a dull, rolling boom. Hafez squeaked and looked apprehensively up at the ceiling, cringing.

"And it appears that the Spaniards have also brought up some of their heavy artillery, sire," Muhammad continued. "At this point the level of supplies inside the city might prove totally irrelevant as the place stands in very real danger of falling before any of us has time to eat another meal."

Abu sat up, swinging his feet to the floor and glaring at Muhammad with Hafez standing at his master's shoulder, adding his own dark looks to the bombardment. Abu opened his mouth as if to say something, then apparently thought better of it, stood up, and began pacing about the room.

"You're quite right, of course," he said after a long pause. "I'll go review the dispositions of the troops at once. In the meanwhile," he added, spinning to face Muhammad, "the very best thing to do would be for you to write one of your succinct and comprehensive reports on the situation for my uncle. We can get some courier, maybe one of our Christian renegades, to slip through the enemy lines to Granada. If we're to have any chance at all, el Zagal needs to put some pressure on Fernando, if not to drive him away completely, at least to force him to divert some of his forces away from the siege lines to watch his own rear."

Muhammad bit his tongue, bowed once more, and backed out the door. He could see that there was nothing more to be gained here.

Back in his room, Muhammad pounded the walls with his fists, stalking about, scattering piles of papers that came within reach, and cursing from the depths of his soul. Yusef quietly entered and stood in one corner, waiting for his master's tirade to subside.

"I have talked to one of the grooms down at the stables," he said once Muhammad had finally flopped down on his bed, holding his head in his hands. "We know that the king didn't go to the walls this morning. It seems that he was right here in the citadel, meeting with a hooded man who came in through the postern gate before dawn."

"I don't need to hear any more," Muhammad groaned, and Yusef just nodded and slipped quietly out of the room.

Later that day, Muhammad duly drafted a report for el Zagal, giving a brief summary of the battle in the mountains, an assessment of the strength of the enemy of the state of the city's defenses without drawing any grand conclusions. He sent it off with a messenger for the king's seal and simply stayed in his room. The bombardment of the city continued well into the evening and increased in intensity as more Spanish troops and artillery came into position. The flight of the burning missiles, which he learned were simply bundles of kindling soaked in pitch and held together with wire around a central core of a melon-sized rock to give them steadier flight and some penetrating power, was quite spectacular against the night sky. He sat, leaning on the windowsill, watching the city below him burn. He did not bother to turn his head when he heard footfalls in his room.

"When will it be done?" he asked.

"In the morning," Fatima replied, standing next to Muhammad's bed, her shawl wrapped tightly around her head and shoulders. "There will be a sudden barrage on a section of the wall that has intentionally been weakened from our side, and when the breach has been made, my son will be able to seek enemy terms with *honor*, having done everything possible to defend this place."

"Which is why Hamet had to be taken out of the battle, of course. And what are the terms? I assume that they have already been agreed upon."

"Yes, they have. Hamet, his troops, and everyone in the population who chooses to will be allowed to leave with all their possessions. My son will remain a prisoner, but that is probably best for his own safety at this point. It seems that his primary purpose in accepting the duty of defending Loja was precisely to be in a position to do a service to the Christians by turning it over to them."

"He said this?"

"Not in so many words, but I know my son."

"Do you really, your highness? I was at the battle in the hills," Muhammad sighed, still looking out over the burning city. "He did not fight like a man about to betray his people. That spear he took through his shoulder was certainly not part of any plan, unless your son is really much more clever than I had ever given him credit for. Or perhaps that was just my tired old eyes seeing only what they had hoped to see."

"But it worked out very well for him just the same," Fatima insisted. "It made him look like a fighter, but the decision had already been made to surrender the town. It would have been more merciful if the spear had pierced his heart."

"So, you are now a partisan of el Zagal too?"

"No, my son is the only true king of Granada, of al-Andalus. The only trouble is that he doesn't seem to realize that he can only gain and keep the throne by acting like a Moor, not as a poor copy of some Christian baron. He has to seize the throne and then fight all comers, to the death."

"It looks as though that decision will be taken out of his hands now."

"Not really. He has been promised some kind of kingdom, including Guadix and Baza, if he can find a way to take them away from el Zagal himself."

"That sounds easier said than done."

"Exactly, which is why, when I leave here, I will be going back to Granada. My family is still powerful there, and many long for a return of the rightful heir to the throne."

"If that were true, mistress, I doubt that we would be sitting here now."

"You will see. There are still millions of Moors in Spain, including many who now live under Christian oppression. They are only awaiting the chance to rise up under the right leader and throw down these idol worshiping barbarians. El Zagal may be a worthy military commander, but he cannot command the loyalty of the people the way someone with a true bloodline can. If we can foment such a rebellion of all the Moors, supported by our own troops, who knows what might happen? The Turks would see that it would be worth their while to send men and ships to break the Christian naval blockade, at least they might. New legions would come over from North Africa as they have done for centuries, and even other Christian kingdoms, like France and Portugal, would leap and the chance to gnaw at the carcass of Fernando's and Isabel's realm, and a new age of Moorish power will dawn here in Spain. I can just feel it in my heart."

"I believe that I will just stay here for awhile," Muhammad sighed. He found nothing quite so tiring as limitless hope based on wishful thinking.

"My son needs you," she said in a tone that, for once, actually sounded like a mother pleading for the good of her son.

"He doesn't seem to think so. He does not take my counsel."

"If you had simply stood aside that day in the marketplace years ago, you would be free to do what you like, but having saved him for the throne, you do not have that luxury to stand aside now."

She did not wait for him to reply, but turned with a swish of her robes and was gone from the room. Muhammad rubbed his eyes, mostly because of the smoke.

Muhammad chose not to attend the formal surrender ceremonies the next day. Yusef reported to him that Hamet el Zagri and his troops had only been informed of the surrender after units loyal to Abu had already evacuated a long section of the city walls, making any further resistance futile. A strong contingent of Spanish troops was then required to provide a cordon, physically separating Hamet's furious men from those of Abu while the former, along with most of the town's population formed a pitiful column and marched out of the city, accompanied by a long baggage train containing most of their movable possessions. Hamet's men had shouted taunts and threats at Abu, most with the message advising him to stay close to the skirts of his Castilian sovereign, Isabel, as they would be eager to settle scores with him if they ever caught him alone. Early that evening Fernando had made his entry into the city and, again, had graciously refused Abu's obsequious offer to kneel before him and kiss his ring, but there was no doubt in the mind of any of those present, Yusef assured Muhammad, of the totality of Abu's subservience to the Christian monarch. Abu's court had then begun hurried preparations for a transfer once more to Velez el Blanco in the north, near the Murcia border, there to await the outcome of Fernando's further campaigns against el Zagal and the Moorish kingdom.

Muhammad, for his part, realized that, ultimately, he would have to rejoin Abu's court. As Fatima had pointed out, he had made his choice years ago, although he had not realized it at the time. He knew that he had been placed on earth to serve the throne of al-Andalus. It was the will of Allah, and it was not his place to decide whether God's judgement had been correct or not. The most he would allow himself was the privilege of taking his time in going about it.

Chapter Two
Sevilla

Raquel stood up from where she had been leaning over a pile of maps and lists of supplies, horses, oxen, and troops that were spread out before her on the wide table in the queen's chambers. She braced both of her hands at the base of her spine and leaned backwards to ease the ache, causing her distended belly to bulge outward and rub against the table. Although her morning sickness had largely subsided, she now felt her gorge rising and, with the efficiency born of long practice, she bent over the chamber pot kept by her side for just such a purpose and threw up, holding her long braid out of the way with one hand. She rinsed her mouth with a cup of watered wine and spat that into the receptacle as well before handing it to a servant who had hustled forward from the next room at the sound. She daubed her mouth daintily but efficiently with her linen handkerchief and then returned to the study of her documents.

Raquel often shocked herself these days with her capacity for mechanically calculating every aspect of her life. After the initial horror of her wedding night, she had been spared further unwelcome advances from her husband by his almost constant absence at the front, and then by her pregnancy, which had seemed to abhor him almost as much as the plague had done at Cordoba the year before. She had enjoyed, of course, the brief interlude with Muhammad and had the memory of that to comfort her in the meanwhile, providing her with the reassuring knowledge that lovemaking was not necessarily a case of animal assault and humiliation. She now knew that the coupling of two lovers could be the most touching, warm, sharing of souls imaginable, although this soothing feeling was tempered with the knowledge that she would never experience it again. This was evidently just one more punishment that God was visiting upon her for her lack of adherence to any faith, a taste of the forbidden fruit never to be repeated. What a tantalizing form of torture, she thought, but so be it. She had never seen the point in bemoaning any fate that one was powerless to alter. Life did have to go on, after all.

Once upon a time, she had dreamed of living a life worthy of her heroines from biblical times, Ruth, Ester, or even Mary Magdalen from the New Testament, women of faith and spirit in times of adversity. Now, she wondered how far she had fallen. While she had never properly come to terms with her double life as a secret Jew in a Catholic world, the new layers of deception and trauma that her marriage had imposed on her soul had warped it in ways that she could no longer determine, and she had to wonder how this would affect the course of her life.

Now she found herself capable of toting up the assets and debits of her life, just as she kept track of the pledges of support in men, money, and goods from the towns, guilds, religious and military orders, and noblemen of the two kingdoms against those that actually arrived at the muster. All in all, she had convinced herself, she was left with a positive balance. She may have been saddled with an abhorrent husband, but it appeared that her actual exposure to him was likely to be strictly limited, and she did have a plan in the back of her mind should he attempt to force himself on her again. She had experienced at least a brief moment of true love, which was more than many women in her society were likely to do in their lifetimes, and she could relive the memory of those nights of passion as often as she liked. And now she was blessed with a tiny ball of pure love that was growing within her, and, as she thought about the baby, she tenderly caressed her abdomen and made a little clucking noise as if to a real child. So she would not simply shrivel up from within, as she had felt herself doing in recent years, devoted only to her work and afraid to share her emotions with anyone for fear of giving away her deepest secret. She now felt her spirit unfolding like the leaves and petals of a flower under a spring rain after a long dry spell. It was a rather small universe, but more than sufficient for her survival, which was all that she had ever asked. It was all the more easy to accept being much more than she had ever expected to have.

Raquel's father's time was now totally devoted to the casting and mounting of new artillery pieces, training their crews, and ensuring a steady supply of powder and shot of adequate quality from a variety of manufacturing centers that had been set up throughout the country. She had just received a letter from him advising her that her suggestion for casting larger bronze cannon in a vertical position, rather than horizontal, with the breech downward, had worked very well. The pressure of the weight of the metal had resulted in greater density in the breech area, which allowed the guns to withstand a larger charge of powder, thus increasing their range and power at no additional cost in gun size. She smiled as she read this as it gave her the idea that her father had been able to lose himself in the minutiae of his work, the constant array of technical problems to overcome, and to forget the unrelenting, nagging fear that, someday, the secret of their faith would come out and doom them all. Good for him, she thought.

Raquel had taken it upon herself, in the meanwhile, to keep the family name before the two sovereigns in a very overt way with her own unstinting dedication to the endless details of the organization of a campaign. Fernando, despite his unrivaled bravery in battle and a certain sense for the tactical advantage, when a cavalry charge would tip the balance or the point of an enemy line that appeared to be wavering, did not have the patience or the overall mental equipment for long-term planning. Isabel had a commanding presence and a persistence of character that enabled her to squeeze the last copper *maravedi* from a reluctant town council or wealthy monastery, and the burly, sweaty, foul-mouthed men-at-arms looked upon her with nearly the same awe as that in which they held the Virgin Mary herself, perhaps even more, since Isabel was a physical presence among them, and in her name they would perform prodigies of courage and stamina that no mere general could draw from them. But someone had to do the day-to-day book keeping, the tallying and the projecting of requirements over time, the exquisitely detailed work of taking general goals and lofty plans and combining them to produce concrete results. And this was Raquel's particular genius. True, she did not sign her name or put her seal, if she had had one, to any orders, and she was content that only a few members of the royal household were even aware that she took a part at all in the work, but she took great pride in the results that her labors achieved, all the more so because every victory gained through her efforts took herself and her family one long step farther away from the horror of the *quemadero* of the Inquisition.

For the Loja campaign, she had taken carefully drafted topographical sketches of the mountains through which the army must pass, compiled from discussions she had had with innumerable merchants and border raiders who new the border territory best, and then had calculated the amount of work that would be required to construct roads over which the artillery could pass. Rather than leave the matter to common sappers, generally little more than day laborers requisitioned by the army from the nearest villages, she had diagramed how steep ascents could be negotiated through the use of switchback roads or sharp ridges overcome by a judicious cutting away of the crest, using the debris to construct a ramp over the low spots in the trajectory with a gentle slope that required only a minimum of work either in digging or hauling of dirt. The sudden fall of the Moorish fortress that had defied Fernando on two bloody occasions was largely a result of this painstaking toil long before the first soldier had even laid eyes on the first Moorish enemy.

Just now she was finishing a similar plan to bring irresistible firepower to bear on the towns of Moclin and Ilora and was shifting her longer range planning to next year's campaign which would be against the key Moorish ports of Velez Malaga and Malaga itself. It sometimes amazed her that the veteran commanders of the army did not come up with the simplest solutions themselves. Since the combined Castilian and Aragonese navies had complete dominion of the waters along the Moorish coast, she planned to transport the heaviest siege guns by sea direct from Barcelona and Sevilla to a convenient landing place near the target cities, allowing the army to travel much lighter overland. This would greatly reduce the number of beasts of burden required for the artillery, as each gun required eight or ten span of oxen or mules for even the smaller pieces, which, in turn, would further reduce the total number for the army since nearly half of the draft animals used by the army were needed to carry fodder for the others, and these, in turn, required muleteers and teamsters to handle them, who also had to be paid and fed along the way. They would need the animals eventually, to move the guns up from the coast and into position, but only for a matter of days, not the weeks and overland trip would have entailed. The army would thus also not need to have an extensive road network built up behind it, as, without the heavy artillery, the army could travel over pretty much any terrain that presented itself, which meant that they would not need to raise the thousands of workers required for road building or to pay and feed them either. Raquel had just finished reading a long column of figures, triumphantly achieving the same total as her first attempt, when she looked up to find the queen smirking at her over her embroidery frame as she sat in a window seat, warming herself in the afternoon sun.

"It does one's heart good to see a young wife so dedicated to her husband's enterprise," the queen said, and Raquel looked up with a crooked smile on her face, assuming that the queen was being sarcastic. She quickly corrected herself, however, as she came out of her deeper thoughts and realized that the queen had no inkling of just how little Raquel cared about her husband's fortunes. Isabel was, of course, projecting her own feelings onto Raquel, as it was well known how deeply and sincerely the queen worried about Fernando's welfare at the battle front and her tireless efforts to support his campaigns. Theirs might have been a political marriage, but it also happened to be one that was crowned with the closest thing to true love that Raquel had ever witnessed at court. It was the one thing that made the queen, normally a terrible and powerful figure in Spain, into a real human being in Raquel's eyes.

"My dedication to the crown and to the prosecution of the war long predates my marriage, your majesty," Raquel ventured to say, "but, yes, it is some comfort to me to think that my little efforts here may in some way serve to ease Don Juan's path and, perhaps, help to preserve him."

The queen nodded, smiling. "We are a strange pair, you and I. Who would have ever thought that two women would play any role at all, much less such a significant role, in managing a war?"

"Now that you raise the subject, your majesty," Raquel continued, eager to get any thought of Juan from her mind, "it has occurred to me that there is something else we might do to help your armies in the field."

"And what might that be, that we are not already doing? We would certainly feel we had done a poor service if there were some stone left unturned that it was in our power to affect."

"It's not something that would have been useful, or even possible, earlier on, your majesty," Rachel added hastily. "I was just thinking that our informants have told us that both Ilora and Moclin have been reinforced by the Moors, while their civilian populations were evacuated, increasing their defensive capability while decreasing their consumption of supplies and the pressure a commander of a besieged city always faces from its inhabitants for an early, negotiated surrender. This implies that the Moors plan to make a test of this battle and to hold out as long as possible, while inflicting the maximum losses on our forces."

"That's true enough," the queen allowed. "We've discussed that possibility with our husband, the king, in our correspondence. But we cannot permit our current momentum to falter, or that will only encourage the Moors to resist all the more. Surely you're not suggesting that we abandon the campaign. We were diverted away from Moclin last year, and a second aborted attempt might give the place a kind of mythical power. You know how superstitious the Moors are about such things. Their weakening morale is one of our greatest strengths."

"Not abandon the campaign at all, your majesty. What I was thinking was that, given the honor in which the troops hold your person, it might put heart into our men if you and your court were to join the king in his camp. Many of our soldiers have been campaigning almost without respite for several years, and there has been talk of poor morale in their ranks. If they were fighting under the eyes of their queen, the only problem we would have would be holding them back, trying to prevent them from running undue risks in an effort to outdo each other for your favor. At the same time the Moors would take the strong message that no

Christian knight would ever consider breaking off battle while his sovereign lady looked on, and they would then be more likely to sue for peace sooner rather than later."

Isabel cocked her head and smiled coyly, considering the proposal. Raquel watched her out of the corner of her eye as she scribbled in the margin of a letter from the town council of Cuenca, arguing that their levy of troops had been too heavy already and pleading for a reduction in the queen's latest demands. Raquel disallowed the request and shifted the letter to another pile. Isabel was one of the most intelligent people Raquel had ever met, man or woman, yet it seemed that no one was immune to an appeal to personal vanity, and the queen was no exception. The fact that Raquel's comments were also true did not alter the fact that the queen longed for the adulation that the troops always lavished on her as they headed out on campaign, and she could well imagine their frenzy should the queen suddenly show up out in the field as if to share their risks and hardships.

Of course, life for the court, even travelling with the army, would hardly be any more arduous than it was in a royal palace. Massive tents would be set up with rich carpets on the ground and silk tapestries to keep out the drafts. The quality and quantity of food would hardly diminish, and, if anything, life out in the field would be arguably healthier and more pleasant than in the dank, clammy confines of even the finest of the royal residences. Still, the men would be literally throwing themselves in the dirt and her feet, battle-scarred warriors weeping openly at the sight of her, and screaming her name as they charged into battle. It was not hard to imagine that such a thing would tend to turn a lady's head.

"The king will certainly object," Isabel argued weakly.

"But I believe that he will ultimately see the wisdom of your decision," Raquel countered, delicately making the entire project Isabel's own. "And there would be the added incentive of his being with your majesty, his wife."

Raquel saw Isabel wince. It was widely known that Fernando freely sampled the charms of the ladies of the court and of any women who happened to be at hand when he was out on his frequent campaigns. He was always discreet about his adventures, although several of his bastard children from before his marriage to Isabel had been formally acknowledged, and a couple of the males had achieved notable rank in the Aragonese military, something that Isabel had accepted in good grace, if with a certain private discomfort. Fernando was, however discreet, also indiscriminate, and Raquel herself had felt the royal hands appreciatively caressing the backs of her thighs at one official function or other. She had always managed to make herself inaccessible during the king's nighttime prowling through the palaces, however, and she believed that Isabel both knew this and appreciated her loyalty.

Isabel, for her part, despite having married Fernando for the best of political reasons, was passionately in love with him and, unlike many of the other ladies of the court, would never have considered taking a lover herself. Furthermore, she was violently jealous, not so much of the physical act of sex, which she recognized as a normal bodily function that men were required to perform in order to remain healthy, but of any possible alienation of Fernando's true affections. Raquel had seen herself that it was definitely fatal for any woman to arouse the queen's jealousy. More than one attractive, buxom, and amenable lady at court had suddenly been banished from the royal presence or had some particularly undesirable marriage arranged, at great distance and with some especially old and ugly suitor just at the moment when tongues had begun to wag that she happened to be Fernando's latest conquest. There had even been instances of a couple of untimely deaths from mysterious causes or cases of investigation by the Inquisition had also coincided with such rumors, although Raquel was unwilling to give these thoughts any credence, not because they were unlikely so much as because she found them too frightening.

From her own observations over the years, Raquel firmly believed that Fernando did love and respect his wife, even deferring to her to a far greater extent than was normal for a Spanish nobleman, but Isabel's love was of such an intensity that the mere possibility of losing Fernando to another woman almost drove her to distraction on more than one occasion. She would fly into violent tantrums, smashing furniture and crockery, screaming at courtiers and servants for imagined failings, and sobbing uncontrollably for hours when such fancies took her. And now, as Raquel had anticipated, Isabel's jaw set in the determined line that she knew so well, her decision made.

"We shall write the king immediately," she announced. "Give the orders for the packing to begin. We will be leaving as soon as practicable."

"Yes, your majesty," Raquel said, bowing as much as her stomach allowed. "But it occurred to me that perhaps I should stay here and continue the planning and organizing of supplies. I believe that my father will be delivering a consignment of artillery to the army about now, and I would dearly love to see him, and to be with *my* husband, of course. But, if you are away at the front, it seems that the contractors and those responsible for levying troops and collecting contributions for the war effort may take it as a sign that they can freely go on holiday. Now that we have the system running so smoothly, it would be a shame to allow it to grind to a halt."

"Of course, you're right, my dear," Isabel said, although she was already moving quickly about the room, pulling dresses and slippers out of a wardrobe and tossing them on her bed in a pile. "In your condition you should, by all rights, be flat on your back in bed. If I cannot prevail upon you to take that sensible precaution, at least I can prevent you from undertaking what promises to be a tiresome journey. It makes me feel a little guilty for running off and leaving you with all of the work, and at a time like this when I should be at least by your side to return the support and comfort that you have given me at more than one lying in of my own. But, as you say, perhaps my presence with the army will do more for the cause than anything that I could accomplish here. And you are doing all of the real work anyway. You will only accomplish all the more once I am out of your way. At least I can comfort myself that you will be left in the best of hands as I will assign my own midwife to attend to you here in the palace."

And with that Isabel fluttered down the hall, calling to Beatriz de Bobadilla and some of the other ladies in waiting to give them the exciting news.

Raquel smiled quietly to herself. It was really almost too easy for her to manipulate the most powerful woman in Spain, maybe the most powerful woman in Spanish history. With the queen gone, and with her all of the long tongues of the court ladies, there would be nothing to hinder Raquel taking advantage of *his* arrival. And she was certain that he would come.

It was not until after Isabel and her court had departed Sevilla for Ilora, amid great fanfare, that it occurred to Raquel that, if Muhammad were intending to come and look for her, he would have no way of knowing that she had not gone on to Ilora with the queen. The endless migration of the royal court was, of course, a matter of common knowledge, even in time of war, but the whereabouts of a particular lady-in-waiting would not be quite so widely known. At the same time, Raquel had no way of knowing that Muhammad was not accompanying his own sovereign's court to Velez el Blanco directly, so a discreet note that she sent by courier to his attention there might never have reached him. It was completely fortuitous that Muhammad's trip from Loja brought him to Sevilla just after Isabel's departure, and his

461

own supposition that a Moor, even an ostensibly friendly one, would not be welcome in Fernando's army camp, caused him to remain in the city, awaiting the return of the court or word that the queen had moved on to another more accessible site. Consequently, Yusef's indefatigable network of humble informants among the serving class was soon able to bring word of Raquel's continued presence in the royal palace, and Muhammad sent a formal request to be received there, as a representative of Abu's staff, of course.

Raquel was waiting for him in a small sitting room that formed part of the queen's apartments in the palace. Muhammad entered, tall and dignified as always in his impeccable white robes and turban, his staff in his hand, and bowed deeply, taking the opportunity to check to make certain that they were alone once the page who escorted him had closed the door behind him. Even then Raquel did not rush into his arms but walked over to him and allowed him to kiss both her hands and press them against this forehead. She watched his eyes travel down her body and take in her swollen middle, and she wrapped her arms about herself as if to try to hide it, but she saw nothing but warmth and understanding in his eyes. So, it would not be necessary for her to tell him at all. He already understood.

At last they embraced, and she buried her face in the hollow of his neck, feeling the rough texture of his beard against her own cheek. They stood for a long while like that, without moving or speaking, just taking strength and comfort from each other.

"When will the baby arrive?" he finally asked.

"Soon, perhaps this month."

"I can wait here that long, and perhaps a few weeks more, until you are ready to travel."

"Travel? Where to?" she almost laughed at the absurdity of the idea.

"Not so much where to but with whom," he corrected her. "To come with me into the Moorish lands, where the Christian laws cannot touch you."

"There is nowhere we could go in al-Andalus that the Christians could not touch us, not with your king certainly, and probably not with el Zagal either. Even if he would have you, your having been a prominent member of his nephew's court for all these years of civil war. And either of them would surely sell us back to the Castilian throne if they were simply asked."

"And are you so beloved by your Old Christian brethren that they would ask?" Muhammad insisted.
"Surely you can't be serious," she said with a frown. "My husband could not stand the idea of any man running off with his wife, much less a Moor. With or without the consent of the crown he would carve a path of death and destruction through the whole Moorish army to get me back, or die in the attempt."

"I can understand how a man would love you that much."

"Love has nothing to do with it. He loves horse more, or any of his other possessions. He could just not live with the disgrace of having something taken away from him. And the royal family would see me as a traitor. They would use all of their influence as well to get me back, as a warning to others, if not for myself. You should know that societies have a certain proprietary view of their women. When a Moorish woman recants her faith and runs away to marry a Christian, it is a beautiful love story. If a Christian woman runs off with a Moor, she is a harlot and an apostate and does not deserve such an easy death as the flames."

"I suppose you're right about that, but you can't expect me to just leave you, and the child, to live with that man, a man like that, without me."

"I can and do. We spoke of this before. There is no hope for our being together now, and there never was. We knew that when we began even if we did not admit it at the time. Now I am to be blessed with a package of pure love through which to remember those days. That is not such a bad thing. In fact, this is the most wonderful thing that has happened to me in my whole life. I had dreaded what I might do if I should have had a child by my husband, whether I could even stand to let the thing live, much less give it the love and attention every child deserves. Now I don't have that worry, and I have done some of my own medical research and have learned methods by which I will not have to worry about having any other child in the future."

"And how can you be certain that this is my child, not his? I know what I feel in my heart, but . . ."

"There are ways to tell," she assured him, rubbing his broad, muscular back with a gentle, circular motion as she spoke. "I am certain that I was not pregnant when my husband left on campaign, and I am certain that I was after our first time. He has not touched me since, as he was away for some months, and by the time he returned, my condition precluded his usual *entertainment* as the loss of the child would have been very hard to explain to the queen. It seems that he is desperate to have a child, at least to have a son, and would do nothing that might jeopardize that, even though he would also probably suspect that the child is not really his. He may be dense, but he can count on his fingers well enough."

Muhammad grimaced at the mention of Juan's abuse of Raquel. She had told him about it in general terms, sparing him most of the details, but this had made Muhammad all the more eager to eliminate Juan when he briefly had the chance in the hills above Loja. And he had failed, just another in a long list of things that he should have done in his life and had not accomplished.

"And won't anyone else suspect that the child is not his?"

"Oh, there will be the usual counting out of months by the gossips of the court. They always do that when a woman's husband is off on campaign, but this will be too close for them to make anything of it. Fortunately, my family is rather swarthy, at least on my father's side, so no one will make anything of dark hair or eyes, if it should work out that way.

"We also know for a fact that the child will be a boy, at least that is what Maria says, she's one of the cooks who also works as a midwife. She's been with my own family for many years, and she joined me when I came to court. She has conducted such scientific tests as taking a drop of my blood and putting it in a glass of water. Since it sank, the child will be a boy. She would also come up to me unawares and demand that I stick out my hand, since I'm right-handed, that's the one I would use, but that is also supposed to indicate a coming son. I also know that she has sneaked into my room more than once during the night to roll me over onto my right side while I supposedly slept to ensure that the child would be a male. If that does happen, there will be all the less reason for anyone to question the paternity, since Juan will violently insist that his own loins had produced the desired result."

"We could go beyond Granada," said softly, after a pause. "The world is wide, and two, or three, people are but grains of sand on a beach."

"I said no," Raquel repeated, raising her voice slightly. "I told you that the king and queen would look for me, and if they can't find me they will take out their wrath on my parents. I could see the Inquisition getting interested in a *converso* girl, someone close to the queen, who runs off with someone not of the faith. Moor or Jew is all the same to them. And there are enough powerful men who resent my father's influence with the king, the changes his innovations are making in the army, to add their testimony to any kind of 'evidence' they might gather. Of course, I don't have to remind you that my family and I really *are* apostates, just the sort of people that the Inquisition was designed to uncover. With jealousy, suspicion, and a liberal amount of torture, they will bring my family down and destroy them if I give them the slightest pretext. My happiness is simply not worth that much."

Muhammad held her out at arms' length, gazing into her face, not in anger or frustration, but with infinite sadness.

"There must be a way," he said flatly. "I cannot believe that God would doom two good people to such a life of deceit and emptiness. What reason could there possibly be?"

"You know the reason very well," she said with resignation. "I have sinned. I am being punished. It is only a shame that you are being punished along with me when you have committed no sin. It is even less fair in that I, at least, will have the child to take away some of the pain, while it will only make matters worse for you."

"If you do not think that I have sinned, you do not know me very well. I have had time to think about this possibility, if not of the baby, at least of loving you and never being able to have you. It has occurred to me that this is His punishment for me for having abandoned my first family. He has offered me another and has taken it away again. Now that I think about it, it seems quite fair, if extremely cruel."

"They were sick and dying."

"All the more reason I should have stayed."

"There was nothing you could have done, other than join them in death."

"Perhaps that was God's will. I understand that He has very little patience with those that go against His will."
Raquel opened her mouth as if to respond, but then shook her head and leaned against his shoulder again.
They stood like that a long while, when, suddenly, a sharp pain caused Raquel nearly to double over. She would have

screamed, but the very air was sucked out of her lungs by the agony.

"What is it? Could it be the baby?" Muhammad asked, scooping her up in his arms and carrying her over to the bed.

"I think it must be. I've been having the pains off and on since yesterday, but nothing like this. Oh, God!" She reached down and pulled her skirts aside to reveal of dark puddle on the coverlet. "It is time! Quick, run down the hall to your left to the kitchens and call for Maria. Tell her what's happening. She'll know what to do!" she gasped in a whisper, holding her bulging stomach with both hands.

"I'm not going anywhere," he said and turned his head to bellow for help, but Raquel clapped her palm over his mouth.

"No! It will look better for you to bring me help, just a casual visitor a passerby, rather than for the servants to come in and find us together on the bed. It's things like that that get the gossiping started. Now do as I say!"

Muhammad shook his head as he bolted for the door. Perhaps this really was the Amazon who was guiding the Christian armies after all.

A fat woman with large dark eyes wearing a clean white apron, with her hair tied up under a matching head scarf, her reddish cheeks liberally dusted with flour, was standing in the kitchen with several younger serving girls, about to pounce on a mound of bread dough, when Muhammad burst into the room calling for help. When he first called out Maria's name, three of the women responded, since this was by far the most common name in Spain, but the fat woman immediately snarled at the others to be quiet, and Muhammad knew he had found the right one. He had no trouble appearing to be distraught and terrified, since he was both. Maria shrieked when he explained what had happened and hurriedly wiped her hands on her apron, barking orders to the other women like a drill sergeant.

"You, go get the birthing chair," she snapped to one maid. "Then I'll need a jasper gemstone, the blood of a crane and its foot, you'll find them in a box under my bed, and a knife to put under the chair to cut the pain," she yelled to another, giving her a firm shove toward the door. "And you run and fetch a priest, just in case. He can't come into the lying in room, but he should be ready at a moment's notice." Maria paused and crossed herself. "And I want you two," she indicated a couple of young pages lounging by the garden door, "to go about the palace and start untying all of the knots you can find, curtain ropes, anything. Understand?"

The boys apparently knew well enough not to question her and rushed out of the room. Maria snatched up a stone jar filled with some kind of ointment whose smell caused Muhammad's nose to wrinkle, and he turned to lead the way back to the room, but Maria shoved him aside, thrusting him painfully against the door frame with a muscular arm, and bustled off down the hall on her stumpy legs at an incredible rate of speed, mumbling prayers under her breath.

Muhammad followed her, rubbing his bruised shoulder, trying to explain that he was a man of medicine and could possibly be of some assistance, but Maria paused in the doorway of Raquel's room, gave him a withering look of disdain, and slammed the door in his face. Other women came running in and out from time to time, carrying supplies, including a bizarre chair with three legs, two in front and one behind, with a partially reclined back, a raised front edge, and a large hole where the seat should have been. Muhammad understood that Moslem women normally gave birth lying flat on their backs even though men were not permitted to attend to births there either, even medical men, but Christians preferred to do the job in a seated position, allowing gravity to help in the process and delivering the baby through the opening in the chair.

Muhammad could hear groaning and, every so often, a muffled scream, coming through the heavy door, and his hands trembled with worry as he ran his fingers through his hair and tugged nervously at his beard. He had been away at the *souq* when his daughter was born, and the entire process had happened so fast and so effortlessly, that, by the time he had come racing up the street and into his house, the child had already been delivered, cleaned, and swaddled, and he had nothing to do but kiss the exhausted, sweaty, glowing face of his wife and take the child in his arms. This time, however, he realized how lucky he had been before as he paced up and down the hall, beating on the stones with his fists, and praying for an end to the torture.

Minutes went by, then hours, or at least so it seemed. Muhammad only noticed that time really was passing, and not just in his imagination, by the lengthening of the shadows cast as the sun moved past the tall windows high up in the wall. Eventually, a servant came by to light the candles held in sconces beside each doorway, and still Muhammad paced. Occasionally he pressed his ear up against the door, but he could only hear the buzz of voices, no distinct words, and he suspected that they had given Raquel a belt or something to bite down on to stifle her screams. Yusef found Muhammad there during the course of the afternoon, having talked his way up through the ranks of the servants in his usual style, and brought him a flask of water, some biscuits and dried fruit, which now sat untouched next to a pillar in the hall. Muhammad had soon tired of pretending relative indifference in front of his servant and chased him off with instructions to seek out lodging for the night somewhere near to the palace.

When the door finally opened, and Maria appeared, strands of hair broken loose from under her bonnet and plastered to her forehead with sweat, her sleeves rolled up to the elbows, and the front of her apron spattered with blood, she took a step back in fright. Muhammad had long since cast aside his travelling cloak and had spent much of the afternoon and evening running tearing at his hair, so he now appeared to be one of the mad prophets, straight out of the pages of the Bible, fiery eyes, panting breath, and disheveled beard and all, just as if he had just had a personal conversation with the Almighty out of a burning bush.

"Well?" Muhammad almost shouted.

"It's a fine, healthy baby girl, sir," Maria stated. "You came and got me just in time, and everything went quite well."

"And the Lady Raquel?"

"She's fine too, sir, just a little tired, as you can imagine, but then again, maybe you men can't imagine. I've never yet met a man who really appreciated what we women have to go through just to keep the human race going. You have no idea of the pain involved, and worry. Will the baby survive? Will the mother survive? Will it be a boy? Of course, in this case it was a girl, but that's the will of God, and there's no arguing with Him about it. He sends what he has it in his mind to send, and you can just go whistle if that's not . . ."

"Excuse me, could I go in to see her, the Lady Raquel, I mean?" Muhammad finally interrupted the torrent of words.

"Well, I should hope not, sir," Maria said in a state of shock, and she pulled the door closed behind her as a precaution. "I'm certain that we're all most grateful that you happened to be visiting just when the lady came into her time, and you did the right thing to come running for help, but, after all her own husband hasn't even been informed of the birth yet, and here you are a virtual stranger and a Moor into the bargain. Why, the queen would have my head on a platter if I allowed her ladyship to be viewed by some strange man just minutes after having gone through what she just did, and I'd be of a mind to hand her the axe. Now, upon my soul, I suggest, sir, that you retire to your quarters, or your tent, or wherever you're in the habit of spending the night, because it would be worth more than my life for me to let you spend it here."

She planted her feet wide apart, crossed her thick arms over her ample bosom, and glared up at Muhammad with absolute firmness. He stood there stupidly for a moment, then finally came to his senses.

"Of course, madam. You are quite right. I was just excited by the event, and the lady has been so kind to me on my visits to court that I felt somehow responsible for her condition." He winced inwardly as these words escaped his mouth, and he saw Maria's eyebrow arch dangerously, but then she broke out into a guffaw that turned her face bright red.

"Oh, I assure you that you are not responsible for the lady's condition, sir!" she cackled. "Oh, that's rich. But I know just what you mean, and I'm sure that the lady will be quite touched by your concern when I tell her. Perhaps if you sent her a note tomorrow, she would most welcome your good wishes."

"Yes, I suppose I could do that," Muhammad muttered in relief.

"And perhaps even some little gift," she went on, ignoring his comment. "A lady always likes a little gift at any time, and Lord knows that she's earned some consideration this afternoon, and no mistake about it."

He nodded dumbly and was just about to turn away in defeat, when another serving girl opened the door, bringing out a large pan covered with a cloth. Muhammad was able to peek over her shoulder into the room, and there he saw Raquel, back in the bed now and propped up against a mountain of pillows, her long chestnut hair loosened and spread across the pillows like a thick cape, cradling a small bundle in her arms. She looked up, her face streaked with tears, but with a broad smile on her face as she raised one hand and limply waved Muhammad away. He bowed to her and to Maria, then finally staggered down the hall and out into the cool night air.

He walked through the narrow cobblestone streets, enjoying the fragrance of the orange trees and taking comfort from the hum of voices the issued from the windows of the houses as he passed. There would be laughter, an occasional shouted word, and the clatter of tableware as families sat down to a typically late dinner. He wandered past the Grand Mosque down toward the river. The city gates were shut for the night, and he found himself heading back up into the Moorish quarter, to the now-deserted site of the marketplace. Sawhorses and boards, which would be assembled again into counters for the day's business in just a few hours when the sun rose, were stacked against the outer walls of the large square, tied together in bundles, and covered with the tarps that were the stall awnings. The ground was littered with fruit rinds and scraps of cloth and paper, and two old women chatted quietly as they patiently swept the market with large brooms made up of dried branches lashed to a pole. In one corner of the square a group of skinny dogs quarreled over some scrap of meat until one of them snatched it up and dashed off down an alley, the others in frantic pursuit.

By the time the first rays of sunlight began to steal in between the crowded buildings, he arrived at the inn where Yusef had rented a room for them. He gratefully accepted a cup of coffee but immediately sent his servant off to the palace with a note for Raquel, nothing compromising, just a formal congratulation on the birth and expression of hope for her well being. Before long Yusef returned with a brief reply scrawled in a cramped hand on a small square of parchment.

> *Sir,*
>
> *I thank the Lord to be able to announce to you the birth of my daughter, who will be called Marisol, after a childhood friend of mine. You have my most heartfelt gratitude for your help yesterday, and I am certain that God will repay you for your kindness. I*

understand that you will soon be leaving Cordoba to return to the service of your sovereign, and I look forward to seeing you on your next visit.

There was nothing more, but he had not expected more. They were both alive and well, and he would have to be satisfied with that knowledge. Now, the only thing that remained for him to figure out was how they would be able to make a life together despite the power of the Spanish crown.

Raquel lay in her bed, letting the baby clutch at her finger while she nursed. She had a full head of dark, curly hair, just like Raquel's father, and her eyes appeared to be the same deep blue of Raquel's, although they might turn brown later. Maria told her that baby's eyes often did that. Raquel's position at court would have entitled her to seek out a wet nurse for the child, and Maria had insisted that this was the only proper thing for a lady to do. Raquel had pointed out that she was not actually of the nobility, but Maria had countered that she might not be so by birth, but her marriage into her husband's family raised her to that status. But Raquel enjoyed nourishing her little girl, and she suspected that Maria let the matter drop to avoid having some other woman around to compete with her for the attention of both mother and child. In fact, although she was not about to explain it to Maria, when the tiny mouth clamped down on her breast and the little fists opened and clenched in the air as she fed, it was almost as if Raquel was drawing as much sustenance from the infant as Marisol was deriving from her, sustenance for the soul that made Raquel's heart swell with love and reassured her that somehow, someday, everything would be all right.

GRANADA

Chapter Three
Moclin

The collapse of resistance at Ilora and Moclin almost immediately after the arrival of Isabel at Fernando's camp had again robbed Juan of any chance of distinguishing himself anew in combat. Not that his reputation as a warrior really needed any reinforcement. He was the Marquis of Cadiz's strong right arm in the field, and everyone knew it. And he had to admit that the sight of Isabel riding into the tent city that had been set up on the plain below the rocky crag atop which sat the fortress of Moclin had been an inspiring sight. She was riding a tall chestnut mule with a silver embossed saddle. She wore a pale green gown with an emerald green cloak, and the mule was caparisoned in a matching cloth embroidered in gold with the yoke and arrow symbol of Isabel and Fernando. Fernando, the Marquis of Cadiz, the Duke of Medina Sidonia and other nobles and senior members of the clergy had ridden out to meet the queen and her entourage at the Yeguas River ford, and their arrival appeared to be that of a whole new army encamping before the walls of Moclin. Juan was certain that he could hear the wailing of the Moors within the town at the thought of their imminent destruction.

But there had been no destruction. After a couple more days' bombardment, which was certainly damaging to the walls and towers of the defenders but had yet to create a viable breach anywhere, the Moors had asked for terms, and Fernando had granted the inhabitants the same terms he had given those of Loja and other recent conquests, free passage for all who chose to leave, with all of their portable possessions, either to Granadan territory or to any port of their choosing for transport overseas at the king's expense. There were no slaves to be divided up and almost no booty to share out among the troops except the modest contents of official buildings and armories and the town treasury. Most important to Juan, there were also no women to enjoy in his own special way, and he was very much in need of such an outlet since his wife was not currently available to him. There would be some lands to share out, of course, but this was a huge army, and his role, frankly had been no more than to stand by drinking wine from a goatskin bag, watching the artillery chew away at the battlements of the town high above, so he could hardly count on much.

And now fall was fast approaching, the traditional end of the campaigning season when the rains would make the roads impassable for the artillery, and even the cavalry, rivers would become torrents, and any camp site the army occupied for more than a day would become a bottomless sea of mud. Many of the men would also have to be heading home soon to help with the harvest, while the king and his officials would want to be back in their own lands to supervise the collection of taxes. It looked like another year wasted, and, with the territory left to the Moors constantly shrinking, it was anyone's guess how many more good years of war there might be for a young knight to make his mark. To be sure, there was talk of voyages of exploration along the coast of Africa in search of gold and slaves and of the elusive

Christian King Prester John, the legendary ally with a realm somewhere in the heart of Africa who would join with the Europeans to crush Islam once and for all, but Juan had never felt quite at home aboard ships and had no desire to see strange lands. He had always considered the idea of a sea voyage as something like a jail sentence with the added possibility of drowning thrown in for good measure. He wanted what his mentor, the Marquis, had had, a lifetime of warring right here at home, carving out a little empire for himself amid familiar sights and smells, where he knew what the land and people were worth and where his achievements would be talked about among his own people. And Juan's thoughts turned briefly once more to his old father, from whom he never received even a note of thanks for the gold and slaves and livestock he continually sent back to what must now be a very considerable establishment on their family lands.

As a result of this thinking, the summons that Juan had received that morning to a meeting of the high command had left him eager and anxious at once. Perhaps they were planning another *coup de main*, a surprise assault on another Moorish castle, as had been done at Alhama and Zahara. With his recently earned rise in rank and stature within the military, he might even hope to command the enterprise himself, rather than serving as a subordinate to one of the great nobles, since the force involved might not be very large. If that were the case, and if he were successful, which he certainly would be or die in the attempt, the entire town or castle might become *his*, bringing with it a proper title of nobility, not the ragged little village that now nominally belonged to him and which seemed to cost him more in the salary for a small garrison than it ever returned in taxes and rents. Now that would be something to rub his father's face in, and his brother's too, when he invited them to visit him in his own great hall, surrounded by his retainers and servants.

Juan could not help letting a satisfied smile spread across his face as he approached the mouth of Fernando's vast tent.

When he entered, he found Fernando and Isabel surrounded by the usual constellation of noble military commanders, the Marquis, the Duke of Medina Sidonia, Alfonso de Aguilar, and the Masters of the Orders of Santiago and Calatrava, along with their clusters of aides and junior officers. Much to Juan's surprise, conversation suddenly halted, and these powerful lords actually stepped aside to open a path direct to the king. Juan approached, a little nervously now, and bowed low to the sovereigns and to each lord in turn.

"We had hoped to be the bearers of glad news, sir," Isabel began, "but it appears from the look on your face that you have already heard."

"Heard what, your majesty?" Juan asked, perplexed. Perhaps word of his new assignment was already making the rounds of the camp. That must be it, he thought.

"About your daughter, of course," the queen replied. "We have just been informed that your wife has given birth to a fine baby girl. They are both in excellent health and send you their love."

"Oh, that," Juan mumbled, still confused, and the buzz of congratulations that had begun died away quickly in the face of his lack of enthusiasm. "Yes, of course," he finally added as the queen scowled at him. "That's wonderful news. Of course, we had been hoping for a son, but perhaps next time, certainly next time."

Isabel shrugged. At least this was a rather typical male response to such a blessed event. Fernando cleared his throat and went on.

"Unfortunately, although we appreciate the importance of this news, it being your first child and all, the original purpose of our summoning you to this council was not in fact about the birth, but about a task we have for you."

Juan's face brightened again, although only Isabel seemed to register the difference in his response to the two pieces of information. Of course, every other male in the room would have reacted in precisely the same way. A daughter was more of a burden than a blessing. A dowry would eventually have to be found, and, unless the new father already had the son of some prospective ally in mind for a match, marketing the girl would undoubtedly be a headache, even if a marriage alliance could offer advantages to a rising young noble that were not to be sneezed at either. On the other hand, the chance for slashing away at one's enemies with the chance of booty and recognition in the offing, was an unqualified good. How could the creation of life ever compare with the pure joy of taking it away?

"As you may have heard," Fernando continued, "we have just concluded a new agreement with the Moorish king, our vassal Mohammed XII."

"Do you mean at Boabdil's surrender of Loja, your majesty?" Juan asked. The intricacies of diplomacy were something he found endlessly boring. All he wanted to know was where and when to show up and whom to fight. Let the kings and priests worry about the wording of agreements.

"No, another one since then, a new one, and he prefers to be called Mohammad XII. Boabdil is just something we Christians call him, so you had better get used to the right name. It seems that the king's mother slipped back into Granada by herself and rallied her numerous family and other supporters of the king against the usurper, el Zagal. She then called on the king to join her, which he did with a small armed retinue, and there has been fighting in the streets of Granada for several days, with el Zagal's men holding the Alhambra and about half of the city, and Boabdil, I mean the king's people occupying the rest."

"All the better for us, your majesty. As long as Moors are killing Moors, there are fewer of them for us to worry about." Yes, this was almost certainly what they had in mind. While the Moors were busy with their civil war, there must be some stronghold that was known to be undermanned and that might fall to a sudden assault. Perhaps it would be a small port city. Now, that would be ideal! His own outlet for trade and the ability to draw taxes on the merchants while sitting on a veranda overlooking a smooth curve of bay!

"Our point exactly!" Fernando agreed heartily. "And what we need for you to do is to see that this situation continues."

Juan frowned again. "And how would I be able to do that, your majesty?"

Fernando cleared his throat and paused for a moment, the way people do when they have to say something that is not likely to be well-received. "By leading a force of men-at-arms into Granada to support the king in his fight against el-Zagal," he said hurriedly.

Juan's mouth dropped open and stayed that way as he stared dumbly at Fernando, who waited, smiling broadly now, as if having every right to expect a gushing, grateful response for this opportunity. It would be suicide. To take an armed body of Christians into the enemy capital, surrounded by heavily armed Moors and with no hope of help if that jackal Boabdil suddenly decided to switch sides *again*. That was why they were offering this plum to him, of course. He was a nobody. There would be no incentive for the Moors to take him for ransom. No one would pay! And if he should happen to be killed along with all of his men, well, no major harm done. A risk well worth the taking, as far as the crown was concerned.

Fernando cleared his throat again and looked around the room. "You understand that we will need this diversion of el Zagal's forces if our main attack on Malaga in the spring is to succeed. That city, and Velez Malaga with it, are the most heavily fortified towns the Moors have, after Granada itself, and they will send every soldier from every corner of the kingdom before they will submit to the loss of their only major port. Apart from the many Moors we expect you and your men to kill by your own hands, keeping the enemy divided will naturally halve their strength. Once we have taken Malaga, the rest of the kingdom will be like a grapevine whose roots have been cut. We will be able to snap off their remaining cities like dried twigs, one at a time, and complete the reconquest that has been the most holy goal of our entire people or centuries!"

So, apart from sacrificing him on the altar of military convenience, Juan thought, they were going to put him aside in a useless diversionary action while the real conquests were going on elsewhere, with lands and titles and booty all going to others whose conquests the risks he was taking would make possible. What kind of benefit could he hope to get out of that?

"It seems that the audacity of our plan has left my young protégé speechless, your majesty," the Marquis growled, nudging Juan roughly and painfully in the small of his back with an armored elbow.

"Well, yes," Juan stammered. "It just never occurred to me. To fight alongside the Moors?"

"You'll be slaughtering Moors," the Marquis corrected him. "That's all that matters. Who cares who else is on your side? You should remember that El Cid did no less in his time."

"But, . . ." Juan struggled for words. "Would it be safe?" Juan was never much of a student of history, but he did recall something about el Cid dying a rather violent death, covered with glory, of course, but dead nonetheless.

"Running up a scaling ladder while a dozen swarthy devils are doing their level best to crush, stab, and shoot you isn't safe," the Marquis reminded him, "and you never had any trouble taking on those jobs. By comparison, this will be like picking flowers in the garden."

Juan stood mute for another long moment and then finally bowed low. "I am my lord's servant. I am honored by your trust in me."

"Excellent!" Fernando bellowed, swatting Juan forcefully across the shoulders. "I'm sorry to say that time is of some importance, so there will be no opportunity for you to return to Sevilla to visit with your new family, but I expect this business to last no more than a few weeks. One side or the other is bound to prevail in Granada. If it's Boabdil, we'll arrange for someone to come and relieve you after awhile. And if it's el Zagal, well, rest assured that we'll get you back somehow," he mumbled, waving his hand vaguely in the air. "Now," he added stepping close to Juan and placing a fatherly arm across his broad shoulders, Fernando being one of the few men present who was big enough not to have to reach up to do so, "we don't mean for you to fight to the death for these heathens. You do what you can to keep the fires stoked, but if things get too hot, send word to us. We'll give you some carrier pigeons for the job if runners can't get through. And you gather your men and make your way out if you feel the time's right. I don't think that el Zagal will have any problem with your *leaving* the kingdom, and we'll make it quite clear that he'll pay dearly for any aggressive action on his part once you decide to retire. And, if things are going that badly for our Moorish friends, they won't be in much of a position to stop you either."

"I understand perfectly, your majesty," Juan said softly, bowing again.

"Good! Then we won't keep you. I want you to pick out about one hundred men-at-arms, your choice from among the whole of the army, and don't take any nonsense from anyone, from the Marquis here on down," he added, frowning theatrically at the assembled nobles. "And then pick another four hundred infantry equipped with the best arquebuses and crossbows in our stocks. Your job is not to be an army, just the point of the spear. It's up to Boabdil to supply the numbers, but you will be the shock troops that will give him the edge in fighting in the city. Neither side seems likely to want to use heavy artillery in their own house, so you won't have to worry about that, and cavalry won't be of much use either, so select men you know who are good for close-in work."

Juan just nodded and bowed once more in turn to the king, the queen, and the other assembled lords before backing out through the tent flap.

It came as no real surprise to Juan that, despite the king's orders, he had trouble raising the necessary force of good men. Although there was a generous salary promised, with a month's wages in gold in advance, the slender possibility of profiting from any plunder or ransom, where the real money was to be made in war, made the prospect singularly unattractive to most of the veteran fighters, and that was even without considering that the troop would be marching deep into Moorish territory with only the most theoretical plan for extracting themselves should events go against them. Needless to say, no one in the Christian army gave a fig for the word of Boabdil, and they all knew that, even with the best will in the world, Fernando might not be able to get to them out if the plan went sour. And even those who might have been willing, the best of them at any rate, were often discouraged by their own commanders and lords, either out of genuine concern for an old vassal's safety or simply out of a reluctance to lose a valued asset when that commander would not directly benefit from it. This has been true of armies since the dawn of time, commanders assign to "special details" the men they are most willing to spare, no matter how glorious the assignment appears to be.

Juan had his usual band of followers of course, the Basque, Gamal, the Castro brothers, Escudero the Minorcan, and about a score of others, some of whom had been with him for years now, and a few foreign mercenaries as well, an Englishman named Castlebury, and a handful of Germans whom no one could understand but who were very efficient with their matchlocks. Fernando was finally obliged to sweeten the deal for the troops by providing at his own expense nearly new suits of armor for the men-at-arms and cuirasses and greaves for the other troops. Since armor was prohibitively expensive for those without independent sources of income from family lands or who had not been unusually lucky in gathering booty in some previous campaign, this offer finally brought in enough bodies to fill up the unit. Armor for the soldier was like the tools of a craftsman, the means by which he earned his bread and butter, and, in this case, also kept himself alive. Still Juan did not have the luxury of being overly selective about the quality of the men who were to go with him.

The trip to Granada was accomplished without too much difficulty. Juan and his men joined a heavily guarded convoy of supply wagons for the garrison at Alhama, which put them a single hard day's march from the Moorish capital. They set out just before dusk from there and were met by a small troop of Arab horsemen near midnight at a crossroads out on the *vega* only a few miles from the city, and Juan recognized the leader of the group, the tall Moor who had been at court with Boabdil and had even had the nerve to speak to Raquel. Juan had not truly expected a warm welcome from these new allies, and he had no special liking for this Moor in particular himself, but the dark, burning hatred that Juan read in Muhammad's eyes took Juan aback. If these are our *friends*, Juan thought to himself, God deliver us from our enemies. Juan could tell that his men shared his anxiety as they fingered their sword hilts and carried their crossbows or arquebuses at the ready instead of balanced on their shoulders as usual on a route march, and he quietly passed the word to spread out the line of march to allow for more flexibility of maneuver if this all suddenly turned into a massive ambush.

But there was no ambush. Juan rode alongside Muhammad through the warm, sticky night as they approached the massive walls of Granada that loomed before them, bathed in the pale, colorless light of the moon. Juan had heard that the walls measured over six miles in length and were studded with nearly a thousand towers. He did not look forward to being on the wrong side of those walls if this treaty should happen to go bad. Muhammad provided Juan with the information that he would need for his assignment in a dull monotone, staring straight ahead as they rode, avoiding direct eye contact.

"We hold the Albaicin district, the working class area in the lower, western part of the city, and the walls adjoining it," he explained. "El Zagal holds the Alhambra palace and its fortress on the high ground, and the eastern part of the city and its walls. We have fortified key positions along the "border" and thrown up walls where necessary, so our position is relatively secure, but there is still a constant flow of people between the two zones, people living in one area and working in the other, tradespeople, merchants, and the like, so there is ample opportunity for both sides to raid into the other's territory. Fortunately for us, el Zagal is aware of Fernando's plans to attempt to capture Malaga in the near future, and he has dispatched the bulk of his fighting men to the south under Hamet el Zagri to defend the port. Consequently, our numbers are more or less evenly matched within the city, but el Zagal has enjoyed a substantial advantage in trained warriors, while most of our supporters are hastily armed militia. My lord hopes that you and your men will help to even the odds."

Juan just grunted in acknowledgement at appropriate pauses. He wondered if this Moor, who certainly had airs of education and intellectual capability, had figured out that his job was precisely to *even* the odds, not to deliver victory to Boabdil. If the opportunity presented itself, of course, he would not turn away from a chance at a clear victory, but the interests of Juan's sovereigns, the only interests that he cared about, would be best served by an indefinite continuation of the fighting within the enemy capital, not by either side finally subduing the other and uniting the entire kingdom under one ruler again. Juan had no doubts that Boabdil would spit on his treaty with Fernando as he had done in the past just the second he felt secure enough on his throne to do so. And Juan had no intention of helping him achieve that goal.

After they had ridden some way in silence, Juan felt the urge to make some kind of conversation.

"I understand that you were present in Sevilla at the birth of my child."

Now Muhammad did turn to look into Juan's face with a curious expression.

"Not *at* the birth, exactly, sir," he began. "I was paying my respects to the lady your wife when it happened that her time came. I beat as dignified a retreat as I could manage and left the women to deal with the affairs of women. I trust that all went well after that."

"Quite well, although it was a girl," Juan sighed.

"I'm certain that God will grant you everything you deserve, and in the near future as well," he concluded, and Juan did not like the tone of his voice at all as he said it.

They were granted immediate entry through the gates, despite the late hour, and rode on and on through the narrow cobblestone streets in almost pitch blackness. What little moonlight there was was almost completely obscured by the tall houses whose balconies overhang the avenue, nearly touching in some places, and runners with flaming torches led the way, although the darkness gobbled up the light like locusts in a wheat field, and only two tiny glowing points could be discerned bobbing along at the head of the column to provide a general sense of direction. But, even though he could see virtually nothing, Juan gradually got the impression of just how large a city this was. The troop rode on for quite some time in a nearly straight line, only bending to accommodate the irregular street, and Juan knew that they obviously must only be keeping to the half of the city occupied by Boabdil's forces. This implied that the whole place must be at least twice the size of Sevilla, the largest city in Christian Spain at the time. He had the added impression that, if the doors and shutters of the houses along the way were suddenly to burst open and issue forth a torrent of gunfire and arrows, he and his men would die in less time than it would take for their bodies to hit the ground. Juan rode intentionally on Muhammad's left, his own shield on his arm to protect him on that side, and a long dagger concealed up his right sleeve. If there were to be treachery, he would have the best blood of this prancing Moor filling the gutter before he died. Of that, at least, he could be certain.

They finally crossed another anonymous narrow street and turned in through a narrow gate in the opposite wall and found themselves in a large courtyard forming the center of an open square nearly two hundred feet on a side with a three-story building wrapping around all four sides. The ground floor was occupied primarily with stables, and the upper floors had interior wooden balconies that looked down on the courtyard. Lemon trees were spaced around the edges of the little plaza, growing in large stone planters, and a tall fountain gurgled in the center. Lights burned in many of the small windows, while torches lit the courtyard, and the enticing smell of cooking wafted on the night air.

"You will find comfortable quarters here," Muhammad said flatly. "After your long trip, we assume you would like to rest yourself and your men, so the king plans to meet with you later this evening, if that is agreeable."

"We did not come here to rest," Juan growled. "We are at the king's disposal and will present ourselves at his pleasure."

"I know," Muhammad said in a voice just above a whisper. "That was just the polite way of saying that his pleasure is that you should meet with him later this evening." Then he just nodded and turned his horse to canter out through the gateway, followed by the other Moors of his troop.

Juan had noticed that a squad of Moorish spearmen was posted as sentries out in the street, but he detailed several of his men to secure the gate and to stand guard inside. Other well-armed men were sent to points on the rooftops to provide an all-around view of the approaches to the barracks, which were actually an extensive villa located in the heart of the city, occupying an entire block by itself, which provided the defensive advantage of having open, if rather narrow, streets on all sides. Juan conducted his own tour of the place immediately, as there was no telling just how soon his men might have to hole up here and fight off an inexhaustible supply of attackers.

Juan and his men found that the Moors had provided for them adequately, if not lavishly. A large kitchen was staffed with a dozen servants, and there were stacks of flat loaves of Arab bread there, still warm from the oven, and trays full of grilled lamb, along with some fruit and cheese. The men complained about the absence of wine, although Juan was just as happy, as the last thing he needed was for part of his little army to be dozing away drunkenly when their survival might depend on the alertness of each and every man. Juan also noted, however, that there were no large stores of food anywhere in the villa, and only a small cistern of water, so he and his men would be dependent on deliveries from the king every day for their sustenance. Mats had been laid out for sleeping, and the place was clean, so there was no good cause for complaint, yet.

Muhammad called for Juan as expected several hours later, and the two rode silently through the streets, accompanied only by the Basque and the Castro brothers, all wearing full armor, as was Juan, while Muhammad wore a simple white robe with a long staff dangling from a leather strap at his saddle bow. They dismounted at an even larger villa not far away which was surrounded by an actual army camp, with dozens of tents pitched in the streets, the entire affair protected by low breastworks thrown up at every intersection and guarded by scores of soldiers and even a few pieces of light artillery.

Abu had chosen to receive his new protectors in the large hall that he had set up as a throne room. There was a raised dais at one end of the hall, and all of the normal furniture had been removed to oblige visitors to hike the length of the room in order to address his majesty, who sat upon a tall chair that had been hastily covered with gilt for the occasion.

Juan and his men approached the dais while Muhammad hung back by the door of the hall, but, before Juan could reach the throne, Hafez, dressed in an elegant white silk tunic and pantaloons with a gold sash and a turban of deep blue, stepped in front of him with an ingratiating smile on his face, the sort of a smile one would use when addressing a dog, but one that just might bite.

"Please receive the most hospitable welcome of my sovereign, King Mohammed, the twelfth of that line," Hafez announced grandly, spreading his arms and bowing, but still effectively blocking the way to the throne. "And please pass along my lord's most sincere gratitude to your great king, his brother Fernando and the most gracious lady, the queen Isabel. We hope that this passage of arms will help cement the friendship of our two peoples for many years to come."

Juan listened impatiently to the speech and frowned. "It is my honor to serve my lord, and you will find that my men and I will bring fear into the hearts of the enemies of your king and mine, as you already have good reason to know."

Hafez jerked his head up and shot Juan a hot glance, but then only smiled pleasantly. Abu sat, slumping slightly in a bored way, upon the throne, and gazed blankly toward the tall windows that ran down one side of the hall.

Juan and Hafez stood there, face-to-face, for a long moment, while the Basque and the Castro brothers cast sidelong glances at each other. Finally, Hafez gave Juan a particularly greasy smile.

"I'm sure that you will be eager to get the lay of the land and begin your military activities without delay, so we will not keep you any longer."

"I thought that I was to be presented to the king," Juan snorted.

"You just were, sir," Hafez responded. "Now, you must understand that his majesty has a great many important matters of state to attend to, and it would be just as well if you were not seen about the palace any more than absolutely necessary for the performance of our duties. I'm sure that you understand."

"I suppose that I should have taken the opportunity for a chat with *his majesty* when we were dragging him out of his citadel at Loja, trying to prevent his own people from tearing him to pieces," Juan grumbled, jerking his head toward the door, indicating to his men that he was the one terminating the interview.

Hafez's hand moved to his belt, close to the hilt of a jeweled dagger, and Juan half turned in his direction.
"Go ahead, puppy," he growled in a voice so low as to be inaudible to anyone else. "Your head will be rolling across the floor before the blade even clears its sheath."

"You'd never leave this room alive," Hafez hissed.

"That wouldn't put your head back on, now would it?" Juan said, pointedly turning his back on the throne and marching toward the door with his men. Hafez withdrew his hand and bowed deeply again, but keeping his eyes on Juan's retreating back.

Later that day, Juan's troop got its first taste of Moorish street politics. He left one hundred men at the villa, barricaded in to provide at least one place of refuge if the rest of the unit had to retreat on its own. Muhammad took Juan up the minaret of a small mosque and pointed out an open market that occupied the border between the two sections of the city.

"We have information that, in about an hour, a strong force of el Zagal's men will infiltrate that market, which we have kept open to allow some trade between the two zones. They plan to overcome the guards at the street intersections on our side of the market and attempt to penetrate our defenses. More troops will push through them with the idea of trying to reach the royal residence and assassinate the king, thus putting a sudden end to the civil war once and for all."

"That shouldn't be too hard to prevent," Juan said. "All you have to do is block off the streets here back from the market. Their force will be bottled up with no way through, and they'll only take heavy losses if they try."

"We were hoping for something a little more dramatic for your debut in the battle," Muhammad went on. "Instead of bottling them up, we want to let them through into an ambush set up by your men. It is our hope that, if we can inflict some really serious losses on them, including possibly the death or capture of some senior officers of el Zagal's army, it might serve to drive the usurper from Granada completely. Since he still has somewhere to go, to Malaga, he is only holding on here for reasons of prestige, and it might not take all that much convincing to get him to move on."

"As opposed to your king, who has nowhere else to go," Juan added.

"Precisely," Muhammad replied without emotion.

Juan nodded and marched down the winding staircase to confer with his officers before returning to the tower to watch the opening of the battle, his big dog Asco plodding along happily at his side.

Just as Muhammad had predicted, just as the vendors and shoppers were beginning to return to the marketplace following their afternoon siesta, an unusual number of fit young men wearing bulky robes that must have been extremely uncomfortable in the warm sunshine of late summer, began to drift in from the eastern part of the city. They looked without interest at the wares out on display, and none of them made any purchases as they moved toward the west, first singly, then in groups of twos and threes. None of them approached the guards along the western perimeter, Abu's men armed with short spears and small round shields, but they began to tuck themselves into out-of-the-way corners behind packing crates and piles of grain sacks, inching closer and closer without appearing to do so. Juan watched as the merchants stared curiously at these disinterested customers and then suddenly, as if all coming to the same conclusion at once, they began to discreetly gather up their produce and other merchandise, to break off haggling with an offended buyer, and to scuttle away, one by one, through the various alleyways leading off the plaza.

With a shout, a dozen of the intruders hurled aside their cloaks to reveal shirts of chain mail or breastplates and swords at their belts. Each of them wore a bright red cloth around their right arm as a sign to others. They fell on the surprised guards with a fury, cutting several of them down at the first onslaught, and forcing the rest into a hasty retreat while their compatriots came rushing up from where they had hidden themselves about the market. It occurred to Juan that this Moorish king he was supporting was a particularly cold fish not to have warned his own men on the gates of the impending attack, but then they might have either spooked too early and given away their advance knowledge or they might have put up too good of a fight and not let the enemy into the trap. He would have to keep that in mind for the future.

A trumpet sounded from a rooftop nearby, and a strong column of heavily armed enemy infantry now charged openly into the market from the east, shoving aside the remaining merchants and their stalls indiscriminately as they hurried toward where their men had already seized control of the barricades that had barred entry into the western part of the city.

Juan stuck two fingers into the corners of his mouth and let out a piercing whistle while he raced down the stairs of the minaret, Asco right on his heels. He quickly joined a body of about fifty men armed with arquebus or crossbow that were formed up across a narrow side street, about twenty yards off an intersection with the main street leading back to the market. Behind these troops Juan took his position, in full armor and helmet, along with his regular followers, likewise armed, the Basque, the Castros, and Gamal, while Escudero took charge of the missile troops.

They could see men rushing past the mouth of their little street, first a few unfortunate shoppers or vendors, then soldiers wearing the green cloaks of Boabdil's guard force. They came in a compact body of men with red arm bands, swords raised high, howling like demons. The front rank of arquebusiers was kneeling, stretching across the narrow street from house to house, and they fired a solid volley that literally blew the intersection clear of the enemy while a blue cloud of smoke partially obscured the scene. They then pulled back through the next rank, this one of crossbowmen, and raced back to take up another position about twenty yards farther on. Juan knew that the attackers would have no choice but to turn down his street, as the guards they had been chasing were routed and no longer a threat, while the enemy could not afford to leave this new force in existence on their flank as they advanced.

There was now a moment of silence, broken only by the groan of a wounded man, then a deep rattling sound that echoed off the houses and made the ground tremble.

Suddenly a heavy two-wheeled cart loaded with hay bales appeared in the intersection and turned to head up Juan's street. The solid wooden wheels crunched over the bodies lying on the cobblestones, and one of the men screamed, not having had the sense to die earlier. A large knot of soldiers clustered behind the cart, pushing it quickly, while others began to fire wild shots with matchlocks from around the corners.

Juan barked out an order and a couple of men ran forward with a long wooden beam which they tossed into the roadway in front of the cart while the crossbowmen picked off any Moor brave or unlucky enough to show himself. The wheels of the cart jammed against the beam, and ground to a halt, spilling bales into the street. The enemy charged around and over the obstacle, some falling under the shower of arrows, but others racing forward, screaming and swinging their swords.

Juan and his men-at-arms stepped forward to meet them, allowing themselves ample room to use their weapons while the Moors were bunched too close together. Juan whirled his long, basket-handled sword with his right hand while using his left for a foot-long dagger with three blades, like a pitchfork, and a small round target strapped to his left forearm. He used the dagger to snag the blade of one attacker and pull it aside, allowing him to hack down through the man's neck. With a back stroke he casually lopped off the leg of another man who was trying to move past him on his right, then spun and impaled a third who was dueling with one of the Castros on the other side.

The Spaniards had been gradually falling back, taking care to keep an even line to cover each other's flanks, and now they had reached the new line of arquebusiers. They stepped between the gunners and allowed them another devastating volley, each gun loaded with charges of jagged metal, nails, or small lead balls, which swept the street clean again back to the cart.

Juan heard a voice from behind him and glanced to see Muhammad, also well-armored and carrying a bloodied sword.

"All of the other streets have been blocked off," he shouted into Juan's ear over the noise of the battle. "There is still a large force on this avenue, and they've advanced farther here than anywhere, so they'll be coming again."

Juan just nodded and pointed to a man standing behind the line with a brass horn. The main lifted the horn to his lips and, at the high, wailing note, Juan and his men turned as one and ran back up the street to where it opened out into a small plaza, about two hundred feet long and a third as wide, with a stone fountain located near the far end. They ran to the fountain and formed their line again on either side of it, the arquebusiers and crossbowmen frantically reloading their weapons. Others quickly dragged out heavy shields that had been fitted with wood frames to allow them to stand on their own and formed a waist-high barrier across the front of the line as the sound of kettle drums and clanking armor echoed from down the narrow street whence they had come.

A column of Moorish infantry now began to issue from the street into the plaza, the men jogging at double time and spreading out quickly to the right and left behind a solid wall of tall shields of wood and leather studded with iron. They wore more armor than was common for the Moors, all with breastplates and helmets, and all wore the dark blue cloaks often used by el Zagal's men. The Spaniards watched them deploy, the men with matchlocks kneeling and resting the heavy barrels on the top of the shield wall, the crossbowmen standing behind them, tracking their targets, while Juan, Muhammad, and the men-at-arms stood spaced along the line in the rear. The Moors now formed a solid phalanx stretching all the way across the plaza and four or five men deep, and both sides stared at each other for a long moment as the final squads of attackers took their positions.

The wailing cry of a *mullah* broke the stillness calling, "*Allah u akhbar!*" and the Moorish infantry roared and surged forward like a wave racing toward the beach.

The Spaniards stood silently, fingers tensed on triggers or flexing on sword hilts as the distance closed, fifty yards, then forty, then thirty. Juan had climbed up on the base of the fountain for a better view of the action, his sword raised above his head, waiting. At twenty yards, he brought his sword down in a slashing motion and bellowed, "Shoot!"

A sheet of flame swept out from the row of arquebus muzzles, and a cloud of crossbow quarrels tore into the packed mass of attackers, but not from among Juan's troop, who held their fire calmly. The volley came from the windows, upstairs and down, and from the rooftops of the houses around three sides of the plaza, cutting down the Moors from every direction, tumbling men into a tangle of weapons, limbs, and blood, their wall of shields buckling and falling to pieces.

"Now! Shoot!" Juan roared out again, and this time his own men fired, now with clear shots into the struggling crowd just in front of them. A pair of light cannon mounted in an upper window of a house just behind Juan blasted the survivors with a shower of grapeshot. There were a few scattered answering shots from the Moorish ranks, but men could already be seen turning and running, or hobbling, back down the street away from the carnage.

"At them!" Juan called out, and he led his own men-at-arms, leaping over the shield wall agilely as if their full suits of armor had been made of feathers, while others poured out of the doorways all around the plaza, hacking their way into the confused enemy ranks like reapers in a wheat field.

Even those enemy soldiers who had not been mown down by the gunfire and arrows were now shrieking in terror, fighting with each other for passage back down the narrow street, not thinking to turn and face their pursuers and thus allowing the Spaniards to butcher everyone they could catch with little or no resistance. A trumpet somewhere in the distance was calling the retreat, but there was no need for orders. Those who could were already running as fast as their legs would carry them, and those who could not, were already dead.

Juan had been watching the performance of the Moor, Muhammad, out of a corner of his eye. From their first contact years ago, Juan had assumed that he was some sort of court intellectual, a bookish, foppish parasite, not unlike the buffoon who had spoken so unbearably to Juan during the "audience" with the king upon his arrival in Granada. But now he had seen this Muhammad leap over the shield wall with the best of his own men-at-arms, hacking his way through the ranks of his co-religionists with great abandon and considerable skill. Juan was particularly impressed with the way Muhammad used his small round shield, equipped with a short spike at its center, as an offensive weapon, deflecting an opponents blow with his sword and then smashing the shield into his enemy's face with tremendous force. He was also not reluctant to use his feet to sweep an opponent off balance or his helmet to butt against an unprotected chin or nose. It was Juan's philosophy, inasmuch as he had any philosophy at all, that a successful warrior must use every part of his body in a fight and not be limited to the traditional weapons or tactics. Yes, for all the Moor's smooth words and haughty vocabulary, he was a warrior at heart. Juan could respect that.

But what prompted Juan to observe the Moor's activities was not an appreciation of his skill in battle, it was the unbelievably hostile glares that he had detected from the Moor when he thought Juan was not looking. Now, Juan did not expect any undue affection from the man, and he himself thought the Moor would look particularly well spitted on the end of a lance, but they were all professionals, and professionals could hardly afford to let their emotions dictate their behavior. Juan fought because that was his job. It happened that, as a devout Catholic and believer in the righteousness of the cause of the reconquest of Spain from the infidel, his duty happened to coincide with his beliefs and he gladly went off to battle with the Moslems. But he had also fought with equal courage and enthusiasm against the Christian French and Portuguese and even fellow Spaniards at one time or another in his career. Now his duty called on him to fight alongside Moors, although his primary mission was to kill other Moors, and Muhammad's lord had ordered him to work with the Christians, something he might find distasteful, but a man of his intellect must surely see the benefit to his own lord from this alliance.

In any event, Juan could not fathom why these black looks should only be directed at him, and apparently not at any of the other Christian soldiers, unless it was just his own imagination. This entire operation was hardly Juan's doing, even if he was the commander of the Christian forces. Juan did recall vaguely unpleasant words between them back in Cordoba when the Moor seemed to be monopolizing Raquel's attention, but Juan had been the one who had rightly felt slighted, so there was nothing for this Moor to be upset about. And Juan had ultimately won that little contest as Raquel was now his wife. Could that be it? Could this Moor have had some kind of designs on Raquel? But that was too absurd even to contemplate, and it gave Juan a little jolt of excitement to think of what he had done with Raquel, *to* Raquel, when he had finally found the key to overcoming her resistance. He wondered how this Moor, if he really did have some bizarre feeling for her, would appreciate how Juan could just *take* her whenever and in whatever way he liked, the more humiliating the better. But, for the moment, Juan decided it to be best to put all of these thoughts from his mind, although he made a mental note to make sure that the Basque watched his back in fights like these lest Muhammad decide to take the opportunity to see that a stray arrow flew in Juan's direction. An accident of that kind would be all too easy to arrange in the heat of battle, and there was no harm in taking precautions.

The Spaniards were granted the modest privilege of rooting among the dead for items of value in the gathering darkness of early evening, and there was a small harvest of gold rings, a few silver coins, and some decent armor and weapons that were shared out among the men, although Juan found it a little humiliating the way Muhammad stood by and watched the Christians scavenging, as if the same didn't occur on every battlefield. Juan was, however, pleased to note that Muhammad politely ignored the killing of a Moorish civilian by one of the men-at-arms when the former sneaked out from a side street with the evident aim of taking part in the spoils. But the handful of prisoners that were taken, most of them badly wounded, were rounded up by a detachment of Boabdil's soldiers and taken away to the royal residence, either for interrogation and torture, death, ransom, or possibly to attempt to convince them to join the young king's cause. That was beyond Juan's caring. He knew that there would be no ransom money for him or his men, and that was the extent of his interest in the matter.

The next day the insufferable sycophant Hafez appeared briefly at the Spanish barracks to convey his master's "undying" gratitude to his Christian allies and his sense of awe at their recent feat of arms. Juan suspected that this large chunk of bait would likely conceal a hook, and he was not disappointed, since Hafez went on to explain, as if in passing, that it had occurred to the king that now might be a convenient time for his forces to turn to the offensive, to take advantage of the disorder in the enemy's ranks caused by their heavy losses, and that it would be his pleasure to grant the honor of leading the assault to Juan and his valiant troops. Juan pointed out that he was his majesty's servant to command, and with his chore accomplished, Hafez swished out of the room in search of more agreeable company.

Juan spent the rest of that day and most of the night closeted with the Basque, several of his other trusted subordinates, and the Moor Muhammad, poring over detailed sketch maps of the city, planning an assault. Since no goal had been set for them, Juan intentionally chose the limited objective of a large house that occupied a high point only some two hundred yards from the existing lines. With this as a vantage point, Juan calculated that he would be able to plan out a route of advance for a later date which might enable his forces to attempt a surprise assault up the steep sides of the hill upon which the Alhambra itself stood. He was very much aware of the advantage to the defense that the closely-packed stone and brick houses provided, turning every narrow lane into a potential death trap, just as his own men had been able to create the previous day for the enemy. He was also well aware that Boabdil would lose no sleep over the slaughter of his band of foreign mercenaries. They were assets to be expended, and if any of them survived to be repatriated to Castile, then Boabdil would likely consider that they had not been used to the full extent possible. Juan was pleasantly surprised that Muhammad shared his reservations about offensive action, and he actually seemed to go to some effort to minimize Spanish casualties, although he explained this in terms of wanting to further his sovereign's goals.

On the day of the attack, Muhammad was able to obtain several small wooden trebuchets which they used to hurl incendiary missiles composed of bundles of oil-soaked rags bound around large rocks into a cluster of houses just upwind of their planned point of attack. Besides distracting the defenders and misleading them as to the point of the real attack, the subsequent fires created a thick wall of smoke that drifted down and allowed Juan's assault teams to rush across the intervening street unseen and gain a foothold in the houses beyond this no-man's-land from the blinded and confused defenders. Beyond that, however, progress was slow, and every foot of ground gained cost Spanish blood.

Juan's men learned to advance by tearing holes in the interior walls of adjacent houses, but, when the houses ran out and a street had to be crossed, they were met with withering fire from guns and crossbows. Juan's solution to the problem would have been to bring up a few light cannon to blast their way from block to block with direct fire, but this was not always possible. It seemed that Boabdil had precious little artillery of any sort, and he specifically prohibited the systematic destruction of *his* city, even if that were the only means of securing it for himself. Juan was finally obliged to break off the attack, having managed to gain perhaps a hundred yards of territory but falling far short of taking the target house or any other position of strategic value in exchange for nearly one fifth of his force killed or wounded. Juan was again surprised when Muhammad and a team of Moorish physicians visited the barracks and attended to the Christian wounded in a most efficient way, saving the lives of a number of men that Juan had given up for lost.

Despite a shower of missives from Boabdil demanding a renewed offensive, Juan insisted on an extended period of rest and refitting for his troops. He noticed that the messages always came through the unctuous Hafez, not through the more sober and reasonable Muhammad, whom Juan had previously assumed was some kind of senior counselor to the king,. The messages ran the gamut from wheedling and pleading to practical ones offering booty and great rewards, to authoritative demands implying terrible penalties for failure to comply, but Juan ignored them all, and it appeared that Boabdil had no desire to open a second front of his civil war within his own lines to force the Spaniards out of their barracks.

The men were more than content to sit idly for awhile. The food free and ample, the duty light, consisting of only mounting their own guard and seeing to the maintenance of their weapons, something most of the men were accustomed to doing whether they were paid for it or not. Hafez had even managed to make himself useful by arranging for some female company for the troops, mostly drawn from among Christian women, slaves or free, of whom there was a surprisingly large number living in Granada. These generally welcomed the business of these lonely, well-paid Spaniards who were able to indulge their tastes with gold and silver coins, not the debased copper *miravedis* that had driven most of the good currency out of the market in what remained of the Moorish kingdom, as anyone with means did their best to hoard their movable valuables against the day when the avenging armies of the Christians came sweeping in to erase what remained of al-Andalus from the face of the earth. That was all well and good in itself, as it kept the men occupied and content, but it did nothing to satisfy Juan's particular wants and needs. He had to rely on the Basque to take care of him in that regard.

And take care of his commander the Basque did. It seemed that a number of prominent Moorish families whose loyalties were known to lie with el Zagal had been caught by the new outbreak of civil violence on the wrong side of the partition line within the city. Boabdil had seen to it that these unfortunates had been rounded up, a few of the more affluent having been ransomed across the lines for considerable sums, and those of the lower classes simply sold into slavery, but there were a number of families whose status prevented their simple sale and yet who did not have the resources to buy their freedom. These were being held as bargaining chips, for possible use in future prisoner exchanges, and generally serving their time in captivity in the role of house servants to Boabdil's key advisors and military officers. The Basque had ferreted out this information and had been able to locate a particular fourteen-year-old girl, the youngest daughter of a modestly successful merchant, and had purchased her "contract" for a substantial purse of gold.

"She's a virgin, sir," the Basque explained as he escorted Juan to his apartment, "or so I'm told. I know that you wouldn't be interested in the common sluts they've provided for the men, and it wouldn't do to, well," he hunted for words, "have something happen to a local Moslem girl, even if she were a whore. This one's unimportant enough that no one's going to be in a position to ask any questions or raise any complaints, and yet her former station in life should give her the kind of attitude that would make things, well, interesting for you."

Juan paused in front of his door and laid a hand on the Basque's shoulder. "My own mother should have taken such good care of me," and the two men laughed. "Of course, I'm not sure that my mother would have gone to this kind of trouble to see to my needs. It takes a man to realize what a man has to do every now and then, especially when he's deprived of the services of his wife for a long stretch of time."

The Basque just nodded and pushed open the door, and Juan entered alone. As much as Juan appreciated the Basque's efforts, he could not help a nagging worry about the simple fact that the Basque knew about the darker side of his life. The Basque was more loyal than any man he had ever served with, and loyal to Juan personally, as no one else had ever been, even Gamal or the Castros, but there could always come a day when it would be in the man's interest to make use of this damaging knowledge. Juan just shook his head and hoped that day never came.

The girl was seated in a corner, busily polishing Juan's breastplate, and, when he entered, she dropped her rag and knelt, touching her head to the floor. Juan smiled cruelly. The Basque must have explained to her that she would be a simple domestic servant to a great Spanish lord, nothing more or less, which would make it all the more perfect. He could feel himself swelling painfully against the tight laces of his britches even as he thought about it. Juan honestly wondered whether the Basque might not harbor some of his own tendencies toward women. How else could he anticipate his commander's wishes so precisely?

The girl welcomed Juan to his home in passable Spanish and expressed the hope that Allah had been kind to him that day. Juan did not reply but merely gestured that he wanted the breastplate stored in the wardrobe.

The girl was tall and willowy, with fair skin, for a Moor, and rich dark hair that hung down her back in a thick rope that reached well below her waist. She moved with the grace of a dancer, and she stifled a shriek when Juan suddenly came up behind her, scooping up the hem of her caftan to reveal her lithe, well-muscled thighs and grasping her firmly around the waist.

"Now we'll have some *real* service," he growled in her ear and bit her neck viciously, drawing blood.

She pleaded with Juan to stop, trying to explain with a voice choked with terror that she was only there to clean and mend, offering to obtain *another* girl, one that could perform the way the lord desired, suggesting that her father would be glad to pay the price himself, that she would pay it with her little jewelry, anything, if he would only stop. But Juan's hands roamed freely under her robe, kneading her small, firm breasts and trying to force their way between her clenched thighs as he chuckled evilly, licking at her ear.

Juan spun her around to the bed, pinning her upper body to the mattress effortlessly with one thick forearm as he knelt on the floor and using his free hand, first to tear away her undergarments, then to pull down his own breeches. All the while she kept on sobbing and pleading, and Juan only hoped that she wouldn't get so tired or dispirited that she would stop. Surrender had never appealed to him quite so much as the conquest, whether on the battlefield or in the bedroom, and when she appeared to be on the verge of accepting her fate, uttering only a pained gasp with each new thrust, Juan began to twist her arm viciously behind her back until she started wailing again. He glanced toward the window where the last rays of sunlight were still filtering through. It looked like it would be a long and pleasurable night.

Muhammad vaguely recognized the old man who stood in his doorway, but he could not quite place the face. From his dress he was obviously Jewish and well-to-do, possibly someone from his days at the *souq*, a merchant looking for some leverage with the palace perhaps. Muhammad was back in his old home in the Albaicin, preferring it to the stifling atmosphere of the court, and his absence was not disputed, since room in the temporary royal residence was already very hard to come by. In fact, with so many refugees flooding into the city to escape Christian raids, even despite the on-going civil war within the walls, it had been only through his lifelong relationship to the local watchman that Muhammad had managed to keep squatters from seizing this place as well, and he had turned down impressive offers of rent from well-heeled refugees on several occasions.

"I am Ysaque Perdoniel," the old man said, waiting for some kind of reaction, then adding, "a relative of the lady Raquel."

Muhammad threw up his hands in recognition. He had met the old man on occasion in the old days the palace, where he had functioned as an interpreter due to his fluency in Spanish and a variety of Arab dialects as well as Greek and Latin, and he remembered that Raquel had mentioned him once or twice, but it had never occurred to him to seek the man out, for fear that this might somehow place Raquel in jeopardy. Muhammad stepped aside and held the door open to the patio where he had been sitting at a small desk working on some official letters.

Ysaque looked around before seating himself on the cushions Yusef quickly brought out. "Yes, this looks like the home of an intellectual," he said in measured tones. "Simple without being austere, quiet without being isolated. She told me that you were an intellectual."

"You've had some communication from the Lady Raquel," Muhammad blurted out, not waiting for the obligatory small talk of a proper Arab conversation. "I trust that she is well," he added hastily.

"Quite well," Ysaque replied, his smile wrinkling his face to the look of the bark of a very old tree. He reached into the sleeve of his robe and withdrew a carefully folded piece of velum, handing it to Muhammad. "I understand that she communicates with her husband through the royal mails," he added, "but she seemed to want both to ensure that this message reached its destination and that the fact of the correspondence be kept discreet. We Jews are used to such tendencies to avoid official attention, and this has come to me through a merchant friend with whom I would readily trust my life."

Muhammad broke the wax seal, unmarked by any signet ring, and read the note greedily. It was not signed, nor did it bear his name. The text itself did not reveal any great meaning either, except that, to Muhammad, the apparent rambling about collecting rare flowers in the hills spoke volumes to him about how their hours and days together still filled her thoughts, and he understood that the healing properties of the plants she mentioned referred to how their connection was a salve for her soul. That was just what he needed, and all that he needed, for now.

"Thank you for bringing this," Muhammad said, carefully refolding the note and tucking it into the pouch at his belt. "Would it be possible to send a reply by the same means?"

Ysaque nodded slowly. "If you had a message of sufficient importance, although I would suggest that you two are playing a dangerous game, a member of the Moorish court and one of that of the Most Catholic Kings exchanging secret missives, but there are so many dangerous games afoot nowadays, that one more hardly seems to matter. If this is of value to my dear Raquel, then anything that I can do in my humble way to ease her road will be done with great pleasure."

The two men sat there in the little courtyard and shared a cup of strong coffee and talked through the afternoon of philosophy, of Aristotle and Plutarch, of Marcus Aurelius and Maimonedes, ignoring the occasional thud of cannon fire and clatter of armor that told of skirmishes a few hundred yards and many worlds away.

As they talked, a small scraping sound came from one of the upstairs rooms. Ysaque looked up, cocking his head.

"You have servants here?" he asked. "I had assumed that you did not, since you answered the door yourself."

"I have one," Muhammad replied, "but he is out running an errand. That must have been my daughter, Miriam."

Ysaque frowned. "I gathered from Raquel's comments that you were, I mean I rather understood that you were not married."

"My wife died some years ago, of the plague."

"I am so sorry, sir," Ysaque said, bowing. "It must be difficult for you raising your daughter alone."

"Oh, my daughter died just before my wife. It was a terrible plague."

Ysaque's frown deepened. "But didn't you just say. . . ?"

Muhammad smiled patiently. "I imagine that you will take me for a madman, but I believe that my daughter still inhabits this house. I sometimes sense my wife's presence as well, but only rarely. It is my little Miriam whom I *know* to be here, watching me, keeping me company. She is very mischievous, hiding things from me and then putting them back just where they had been, tapping me on the shoulder when I'm working, laughing in some far corner of the house, but never being there when I go to look."

Ysaque shrugged his shoulders and smiled sadly. "I have heard of worse forms of madness."

Muhammad nodded. "It is my opinion that, if this little bit of insanity allows me to remain sane and functioning in all other areas, well, it's a small price to pay. You see, I don't have to deal with the loss of my daughter, because I haven't really lost her at all, although it would have been nice to have her here in the flesh, to watch her grow and learn, but Allah knows best. He has given me this little gift to ease my pain, and I am eternally grateful for it."

Ysaque smiled, raising his cup of coffee toward the corner of the house from which the sound had come. "I know just what you mean, my friend."

Book Five

1487

GRANADA

Chapter One

Granada

The fighting in the city continued in a desultory fashion through the fall and winter and into the early spring of the next year with neither side being able to obtain any lasting advantage over the other. It was not until word of a vast new Christian army gathering at Cordoba for an advance on Velez Malaga that significant movement could be detected in the enemy camp. As important as occupation of the Alhambra and much of the capital was for el Zagal's position as pretender to the throne, he apparently realized that the loss of Malaga, the Moorish kingdom's last remaining major port, would spell the death knell of his regime and that the campaign for Velez Malaga was a first step in that direction. It would be theoretically possible for him to hang onto a rump kingdom based along the coast, even if he had to sacrifice Granada temporarily, and a sudden change in the fortunes of the Spanish, such as a new war with France, another civil war, and/or the death of one or both of the monarchs, could distract them long enough to

511

enable el Zagal to regain any lost ground in al-Andalus. The old fighter thus began to send columns of his best troops south, thinning his defenses throughout the city and even abandoning some salient positions that had proven difficult for him to hold. The transfer of el Zagal's troops was not apparent immediately, and the militia with which el Zagal replaced his veteran forces in the front lines did a creditable job of holding off the opposing forces for some weeks, but then they finally began to crack, and Juan's infantry began to capture important local objectives with relatively light losses, and the pace of their progress became increasingly rapid.

Muhammad sat idly in the conference room of the royal residence while Abu's military commanders and courtiers plied the king with differing advice on his best course of action at this time. Some, led by the ever-present Fatima, preferred using all of their existing forces to support the Spanish mercenaries in a final drive on the Alhambra to take advantage of el Zagal's absence. Others commented that el Zagal's decision to take the field against the Christians, abandoning his strong defensive position in Granada, had made him immensely popular with many of the people, and it would make Abu look all the more like a traitor to launch an attack now while he was off fighting the infidel invaders. Muhammad listened but made no effort to join in the debate, preferring to stare out the double-arched windows at the distant silhouette of the Alhambra, gleaming in dark gold against the light of the rising sun. Suddenly, however, he noticed that the buzz of conversation had stopped, and he turned to find Abu, Fatima, Hafez, and all the others staring at him.

"And what does my learned secretary have to say on this matter?" Abu asked in an airy tone, as if they'd been discussing the menu for a dinner rather than the fate of his kingdom.

Muhammad sighed and slowly rose from his chair, bowing stiffly. "Our intelligence is that Fernando is moving on Velez Malaga with a force of over 20,000 horse and 50,000 foot, by far the largest army he has ever put into the field, while the combined Castilian and Aragonese fleets under the Count of Trevento have completely sealed off the coast and all the waters between here and North Africa. El Zagal has taken with him perhaps a thousand cavalry and 20,000 infantry, and he will probably gather more en route to the south, but there is no chance that he will be able defeat the Christian army, even with the support of the troops Hamed el Zagri has in and around Malaga.

"What concerns me a little," Muhammad went on, striding closer to the group and looking into Fatima's eyes, while she glared back at him in defiance, "is that I have heard a rumor that a messenger arrived during he night from el Zagal with the purpose of proposing a truce between us and offering for our forces to join his in a combined attack on the Christians. I have not heard your majesty comment on that possibility, any more than I have been officially consulted about the visit."

"What messenger?" Abu asked, and he followed Muhammad's gaze to his mother's face.

Fatima was unveiled, as was her custom when in council, and her airy silk robes did more to enhance than to conceal the delicious curves of her body. She was someone who knew very well how the sight of a beautiful woman disconcerted men, particularly Moslem men who were unused to seeing so much as a patch of female skin, and she used this power blatantly.

"I understand that he was killed attempting to cross the lines," Fatima said with a shrug, "which makes one wonder how the *katib* knew of the nature of his mission. It is of no matter in any case. We have a treaty with Fernando and Isabel. It would be foolish to break that treaty simply in order to secure the throne for el Zagal, for he would certainly be the one to emerge the hero in the event of a victory, not you, my son. We would, of course immediately lose any support we are now getting from the Christians, support we desperately need, in addition to earning their undying wrath so that when they come back with an even larger army, next year or the year after, it would be our heads they would be after, not el Zagal's. We have turned on them before, in their eyes, and it would be impossible for them ever to trust us again, should this massive horde of theirs prevail, despite our help for el Zagal. There would never be another agreement with the Christians short of total surrender."

"I had heard that the messenger had made it as far as this very building, even to have met with officials of this court," Muhammad cut in, "although I do believe that there was some sort of accident that ultimately deprived him of his life."

Abu frowned at his mother for a moment, and his eyes narrowed, but then he shrugged in his turn. "It is of no matter. My mother is quite right. We could only add a few thousand men to el Zagal's forces, certainly not enough to overcome this vast swarm of infidels, so there's no point in even considering such an offer. But given the facts of the case as they stand, *muhtasib*, what should be do now?"

"Nothing, my lord," Muhammad replied, noting his implied demotion back to supervisor of the marketplace. He only wished that the king would make that assignment permanent and leave him to his old life.

"Nothing? All of your years of study, all of your analysis of history and the products of your famous network of spies, and that is the best advice you can give me? Nothing?" Abu cackled in a way designed to make his courtiers join in the laughter, the way a group of trained dogs will bark on command.

"For the moment, sire, that is precisely what I advise you to do." Muhammad spread his arms wide, allowing the long sleeves of his robe to hang down like the wings of an angel. "The queen your mother is quite right to believe that el Zagal will be beaten by the Christians and that there is little we could hope to do to alter that outcome. It is also true that el Zagal's sortie has greatly enhanced his popularity with many of our people, our *own* people, my lord, and a serious offensive against his holdings at this time would only disgrace us in their eyes. But, if we wait for him to lose on his own, there will be little harm in it for us. We are, after all, engaged in a civil war against him, and most people do not expect us to aid him, even in a fight against the infidels. When his army is defeated, and the wounded start coming home, or letters to the newly made widows start to arrive, more and more people will begin to see that to follow el Zagal means only continued warfare and endless deaths, while our way, that of conciliation with the Spaniards, has at least the promise of peace and some kind of survival for most of our people. The way will then be open for us to take Granada, not by storm, but through negotiation with el Zagal's lieutenants, before he can return from Malaga, and he will be faced with a double defeat that will, in all likelihood, convince him to surrender the throne once and for all."

Abu pursed his lips and thought for a moment. "That makes a certain amount of sense."

"I would recommend that your highness do something immediately, however," Muhammad added.

"And what might that be?"

"Send back the Spanish troops to Fernando. We will have no more need of them now that el Zagal's strength has been diverted from here, and if you agree to forego an immediate assault on the Alhambra, we will have no real use for them. Our current position in Granada is not threatened, and, if we are not going to attack, our own forces are more than adequate for protection of our territory. It is, of course, no secret that they have been here, fighting for you against our fellow Moslems, and that has and will hurt your image for some time, I'm afraid, but the memory of the crowd is notoriously short. As long as they are not present with us when you do take over the citadel and the throne, then it will be that much harder for your enemies to claim that it was the Spanish who installed you in power."

"I rather hate to do that," Abu argued. "After all, Fernando gave them to me, and as long as any of them are alive, you could say that we haven't quite gotten everything out of them that we might."

Muhammad had considered this possibility almost every moment since he first realized that Juan would be leading the Spanish contingent supporting Abu. Whatever the cultural and political obstacles to Muhammad and Raquel ever coming together as they wished, if Juan were dead, at least Muhammad would no longer have to worry about the abuse he might visit upon her. Raquel had assured him that she had a plan in hand to deal with her beastly husband, and Muhammad had learned to place some faith in her judgement. However, he could not be entirely certain that she had not made such statements merely to ease his mind and that she would not simply be subject to beatings, violation, and worse if this animal ever got her back within his grasp. Still, Muhammad had to consider his role as an advisor to his king, and the return of the Spanish troops to their homeland was a sensible and important step that Abu must consider. There was always the chance, of course, that Juan would still manage to catch an arrow or a bullet before he could leave the city, that he would succumb to some disease on the way home, or that he would simply go on to another campaign and not be in a position to bother Raquel at all, which was by far the most likely outcome.

"Exactly, your majesty," Hafez chimed in. "Rather than give up the Spaniards, we should use them up. Even if we don't storm the Alhambra itself, we can use them to spearhead attacks on other parts of the city and other outlying towns as well. Better to have their men fall in battle than ours."

"No," Abu said, waggling a finger in the air. "I think that the *muhtasib* has a point. I'm sure that Fernando will be delighted to have his men back for his drive on Malaga. It will almost be as if *we* were making a military contribution to *his* campaign, kind of canceling out our debt to him in this regard."

Hafez, never one to contradict his master, just bowed, holding his open palms in front of him, while he cast Muhammad a hot glance over his shoulder.

"So, it's decided then?" Abu went on. "We sit tight, maybe expanding our base a little as well as we can on our own but without provoking a major battle with el Zagal's people until the campaign down at Malaga plays itself out, and only then make our move on the Alhambra. In the meanwhile, we will send a suitably obsequious note to our dear brother Fernando, blessing him for his support in our time of need and returning his beefy, evil-smelling killers to his control for use against our mutual enemies in the south?"

There was a general murmur of consent, and Muhammad could see a sly smile spread across the face of Abu's mother as she affixed her veil anew with a modesty proper to a good Moorish mother.

Muhammad drafted an appropriate message for Fernando and Isabel, praising the valor of Spanish chivalry and the generosity of the crown of Castile for lending the fighting men to the true king of the Moors during this crisis, and it took several days for the couriers to reach the Spanish camp before Velez Malaga and return with an answer. Not surprisingly, Fernando did welcome the return of his forces and congratulated Abu on the success of his arms against the usurper el Zagal. By this time, el Zagal's inadequate army had reached the vicinity of Velez Malaga as well, and the old warrior planned a night assault on the Christian camp. This might well have succeeded, but the courier carrying word of his plans to the defenders of the city, who were to time a desperate sortie to coincide with el Zagal's attack from without, was captured by a Spanish patrol, and, not only was there no supporting effort from the city when el Zagal launched his assault, but the Spaniards had laid an extensive ambush that cut down thousands of Moorish troops out in the open. When the sounds of battle were detected within the city walls, a belated raid by a small force of cavalry was attempted, but it was too little and too late to help el Zagal, who retreated into the hills with his battered survivors.

The defenders of Velez Malaga had already been demoralized by the obvious defeat of the only possible relief army. They could see Moorish bodies strewn over the fields for acres around the city, and the heads of prominent Moorish nobles who had fallen in the battle were displayed on pikes mounted on the Christian earthworks. To make matters worse, the Christian heavy artillery arrived the next day over a network of roads that had been constructed by huge teams of laborers through the mountains from Antequera. The garrison did not wait for the bombardment to start and immediately surrendered on the generous terms Fernando had made it a habit of offering if such could preclude a costly and time-consuming siege. As with other cities, the garrison was allowed to march away with full honors of war and carrying its arms, while the citizens were permitted to emigrate with all their moveable possessions or remain in the city with the guarantee of the Christian sovereigns as to the security of their property and the practice of their religion. With the fall of Velez Malaga, no fewer than two score other towns and villages in the surrounding area also opened their gates to the Christians, thus carving a massive chunk from the flank of what remained of the Moorish lands.

El Zagal escaped through the hills, first to Almeria, then finally settling in the city of Guadix, far to the northeast to await developments. Meanwhile, Fernando was able to garrison Velez Malaga and the surrounding area and move his massive army, still virtually unscathed in the campaign, toward the true goal of the offensive, the port of Malaga itself, where they arrived on the 7th of May.

Muhammad had observed the departure of el Zagal's army for Velez Malaga with some concern. Although he was not surprised, the fact was disturbing that hundreds of people from Abu's sector of the city, including some prominent members of the Abencerrajes family itself, had poured out of the city gates controlled by Abu's army and had lined the road leading to the south, cheering on el Zagal's troops, shouting out prayers for their safety and success, and with the women making their shrill ululation to encourage the warriors. Several hundred of Abu's men even joined the column, making their own personal peace in the civil war in order to devote their efforts to the fight against the infidel. Within the city over the succeeding days, Abu wisely stayed off the streets, but some of his more prominent courtiers had been accosted, insulted, even set upon by bands of young men, and Hafez himself had barely escaped back into the royal compound, sobbing hysterically, his expensive robes in tatters, and with a large gash near his temple from an accurately thrown paving stone.

The departure of the Spanish troops was to be effected in the dead of night, to minimize the public spectacle. Muhammad rode alongside Juan at the head of the column, followed by the mounted men-at-arms and the infantry, with a small troop of Moorish lancers riding on ahead and another bringing up the rear. Torches burned at every street corner providing some illumination in addition to that of the crescent moon, but the houses along the route were closed and shuttered and dark. Muhammad rode in silence, with only the clopping of the horses' hooves, the tramp of boots, and the rattle of armor to mark their passage.

As the column entered the small plaza just in front of the city gate, the lancers in the vanguard pulled off to one side to wait in a side street while Muhammad and Juan took up a position next to the guardhouse. The drawbridge was down and the portcullis up, and Muhammad began to have a very uneasy feeling. A large bonfire was burning near the gate, and sausages were still grilling on spits propped up around it, but there were no guards present other than a pair of spearmen Juan could just make out in the shadows at the far end of the drawbridge.

Suddenly, one of the Spanish riders let out a yell as a piece of rotten fruit slapped into the side of his visor. His horse lurched to one side, colliding with another, and in a moment there was a tangle of men an animals as a shower of objects began to pepper the column from all sides. Apparently, word had somehow slipped out about the departure, and a crowd of young ruffians had positioned themselves atop the walls near the gate and on the roofs of nearby houses. From the heights they now rained down a storm of rotten fruit, animal (and human) dung, and broken crockery on the Christians while screaming epithets and curses in Arabic and Spanish. The guards on both the gate and walls had either disappeared or were joining in the fun, and Muhammad's lancers sullenly sat their horses, ignoring the shouted orders of their officers to dismount and chase the rioters away. It was only with some difficulty that Muhammad and Juan managed to restrain the Spaniards from loosing a much deadlier volley from their arquebuses and crossbows or from storming the walls themselves and massacring the miscreants on the spot. After a few minutes, the Spanish riders had cleared the gates, followed by the infantry, holding their shields over their heads.

"This is the thanks we get for spilling our blood for their damned king!" Juan growled swiping off of clod of either dirt or excrement from his shield with a mailed fist."

"They didn't invite you," Muhammad said calmly, delicately picking bits of rotten apple from the front of his tunic, "and your work here did nothing for them. Go home now. You have done your king's bidding."

Juan just snorted and wheeled his horse and cantered across the drawbridge to follow the last of his infantry.

Muhammad sighed. He had let slip another chance to kill the man. He could have anticipated this kind of scene, and it would have been so easy for Yusef or some hired assassin to have been up there on the walls with a crossbow. And then Raquel and their child would have been safe from this monster once and for all. But then the Spaniards would have turned on them, and they would have had a full-fledged battle. There were only about two hundred of the mercenaries left, barely half their original number, and Moors would have come swarming from all over the city to take part in the slaughter, but then Fernando's rage would have been turned on Abu, whom he would undoubtedly have seen as a traitor and a murderer. Muhammad could simply not justify putting his king in that position, no matter how good the cause.

Still, the Spaniards were gone now. They would be marching first north into Christian territory before turning to head southwest to join Fernando's army in the field, and, with any luck, he would never see any of them again.

The news of el Zagal's defeat caused the entire city, Abu's sector included, to lapse into a period of deep mourning. Of course, many families on both sides of the dividing line of the city had actually lost loved ones in the battle, which accounted for the wailing that shattered the night's silence for nearly a week, and the deserted look of the streets, except for the occasional woman in white mourning clothes slouching along to the market to buy the bare necessities for her family. But the local population had become more than a little inured to loss and defeat, and, within a few more days, the markets were back up to their normal level of activity, and the streets were again crowded with craftsmen, peasants, and soldiers coming and going.

Of greater importance was the fact that Yusef's informants reported to him that the guards on el Zagal's side of the city had become increasingly restive and were openly fraternizing with Abu's men. More than a few had actually come over, claiming that the army had lost all faith in el Zagal and his chances of either leading the kingdom to victory over the Christians or of establishing any kind of peace within Granada. The consensus was, according to the deserters at least, only Abu's policy of conciliation and negotiation with Fernando and Isabel had any chance of securing the survival of Moorish Spain. Above all, they wanted an end to the internecine warfare that was crippling the cause. With el Zagal's decisive defeat at Velez Malaga, the only person who seemed capable of reuniting the kingdom was none other than Abu, his highness, Muhammad XII, no matter what sort of reputation he had earned for himself, and all thought of his past collaboration with the Christians was forgotten, at least for the moment.

Muhammad conducted negotiations discreetly with the commander of the garrison of the Alhambra, a portly, dark-skinned man of short stature, but a soldier of long experience but also a man of considerable education, which Muhammad found refreshing. On Abu's behalf, Muhammad promised that there would be no reprisals against the followers of el Zagal, that those who chose to leave Granada for Guadix or some other of el Zagal's remaining territories would be allowed to do so with all of their property, and that the change of administration would be effected as discreetly as possible. The pact was sealed in the presence of an aged *mullah*, serving as God's witness, although Muhammad had the distinct impression that the old man would have much more enjoyed presiding over Abu's funeral. But, the deed was done, and Muhammad returned easily through the lines to Abu's residence with the good news.

The first phase of the changeover went off without any problems. At first light on the next morning, Abu's troops moved forward all along the line dividing the city and found the enemy positions unmanned and the street barricades demolished and neatly cleared out of the way. The streets were deserted, the houses all locked and shuttered, as columns of Abu's men jogged through the city, taking possession of the entire circumference of the city's walls and the various strongpoints scattered throughout. Abu then led a solemn, silent procession of mounted men, all heavily armed but with swords sheathed, up the winding road that led to the Gate of Justice, which stood open for them, a small delegation led by the garrison commander, kneeling in the roadway at the entrance awaiting Abu's approach. Abu allowed the commander to approach and kiss his hand while a squadron of cavalry cantered through the gate, quickly followed by a long column of infantry who occupied the gatehouses and towers. When a bright blue flag could finally be seen waving from within the Alhambra, Abu nudged his horse forward and into the palace grounds.

Muhammad stayed at the gate, chatting amiably with the garrison commander, who had made plans to take ship from Almeria for Egypt, having decided that the Moorish cause in Spain was lost. He had already sent his family on ahead and spoke of how much he missed his precocious little daughter, the youngest of fourteen children by three wives, all of whom would be waiting for him in

Alexandria. He showed Muhammad a little cloth doll that the girl had given him "to keep him company" while they were apart so that he wouldn't cry. The old warrior laughed and shook his head and tucked the doll back inside his breastplate, but Muhammad could detect the slightest glint of moisture at the corners of his eyes, just beginning to trickle down through the network of creases in his leathery skin.

As they talked, Muhammad saw a group of soldiers marching in a double file down from the palace toward the gate. He assumed that they were coming to mount guard until he noticed that Hafez was with them. Although Hafez often accompanied Abu when he went into battle, usually managing to keep unobtrusively but securely away from the hottest of the action, he never accepted the more routine soldierly assignments like patrolling or standing sentry duty. Worse yet, Muhammad could see that Hafez had a curious smile on his face as the soldiers spread out to either side of the gate. Muhammad was just about to ask about his purpose there when the two nearest men rushed forward and seized the commander from behind, pinning his arms, while Hafez stepped up and bashed the old man on the back of the head with the hilt of his sword, causing him to collapse as the soldiers dragged him away. Muhammad tried to shove one of the soldiers aside, but two more seized his arms and held him back.

"What are you doing?" Muhammad shouted. "Are you out of your mind?"

Hafez turned to him, walking backwards to keep up with the soldiers and their prisoner. "We are only complying with the orders of the king," he said, spreading his arms wide and shrugging.

"But he gave his word," Muhammad argued.

"I'm sure that this is just a precaution," Hafez continued. "I can assure you that your new friend won't be in custody for long." Hafez made a little jerk of his head, and the soldiers began to pull Muhammad along in Hafez's wake.

They continued through the palace grounds and into the Alhambra itself. They passed through a series of rooms and out into a courtyard surrounded by colonnades, the centerpiece of which was a large stone fountain supported on the backs of carved lions standing shoulder to shoulder and facing outward, the Court of Lions. The open area was crowded with soldiers of Abu's personal bodyguard, mostly North Africans and Christian renegades, all heavily armed. Besides the garrison commander, who had been thrown to the ground in an unconscious heap, there were three other nobles of el Zagal's faction, each of whom bore some mark, a bloody mouth, a swollen eye, or a limp, dangling arm bathed in blood, demonstrating that they had been brought by force. Abu sat idly on a small folding chair of leather and wood at one end of the courtyard, delicately eating grapes from a plate held by a servant. Muhammad knew in a moment what would happen, as this was the very spot on which Abu's father had massacred dozens of the Abencerrajes clan years before in an effort to exterminate his son's primary group of supporters.

"Your majesty!" Muhammad yelled out, but Abu ignored him, gesturing to one of his Christians, a large man-at-arms in a chain mail shirt, bareheaded with long, matted blonde hair cascading halfway down his back and with a great two-handed sword worn in a sheath across his back. "For the love of Allah!" Muhammad insisted, but his guards pushed him back against the farthest wall of the courtyard, although he still had an unobstructed view of the prisoners at its center.

Hafez, as always, dressed elegantly in brilliant white robes embroidered with gold thread, a pale green turban on his head, stepped out in front of the fountain and took firm hold of the chest-length beard of the first prisoner, pulling it taut and extending the man's neck as he knelt on the paving stones. The Christian bodyguard stood off to one side and, at a nod from Abu, brought his sword out in one swift motion, swinging the blade around and down in a vast arc, taking off the man's head at a single stroke, leaving it dangling by its beard from Hafez's hand. Holding the head out carefully to one side to avoid getting blood, which dribbled onto the ground while much more pumped from the neck stump of the twitching corpse, Hafez did a slow pirouette, displaying the grisly trophy to all present.

The next man was sobbing loudly and pouring out a string of prayers to God and pleas to the king, to Hafez, to the executioner, to anyone present who would listen, and Hafez kicked him firmly in the mouth to silence him before proceeding. Hafez scowled at his fine suede boots that now had a bloodstain on the toe and made a clucking noise with his tongue. He jerked the man's beard and twisted it hard enough to make him scream before the sword blow fell. After dealing with the third prisoner, Hafez felt obliged to slap the commander's face several times, ordering the two soldiers to hold his arms firmly, until the man was fully conscious again. Muhammad met the commander's accusing stare just as the bodyguard raised his sword, and he had to turn his head and vomit noisily.

Once the "ceremony" had been concluded, the soldiers began to file away, leaving the bodies scattered in a rough semicircle around the fountain, some of them still twitching and oozing blood. The guards released Muhammad's arms, stepping back quickly and letting him drop to his knees, and then departed with the others.

"You disapprove of my decision, *muhtasib*?" Abu asked absently, his mouth half full of grapes as he smacked his lips loudly.

Muhammad slowly pulled himself to his feet and shuffled toward Abu's chair. Hafez lounged to one side, leaning on the back of the chair, and two tall Berber guards stood behind them, thumbs casually hooked into their belts, conveniently near their sword hilts as their eyes followed Muhammad's every move.

"Defenders of the True Faith will undoubtedly rejoice at the news that the word of the king of Granada is such a flexible thing," he intoned grimly, raising his hands toward heaven.

"And how is that?" Abu asked.

"If your highness' oath were worth even a plate full of warm pig turds, then truly the kingdom of al-Andalus must be nearing its final days."

Hafez snarled and reached for his dagger, and the two guards took half a step forward before Abu halted them with a languid wave of his hand.

"You're making no sense," Abu snapped. "Time was when you were merely boring, but I must admit that, when I did pay attention, you at least had some logic to your arguments. Now you have become both boring and incoherent."

"I am merely referring to your agreement with Isabel and Fernando," Muhammad explained. "By your oath to them you are bound, in exchange for your freedom after the siege of Loja and for the help they have provided you since then in your war against el Zagal, you are obliged to surrender this very city to them upon demand as soon as the last of el Zagal's resistance has been stamped out. I think it is clear that Malaga must eventually fall and that el Zagal cannot hope to hold out indefinitely in his other territories as the Christians only get stronger and stronger. If that is the case, then soon you must surrender this palace, your lands, and what remains of Moorish independence. Fortunately, that would only occur if your word were your bond. By your action today all true Moslems can rejoice that your word is worth nothing whatsoever, so you must not be planning to surrender Granada to the infidels. Praise be to Allah!"

"Fernando and Isabel would never expect me actually to give up my throne," Abu replied testily. "It may be true that I swore to become their vassal, in simple recognition of the balance of power here in Spain, but that is not the same thing as giving up my ancestral rights."

"Your majesty swore to more than that," Muhammad insisted. "You accepted the title of Duke of Guadix, once that city is conquered from el Zagal, and you placed all of your lands and power at their disposal. It cannot now be much in doubt that Guadix will, one day, be conquered, not by your armies but by those of the Christians. Once that has occurred, Fernando will be completely within his rights in ordering you to move your court to that city and in taking possession of the Alhambra itself. But, perhaps your majesty was unaware that word had gotten out about your subsequent secret agreement with Fernando and Isabel promising precisely the surrender of Granada, once it was in your power to do accomplish this, if only they would capture Graudix and Baza for you instead of obliging you to take those cities yourself from el Zagal."

Abu now turned to Muhammad, frowning, with his mouth hanging open.

"But," Muhammad continued, "as I just said, it matters very little what your majesty may or may not have promised, since there does not appear to be any compulsion on your part to fulfill your word. Consequently, I have every confidence that, when the time comes to turn over to the Christians the keys to this fortress, your majesty will simply ignore their demands, just as you ignored your promise to guarantee the lives and security of the men you just had murdered."

"Of course I will," Abu said in an uncertain tone. "They were traitors, and they would soon have taken up arms against me again if I had let them go. And, as for my promise to Isabel and Fernando, this is my kingdom, and no one has the right to take it from me. I see no reason for apologizing for avoiding further fighting between Moslem brothers, as would happen if we were to try to take Guadix from el Zagal ourselves. This way, we let the Christians do the fighting, which they would do in any case, and we retain control of those cities afterward. Without that agreement, the Christians would just conquer them and keep them for themselves. How is that wrong?"

"As I imagined, your majesty," Muhammad concluded, bowing low and backing toward the arched doorway behind him, "you have an answer for every objection. In that event, sire, I strongly urge you to look to your armies, for the day will be coming soon when all debts will be called due."

GRANADA

Chapter Two
Malaga

Juan was disappointed to have missed the capture of Velez Malaga, although the anticlimactic nature of the surrender, with no bloody final assault and no vast horde of prisoners to divide, made this largely a moot question. The port of Malaga would be the key of the campaign, not only of this year, but perhaps even of the whole of the reconquest. It was an immensely rich city, handling trade for both Moorish and Christian Spain with all of North Africa and the Levant for centuries, and its warehouses would be stuffed with spices, silks, and precious goods that would have to be divided among its conquerors. At least Juan and his men would not be robbed of their share in those spoils. Furthermore, Hamet el Zagri was reported to be in personal command of the garrison, which was composed of his fanatical Berber tribesmen who would never agree to surrender on terms, no matter what the fat merchants in the town might prefer, all the better for the granting of free rein to the Spanish assault troops when they clambered over the city walls.

Juan's little army had traveled north into Christian territory after leaving Granada, having been physically restrained by the Basque from turning back through the gates to massacre the damned Moorish eunuchs who had had the nerve to insult his men and then bombard them with garbage and worse upon their departure. And this after these same bearded mice had spent the preceding months hiding safely away in their homes while Juan and his men fought for the glory and honor of their mewling little "king" Boabdil. The Basque had whispered soothingly in his ear as they rode away that they could not hope to win a fight against all of the Moors of Granada combined, which is what they would have been faced with, and he added that Juan would have his revenge soon enough when they returned to storm this same city and put to the sword every man, woman, and child from the king on down, as they undoubtedly would do in the end. Now all of his men were mounted, mostly on mules unfortunately, but it was still better than walking, and although Juan had pressed them hard to cover the ground, Fernando's army was already well ensconced in its camp at Malaga by the time Juan's troop arrived.

Juan had served with large armies before under Fernando's command, but the sight of the immense tent city that engulfed the plains around the city walls, like the surf around an isolated rock out in the sea, had truly taken his breath away. The logistical wizardry of Isabel, aided Juan knew, by his own wife Raquel, had enabled the Christians to put larger and larger forces into the field. Fernando had with him well over 20,000 heavy cavalry and more than twice as many infantry, and this was without counting the thousands of laborers who had been conscripted to work on the quickly extending network of roads over which he now moved in company with long columns of supply wagons, herds of horses and cattle, and still more phalanxes of troops moving up to the front.

In the soft light of a setting sun the sand-colored walls of Malaga were a gilded shield around the brilliant white of its houses with their red tile roofs, the skyline punctuated by the delicate minarets of more than a dozen mosques. Above them rose the elongated hill which was crowned by the city's two fortresses, the Alcazaba on the western end, and the Gibralfaro (lighthouse hill) on the other, both connected with a second belt of thick walls studded with towers. Double arms of breakwaters enclosed the inner and out harbors, also shielded with forts and gun emplacements with the entrance to the outer harbor blocked by a thick chain stretched across its mouth. Within the harbors rode a handful of graceful galleys, their sails furled, but beyond the mole Juan could see the dark shapes of dozens of large and small men-of-war, the fleets of Castile and Aragon, effectively sealing up the port against the outside world, and every now and then a white puff of smoke would appear from the side of one of the larger ships, to be followed several moments later by a dull report, as the navy began to pound away at the coastal batteries defending the city. Even from this distance, Juan could easily make out the cluster of huge tents, made of the most brilliantly colored silks, instead of simple white cotton, that marked Fernando's headquarters around which all of the noble commanders were congregated. There would be no chance for him to stake out a claim to a choice piece of real estate this time to ensure access to the king, so he would have to make a serious effort to reestablish his own notoriety through his actions, and this Juan resolved to do.

It was early evening by the time Juan and his troops had reached the camp and been assigned a place to pitch their tents by an officer of the quartermaster, and stewards were already going through the camp lighting torches that barely provided enough light, with that of the partially cloud-covered moon and the small cooking fires, for Juan to make his way over nearly a mile to Fernando's tent, picking his way carefully over the tent ropes, cursing periodically as he stubbed his toes painfully against a stake. During this journey, Juan was impressed by the wide variety of languages he heard around the campfires. There was the usual assortment of accents in Spanish, slower for the northerners, faster and clipped for the Andalusians, Portuguese, even some Arabic of groups of scouts, and some sing-song Italian, probably troops from Fernando's possessions in the Kingdom of Naples. But there was also the harsh tone of English, guttural German, and the smooth French to say nothing of half a dozen more tongues that Juan could not begin to identify. No wonder the Moors were losing heart in the struggle. They were not just fighting the combined might of Castile and Aragon, but all of Christendom.

Juan finally arrived at Fernando's tent to find the king surrounded by his usual gaggle of military advisors, the Marquis of Cadiz, the Duke of Medina Sidonia, the Masters of the Orders of Calatrava and Santiago, the commander of the combined fleet, the Count of Trevento, and more than a dozen others of somewhat lesser rank. Fernando was lost in conversation with his admiral, but the Marquis spotted Juan entering and rushed over to greet him with a huge bear hug.

"Hail to the first man over the wall of Granada!" the Marquis bellowed, but only a couple of heads turned in their direction, all being intent on following Fernando's discussion with Trevento. "And how went your war?"

Juan shuddered and shook his head. "Please don't let's talk about that. If it weren't for the fact that I was able to make myself useful killing Moors, I don't think I could have tolerated living with the pigs. In fact, I now understand why they don't eat pork, it would be too much like cannibalism."

"It can't have been as bad as all that," the Marquis chided him, chuckling deeply. "Going out and whacking away at the enemy all day and then back home to clean sheets and a nice little bed warmer every night, regular meals, good wine, and a sound roof over your head. Certainly beats slogging your way through the mountains or fording an icy stream with the chance that the blasted Moors will come popping up around every bend or from behind every boulder and start flinging arrows at you."

"And no prospect of any real booty to make it all worthwhile either," Juan added. "I swear that it was all I could do to keep from massacring that worm Boabdil and all his filthy brood while I was at it and then seeing what I could do about chasing el Zagal out of the city by myself."

"But Boabdil is now our faithful vassal, that is, Fernando's vassal," the Marquis corrected himself. "And he is in firm possession of his capital, while el Zagal is crippled. We took not only Velez Malaga but a huge swath of territory with it and handed el Zagal a bloody defeat in the field to boot. Now, if we can just crush the resistance here, I think it will be safe to say that the war will be, for all practical purposes, over."

"And how is it going?" Juan asked, straining to peek over the shoulders of some of the men crowded around the map table.

"We're off to a slow start, I'm afraid. There was no real opposition to our approach march, and we've got most of the heavy batteries emplaced around the city, but so far we've only managed to overrun some of the outlying suburbs. We've had reports that some of the merchants inside the city wanted to sue for terms right away. It seems they're more concerned with saving the stocks of goods in their warehouses and avoiding the possibility of missing a meal or two in the course of a prolonged siege, but that old bastard Hamet el Zagri is in command of the garrison, and that's mostly composed of his blood-thirsty North African *gomeres.* He's announced that anyone found trying to negotiate with us will be put to death, and there are a few bodies hanging from the ramparts of the citadel that imply that a few have tried it, '*Pour encourager les autres,*' as the French would say."

"I'd heard all that on the road. Well, no one can seriously have expected that the Moors would give up Malaga without a fight," Juan snuffed.

"There was always that hope," the Marquis replied, shrugging his shoulders. "After all, their cause is lost, and Fernando has been most generous in the terms he has offered the cities and towns that have surrendered quickly. Why shouldn't the merchants be looking ahead to continuing their fat and happy existence serving as go-betweens for Spain with the Levant in their trade in spices and silks?"

"You know very well what we'd do to any of our own people who tried to make a deal with the enemy in such a situation. There's no reason to suppose that the Moors would react any differently. And seven hundred years ago it was us Christians who were hanging on to a couple of little enclaves in the mountains in the north against the tide of Islam. Now look at us! The Turks are incredibly powerful and they have been pushing into Europe from the east. Constantinople fell only a generation ago and now the Turks are knocking at the gates of Vienna. Who's to say that they won't be part of a general resurgence of Islam all over?"

The Marquis paused for a moment and examined Juan closely. "I can see that, besides gathering a few new scars on that ugly head, you seem to have stuffed some new knowledge inside it as well. In any case," he went on, "you'll be pleased to know that there doesn't seem to be any chance of a peace short of storming the walls and slaughtering the inhabitants," the Marquis smiled, and Juan joined him. "But we're not making the kind of progress we've gotten used to of late," had added.

"Do you mean that the magic artillery hasn't stunned the infidels into submission at the first volley?"

"Not only that, but the Moors here are better equipped with artillery than we've ever seen them, forcing us to keep our own guns out at maximum range. We've got some big German monsters that can out reach any of theirs, maybe out to three or four thousand paces, but only a few of them, so we can't concentrate firepower of any weight to bring down whole sections of the wall. And the Moors have mounted half a dozen floating batteries out in the harbor that have managed to keep our ships at a respectful distance, and can then turn their fire on our entrenchments closest to the shore. Needless to say, their artillery could smash any old fashioned kind of siege tower we might be able to move up against the walls, and they've apparently got an inexhaustible supply of arrows and gunpowder and shot to keep storming parties from getting within striking distance."

"How about mining underneath the walls if we can't go over them or bring them down?"

"We've been working on just that for over two weeks," the Marquis said in a quiet tone, taking a furtive look around for stray servants who might have large ears and loose tongues. He turned and shouldered his way through the crowd of officers, dragging Juan with him to the map table.

"Your majesty," Juan said, bowing to Fernando, who looked up briefly and snorted absently in reply.

Fernando then glanced up from the map again and smiled broadly in recognition. "It's about time you were getting back to fighting with *my* army. None the worse for wear, I see, or at least hardly any," he added pounding Juan on the shoulder with a thick forearm and with enough force to make the younger man stagger. He jabbed at the map with one stubby finger.

Juan could only really read a few words, his name, of course and a few things that tended to crop up on bills of sale and other documents, like "horses," or "sheep," but he had become adept at interpreting the rough, highly stylized maps often used by commanders in the field. He could identify the curve of the coast, with wavy marks to represent the sea, and the crenellated line that indicated the city walls. He also recognized the coats of arms of the most prominent noblemen, artfully and accurately drawn into little flags placed in a rough semicircle around the city to denote where the commanders had their headquarters. Another set of zigzag lines marked the lines of approach trenches that encompassed the city, with occasional boxes filled with heavy bars that probably showed the position of the major siege gun emplacements. There were lines of text here and there that were completely unintelligible to Juan, but they mattered little. He could see a dark hash mark extending from the trenches up toward the city wall on the western side, and this was where Fernando was now pointing.

"We've got a batch of Asturian iron miners with us, and we've set them to work tunneling from the near side of a hillock about here over two hundred yards to the city walls," Fernando explained. "Our original idea was to actually open up a route inside the city for an assault party, but we've had indications that the Moors have learned about our efforts and have positioned units to massacre anyone who tries to poke his head above ground on their side of the lines."

"That's one of the problems we've been having," the Marquis broke in. "I can't explain it myself, but we've had a number of deserters cross over into the city, giving the Moors information about the army and our strategy. I personally suspect that most of them are *conversos*, or more exactly apostates, who are trying to escape the Inquisition, so good riddance to them. The real damage, other than losing a few men from our army and a leak of intelligence to the enemy, is that they've apparently been spreading stories that the army is on the verge of collapse, that hundreds of men slip away every night to sneak off home. That's given old Hamet the chance to convince his people that they only have to hold on a little longer, a few days or weeks, and we'll eventually just pack up our tents and wander away."

"And is it true, about the desertions I mean?" Juan asked, cocking an eyebrow. The mention of the false *conversos* raised the hair at the back of his neck, as it suddenly came home to him that, although this whole idea was exactly what had given him the power to possess Raquel and added the spice he craved in their relationship, the Inquisition was a very real threat, not just to her, but to him as well. He had never been one to experience much fear, not in battle or tournament certainly, but this was the kind of threat that he would be powerless to resist, and *that*, the idea of himself being as powerless as the women he loved to abuse, that turned his bowels to water at the very thought.

"Of course not," the Marquis snorted. "Oh, we lose a few men now and then, as any army does, but we're *winning*, and the chance of booty is more than enough to keep most of the men with the colors, especially now that planting season is over. No, it's just the deserters telling their new masters what they want to hear to ingratiate themselves, but it's doing the very real harm of allowing Hamet to keep the defenders going when their cause is obviously lost."

"Which is precisely why we need a breakthrough," Fernando continued. "Something to shake them up, to show them that their days are numbered, and are getting very short at that. At least a breach of the outer city walls at some point, even if they manage to build up a secondary line to seal off the breach, some kind of real progress. The artillery just isn't working fast enough. It's all very well to knock a hole in the walls of an isolated mountain town that would have been hard to assault in the old way, but when you're dealing with a proper city, with massive walls and artillery of its own, we just don't have the firepower to overwhelm them, yet."

"And since we can't expect much success from an assault, even if we make it all the way under their walls and into the city," the Marquis went on, "we're going for the more traditional and simple undermining of the walls to create a breach. If we can do that, our light artillery can keep the Moors' heads down while we launch a powerful attack through the opening and roll up their defenses on both flanks, or at least have a chance to do so."

Juan frowned. "I could see my role if we were going to attempt a sneak assault through a tunnel. That's just my meat, but if we create a breach, that will mean a major offensive, and I'd just be one of the minor captains under the command of one of the main warlords," he added obsequiously, nodding in the direction of the Marquis. "Although I would, of course, be honored to take part in such an action at any level," he added hastily. Actually, his mouth was watering at the possibility that they did have in mind for him to lead the charge, even if only in command of a picked assault force to spearhead the attack and then hold open the breach for the main army. It would be Alhama all over again, but on an even bigger scale as Alhama had been, after all, just a minor town and nothing like this, the second city in all the Moorish kingdom.

"It's because," the king said in a slow voice, like someone reluctant to break unwelcome news, "as we mentioned, the Moors know about the tunnel, and we expect that they will be countermining."

Juan's face fell, and the Marquis quickly joined in.

"It's an absolutely vital mission," he said, placing his hands on Juan's broad shoulders and turning the younger man to face him. "Those Asturian miners are a precious commodity. If they get killed off, we've got no one on hand with the skills to take their places. It's not nearly as easy as you might think, grinding your way through mud and rock, keeping on a straight path and preventing the roof from caving in on you at every step. We need someone to lead a small company down into the tunnel, to stand by, if and when, the Moors make contact. Naturally, if they don't, the miners will just carve out a big space under the walls, prop it up with timbers and fill it with kindling and flammables, set it on fire, and pull out, letting the whole thing come crashing down, bringing a good chunk of the wall with it. If we're lucky, enough of the wall will come down that the secondary line the Moors have been working on will also be outflanked, and we could take the whole city."

Fernando stood up and smiled broadly, spreading his arms as if to ask, "What better opportunity for glory could a soldier ask for?" Juan just hung his head and sighed deeply. He did not think that his reputation as a fearless warrior would be enhanced if he told his lords and sovereign that, if there was one thing in the world that terrified him more than the invisible, unstoppable onslaught of the plague, it was the thought of being confined in tiny, cramped spaces with no way of escape. So, the idea of being buried alive really didn't appeal to him all that much.

Juan guessed that it must be mid-morning, but there was no telling the time underground. He grunted and rose from his sitting position on the cold, damp ground, but there was no room for him to stand erect, and he grunted again when he banged his forehead on one of the support beams to remind himself of that. He looked up nervously at the beam, steadying it with his hand, suddenly fearful that the collision might have provided just the shock needed to bring down the entire roof, but all was still.

His eyes had long become accustomed to the faint, wavering light of the torches placed every ten paces along the tunnel, but he could still barely make out the shadowy outlines of his men as they sat, packed against the walls of the tunnel and the small alcove the miners had carved out for them near the mine head just a few yards away. Juan could readily understand that miners did not give themselves the luxury of digging spacious halls and rooms, as every square inch of soil and rock had to be wrenched out by their sweat and then dragged out in wicker baskets hauled by sturdy-legged boys of no more than twelve or thirteen years of age. In fact, the approach tunnel had been much more cramped than this, barely three feet in diameter, and they had had to come forward on hands and knees for what seemed like hundreds of yards. Now that they estimated that they were getting close to the city walls, however, the stocky little miners, caked with mud and working nearly naked in the still, smoky air of the mine, had taken the time to hack out a larger space, since it would ultimately serve to weaken the walls that were supposedly above them. That thought gave Juan little comfort as there was still inadequate room for someone of his bulk, and because the idea of consciously trying to cause a cave-in did not seem completely logical to him.

He moved forward, squeezing past the boys waiting for their baskets to be filled, to where a team of four men were pounding away at the wall of dirt and rock before them with short-handled picks in a sophisticated ballet, carefully timed out to allow all of them to work in the cramped space. The staccato clinking of their metal blades against the wall creating a rapid rhythm interspersed with their grunting and wheezing. Juan approached the foreman and laid a mailed hand on his shoulder.

"Hold up for a moment," he said, and the miners simultaneously stopped, dropping gratefully to one knee and staring blankly at the wall. "Silence!" Juan growled, and the dull hum of conversation among the waiting teams of miners, the boys, and Juan's soldiers also stopped.

Juan could hear water dripping somewhere and the dull rasping sound of a basket being dragged of back up the tunnel, but nothing else. He closed his eyes and listened a moment longer, and then he heard it, a thin, tinny clink, then another, and another. He looked at the foreman, red-rimmed eyes staring out at him from a uniformly dirt-colored face. The man gestured with the knife edge of his hand, slightly off to the right of the direction of the tunnel.
"How far?" Juan whispered.

The man shrugged and extended his arms out to their full length from side to side, then shorted the distance a bit to indicate four, or maybe only three feet.

"Coming this way?" he asked, dipping his head even closer to the man's ear.

The miner listened for another moment, then nodded, reaching out to pat a section of the tunnel wall just to the right of the face where he and his men had been digging.

Juan moved quickly chasing the boys and other miners back out of the tunnel with a message for the Basque to come forward. He then placed the foreman, two men on either side of the indicated spot on the wall.
"When they break through," he explained in a rough whisper, "I want one good blow from each of you to widen the hole. Then jump back out of the way as if your lives depended on it, because they will."

The foreman nodded casually. Juan noticed that, at about thirty, the foreman was by far the oldest among the miners, and he suspected that rank air, cave-ins, and floods probably worked against men in such a line of work achieving great old age. Thus the added possibility of underground combat would only add a bit of novelty to their existence without unduly increasing the inherent danger.

The Basque finally appeared, accompanied by half a dozen men, each carrying a thick-barreled arquebus, the heaviest variety. Each gun was set up, its barrel supported by an iron pole with a forked top, while the gunners checked the powder in the priming pans for dryness and pointed their weapons at the wall at Juan's direction. Behind them a solid phalanx of men-at-arms pressed close, each armed with a sword or short thrusting spear and wearing shirts of mail, but no bulky armor or shields. Juan held up his hand for silence.

Juan was very conscious of his own breathing, which sounded like a massive bellows in a forge, and of every shuffle and creak as his men fidgeted in the tense, close atmosphere as the minutes crept by. But beyond this, he could distinctly hear the scrape and tap as somewhere, beyond the blank, dark wall in front of him, Arab miners were working steadily toward him. Every now and then the sound of digging would stop, probably to allow the enemy the chance to listen for the Spaniards at work, but then it would resume, each time just a little louder than before. Finally, he thought he could make out the vague murmur of conversation, unintelligible even if he had spoken Arabic better, but human voices nonetheless.

The torches in the tunnel had been replaced with iron lamps, each fitted with shutters, and Juan now lowered his arm, signaling for the shutters to be closed, dropping the chamber into near perfect darkness, illuminated only by the faint glimmer that emitted from around the edges of the shutters and the merest suggestion of light that filtered in from the tunnel mouth, hundreds of feet to the rear. The red tips of the arquebus matches glowed red in the shadows, like the eyes of evil beasts. There was a general shifting of feet and an almost inaudible mumble from the men, but Juan hissed at them, and all was still once more.

The sound of hacking and shoveling now seemed thunderous, almost as if the diggers were with them in the chamber with them but invisible in the dark. The foreman pressed his ear up against the wall, moving slowly from left to right until he paused at one spot and patted it with the palm of his hand, nodding to Juan and then pulling back to one side. There was another moment of digging by the enemy, and suddenly a large section of the wall collapsed toward the Spaniards, simultaneously flooding the chamber with torchlight from the other side. The foreman and his workers swung their picks as one at the edges of the hole, bringing down still more rubble and them crouched down and rolled out of the way.

"Shoot!" Juan bellowed, and a dozen tongues of flame reached out toward the breach, instantly filling the tunnel with thick, blue smoke and the screams of the wounded and dying as a cloud of shot swept away the front rank of Moorish miners. A second rank of arquebusiers pushed forward past the first and fired another volley into what could now be discerned as a writhing mass of men beyond the wall. Each gun barrel had been packed with small lead pellets and jagged bits of metal that scoured the walls and tore through the flesh of the enemy miners.

"Forward!" Juan shouted, coughing in the gunsmoke, but pushing his way toward the breach as his own miners now continued to hack furiously at its edges to enlarge the opening. He thrust his sword blindly ahead of him, slashing to left and right and feeling the blade rip through bone and flesh. The Basque was beside him, jabbing with a boar spear and pinning a wiry little Moor to the tunnel wall with a grunt. They climbed through the breach and into the body-clogged tunnel on the far side, and Juan could hear frenzied screaming coming from off to his left as the surviving enemy miners attempted to escape back through their own tunnel.

Clearly, the Moors had not expected to come upon the Spanish tunnel quite so soon, or their own contingent of soldiers had taken to their heels even faster than the miners, for there was no one left on hand to fight. Juan climbed over the bodies, his feet slipping in the blood, and made his way toward the dark mouth of the Moorish tunnel. It might not have been part of the plan, but, if he could drive through into the city itself, there was every chance that the panic in the Moorish ranks would have infected any force they might have waiting on the other side. If he and his men could break through, and possibly seize a house or other strong place, and hold out against the inevitable counterattack, there might be time for Fernando to send reinforcements through the tunnel while mounting a full-scale assault on the nearest section of the walls. Taken from two sides, the Moorish defenses might crumble, and the city might fall before the defenders could be rallied.

But just as Juan was about to plunge on through the gloom, he was gripped firmly by the shoulder and spun around with amazing force, and he found himself facing the grimy little foreman, barely half Juan's size but with muscles all over his spare body like knotted ropes. Juan was about to bat the nuisance away with the flat of his sword when the little man held up both hands, palms outward.

"Stop! For the love of God!" the foreman screamed, and he reached out and grabbed Juan's free hand and pressed it firmly against the tunnel wall. "Feel that?" Juan could barely hear the man over the roaring of his soldiers, the clatter of their armor, and the occasional shriek of a wounded Moor as one of his men dispatched him with a dagger thrust, but he could clearly feel a throbbing, pulsing through the tunnel walls.

"What is that?" Juan asked.

"They're battering out their own tunnel supports!" the foreman yelled. "We've got to get out of here."

"What do you mean?"

"They're going to start a cave-in at their end, but there's no telling where it will stop once the supports start to topple like a row of dominoes."

"Can't we stop them?" Juan asked.

"Not in time. This must have been their plan from the start. That is why they didn't have a company of soldiers waiting on their side. We've got to run, NOW!"

With that the foreman turned to his own men, who had apparently already guessed their leader's conclusion and were clustered back at the far end of the Spanish chamber, and with a jerk of his thumb, they disappeared down the tunnel, running at full tilt even though bent over nearly double, weaving their way past the larger soldiers who were still coming forward.

"Pull back!" Juan shouted, grabbing the Basque by the collar of his shirt as he began to move past him in pursuit of the Moors. "Get out of the tunnel! Run for it!" Juan's breath was coming in painful gasps now as the walls began to close in on him, the immense weight of earth above them already feeling as though it were crushing the air from his lungs even while the walls still stood.

Several of the men had paused to pick over the corpses of the fallen Moors, hoping for some loot, but the men were all obviously poor laborers, and they now looked up at Juan in bewilderment.

"Run for your lives, by the Blessed Virgin!" he screamed. "Or you'll be buried alive!"

They took no more convincing but turned in a body toward the tunnel mouth, quickly creating a logjam with their bodies. Juan waded through them, pulling men aside bodily until one at a time could begin to make his way back up the tunnel. He longed to be the first of them, to get through that horrible, narrow tube and out into the fresh air once more, but he could not bring himself to turn coward in front of his men, even now with his knees shaking and cold sweat streaming down the back of his neck.

"Leave your weapons, drop your armor!" he yelled, although he kept his own sword clutched firmly in his fist, the one that Fernando had given him at his knighthood ceremony. There was the relic of some saint in the handle, and maybe that would be what would pull him through, he thought vaguely, but it was mainly that he could not bring himself to emerge from combat without his weapon. He had never done so before, and would not do so now. He could feel a dull rumbling coming up through the floor now, and a cloud of dust was drifting into the chamber from the Moors' tunnel, but there were still half a dozen men crowding about, anxiously waiting their turn to press through the narrow exit.

Finally, the Basque dove into the tunnel, shoving the man ahead of him, and Juan followed closely. He could hear the roar of falling rocks and earth now and the shrieking of heavy timbers as they were torn and shattered. The dust was so thick now that he could see nothing at all but hung onto the cuff of the Basque's trousers as they moved forward, crawling now, their lungs clogged and burning. Then something hit Juan in the small of his back and he was knocked flat on the tunnel floor, something heavy pressing down on his legs. He kicked frantically and clawed with his fingers, and he realized that he was no longer holding his sword, lost in the darkness, but he was only able to crawl a few inches at a time, using his elbows frantically as the dirt poured down around him, swallowing him up like a vast, greedy snake. His mouth and nose began to fill, not just with gritty dust, but with dirt, and he knew that he was going to die. He would have screamed, but there was no air left in his burning lungs.

But most frightening of all, the total darkness was replaced by a horrible red glow in Juan's mind. He could see images, although he knew that he was not seeing them at all, as real as they might appear to him. There were people, hundreds of them, men and women, crowding around him on all sides. They wore tatters of clothing and had dark, vacant eyes, and their mouths hung open wordlessly. He tried to push them away, but his arms were pinned, and he tried to run, but his legs could not move. Then he began to recognize them. He saw the face of a French man-at-arms he had gutted in a skirmish years ago near Montpelier, and a sentry from the walls of Alhama, still wearing the surprised expression he had had when Juan had cut his throat. And there was that first prostitute, what was her name? Had he ever known? The one in Trujillo he had killed, practically by accident. And they were all pressing against him, clutching at his clothes and hair, trying to smother him with their gaunt, bony hands, and he thought he could vaguely hear the sound of laughter over the pounding of his own heart.

But then, just as he began to feel his body grow limp, he felt strong hands clasp onto his wrists and haul him forward while he twisted and flailed anew with his legs to break them free of the clinging earth, and then they all tumbled out into the daylight, coughing and gasping for air. Someone dumped a gourd of water over his face, and he sputtered gratefully as the dirt and terror were flushed from his throat. He rolled over on his back and opened his dust-caked eyes to the pale blue sky that he had thought he would never see again, and he wondered if what he had experienced in the tunnel had been a foretaste of what awaited him when he did die, an eternity of torment at the hands of his many victims in this life.

Behind him the mouth of the tunnel belched a thick cloud of brown dust, and the trembling of the ground made Juan dizzy, preventing him from getting to his feet. He sprawled there, half lying atop the Basque, and with the little foreman still firmly grasping Juan's arm. The

Marquis finally came striding up, fanning at the dust in the air with the broad sleeve of his tunic.

"We half expected something like this," the Marquis said, his voice raspy with the dust.

"And when was *I* going to be told about it?" Juan coughed.

"Well, it goes with the territory," the Marquis sniffed. "You've had almost as much experience with sieges as I have. You know how this mining business works. Lord knows we saw enough of it at Ronda and other places. We try to knock the ground out from under their walls, and they try to collapse our mine on top of us. Pretty much the traditional thing. At least you seem to have gotten out of there with all your limbs and all your men, that's better than one could have expected." And the Marquis turned to climb up the berm of earth that had shielded the mine entrance from view by the city defenders. He stood atop it, shielding his eyes against the sun and surveying the city walls beyond.

Juan painfully dragged himself to his feet and staggered up the slope to stand beside him.

"There, you see," the Marquis was saying, pointing to the sand-colored walls against which a battery of heavy lombards was sporadically pounding without much apparent effect. "There's a slight dip in the wall just there. You can see where the line of the battlements bow under just a bit. That must be where the tunnels collapsed. Not enough to do any good, though. I'd guess that little hollow there in no-man's-land about twenty yards short of the wall must be where we had carved out that chamber for you and your men. If that had been right under the walls, then maybe it would have done some damage, but not as it is."

"So what are we going to do now, sir?" Juan called after him. "Try another mine?"

"Oh, I don't think so," the Marquis said. "They seem to have that one figured out all too well. But don't worry, his majesty has decided to employ his secret weapon."

"What secret weapon?"

"Why, the queen, of course. He's sent word to her to bring her court right down here to the camp, just as he did at Loja. If anything will convince the Moors that we're in this until the bitter end, that will. Our men always fight better under the eye of their lady, and the Moors know that we'll never just give up once Isabel is on the scene. She should be here in a week or two."

And then, so will Raquel, Juan thought, smiling to himself despite the aches all through his body and the burning in his lungs, and he started to feel a sudden stirring in his loins that he had not felt in some time. He smiled inwardly. Perhaps he had seen a vision of what was to come, but surely his fate was already sealed. There was certainly nothing he could do now to bring those people back to life or to mitigate the agony that he had put many of them through before he had deigned to kill them. So, he might as well enjoy the time that remained to him on this earth in the only way that the all-knowing, all-merciful God had seen fit to allow him.

The arrival of Isabel's court at the army's camp was designed to create the maximum impact, both on the Spanish troops and on the Moorish onlookers who crowded the battlements in dark, silent masses. Fernando and a large entourage of nobles, along with an escort of several thousand mounted knights, had departed the camp the night before to escort the queen and her court on the final miles of their journey. In the late afternoon the procession appeared, winding its way down from the foothills and onto the coastal plain. Isabel was, as was her habit on formal state occasions when she hoped to impress an audience, lavishly dressed, wearing a gown made of cloth of gold inlaid with thousands of pearls and brilliant gems, a tall golden headdress, and a sweeping veil, with her tall white mule caparisoned in similar gold cloth embroidered with the yoke and arrows of the royal household, and Fernando rode beside her on a prancing black charger, his full suit of armor, embossed with gold, gleaming in the long rays of the afternoon sun. The several dozen ladies rode matching white mules in a solid phalanx around the king and queen, each dressed in a gown of ivory-colored silk, and beyond them rode ranks of knights, each in his most elaborate suit of highly polished armor with colorful pennants snapping in the breeze at the tips of their lances. Before and behind the column rode bodies of mounted musicians beating huge kettledrums hung on either side of their saddles or blowing long brass trumpets. At the head of the entire column rode a squadron of noblemen carrying silken banners of the Holy Virgin and the coats of arms of the many aristocratic houses represented in the army. Behind them came a long, broad column composed of more cavalry, several thousand fresh infantry levies from Northern Spain, endless columns of supply wagons, and herds of livestock both to replenish the army's stores and to help convince the Moors of the irresistible power that was being brought against them by the Christians.

It was possible that the population of Malaga had been informed of Fernando's departure with a portion of his army and had taken this as a sign of an imminent retreat by the Spaniards, but the arrival of the queen was now greeted with a pitiful moaning sound that came from the city walls and echoed across the plains. Occasional jeers were shouted out by the Moorish soldiers, but these were half hearted and were drowned out by the lusty cheers emanating from tens of thousands of Spanish throats as the besiegers stood atop their barricades and along the route of march, waving banners, their weapons, or even old rags and blood-stained bandages to welcome their sovereigns. The many priests and monks who accompanied the army, whether in the role of chaplains or as actual combatants, stood out in their robes and cassocks, sprinkling the passing column with showers of holy water and intoned prayers for the protection of their lords and the success of their enterprise.

Raquel rode several rows behind the queen, with Juan riding beside her, while little Miriam followed under the care of Maria in one of the wagons at the rear of the column. She had seen the leer on Juan's face when the two royal parties had met early that morning, a look that spoke of the horrors he expected to inflict upon her as soon as they were alone, but she had met his gaze with a calm and even impertinent smile that caused him to frown in anger and confusion. As his discomfiture became more and more apparent, Raquel's smile had broadened, causing the color to rise in Juan's cheeks, and his nostrils to flare and his eyes to widen like a horse spooked by thunder and lightning. He had growled their few words of formal greeting and had become all the more enraged at Raquel's casual, playful tone.

"We'll see how much you smile tonight in my tent," he hissed into her ear, and his whole body trembled with her reply.

"Exactly."

Now, he kept casting glances in her direction, sometimes angry, sometimes confused, sometimes simply nervous, as she gaily chatted with Beatriz de Bobadilla who rode on her left, but he said no more, merely snorting occasionally and grinding his teeth. Raquel found it immensely amusing how easy it had been to disconcert this mountain of a man, all encased in iron and carrying enough weaponry to equip a small army, and all simply because she did not cower before him. She only wished that she had taken her decision much earlier on. It might have saved her a great deal of pain.

After taking a leisurely ride about the camp, allowing Isabel to receive the acclamation of "her loyal crusaders," the royal party finally dismounted and prepared for an evening of dining and entertainment. A vast pavilion had been set up near Fernando's tent, actually a series of huge tents arranged side by side with no walls between them, and under this dozens of trestle tables had been laid out, now all loaded down with platters piled high with roast boar, bear, and fowl, boiled fish, mounds of fresh bread, tureens of soup, and casks of wine. A small orchestra had set up in one corner of the pavilion and was playing light tunes on a collection of flutes and stringed instruments to accompany a young boy with a pure, clear tenor voice.

The men had been led to their seats as Isabel and her ladies performed the role of serving maids, bringing trays of food and drink to their valiant warriors. Fernando found this thoroughly charming, although he had originally protested that such activities were beneath the dignity of his queen, but Isabel had insisted. It never occurred to anyone that Raquel, who was busily doting upon Juan as he sat, eyeing her morosely, had suggested this little extravagance to the queen for a particular reason. Isabel, Raquel, and the other ladies of the court danced across the floor, bringing platters of food to their men, although Isabel finally allowed herself to be persuaded to take her seat at Fernando's side after one symbolic trip. The married ladies whose husbands were with the army catered to them, while the maidens or others with no spouse or close relative present chose a champion at random to attend throughout the evening, and it was widely assumed that the liaisons established at the table would be continued long after dark, after all had retired for the night.

With exaggerated obsequiousness, Raquel placed a large silver plate laden with a fat capon swimming in gravy in front of Juan, intentionally bending low over the table to display her cleavage to him, and then turned to fetch some wine. When she returned to the table, she found the capon untouched, with Juan scowling at her over it, his thick arms braced against the table while all around him ate, drank, laughed, and chatted totally disregarding him. Raquel simply smiled slyly at Juan and reached out to rip a drumstick off the bird, taking a large bite before tossing the leg back onto the plate and licking her fingers lasciviously. She then took a deep draft of the heavy red wine in the goblet she carried before placing it delicately near her husband's hand. She took a step back from the table, her hands on her hips and smiled at him again, raising one eyebrow and turning a bare shoulder toward him in challenge. She could see his huge dog, Asco, sitting just behind his right shoulder, looking back and forth between them with an expression of mixed anticipation at the scraps he hoped to receive and concern over his master's apparent reluctance to get his part of the eating done in order to produce the aforementioned scraps.

Juan scowled again, snorted, and then snatched up the goblet, draining it at one go before holding it out to her to refill. Then he reluctantly began pulling the capon apart and shoving the meat into his mouth, the rich juice running freely down his chin and over his hands. Of course, it was only natural that Juan would have some suspicions about the possibility of poison in his food. Everyone connected with the court had such thoughts in the back of his or her mind after the mysterious and conveniently timed deaths of the old king Enrique and the influential royal advisors Luna and Pacheco years before. It was not at all unusual for someone who had earned powerful enemies at court to suddenly be taken ill with vomiting and diarrhea, in a form not associated with any common plague. The victim's nails might suddenly blacken and fall out, along with the hair, or he might appear to have returned to complete normality and good health after the initial bout of abdominal pains, only to collapse and die in a matter of moments a few days later.

And it was well known that poison was a woman's weapon of choice.

Juan's suspicions would undoubtedly have been fed by Raquel's flirtatious and totally uncowed attitude since their reunion, and this would have been further reinforced by her enthusiastic participation in the serving of his food, also very much out of character for her. So her ostentatious sampling of his food and wine were consciously meant to put his mind at ease, at least on that score, and she now watched contentedly as he continued to gorge himself on roast fowl and boar, broiled river fish and mutton chops, interspersed with great slabs of buttered bread and cheese, handfuls of grapes and cup after cup of wine. He kept a close watch on Raquel, and she continued to grin at him innocently, coquettishly, but there was nothing in her movements that implied that she might be attempting to introduce a foreign substance into his meal, and she showed no ill effects herself from what she had sampled. What Juan found so disconcerting was Raquel's playful, yet intense, gaze, watching him eat and almost willing each morsel of food into his mouth.

Once even the traditionally insatiable knights had begun to slow the pace of their eating, all of the ladies took their places beside their respective husbands, lovers, or escorts, and the large open area in front of the royal table was cleared to allow a troupe of dancers to perform. Dressed in bright silks, they executed elaborate figures, lines of men intersecting with lines of women, and each outdoing the other with fantastic leaps and tumbles in time to the lively music of flute and tambourine. These were followed by jugglers and a children's choir, by which time the evening was well advanced, and many of the overfed guests were already snoring loudly, slumped in their seats, women as well as men.

It was hardly unusual, therefore, that Juan's eyelids had grown heavy, drooped, and finally closed, and that his breathing had become deep and regular, his head lolling back, and his mouth open with a string of drool bridging the gap between his upper and lower teeth. Raquel silently gestured for two pages to lift the sleeping man from his chair, a task that would have required a winch had he not followed the example of Fernando and other knights in doffing his heavy armor before dinner. Even so, it was only because Juan had come halfway back to consciousness and aided in their progress with stumbling steps that the two boys were able to support him, one under each arm, as they wove their way between the treacherous tent pegs and ropes back to Juan's quarters in the dark.

The Basque was lounging with the Castro brothers by the fire in front of Juan's tent, and they all rose as Raquel approached, followed by the pages with their burden. They quickly moved forward and took hold of their commander, carrying him into the tent and lowering him gently onto thick pile of blankets covering a straw mattress that served as the bed. The Castros and the two pages bowed their way out of the room, but the Basque lingered, as did the dog, Asco, who flopped down at the foot of the bed with a contented groan.

"Shall I help you get him undressed, lady," the Basque asked with a mildly suspicious tone in his voice.

Raquel smiled sweetly at him, raising one eyebrow suggestively. "No, thank you, I'll take care of *everything*. Oh, and take the dog with you," she added as the Basque moved toward the tent flap. It took some doing for the Basque to haul the animal out by his spiked collar, with the dog passively resisting by going limp and loosing a noisy fart in protest. Halfway to the entrance, Asco wrenched his neck free of the Basque's grasp and trotted back over to the bed, flopping down in his former spot. The Basque took a couple of steps toward him, but the dog raised his head and let out a deep, menacing growl.

"Oh, never mind," Raquel sighed. "Just leave him."

The Basque nodded, shrugged, and pushed out the tent flap.

Raquel followed him to the entrance, fanning the air and squinting at the odor, and then she pulled the flaps closed, carefully beginning to knot the leather laces to secure the opening. The tent was roomy, about ten feet square with vertical sides with supports in each corner and one large center pole. It was lit by a candleholder containing half a dozen stubby tallow candles on a small wooden table near the entrance, an extravagance that Juan would have never been able to afford in his youth but to which he had become accustomed of late. Raquel slowly moved around the perimeter of the tent, making certain that the side flaps were snug to the ground and that there were no openings at the seams.

She stood silently watching Juan for a long moment. He was on his back, snoring loudly, a trickle of drool running down from the corner of his mouth onto the blanket. Raquel smiled as she blew out one candle after another, leaving only a single one burning that barely lit the interior space. She moved to the bed and pulled off Juan's felt boots with some effort, then unlaced the laces holding on his britches, and pulled them down over his hips, then grabbed the cuffs and wrestled them off his legs. He wore no undergarments, and she pulled aside the tail of his shirt to look at his member lying limply against one of his hairy thighs. She smiled again.

She knelt down and reached underneath the mattress to withdraw a handful of leather thongs. She tied one tightly around one of his ankles, then the other, pulling roughly on the thong and watching it bite into his skin. He snorted once, but his breathing continued to be slow, deep, and regular. The powder Raquel had prepared according to the formula given her by Muhammad had been described to her as a sleeping potion, ideal for dealing with the sick and wounded as it dulled all sensation, even of the removal of an arrow or the stitching up of a deep cut. Raquel had given him a large dose, dividing it up between some concealed in his food and more in his drink, considering his size and knowing that the effects would be amplified by large amounts of wine. The small bit she had consumed when she had tasted his food and drunk from her cup might have made her drowsy except that she had taken the precaution of drinking several strong cups of the Moorish coffee Muhammad had also given her, having already proven to herself the truth of his claim that the drink tended to combat sleepiness. Besides, she was far too energized for any drug to affect her tonight.

She bound his wrists behind his back tightly, then the forearms almost to the elbow before slipping another leather strap between his ankles and finishing off by securely tying both wrists and ankles together and then stuffing a damp rag into Juan's open mouth. He grunted once or twice more, but nothing in this operation woke him. Raquel's gown was bound at the waist by a thick belt of woven silk cords of a golden color, set off nicely against the ivory of the material and the gold necklace and bracelets she wore. From under the belt she now withdrew a small, flat porcelain jar and a tiny little dagger with a narrow, double-edged blade. With the blade she peeled away the wax seal that covered the top of the jar and dabbed a little of a pale ointment out of the jar with her forefinger. She flipped aside the tail of Juan's shirt and, holding the jar and knife in one hand, carefully began to apply the ointment around the head of his penis, laying on a thick coating and rubbing it in gently. She could feel the member twitching slightly, and she thought she saw it beginning to swell, so she worked faster. She had never even witnessed a circumcision ceremony, but she had an idea that it would be harder to accomplish her task if he were erect and the skin drawn taut and did not want to take that chance.

Once the ointment had been applied, she waited for a moment, as she had been instructed, placing the jar to one side. Then, taking his foreskin gingerly between her fingertips, she inserted the point of the knife from the inside and poked it through. The blade was razor sharp, as Raquel had developed a ritual over the weeks and months past, ever since she had decided on her course of action, of spending nearly an hour each night honing the edges on a whetstone or stropping them on a leather belt. She ran the blade in a quick circle around the head of the penis, and in an instant, the job was done, and she was left holding a thin circle of skin between her fingers. She quickly rubbed more of the ointment into the cut, but, as she had hoped, the medicine not only deadened sensibility, it also restricted bleeding, and only a thin line of red could be seen where the foreskin had once been connected. Juan moaned and writhed once, but just let out a muffled belch and continued sleeping.

Raquel grimaced at the grisly trophy in her hand and then turned to find Asco staring at her with an intensely curious and vaguely hopeful gaze. A wicked smile spread across Raquel's lips, and she made a little kissing noise at the dog before tossing the bit of skin into the air, where the animal caught it effortlessly and gulped it down, rewarding her with a slobbery smile and the faint thumping of his tail on the carpet floor of the tent. Raquel then sat down on the floor next to him, scratching absently at a spot under one ear, half of which was missing, evidence of one of his many battles, and wordlessly watched her sleeping husband.

The dawn came, and the canvas walls of the tent began to glow a deep golden color. The candle had long since burnt out, but Raquel had not slept. She had cleaned the wound several times during the night, reapplying the ointment each time, and now there was virtually no trace that she had done anything. Juan had begun to stir, whimpering softly through the rag that still filled his mouth, and attempting to roll over, only to be stopped by the awkward position of his arms and legs.

Suddenly, his eyes popped open, and he let out a stifled scream that could not have been heard outside the tent. He struggled frantically, the huge muscles of his shoulders and upper arms bulging and the veins standing out along the sides of his thick neck and at his temples. His squealing became higher and higher pitched as Raquel slowly got to her feet and walked over to the bed. Asco sat up partly and grinned, letting a glob of saliva plop to the floor loudly as he thumped his tail in greeting.

Juan was looking desperately about the room, his eyes red-rimmed and wide, a jumble of sounds coming from his throat that were probably threats of the most terminal kind, but Raquel just sat casually next to him on the bed, then reached out and grabbed a handful of his matted red hair, twisting her face toward hers.

"Good morning, husband," she spat. "I have a little surprise for you."

She reached down for the edge of his shirt, and Juan instinctively jerked backward, trying to double over to protect himself, but the bindings behind his back prevented him from moving more than a few inches.

"Now, now," she cooed. "Don't be such a big baby. Here, look."

She pulled the shirt back and grabbed his penis with her free hand, waggling it toward his face.

"See? Now doesn't that look much better?"

Juan shrieked once more into the gag, but Raquel tightened her grip twisted his hair painfully.

"Shut up and listen to mama," she hissed into his ear. "You have no idea how much of a temptation it was for me not to cut it *all* off and be done with it while I had the chance, so count yourself lucky. You see," she went on, releasing him and standing up, "I just had this idea that, in order to make this a real marriage, we should have something in common, something to share. Now, I know that my little secret was something that we shared, but it just didn't seem like enough somehow, a little too one-sided. So then this wonderful idea came to me. Wouldn't it be just perfect if *you* became Jewish too? That way we wouldn't have this burden hanging over us of you possibly denouncing me someday, whenever it suited your fancy. Of course, this will mean the end of those magical nights of love-making we both enjoyed so much, but if priests and nuns can do without, I suppose we can too. You see, if you were to talk to the Inquisition now, no matter what sort of story you concocted, I would just be able to make my confession, beg for mercy, and as a token of my repentance, surrender my own dear husband, who has been a secret Jew for many years. I assure you that this little bit of physical evidence will convince them. You can tell how nicely it's healed already. You really must take some of this ointment I found with you on your next campaign. It's absolutely marvelous in its healing powers. Of course, I should apologize to you," she added hastily, chatting in a gay tone. "This all should have been done with proper ceremony, with a rabbi present, with prayers and candles, and a nice dinner afterward for close family members, but I'm sure you understand that that just wouldn't have been possible under the circumstances, so your induction into the ranks of God's chose people had to be something of an impromptu affair, just the two of us, and Asco, of course. Although I did arrange a little snack for him." She started to giggle and covered her mouth with one hand.

Juan had stopped making noise, but his breath was now coming in tortured gasps through his nose, and he could not take his eyes from his suddenly altered manhood. Raquel stooped over him and delicately pulled the rag from his mouth.

"You bitch!" he wheezed, between gulps of air, but Raquel only smiled when she noticed that he had already realized his own need to remain quiet. "I'll kill you! I swear to God that I'll rip your heart out and eat it!"

"Oh, I don't think so, dear," Raquel said, shaking her head. "That's the sort of thing that can get you garroted. I know that you've had your heart set on a glorious death on the field of battle, so it would seem a waste to ruin your chances for that when we still have a perfectly good war going on just over the next hill. I suspect, and I think that you'll agree with me, that no matter what sort of story you came up with, especially if it had anything to do with your present *condition*, wouldn't absolve you of my murder. The most that it would get you would be the attention of the Inquisition and rather worse treatment than you'd get from the king's justice. So let's just not talk about such unpleasant things, shall we?"

"Then what do you want?" he growled. "Aren't you just going to denounce me yourself for the satisfaction of watching me burn before you? That's your little plan, isn't it?"

Raquel placed her fingertips over her breast in horror. "Why, Blessed Virgin forbid!" she giggled. "I certainly don't want to burn. I've seen it done, and I didn't enjoy even that! And we have our little daughter to think about. There are far too many orphans about in this country as it is. Now, this is what I propose." She bent down, her fists planted on her hips, her nose almost touching his. "As far as the rest of the world is concerned, nothing has happened. We are married, but, unfortunately, your call to the duty of your lord keeps you endlessly busy off on campaign, first against the Moors, then against whomever else you choose to slaughter. And during those times when, like now, we are inadvertently deposited by fate in the same place at the same time, we will appear to take up lodging together, but you will keep your filthy hands off me, like brother and sister, like mother and son. Is that quite clear?"

Juan made no reply, but his entire body quivered with rage, and sweat streamed down his face, a large drop of it collecting at the tip of his nose. With a single swift motion, Raquel pulled her little dagger from her belt and pressed the blade against Juan's neck, delicately shaving a patch clean of the ruddy stubble that covered his face.

"And if your *desires* should ever get the better of you," she added in a voice barely above a whisper, "you had better kill me, because I swear by both our Gods and every saint and prophet in heaven that the best you will be able to hope for from life will be that the Inquisition will get its hands on you! With your inspiration, I have learned ways of killing a man that you could never prevent, and no one will ever detect, but which will rot you from the inside out, turn your guts to jelly, your bones to water, and your brain to fire! Now, do you understand me, husband?"

Juan paused a long moment before nodding his head, almost imperceptibly, since the little dagger was still hard against his throat.

"Wonderful!" Raquel chirped twirling about him and using the blade to slice easily through his bonds. "I knew that we could work things out if we only put our hearts into it."

Juan groaned as he painfully brought his arms around in front of him, gingerly flexing his muscles and rubbing his wrists and ankles where the thongs had left deep imprints in his skin. Raquel knelt to help massage the sore areas, but Juan jerked away.

"Now, don't be that way," she chided him. "We don't want your men or anyone from the court to see these marks. They'll think we've been very naughty indeed!" She laughed carelessly and went back to rubbing one of his ankles vigorously between her palms, and this time Juan let her.

After a few minutes of this, Raquel stood up and went to the tent flap untying the fastenings one by one.

"I'm off to attend the queen," she called over her shoulder. "I trust that you won't forget what we've talked about. Oh, by the way," she added, touching a finger to her temple, "I heard once that there was an operation of some sort you could have done by a physician to have things put back the way they were, but I wouldn't know whom to ask about it. Also, I wouldn't recommend it as I've heard that it doesn't always work. I mean," she started to giggle again, "*it* doesn't always work afterwards, if you get my meaning. Bye-bye, my husband," and she blew him a kiss over her shoulder.

Juan just glared at her, and Raquel smiled as she swung out into the sunlight. The Basque was sitting some yards away, eating oatmeal out of an earthen bowl with his fingers. He looked up at Raquel as she walked by, smiling at him, and his eyebrows twisted into a complex frown of confusion. As soon as she was out of sight, he rose and strode into the tent. Juan was sitting on the bed, one hand covering his face, the other gently rubbing his groin, oblivious to his lieutenant's presence. The Basque paused for a long moment before speaking.

"Is everything all right?" he finally asked. "I didn't, uh, *hear* anything during the night, and I was worried that something might have happened." Both men knew that Juan's bedroom habits normally resulted in a great deal of noise, whether the thud of blows, the crashing of furniture, or the sobbing and screams of his partners.

A look of intense rage came over Juan's face, distorting his features, and turning his skin a deep crimson. "Get out! Get out, you imbecile!" he screamed, half rising, but still clutching the tail of his shirt about his genitals, and reaching for his sword.

The Basque backed away, both hands up. "Good God!" the Basque exclaimed, pausing when he saw that

Juan was apparently not planning to cross the floor. "What did that bitch do? Give you some disease? Do you want a physician?"

"No!" Juan shrieked at him. "Don't do anything. Don't call anyone. Just get the hell out of here and leave me alone! And take that filthy, traitorous animal with you," he added, aiming a clumsy kick at Asco and wincing at the effort, while the dog easily sidestepped the blow, his tail wagging, more than happy to join in the game.

"Jesus, Mary and Joseph!" the Basque grunted, taking the dog by his collar and heading toward the door. "I told you that married life was not for the likes of you and me. Look what it's turned you into! You're as touchy as a young maid who's just had her first good reaming!"

Juan could not see. His vision was blurred by a red fog of pure hatred and rage. His privates at least didn't hurt terribly, no more than if he had landed too hard on his saddle. But he was a ruined man. It wouldn't be that hard to disguise his condition from his men, since, Lord knew, they didn't bathe all that often, and he could always step off into the bushes to do his business out in the field. But there was no denying that the hold he had had over Raquel was gone for good. The bitch was more than able to turn him in to the Inquisition. A woman who was capable of doing what she had done was obviously capable of anything. Not that she'd just turn him in. She was telling the truth when she said that she didn't want to burn, along with her father and mother, but she had also made it clear that, if it came to a choice between yielding to him as he wanted and the stake, she'd take the stake.

Juan suddenly felt a great emptiness inside him. Surely he could find women to use as he needed to use them, but that wasn't it. There was something about Raquel, there always had been something about her, that obsessed him. Not that they had ever been just man and wife in the proper sense, not the way they talked about it in the poems that the traveling bards always told. They could never have just sat together by the fire and talked about their lives, their children, or anything else. But he had wanted her above all women, from the moment he had first seen her, and now she would never be his again. And that hurt more than the pain in his groin.

Chapter Three
Granada

Muhammad sat his horse amid a small clump of trees atop a round hill flanking a long, narrow valley several leagues to the southeast of Granada. The late afternoon sun was warm, and a slight breeze moved the branches of the trees, dappling the ground with a pattern of light and shade that danced about him constantly. But Muhammad was not enjoying either the view or the pleasant weather.

Down the center of the valley straggled a ragged column of soldiers, about two thousand men, he estimated, between horse and foot, banners hanging limp down where the breeze did not reach. A cluster of horsemen rode at the center of the column, and the glinting of the sun on metal showed that they were more heavily armored than most of the others, many of whom wore only padded cotton or boiled leather jerkins and carried wooden shields as their protection. That would be el Zagal and his commanders as the old warrior led a pitiful remnant of his former power to attempt to relieve the Moorish forces under siege at Malaga. There was no chance that an army this small could

569

defeat Fernando's host, but they might divert some of his strength for awhile, and possibly even break through to the besieged city to reinforce the garrison. This would be a mixed blessing, of course, as word had spread through the kingdom that Hamet el Zagri, the commander of the garrison, had cut rations to only four ounces of questionable bread in the morning, and two more ounces in the evening, and this only for the soldiers. Famine already stalked the streets of the port city, and there were reports that many of the civilians had already died from hunger. A few hundred more mouths to feed might not be as welcome as all that after all.

Muhammad heard the other horses approaching and did not bother to turn his head as a pair of Numidian light horsemen took up a position farther down the slope. He knew that there would be others posted in a rough circle around his little hillock.

"You are not riding with my son today?" a woman's voice asked, coming like the buzzing of the large black bees that hovered near the tops of the wildflowers that speckled the grass on the slope.

"Not today, your highness," Muhammad replied wearily, only just turning his head in Fatima's direction and bowing slightly. She was mounted on a small gray mule, awkwardly perched sidesaddle, and was wrapped from head to foot in heavy blue robes, with only her dark, penetrating eyes visible. Muhammad wondered idly how women could stand the heat in such attire when he could feel a thin trickle of sweat running down his temples while he wore only a light silk tunic above his riding breeches. But then, perhaps, the sweat was not entirely due to the warmth of the day.

"You do not approve of his plans?"

"He did not consult me, probably because he knew that I would object. My lord was gracious enough, and considerate enough of my feelings not to put me in the position of having to disagree with him publicly."

"Again," she added.

"Yes, again, your highness."

"You do not feel that my son has a right to defend his throne?"

"I fought for him these past months in the streets of Granada because I did feel that he had a right to defend his crown, but this is different."

"No, it is not," she insisted, and he thought that he could hear the tone rising in her voice.

A bugle call could now be heard, rising up to them slowly, reluctantly on the heavy warm air. Movement was now visible in the advancing column, men turning in their saddles, wheeling their horses in the direction of the sound, but it was too late. A thick cloud of horsemen came charging out of a heavily wooded gully flanking the valley and struck the column solidly in the flank, scattering the marchers in all directions. A few men tried to ready their crossbows or draw weapons, but that only made them easier targets for the charging lancers. At the same time, a line of infantrymen also advanced out of the woods on either side of the gully wearing green capes that identified them as Abu's men, took up a position within fifty yards of the road, and poured a volley of arquebus fire into the milling defenders. A thick cloud of white smoke now fringed the column and partially obscured Muhammad's view. He was grateful for even this small favor.

Near the head of the column, el Zagal's party formed up and turned, drawing to it riders who had dispersed at the first enemy onslaught. They charged back up the road, overpowering the first attackers they encountered, but now a second squadron of cavalry emerged from the gully, hurling javelins while advancing at the gallop, and a number of el Zagal's men went down.

El Zagal's infantry had obviously not been prepared for combat, their shields slung over their backs, their bows unstrung, and their firearms unloaded. Most of these now panicked and either raced off back up the road whence they had come or dropped their weapons and fell on their knees, raising their hands in surrender. Muhammad was relieved to see that most of them were at least being taken prisoner, rather than massacred on the spot, but this was cold comfort.

A small party of brilliantly dressed and accoutered horsemen now cantered out of the woods to a position just behind the fighting against el Zagal's vanguard. Muhammad could see Abu's green banner and the figure of Hafez prancing about on a white stallion, waving his sword in the air ferociously without actually coming into contact with the enemy. Abu had at least double el Zagal's numbers, besides benefiting from the element of surprise, and el Zagal now apparently realized this, pulling his few remaining troops slowly back up the slope on the far side of the valley, and then suddenly breaking contact and galloping off toward the east, back toward Guadix and safety.

"You do not appear to rejoice in my son's victory," Fatima commented as a cheer went up from the ranks of Abu's men. They busied themselves in gathering the prisoners and herding them back in the direction of Granada without bothering to pursue the fleeing el Zagal and his party.

"I fear that this *victory* may cost your son more than many a defeat, your highness," Muhammad sighed. "It was one thing to fight against el Zagal in a straight up civil war. Our kingdom has, unfortunately, become accustomed to that sort of thing, but to blatantly go out to attack his uncle when all he was trying to do was to bring succor to a city that was being besieged by the Christians? I fear that our people will not appreciate the political nuances of such an action, and they will turn their faces from him."

"If el Zagal were to defeat the Christians, somehow," Fatima argued, "they would turn their faces from him in any case."

"We both know that there was little chance of that happening. El Zagal's was a vain but honorable effort with no hope of success. I suppose it then just becomes a question of how many wrong things a man is entitled to do in order to achieve his ends, no matter how lofty those ends might be," Muhammad went on, "before God Himself turns his face away as well."

Fatima opened her mouth as if to continue, but Muhammad turned his horse's head and began to ride slowly back to the palace alone.

GRANADA

Chapter Four
Malaga

Raquel leaned against a tent rope, fingering its braids with one hand, while she looked down the hillside toward the walled city below. The land all around the city, for hundreds of yards away from the sand-colored walls, was barren red clay, scarred with trenches and pock-marked with the dark mounds that were the forward batteries of falconets and other small cannon. Outside of that ring were larger emplacements for the massive lombards and culverins, each one teemed over by small dark figures, like termites on a rotting log, and sometimes adorned with a fluffy white cloud of smoke just after the piece had been fired. Several fires were blazing within the city walls, thick columns of greasy black smoke rising up to heaven, and at several points the walls had been battered into piles of rubble by the big guns. Out in the harbor, the Moors had floating batteries that traded shots with the Castilian fleet offshore, while nimble little feluccas with brightly colored sails, busily plied back and forth from the batteries to the shore bringing fresh ammunition and relieving the crews.

There was a stiff breeze blowing from behind Raquel toward the city, so the sounds of the battle were carried away from her. She could see the swarms of Moors who had come pouring out of several sally ports in the walls clashing with the companies of Spanish infantry in their trenches and the columns of reinforcements that had now moved up to the line, but the clash of steel and the battle cries were missing at this distance. Only the occasional note of a horn or thud of a gunshot would suddenly make its way up to her position on a random gust of air. She knew that Juan was down there somewhere, that his company had been in reserve behind that section of the line when the Moors had attacked, and he must be in the thick of the fighting, slashing about him with a great two-handed sword, probably hoping for a quick and glorious death in battle. She prayed that he would get his wish.

It suddenly occurred to Raquel that, if Juan did happen to be killed on the field, it was entirely possible that his new *condition* might well be discovered in the course of retrieving his body and preparing it for burial. If that were the case, the Inquisition would need no more evidence than that to launch an investigation of Raquel and her whole family. Hers was known to be a *converso* family, after all, while Juan's was an old Christian family. The assumption could well be that she had managed to convert him to her faith, and the burden of proof would be on her to establish otherwise. That could mean imprisonment, torture, and death, but Raquel found herself to be surprisingly apathetic about the entire matter. If it happened, it happened. The issue was out of her hands one way or the other, whether he lived or died, whether they were discovered or not, and it might, in a way, be something of a relief for the entire charade to finally be over, even in that way.

She watched the battle with that in mind. The Moors had surged over the first line of trenches, the first of a triple ring of fortifications that the Spaniards had built surrounding the town on the landward side, but they had been held at the second by the timely arrival of several hundred men-at-arms. These heavily armored infantry, each one a miniature fortress equipped with long two-handed sword or battleaxe, positioned themselves behind the trenches, not in them, protected from missile fire from the city walls by the presence of the attacking Moors themselves. The Moors then had to try to scramble into and then out of the trench under the swinging blades of the knights, who were spaced well apart to give them room to handle their weapons. Another line of Spanish troops, these armed with crossbows and arquebuses, backed up the men-at-arms, firing into the ranks of the Moors beyond with a steady rhythm that thinned out the attackers and disrupted their formations.

Still, the Moors pressed on, for more than an hour, flinging wave after wave of men against the Spanish lines that did not bend or buckle. The Spaniards had the luxury of numbers that allowed them to relieve their fighters at the front periodically, when their sword arms wearied of the harvest, while the Moors, already weakened by hunger and demoralized by the news that had recently come in of the defeat of el Zagal and his relieving army by his own nephew, Boabdil, had to fight on until they were killed or disabled, or until they broke and ran for the safety of the walls. Finally, as the sun began to set, trumpets blaring from the nearest Moorish tower called off the attack, and the Moors retreated back through their gates, pursued energetically by still more fresh Spanish troops who continued the slaughter until arrows and bullets from the walls drove them back to their own lines.

Raquel continued to watch as the thick columns of Spanish infantry gradually dispersed, and the golden points of light that were the squad campfires began to wink on in the gathering darkness, soon covering the plain around the city with a galaxy of stars reflecting those that soon came into view in the sky above them. She turned and headed back to the royal tents, wanting to pay her respects to the queen before returning to her own tent, that Juan had not visited since *that* night, to put little Miriam to bed with a story and a kiss.

She came around the corner of the vast royal tent to find a small commotion taking place in the open space before it. A dozen mailed riders had just ridden up escorting a small, dark man in tattered, dirty robes, riding a donkey whose ribs could clearly be counted and whose head hung down , vainly poking in the mud of the camp for a blade of grass. A number of courtiers, men and women, and idle soldiers had gathered about to observe the goings on, and Raquel joined them. The captain of the troop was explaining the situation to the head of the queen's bodyguard, a massive Catalan knight who towered over them all, a mass of muscle and iron, wearing a tall conical Norman helmet with steel nose guard, a shirt of chain mail that hung to his knees under his tunic, and the red cloak of an officer of the *Santa Hermandad*.

"We found this old relic picking his way through our lines on the far side of the city," the captain was saying. "No one knows how he got through to the third line without having been seen, but he claims to be a holy man and to have come from the city with an offer of a surrender on behalf of the citizenry. He says that people are starving in the streets, and most of them want to surrender, but Hamet el Zagri and his *Gomeres* soldiers have threatened them and murder anyone who even talks of making a peace. He says that he can arrange to have one of the sally ports guarded by the local militia opened for us, but he insists on meeting with Fernando and Isabel themselves to get their word that there will be no slaughter and that the inhabitants will be allowed to take their belongings and leave the country if they want."

The Catalan scowled, first at the captain, then at the Moslem holy man without speaking. The old man's arms and legs, which hung out from the folds of robe, were like broomsticks, his skin like cracked and aged leather, and his beard and hair were matted with dirt and stood out from his head at crazy angles. The guard finally grunted and disappeared into the tent. A few minutes later, he stuck his head out from the tent flap and growled at the captain. "The king and queen will receive him in a moment. Bring him in here."

The captain beckoned to the old man with two fingers, and he dismounted, bowing repeatedly to all present, and made his way toward the tent, his hands clasped before him, his shoulders bent in humility, but Raquel noted a burning intensity in his dark eyes that did not imply either fear or subservience. She picked up the hem of her skirts to protect them from the mud and quickly went around to a side entrance to the tent and went in herself.

Inside she found, not the king and queen, but Isabel's confidant, the Lady Beatriz de Bobadilla and the visiting Portuguese nobleman, Don Alvaro de Braganza, seated on some low cushions on the elegantly carpeted floor of the tent where they had apparently been eating some stuffed dates from a copper plate set out before them. Raquel assumed that Beatriz had sent a messenger for the royal couple and planned to entertain the envoy from Malaga in the meanwhile.

The Catalan officer led the Moor into the center of the tent, then merely indicated that he should stand there by pointing at the spot and then retired to the tent entrance, standing there with his thick arms folded across his chest, his right hand hanging conveniently near the hilt of his sword. The Moor kept up the bowing he had begun outside, to the guard, to Raquel, who stood off to one side where a couple of pages were mixing wine in a large bowl, and to Beatriz and Don Alvaro. Raquel realized that the sumptuous attire of this noble couple, both of them decked out in brocaded silks and with ostentatious jeweled rings and gold necklaces, probably had convinced the scruffy Moor that these were the king and queen themselves, and she smiled at what would be his confusion when the real monarchs entered, even more richly dressed than these two. Suddenly, however, the Moor let out a screech, *"Allah u akbar!"* and reached into the folds of his cloak, drawing out a long narrow dagger and rushing at the two seated figures. He slashed downward at Don Alvaro first, who raised his arm to protect himself and received a deep gash from elbow to wrist that gushed blood over the pale green of his tunic. The Moor then rushed on toward Beatriz, who was petrified with fright, her eyes huge, and her mouth open in a soundless scream. The Catalan's sword hissed as he jerked it from his scabbard, but he was at least six long paces away.

Raquel snatched a tall earthenware wine pitcher out of the hands of the nearest page, who was also standing, paralyzed, with his jaw hanging open, and hurled it with all her might at the head of the assassin. The pitcher shattered against his skull, causing him to stagger to one side, but the Moor did not stop. With another scream, he raised his dagger again and lunged at Beatriz, but that second of hesitation had been enough. Now the guard had crossed the floor, and the blade of his sword whipped around in a flat arc, neatly lopping off the upraised arm and burying itself deep within the old man's neck. The severed arm flopped onto the cushions at Beatriz's side, and she kicked and scrabbled to get away, finally now able to give voice to a shrill scream of terror and disgust. The old man simply collapsed onto the floor with a sigh, like a pile of rags, but

Raquel could still see the burning commitment in his eyes as they stared sightlessly up toward heaven.

Raquel tore the scarf from about her neck and rushed over to wrap it around Don Alvaro's arm just as the captain and several of his men charged in through the front of the tent, swords drawn, and Isabel and Fernando came walking in through the other entrance, looks of confusion on their faces.

"The old bastard must have taken them for your highnesses," the Catalan explained to Fernando while Isabel and Raquel attempted to comfort the hysterical Beatriz.

"And didn't anyone think to search him for weapons?" Fernando bellowed.

The Catalan looked to the captain, who raised his arms over his head. "We took the old man from a troop of Estremadurans who found him. I assumed that they had searched him thoroughly. I did check under his robes and found nothing, but he must have had his dagger down between his legs. I admit that I did not think to look there, sire, and I accept full responsibility for this failure," he added, hanging his head with the most miserable expression on his face that Raquel had ever seen.

Fernando snorted, then let his face soften. "Well, this isn't the first time they've tried something like this and won't be the last I suppose. Thank you for your quick action," he said to the Catalan, who bowed.

"I would have been too late if it were not for the jug of wine that the lady served him," he said, nodding in Raquel's direction.

Fernando laughed heartily, his fists planted on his hips. "Oh, that goes without saying. Little did the Moors realize that they were going up against our secret weapon, Lady Raquel, our Amazon warrior maiden."

Raquel just blushed and continued, stroking Beatriz's hair.

"Now load that old bastard up in a catapult and return him to his people," Fernando roared. "And see to it that he's sewn up in a nice fresh pig skin first, just as our way of expressing our appreciation for their interest in peace."

The next morning, several dozen Christian prisoners were marched out onto the city walls and beheaded by the *Gomeres*, who threw the bodies and heads into the nearest Spanish trench. Still, with all hope of relief gone, the city finally surrendered unconditionally several days later. One third of the population was sold into slavery to pay the costs of the campaign, another third was used to exchange for Christian captives elsewhere in the Moorish kingdom or in North Africa, and the remainder divided up among the army as booty, along with virtually everything of value in the city. Juan received four adult slaves and two children, which he dutifully sent home to his father. Four hundred of the fierce *Gomeres* were sent as slave-soldiers to the Pope in Rome, where they performed faithful service for years, fifty ladies to work as servants for the queen of Naples, and 450 Jewish inhabitants were ransomed by various wealthy Spanish Jewish tax farmers and allowed to settle elsewhere in Spain. Thus the last great Moorish port was lost.

Book Six

1490

GRANADA

Chapter One
Near Sevilla

The stone wall was cold and hard against the back of Raquel's head as she sat on the wooden pallet that served as a bed in the tiny cell. The room was perhaps six feet on a side with the bed hung from the wall opposite the heavy oak door with its little Judas hole for the guards to peek through as they walked by, but the ceiling was at least thirty feet high, the outer wall arching in to meet the inner one high above her head, with a small round window about twenty feet above the floor providing the only dim light available. Raquel was in a monastery on the outskirts of Sevilla, probably the Santiponce to the northwest of the city, although she was not certain of this, having been transported there in the dark of night inside a closed, curtained wagon. She only knew that the trip had taken something over an hour of fast driving.

Isabel's court had been visiting the city and planned to stay through most of the year although Easter Sunday was only just coming up. The court had been in a frenzy due to preparations for the marriage of Isabel's eldest daughter, also named Isabel, to Prince Afonso of Portugal, putting to rest once and for all the possibility of a renewed armed conflict between the royal houses of Spain and Portugal, at least during the lifetimes of the reigning monarchs. Given the queen's commitment to the concept of the political value of protocol and public display for the royal house, the planning for the wedding, actually a proxy wedding without the groom, as the formal ceremony would take place in Portugal, had been only slightly less complicated than that for the logistical support for a major military campaign, and Raquel had spent many late nights with the queen plotting seating charts, menus, entertainments, and guest lists just as they would provide for artillery ammunition and reinforcements for the army.

The expenses incurred in putting the wedding together had been staggering. Naturally, in addition to crown lands that Isabel and Fernando conferred upon their daughter and her husband, lands whose revenues would no longer be coming into the royal coffers in the future, the queen had to provide her eldest offspring with a suitable set of gold and silver plate, which ran to over three million *maravedis*, roughly the income of two thousand working class men for a full year. Another half million *maravedis* went toward the rich trappings for the mounts of the ladies of the court during the obligatory processions and tournaments during the two weeks of festivities, 100,000 for the harness and caparison for Prince Juan's horse alone, and endless amounts for the lavish food and drink offered to hundreds of noblemen and women from Castile, Aragon, and Portugal who attended, with lesser quality viands for the townspeople to keep them in a suitably celebratory mood during the entire show.

Ostensibly, it was Prince Juan who, as heir apparent to the united thrones of Castile and Aragon, was sponsoring the spectacle on behalf of his sister, but the money came directly from the royal treasury, which had already been drained by the constant campaigning against the Moors during the previous years. Isabel was a firm believer that this show of largess would convince the crowned heads of

Europe that the Spanish royal family was indivisibly united and literally awash in gold, thus damping down any possible consideration of foreigners fomenting new civil wars in Spain like those that had troubled the country during Isabel's youth.

The entire extravaganza was timed to finish on Easter Sunday with the proxy ceremony presided over by Cardinal Mendoza. All of the great nobles of the realm were on hand decked out in cloth of gold and festooned with gold chains and studded with jewels along with the one hundred gentlemen of the court and a similar contingent of ladies in waiting, all desperately, if discreetly, competing with each other for the most lavish display of personal wealth and beauty. A vast jousting field had been set up along the banks of the Guadalquivir River, just outside the city walls, at which the elite of Spanish society watched days of races, tournaments, jousting, and armed melees that lacked little to be simple battle between gangs of heavily armed men and that resulted in several deaths and innumerable serious wounds. There were other entertainments as well, such as dancing, juggling, plays, and musical recitals that the court could observe from the comfort of a massive set of wooden bleachers shielded from the brilliant spring sunshine by a silk canopy embroidered with the yoke and arrows of Isabel and Fernando. Thousands of common folk crowded around the barricades set up along the edges of the field, elbowing each other for a better view of the goings on, both of the competitions on the field and of the awe-inspiring show of pomp in the stands, while squadrons of food vendors, mountebanks, singers, and pick-pockets plied their trades among them, and a group of enterprising prostitutes even set up shop underneath the viewing stands until they were discovered and ejected by the royal guards.

Even though the capture of the fortified city of Baza the previous year had brought the surrender of el Zagal and a virtual end to the war, at least in the eyes of most of the people, Isabel and Fernando, along with their commanders, knew that there would still be fighting to do eventually to rid the peninsula of the stain of Mohammedism and that this would all cost money. The fall of one Moorish city after another had brought immense wealth into the royal treasury in the form of tribute, slaves sold, and property confiscated, even after the soldiers had been given their fair share of the spoils, but the cost of the campaign, the armies of laborers, the mountains of supplies, and the massive parks of technologically advanced, and very expensive, artillery, had still served to drive the crown deeply into debt. Fernando's policy, as wise as it was, to grant lenient terms to Moorish cities that surrendered with a minimum of resistance limited the amount of fighting to be done, and those cities would ultimately contribute their share to the wealth of the state, but, in the short term, such generous provision had prevented the systematic looting of the conquered territory which would have eased the debt burden considerably.

The capture of Baza, one of el Zagal's last major strongholds, had been hard-fought, with the siege lasting over six months, but the city's commander, el Zagal's faithful lieutenant Sidi Yahye, had finally surrendered on terms in December of 1489. He had even gone so far as to convert secretly to Christianity, convinced as he was that the victory of Spanish arms must have been due to the favor of God for their religion, and to go to el Zagal himself and convince him to lay down his arms and submit to the authority of the Spanish crown. El Zagal had finally agreed and had been named "king" by the Spanish sovereigns of the tiny principality of Andarax with a token army of two thousand men and a stipend provided by Fernando of four million *maravedis* per year, a further drain on the royal treasury.

The news of el Zagal's submission had been greeted with widespread celebration throughout Spain, but the expectations of a final peace had proved to be short-lived. According to the Treaty of Loja, Muhammad XII, or Boabdil as the Christians called him, had agreed to surrender Granada once Guadix, Almeria, and other Moorish cities had been captured from el Zagal, providing a basis for a truncated little kingdom over which Boabdil would be allowed to rule. It had originally been envisioned that Boabdil himself would have been the one to conquer these lands, but Fernando and Isabel had recognized his inability to do so and had thus been willing to exchange these cities, captured by their own armies, for the much more important city of Granada, thus formally putting an end to an independent Moorish realm on the Iberian peninsula.

Boabdil, however, had apparently had other ideas. When emissaries from Fernando and Isabel traveled to Granada with piles of lavish presents and many gracious words on their lips to ask for the keys to his citadel, Boabdil put them off. At first, he claimed that to surrender to the Christians at that time would be more than his life was worth, that he would be torn to pieces by the Granadan mob as a traitor to the faith, especially after his own attacks on el Zagal's forces during the siege of Malaga in dutiful compliance with his treaty of alliance with his Christian overlords. He begged for time to prepare the ground for such a move, claiming that the most Catholic kings owed him that much consideration for his past service, and the ambassadors reluctantly agreed. Time went on, as it tends to do, but there appeared to be no effort on Boabdil's side to surrender the city as promised. In fact, rumors abounded about Moorish foundries working through the night to manufacture new swords, lances, and arrows and to cast artillery and of diplomatic missions sneaking abroad to the Berber kingdoms of North Africa and to the Sultan in Constantinople, pleading for military intervention to support the Moorish kingdom in a renewed war against the infidel in Spain. Still, Boabdil procrastinated, claiming that, while he and the majority of the merchant class in Granada were more than willing to accept Fernando's terms and to help bring a new prosperity to the region through expanded trade between East and West working in peaceful harmony, he was being held a virtual hostage by hordes of fanatical Moslem refugees, survivors of the battles for other cities in the old kingdom who had now clustered in Granada and refused any sort of accommodation with the Christians. He went so far as to chastise Fernando for having been perhaps too generous in his treatment of the survivors of the battles for cities like Malaga, former supporters of el Zagal who had no love for Boabdil, and whom the Spaniards would have been better off to have killed outright when they had the chance.

Fernando's patience finally came to an end, and he was now in the process of putting together a vast *cabalgada*, a mounted raid deep into what remained of Granada's territory on the fertile *vega*. During the late summer of 1490 Fernando planned to strip Boabdil's realm bare of livestock and crops, to burn isolated villages to the ground and to storm what smaller strongholds he might. This would be much less costly than a formal campaign to reduce Granada itself by siege and would at least partially pay for itself in the loot gathered by the raiders. Ideally, it would also put the fear of God and Spanish steel into the hearts of both Boabdil and his subjects and force them to come to terms. If that failed, the raid would certainly undermine the ability of Granada, the greatest of the Moorish fortified cities, to withstand any subsequent siege after a winter of privation, and the Spanish army could then move in during the coming spring, enclose the city, and grind it into the ground.

The upshot of all this was, however, that there would be no respite from the immense expenses of the war. Fernando would have to ensure that the army he took with him would be invincible. A defeat at the hands of the Moors, even a relatively minor one, would reinforce the decision to resist in Granada, and it might well encourage the millions of Moorish subjects, only recently and imperfectly subjected, throughout southern Spain, to take up arms again and attempt to throw of the Spanish yoke while there was still a viable Moorish kingdom on the continent that could support them. A violent uprising had already occurred in el Zagal's former stronghold of Guadix and had been bloodily repressed by the Marquis of Cadiz but not before hundreds of Spaniards had been slaughtered and important army contingents diverted from Fernando's army for far too long a time. A major defeat might even convince other Islamic powers to send support to Boabdil after all with ships, men, and gold.

Tens of thousands of men would have to remain under arms, living off the royal treasury, consuming mountains of grain and herds of livestock on a monthly basis, even considering the food and treasure that could be captured from the Moors. Unfortunately, years of warfare had already impoverished the Moorish lands, and the Spaniards could not count on being able to live off the land for weeks at a time. Furthermore, the free flow of trade in a large portion of the peninsula would continue to be disrupted by war, depriving the crown of the taxes and revenues that would result therefrom, and relations between Christian Spain and the Moslem kingdoms of North Africa and the Levant would remain tense or even openly hostile.

Isabel, strongly supported by Raquel's efforts behind the scenes, made her now legendary appeals to the *cortes* of both Castile and Aragon, to individual townships, to the professional guilds, the immensely rich noble military orders like Calatrava and Santiago, to the Jewish community, and to the Pope in Rome, and through the Pope to the rest of the monarchs of Christendom, to support this final crusade with men, money, and equipment. And her pleas had not gone unanswered, with substantial amounts in money and kind coming in from all over Spain and the rest of Europe, and thousands of men, both knights and common soldiers, flocked to the peninsula in search of glory and plunder. But it was still not enough. It was never enough to fill the vast maw of war, it seemed to Raquel. As she had done more than once during her reign, Isabel had been obliged to put up her royal jewels as collateral for a loan with merchants in Valencia and Barcelona. This was not such a drastic move as it might have sounded, since the royal jewels, apart from serving the function of dressing up the queen during state occasions, also functioned as a sort of portable, easily tapped royal treasury. Still, such a step was only considered when all other means of raising funds had been attempted and found wanting.

The crown was also forced to put aside all other projects requiring financing, no matter how necessary or promising. Roads, canals, walls, and mills throughout the kingdom were disintegrating rapidly, and brigandage was on the rise as virtually every able-bodied man had been conscripted to serve in the army, stripping the local *Santa Hermandad* gendarmerie of its best manpower while thousands of deserters from the army roamed the country in search of victims.

Even though Isabel was particularly interested in Spain's entering the competition with the Portuguese for opening a trade route to the Indies by-passing the Moslem-dominated land road through the Levant, there was no money for this either. Raquel had joined Isabel in listening to a proposal from a very animated, but not very realistic would-be explorer, one Cristobal Colon, for a means of reaching the Indies by sailing west across the Atlantic, thus avoiding the southern route around Africa in which the Portuguese were already predominant. He was not a Spaniard, but a Genoese, although Raquel suspected from his use of the *Ladino* dialect that his family was a *converso* one, probably among those who had escaped from Spain to the more tolerant lands of Italy in the previous century, and she had vaguely wondered whether he might have known something about the fate of her older brother, but had been afraid to ask.

His theory was quite plausible, of course, since everyone since the days of the ancient Greeks knew that the world was round and that, by starting at any point, one would eventually reach the opposite side and ultimately return to the source by traveling constantly in one direction. Whether this would be possible in a practical sense was another matter, however. Raquel had patiently pointed out to this Colon person that he had grossly underestimated the circumference of the earth by arbitrarily substituting shorter Arabic miles for the longer statute miles used by Ptolemy in his calculations some two thousands years before. She cited the works of various Greek and Arab astronomers and mathematicians in this regard, but Colon had insisted that his figures were not only correct but that he was willing, literally, to bet his life on them. She also noted that perhaps he was being overly optimistic about his likely sailing speed in unknown waters with unknown currents and winds, especially as the speed of any ship would gradually be reduced as seaweed and marine life attached itself to the hull during weeks of sailing. She concluded by stating that, unless he were fortunate enough to encounter a chain of habitable, and preferably inhabited, islands like the Canaries strung out like a belt around the earth, he and his men would inevitably run out of food and water before they had made it halfway around the globe and would die out in the vastness of the ocean. Scribbling on a scrap of parchment, she estimated the circumference of the earth according to the leading authorities and the estimated land distance from Spain to the Orient from travelers' reports and triumphantly demonstrated the physical difficulties of such an endeavor.

Isabel had thought that the potential gain was worth the investment, since Colon was only asking for enough to equip a handful of little caravels, and he and his men would be assuming the personal risk voluntarily. The cost in Europe of spices and silks from the Orient was astronomical, mainly because of the fees and tariffs charged by Moslem middlemen along the land route from Asia. If a way could be found to detour around the Moslem lands, any European power that could accomplish this would be awash in wealth, and Islam, simultaneously, would be similarly weakened by depriving it of this vast source of income, so the thought of such a sea route had intrigued for years the two powers best positioned to launch expeditions of discovery to the west, Spain and Portugal. But there was simply *no* money for any project that did not directly relate to the war. Isabel had ultimately been obliged to turn the enthusiastic Italian away with the vague suggestion that he come back again once Granada had fallen or that he seek sponsorship elsewhere, which he had apparently done without much success.

In any event, Raquel now blamed herself for not making the connection between the dire financial straits, of which she was only too well aware that the royal government now found itself in, and the sudden increase in the frequency and intensity of meetings between Torquemada and Isabel. It had been some years since the gaunt, humorless Torquemada had been Isabel's confessor, a role now still played by the must more jovial and humane Hernando de Talavera, yet it was hardly unusual for the queen to be closeted with senior Church officials on a variety of religious and secular matters. The Inquisition that Torquemada was responsible for overseeing, was still active in different parts of the realm, setting up shop in one city after another, issuing its appeal for miscreants to take advantage of the period of grace to make their confessions, and then pursuing those who did not with now legendary diligence and even ferocity. Raquel knew that, although only one source out of many, the Inquisition had provided millions of *maravedis* to the royal coffers in terms of fines imposed on those who confessed, and who were generally glad to buy their way out of the Inquisition torture chambers at any price, and even more in terms of property confiscated at the outset of an investigation, property that might or might not eventually be restored to a suspect who was later proven innocent, as some occasionally were. In any case, the property was considered the crown's own from the moment of confiscation and subject to sale or mortgage as the crown saw fit, with any repayment to come in the crown's own good time, possibly years later, if ever.

But, even with her intimate knowledge of court politics and the history of the sudden rise and fall of even the most prominent courtiers, Raquel had allowed herself to become complacent in a life that had taken on many of the trappings of normalcy. The constant campaigning of the royal armies had kept Juan away for months on end, along with hundreds of other noble warriors, and, even when he did find it necessary to put in an appearance in the city where Isabel happened to be holding her court, the visits were mercifully brief. Raquel had status enough at court to merit a modest apartment, and Juan would take up lodging in one of the spare rooms without question or protest and never attempt to communicate personally with Raquel, even when both were present at unavoidable official functions. Juan made no special effort to have contact with little Marisol either, almost as if he had guessed that the child was not his. This sort of arrangement was common enough in many of the planned, political marriages at court and hardly raised an eyebrow among the ordinarily perceptive and gossipy ladies in Isabel's entourage.

The one thing that had struck Raquel as odd over the past several years since the *operation* was the look in Juan's eyes when she did see him across a crowded hall or seated among the army commanders at a state dinner. She had fully expected thinly disguised expressions of hatred and disgust, the same look that he had directed at her the morning he had awakened to find his manhood altered, but instead she now detected what appeared to be a deep longing and a sense of hurt that she was hard-pressed to explain, and she had to assume that she was simply misreading him. She could not imagine that this man, this animal, felt anything toward her remotely approaching what most people understood as love. No one could possibly treat another human being as he had treated her and pretend to claim even the vaguest affection or respect. Yet, it could hardly be that he simply missed the excitement and pleasure that he got from her in his perverted way or that he merely regretted the loss of such a valuable piece of property, as many Spanish men considered their wives. There would undoubtedly be an ample supply of captured Moorish women, slaves, and prostitutes available to him as he fought with the army to satisfy those horrible needs and desires. And still, there it was, and almost child-like sense of loneliness and emptiness in his eyes that froze the ironic smile Raquel had practiced in front of her mirror, even before she could form it on her lips when she saw him.

In any event, life had gone on for Raquel relatively uneventfully. She immersed herself in her work as always, and now had the added diversion of watching Marisol grow and learn from day to day. In fact the greatest worry that lay upon her mind at this point was at what age she should tell Marisol about their *true* faith and her *real* father. She corresponded with Muhammad on a regular basis now, using her uncle in Granada as their go-between, and she even contemplated how they might ultimately come together, once the war was over and he would be just another one of the Spanish crown's tens of thousands of Moslem subjects. She envisioned simply disappearing from the court one day, on an ostensible trip to visit family or friends in some other part of the country, and never return. She could have word sent back that she and the child had died of some mysterious but all too common malady, and that would be the end of it. Then she could turn up on Muhammad's doorstep and live with him as his wife. To anyone else she would merely be an anonymous Jewish woman and her child married to a Moor, not that unusual an event, as she understood it, and she would not even mind posing as a Moslem, if that proved necessary. After all, the differences between Islamic practice and Jewish were relatively minor, and there was no Moorish Inquisition for her to worry about. The only question was whether

Muhammad would have her, and she could not believe that there was any real doubt on that score.

All these thoughts flew from her mind like a cluster of bats fleeing the light of a torch when she had opened the door of her apartments at the palace several nights before and found three men standing in the corridor. Two were junior officers of the *Santa Hermandad* that she did not know, and they stood silently flanking the third, a tonsured monk, a Dominican who identified himself simply as Brother Jaime. The clean-shaven young monk wore only the plain brown cassock and rope belt of his order and could not have appeared more benign. His face was pale, and his soft, thick hands did not have the look of familiarity with hard work, but there was the same intensity in his pale green eyes that Raquel had seen and feared in Torquemada's, although the two men could not have otherwise been more different. The soldiers wore no armor or mail under their red cloaks, but they did both carry swords at their sides, just in case, but then so did most of the gentlemen of the court.

"My child," the monk began in the dull, sweet tone used by priests in the confessional as one of the soldiers pushed the door open and all three walked into the room uninvited, "it is my sad duty to inform you that you are under arrest by the order of the Holy Office. I will give you a moment to gather some things to bring with you, but we must be on our way fairly quickly and may not return for some days."

Raquel did not respond immediately but glanced to one side and saw Maria, peeking around the edge of the door leading to one of the bedrooms, holding Marisol by the hand. Maria appeared about to open her mouth to say something, or perhaps to cry for help, but Raquel silenced her with a firm but barely perceptible shake of the head and a jerk of her chin indicating that she should step back into the room, out of sight, and Maria silently retreated, putting a hand gently over Miriam's mouth as she went.

"And what am I accused of, may I ask?" Raquel finally asked, taking pains to keep her voice from quavering, and not moving from the spot. "And by whom?" She knew that the Inquisition must already have damning information, and she also knew that she was quite guilty, but it would cost nothing more to play the game out to the end. An innocent person, she figured, would never just hang her head and go along quietly, and there was always the chance that the evidence against her would not hold up. This had happened before, and people had actually been exonerated by the tribunal. She had no property to speak of, so there would be no incentive for the Inquisition to hold her merely for her wealth.

She also knew that the Inquisition never revealed the names of its "witnesses," but it seemed a logical next question to ask. After her years at court, and with the jealousy of many courtiers over her close relationship with the queen, there would be no shortage of persons who would gladly perjure themselves to have her removed. On the other hand, if the testimony had come from Juan himself, or from one of her parents under torture, all was lost in any case.

The priest smiled. He was a young man, not more than twenty years old and had an innocent look about him like a little boy trying to gather the nerve to ask for an extra serving of desert, and the tautness of his robe over his thick body implied that he had done that more than once in his life.

"My dear lady," he began, spreading his arms wide, his long sleeves hanging like the wings of an angel, "I'm sure that you know that it is the practice of the Holy Office not to reveal the names of those who testify to us, otherwise people would be too frightened to bring charges against the unfaithful. Obviously, anyone who would not have any scruples about pretending to practice the True Faith and, in secret, continuing to practice devilish rites, even to the defilement of the Host and the bloody sacrifice of poor Christian children, would hardly have a problem with murdering someone whose testimony could put them in prison or bring them to the stake. In any event, you have been accused of being a clandestine judaizer, along with your father and mother. Do you have anything that you would like to say to me about that at this time?"

"I do not," she said coldly, raising her chin a little and holding the monk in her gaze. "This is clearly a false charge brought against me and my family by a person or persons jealous of our position at court, and I demand to see their proof."

"This is a very common occurrence," Brother Jaime said nodding, as if he could not have agreed more, then added hastily, "not false accusations, that is, but people denying the charges and claiming that they come from personal enemies. It really would be so much easier if you were to confess of your own free will. A full and complete confession, along with true repentance, would undoubtedly move the Inquisition, and it is quite possible that you would be accepted back into the faith with only the most modest of public acts of atonement."

"I must inform the queen of this," she stated abruptly. Usually, in Raquel's experience, mention of the queen and the heavy implication that Raquel was not only able to meet with her whenever necessary but was actually *obliged* to meet with her, would tend to put the fear of God, so to speak, into most anyone.

The monk smiled again and nodded to the soldiers who moved around behind Raquel, one on either side. "Do you think that we would consider arresting a member of her royal highness' court without consulting with her first?"

"I cannot believe that the queen has authorized this outrage!" she insisted, but the two soldiers each took a grip on her arms, not painful, but quite firm, and began to propel her gently but irresistibly toward the door. Raquel attempted to plant her feet, but they easily moved her along, their gaze never diverting from straight ahead.

"I assure you that she has, my lady," the monk said, falling in behind them. "She was shocked at our revelations, but she was, nonetheless, adamant in her support of our mission and of the necessity of rooting out iniquity wherever it might be found, *especially* within her own court. In view of your attitude, perhaps it would be best for us to be on our way directly. You will be provided with anything that you may need in the short term, and you can always send for any other items you require."

Those were the last words anyone had spoken to her. Her attempts to question the guards as to her destination on the long ride to the convent had studiously been ignored. She had not bothered to ask to communicate with her father, for, if he were not already a prisoner himself, the last thing Raquel wanted to do was to draw attention to him as well. The thick oaken door of her small cell was opened periodically, and a silent nun would take away and replace the chamber pot each morning and would bring a tray of simple but ample food, usually a half loaf of coarse bread, a bowl of gruel, and a couple of pieces of dried fruit, taking it away again an hour later, as yet untouched as Raquel hardly had much of an appetite.

She had no doubt about who had informed on her. How Juan might have done so without incriminating himself, she had no idea. It was entirely possible, of course, that a deranged mind like Juan's would not be overly concerned with escaping punishment as long as she was brought low in revenge for what she had done to him. Perhaps he was sitting in a cell somewhere, perhaps even in this very convent, awaiting trial. The more she thought about it, the more it seemed plausible to her that he would gladly sit beside her in the tumbrel, and smile at her with that wicked, evil smile of his from his own stake as the flames leapt higher and higher around them both.

Still, Raquel found herself to be surprisingly calm as she sat there. She was concerned, of course, about what might be happening with her parents. Her father's strategy of making himself, and her, so indispensable to the crown that they could not be touched by the Inquisition had clearly failed, but that had been a calculated risk from the outset, and it was not as if they had had any choice in the matter. It had been a conscious decision by all of them to maintain their Jewish faith, with all the dangers that implied, and then they had decided that, rather than make themselves as inconspicuous as possible, they should actually seek out important positions and work most industriously as the only kind of protection that they could hope to have in this world.. Now, they had been found out, and there was nothing they could do, or could have done, to avoid this situation. At least, she thought, Marisol would not be persecuted, and she would undoubtedly be taken care of by Beatriz de Bobadilla, or perhaps the queen herself, as a ward of the court, educated in fine style, and found a good match with a suitable dowry. She would be raised as a Christian, and her young memories of her mother might eventually fade and be erased, but she would come to no harm, and Raquel had faith that they would be reunited in heaven and that God would ultimately judge her actions mercifully. Still her arms ached to hold her little girl just once more, to kiss her soft cheek, and brush the hair back from her brow. Would that have been too much to ask? In spite of herself, tears began to trickle from the corners of her eyes and she brushed them away impatiently with her sleeve.

As she sat in her cell, in the near darkness, Raquel could hear sounds coming from throughout the monastery. There was water dripping somewhere, and the clanking of metal, possibly coming from a kitchen somewhere, which would explain the vague smell of food that wafted in under the door. She could hear muffled chanting and the shuffling of feet as the tenants of the convent came and went to Mass, Vespers, and Matins, and from the tiny window high up in the wall, she could sometimes hear the singing of birds and the rush of the wind, and she wondered whether she would ever have a chance to stand in the sun again and feel the breeze on her cheek. Well, there would be that one chance, the day they took her to the *quemadero*, and they would probably pick a fine day for it as rain would dampen the wood. There were no screams of agonizing inmates, no hissing of whips or the creak of infernal machinery of torture, but Raquel knew that this did not mean that, deep in the cellars underneath the convent, all the torments of hell were not being inflicted on some hapless victim, perhaps even her own father, and she shuddered.

There was a squeak of metal on metal, and the door of the cell swung open slowly causing Raquel to jerk her head forward, realizing that she had dropped off to sleep. She expected to see Brother Jaime, but instead she found herself facing the slender frame and deep-set dark eyes of Torquemada himself.

"I cannot tell you how much it distresses me to come to you here, my daughter," Torquemada said in a low tone that positively breathed sincerity and compassion, thus implying just the opposite.

"Your apology is accepted, father," Raquel smirked. "I assume that you've come to explain that the charges against me and my family have been found to be without basis and that you will release me immediately. I will require a horse or wagon to take me back to the palace, and I will expect something in writing exonerating me of all wrongdoing."

Torquemada chuckled softly and shook his head. "I only wish that I could do that. I want you to know and to believe that I take no pleasure in this. I would be much happier if all of my investigations and inquiries were to prove that all of the Christians in Spain are what they profess to be, true believers and keepers of the faith. It tears at my very heart to find so much evil and deceit, even among people in positions of great trust in the court of our most Catholic sovereigns."

Raquel did alter her stern expression. "In that case, I demand to hear what the precise accusations are against me and who has made them."

Torquemada smiled again. "Ordinarily, that would be out of the question, as you well know, but," he went on, "in view of your standing at court and the fact that your accuser is a confessed judaizer himself, not some envious neighbor or disgruntled servant, as is often the case in such matters, I see no reason why you should not be allowed to confront him, even as we are in the process of *interviewing* you."

Torquemada stepped back and gestured toward the open door where two tall soldiers, these dressed in dirty leather aprons, the kind blacksmiths and Raquel's own father often wore at the forge, and equipped with the iron-shod wooden staves typical of jailers had now appeared in the hallway outside. Both men had long, matted hair and thick dark beards and expressions that were at once studiously blank and somehow deeply sinister. Raquel rose gracefully and walked erect past the priest, taking care not to brush against him, and followed one soldier down the long barren corridor, the other soldier falling in behind Torquemada.

As she expected, their route led down a flight of narrow stairs, taking them below ground level, and the way here was lit only by occasional torches in wall sconces. They made their way through a maze of passages, turning this way and that for several minutes, leaving Raquel confused and disoriented as much as she had tried to mark their route, before coming to a small door made of thick oak planks and braced with iron studs. The lead soldier unlocked it with a huge iron key from his belt and motioned for Raquel to enter with a jerk of his thumb.

Just inside the doorway, Raquel found herself facing a thick quilted pad hung like a curtain which she had to push aside, and she could now hear a strange, low moaning sound, like a cold wind moving down a narrow valley. She found herself in a low-ceilinged room, again lit by torches and by a blazing fire in a large hearth set into the far wall. The walls were all covered with the same padding that had blocked the door, and Raquel realized that this was why no hint of sound escaped from this room, and she shivered to think of the reason for such precautions.

If she had not known better, Raquel would have suspected the room was some kind of metal worker's shop. There were a great many iron tools laying about on the floor or propped against the walls, tongs, hammers, and sharp implements whose purpose she did not care to guess, and there were several braziers filled with glowing coals and even a small leather bellows near the hearth, but she knew that these tools were for creating pain, not for shaping metal.

Near one wall was a simple wooden frame, about six feet in length and half as wide, just four wooden beams raised up from the floor to about waist height. At each end stood a windlass and a collection of ropes. But the piece of furniture that immediately captured her horrified attention was a straight-backed chair in the center of the room, all made of iron, with the figure of a heavy-set, naked man sitting stiffly in it. The back of the chair faced the door, and Raquel found herself involuntarily walking slowly around it to see its occupant. The dark hair and beard were matted with sweat and filth and in wild disarray, and she could see at a glance that it was not Juan, but her throat seized at the thought that it could possibly be her father, judging by the man's size. Step by step, she moved around the room, staying as far from the chair as possible until she could see the face, and neither Torquemada nor the guards made any objection. The man's head lolled to one side, and there was a look in his red-rimmed eyes that pleaded for pity, but there was no sign of recognition, or even a sense of consciousness in the face. It was he who was making that low moaning sound, not a scream, not words, just a constant whine, broken only when he took in fresh breath.

It was not her father, though, it was Tobias, the *converso* tax farmer, their neighbor from the old house in Cordoba, her father's partner in the cannon foundry, the last person Raquel had expected to find here. Raquel could now see that he was strapped into the chair with leather belts around his chest, arms, and legs, and that a large iron brazier was sitting on the floor between his feet, filled with brightly glowing coals that had turned the iron bands of the brazier and the legs of the chair itself red hot. His legs were shriveled and the color of well roasted meat, a deep mahogany, and another man wearing a leather worker's apron and a black hood over his head was carefully ladling melted lard onto Tobias' skin, much as one would baste a roasting fowl. The air in the room was filled with an aroma vaguely similar to baked ham.

"But this man is a true Christian," Raquel whispered feebly, not directly to Torquemada, who had come to stand beside the chair and was gently stroking Tobias' hair back out of his face. "I've known him all my life, and I would be willing to swear that he is."

"That's exactly what *he* said at first," Torquemada agreed. "Don Tobias apparently earned the enmity of a great many people in the course of his duties collecting the crown's taxes, a dangerous weakness if you have a terrible secret to hide. One of them turned him in as a secret practitioner of the vilest of Jewish rites, and we naturally opened an investigation. Initially, he insisted that he was innocent, although he was glad to offer up most generous financial donations to the Holy Office and then to provide us with your name and those of your parents as people he knew to be guilty of that crime. We naturally took this as a very positive sign of repentance, but, in order fairly to do our duty to God, we of the Holy Office must insist on a true and full confession, due to the gravity of the charges that had been brought against him. Unfortunately, given the deceitful nature of man, the only way to get that kind of soul-cleansing release, is through the judicious application of physical incentives, such as this, which is called 'the Spanish chair,' although I seriously doubt that we invented this device ourselves. It is with great reluctance that we undertake such measures, but it is really the only way, and now Tobias has assured us that he, too, secretly avoided the eating of pork, often thought in Hebrew, and did *not* truly believe that he was consuming the body and blood of Christ during Holy Communion. You see that we are putting oil on his burns in order to keep him from dying of his torment, it prolongs the process without lessening the pain. He will eventually be pardoned for his sins now that we are convinced, *almost* entirely convinced," Torquemada added, nodding toward the coals and the horribly burned legs, "that he has no further secrets to confide. He will be given an appropriate penance, his considerable wealth with become the property of the crown, and he will be allowed to go forth and live a pure and irreproachable life in the future."

"But it's not true," Raquel insisted, still in a whisper barely audible above the sound of Tobias' whimpering. What Raquel found the most frightening was the look of almost sincere pity and reluctance on Torquemada's face, one that told her that no one could expect any kind of mercy from this man.

"That's precisely why we must resort to these tactics, my child," Torquemada went on. "We must prove that his confession *is* true, before God. Now, to make absolutely sure, the gentleman will be allowed a period of repose tonight before his formal hearing before the council tomorrow. At that time, he will be given the opportunity to repeat his full confession, of his own free will."

"And if he recants, he will be brought back here for more torture," Raquel argued.

"Well, of course," Torquemada shrugged. "Oh, excuse me." He turned toward the hooded man. "I think that will be sufficient."

The man nodded and used a large pair of iron tongs to pull the brazier away from Tobias' legs. He then took wooden a pail of water and dumped it onto Tobias' lap, raising a cloud of steam from the glowing chair and a scream from the victim that might have been of relief, but was probably was of renewed agony. Two other hooded men appeared from a side door, and between them they unstrapped Tobais, lowered him onto a flimsy stretcher which they carried from the room. Tobias kept on screaming in an insane, animal way until the padded curtain dropped, the outer door closed, and the shrill sound was finally lost.

Raquel stood staring after them for a long moment. "Are my father and mother here as well?" she asked without looking at Torquemada.

Torquemada did not respond immediately, and Raquel finally turned toward him to find him frowning pensively. "I regret to inform you that your mother has died." He shook his head in disgust. "While we try to be discreet about the affairs of the Holy Office, word sometimes leaks out, and it would appear that your mother learned of the charges against her and took her own life by drinking poison, just as our officers were arriving at her door in Cordoba. A subsequent investigation indicates that she had a lethal mixture prepared and on her person at all times for just such an occasion." Torquemada crossed himself. "May God have mercy on her soul."

Raquel covered her eyes with one hand, but tears did not come. "And my father?"

"As I said," Torquemada went on, "word apparently leaked out. We have reason to believe that it was your father who had cultivated people connected with the Holy Office, or perhaps he took warning on his own from the arrest of his partner. It was probably he who sent word to your mother.

We believe this because we intercepted one of his servants, a supposedly converted Moor who was on his way to you with the same news. In any event, your father escaped. The *Santa Hermandad* is looking for him now, and we expect his apprehension at any moment. He may have crossed over into Moorish territory, or he may have gone abroad as there were reports that he was seen heading toward the port of Valencia."

Now the tears did come, but they were tears of relief. Her father was alive and these bastards didn't have him!

Torquemada nodded sagely. "I can easily see the reason for your tears, my child. The suicide of your mother and the flight of your father certainly do not speak well for your own case. Obviously, what reason would they have to escape, each in their own way, if they were not absolutely guilty."

Raquel did not bother to correct his interpretation. She considered herself now to be lost, and the only solace she now had was that her dear father was probably safe, and her mother, at least, was beyond anything that they could do to her.

"And my husband?" Raquel asked, out of curiosity.

"Your husband, the valiant Juan Ortega de Prado, was not mentioned in the original charges," Torquemada sniffed. "Naturally, he was not arrested. We are not conducting some sort of witch-hunt here. We have our procedures, and we follow them to the benefit of all. Of course, it would not be unusual for *you* to bring his name up during the course of our investigation, unless you would care to do so right now. It is hard to imagine that a wife could be a practicing Jewess without her husband at least knowing of it, if not taking an active part in the blasphemy. So, naturally, he will have to be investigated as well, as a matter of course."

"My husband is a Christian," Raquel found herself saying. "His family is not even of *converso* origins." Why she would make even the slightest effort to protect the man simply escaped her. In fact, now that she thought about it, if the Inquisition were to torture and kill him, especially with the physical evidence that Raquel herself had provided for, it might be the one real positive contribution to society of the entire institution. Still, something prevented her for turning over even Juan to the mercies of these animals.

"Again, I put it to you, my dear," Torquemada continued after a long pause. "It would be infinitely better for you to cleanse your soul now and make a full confession of your sins."

"Like that man Tobias did?" Raquel snipped at him between her sobs.

Torquemada sighed. "Have it your own way," he said, and he gestured to the two hooded men who had now returned to the chamber.

They came up behind Raquel, one on either side, and suddenly grabbed at the neck of her gown and tore it away in one violent tug. Raquel shrieked and clutched at her garments, but the third hooded man had also rushed forward and pinned her arms at her sides while the other two men pulled away her stockings and underwear, leaving her totally naked as she writhed in their iron grasp, then, just as suddenly, they released her to stand, trembling from cold, fear, and rage between them. Torquemada turned his face away ostentatiously, shielding his eyes with his hand. Now Brother Jaime also appeared, also with his face averted, and he tossed Raquel a folded piece of cloth. She clutched it to her breast and found it to be a simple cotton shift that came down to her knees, which she quickly pulled it on over her head but continued to shield both her breasts and her loins with her hands as the thin material was nearly transparent.

"I apologize for this," Torquemada said, still facing the far wall of the chamber, "but it is generally required that prisoners be deprived of their clothing during the investigation, although we do allow females this simple dress out of modesty.

"And I suppose that it would have been unacceptable to simply have given me this in my cell and allow me to change there?" Raquel asked with no attempt to conceal the irony in her voice.

"We must follow our established procedures," Torquemada shrugged.

Raquel was about to say something else, but two of the men pulled her roughly over to the wooden frame where one of them bent down and grabbed her by the ankles while the other picked her up in a bear hug and dropped her on the floor on her back. The third man quickly looped the noose ends of two ropes over her ankles, passing the ropes over one end of the frame. He then ran to the windlass on that end and turned the spokes, taking up the slack. The first man now straddled her and jerked her arms up over her head, holding out her wrists to his colleague who similarly tightened rope nooses around them and then spun the windlass to pull those ropes taut, leaving Raquel with her arms and legs stretched upward but with her bottom still resting on the floor. She wriggled briefly, her primary concern being that the shift had slipped way up almost to her waist, but she soon realized that this exercise was both futile, and even ridiculous, in view of her situation.

"All I can suggest to you, my child," Torquemada said, turning toward the door, "is that you look deep into your soul and reveal everything, without restraint or modesty. It is now beyond the point where you could hope to avoid this kind of pain, but it will make your ordeal end all the faster and will serve the far greater good of helping to redeem your immortal soul, and that is my greatest goal." He waved one hand in a gesture of resignation, lifted up the curtain flap and disappeared.

"Please do confess, my child," Brother Jaime whispered, almost in Raquel's ear, in a honeyed voice.

She turned to him and found an expression, not of compassion or even of cold objectivity, which she might have expected, but one of intense interest as his large brown eyes ran up and down her body, lingering on the smooth skin of her exposed thighs, and she twisted her body slightly to help shield her barely covered loins. There was something in his eyes that seemed to beg her *not* to confess, at least not for awhile. At the moment, Raquel was extremely uncomfortable, apart from her shame over her exposed flesh, with the ropes already chafing her skin and cutting off circulation to her feet and hands, but she had no illusions that this would be the extent of the procedure.

Brother Jaime turned to the hooded men and nodded. One man operated the windlass on each end of the frame, and both now turned the spokes a quarter turn in opposite directions, pulling the ropes tighter and lifting Raquel's body clear of the floor. She felt a sharp pain in her shoulders and legs that caused her to gasp, and she saw the shadow of a smile dance across Brother Jaime's lips. He nodded again, and the men have the wheels a half turn each, pulling her body higher still, almost level now with the top of the frame. The pain redoubled, and Raquel gasped as she felt sure that one of her arms had been dislocated. She screwed up her face, closed her eyes, and felt the sweat beginning to collect at her temples despite the clammy coldness of the room. She did not want to give them the satisfaction of hearing her cry out.

"Are you a Jew, my child?" Brother Jaime asked in a sweet, low voice, bending down to put his lips next to her ear.

Raquel did not answer. She was concentrating all of her force on keeping the ropes from pulling her body apart, although she had no idea whether it would be better for her to relax and go limp or to resist as strongly as possible. It was the natural reaction, and she pulled with all her might. She expected them to tighten the ropes further at any moment, but no one moved. Brother Jaime just continued to look into her face from just a few inches away.

"There are many misconceptions about how this device is designed to work," Jaime whispered into her ear. "While the actual hauling of the ropes is a key element, it is only one aspect. It is actually the weight of your own body that does most of the work, eventually tearing muscles and pulling the joints from their sockets, which is why there is no table underneath you on the frame. The same could be accomplished by simple brute force, aided by the mechanism of the windlass, but that would be far too quick to have the desired effect. You see, the point is not just the inflicting of physical pain, but working on your mind, giving you time to think about how much it hurts and how much more it will hurt in the near future. Ideally, that is what will convince you to cooperate, not just ripping your limbs from your body. Nobody wants that," he added, casting another appreciative glance at her thighs. But it was clear that he did want that very much. Raquel had the distinct impression of the similarity between Brother Jaime and her own husband when he was in the throes of exercising his own particular passion. Raquel just gritted her teeth and tried to focus her mind through the waves of pain that washed over her like a red tide. She hung there suspended, her arms and legs beginning to tremble uncontrollably with the effort.

"Are you a Jew?" he asked again, softly, almost sweetly.

He waited for what seemed like a very long while, but he finally stood up and waggled a finger at the two men. They each knocked aside a wooden chock, and the wheels of the two windlasses spun free, dropping Raquel to the floor with a thud. She expected the pain to stop, but a whole new kind of pain engulfed her shoulders and legs, and she screamed aloud, rolling herself into a tight ball as her limbs convulsed. She had lost all sense of time. The ordeal seemed to have lasted forever, but it occurred to her that it might have all been over in a matter of minutes. Then she noticed that the fire in the grate, that had been burning high when she arrived, was now down to a bed of crimson embers, which implied a lapse of at least a couple of hours.

"This phase of the procedure," Brother Jaime went on in a professorial tone, "is meant just to give you a *taste* of what you can expect. Now you will be given a night to think about things. I assure you that no permanent damage has been done to you, yet," he added meaningfully. "The pain will subside in a couple of hours, but its memory will stay with you far longer. Hopefully, tomorrow, when we reconvene to continue with the investigation, the very feel of the ropes being cinched up on your wrists and ankles will be sufficient to jostle those memories, even before any other action is taken, and help to convince you to change your mind and cooperate as you should."

He bent down low over her again and waited a long while, then snorted and waved toward the door with impatience at her continued silence. The two men unfastened the ropes and, with one supporting her under each arm, nearly carried her from the room, her limp, bare feet dragging along the rough flags of the floor.

She lay on her back on the hard wooden pallet that served as a bed in her cell and watched the pale ivory arch of moonlight passing through the tiny window as it drifted along the wall. The muscles in her arms and legs twitched spasmodically for some time but gradually relaxed, leaving her with a dull, burning ache throughout her body. Now only her chest heaved as she sobbed silently, her hands pressed tightly over her mouth, so as not to give the guards the enjoyment of hearing her cry.

She heard a faint rasping noise of metal on metal, and the door of her cell opened slowly. A dark figure slipped into the cell and closed the door firmly after. Raquel squinted, but all she could see was a darker patch against the near black of the corner of the room.

"Have you had a chance to think, Raquel?" came the hoarse whisper of Brother Jaime. "Are you willing to talk now?"

"I have nothing to say to you," she replied, doing her best to keep her voice from cracking.

"You're not going to make us go through that horrible scene again tomorrow, are you?" He crossed the room slowly and knelt by the side of her pallet. Raquel could detect the smell of sour wine on his breath.

"I'm not in a position to make you do anything," she snapped. "And while we're at it, I find it interesting that your men find it necessary to hide their faces, as if I were the one who posed a threat to them. From my point of view, I have to say that I could not feel more helpless to do them any harm."

"Church libraries are filled with books about the thousands of martyrs to the faith who have fallen to the forces of the devil over the past fifteen centuries," the monk argued, resting back on his heels, "so don't tell me that there is no danger to the Church or its officers for the carrying out of their duties. Even here in Spain, we've had cases of people, undoubtedly those who knew very well that they were guilty of blasphemy, heresy, and apostasy, who armed themselves and planned assassinations of members of the Holy Office, and some of them succeeded in their plots, even if they were later caught and punished." He paused for a moment, then leaned closer to her. "But that is not why I have come. I have no desire to argue Church policy."

"Then why have you come?" she asked, sliding back, wedging herself farther against the wall.

He leaned closer still, his face barely an inch from hers. "I think that I can help you. In fact, I know I can, if you will only let me."

"How can. . .?" she began, but then he felt a cold, clammy hand in her bare calf, sliding slowly up past her knee.

She jerked her legs up to her chest and swatted at the hand, but Brother Jaime reached across her body and pinned her arms while again beginning to push the material of her shift up toward her waist.

"Please!" she hissed. "Stop or I'll scream!"

Brother Jaime let out a low, sinister laugh and began to nuzzle Raquel's neck, licking at her ear lobe. "A scream in this place would attract no more attention than a prayer in Church at High Mass. But you shouldn't worry. I won't hurt you. In fact, I can do a great deal to keep the others from hurting you. If you will only confess and provide me with the names of a few people that you must know to have been involved in Jewish practices, even if they weren't, just people you know who have done wrong, any wrong. There must be plenty of those about the court. And you will be free, with my support," he added significantly.

He tried to slip his fingers in between her thighs, which she pressed together tightly, then slid his hand around toward her buttocks, but she pressed herself firmly against the bricks of the wall, and he had to content himself with caressing the curve of her waist and probing the small of her back. He planted his mouth over hers, trying to insert his tongue between her lips, but she kept twisting her head from one side to the other violently, then reared backward and brought her forehead down with as much force as she could muster against the bridge of his nose.

Brother Jaime let out a grunt of pain and released her, staggering to his feet, grasping his nose with both of his hands, and even in the dim light Raquel could see a dark stain of blood spreading down over his chin.

"You bitch!" he shrieked. "I am going to break you into pieces. I don't care how much you confess. You will be howling like an animal and beg for mercy before I'm done with you. And I'll fuck you while your screaming. You'll never even live to burn at the stake. Many people die during the process of the investigation, and I promise you that you'll be one of them. You're *mine*! You'll never see the sun again. And when I'm done with you I'm going to get that little whelp of yours and skin her alive. Maybe I'll even do that before you die, so you'll get a chance to watch. Yes, that's what you need, to watch your child scream and cry and die covered in blood!"

As he shouted, Brother Jaime did not hear the latch of the door as it squeaked slightly, but he turned when the heavy door slammed into the wall. Raquel's view was blocked by the monk, and she could only see him double over and stagger backward and the momentary glint of light on metal as the tip of a sword suddenly emerged from his lower back, then disappeared again with the hiss of steel rasping against bone. The monk slumped to his knees, then slowly bowed forward until his forehead rested on the floor, like a Moslem at prayer, and a soft sigh escaped his lips ending in a gurgle.

Raquel jerked herself into a sitting position, her knees clasped tightly to her breast, expecting the sword to swing in her direction next, but instead a familiar, gruff voice came out of the darkness.

"Help me get him out of his cassock," Juan growled as he bent over the still trembling and twitching form of the monk.

Raquel did not move, but Juan managed to pull the skirts of Brother Jaime's robes up around his waist and then, with a great tug, strip him of it entirely, sending the pale body rolling halfway underneath Raquel's pallet. Juan held out the robe to her.

"Put this on," Juan said in an almost casual tone. "We're not going out the front door, but there won't be any questions in the halls of a man-at-arms with a monk, where a half-naked woman might attract attention."

"What are you doing here?" she asked.

"What does it look like?" he snorted. "I heard about the order for your father's arrest, and I knew that they'd take you as well, so I've come to get you out."

"But why? I didn't betray you, if that's what you're thinking."

Juan paused for a long moment, and even in the darkness Raquel could sense a deep frown passing over his face.

"If I'd feared betrayal, I'd be on my way out of the country by now. Coming here will only convince them that I'm a Judaizer just like you."

"Then, why?"

"I don't blame you for asking that, but all I can tell you is that you don't know me, certainly not as I've become this past couple of years. Let's just leave it at that. I've come to set you free, because it is something that I have to do, nothing more, nothing less. I expect nothing from you for it. Just do as I say, and all will become clear. I've sent the Basque to collect Miriam, and I don't suppose he'll have any trouble doing that. They'll meet us on the road."

Raquel reached out a hand and took the robe and began to pull it over her head. The front and back were damp and sticky with blood. She let out an involuntary groan of disgust.

"Don't worry," he said, stepping to the door and peering up and down the corridor. "No one will notice the blood stains on the dark cloth, especially not tonight. And it's just starting to rain outside, a big storm coming in, so we'll probably meet few travelers on the road and those won't be noticing our clothes. Hurry up."

Raquel stood up and tiptoed behind Juan out the door and down he hall. He had sheathed his sword and strode down the passageway as if he owned the convent. He glanced over his shoulder at her.

"Straighten up and pull that hood over your face," he snarled. "People who have nothing to hide don't skulk about, and crouching won't make it any harder for someone to see you."

Juan walked briskly along, and Raquel staggered to keep up. Her legs ached viciously, and her stomach was still churning, threatening to make her vomit at any moment after the incident with Brother Jaime, both what he had attempted to do to her and what Juan had done to him.

As they moved through the corridors, Raquel had a better chance to look at her husband in the light of the torches in their wall sconces. She had hardly seen him in the past two years, and he had aged. He had always had a ruddy complexion, but his skin was now like tooled leather from constant exposure to the sun and weather. There was a large bare patch on his scalp, just above the ear where some sword or axe had apparently grazed his skull, and only a few tufts of stiff hair sprouted through the puffy pink scar tissue like clumps of weeds in a vacant lot. He walked with his right hand swinging free, but his left rested on the hilt of his sword, and she had seen him practice for hours at flicking the heavy blade from its scabbard with his left hand, catching it with his right, and whipping about in a series of violent, pre-planned strokes against which she could not imagine anyone defending.

She had expected him to lead her out into the convent's courtyard, the only access she knew of to the main gate, but instead he led her up a series of stairs until they emerged on a walkway atop one of the convent's walls. He continued to a point halfway down the wall where she noticed a grappling hook anchoring a rope that dangled out over the exterior of the wall. She leaned against the wall and peered downward into the darkness and could see a drop of at least forty feet.

"You're not planning to climb down that, are you?" she asked hesitantly.

"That's the way I came in," he replied, kicking the prongs of the grappling hook deeper into the mortar between the heavy stones and tugging at the knot. "Fortunately, they don't bother to post guards here on the walls in a place like this, just at the main entrance. This is convent, not a fortress."

"But I can't do that," she whispered.

"No need to," he said casually, and without another word, he whisked her off her feet and over his shoulder with no more effort than if the monk's habit she wore had been completely empty.

With a graceful spring, totally unexpected in a man of his bulk, Juan leapt to the top of the wall, spun about, and began to walk backwards down the face of he wall, sliding the rope through his gloved hands and moving almost as fast as if he were striding on flat ground. They landed at the base of the wall, and he lowered her to the ground, then held her hand as they stumbled and slid down the steep slope of the hill atop which the convent was perched, but there was no hint of intimacy in his touch. He was just taking her along as he would hold the reins of a horse.

They reached level ground and she sprinted after him to a small copse of trees where two horses were tied. Asco, slower and heavier than Raquel remembered him, shuffled out of the shadows and nuzzled her hand, leaving it slick with drool. Juan effortlessly heaved her into the saddle of one, a small bay that turned to inspect the new rider and shook its head in apparent disapproval. Then Juan vaulted into the saddle of his own mount, a tall chestnut gelding that Raquel recognized at once, without bothering to use the stirrups, jerked both sets of reins free of the bush to which they were tied, tossed Raquel hers, and put spurs to his horse's flanks, and they cantered quickly down a road leading off to the east with Asco resolutely trotting alongside.

Although the sun was up by this time, the cloud cover had closed over, laying a lead-colored roof over the world seeming to rest on the tops of the trees, leaving only a thin band of pale gray along the distant horizon. The rain began to patter about them, kicking up little clouds of dust in the road, then turned into a steady drumming, drawing a thick curtain all about them and limiting visibility to only a few yards, and Raquel could see little more than the dark shadow of Juan's back just ahead of her and the smaller shadow of Asco running along just beside her stirrup.

Raquel was grateful for the rain. Her escape would undoubtedly be discovered soon, if it had not been so already. It was debatable how desperately the authorities would bother to pursue a simple evader of the Inquisition, but with the murder of a cleric added to the equation, there would undoubtedly be a major effort undertaken to bring her to "justice." The downpour would quickly eliminate any tracks that might give an indication of the direction they had taken, and there would be no hint whether they had headed west toward the Portuguese border, northeast toward the Mediterranean ports, or due north toward French territory. Juan had not bothered to tell her their destination, but she noticed that they had passed several crossroads already, and he had always picked the route that tended toward the southeast.

She was also grateful fot the rain, which was now so heavy that it almost interfered with her breathing, had not been for the cowl of Brother Jaime's robe that shielded her face to a limited extent, because it prevented her from speaking to Juan. Not that he had shown any inclination to speak to her, but it seemed more than a little awkward to Raquel to have nothing to say to a man, her own husband, who had just risked his own life to save hers, even given their unpalatable history together.

They rode on through that day, pausing only twice, briefly where rock overhangs provided some protection from the rain, to eat and rest the horses. Juan produced hunks of hard, crusty bread and ripe-smelling cheese from his saddlebag and a skin of rough red wine that made Raquel's mouth burn. They ate in silence, sitting with their backs to the rock face while the horses' bodies shielded them as they munched grain from bags Juan hung over their muzzles, the warmth of their steaming flanks providing a little comfort, although Raquel still shivered under her sodden cassock. That night they slept in a small, abandoned shepherd's hut that provided some protection from the wind, although the collapsed roof did little to ward off the continuing rain. Juan wordlessly piled some reasonably dry straw in the one dark corner where the roof was still more or less solid and jerked his chin in its direction for Raquel's benefit while he sat down with a weary grunt, his back against the mud and wattle wall, his sword in one hand, and his legs stretched out across the single doorway. Raquel was completely unused to sleeping in such conditions, softened by life at court, and she could feel armies of lice working their way up through the straw and under her garments, but, even so, she soon drifted off to sleep to the regular sound of Juan's snoring across the room, and she did not awake until she heard him shuffling about outside, saddling the horses and noisily washing his face in the icy water of a stream that ran past the front of the hut.

She inched her way out of the cabin into the blue half-light of dawn. The rain had moved on, and she could see the last stragglers of the night's stars still twinkling off to the west. They could not risk a fire, and her breath condensed into little clouds in front of her face as she rubbed her arms to try to get some warmth into them. Juan thrust another handful of bread and cheese at her, tore a huge mouthful off the loaf for himself, and then swung easily into his own saddle.

"Where are we going?" she asked finally, nibbling at the cheese as she scanned the unfamiliar hills that now surrounded them.

"To meet with the Basque and pick up the child," he mumbled around the food in his mouth. "Probably later this morning."

"I mean after that," she went on. She expected him to snap at her, to tell her that he had done enough, more than

621

enough, and that she was on her own along with her little half-breed daughter, but his tone revealed no anger, no bitterness, only a great weariness and resignation.

He jerked his chin toward the horizon, a little to the right of where the sun had just begun to peek over the tree line. "The only place we can go, to Granada."

"How can we go there?" she gasped. "That's enemy territory. We'd be taken prisoner and sold as slaves! How would that be any better than our condition now?"

"At least we're not likely to be burned at the stake," he grunted. "And besides, I have my own contacts among the Moors now. Remember that I fought for them, and I would not be the first or the only Christian soldier in their army. I have already sent a message to them to expect us, to someone I believe is a mutual friend, that secretary of the king's, Muhammad."

Juan did not look in her direction, but Raquel could feel her cheeks burning pink and her heart racing. Could she hope for anything that good? Not only to escape with her life, to be free at long last from the burden of living a lie, many lies, but to be free to be with the only man she cared about in the world, now that her mother was dead and her father was effectively lost to her, that is. And to think that this had been arranged by the man she hated the most in the world.

The sun had nearly reached its zenith in the clear sky, and the road had dried with amazing speed, leaving only occasional dark spots of mud here and there. They made good time as they pressed east and south, and Raquel's robes had not only dried but had almost become too warm for this weather, but she ignored the heat as she ignored the continuing aches in her muscles, her bruises, and the hellish itching of the rough robes on her nearly bare skin, now liberally gnawed by lice and other new tenants. They crested a low rise and came into view of a muddy crossroad in the middle of a small valley. There she could see a covered, two-wheeled cart drawn by a pair of mules, with Maria's anxious face peering from behind the driver's shoulder. The Basque sat on the driver's seat, his own horse tied to the back of the cart, and Raquel recognized the faces of the half-dozen heavily-armored men who sat their horses patiently in a rough circle around the cart, the Castros, the Minorcan, and Gamal, besides a few she did not know. Juan's horse broke into a canter, and hers followed suit as they descended the hill, and Juan raised his hand languidly in greeting, replied to with nods from his men.

"You didn't even bother to set up camp?" Juan chided the Basque, who stiffly climbed down from the cart and stared up into his commander's face, shielding his eyes against the sun that was high over his shoulder.

"You said you'd be here about this time, and here you are," the Basque grunted. "Why pitch tents and start a fire if we're going to be pounding off over the horizon before the soup comes to a boil?"

"I could have been detained."

"By a couple of monks? I didn't think so."

"There was the *Hermandad* to consider," Juan responded. "After all, *we're Hermandad* ourselves."

"We're *old Hermandad*, not these new levies that know no more of fighting than they do of fucking. They're just working for the Inquisition to take a share of the confiscated goods, and they're not used to having to fight anyone for it. No, I didn't think you'd have any trouble."

"And you had no trouble getting the child out?"

"No one even tried to stop us, or even asked any questions. The only problem we had was with that old hen in the cart. Wouldn't let the child out of her sight, so we just brought her along. Less work for us anyway." The Basque snorted up a huge wad of snot and spat across the road, splattering a large flat rock and smiling with his achievement. "So now what? I understand that the Austrians are paying top price for veterans to fight against the Turks, and they won't ask too many damned questions about where we came from or why."

Juan just shook his head and gestured for his men to draw closer. They had been discreetly straining to hear the conversation but had refused to abandon their posts around the cart. They now trotted up, letting the reins hang loose in their hands.

"We're not going to Austria, or France or Italy either, and it's time for each of you to make a decision on your own future."

"I don't like those sausage-eating, beer-swilling bastards anymore than the next man," the Basque argued, "but their gold spends just fine, and they've got plenty of it. And I understand that Turks are real easy to kill with your hands." The other men chuckled hoarsely.

"That's not the question," Juan continued. "You know that my wife has run afoul of the Inquisition, and it's deadly serious business these days."

"It's her old man that they were after," the Basque insisted. "Everybody knew that some of the nobles hated the idea of his artillery taking over the battlefield and killing their power over the king. I wasn't too crazy about it myself. Almost like doing ourselves out of a profession, but he's long gone from all accounts, so they won't go to too much trouble to bring her back, even if they could find us."

"You haven't been following Torquemada's progress as closely as I have, old friend," Juan replied. "I believe that my wife was a target in her own right as a *converso* with very close access to the queen, just the sort of person whose influence Torquemada wanted to replace. By stirring up a scandal about her escape, he can keep the issue alive and help to undermine any confidence the queen or the king might have in other *converso* figures at court. It will be even easier to do since I had to kill one of his investigators during the escape."

"You killed someone, an official of the Church?" one of the Castros asked. "I thought that we wouldn't be doing anything more than knocking the odd guard over the head." His brother and the Minorcan nodded at each other while the Basque rubbed his beard thoughtfully.

"It was a Dominican and he was busy trying to rape my wife, so it seemed like the thing to do at the time," Juan answered off-handedly, and the men all reluctantly nodded their consent. "So," Juan went on, "I believe that we will not be safe in any Christian country, no matter how far away. We will be tracked down and brought back, one way or another."

"Then what's the plan, *jefe?*" the Basque asked.

"There's only one place we can reach that offers any kind of safety, and that's Granada."

The Basque took in his breath suddenly, and the Castros shook their heads, frowning. Only Gamal held an impassive look on his face.

"I know what you're thinking," Juan said in a calm voice. "We'd be traitors, renegades, but how much worse could it be? We're under a death sentence as it is, and we've fought for Boabdil before, after all."

"That was different," the other Castro brother chimed in. "We were under orders from Fernando himself then. And *we* aren't under any death sentence now. We're just soldiers backing up their commander. Nobody would hold that against us, or not much anyway. I could stand a few stripes of the lash if it came to that, but if we cross over the line and fight for the Moors, we'd each earn our deaths in our own right. You remember what they did to the Christians they captured fighting for the Moors in Malaga, used them for target practice for the lancers. I don't mind dying. In fact, I've been planning to do it eventually all my life, but I'd kind of like to be over pretty quickly once I get around to it. Those bastards can make the experience last."

"And you know that Granada is going to fall," the Minorcan added. "Sooner rather than later. Fernando has his heart set on it, and that goat-fucking turd Boabdil won't lift a finger to protect the likes of us when time comes for him to make his peace with Castile. He'll just forget about us. He's done the same with his own people, with his own blood for that matter. No, this is more than we ever signed up for."

"That's why I'm not asking you to go with me," Juan said with finality. "You're absolutely right that no one will hold anything that you've done so far against you. It's only from this moment that you'd be crossing the line. It might be wise of you to take your swords off to sell them to the Austrians after all, but even if you stay in Spain, you could easily deny any knowledge of my plans, since you don't really know what they are. In fact, up until the other night in the monastery, I wasn't even wanted by the Inquisition myself, and you had no part in what I did there."

Raquel noted that, while the Basque was minutely studying the hoof prints in the mud around his feet and the Minorcan had a look of dismay and sorrow, like a child who had been beaten unjustly, the Castros were fuming, gritting their teeth, and casting murderous looks at both Juan and Raquel.

"So that's it then?" the first Castro brother snarled. "After all these years, after seeing so many of our men die in the wars, you can just turn your coat inside out and go off and fight on the other side?"

"The decision has been forced on me," Juan replied quietly. "You know that. If there were any other way, I would take it, but there isn't. Even without freeing my wife and killing that raping monk, I'd have been done for. The Inquisition would have had me one way or the other. For me it's fight for the Moors or die."

"Die then!" both of the Castros screamed in unison. They wheeled their horses and spurred off up the road to the north, followed almost immediately by the Minorcan who shook his head sadly as he went.

Gamal simply shrugged. "For me this is obviously not quite so hard a decision. If Boabdil does not hold it against me that I have fought on the Christian side for so long, then it is much less difficult for me to march under another flag, especially when it is the green flag of Islam, even if of a blasphemous sect of Islam, than it would be to find a new captain to follow, one that I could trust."

The Basque stood for a long moment staring at his feet, kicking at the little ridges in the mud made by the horses' hooves. Finally he looked up into Juan's face.

"I can't do it, brother. I just can't," he said in a hoarse whisper, and Raquel could see the tears glistening on his scarred cheeks as they ran down into his matted beard. "I've killed my share of Spaniards over the years, not to mention French and Portuguese and other Christians, and, like you said, we did fight under Boabdil's banner before, but it *was* different. I just can't make myself fight with the Moors against our own king and queen, now that we've finally got a good pair. I know that I'm going to burn in Hell for all the sins I've done in my life, and there's no amount of absolution that a hundred priests could give me that would change that, no matter what the Church says. But I believe that there must be a special corner of Hell reserved for real traitors. You've got your family to think about, and maybe the Lord will take that into consideration, but I don't think that he'd stretch the point to include a man like me just sticking by a friend."

He reached under the rough woolen poncho that he wore over his armor and withdrew a leather purse.

"Here," he said, handing the purse up to Juan. "I sold off your horses and spare armor and weapons and even got a Jewish merchant to advance me money on the sale of those slaves we got from the capture of Baza."

627

Juan took the purse and hefted it. "I can't believe that you got this much gold from those broken-down animals and what little equipment you found around the camp."

The Basque smiled. "I can remember when we didn't have enough copper maravedis between us to fill your palm, let alone gold, but you're a lord now. They'll be taking your lands. That's for certain, and all your other property, but you can't just go back to being a poor swordsman, trading blood for a little bread and wine. You've got an image to maintain, and that costs money."

Juan vaulted down from his horse, and the Basque started to back away from him.

"That's all," he growled. "I've done what I came to do, and now I'm off. May God grant that we never see each other again, because, if we do, it will probably be in the pits of Hell, roasting over the same fire. Or across a battlefield," he added after a pause, "which would be worse yet."

Juan tried to grasp his arm, but the Basque turned away and hustled to untie his horse, swinging up into the saddle. Without looking back, he galloped off in the same direction the others had gone.

"God protect you, brother!" Juan called after him, and he buried his face in his hands and sat that way for a long while.

Raquel now gingerly steered her horse up to the cart and pulled the canvas flaps open. Marisol squealed with delight at seeing her mother and leaped into her arms. Raquel cradled her there and turned to Maria.

"And what about you?" she asked. "You heard what my husband said. We're going to live in Granada among the Moors. It's the only safe place for us, but we can't ask you to go. If you hurry, you can catch up to the men. I suspect that they'll be waiting for you just up the road."

"You shouldn't even ask me that, ma'am," Maria sniffed. "You know that I lost my own children to the plague these many long years ago, and this one's all I've got left in the world. What do I care about Inquisitions and Churches and Moslems? The Lord loved little children, and I suspect that he'll not think badly of anyone who spends her life caring for them. I'll be going along with little Miriam, if you don't mind."

Raquel just smiled and reached down to caress the portly maid's chubby cheeks as tears welled up in her own eyes.

With that, Maria took the child back into the cart and took the Basque's place on the driver's seat, clucking to the mules and following Juan down the trail to the southeast with Raquel riding alongside and Gamal silently bringing up the rear, periodically turning in his saddle to survey the ground behind them.

GRANADA

Chapter Two
Granada

Muhammad hardly ever left his house anymore, not even to visit the *souq*. He had not exactly become a recluse. He still received visits from his old acquaintances from his days as *muhtasib*, merchants and artisans and the occasional local intellectual, and from Raquel's uncle Ysaque, and Yusef served to keep Muhammad fully informed of the secret goings on within the city. He received regular stacks of correspondence from the Alhambra, letters that the king wanted him to answer, reports that he wanted him to analyze, and even occasional personal notes from the king, chatting about court gossip as in days gone by. But Muhammad had no illusions that any of his advice was seriously considered up in the hilltop palace, unless it happened to coincide with what the king and his true advisors, like Hafez, had already decided upon, and this happened very infrequently. Muhammad now did what was asked of him, no more, no less, and he knew that the days of the Moorish kingdom were numbered.

The only official visitor that Muhammad received anymore was the queen mother, Fatima, who now made it a practice of appearing, unannounced and heavily veiled, escorted only by a pair of African slaves and a single lady-in-waiting late at night. Muhammad would offer her a cup of strong coffee, and they would sit for hours in his patio talking about politics and strategy, both of them now having largely been marginalized in the councils of the king. It was as a result of one of these visits that Muhammad had begun what he believed would be the culmination of his life's work, just as he had always imagined. For several weeks he had been engaged in the writing of a letter, but more than a simple letter, it was a piece of literature, embodying the essence of the Arabic court language, poetry, and prose, something that would last, if properly done, for centuries, regardless of any effect it might have on the present day world.

The primary purpose of the letter was to plead with the king of Fez in North Africa for a military expedition to reinforce Abu's army and possibly reverse the tide of war against the Christians. During the seven hundred years of Moslem presence in Spain, on more than one occasion the Moorish realm had been saved by waves of hardy Berber and Arab warriors from the Sahara sweeping across the straits to do battle for the faith. On two of those occasions, rigorous religious fundamentalists from Morocco had taken it upon themselves to overthrow the existing, decadent Moorish dynasty in al-Andalus and install one of their own, the Almohads and the Almoravids, only ultimately to become seduced by the opulent lifestyle in southern Spain and to turn into a parody of the very regime they had sought to replace. To Muhammad's way of thinking, the installation of a pure, spiritually committed leadership would be all to the good, especially if it brought with it enough military force to push back the Castilians. Such a movement might well encourage the hundreds of thousands of Moslems now living under Christian domination to rise in rebellion, thus multiplying the armies of Islam and simultaneously diverting important Spanish forces from the main battle front.

This was Muhammad's purpose, and he spent hours every day, and sometimes well into the night, pouring over his work, searching through his own library for the appropriate quotation, constantly editing and rewriting. He knew that the practical aspects of such a venture would not be very appealing to the king of Fez. He already had a treaty of peace with Fernando, although any accord with an infidel was easily broken. The sticking point would be the military difficulty of getting an army across the straits from Africa, now patrolled heavily by Castillian and Aragonese ships. The practical argument would be that, as long as the Christians were busy struggling in their own land to reconquer Spanish territory, they could not afford to divert forces to attack and seize enclaves along the African coast, which the Portuguese were already starting to do. But it might also be argued that, by intervening in the war in Spain, the king of Fez might well attract Spanish retribution all the sooner, while his armies might be massacred on the seas, leaving him vulnerable to a vengeful response by Fernando. Muhammad saw his only hope in writing a missive of surpassing literary mastery that the king's advisors, who would see it first, and then the king himself, would be obliged to read and study it, that the elegance of the words and even the calligraphy in which it was written would surpass the text of the message itself and carry the day where simple logic and cold calculations never could.

So obsessed with his writing had Muhammad become, that it took several attempts before Yusef was able to snap him out of his reverie to pass on the message he had just received from Ysaque. Muhammad would normally have jumped at the mention of the old Jewish scholar's name as it usually meant that a letter had arrived from Raquel, for which he would drop whatever he was doing, day or night, set aside his work, and accept the small packet of papers into his hands as if it were the most delicate of flowers. He would untie the ribbon with which it would be bound most lovingly, carefully storing it in a pocket, and then read the letter through three, four, or more times without pausing, soaking in the least mention of little Miriam's growth and learning and stroking his beard pensively as he tried to evaluate how Raquel was holding up under the pressure of her double life. He would then hold each page close over the flame of a candle, searching for secret writing that he had taught Raquel to perform, using the juice of a lemon, writing perpendicular to the open text of the message. This procedure was reserved for the most sensitive thoughts, usually referring to the Inquisition or court politics that, if the letter fell into the wrong hands during its transmission, might be construed as treason in the paranoid atmosphere of the Spanish court. Not that Raquel ever revealed anything about Spanish military plans. This had been an unspoken agreement between them, and Muhammad had never asked for such information, nor Raquel ever volunteered it. As ambivalent as her position in Spanish society might be due to her religion, Raquel had a deep and abiding loyalty to Isabel, and Muhammad would never have presumed to ask her to abandon it.

But this time Muhammad happened to be in the midst of framing a particularly eloquent passage of his missive, tying in phrases from the Koran to make his argument appear to be the revealed word of God himself, and Yusef had to grab him by the shoulder and shake him before he turned to face his servant.

Within moments, however, Muhammad had mounted his horse, which Yusef had already had the prescience to order saddled and was pounding down the cobblestone streets, scattering early morning travelers on either side amid a shower of curses and screams as he upset bakery trays and sent nervous donkeys bucking and twisting in their harnesses. An officious soldier at the city gate attempted to bar his passage, either disapproving of his rate of speed within the city walls or suspecting that Muhammad might be a desperate criminal escaping from the scene of a robbery, but Muhammad brushed him aside with a sweeping stroke of his staff, sending him tumbling helplessly backward over a pile of baskets filled with fruits and vegetables, and he raced off up the road leading out of the city toward the northwest.

Muhammad came across the little caravan on a lonely stretch of road several miles farther on. The message had only stated, in the most cryptic terms, that Raquel and her family had been forced to escape the Inquisition by fleeing to Granadan territory, and he had not stopped to think about what road they might be on or when they might be arriving. Had he not encountered them so soon, he probably would have come to his senses and gone back home to await their arrival, but, as it was, he spotted the tall figure of Juan leading a small cart at a considerable distance, and it was only his instinct that told him that Raquel was there. He had paused for a moment when he saw Juan, as he had vaguely assumed that it would be Raquel with her parents and Miriam, not the Christian warrior who had actually blackmailed Raquel into marriage years before, but even this thought could not slow his pace, and he only reined in his horse when he reached the cart itself.

There was an awkward moment as Muhammad sat there staring at Juan and Raquel, unsure of whom to address first, and Raquel and Juan also sat there, looking stupidly back and forth from one to the other, waiting for someone to speak. Finally, Juan cleared his throat.

"I am glad to see that my message was received," he said flatly. "I understand that I am to be given an audience with the king immediately upon my arrival, and I was hoping that you would be on hand to see that my family are shown to suitable quarters so that I would not keep his highness waiting."

Muhammad stammered for a moment, then replied. "Yes, yes, I was told that my lord had agreed to accept you into his service and would like to discuss the plans for his upcoming campaign season at your earliest convenience. Naturally, if there is anything at all that I can do to help the lady to get settled in the city, it would be my honor and my pleasure."

Juan nodded briskly at Muhammad. "Then, if it would not appear rude of me, I will be riding ahead to speak with the king and will be much obliged to you if you will escort my family the remainder of the way into the city and help them get established in their new quarters."

Juan turned briefly to Raquel, who sat perfectly still on the driver's seat of the little cart, and gave her the most plaintive look she had ever seen, like a child hoping for a parent's approval but not really expecting it. But, in an instant, the look was gone, replaced by an impenetrable mask of stone. He bowed to her stiffly, and spurred his horse down the road as Gamal kicked up his horse as well and followed, giving Muhammad a casual "heart, lips, and head" salute as he rode past.

Muhammad sat there for a long moment, watching the two figures gradually disappear in the dust of the road, frowning after them, before turning to Raquel. He was just about to dismount and take her in his arms when the round face of a florid woman, one that he recognized from that night in Sevilla when the baby was born, his baby, appeared between the canvass flaps of the cart's cover behind Raquel's shoulder, and Muhammad limited himself to a deep bow in the saddle.

"The city is jammed with refugees from all the captured Moorish cities, my lady," he began. "For that reason, I hope it will be acceptable to you if I lodge you in some rooms in my own home."

Raquel was still troubled by Juan's departure, although she could not honestly say why, but Muhammad's discomfiture at the sight of Maria brought a smile to her face. She bowed in return.

"That would be most gracious, sir," she responded. "I only hope that we will not be putting you out too much."

"It will be an honor for my household," he announced, a little too loudly and far too stiffly.

Then he turned his horse and led the way back up toward the city, allowing the cart to catch up so that he could ride alongside and steal glances at the profile he had longed to see for so many months, with the creaking of the cart wheels and the plopping of the animals' hooves as the only sound on the air. After they had gone a little way, another face, a smaller one with large green eyes and a playful smile on her lips, peeked around the edge of the canvass. She must be five years old by now, Muhammad thought as he drank in the beauty of her little face and the warmth of her smile, and he could feel tears welling up in his eyes.

"Are you a heathen?" the girl asked. "My Maria told me that we are going to live among the heathens now." Muhammad could see chubby hands trying to pull her back inside the cart, but the girl shrugged them off. Raquel just turned her face away to hide her smile.

"I am a Moor, my child," Muhammad replied gravely. He was pleased to note that she had phrased her question in very passable Arabic, not exactly classical, but for her age very well done, and there would now be all the time in the world to teach her. "You speak my language very well, if I might say so."

"My mother taught me," she said proudly. "I can speak Castillian and Latin too," she added and began to recite a poem in Latin when Raquel finally reached back and put her fingers to the child's lips to quiet her.

"There will be plenty of time for that when he reach our new home," Raquel said in a soothing tone.

"Will we live there for very long?" Marisol asked, and Raquel looked up at Muhammad. Having spent her life traveling with the royal court from city to city, Marisol had obviously taken the sudden move very much in stride.

"That is my greatest wish, my child," Muhammad replied, bowing to her and smiling.

Although he had only been gone a few hours, Muhammad was astonished at the transformation that Yusef had worked on his modest home. Although the house was typically quite clean and orderly, it had always been, at least for the past decade, a decidedly bachelor residence, a little Spartan and primarily functional in style. When Yusef now pulled open the tall double doors that allowed the little cart to pass directly into the patio from the street, the party was greeted by a fragrant breeze provided by the drifts of freshly cut flowers that now filled every available nook in the house. Even though it had not been certain, in the slightest, that Raquel would be staying at Muhammad's home, Yusef had laid out fresh bedding for Raquel and Marisol in Muhammad's rooms at the front of the house, moving his master's things to a smaller bedroom at the back, for propriety's sake. Through his network of informers, Yusef had even managed to learn of the presence of the nanny, for whom he had also prepared a small alcove near the child's bed. And in the room, a table was laid out with a tall brass pot of steaming coffee and a tray of the sweet almond cakes that were Muhammad's favorites, to which Marisol rushed the moment she was set on her feet by Maria.

While Maria busied herself changing Marisol out of her traveling clothes and Yusef bustled off to the kitchen to prepare a proper dinner, Muhammad took the opportunity to give Raquel a tour of the rest of the house. They walked slowly, and, as soon as they were out of sight of the others, Raquel took his hand in hers.

"I have dreamt of this day for a long while," Muhammad whispered softly as he paused to show Raquel his small library.

"And I had dreamt that you were dreaming it," she replied and kissed him gently on the cheek.

"I was a little taken aback by your husband's attitude," Muhammad said finally. "You had written that he had changed, but it had never occurred to me that a man could change that much in one lifetime."

"I don't pretend to understand it myself," Raquel admitted, "although I have hardly seen him over the past several years. It's almost as if, when I sliced off that bit of skin, I cut out something of his soul, or not his *soul* exactly, but something that made him what he was."

"Scientifically, I believe that that is impossible," Muhammad mused, "but the change is there nonetheless."

"It only remains to be seen whether it will be as permanent as the alteration of his body," she added. "But we should enjoy the respite while it lasts and give thanks for it without asking for explanations. Speaking of which, there is something that I very much want to do, now that we are here."

"I thought that you might," Muhammad said, holding up his hand. "Your Uncle Ysaque is waiting for us there."

Calling out to Yusef that they would return before dark, Muhammad led Raquel out into the street and through the milling crowd toward the *souq*. He pointed out his favorite spot when he had been *muhtasib*, the little café at the corner of the marketplace, and many of the shopkeepers greeted him with that title as they passed, as he paused occasionally to examine a piece of brass work or to smell a bit of fruit. They continued on out the other side of the market and finally wound their way through the narrow streets to a small building with an arched doorway above which a Star of David was affixed to the wall. The slightly stooped figure of Ysaque stood next to the door and embraced Raquel warmly when they arrived.

"I will leave you now," Muhammad said. "Ysaque knows my house and will bring you back when you have finished."

Raquel embraced Muhammad in turn and kissed his hand as he turned away. She faced Ysaque and touched the patch of yellow cloth that was worked into the shawl he wore over his shoulders.

"I will want one of those," she said with determination in her voice.

"It is a requirement of the law here, as it was in Castile, for Jews to be marked by their clothing," Ysaque said with a sigh. "At least here it does not carry with it the threat of violence by any gang of toughs on the street. Still, it's a shame that such things exist even here."

"After all these years of hiding, I will consider it a badge of honor, uncle, to at least be able to profess my faith openly," she said as she took his arm and he led her into the temple, and tears stood in her eyes as she caressed the door post as they entered.

Juan had not realized just how dependent he had become on the technological advantages that the Spanish armies had over their Moorish opponents, advantages he disdained as almost unmanly and certainly not comparable to a good warrior's strong right arm and a reliable piece of steel. But over the months since he had been made a captain in the armies of Muhammad XII of Granada, he had come to sorely miss the powerful artillery that not only turned enemy walls into rubble but also demoralized the defenders to the point that the final assault of a fortified town, on the occasions that it did come to an assault before the surrender, had hardly been more demanding than the work of a reaper at harvest time. He had made his own name by the art of the sudden, unexpected attack, the scaling of impossible cliffs and walls and then holding open a breach or defending a section of captured wall with nothing more than his sword until relief could arrive. But he only now realized that his achievements had been all the easier by the simple fact of the existence of the massive Spanish artillery park against which the enemy had always to calculate, keeping large numbers of troops off the walls to prevent their destruction by the hurtling missiles and the diversion of even more troops to the repair of fortifications shattered by the bombardment. His record during this campaign for the Moors had proven that much could still be accomplished by dedicated men-at-arms, even without the sophisticated network of supplies and reinforcements that Isabel had established for the Castilian armies, but it was much, much harder, and Juan had to admit that it had only been possible because they were confronting, not the main force of Fernando's armed might, but merely small Moorish towns whose populations had gone over to the Spanish side together with their minimal Christian garrisons. He knew that it would be different when Fernando was finally ready to take the field against Granada, making this work look like child's play, and just the thought of what was to come made Juan absolutely bone tired.

Juan had found the court of the king, whom he still thought of by his bastardized Spanish name of Boabdil, reduced to a small circle of courtiers dominated by the obsequious Hafez, whom Juan remembered from his previous visit to Granada and whose flinch at the sight of the burly Spanish knight proved that Hafez had not forgotten their last encounter either. The mood at court was somewhere between panic and dementia, with the wildest projects and prophesies floating around from mouth to mouth, plans for a sudden dash to liberate Cordoba, a raising of rebellion among all the hundreds of thousands of Moors throughout the southern part of Spain, of massive and evidently mythical armies of Berbers swarming across the straits from North Africa once the Turkish fleet, which was expected over the horizon at any moment, had swept the Castilian and Aragonese navies from the seas. Juan had never deluded himself into believing that he had a very deep understanding of high politics, not like Raquel or even that

Arab Muhammad, but it did not take a genius to realize that the entire court at Granada was living in a fantasy world.

Although tens of thousands of Moorish refugees had flocked to the one remaining enclave of Moorish Spain, including thousands of warriors from the many towns and fortresses captured by Fernando over the preceding years, Boabdil could still only field a force of a few thousand cavalry and perhaps fifteen or twenty thousand infantry for field operations after ensuring a proper garrison for Granada itself, a vast city with miles of walls that required thousands to properly man them. Compared with this, the Spaniards could easily garrison all of their frontier fortresses adequately and still put twenty thousand heavy cavalry and more than fifty thousand infantry into a major campaign, to say nothing of the endless train of artillery, from small falconets to the huge bombards and culverins that could throw stone balls weighing hundreds of pounds nearly a mile, of which the Moors had nothing of the kind.

Even so, after a cursory examination of the dispositions of the Moorish forces and with his knowledge of the current deployment of Fernando's armies and of Castilian defense priorities, Juan was able to produce a proposal for an active campaign that promised, if not a complete reversal of fortunes, at least the possibility of retaking the initiative and that might force the Spanish to react to Moorish threats rather than allowing them to plan their own offensive moves and execute them at their leisure.

Juan suggested that a relatively small force of light cavalry raid far to the northeast, tens of leagues behind the Spanish lines to the vicinity of the town of Quesada and even beyond to the Guadalquivir River near Baeza, burning crops, stealing livestock, and generally causing as much trouble as possible. Juan was aware that the main Spanish forces that Fernando and Isabel were gathering for the final push against Granada were concentrated well to the west, which would leave the target area largely denuded of troops. At the same time, even though the raid would not have the manpower or the equipment to seriously threaten the capture of any sizeable fortified Christian towns, Fernando could not afford to ignore this pinprick and proceed with his own campaign, thereby eliminating the source of Moorish power once and for all. The local nobles in the region would be screaming for protection, and Fernando would have to detach troops, probably out of all proportion to the size of the Moorish raiding party, with a view to containing and eliminating them quickly.

Meanwhile, the *real* Moorish offensive force would leave Granada and head in the opposite direction, toward the southwest and the coast. Muhammad had consistently advised Boabdil to pay heed to Juan's ideas, and his support to Juan's proposal was key at this point, although Juan had his suspicions that Muhammad would have endorsed any plan that called for Juan leaving the city and placing himself at the front of a battle line. Muhammad had argued that only a lifeline to the coast and control of a viable port, gave the Moorish kingdom any chance of survival over the long term. It would be too much to hope for the recapture of any of the major coastal cities like Malaga or Almeria, but there were many small ports that would serve to receive reinforcements from North Africa, if Muhammad's pleas for support were successful, and these were often only lightly garrisoned by Spanish troops, if at all, and local Moorish militia would not likely fight hard against Boabdil's army if it appeared in the area in any strength. More importantly, a series of quick successes on the battlefield might well spark the kind of uprising among the hundreds of thousands of Moors now living under Spanish domination that Boabdil dreamed of, forcing Fernando to concentrate on recapturing or defending his current holdings and giving Granada a new lease on life, possibly even prompting Fernando and Isabel to overlook Boabdil's past infidelities and allow him to keep his kingdom after all in a new peace treaty that would recognize his independence.

The campaign was ultimately adopted by the king and had scored some initial successes, with the raid toward Quesada performing its duty extremely well, drawing off most of Fernando's forces that had been operating to the west, burning crops and stealing livestock to weaken the Spanish economic base, and replacing some of the losses the Moors had already suffered. The main Moorish force, under the command of Boabdil and his new leading general, Musa Ibn Abu'l-Gazin, marched to the small castle of Alhendin, with Juan reprising his role as commander of the *escaladores*, now a mixed bag of veteran Christian renegades and Moorish warriors, and capturing the place in a single day. This opened the road to the coast and was quickly followed by the fall of other small castles at Maracena and Bulduy, securing a large swath of territory around Granada itself as the towns in the neighboring territory immediately renounced their forced allegiance to the Christians and declared their loyalty to Boabdil. Of far greater importance was word that arrived of a large-scale uprising that had occurred among the Moorish population of the major city of Guadix to the northeast of Granada, exactly the result that Boabdil had hoped to provoke, although, with his army now ranging along the southern coast, he was in no position to help the rebels.

Despite these achievements, Juan had not been impressed by the army overall. The several thousand cavalry that rode with Boabdil were of high quality, mostly North African mercenaries who also displayed an intense religious fervor that was normally lacking in troops fighting only for money or feudal obligation, and this fervor was unfortunately also evident in the bulk of the Moorish population, as Juan had observed. The infantry, however, was little better than raw militia, ill-equipped with firearms or artillery and all too quick to turn and run at the first sign of trouble on the battlefield. Their main weakness, though, was typical of inexperienced infantry, slowness and straggling on the march and a tendency to turn aside to looting at the least opportunity, which both antagonized the inhabitants of the countryside that Boabdil was desperately trying to rally to his cause, and made the troops vulnerable to counterattack by any enemy forces in the area.

Now, as August was coming to a close, Juan's most dire predictions had come true. The raiding force in the north, after stirring up much trouble behind Spanish lines, had been ambushed and largely destroyed by the Castilians on the way back from Jaen. Down on the coast, Juan had led storming parties over the walls of the small port of Salobrena, but the Spanish garrison had retreated to the citadel, where they were able to hold out, receiving support and reinforcements from Aragonese ships and making the port unusable for the Moors, even if there had been a friendly fleet standing by to come in, which there wasn't. Lacking the artillery to reduce the citadel, Boabdil was obliged to withdraw his army which then raced eastward in an attempt to secure another port, Adra, where the local population had risen in his favor, but the slow-moving Moorish army arrived only in time to see the banner of the Marquis of Villena rising over the fortress while the bodies of dozens of Moorish notables dangled from the battlements. With that, and news that Fernando was moving south with a force of five thousand cavalry and twenty thousand infantry to cut him off from Granada, Boabdil turned his column back to the north, arriving at his capital just ahead of the Spaniards, who spent the remaining weeks of good campaigning weather ravaging fields right up to the walls of the city before retiring to their own territory for the winter.

During the long retreat through the rough mountain country to Granada, Juan had time to think over his situation as he rode, dozing in the saddle. Since his mutilation, as he still thought of it, at Raquel's hands years ago, he had gone through the motions of life, vaguely hoping for a quick death in battle. He had far too great a fear of the eternal fate of those who consciously committed suicide to consider that road, even though he had little hope for salvation for himself given the kind of life he had led. His situation had hardly been improved now by betraying his own faith and now living in a state of excommunication, without a chance either at taking communion or of receiving last rites from the Church, but that was really the least of his troubles and only recently added on. Then, one evening while strolling through the army's camp during the siege of Almeria two years ago, he had stumbled across the amiable priest Hernando de Talavera, the queen's former confessor, and one of the few clerics whose company he found tolerable.

It was almost as if the priest had been looking for him, and perhaps he had been, but before the night was through, Juan found that he had confessed *everything* to the man, from his first, largely accidental, killing of that whore years before, through all the others since, his discovery of Raquel's secret and his blackmailing her into marriage and then his ultimate disgrace. Juan could not remember how long it had been since he had cried, many years before certainly, probably at the hands of his father in the face of the old man's constant disapproval and derision, but now he had broken down and sobbed like a baby for what seemed like hours. Even though someone used to hearing the confessions of members of the Spanish court must have been largely inured to excesses and violence of all sorts, Juan still had to smile through his own tears and shake his head at the look of astonishment on the holy man's round face when he had finished his story. Hernando had held his head in his hands for a long time, and Juan had been afraid that he would rush off to the officers of the Inquisition and have him hanging from a rack before the sun came up. But when the priest finally raised his eyes, there was no look of rage or disgust on his face, just one of the deepest, most sincere concern.

"You could probably find yourself a priest who would grant you absolution for a substantial sum of money, and you can afford that sort of thing now," Hernando had said, shaking his head sadly, "perhaps along with some public atonement or even a commitment to enter a monastery as a means of compensating for your deeds, but that is not my way, I'm afraid."

Juan could not keep himself from laughing at the thought. "Do you mean that there is *anything* I could do to atone for my sins, father? Perhaps you weren't listening very carefully. I am lower than the beasts of the forest. They kill for food. Other soldiers kill for God and country or for self-defense. I have killed God's own people, killed them and made them suffer first, for *pleasure*."

"I do not pretend to condone anything that you have done, Juan, but the mind of man is not capable of conceiving of a sin that the mercy of Our Lord could not encompass. It is only that something of this. . ., magnitude, requires more than just a few Hail Marys. I would say that the commitment of your entire life would be a very small price to pay to mitigate the penalty your soul will ultimately pay throughout eternity, and I expect that you will still have to pay a price, but what you do here will have to be a commitment more complete than simply devoting your remaining days to poverty and prayer."

"More than that?"

"Oh, yes. A life of prayer and simple living can be rewarding and fulfilling, not as much of a sacrifice as this case clearly calls for."

Juan nodded toward the priest's ample belly that forced his cassock to bulge outward as they sat on a pile of sandbags at the edge of the camp, far from the nearest sentry. "And there are all degrees of simple living, I suppose."

Hernando patted his stomach. "There are orders with much stricter regimes than those dictated by life at court, but even so, I had something else in mind. The sanctity of the confessional and the dictates of my own heart prevent me from taking any action against Raquel, and I can hardly imagine the enormity of the sin that *she* has been committing all these years," Hernando shook his head again and let out a deep sigh. "But we are talking about your case, and it is against her that you have done the greatest harm, so I would suggest that God would be looking for you to take some action to repair that damage. Naturally, from this moment on you will have to give up these, um, *activities* that you have told me about in relation to any woman, if you hope for some kind of redemption, but you will have to do much more. It is my view that you must not only leave Raquel in peace from now on, but you must do everything in your power to make her *happy*, and your child as well, the exact opposite of what you have done to date. You must deny yourself and your own desires completely, not look for her forgiveness or anything else that would simply make you feel better in this world and hope for the mercy of the Lord to take consideration of this when you enter the next."

"I thought I was doing that now," Juan had replied. "I'm dozens of leagues away from her most of the time and offering a distinct possibility of getting killed at any moment. What more could she ask for?"

"Perhaps for the moment, nothing more, but God has a way of telling us what additional sacrifices he wants. He's never been very shy about that. And when he does send that message, you have to be ready to receive it."

It was just a couple of weeks later that word had come to him about Raquel's arrest. In fact, it had been Hernando who had informed him, with a sly look of triumph on his face, although the priest certainly did not suggest anything more, and probably did not have in mind that Juan would mount a rescue operation, and certainly had not had in mind the killing of a member of the Holy Office in the act. Still, the divine message there could not have been clearer to Juan. It had all come like a revelation, and he had experienced something like what he imagined the old time prophets had felt when God had spoken to them out of burning shrubs and things. At one stroke he could save the woman he loved, in his own way, and deliver her into the arms of the man she loved, at least as he had long assumed. He would even be on hand to watch the whole process. What more perfect sacrifice could there be? How much more could he be expected to suffer? What more could God want of him? So he had taken his decision, thrown away everything he had worked for in this world, property, respect, position, and power, to say nothing of his personal desires, and here he was, deep in the heart of enemy territory, fighting as a renegade against his king and queen. He could even imagine the self-satisfied smirk that would spread across his brother's face when word reached him, as the fat slob sat at table, gorging on food paid for with the fruits of Juan's campaigns in the new manor house that Juan had ordered built on the family lands. The only minor respite God had granted Juan was that his father had died the year before. At least he had not lived to see his son disgraced, and Juan had been spared the look of reproach on the old man's face.

Juan had expected to find the mood in the Alhambra to be grim on his return to Granada after the campaign had collapsed. After all, the raiders had suffered considerable losses in the field, and the main army had failed to capture a single port, the primary mission of their expedition. To make matters worse, a powerful Spanish force had crushed the rising in Guadix in bloody and brutal fashion, and all Moorish residents of the city had been expelled whether they had taken part in the rebellion or not, at least those who had not perished in the fighting or been executed immediately thereafter as ringleaders, and there had been no signs of any significant resistance to Spanish rule anywhere else in the occupied territories. Still, when Juan entered the palace, having taken time to see to the care of some of the men wounded under his command, he found the king and many of his courtiers celebrating as if coming off some major victory. A festive banquet had been laid out in one of the large reception rooms of the palace, and a troop of Turkish dancers in tall white hats and long skirts (even thought they were all men) were spinning and gyrating insanely in the center of the floor as a small orchestra played a shrill, discordant tune in one corner. Juan saw Muhammad standing alone, the only solemn face in the crowd, and walked up beside him, swallowing his pride as he went and casting his eyes heavenward as if to check to see if God were watching and enjoying this.

"Is there some good news about that I'm not aware of?" Juan asked. "What's the celebration for?"

Muhammad bowed slightly but did not meet Juan's eyes. He kept his gaze on the king, who was whispering in Hafez's ear, after which they both began giggling uncontrollably. Both Juan and Muhammad noticed that the king and his confidant were looking in their direction as they laughed.

"There is some news," Muhammad admitted, "but not such as would justify this sort of display. It seems that the king's uncle, el Zagal, who made peace with Fernando some time ago, actually led a company of horsemen to support Fernando's latest campaign, something that has driven the population of Granada wild with anger and boosted our king's support at home, even though he had done the same thing often enough himself against el Zagal. The *mullahs* throughout southern Spain have been preaching *jihad* against the Christians, and a few small towns, those without permanent Spanish garrisons, have declared for the king. Hundreds of men have come in, mostly individually, from the Spanish-occupied territories to join our army, although not nearly in sufficient numbers to give us any chance of meeting Fernando on even terms. Taken all together, this has meant a considerable improvement in the king's fortunes from the days when he did not dare to set foot outside the palace without an armed escort for fear of being set upon by his own people. But the favor of the mob in Granada changes like the wind, and the first serious setback will have the people howling for his blood once again, I'm afraid."

"Then there is no hope of holding the city if Fernando comes here in force?" Juan asked.

"There is always hope," Muhammad shrugged. "I have drafted what I consider to be a most moving letter to the Moorish king at Fez begging for an army to come and relieve us, and the Turkish Sultan has spoken more than once of sending his fleet into the Western Mediterranean to attack the Castilians and Aragonese, which could open up our lines of communication with North Africa, but he has yet to carry through on this proposal. There is also always the chance that the Spaniards will become embroiled in another war with the French or Portuguese or with each other, which might draw off their forces for a time. But of our simply winning the battle on our own account, no, I do not believe that there is any hope of that."

That winter was a grim one in Granada. Although there was no actual shortage of food or other basic necessities in the city, virtually all trade with the world outside the small compass of towns owing allegiance to the Moorish king had been cut off by the Spaniards. So, the bolts of silks and jars of spices from the Orient had been replaced in the market by the more mundane staples like olives, barley, and wheat that would keep body and soul together but did little to uplift the soul of the sophisticated Granadan shoppers.

There were still individual travelers, of course, as the Spanish blockade was a relatively loose one, and they brought news from across the seas. It was learned that el Zagal, disillusioned with life as a Spanish puppet king, had sold his little realm back to Fernando for five million maravedis and had emigrated with his modest fortune and his family to Morocco where the king of Fez, irate at el Zagal's dealings with the infidels, had arrested him and had his eyes put out, leaving him to spend the rest of his days as a blind beggar in the streets. There had been some rather unseemly jubilation in the Alhambra at word of this sad end to a valiant warrior for Islam, as most of those outside of the king's immediate circle of courtiers still considered him, but el Zagal's removal did eliminate the last possible contender for the much-reduced throne of Granada, leaving Muhammad XII, or Abu or Boabdil, however one carried to refer to him, with only the problem of surviving in the face of a determined onslaught by the most formidable military force in all of Christian Europe.

Still, there was a pall of gloom that hung over the city. Occasionally, one could see a column of smoke off on the horizon, evidence of a raid by Christian marauders destroying some hidden store of grain or an isolated village out on the *vega*. The market was particularly subdued, with only trade in basic foodstuffs taking place, and that at increasingly steep prices as each family sought to stock up as much as possible against the siege that all knew was inevitable. Piles of fine silk cloth that still remained collected in the merchants' stalls, attracting no attention from the customers, when the sellers bothered to bring out their merchandise at all. Gold, too, had largely disappeared from circulation, being replaced by the basest copper coins that could be found as everyone sought to convert as much of their wealth as possible to the most portable and easily concealed form. Meanwhile, abandoned market stalls were taken over by private individuals trying to sell off richly embroidered rugs and hand-carved furniture, all for a tiny fraction of the true value in gold, jewels, or even, as the winter wore on, in grain.

Juan was able to keep himself occupied almost constantly by organizing patrols far out onto the plain surrounding the city in search of enemy raiders to drive off. With the exception of Gamal, Juan was surrounded now largely by strangers, mostly demoralized refugee Moslem warriors from other cities who spoke vaguely about returning home someday, after the unlikely defeat of the Spanish, and a handful of other Christian renegades. Juan had always loathed turncoats and had participated enthusiastically in their extermination when they had fallen into Spanish hands after the surrender of some town or fortress, and he did not now consider himself one of them. His, after all, was a different case. Most of the renegades were men who had fled into Moorish territory to escape punishment for robbery or murder and were only fighting now in exchange for room and board. Juan was here for a much loftier reason, that of cleansing his immortal soul. He had never really believed that God particularly favored one army over another, even in a conflict between Christian and heathen. In any case, any such preference that God might have would certainly take second place to what had amounted to Juan's compliance with the expressed wish of the Lord, so he had no reason to worry about his soul on that account. His problems with God were entirely of his own making.

Juan's closeness now to the Moorish members of his troop opened his eyes to a strange point of view, however. Even though he knew very well that the Moors had been in Spain for the better part of seven centuries, as the stories and epic poems told and retold by traveling troubadours over the years had constantly reminded him, he had always considered them to be invaders in a foreign land, his land. Only now did he fully realize that these men with whom he now rode truly looked upon Spain, their al-Andalus, perhaps Malaga, or Ronda, or Guadix, as their family home, often for much farther back than any of them could possibly trace their lineage. That their forebears might have come from Arabia made them aliens no more than the possibility that Juan's own ancestors might have been Romans or Gauls or Visigoths made him an Italian or a Frenchman or a German. And he began to understand why they fought on, when their cause was obviously lost. They could not just pack up and go *back* over the seas to their homes. Most of them had never been over the seas to begin with. Their homes were here, just as his had always been! And their bones would lie here after they were dead.

During this same time, Muhammad and Raquel were spending what seemed to be the most wonderful times of their lives. Juan had never explicitly outlined his plans for the future to either of them. He had merely left Raquel with all of the money he had obtained from the Basque and had ridden off. Even on the rare occasion when he was within the city, he tended to take a room within the palace complex and did not call on Raquel, and it was only his infrequent contact with Muhammad at court that told them that he was present in the city at all. Juan knew that this lack of communication must have left the lovers with a certain amount of trepidation as to when he might suddenly turn up and attempt to claim his rights as a husband, but his own pride could not allow him to put their minds at rest on this one minor point. He would leave them in peace, but he did not feel obliged to inform them of that fact.

Out of a vague sense of delicacy, Muhammad and Raquel kept their separate beds in his home, although on most nights she would silently slip down the hall and into his chamber, returning to her own room long before dawn. Other than that they led what appeared to be a normal life of a normal wedded couple as far as the neighbors might have been concerned. Muhammad spent several hours a day at the palace, but he spent most of his evenings sitting and talking with Raquel in the patio or telling Marisol stories he had heard on his travels to the East, even on chill winter days when Yusef would have to bring out a small brazier filled with glowing coals to set near their feet. He had even explained that the occasional rustling of a curtain or the scraping on a floor in a room where no one was present was due to his own little daughter, and Marisol nodded earnestly and said that this must be the little dark-haired girl that she sometimes played with when everyone else was busy. Muhammad and Raquel and stared at each other wide-eyed for a moment, and, when Marisol suggested that Muhammad tell his stories in a louder voice so that her friend could hear better, from where she usually hid upstairs, Muhammad had to excuse himself to rub at his eyes in private.

Ordinarily, the coming of spring was greeted with celebration and feasting in Granada as in most of the world. Although the winters in Spain were not normally very harsh, even here among the snow-capped mountains, the winter months were, for most families, a time of tightened belts and concern whether the food stored away in the autumn would be sufficient to last until the next harvest. There was only occasionally snow down at the levels where most towns and cities were located, although it could clearly be seen dusting the peaks of the sierra, but the brown stubble in the harvested fields and the dead grass and bare trees left a rather bleak landscape that the opening of the first pale green buds of spring banished every year with a sudden shout of fresh new life with musical accompaniment by the hordes of birds passing through Spain on their migration from North Africa back to their summer homes in Europe.

But this year the drying out of the roads and the melting of the snow and ice in the mountain passes brought no celebrations of new life but did bring hundreds of the city's residents up onto the battlements of the city walls to peer off to the north and west, shading their eyes against the sun, trying to catch the first glimpse of movement, the coming of the doom they all expected. By early April, word had come in from the border towns that the Castilian army was on the move. A new flood of refugees entered the city, bringing tales of burning and destruction by a Christian army far too vast to count, although Moorish scouts put its numbers at over 40,000 infantry and 10,000 cavalry, certainly several times the force that Granada could put into the field. Finally, on April 23, a dark smudge appeared on the horizon to the north that was soon identified as a dust cloud raised by the approaching horde. Marching in several parallel columns, thick ranks of infantrymen slowly poured across the *vega*, shielded by clouds of horsemen and followed by ponderous trains of baggage wagons and artillery, gradually nearing the city walls, then parting and spreading around them like a torrent of water engulfing a rock in midstream. No effort was made to mount an immediate assault on the city's defenses, and this was perhaps the most terrifying aspect of the advance. The citizens watched in horror as the endless might of the Spanish kingdom paraded below the walls and acres and acres of white tents sprang up like poisonous mushrooms on the surrounding hillsides, finally choking off the last of the roads leading out of the city, and a low, mournful moaning sound could be heard rising up from the different quarters of the city as its fate was deliberately sealed.

Juan watched them march past with a practiced eye. He noted the stolid companies of pikemen from Old Castile and Aragon, stocky little Asturian crossbowmen, arquebusiers from Zaragoza, troops of heavy northern cavalry in bright armor, and squadrons of light Andalusian horsemen with their javelins and round leather shields, both Christians and Moslems. He saw the light falconet cannon carried along on carts drawn by several pairs of oxen, and he knew that the heavier bombards would take some weeks yet to arrive, during which time trenches would be dug and gun pits prepared for them within range of the city walls. He squinted and shielded his eyes to make out the banners of the noblemen, identifying those of the orders of Calatrava and Santiago, of the Duke of Median Sidonia, and many foreign nobles as well, French, English, Portuguese, Burgundian, and, of course, the tall white banner of Fernando himself with the yoke and arrows worked in gold embroidery. He saw the familiar colors of the Marquis of Cadiz, although he could not make out the old man himself or any of his old comrades-in-arms, but he had no doubt that there were there, that they would never miss this last great confrontation of a war that had lasted seven centuries. He had started to keep count of the invaders' numbers, but he gave that up when he realized that there were more than enough for the job at hand, far more than enough.

The Moorish king and his advisors, who now included Juan and Muhammad in their number, watched the arrival of the Spanish from the towers of the Alhambra in silence, then solemnly adjourned to the king's apartments to confer. Juan found it amusing that those who had most vociferously advocated warfare to the death during the preceding months now suddenly saw the possible value of negotiations, notably Hafez and his small clique of courtiers, but Muhammad and most of the military commanders, notably the aged veteran warrior Musa Ibn Abu l-Gazan, had argued against this, at least at this stage of the campaign. Muhammad had pointed out that, after a long string of relatively easy victories, Fernando was not currently offering any kind of incentives for the surrender of Granada. Indeed, word from the Spanish camp was that, given the Moorish king's pledge of fealty to the crown of Castile and his promise to surrender Granada at the command of the Spanish crown, his refusal to do so was tantamount to an insurrection by a rebellious subject. Consequently, Fernando would be justified in enacting the harshest punishment upon the Moors, the confiscation of all their property and the enslavement of all of the population that proved unable to purchase its freedom with generous bribes to the victors. It would only be after Fernando had become convinced, through weeks and months of fierce resistance by the city's defenders, in the face of mounting casualties among his own troops, and skyrocketing costs of the campaign that the Christians could be convinced that the most efficient course of action would be to negotiate a merciful peace, perhaps even leaving Muhammad XII in control of the city of his birth, if little else. As reasonable as this had seemed, it was the shrill wailing of the queen mother, Fatima, denouncing her son as less than a man, unable to defend the birthright that she had placed in his hands and had had to rescue for him herself on more than one occasion, that finally won the day for continued resistance. Juan could well imagine that the prospect of facing a few thousand Christian knights in mortal combat would pale in comparison with doing battle with this formidable woman.

The Christians worked quickly in setting up their string of camps, including one huge, fortified camp at Los Ojos de Huescar, just to the west of the village of Zubia, about a league south of Granada itself. Other Spanish garrisons were reestablished at the castles of Alhendin, Marchena, and Bulduy, which had been quickly recaptured from the Moors after their initial offensive of the previous year. Ordinarily, with the massive forces available to Fernando and an almost unlimited supply of forced labor that could have been obtained from surrounding Moorish villages now under Christian control, the next logical step would have been a circumvalation, the construction of trenches and ramparts completely surrounding the city walls, just out of range of the defenders' guns. Behind these works would have been constructed the firing positions for the heavy bombards, safe from sorties by Moorish infantry and cavalry, while other trenches would have begun to zigzag forward toward the city walls to provide jump-off positions for assaulting troops. But this time the Spanish appeared content to fortify their main camps, leaving much of the ground around the city essentially open, as if inviting the defenders to come forth and accept battle in the field. It was painfully obvious that the Spanish did not have to worry about the sudden arrival of a large relieving army of Moors at their backs, something a besieging army would normally have to defend against. Apart from occasional patrols of Spanish cavalry, the land to the east of the city, thinly covered with woods in the Genil River Valley, not even a proper blockade existed, and a tenuous trickle of food and reinforcements still found their way into the city even weeks after the arrival of the besieging army from the few towns elsewhere that still owed allegiance to Boabdil.

Hafez claimed that the Spanish must have become overconfident and careless now that they were embarked on what must be the final campaign of a centuries-long war and that the time was ripe to arm every man who could carry a weapon and surge out across the open ground and launch a surprise attack that would send the Christians reeling back toward the border. Juan argued that this was precisely what Fernando wanted, that there was no chance that the outnumbered and outgunned Moors would be able to defeat the Spaniards in the open, even if they were to catch them by surprise, which he thought highly unlikely. On the contrary, Musa, while agreeing with Juan, suggested that some of the city gates be left open, also as an apparent act of carelessness, in the hope of luring an impetuous Spanish force into attempting to take the city by *coup de main*, at which time Moorish infantry lying in ambush would cut them off and slaughter them. While Juan considered this to be more than a little risky as well, he also appreciated his lack of real status at this Moslem court, and he chose to remain silent.

Muhammad, meanwhile, had been given the task of putting the city itself into a state of defense. His first task was to take an inventory of all of the governmental holdings of grain and other foodstuffs after which he confirmed that sufficient supplies were on hand for several months of siege. He then organized flying squads of heavily armed troops whom he led through the city, searching the private warehouses of the local merchants and discovering and confiscating hidden stores of grain nearly equal to those held by the government, which had been carefully hoarded against the day when hunger would drive the price of food rapidly skyward. Muhammad also organized neighborhood committees to oversee the clearing of land and planting of grain and vegetables in every square inch of vacant ground in the city, the uprooting of ornamental flowerbeds, even within the grounds of the royal palace and to encourage the raising of chickens, pigeons, and every sort of animal that might be used for food in case of need. Virtually the only flowering plant that survived this purge was his own beloved bougainvillea in the corners of his patio, but he ascribed this one minor lapse as the only real benefit he would ever receive from his position of authority.

Muhammad's second area of responsibility was the organization of the city militia. The regular army, including the royal guard, the retainers of the principal nobles, fighters contributed by the *ribat* monasteries run by the religious orders, and the mercenary troops paid out of the royal treasury, were under the direct command of the king and received their training from their established leaders. However, all able-bodied males from the ages of fifteen to sixty were subject to military service now and had to be grouped into fighting units, provided with whatever weapons could be scrounged up, and given at least rudimentary training in their use.

Among the thousands of men and boys who turned out at the musters held by Muhammad in each section of the city there was always a substantial percentage of refugees from the countryside, where there had always been a tradition of competition in the martial arts of archery, horsemanship, and swordplay. The city dwellers, however, by far the largest portion of the men available, had long since lost interest in such activities, preferring the pleasures of urban life and a dedication to earning money. Muhammad could not help but draw a comparison to the citizens of Rome during the last days of the empire described in his readings of the great Roman historians, as their civilization was about to be engulfed by a tide of barbarians and the Roman army was composed mostly, by then, of foreign mercenaries. Rome had not survived then, and he held out little more hope for the Moorish empire in Spain now. He concluded that, when a nation surrendered its own defense to strangers and its own citizens considered themselves too good to sacrifice for their country, that nation was doomed.

In any event, Muhammad mobilized every metalworker in the city, including a number of very irate and resentful jewelers, and scoured the city for every scrap of usable iron or steel, setting of forges and workshops in every available corner to turn out swords, pikes, and arrows by the thousands. He had to issue strict instructions, with dire penalties, to the more upscale artisans, prohibiting them from spending time and effort to produce the elegant armor and weapons preferred by the nobles (at a correspondingly high price) instead of simple, sturdy equipment that could be produced in bulk.

The men were gathered in companies of one hundred, each centered on the district in which they lived and given responsibility for the segment of the city walls immediately adjacent, thus, Muhammad hoped, giving them something of an advantage over an invader at least in their intimate knowledge of the narrow alleys and interconnecting gardens and the knowledge that their own homes would be the first to be destroyed if they failed to hold their lines. These were drilled for hours every day by elderly veterans in the use of weapons, even if many of them had to practice with sticks until swords and pikes became available. Then, after drill in the afternoon, these same companies were marched to places on the walls in need of repair or bolstering, and they worked far into the night, the better to avoid the harassing fire of the Christian cannon that now began to stud the opposing earthworks. Many of the city gates were not only closed permanently, but were walled up on the inside, and teams of laborers built hoardings along the tops of the city walls, miles of wooden balconies that hung out beyond the walls to allow the defenders to drop stones, burning pitch, or to shoot weapons down on to any enemy troops who gained the base of the walls. There was considerable grumbling, but Muhammad made a point of having his lieutenants take each company up onto the walls once each day for a good look at the vast army that surrounded them, indicating each new enemy contingent as it arrived, and of having the old veterans and refugees tell the most gory stories imaginable about the horrors that conquest by the infidels implied, to keep them focused on the importance of their assignment.

So, defensive preparations went forward, and the days wore on. April passed into May, and the Christian army only grew larger and stronger. There was no sign of sickness within the lines of the besiegers, although it was too early really to hope for that. Food was still readily available within the city, but little was for sale, and that only clandestinely and at exorbitant prices from a handful of speculators who had evaded Muhammad's sweeps. There was no massive Christian assault on the city, as Fernando had apparently decided not to waste his soldiers' lives when the ultimate fall of the city was hardly in question, but there was no indication of a willingness by either side to engage in serious negotiations. In fact, the only event of any note during these first several weeks of the siege was a raid by a small band of Christian knights who, countermanding Fernando's orders to avoid wasteful and pointless acts of individual gallantry, had taken advantage of one of the gates left open in the city walls on Musa's orders and had dashed into the city under a hail of arrows and musket balls and had hurriedly nailed a sign with the words "*Ave Maria*" to the door of a mosque before beating a hasty retreat. While Musa's planned ambush had largely misfired and there had been few casualties during this raid on either side, other than the pride of the commander of that section of the city defenses, morale within the walls continued its decline.

Then, one morning in early June, Muhammad was awakened out of a sound sleep by a deep moaning sound. He had been up nearly all night checking on sentries along the walls and supervising the reinforcement of a key section of the wall, and the curtains of his bedchamber were drawn tight to allow him to rest. He threw them open and jerked aside the shutters to listen better.

"What is that?" Raquel was asking as she emerged from her room, holding Marisol by the hand.

"I have heard this kind of commotion once before," Muhammad said glumly. "Isabel is here."

They walked quickly through the streets, where people were beginning to gather, streaming out of their homes and talking in nervous clusters in the little squares and every intersection. The guards at the door to one of the towers in the city wall saluted Muhammad and stood aside as they entered, and Muhammad led the way up the narrow, winding stairway and out onto the battlements. The walkway was already crowded with soldiers and city dwellers, all peering out over no-man's land and howling in dismay. Some of the men tugged at their beards or pulled their hair in desperation, pointing out at the Spanish camp beyond the walls.

Muhammad could see a thick column of troops winding down from the hills to the northwest of the city. Strong contingents of knights preceded the column in brightly polished armor with the banners of all the noble houses of Spain prominently displayed. On the flanks came phalanxes of pikemen, their long spears carried over their shoulders as they swung along. And in the center, he could just make out a solid block of women, mounted on richly caparisoned horses and dressed in white silk gowns that shone in the morning sun, sparkling with gems and pearls even at this distance, all surrounding a pair of figures riding prancing black horses, taller than any of the others, with the banner of the yoke and arrows held just behind them as they came on.

Raquel's hand went to her mouth, and she involuntarily ducked partially behind a corner of the wall at the sight of her former queen.

"I don't think she saw you," Muhammad chuckled softly, but the look of fear in Raquel's eyes stilled his laughter. "This *is* a bad sign, though, I'll admit."

"It could not be worse," Raquel groaned. "Isabel and I worked out this strategy years ago. The men in the army worship her. They might respect Fernando as a military commander, and they trust him, but it is Isabel that they love. Fernando orders them off to their deaths. Isabel sets up hospitals to take care of them if they are wounded. She sees that widows and orphans are cared for. She is the one who makes sure that they get paid and that they get fed. They will gladly march into the mouth of the cannon for her before they would let her see them retreat. It is victory or death for them now."

Muhammad had nothing to counter this with, since he understood exactly what she was saying and had analyzed the Spanish tactic when he had first seen it himself at Loja years before. "I must talk to the king about this."

The buzz of conversation in the king's reception hall, the Hall of the Ambassadors, could be heard even out in the gardens when Muhammad finally pushed his way through clusters of anxious courtiers who crowded the hall and made his way toward where the king was standing near one of the all arched windows, arguing loudly with a small knot of advisors, his arms flailing desperately about his head.

"I told you that we should have negotiated before the Spaniards got their camp established," Hafez was saying. "Now it's too late. It will be unconditional surrender, and nothing less. We'll be lucky if Fernando lets us keep our heads."

"And do you think they would have offered us anything better a month ago?" the king screamed back at him. "They would have given me some damned goatherd's shack as my new 'kingdom' and then, once my army was gone and my retainers disarmed, they would have come and burned that to the ground! What kind of limp reed are you that the presence of a woman in the enemy camp has you wetting yourself without a blow being struck?"

A captain of the royal guard strode into the room and saluted the king. "The watchtowers report that a strong column of enemy troops is moving in the direction of Zubia from their fortified camp, a mixed force of cavalry and infantry. It would appear that the Spanish king and queen may be with them."

The king's eyes burned with unquestioning rage. "They are coming to accost me in my own capital!" he shrieked, waving his fist in the air. "This cannot be tolerated. I want every man with a horse to arm himself and mount, and I want ten thousand infantry, more if possible, to support an attack." He leaned his head out the nearest window. "It is nearly noon now, if we move quickly, we can hit them just before dusk and throw them into confusion before any reinforcements can reach them in the dark."

Musa shook his bearded head and cast a sidelong glance in Muhammad's direction, frowning. "You majesty," the older man objected, "we will barely be able to field two thousand cavalry now, none as well armed as the Christians. They must have ten times that number. We cannot hope to meet them in the open field. And they cannot be planning an attack themselves if they have their queen and her entourage in among the column. I would surmise that they are just going to the high ground near Zubia to have a view of the city, little more than a picnic outing really. They pose no threat to us, my lord. Why risk what forces we have when it is not in the least necessary?"

"Their forces are spread out all around the city," the king countered, already striding toward the door. "They won't have much more on hand than we have, and they won't be expecting us to attack. They're expecting that we'll just sit here and wait to starve to death. If we can strike hard enough," and the king paused as he began to see the implications of his own plan, "and the royal couple will surely be surrounded by all their nobility. If we can drive through their covering forces, we could kill or capture some of their key leaders, maybe even Fernando and Isabel themselves!" He smacked his forehead with his palm. "This could be their greatest mistake ever! If we only had them, or either one of them, in our power, we could make them take back all the humiliating treaties they forced on us during our own captivity! We could reverse the entire course of the war, regain all the territory lost in ten years, or a hundred years, and all with one lucky stroke! This is truly a vision from Allah!"

Musa appeared ready to argue some more, but the king marched through the door and off toward the stables as dozens of aides rushed on ahead of him to order prepare his horse and armor while others raced throughout the palace calling out the other nobles and their retainers.

Muhammad sighed and looked at Raquel, shrugging his shoulders.

"You're not going with them?" she asked, clutching at this arm. She knew that he had been in combat many times in the past, but this was the first time since they had been together, *together*, how strange that word sounded to her! She had always learned of his battles after the fact, so there had never been anything for her to fear, but now her knees quaked at the thought of watching him ride off with no way of telling whether she would see him again. She had seen Juan do that often enough, but her barely concealed wish then had been that he would die. This was quite another sensation.

"No," he replied, patting her hand and then prying the fingers painfully from his arm. "My job is with the militia. I will be commanding a force of them on the walls, to cover the withdrawal, if there is one, although I have to admit that the king's plan, even if arrived at suddenly, has some logic to it. But *he* will be going," he added, jerking his chin toward the retreating bulk of Juan's broad back, his helmeted head bobbing well above those of the king's entourage.

Raquel frowned. She had only just been thinking of Juan, but that had been another man, at another time. She could certainly not say that she bore any truly warm feelings for him, after all that he had done, but, she had to admit, he had given her what she most deeply desired in the world, and he had done it knowing that it would cost him his position, his honor, everything that seemed to be important to him. Suddenly she did not want him to die. She certainly never wanted to be with him again, but she no longer believed that the world would necessarily be a better place without him in it.

Juan turned in his saddle, lifted the visor of his helmet, and barked at the men clustered behind him in the tight column of heavily armored horsemen crowded into the narrow street leading up to one of the city's sally ports. Other companies of cavalry and infantry were crammed into every alley and side street, all waiting, watching the signalman posted atop the tower above the gate for the order to advance.

"Stay close together and throw your javelins at no more than ten paces, and aim for their horses. Don't try to joust with them, they've got more weight and armor, and their lances are twice the length of ours. If they're moving, try to hit the horse of the man in the front of a pack. That might topple the whole bunch. Then go at them with the sword. Don't slow down, just ride right through them as fast as you can, then wheel, reform, and rally on me. When the battle's the hottest, we'll go on to do our job. Understood?"

Half of his ragged collection of Christian renegades and Moorish mercenaries nodded. Then, when Gamal had translated the tirade into Arabic, the other half nodded, and all began to check their weapons, wrap their reins more tightly in their fists, and bend down to calm their horses.

Suddenly, a bright green banner began waving frantically atop the tower, and the heavy oak gates crashed open while the soldiers who had pushed them scrambled to get out of the way. Juan lowered his visor and dug his spurs into his horse's flanks, leading the way through the narrow gate and out onto the downward slope leading to the southwest. Teams of workers had already surreptitiously thrown piles of fascines, bundles of branches, into the dry moat protecting this face of the city wall, and dumped hundreds of basket loads of dirt on top of this without attracting the attention of the Spaniards, who were quite engrossed in watching the progress of their own sovereigns around the siege lines. These bundles formed a narrow, temporary bridge over which the Moorish army now poured. The bridge could then be burned relatively quickly, in case of need, to prevent the enemy from using it to approach the walls in their turn.

Juan's troop advanced at a slow trot. This would give the following units time to form up and join them, if they hurried, and still they would be able to cross most of the deadly open ground before the Spaniards could react without unduly fatiguing their mounts. Juan stood tall in his stirrups, craning his neck to see over the earthworks of the nearest enemy fortified camp. He could make out a handful of sentinels, now frantically waving their arms and blowing trumpets as a call to arms, but most of the long-barreled falconets sat in their pits unmanned, their crews having rushed off to cheer the arrival of their queen. With luck, the attackers could overrun these forward positions and then take on the Spanish army in the open, without having to withstand the withering fire of their cannon and without the Spaniards having had time to form up properly for battle. Juan had seen from the city walls that the knights of the royal escort were wearing their decorative armor, elaborately etched and polished, but not necessarily designed for maximum protection and ease of movement, and many of the common soldiers on the enemy works had taken off their mail coats in the heat of the June day, not expecting a major attack at this time. Juan had also seen from the banners on display at the head of the Spanish column that the formidable Marquis of Cadiz was leading the escort of the royal couple. Juan would have to be very careful indeed today. He did not know how he would react if he should find himself facing his old patron across the battlefield, but he knew that he would have no choice but kill or be killed.

Hundreds of Moorish infantrymen now rushed forward between the compact groups of cavalry, emerging from several smaller hidden gates in the city walls on either side of the main sally port with their large round shields held loosely in front of them, their javelins low as they sprinted down the slope. They all appreciated, as Juan had, the importance of reaching the Spanish guns before their crews did, and they scrambled up the earthen walls of the Spanish camp, roughly hacking away and pushing aside the sharpened wooden stakes that had recently been installed as a defense. Juan spurred his horse up the slope alongside them just in time to see a mob of Spaniards, most without armor or even weapons, running toward them, desperation in their eyes. They would be the gunners, most of whom were not technically even soldiers, but civilian specialists under contract to the army, whose job was to perform their function normally at a safe distance from the enemy under the protection of their own army, and now they skidded to a terrified halt as the Moors poured over the low dirt wall, screaming and singing the praises of Allah, swords and spears waving over their heads.

A cloud of javelins streamed out from the Moorish lines and a ragged volley of arquebus fire rattled from men who had gotten into position along the top of the wall. Dozens of the Spaniards fell under this hail, and Juan quickly rallied his troop to charge through the disrupted ranks of the enemy. Beyond the panicking Spanish infantry and gunners, he could see a cloud of dust as the Spanish were undoubtedly hurrying the queen and her retinue back out of harm's way and forming up their own cavalry to counterattack. Juan circled his javelin once over his head, pointed it at the enemy, and charged without looking to see if any of his men were following. In his years of experience, the only warrior he had learned that he could be certain of was Asco, who was galloping along on his right side, as always, teeth bared, the fur along the back of his neck standing up in bristles on either side of his spiked collar. Asco, and perhaps the Basque, but the Basque was not here, or, if he was, he would be on the other side.

Juan simply rode the Spanish infantrymen down. Occasionally he would lash out with the edge of the leaf-shaped blade of his javelin, hacking into an exposed face or neck, but his target was the cavalry ahead, and now he could hear the thunder of hooves coming up on either side of him as his men caught up. He spotted a young Spanish knight just ahead of him, probably in his first battle, having trouble getting control of his mount and trying to draw his sword at the same time, and he marked him as his first prey. Just as the young man, all decked out in gold-plated armor worked in the shape of autumn leaves that must have cost his father the equivalent of the yearly wages of an entire village, finally wrenched his sword free from its scabbard and turned to face the onslaught, Juan rose up in his saddle and hurled his lance. It pierced the young man's side, just beneath his raised sword arm, the point protruding near his left hip. As Juan thundered by, he saw a look of perplexed embarrassment on the young man's pretty face, probably wasting his last seconds of life wondering what he was going to do with this bothersome shaft sticking out of his chest, wondering in embarrassment if anyone had been watching when he made his fatal mistake, just before he toppled from his saddle.

Juan had his long sword out now, hacking to left and right, indifferent as to whether he cleaved the flesh of man or horse. Off to his left he could see the green banner of the Moorish king Boabdil right in the front line of the charge, and he glimpsed the fine chestnut Arabian that Musa rode, also well to the fore. At least, Juan mused, he would not be dying in the company of cowards, even if he were in with a band of infidels. He rode on, fighting all the way through the Spanish column and into the clear on the other side. He had purposely avoided the Marquis of Cadiz's banner, and he now saw that the entourage of the queen had raced back toward the main Spanish camp, barely visible in the rising cloud of dust, with a thick phalanx of pikemen now drawing up to block the way between the advancing Moors and the queen. There would be no catching that prize today.

But Juan had never expected to accomplish that. Instead, he turned and found Gamal, right where he expected him, not ten yards away, his right arm and sword bathed in blood, whether his own or some victim's, Juan could not say. Juan pointed his sword at him and bellowed, "Now!"

Gamal nodded and rose up in his saddle, letting out a shrill, warbling cry that drew to him all the Moslem members of Juan's troop. They formed up and charged back through the milling Spaniards in the direction of the city.

Juan gathered to himself the surviving Christians of his band, only eight were remaining. Fewer than he had had at the start, but enough to carry out his own plan. They quickly followed his example and tore away the green tunics they had worn over their chain mail, revealing white tunics with a bright red cross on the breast and back hidden beneath.

They then fell into line behind Juan and rode at a casual trot in the direction of the Spanish camp.

Juan and his men fell in behind a mob of retreating Spanish infantry, letting them use the weight of their numbers to force a passage through the gateway into the camp against a thinner stream of reinforcements trying to make their way to the scene of the fighting. Since the incentive to reach safety is naturally stronger than that of attempting to do one's duty by seeking death in battle, he had no doubt that the retreating troops would ultimately win out and open the road for him to slip through. It was nearly dusk as he passed into the camp without being challenged in the confusion, and he directly led his men away from the main avenue between the long rows of tents and off to one side where they dismounted, leaving their horses tied and moving out on foot.

The camp covered acres of ground, all now crowded with tents and small huts, open corrals for the horses, mules, and oxen, and small stockades built of vertical poles embedded in low raised earthen walls for the storage of food, fodder, and munitions. These latter were designed primarily to discourage random pilfering by the troops rather than for proper defense, since the whole camp was protected by an earthen wall twelve feet high and nearly as many thick, which was stoutly garrisoned and provided with raised towers for light cannon at various points. Of the stockades, only those containing food (and wine) stores boasted a proper and vigilant guard as there was little reason for individual troops to bother stealing powder, shot, or arrows that they were freely provided with anyway. It was toward the primary munitions stockade that Juan and his men now made their way, picking through the tangle of tent ropes quietly in the gathering dark.

The sounds of battle had now died away, and more and more men were filing back into the camp. With a force this large and this cosmopolitan, with contingents from all over Spain and much of the rest of Europe, a handful of unknown men hardly raised an eyebrow. Juan and his men kept their visors down and stuck to the shadows without appearing to be trying to do so. Only Juan's face was truly well known among many of the veterans of Fernando's army, although he wore nondescript armor that no one would identify with him, so the risks there at least were minimized. The rest of his men were all fighting on the side of the Moors because they were on the run from the law in Christian lands, for murder, for stealing the wrong man's wife, or for simple robbery, and as all were Spanish, they could return the casual greetings of passing soldiers without raising any suspicions.

There were only two soldiers lounging near the flimsy wooden gate to the munitions stockade. It was dark here by now, as open fires were not permitted within fifty yards of the gunpowder stores, and both men squinted, half rising from their seats as the column of dark men-at-arms approached them led by someone who was obviously an officer. The guards were just about to ask his business when Juan's arm shot out, a razor sharp dagger in his hand, slashing across the throat of the first soldier. Before the second could open his mouth to scream, Juan had grabbed him by his long hair and plunged the dagger up under his chin to the hilt. He twisted the blade as dark blood gushed down the front of the man's breastplate and his body twitched convulsively in Juan's grasp. One of his men lifted the leather strap that held the gate, and they dragged the bodies inside, leaving two of their number in place at the entrance.

Juan quickly marched through the stockade, which was crammed with stacks of powder kegs, pyramids of iron and stone cannon balls, and sheaves of arrows. He pointed to a stack of kegs from which each of his men grabbed one, while with the pommel of his sword he broke in the lid of a large barrel, tipping it over and spilling the glistening black powder out onto the ground at this feet. He took another smaller keg and broke in its lid as well and began to lay a trail of powder toward the back side of the stockade where one of his men had already cut away the lashings that held some of the poles in place, making a new exit in the surrounding wall. Juan gave a low whistle and his two replacement guards quickly latched the gate behind themselves and followed the party through the stockade and out the back.

They found themselves in a narrow, shadowy alley between the stockade and the outer wall of the camp, and Juan used up two kegs of powder laying a trail to a huge stack of hay bales standing next to a large corral. His men broke open the remaining kegs and strew powder all around the area while Juan walked over to an untended fire and pulled out a burning branch. He lit the straw at a dozen places out of sight of where the nearest soldiers were setting about cooking their evening meal and then tossed the branch onto the trail of powder leading back to the magazine.

He and his men raced to a ladder propped up against the camp wall and quickly climbed up. A sentry with a crossbow turned to question them, but one of Juan's men silently ran him through and shoved his body over the wall. Flames could now be seen licking up around the stack of hay and scattered shouts rose up nearby. A loud hissing noise could also be heard, and Juan watched as a bright yellow glow raced along the base of the wall and disappeared into the shadows of the munitions stockade. Juan vaulted over the low parapet, and he and his men hung by their arms and dropped to the ground outside just as a rumbling explosion began, quickly followed by others, and kegs began soaring into the night sky, trailing sparks like miniature comets.

Juan and his men ran flat out across the broken ground toward the city, and he turned to glance over his shoulder to see the entire Spanish camp bathed in the red glow of a massive fire. A steady, warm breeze was blowing, carrying sparks throughout the camp, and soon these landed on tents and other piles of straw and bedding that started a hundred other fires before any thought could be given to attempting to put out the first conflagration. Trumpets were calling, drums beating, and screams could be heard above it all as the raiders disappeared into the darkness.

The initial euphoria within Granada with the destruction of much of the main Spanish camp in the fire had dimmed even before the last of the sparks had been stamped out. At dawn, while the camp still burned, the Marquis of Cadiz had led a heavy assault on the city walls to prevent the Moors from taking advantage of the disaster. The Moorish king had led a countercharge with every man that could be armed, in the hope of finding the Christians demoralized by their misfortune, but such was not the case. In a day-long battle under the walls of the city, the Moors had at first gained the advantage and pushed to within a few yards of the smoldering ashes of the Spanish camp, but thousands of fresh enemy cavalry had charged down onto the plain from some of the other camps, driving the Moors back, and volley after volley by hundreds of Spanish arquebusiers tore into the Moslem infantry, who were largely helpless to reply. Finally, as the sun had lowered in the west, the Moorish king himself was felled by a crossbow bolt, causing panic in the Moorish ranks and sending them streaming back to the protection of the fire of the guns on the city walls. While the king's wound was not serious, this would be the last major foray of the Moors out into the open field.

Days stretched into weeks, and the summer waned. The mood of the population of Granada gradually improved as the weather cooled, even though food became more and more scarce within the city. Everyone knew that winter tended to come early in the mountains, and the Spanish army would have to retire to summer quarters in Andalusia well before the heavy autumn rains made the roads impassible to their artillery. The besiegers had fairly quickly made good the damage to their camp, but the destruction of a large portion of the gunpowder that had been accumulated precluded the kind of heavy bombardment that had crushed one Moorish city after another in previous campaigns. And the Spanish seemed to have no stomach for a direct assault on the walls. It was unlikely that the city could be starved out before the winter set in, and, without the option of smashing down the city walls with their heavy bombards, it appeared that Fernando's campaign would be a colossal failure. Even the meanest workman and shopkeeper in the city knew that the Spanish crown had gone heavily into debt to finance this campaign, and, with nothing to show for it, there might be several years of respite before such an effort could be made again, if ever.

But then, even as early autumn came to Granada, a bustle of activity in the Spanish camp brought hundreds of curious spectators up to the walls and towers every day. Men, women, and children shielded their eyes and squinted, and the military commanders sent daring scouts on night patrols right into the enemy's lines to observe or even to attempt to capture a prisoner who might tell what was afoot.

Then it became obvious. In the place of the burned out tent city, the Spaniards were constructing an entire town! With stone, mud bricks, thatch and tiles, row after row of little houses began to arise. Larger barracks, headquarters, and storehouses, even a church, also appeared within a protective wall within sight of the city on its hill, with streets laid out in the form of a massive cross plainly visible from the city walls. Prisoners told the Moors that the new city was named Santa Fe, christened by the queen herself, and it was proof that the Spanish had no intention of leaving for winter quarters at all. They were importing thousands of head of cattle, wagonloads of wheat and other grains, and assigning armies of workers to carving permanent roads back through the mountains to ensure a steady supply of food and munitions throughout the winter. The prisoners swore that Fernando had issued orders that the army would remain in position until Granada fell or the last Spanish soldier was slain, and they stuck to this preposterous story even when tortured to death.

Muhammad could see the change in attitude within the city as the walls of Santa Fe rose from the mud of the camp. Men and women dragged themselves through the streets, barely going through the motions of daily life. Haggling in the marketplace, when there was anything to sell, was languid, but arguments quickly flared up and blows were struck over the slightest matter. He suffered for his people, all the more because he knew that they were not aware that word had finally come from the King of Fez that, despite the eloquence of Muhammad's written plea for military support, no such reinforcement could possibly be raised or transported to Spain from North Africa. There would be no rescuing army. The fate of the city was sealed.

Muhammad found the scene in the Hall of the Ambassadors to be more than a little chaotic. The long room, with its rows of slender columns of pink limestone, had a soft glow with the light brought in through the lobed, arched windows along the outside wall, but it was filled with a mob of arguing, shouting, and wailing courtiers, nobles, soldiers, and civilian merchants, all demanding to be heard, none the least interested in listening. Hafez was engaged in a yelling match with Musa close to where the king slouched on his gold leaf throne on a raised dais at one end of the hall. Hafez stood to one side, flailing his delicate hands about his head and glancing frequently for support to the king, and Musa stood on the other, his burly arms crossed over his barrel chest, his jaw set in a grimace, snarling back in return, and a long-haired, wild-eyed holy man in tattered robes stood with Musa wagging his finger in Hafez's face, spittle from his lips sprinkling down on the royal lap, but the king did not appear to take notice. As usual, the king's mother, Fatima, was the only woman in the room, sitting quietly next to the throne, her head resting against one of its arms, her mouth only inches from her son's ear.

The king did not appear to be following the argument. He had not fully recovered from the wounds he had suffered in the fighting after the burning of the Christian camp, and an angry pink scar now ran from near his right eye, down his cheek and disappeared under the collar of his white silk tunic. His face was gaunt, and his eyes were sunken, with dark rings underneath them as a sign of his recent difficulty in sleeping. He had resisted Muhammad's suggestions to take a sleeping potion, and he appeared to be avoiding all food that his mother did not taste first as a precaution against the poison of assassins he recently had begun to imagine lurking all about him. Muhammad had to agree, however, that poor Abu was probably not being unreasonable in this. Too many people now saw him as the main stumbling block on the road to peace for Granada, even if that involved total submission. Muhammad approached the throne, weaving between the clusters of arguing men, and listened to the discussion.

"But we have food for less than two more months," Hafez was saying. "What are we going to do then? Better to make a treaty now while we still are in a position to resist than to wait until the enemy knows that we're desperate."

"And what kind of deal will you make with the devil?" the holy man shouted back. "The blessings of paradise will be assured to him who fights for the true faith. Would you sacrifice all of eternity for a little comfort in the here and now?"

"And what of our honor?" Musa joined in. "Will we become like el Zagal, the tame lap dogs of the Christians, living in some little shepherd's hut and calling it a palace, wandering the mountain valleys and calling it a kingdom? No wonder el Zagal lost his mind and went off to Africa. He probably welcomed the punishment the King of Fez handed him as a way of atoning for his lack of faith."

"We have had treaties with the Christians in the past," Hafez countered. "They want this war over quickly, and they will offer generous terms to make it so. Granada is theirs, whether we die first or not. The only difference will be whether every man, woman, and child here is sold into slavery or whether we can live out our lives in some dignity and, yes, comfort. What's the harm in that?"

The king finally waved a languid hand in their direction, closing his eyes and frowning as if in pain.

"You can stop your squabbling like fruit sellers in the market," the king growled at them. "It is done."

Conversation suddenly stopped in the hall, and all eyes turned toward the king. Muhammad had long since become accustomed to the idea that he would be cut out of any negotiations with the Christians, but it still came as a surprise to him that even Yusef's network of informants had provided no warning that serious talks had apparently been taking place. He was also surprised that it did not appear that any of the factions at court had been privy to the talks either, obviously not Musa, who was known to advocate a fight to the bitter end, but it even appeared that Hafez had been left out in the cold as well. Muhammad studied Fatima's face carefully now. She, too, had turned toward her son, but her expression was not one of surprise, neither was it of foreknowledge, but it carried a look of weary resignation. She had not *known* of the talks, Muhammad concluded, yet, in her heart, she had known very well.

"I have the terms from Fernando," the king went on, "and I have communicated my acceptance this morning. The lives and property of all residents of Granada are to be respected. None will be forced to leave, nor will any be sold into slavery. Our religion is to be protected, and Moslem clerics and local administrators will retain their positions. My court will remove to the Alpujarras Mountains where I will have a small kingdom, and Fernando will pay a sum of

30,000 *castellanos* in gold upon my surrendering the keys to the city."

"That's disgraceful," Musa snorted. "And what if the Berbers or the Turks have gotten together an army and are coming to our aid? We haven't had word from the outside world for weeks. Our own people would tear us to pieces if that were to happen."

"I have thought of that," the king said, finally raising his head with a sarcastic smile on his lips. "Fernando has granted us a period of grace of two months, until the end of this year, 1491 by the Christian calendar. Only if no relief is seen by that time will the formal capitulation take place. In the meanwhile, there will be no bombardment of the city nor any assault on the walls, nor will there be any attack by our forces on the Spanish."

"So we are just to sit here and starve?" Musa asked. "To what purpose?"

"Why, to serve our honor, I suppose," the king replied, shrugging, and he turned his head to stare blankly out the windows.

Musa turned on his heel and strode toward the door followed by a small knot of his officers, without bothering to bow to the king, the crowd parting before him like the waves before the prow of a heavily laden ship with the wind astern, and the holy man scurried along in his wake, glowering back in the direction of the king. "You can't serve something that doesn't exist!" he roared over his shoulder as he disappeared through the tall double doors.

Muhammad did not wait to observe any further reactions but made for the door quickly himself. He found Yusef in the hall, pretending to talk to one of the guards but certainly listening in on the proceedings.

"Go to the barracks and find Don Juan," Muhammad whispered, taking Yusef by the arm and dragging him along the corridor with whim. "Bring him with you to my house in the Albaicin."

"And if he won't come?" Yusef asked.

"Tell him what you just heard, and he'll come," Muhammad said, then turned out into a patio while propelling Yusef down a different corridor with a shove.

Muhammad hurried out of the Alhambra through the Gate of Justice and trotted down the steep road, through a series of switchbacks, that finally took him over a bridge over the Genil River and to the suburb of the Albaicin. He noticed nervous glances from passersby along the narrow streets. He was wearing the fine robes of a member of the court, and the common people knew that the only time when members of the ruling class moved quickly anywhere was when something was very, very wrong. But Muhammad ignored them and burst through the doors of his own house and into the patio.

Raquel was there, playing cat's cradle with Marisol with a piece of red yarn. She looked up happily at his arrival, but her own expression froze when she saw his face.

"Has the city fallen?" she asked flatly.

"We have two months," he replied, taking her hand while Marisol hugged his knees fiercely. "Go to the kitchen, child," he said in a quiet voice. "See if there are any oranges left."

"There are none," Raquel whispered as the little girl skipped out of the patio.

"I know, but it will take her some time to look."

"What happened? There hasn't been any serious fighting. We would have heard it."

"No, it's just my protégé, working things out on his own again," Muhammad sighed. "Although, this time I can't really blame him. There is no hope, and people are starting to die, not from hunger, but from the sickness that seems to precede the worst of the hunger. There is no one to help us, and the Christians are not going away, so he made the best arrangement he could."

"For himself, I suppose," she added bitterly. "But what will happen to . . ."

Just then the street door creaked open again, and the bulky figure of Juan blocked out the sunlight from the street.

"I was told to come here," Juan said, almost meekly, pausing in the doorway.

"Yes," Muhammad said, while Raquel looked nervously back and forth between the two. She had not seen Juan in months. Despite his still-imposing size, she could tell that he had lost weight, and there were new scars on his face and his sinewy, bare forearms. Asco impatiently pushed past him and shuffled up to nuzzle Raquel's hand. "You need to hear this too. We are all in this together."

"I have heard already," Juan said. "Musa just rode out the main gate with a dozen men and charged the Spanish lines. They were cut down in a moment. I watched from one of the towers, and I knew what must have happened."

"When the Christians come, they will not take out the whole population, but there will certainly be a search for renegades," Muhammad said, almost biting off the last word in embarrassment.

"There must be some way to escape," Raquel said, looking toward the kitchen to make sure that Marisol had not returned.

"Not while their army is still camped all around the city," Muhammad said. "There are enough loose tongues at court that they will know to look here for you," he said to Raquel, still holding her hands in his, "and I'm sure they will look even harder for those who fought against them, especially if they hear of your fame as the one who burned their first camp," he added, turning to Juan.

"Eternal life is not something I ever expected," Juan said, shrugging. "I'll give them some exercise before they take me, though. Perhaps I'll give them something to write a song about after I'm gone."

Muhammad shook his head. "If we can just keep you both hidden for a little while, a month or two perhaps. Their army will be gone. Merchants and travelers will be back on the roads in large numbers, and then we can look to getting away from here. All we need is a little time."

"But you just said that they would probably look here," Raquel said.

"Here, yes, but I don't think they'll bother the Jewish quarter. I stopped on the way here and spoke with your Uncle Ysaque. He is willing to take all three of you in."

Juan planted his fists on his hips and threw back his head, letting out a deep, echoing laugh. "Who ever said that God doesn't have a sense of humor?" He doubled over, shaking his head. "Just when you think you've hit bottom, God hands you a shovel and tells you to start digging." Then his smile disappeared, and he turned to Raquel, whose eyes had grown wide with fear. "I will accept this penance, because it is the will of God, and I will swear to you that I will not touch you, or even speak to you, if that is your wish. But I will lay down my life to protect you and your daughter. That is little enough, but it is all that I can do, and sometimes all has to be enough." He drew his sword and held it up, hilt skyward, and kissed the crosspiece.

Muhammad reached over and placed a hand on his broad shoulder, while Raquel covered her mouth, tears streaming down her face. Just then Marisol came running back into the patio.

"No oranges!" she announced in an official tone. Then she noticed the visitor, hardly having seen Juan since infancy, except for their escape months before, and saw that her mother was crying. She frowned.

"Don't worry," Juan said, planting the tip of his sword on the ground and kneeling to her. "Everything will be all right. I promise." She smiled at him.

Muhammad watched from the city walls as the king and a small mounted party of Moors met the massive entourage of Fernando and Isabel down by the banks of the Genil River on the second day of January, 1492. Muhammad had finally been allowed to join in the last of the negotiations and had spent endless hours haggling with Spanish courtiers over the protocol of the surrender. Fatima had been adamant that her son not be obliged to kiss the hand of either Fernando or Isabel, or to dismount from his horse. Muhammad had all he could do to keep from laughing out loud at the ultimate formula agreed upon which called for poor Abu, so consumed with the trappings of the kingdom he had already lost, to rise up in his saddle and lift one leg partially over the seat, as if to dismount. At this point Fernando would tell him to stop, thus demonstrating Abu's willingness to make obeisance before the conqueror but not actually to have to do so. That morning, as the party was just setting out for the ceremony, Abu had broken down in tears, and Yusef, who had been helping with the horses, later told Muhammad that Fatima had chided him that, "You may as well cry like a woman for what you could not defend like a man," but Muhammad knew that Yusef had a love for the dramatic, and he doubted that such had ever happened.

The friar, now Cardinal Hernando de Talavera, led the Spanish column of one thousand cavalry and five thousand foot into the city and up to the Alhambra, but Muhammad knew that, fearing an uprising by his own citizens, Abu had begged for and received a garrison of Spanish soldiers the night before, making the actual surrender of the citadel something of an anti-climax. As the endless procession of elegantly dressed Spanish courtiers flowed past into the last bit of Moorish Spain, Muhammad watched as Abu sat on his horse to one side of the road. When all had gone by, he turned and led his own little group, including Fatima shrouded in dark robes from head to foot, off toward Val de Purchena, the hill town that would be the capital of his new "kingdom." Abu turned in his saddle at the last rise in the road, and Muhammad raised his staff in farewell, but, if the king saw him, he made no sign but merely bent his head and continued on his way.

GRANADA

Book Seven

1492

GRANADA

Chapter One

Granada

The early days of Spanish occupation in Granada were largely uneventful. A powerful garrison had been established in the Alhambra and Generalife citadels under the command of Iñigo Lopez de Mendoza, and Spanish troops also occupied the towers containing the gates in the city walls while the rest of the army dispersed and returned to their homes. Prior to this, a formal procession by Isabel and Fernando was held through the city, escorted by thousands of troops and the entire court in their most elegant dress. They solemnly received the release of hundreds of Christian prisoners who had been languishing in the dungeons, some of them for years, and these pitiful, ragged, wasted wraiths were each given a handful of coins, some clothing, and sent off to their respective homes with the blessings of their sovereigns. A number of the mosques were consecrated as Christian churches, and the moderate and merciful Hernando de Talavera was named Archbishop of Granada, a promise of a tolerant administration regarding the new Moorish subjects of the crown.

Apart from the few thousand Moorish troops that accompanied the former king into exile, most of the Moslem army was demobilized, with the North African mercenaries being given the option of returning to their homeland or taking up residence in Spain as *mudejar* farmers and artisans. The remainder surrendered their weapons, dumping them in a huge pile outside the city walls, and the Spanish took command of the larger artillery pieces emplaced around the city. There was a cursory search for hidden weapons, but the amount of armaments turned in, and the apparent eagerness of the bulk of the population to put the war behind them and get back to the business of making money encouraged the new sovereigns to minimize the danger of any sort of armed resistance.

Spanish troops did enthusiastically hunt down the renegade Christians who had fought in the Moorish army, most of whom were apprehended attempting to escape the city in a variety of disguises. These were taken to a row of stakes planted in the ground outside the city walls, and a crowd of noble young Spanish cavaliers used them for target practice with light reed lances, racing past on galloping horses and skewering the writhing prisoners on the run. Betting was furious as to how many hits a rider could score on a target without killing the prisoner, and most were studded with upwards of a dozen lances before finally succumbing. Muhammad watched the spectacle from atop the walls, along with hundreds of other Moors, shuddering at the screams of the victims and saying silent prayers of thankfulness that the conquerors' rage was diverted onto their own countrymen rather than the city's population.

But there was no systematic search, house-to-house, for Juan and Raquel, as they had all feared might happen. It appeared that, despite the notoriety of their escape at the time in the Spanish court, and rumors of Juan's role in the city's defense, confirmed by testimony of those like Hafez, who sought to ingratiate themselves with their new masters by eager cooperation, it had been assumed that Juan had escaped along with his wife. Muhammad's seclusion of the couple in the Jewish quarter some time before the actual fall of the city gave rise to the assumption that Juan had slipped away before the blockade of the city had become complete and that they were now likely living in exile, under assumed names, elsewhere in Europe. Muhammad had helped to ensure this outcome by having Yusef use his network of informants to put this rumor about in court circles, thus allowing the Spaniards to hear of it on their own.

Within a few days of the occupation, Raquel felt secure enough to return to Muhammad's home, when it became apparent that they would not be discovered there as long as she maintained the dress and bearing of a Jewish woman and generally stayed off the streets. Muhammad would spend his days reading and writing in the patio, with Raquel seated nearby sewing or knitting, or reading herself, while Marisol played joyfully, oblivious to the events in the world outside the walls of the house. Juan, however, took up residence in the small apartment owned by Ysaque in the Jewish quarter and found himself spending many hours just sitting with the old man, talking about their respective lives, sipping sweet wine in his study until long after dark, even after the candles had burned themselves out. With the small pension that Muhammad still received from his former king and with the money Juan had managed to bring with him into exile, they were able to meet their modest needs while, slowly, the economic life of the city began to return to normal. There would be plenty of time to decide what to do and where they might go later on.

The only worrisome aspect of the new situation in Granada was that Isabel and Fernando apparently intended to make the conquered city their temporary seat of government for the indefinite future. For weeks after the surrender, they maintained their residence in the siege camp/city of Santa Fe, only visiting Granada itself during the daylight hours until the territory could be declared definitely secured. A brief armed uprising by religious fanatics in one of the working class quarters of the city, which was immediately and brutally suppressed by the Spanish garrison, testified to the wisdom of this policy, but, by April, it had become evident that the monarchs would be as safe in the Alhambra as they would in any other palace in their kingdom, and the royal couple moved their entire court up onto the russet hills overlooking the city. With the departure of the Moorish court and thousands of other Moslems, either to return to towns they had abandoned in the face of the Spanish offensive the previous year or to go into exile overseas, there was ample room for the new tenants, and overcrowding in the city that had been common during the final several years of the reconquest was largely relieved. Meanwhile, Spanish and Moslem workers systematically went through the city removing official symbols of Moorish authority from walls and public buildings and installing plaques and engravings featuring the yoke and arrows insignia of the new royal house.

The presence of Isabel and Fernando, and many members of their usual court, within the city walls greatly increased the chances that either Juan or Raquel would be observed or that word of their hiding would leak out. For that reason, Muhammad dictated that both must even more strictly limit themselves to either his or Ysaque's home and venture out into the streets only after dark and, even then, in heavy disguise and only in the case of absolute necessity. Word had it that patrols of the *Santa Hermandad* were still scouring the countryside in search primarily of Moorish nobles who were supposed to have turned themselves in to the Spanish authorities as hostages for Boabdil's continued good behavior or to have paid a substantial financial guarantee in lieu of actually surrendering their persons. Many of these nobles had foregone the honor bestowed on them by their former king in naming them to the Spanish as hostages and had gone into hiding instead or were attempting to flee the country for North Africa with whatever moveable wealth they had managed to gather.

Consequently, the time was still not ripe for Juan, Raquel, and Muhammad to attempt their own flight from the occupied city, for they had taken it as a foregone conclusion that they would all make the attempt together without actually having sat down to discuss the matter. But with the court present in Granada, there were literally hundreds of individuals now walking the streets, both Spanish courtiers, and members of the Moorish court who had chosen to remain in the city, who knew either Juan or Raquel, or both, by sight and were fully aware of their status as fugitives. Raquel was able to hide her appearance by the simple expedient of adopting the heavy veil of strict *chadour* for a Moslem woman. Juan had carefully shaved his beard and moustache, and Muhammad had supplied him with a lotion that died his reddish hair a deep black and his skin a rich mahogany, allowing him to pass, on cursory inspection, as just another Moor, although he could not sustain the disguise if obliged to speak. While he had mastered a basic conversational Arabic, his Spanish accent was so thick as to give him away immediately to any native speaker, or even to another Spanish Christian accustomed to the lyrical tone of the Moors. In any event, the pair now spent virtually all of their time in their respective lodgings, Raquel with Muhammad and Marisol, and Juan with

Ysaque, as the weary, nerve-racking days dragged on. But not as many of them as everyone later would have wished.

At the end of March in the late, chilly, blustery afternoon, Muhammad, Raquel and Marisol had bundled themselves up, both against the cold and to prevent recognition, for the walk to Ysaque's home to celebrate the Sabbath. When they arrived, quickly passing through the door and checking the narrow street behind them to see if they had been followed, they found only Juan present with one elderly servant, the two of them quietly sharing the chores of setting out the candles, cloths, and other details of the ceremony, a sight that still made Raquel shake her head in disbelief.

"Where is Ysaque?" she asked. "It's almost sunset."

"He was called to the synagogue," Juan replied, shrugging. "Something about an official notice having been posted on the door, but I'm sure he'll be back in time."

Raquel frowned. "That's not good. It's never good news for Jews when official notices are posted on the synagogue doors."

"It's probably something about some new tax," Juan offered as he poured sweet red wine into pewter cups and offered them to the guests, with a cup of orange juice for Marisol. "You know how desperate the government is to recoup the cost of the campaign, and they can't get it all from the Moors with the agreement they signed with Boabdil, so the Jews would be the next best thing."

Just then Ysaque burst into the room, turning to bolt the door behind him. His face was clouded with worry. He looked up and appeared surprised to find himself surrounded by curious faces.

"We have four months to leave Spain!" he announced flatly, tossing his dull brown cloak onto a table near the door.

"We expect to be gone in less time than that," Raquel chided him, "if we've worn out our welcome that badly."

"Not just you," Ysaque corrected her. "All of *us*," he said, tapping his chest with a gnarled knuckle. "All of the Jews of Spain. Your Queen Isabel has just issued a decree to that effect. Within the next four months, all Jews living in the kingdoms of Castile and Aragon and their territories, must either convert to Christianity or leave the country. It's as simple as that."

"But that would ruin the country!" Raquel protested, her preparations for the Sabbath temporarily forgotten. "The crown *needs* the Jews to provide financing for the government. Where else are they going to get it? The bankers in Florence and Venice have always been too tight to rely upon, and they could be influenced by the French or the Holy Roman Empire if those leaders saw an advantage to seeing our sources of credit dry up. I can't believe that Isabel would advocate such a stupid policy!"

Ysaque shrugged. "I received an enciphered message from Isaac Abravanel, who is still apparently one of Isabel's closest advisors on financial matters at court. It arrived at the same time as the official decree, which implies that he did not have much advance knowledge of what the queen was planning to do, which is worrisome in itself. He was aware of the movement in the direction of expulsion, although only at the last minute, and he was fighting against it. This would have been about a week ago," Ysaque added, "as our methods of communication are more roundabout and so not so quick as the royal messenger services. He said that Isabel was quite aware that, in the long run, it would be inconvenient for the crown not to have Jewish financiers to turn to for loans, but, at the moment, the war is over, and they are already mortgaged to the hilt with the Spanish Jews, besides having squeezed every copper out of us that they could through special taxes and 'contributions' over the past several years.

"Apparently someone has gotten the queen's ear, and the rumor is that it is Torquemada himself, "Ysaque added dramatically, "and this person has convinced her that, if the Jewish community in Spain is destroyed, the existing debt will be destroyed with it. Besides that, the Jews will be forced to put up all of their property for sale, obviously at bargain prices, which will benefit immensely the only people with the money to buy, the Spanish nobility, so Isabel is cleverly buying their continued loyalty at no cost to herself. And, lastly, we will only be allowed to take a pittance in terms of money or other possessions with us when we go into exile, so substantial fortunes will ultimately become the property of the crown by default."

"But, in the long run," Raquel argued, "this will cost Spain dearly."

"No one but scholars ever worries about the long run," Muhammad said, shaking his head. "Your uncle is quite right. The crown is faced with massive debts right now, and this is a way of getting out from under them without challenging the power of the nobility by attempting to get them to pay taxes themselves. It's a perfect politician's solution to the problem."

They were interrupted by a nervous cackle that erupted from Juan, who buried his face in his hands, tears streaming down his face.

"There is nothing funny in any of this," Raquel snapped at him, but Juan kept on laughing breathlessly for a long moment before he could reply.

"This is not about finances or about the Jews," he said, wiping roughly at his eyes with the palms of his hands. "Torquemada wants a Spain that will be purely Christian. The Jews are the first, but he'll see to it that the Moors are all kicked out too in their turn, when he gets around to it, but it's not even about that. It's God's work, and it's me he's after."

"Some people could take that as a certain lack of humility," Ysaque said, frowning quizzically. "You really think that God would destroy a whole people just to get at you? I think He's got enough of an imagination to be a little more discreet than that."

"One person, ten thousand, a million," Juan went on. "What difference does it make to God? No, he saw how I had sinned. He saw my pride and my violence, and all the dark, dirty little thoughts that were in my heart. So he gave me power and position and then stripped it all away. He made me humble myself before a woman. He made me live as a Jew. Now he is going to show me how the Jews have suffered in my own flesh. Perhaps he doesn't think you'll mind," he continued, shakily pouring himself a cup of wine and tossing it off at one gulp. "After all, he's done it to you before often enough. Perhaps all those other times, the destruction of the Temple of Jerusalem by the Romans, the massacres of the Jews all over Europe for centuries, even the pressure that forced your family," he nodded toward Raquel, "to pretend to convert to Christianity here in Spain years ago, perhaps every one of those events was simply an effort by God to get even with one poor sinner!" He shook his head again and took another drink.

Raquel rolled her eyes, but Muhammad just stroked his beard thoughtfully and held out a cup for Juan to serve him some wine as well.

"But why now, why all of a sudden?" Raquel asked.

"It was not so sudden after all," Ysaque explained. "Apparently, last November, there was an incident in Avila in which charges were brought against the local Jews and some *conversos* as well regarding an incident in which a young Christian boy was allegedly kidnapped and ritually sacrificed in some kind of diabolic ceremony using a stolen communion wafer. It was all fabricated, of course, but the local office of the Inquisition had been hammering on the Jewish community for not turning in people they suspected of being secret practitioners of the Jewish faith, and this was seen as a way of putting more pressure on them with an offer of dropping the charges if a sufficient number of Judaizers were surrendered to the Holy Office. The rabbi refused, and deacons began recounting the story from their pulpits, with the details getting more bloody and lurid with every telling until crowds were roaming the streets stoning any Jews they found, and the bishop put the stamp of official approval on the whole thing by convicting six Jews and six *conversos* for the murder. This gave the crown a pretext, in order to ensure tranquility within the kingdom, to order the expulsion. We just didn't hear about the plans here in Granada until the decisions had already been made because of the siege cutting off our communications with the rest of the country."

"You know?" Muhammad began, talking slowly as he sorted out his own thoughts. "Not to minimize the suffering that this is going to cause the Jews throughout Spain, but for our own strictly selfish purposes, this might not be such a bad turn of events after all."

"It is truly comforting that you can find some benefit to come out of the destruction of a people who have lived in this land for more than one thousand years," Ysaque grumbled with a bitterness that none had ever seen in him before.

"Please forgive me," Muhammad quickly replied. "I really do not mean to make light of the loss to your people or to Spain, and I believe that Juan is quite right in believing that this is just the first step, that the Christians will soon move to expel us Moors as well. They are a selfish people, so sure of the rightness of their belief and their cause that they see anyone who differs from them as essentially evil. All I meant was that, since we, that is myself, Raquel, Juan, and Marisol, will eventually have to leave the country in any case, it might work out well that thousands of others are taking the roads to the coast at the same time. It will be that much easier to mix in with the crowd and go unnoticed."

"I wouldn't count on that," Juan said gravely.

"What do you mean?" Muhammad asked.

"Don't forget who I am, or who I was," Juan said, carefully fingering the material of one of the white cloths that covered the table where they had been about to celebrate the Sabbath. "Word of this exodus will spread rapidly throughout the country, and every brigand in this part of Europe will be swarming the roads in search of easy booty. Everyone knows that Jews have all the money in the world and that they will all be carrying tons of gold and jewels into exile with them, and the country is teeming with men just released from the armies, men who kept their weapons and know how to use them. They will also know that no local authorities, not the *Santa Hermandad* or anyone else, will raise a finger to protect them. Indeed, I would be very surprised if the men of the *Hermandad* were not leading the charge in attacking the refugees. They are not noted for their love of the Jews, but they are noted for their love of money. To make matters worse, it won't do us any good to disguise ourselves as anything other than Jews as everyone will assume that the escaping Jews would do just that, so anyone traveling on the roads will be assumed to be Jews unless they can *prove* otherwise," and he casually hitched up his belt, casting a knowing glance at Raquel, who lowered her eyes. "The road to the coast is likely to prove a very long and a very hard one for all of us."

"But, surely," Raquel objected after a moment, "if we get a large enough group of travelers together, we can defend ourselves on the road."

"You forget," Juan cautioned her, wagging his finger, "we're subject people now, not Christians. Jews aren't allowed to carry swords or crossbows, and neither are Moslems since the surrender. I'd be willing to bet that there will be 'official' patrols out checking the identities of any armed parties, other than brigands that is. If they turn out to be Jews, the *Hermandad* or whoever is conducting the searches, will simply confiscate their weapons and then pass word along to the nearest bandits about the easy prey, in exchange for a cut of the profits."

Muhammad stroked his beard thoughtfully. "Well, I don't suppose that it will be particularly easy, but we have no choice. In that case, we might as well try to move sooner rather than later. It will still take time for word to spread throughout the country and for the wolves to gather. The closer we get to the deadline, the more Jews will be on the move who tried to take every minute to sell off their property, so they'll be the richest prizes of all. If we move quickly, we might still miss the worst of it."

"That, at least, makes some sense," Juan allowed. "After all, we don't have much in the way of property to dispose of."

"And it won't be worth more than a few coppers anyway, once all the Jews start selling things off," Muhammad added.

"What the edict prohibits is only the exportation of gold or silver," Ysaque went on. "So most Jews will be trading their property and their cash for commodities like woolens or wine, anything that they can sell abroad. Unfortunately, that will make for some bulky caravans, all the more vulnerable to attack if the authorities aren't going to do anything to protect them. But there are those who will have special treatment," he added with a crooked smile.

"What kind of special treatment?" Raquel asked.

"Well, I suspect that most Jews, this time, will simply convert. I know that Abraham Senior, one of Isabel's advisors, has already done this, but Isaac Abravanel has been given special dispensation to take his wealth with him, and it is considerable wealth at that, and, of course, myself."

"You?" they all asked at once.

"I was not made aware of it at the time, but apparently our former king, Muhammad XII included a special little paragraph in his surrender treaty with Fernando that, anticipating some kind of action to be taken against the Jews, I would always have be able to take my gold and other valuables with me, in gratitude for my years of humble service to his court. I only wish that I had known, so that I could have thanked the king properly. The only problem is that I have so little that the concession is hardly of consequence."

"At least we can all go together and you can carry what gold we have for us," Raquel said, brightening considerably.

"That's assuming that any ruffians we run into on the road care a fig about a diplomatic agreement with Boabdil," Juan added grimly.

"That is quite true," Muhammad agreed. "That fact will be of use to us in dealing with officials at the port when we actually get to board a ship, but not before then. It will also not be of any use to us to attempt to disguise ourselves as anything other than a band of escaping Jews. As Jews you will only have to worry about robbers. As Christians you are wanted by far more dangerous characters who have the whole power of the state behind them."

"So, what shall we do now?" Raquel finally asked.

"I believe that we should immediately start gathering and preparing food and other supplies for the trip. I have two good horses, but we'll need to buy others, and the prices for them will only go up once the exodus starts.

Since I'm technically the only non-Jew among us," Muhammad cocked his head at Juan who responded with a silly smile and a shrug, "I'll probably get better prices on things that Ysaque would, and I'll also have to see about buying a stock of goods with our savings, perhaps some fine silk cloth, something that's worth good money but won't be too bulky to transport."

"Yes," Juan agreed. "It may mean an extra pack horse, but if we do get stopped and don't have some goods for the thieves to take, they'll cut us open looking for gold and jewels."

"And we'll have to start looking for buyers for this house, Ysaque," Muhammad went on, "and for mine as well."

"Your house?" Raquel gasped, her hand going to her throat. "But how can you sell it? Your, well, your memories are all there."

Muhammad smiled calmly and patted her arm. "I'm taking my life with me, and my memories," he tapped his forehead with a finger. "I'll never be coming back here. It's sad, but there it is, and there's nothing we can do. We'll need every *maravedi* we can raise to help us start over somewhere else."

"And where is it that we're supposed to be going?" Juan finally asked.

"An excellent question," Ysaque said. "I'll admit that I have already given the matter considerable thought. While I did not know of the actual plans for the expulsion of the Jews, any Jew who has a sense of history must live with his bag packed and never leaves his cloak far out of reach. It has occurred to me that perhaps the only place that this might not be true, the only place where we all could live in peace together, Jews, Christians, Moslems, all of us," he took the group in with his arms outstretched, "is the Holy Land itself."

Juan frowned, but Muhammad pursed his lips, wagging his head from side to side. "You have a point there. The place has certainly seen its troubles over the centuries, but now it does seem to be the one spot where God has perhaps drawn a ring around hallowed ground and said, 'No more fighting, not here, not ever.'"

"One place is as good as another as far as I'm concerned," Juan grunted, "as long as it's beyond the reach of the Inquisition and the Spanish crown."

Raquel nodded, tears glistening at the corners of her eyes. "It would be nice to be able to walk those ancient streets and think back on the days of the prophets, of all our faiths. Let's go!"

"Right!" Muhammad shouted, clapping his hands together loudly, and Marisol came running in from the kitchen with telltale crumbs hanging from the corner of her mouth as she tried to clean her hands on her skirt and forcibly swallow a large piece of the biscuit she had been sneaking. "Let's get to work," Muhammad added and rushed toward the door.

"Oh," Juan called after him. "If I can't take my sword, at least not where anyone can see it, I wonder if you could keep an eye out for a staff like yours. It might come in handy." Muhammad nodded and was gone.

It took several days of frenzied work to make preparations for the exodus. Both Ysaque and Muhammad were able to sell their respective homes quickly and at reasonable prices as the market had not yet become flooded since most prosperous Jewish property owners had not exhausted their efforts to lobby for special treatment in their cases and accepted the inevitability of exile. Muhammad was able to use the money to lay in a stock of fine silk cloth and exquisite damascene work, black enameled plates and cups inlaid with gold that would bring a good price abroad and involve relatively little bulk, while

Juan spent his time carefully examining the horses and mules purchased for the trip to the coast by Yusef.

In less than a week from the original notice of the royal decree of expulsion then, they stood ready in the courtyard of Muhammad's home. Juan, Muhammad, Ysaque, Raquel, Maria, and Marisol all mounted on sturdy but unostentatious horses, with a train of half a dozen pack mules beside them piled with their clothing, food, cooking utensils and trade goods, and with big, drooling Asco standing by Juan's side, smiling expectantly. The horses and mules pawed at the paving stones or nibbled at the grass on Muhammad's small patch of "lawn" around his fountain, small clouds of steam forming at their nostrils as they huffed and puffed impatiently, and all of the riders gripped their reins tightly, staring only at the tall double doors that lead out onto the narrow street. Maria was seated in a special double saddle that allowed Marisol to ride in front of her, and she hugged the child fiercely, as if to reassure the child, although her own wide eyes and quivering lips told of her own anxiety. Muhammad and Raquel had offered her a generous pension if she had decided to stay, but she had insisted that she was not about to allow *her* babies, taking both Raquel and Miriam by the hands, to wander off to parts unknown without her protection, no matter what the circumstances, and if the world thought that she was a Jew, well, wasn't the Lord himself a Jew, at least before he became a Christian?

Finally, the clatter of hooves could be heard just outside the gate, which was pushed open a crack, enough to allow Yusef to stick his head in.

"The city gates are opening just now, and there is already considerable traffic heading out of the city," Yusef announced.

Juan nodded to the servants who pulled both halves of the gate open, and the little column rode out now, Juan in the lead, with Yusef just behind him. Muhammad waited until all the others had filed out, then paused to take one last long look around his little corner of the world. He plucked a blossom from the bougainvillea in one corner, and slipped it inside his tunic, next to his heart. A gust of wind stirred the hem of a curtain that waved briefly in an open doorway on the second floor, and Muhammad blew a kiss in that direction, turned his horse's head, and rode slowly out into the street. Raquel was waiting for him just outside the gate and handed him a handkerchief from her sleeve with which to dry his eyes.

Despite the early hour, the streets were already crowded with people heading toward the marketplace, and many of them eyed the riders suspiciously. Although most of the population of Granada was still Moorish, hundreds of Christian Spaniards had moved into the kingdom, either as soldiers or hangers on with the army, or as settlers to work the new lands that had been granted to Fernando's favorite nobles at court. The Moors looked upon the riders, all of whom except Muhammad and Yusef were identified by their clothing as Jews, with pity, but the faces of the Christians were twisted in expressions of hatred and contempt, and there were frequent grumbles from the crowd about the "rich pigs" stealing off with their hoards of gold. Had it not been for Juan's size, and the stout staffs that he, Muhammad, and Yusef carried loosely across their saddlebows, it is likely that some of the less cowardly might have tried to lay hands on them right there in the city.

The group had made its way to within sight of the gate in the eastern wall of the city when a horseman suddenly pulled in front of them from a small alleyway. Muhammad raised his staff and spurred his horse forward, but Juan waved him to a stop.

"Ho, Gamal," Juan said cautiously. "I would have thought you'd have long since left this place."

"And where would I go, my captain?" the tall Arab asked. "I am a warrior by trade, and I have long since been used to fighting at your side. I am far too old to try to break in a new captain now, and I assumed that, if you had not already slipped away, as rumors said that you had, I might yet find you and join you on your travels. There is no doubt in my mind that, wherever it is that you go, there will be violence enough for any appetite." Gamal smiled broadly, but Juan grimaced and hung his head for a moment.

"I'm sure that I'll have a sword in my hand again before too long, old friend," Juan replied, "but for the moment we are on a dangerous journey from which there will come no profit at all, and I would not presume to ask you to join us, especially because you have been a good friend."

"I was willing to overlook the fact that you had not bothered to invite me," Gamal went on, "but I was hoping that my company had not become such a burden that you would seek to stop me from following the same road if I had a mind."

Juan laughed loudly and shook his head. "If a mind is what you call it, you are more than welcome." The two men shook hands, and Gamal turned to follow behind his leader.

On the plain just outside the east gate was an open ground that was the traditional forming up place for caravans taking goods and people to other parts of the kingdom. One long column of oxcarts hauling casks of olive oil was already moving off to the northwest under escort of several mailed horsemen, but Juan and Muhammad ignored this one as heading in the wrong direction. They continued to receive angry stares from the Christian merchants and passed them by as well until they came to a train of about a dozen pack mules under the direction of a pair of tall, slender Jews, apparently identical twins. Ysaque kicked his horse to the front of the column and greeted the men in Hebrew.

"Are you heading for the coast, brothers?" Ysaque asked.

"And where else would we be going in these dark days?" one of the merchants countered. He gestured toward a small cart in which several heavily veiled women and a couple of runny-nosed children stood staring. "One last run to Almeria for old times' sake, and then to find us a boat to take us away over the seas."

Juan and Muhammad had moved up on either side of Ysaque and now leaned their heads together.

"Almeria would be a good choice," Juan said.

"I agree," Muhammad joined in. "My sources tell me that most Jews are either heading overland to Portugal to the west or to Valencia in the east, and there have already been many reports of attacks on the roads."

"Exactly," Juan went on. "This way we can move up the valley of the Genil and then down that of the Andarax River to Almeria without either having to cross the highest mountain passes where ambushes would be too easy or to enter Christian territory, as I figure that our greatest risk of attack would come from them."

"I am Ysaque Perdoniel," the old man said in a loud voice to the other Jews, "and my family and friends and I are traveling to the coast as well, for the same reasons as yourselves. We wonder if you might not accept our company on the road, both for the conversation and for mutual protection."

"We are Joshua and Benjamin Israel," the two Jews said, bowing simultaneously from their saddles, "and we have heard of you, sir. We would welcome the conversation, but we have already arranged for our own protection." They both jerked their chins in like manner toward a cluster of mounted lancers in the armor of Fernando's former army lounging on their horses near the lead mules and casting furtive glances about them. "If you want to accompany us, and enjoy the protection of our little host, it would seem only fitting that you share in the expense."

Juan frowned and whispered to his companions. "I don't like the looks of those men. They haven't stowed their gear like soldiers, so they're probably just layabouts who have picked up some cast-off armor and weapons. They'll either be of no use in the fight, or they'll be the ones who will try to rob us themselves. We might be better off going it alone," he added, scanning the field for signs of another convoy of Jews, of which there were none.

But Ysaque had begun to answer the others even before Juan finished speaking. "I can see that it would be very wise to employ guards such as these, and we would certainly have done so ourselves, but what little fortune we had we have sunk into our poor trading goods, and that will be little enough for us to start our lives over in another land."

"You certainly don't expect to share the protection of our guards for free?" Benjamin snorted.

Joshua quickly added, however. "Perhaps we could make a gentleman's agreement for you to give us a small portion of your trade goods. There's no need for cash, since none of us can take gold abroad anyway."

"I'm sorry, my brothers," Ysaque replied. "I congratulate you on your wisdom in choosing these fine looking soldiers," he said nodding at the horsemen who were now passing around a wineskin and laughing uproariously at some joke, "but if contributing to their salary is a condition of our joining you, I'm afraid that we will have to make our own way and trust to the goodness of God to protect us from harm."

The twins were now casting nervous looks in the direction of their own guards and whispering busily between themselves as Ysaque nudged his horse forward toward the road. He bowed to the two Jews as he passed, as did Muhammad and Juan in their turn, but then the twins called out to them.

"Wait!" they both said before Benjamin took over. "This is foolish. From the look of your companions' scars," he nodded at Juan and Gamal, "it might be safe to assume that you know how to defend yourselves, and it might be considered that you are guards in your own right. So, maybe both of our companies would benefit from riding together and presenting that much more of a deterrence to any possible brigands."

Ysaque bobbed his head. "That was my thinking exactly."

"I hope we haven't offended you," Joshua went on. "It just would not have been businesslike for us not at least to have asked for a contribution."

Ysaque waved his hand graciously. "Absolutely. You were within your rights, and now I think we can all proceed with a little less trepidation as we set out on this adventure."

"Not an adventure of our own choosing," Benjamin growled.

"Since when have Jews ever had need of going out of their way to find adventures?" Ysaque laughed, and the two groups both moved down to the road and began heading eastward, the little troop of cavalry spurring on ahead about fifty meters to lead the way, and they all noticed the frowns and harsh whispers that the men gave each other as they sized up the new additions to the caravan.

The valley of the Genil River was flanked on the south by a solid wall of massive gray mountains, now covered almost down to the foothills with a thick mantle of snow and patches of forest. Occasional goat tracks wound their way up the sides of the mountains, but there was no break in the line of hills that promised a viable pass through to the sea to the south.

The more common route from Granada to Almeria would have led the party along the well-traveled road to the northeast to the city of Guadix, thence southeast down the valley of the Andarax the coast. Juan and Muhammad, however, had come to the conclusion, in which the Israel brothers had agreed, that their best bet of avoiding trouble would be to take the narrow trail that led to the southeast up the Genil River Valley, then turned west and hugged the skirts of the mountains to the small town of Lacalahorra at the headwaters of the Andarax. Although this route would shave miles off the total trip, the going would be much rougher, and the convoy would have to make its own shelter most nights. The advantage lay in the fact that this area was very thinly populated, with no influx of Spaniards yet to worry about, and any brigands who might already be gathering to prey upon the escaping Jews would most certainly be concentrated along the most likely avenues of egress. After Lacalahorra, there would be no option but to descend the river valley to the coast, following the main highway, but they might be able to cover this distance in a few days of fast travel.

In any event, the column moved steadily, making at least fifteen miles a day, sometimes as much as twenty, and pulling well off the road each evening, back into the woods where their fires would not be visible at any distance. The mercenaries posted a sentry each night, but he was usually asleep long before dawn, and Juan, Muhammad, Yusef, and Gamal took turns standing their own watch, mostly being concerned with keeping an eye on the soldiers. They were able to purchase simple food at isolated farming villages they encountered along the way, but there were no other travelers besides an occasional shepherd moving his flocks to higher pasture as the spring thaw was coming on.

By noon on the fifth day, they had entered the valley of the Andarax and turned toward the south, with a view of the town of Lacalahorra, perched atop a rocky crag and surrounded by pale gray walls off to their left. Juan had hoped to keep to the western side of the river, precisely because the main road ran along the broad plain on the far side, but Muhammad, who had traveled this route before, pointed out that they must cross the river at the town of Abla because the mountains of the Sierra Nevada crowded closely up to the river on this side with sheer cliffs, leaving no room for their convoy to pass. They would then have to cross the river again farther downstream at the town of Alhama de Almeria as the port itself was on the west side of the river's mouth. Juan grumbled that he didn't like the idea of being caught at either a bridge or a ferry, but he accepted Muhammad's reasoning that there was no other option.

After their first night on the road had passed uneventfully, the Israel brothers and their families lost their initial nervousness and began to look on the journey as a kind of extended weekend outing. The party included both their wives, Benjamin's twelve-year-old son, and Joshua's own twin daughters of about ten besides an elderly female family retainer who took charge of the cooking for their group and became openly hostile when Maria, Yusef, and Raquel offered to help with any of these chores. The two parties tended to keep apart, with one bedding down on one side of the fire, and the other opposite them, with the soldiers usually setting up their own camp a few yards off with the livestock. In the evenings, the Israel family would gather around the fire and tell raucous stories, sing songs, and the two brothers would drink far more wine than Muhammad and Juan thought prudent, given the very real danger they all still faced. The soldiers did not join in either the conversation or the singing, but they also indulged in impressive amounts of wine that Benjamin saw fit to supply them from his stores. Muhammad, Juan, Raquel, and their party, meanwhile, kept largely to themselves and did what they could to try to keep the others from getting too loud and possibly attracting unwanted attention, although their pleas normally only met with scoffing laughter.

With the prohibition on "noble" arms for Jews and Moslems now likely to be enforced strictly, the Israel brothers carried no weapons whatsoever, complaining loudly to Ysaque that it would be foolish of them to have spent good money to hire professional soldiers for protection and then assume that they could do the job themselves and, besides, that it would be an insult to the soldiers if they were to demonstrate a marked lack of confidence in them by presuming to usurp their function. They laughed at Muhammad, Juan, Yusef, and Gamal for insisting on carrying their stout staffs, besides daggers in their belts, which were allowed by the law. Muhammad, of course, had his well-worn staff, and Juan had equipped himself with an especially massive one, almost as thick as a man's wrist and capped at both ends with knobbed iron caps, and he and Muhammad frequently exercised during rest stops by sparring brilliantly, which caused the soldiers to glare at them from a distance and grumble among themselves.

There was no bridge over the Andarax at the town of Abla, a collection of low huts crowded up against the muddy bank of the river. However, the travelers were able to negotiate passage across on a run-down ferry, actually just a flatboat poled across the stream by several small but surprisingly wiry Moors. The passage should have cost no more than a few copper maravedis a head, but, with the now common knowledge that the Jews had been expelled from the country, the ferrymen insisted on a gold florin for each person, including the children, and an additional fee for the pack animals, a price that sent the twins howling with rage at the injustice but which all were ultimately obliged to pay, thus making serious inroads into their already thin purses. Food also became increasingly expensive, and they were soon reduced to subsisting on stale bread, flavored with a little olive oil that Ysaque had included in their supplies, since there was no way of telling what other tolls or bribes they might have to pay on the road to Almeria or what the passage on a ship out of the country might cost in this sellers market.

The road that paralleled the river toward the south was at least a proper road, flat and level, although a little muddy now that the spring thaw was beginning to set in this close to the sea, and easily wide enough for two wagons to pass each other. There was also a good deal more traffic here than they had seen for the past few days, heavy oxcarts laden with imported North African brass work or with piles of fresh fish packed in mountain snow heading north or loads of oranges and carded wool heading south where ships would take them across the Mediterranean or even up into the Atlantic. They did not see any apparent convoys of escaping Jews, however, which suited them well as they had hoped that most of this kind of traffic would have gone north, taking the most aggressive brigands with them, but then they came across the first evidence that some Jews had passed this way, or tried to.

It was near dusk on the second day after crossing the river, and Muhammad and Juan had ridden ahead with Asco to scout out a camp site, angling well off the road toward where the foothills of the Sierra Nevada, which continued on this side of the river, began to rise from the valley floor. In a small copse of trees, they came across the ashes of a large fire and tracks that indicated a caravan had camped here, probably within the past day or two. Juan rode over to the fire while Muhammad went on to check if a nearby gully might have a stream that would provide them with fresh water. It did, but no sooner had Muhammad arrived there and was about to lean down from his saddle to scoop up some water to taste, than a nervous call from Juan sent him cantering quickly back.

"Look at this," Juan said, poking around with his staff among the large pile of black and white ashes. He turned up a long white object that he flicked out onto the ground where Muhammad could see that it was a bone, a human leg bone. Asco stood nearby, the fur on the back of his thick neck bristling as he let out a throaty growl and suspiciously eyed the woods farther up the hillside.

Juan got off his horse and felt around in the ashes. "This fire is from the night before last, but I don't think it was a campfire, too big."
He stalked around the clearing making a large circle, bending low to the ground, while Muhammad scouted the taller grass farther from the fire.

"They had three mules, and about four people on foot, two men, a woman, and a child," Juan read from the tracks. "They came up from the road and tethered the animals over here. Then some riders and men on foot came down from the trees, maybe twenty of them in all." He used the end of his staff to turn over the dirt like a plow. "Yes, here are signs of blood."

"Over here," Muhammad called from the crest of a low hillock about twenty yards from the clearing. Juan led his horse over, scanning the ground all the way.

"Yes," he continued. "They were dragging things this way."

Muhammad had dismounted and was digging at some loose earth with the end of his staff. He struck something and probed around it, then pried up what looked like an arm, but all of the fingers had been chopped off the hand.

Juan nodded gravely. "They were probably asking about the money," he said. "They must have burned one of them in the fire and cut up the rest looking for hidden gold."

"Why would they have gone to so much trouble to hide the bodies?" Muhammad asked. "They can't be worried about the authorities. Why bother to bury them at all? It can't have been their sense of honor either."

"No, it's the vultures. We would have seen vultures and crows circling from a long way off if they'd left a meal out on the ground for them. They couldn't hide all traces of what they'd done, but they didn't want us to be on our guard too soon."

"You mean until it was too late?"

Juan was already vaulting into the saddle of his horse, and Muhammad spurred his own on to a wild gallop as Asco tore along, outdistancing them both. They crested the hillock and could see the leading soldiers of their caravan just now riding into view through some thin trees. The clearing where the old campfire lay was about thirty yards across, shielded from view of the main road by a low rise and bordered by heavier woods and steeply rising hills studded with large boulders to the north and east. The shadows of the trees now stretched all the way across the clearing, and a low overcast of clouds made nightfall appear to be coming all the faster. Muhammad squinted hard and thought he could just make out dark shapes moving quickly through the trees.

Juan let out a shrill whistle and pointed to Gamal, making a broad circling motion over his head with his staff as they approached, and the Arab steered the column into a jumble of large rocks at the edge of the clearing, quickly dismounted and reached up, pulling Maria and the child from their saddle at the same time while calling to the others to close up and get their mounts into a circle, forming a wall of sorts with their bodies in the gaps between the rocks. Muhammad was pleased to note the surprise and concern on the faces of the soldiers. Whatever might be happening was apparently not of their doing, and they might now fight to defend their own lives, even if their commitment to the protection of their charges was still in question.

At the sight of the sudden movement of the caravan, a shrill cry went up from the woods, and a flurry of arrows sang out, most glancing off the boulders or sticking harmlessly in the packs on the mules, although one did find its mark in the neck of the Israel brothers' servant, and the woman let out a gurgle as she slipped from her saddle and lay still in the dust. Gamal thrust his arm into a space between the packs on one mule and drew forth a long, curved bow and a quiver of arrows that he tossed to Yusef before extracting a crossbow for himself. The two of them immediately set about shooting at the approaching shapes, dropping one or two in their tracks as Juan and Muhammad rode straight into the flank of the attacking band. All of the soldiers had dismounted, and most of them had fallen back into the circle of rocks where one of them added his crossbow to the barrage offered up by Gamal and Yusef, but two of them stood their ground in the open, and the clash of steel rang out over the yelling of the attackers.

The two riders swung their staffs like bats, crushing skulls and snapping arms as they raced through the mob that now numbered nearly twenty men, but they did not slow down, not wanting to be cut off and surrounded by men much better armed than they were. They broke through and Raquel pulled one of the skittish mules aside to allow them into the ring of stones along with the two soldiers from the clearing, while the attackers, apparently not expecting any resistance at all, pulled back to the nearest trees to consider their next step.

Juan dug into the load of one of the pack mules and pulled out several swords and a pair of small round shields that had been hidden there. He handed them out to

Muhammad, Yusef, and Gamal, and buckled one on himself.

"I thought these might come in handy, as long as we didn't parade about with them on," he grumbled. He offered a short sword to Benjamin, who took it grimly, but Joshua shook his head when offered the use of Yusef's staff.

"What use will that be?" he asked. "I'm not a fighting man, and I've hired others to do it for me."

Juan looked over at the soldiers, several of whom had gathered together and were talking in low voices. "When men fight for pay, you can't blame them if they recalculate the value of their labor if death looks like a fair prospect," and he tossed the staff to the older man, who caught it and then braced himself in front of where the women and children from his group, along with Maria and Marisol, were huddled together in a narrow cleft in a large boulder. Asco took up a position at his side, directly in front of Marisol, blood already dripping from his muzzle from the men he had bitten out in the field, and when the small child patted his heaving sides, he turned and gave her a quick, sloppy kiss, then returned to face the danger he knew was coming.

Raquel had taken up Juan's staff, but she found it almost too heavy to hold, and she had traded it for Muhammad's, then took a few practice swings and parries that drew a respectful nod from Juan. She then joined Muhammad and Juan as they peered into the gathering darkness under the trees.

"Will they come again?" she asked.

"There's a chance that they'll just pull back and wait for some other prey that can't defend themselves at all," Juan grunted. "On the other hand, if there are enough of them, they might assume that we've got a real treasure here if we've got soldiers to protect it."

"Do we?" Muhammad asked, jerking his chin to the far side of the circle of stones.

Four of the soldiers had mounted their horses and were pushing their way past Joshua, who was trying to bar their path around the mule cart.

"This is what we paid you for, damn you!" Joshua shouted, but one of the soldiers slashed at him with the flat of his sword blade, knocking him to the ground with a deep cut across his forehead.

Juan snatched the crossbow from Gamal's hands and sent an iron quarrel into the back of the soldier's skull, toppling him from his horse, but the others spurred on their animals and disappeared around the outcropping of rocks back up the road toward Abla. Juan quickly reloaded the crossbow and turned on the two remaining soldiers.

"Make up your minds now!" he roared. "Are you with us or not?"

"If we weren't, we'd be gone with them, wouldn't we?" the taller of the two snorted. He was a lanky individual with a shock of dark hair and a beard that, while very short, began just under his eyes and covered his entire face, running down over his neck and disappearing under his collar like a kind of wolf man. His colleague was short and stocky, nearly bald, with part of one of his ears missing from a knife fight at some point in his life. These were the two who had stood and fought against the attacking bandits from the first. "We have nothing to do with those others, and certainly not with that one," he spat at the twitching corpse near his feet. The shorter soldier just nodded and spat. "They just hired us at the same time. That's all. We were in the army from Malaga on, and we don't run."

"Good," Juan said, and he stooped to pull the round leather shield and steel helmet from the fallen man. "I doubt that they'll get far in any case."

Just then the sound of a scream reached them and the sound of tumbling rocks from back up the road in the direction the soldiers had fled. Juan cocked his head and listened for a moment.

"An ambush," he said flatly. "As they should have expected. They would have stood a better chance of running down toward the coast. The bad part is that the bandits now have horses."

"And they didn't before?" Benjamin asked as he daubed at his brother's wound with a damp cloth.

"I don't think so. The only ones we've seen have been on foot, and I don't think they've got more than a couple of bows either, which is good news. At least this bastard that I dropped here was the one with the crossbow, so they didn't get that," he added, handing the weapon from the soldier's saddle to Gamal. "Let's just hope that our deserters managed to take one or two of the enemy with them, although I doubt that from the sound of it."

Muhammad turned to scan the field before them. Several dark shapes lay still on the grass, but more could be seen moving stealthily between the trees and working their way forward between the rocks and bushes toward the caravan.

"I think they're coming," he whispered to Juan.

"Let them come," Juan replied. "Can you handle this?" he asked Raquel, handing her his crossbow. She nodded, placed the stirrup under her foot and hauled the bowstring back to the cocked position with its lever before loading another arrow. "Good. I want you bowmen to stay here and let them cross the open ground, but as soon as the leaders get to the ring of rocks, start picking off those behind, but stay behind cover yourselves, he added, looking directly at Raquel. Their own men will block their shots against us. You," he pointed to Muhammad, the soldiers, and Benjamin, "follow me and we'll fight them in the open just in front of the rocks. If you get hurt, pull back inside, and if they run, don't chase them, but fall back in here as well, or their archers will have a clear shot at you. Understood?"

They all nodded, and a shrill whistle came out of the forest followed immediately by a series of shouts and battle cries. There were about two dozen of them, dressed in an ragged clothing, random bits of armor, and armed with an odd assortment of weapons, mostly hunting spears and short swords, although a few carried only pitchforks or even wooden clubs. They raced forward without any plan, even bumping into each other as each man sought to pick out the easiest looking target among the defenders.

Juan smiled grimly and spaced his men out to give each room enough to use his weapons. Muhammad was armed with a sword in one hand and a dagger in the other, while the two soldiers both had shields and short thrusting spears, and they and Juan all wore chain mail shirts under their tunics. Benjamin had joined them, also armed with a short sword, and his nervousness at handling the weapon had now been replaced by a dark look of anger, and Muhammad saw him casting worried glances over his shoulder at where his wife and children stood, clustered around his wounded brother.

But Juan was in his element, and as the first attacker approached him, he rushed forward himself, dodging a poorly aimed blow and slashing the man across the belly with a swipe of his sword, bringing it up with the same stroke to crash into the skull of the man behind him, and both men collapsed to the ground spouting blood. Then, with a roar like a wounded bear, he carved his way through the ranks of the bandits, his sword becoming a flashing blur in the blue light of dusk. Muhammad moved up on his right, hooking one man's pitchfork with the blade of his dagger and lopping off both his arms with a downward chop with his sword, leaving the man staring stupidly at his bleeding stumps as his blood gushed out of them. The two soldiers were fighting back to back, like a pair of street dogs, and Benjamin was blocking the gap between the rocks with his body, fending off two attackers, grasping one by the throat with his meaty left hand while he dueled with the other with his sword.

Now arrows began to sing from behind the rocks, and several thudded home in the bodies of attackers in the rear ranks, causing them to cry out in panic. This distracted those in the front, and Muhammad and both soldiers were able to drop one man each as they turned imprudently to see what was happening. A shout went up from the woods, and the attackers began to pull back, slowly at first, but when Juan cut down two more, the remainder turned and ran.

"Back to the rocks!" Juan bellowed, and all turned to run, but now arrows began to fly out from the shadows of the trees, and the shorter soldier was caught in the small of the back as he clambered over the boulders. His friend grabbed him by the arm, but two more arrows hit home in his shoulder and neck, his hand went limp, and he slid to the ground while other shafts clattered against the rocks.

"Where's my Benjamin?" his wife shrieked as Muhammad ducked behind a boulder, panting and fell into Raquel's arms.

They found him sprawled across the gap in the rocks, an arrow protruding from his throat, and his thick fingers entangled in the hair of a dead bandit. His wife keened bitterly and tried to run to him, but more arrows caromed off the rocks nearby, and Yusef pulled her back.

"We can't stay here," Juan grunted, wiping the blood from his sword with a rag. "With full dark they'll be able to creep up close and come at us from all sides, rocks or no, and there are just too many of them."

"But we must have killed a dozen," the soldier protested. "Surely they can't be that hungry!"

"Now they're just angry," Juan argued. "God only knows how many brothers or sons we gutted out there, and

I could see still more moving around in the woods, working up the courage to come in. No, our best chance is to get mounted. We have enough horses to carry everyone who's left, if we leave the cart, and that might attract the attention of some of them. We'll keep the pack mules with us, since they won't slow us down, and might give the impression of greater numbers. If we get off quickly, and head straight back to the river, I don't think they've got the wind to keep up with us for long."

"No!" Benjamin's widow screamed as she clutched her two young daughters to her breast. "We can't leave him."

Joshua crawled over to her, one side of his face caked with blood. "He gave his life for you, Esther. We must take it as his last wish that you and the children live. I will take care of you, please."

She jerked away from him, but no longer protested, just sobbing quietly into the hair of her girls.

Yusef and Gamal quickly began to gather the horses and pack mules. The party was down to fifteen now. Juan, Muhammad, Raquel, Yusef, Gamal, Ysaque, Maria, and the baby, the one remaining soldier, Joshua, the two wives, and three children between them, with each of the children mounted double with one of the women, and half a dozen pack mules. They all mounted, staying bent over in the saddle below the line of the rocks, and Muhammad led the way toward the gap with Juan bringing up the rear with Gamal and the soldier. They paused and listened. Above the pawing and snorting of their mounts and the whimpering of the children, they could hear groans coming from the field of battle from the wounded, and an occasional unintelligible shout from the woods along with the rustling of feet, many feet.

"Now!" Muhammad whispered, swatting his horse's rump with the flat of his sword, and they all spurred on into the darkness. The fastest they could travel was a canter, as there was no road yet, and the women and children were already squealing with each new bump. A cry went up from behind them, followed by others, then a horn sounded.

"Faster!" Juan shouted from the rear of the little column, and arrows began to sing past them, fired blindly into the dark. They picked their way down a steep slope and soon found themselves on flat ground, the river glinting in the moonlight half a mile ahead. Muhammad turned in his saddle, and he could now hear the occasional ring of steel on steel and the sound of many running feet all around them. A dark shape loomed up out of the shadows to his right, and he slashed it down with his sword. Unseen hands reached up to grab his bridle, but he stabbed in their direction, and a man screamed and his horse was free again.

"Yusef," he called. "Lead them to the river!"

Yusef waved to him, and Muhammad could see that he was leading another horse by the reins. Someone was hurt, and a cold feeling suddenly went through his heart, but Raquel rode past him swinging a hunting spear. He wheeled his horse and charged back the way they had come.

The moon was up now, and Muhammad could make out the Juan's tall figure, sitting atop his horse as he hacked and thrust all about him. Gamal was at his side, and a riderless horse was there, with several dark shapes gathered around the fallen man, jabbing at him with their spears. Muhammad spurred through the group, cleaving the skull of one as he passed, then turned to join Juan as the attackers backed away.

"Get out of here!" Juan shouted. "There are more of them coming!"

"Then let's go!" Muhammad replied.

"No," Juan argued. This is the only open place for nearly a mile for them to get down to the river with horses, and I can hear them coming. Take the women and get away. We'll hold them here. If you ride hard all night and tomorrow, you'll be in Almeria."

Muhammad paused, and Juan screamed at him. "For the love of God, take her and go!" and Muhammad could see in the pale light that Juan's face was streaked with tears. Juan reached down and pulled his thick staff from under his bedroll, tossing it to Muhammad.

"Take this, you may need it," he said.

The staff was extremely heavy, far too unwieldy for Muhammad, who had his own staff, but he took the gift and saluted Juan.

A horn rang out, and Muhammad could now hear the sound of hoofbeats approaching. He turned to Gamal who saluted him in the Arab fashion.

"Go with God, my brother. We will meet in paradise."

"If God wills," Muhammad answered.

"Truly, God is great."

Muhammad turned back to Juan, speechless.

"Tell her I'm sorry," was the last thing the tall Spaniard said as Muhammad raced after the little caravan. He heard Asco bark once in farewell as he rode away.

Muhammad caught up to them on the river road and hurried them along. He counted heads and saw that it had been the soldier who had fallen, but he also saw that Marisol was riding alone, with Yusef leading her horse. Raquel rode by her side, sobbing quietly.

"She must have been hit by an arrow," Raquel gasped, "but she tied Marisol to the saddle before she slid off." Muhammad reached over and stroked her cheek with his rough finger. "Where are the others?" she asked, turning to look over her shoulder.

"They won't be coming," Muhammad whispered, and Raquel looked into his face with an expression of deep sadness. "He said that he was sorry."

Raquel nodded. "He'll be at peace now, at last."

"Where's Maria?" Marisol was asking Yusef insistently, "and Don Juan?" She had never called him father, although Raquel had never told her anything and had assumed that it was just because Juan had been around so little and paid so little attention to the child, until these final months, that Marisol had simply called him what the other adults did.

"They're busy now," Yusef told her. "You must be quiet and pay attention to your horse."

"I like horses," Marisol informed him, patting the neck of her animal, and rode on in silence.
Muhammad stayed at the rear of the column, pausing frequently to listen and watch for pursuers, but none came. No, he thought, he would not have let anyone get past him.

The port of Almeria was filled with sailing ships and galleys of all sizes and descriptions, and the busy marketplace by the wharves was so crowded that one would never have imagined that a war had ever occurred in the land. The sunlight sparkled off the blue water in the harbor and made the brightly colored sails glow. Marisol clapped her little hands in delight as she instructed Yusef very seriously on which ships she had chosen to ride in. Raquel could not help but smile herself, despite the weight upon her heart. The night ride had been terrifying, but there had been no more trouble then, or the next day, and now they were almost at their journey's end, at least the most dangerous part of it.

The docks were crowded with people, more people than merchandise, and Raquel could tell that most of them were Jews, all haggling noisily with ships' captains over the fare to Lisbon, or Naples, or Alexandria. Joshua had taken his family as soon as they had reached the port and was looking for a ship bound for Genoa, where he said that he had relatives, and Raquel now waited with Yusef and Marisol seated on their bundles of trade goods, tucked into a corner of the market, out of the flow of traffic, while Muhammad and Ysaque searched for a boat of their own. They had already sold their horses and pack mules, although for virtually nothing as transport animals, wagons, and carts were being dumped on the local market in large numbers by the escaping Jews, and Raquel could tell from the wailing and loud bargaining that was taking place all around the docks that space aboard departing ships was going at a premium as well.

She sat there, turning Juan's staff over and over in her hands, feeling its great weight and marveling at how even a man as strong as Juan could have hoped to handle it easily in battle. They had managed to convince a troop of the *Santa Hermandad* that they had encountered on the road during the night of their escape to ride back up to the ambush site, but these had now sent word to Almeria that they had found only dead bodies there. From their description, they had found Maria along the road and Juan and Gamal side by side in the pass, with the body of a huge dog next to them, surrounded by the bodies of over a dozen bandits, with numerous blood trails leading off into the mountains. Raquel let her tears fall for the man she had hated so desperately for years but who had redeemed himself, at least to some degree, in the end.

She then noticed that Juan had carved a message into the wood of the staff itself, reading: "For a new start." She had no idea what this meant until she happened to examine one of the iron end caps of the staff and realized that it had not merely been hammered on but that there was threading, that it had been screwed on. She grasped the cap and twisted with all her might, but it would not budge. She was busy whacking the cap against the corner of a stone building to loosen it when Muhammad and Ysaque returned, their faces dark with worry.

"We don't have enough for the passage," Muhammad groaned as he sat heavily on one of the bundles of cloth. "Even if we were to sell all our goods here, and we wouldn't get much for them in this market, it still won't meet the fees these bloodsuckers are charging."

"And the price goes up with every day that passes with the deadline getting closer," Ysaque added. "I just don't know what to do," the old man said, shaking his gray head.

"We could try to work our way up the coast to Portugal," Muhammad offered. "It's not too far, and they say that the King of Portugal is welcoming Jews, at least for the moment."

"And what would our chances be of surviving that trip?" Ysaque asked. "We barely made it this far, and we had the advantage of starting earlier than most."

"You could sell me, master," Yusef said flatly, and Marisol grabbed at his hand possessively.

"No!" she screamed, but Muhammad was already shaking his head.

"I couldn't do that, my friend," Muhammad said, placing a hand on Yusef's shoulder. "Even if it would make the difference, which it wouldn't. I did consider freeing you and allowing you to work your own passage, which would cut the cost a little, but none of the captains would go for that either. Every Jew that's able to walk has already spoken for every available seaman's berth on every available ship, and it's a buyer's market there too."

During this conversation, Raquel had been paying only scant attention, being much more interested in her struggles to undo the cap on Juan's staff. The cap finally came off in her hand, and she gasped.

"About how much gold would we need?" she asked casually.

"About twice as much as we could possibly raise," Ysaque replied sadly.

"Would six feet be enough?" she asked, and she tipped the end of the open staff into Muhammad's cupped hands and a stream of small gold pellets poured out filling them completely before Raquel lifted the end to stop the flow.

"For a new start, he said," Raquel announced giddily. "He had this staff hollowed out and filled it with gold, probably every *maravedi* he had gotten from the sale of his property and his payment from Boabdil for his services."

"No wonder the damn thing was so heavy!" Muhammad laughed, and he pulled out his own leather purse, nearly empty now, and began filling it with gold.

Muhammad stood at the stern of the galley as the oarsmen pulled toward the open sea. The sun was dipping toward the horizon behind the blinding white walls of Almeria, and stiff breeze was kicking up whitecaps on the blue water. Raquel could see that his dark cheeks were streaked with tears.

"Seven hundred years is a long time," he said finally as she leaned her head on his shoulder and followed his gaze back to the land. "There will never be another land so beautiful, so cultured, so rich as my beloved al-Andalus."

"In a way, we're just going home," she whispered, "both of us."

"To a home we never knew," he sighed. "And it won't be the same. We are Spaniards, both of us, just as Juan was. We came from different cultures, different peoples, but we were all Spaniards, and I think that those that remain will find their land the poorer for keeping it all for themselves. But I will miss it dearly. I will miss the scent of orange blossoms, the cool dark among the columns of the mosque, the babble of languages in the *souq*, in my *souq*."

"But we will be free where we are going," she insisted. "No more hiding, no more pretending, and no more bloodshed."

"That's true enough," Muhammad nodded. "At least in the Holy Land we can all live together as God intended, Jews, Moslems, Christians, with nothing to argue about except who reveres the land more. That, at least, will be a relief."

He bent down and kissed her on the temple, then, hand in hand, they turned to return to their cabin.

GRANADA

Selected
Bibliography

Amador Sanchez, Luis. *Isabel la Católica.* Mexico: Ediciones Coli, 1946.

Arié, Racel. *España Musulmana (Siglos VIII-XV).* Barcelona: Editorial Labor, 1984.

Fletcher, Richard. *Moorish Spain.* New York: Henry Holt and Company, 1992.

Irving, Washington. *Alhambra.* Chicago: Belford-Clarke Co.

Le Flem, Jean-Paul. *La Frustración de un Imperio (1476-1714).* Barcelona: Editorial Labor, 1984.

Netanyahu, B., *The Origins of the Inquisition in Fifteenth Century Spain.* New York: Random House, 1995.

Nicolle, David. *Granada 1492: The Twiglight of Moorish Spain.* London: Osprey, 1998.

O'Callaghan, Joseph. *A History of Medieval Spain.* Ithaca, NY: Cornell University Press, 1975.

Plaidy, Jean. *The Spanish Inquisition.* New York: Barnes & Noble, 1959.

Prescott, William H., *The Art of War in Spain: The Conquest of Granada 1481-1492.* London: Greenhill, 1995.

Reston, James, Jr., *Dogs of God: Columbus, the Inquisition and the Defeat of the Moors.* New York: Faber and Faber, 2005.

Valdeón, Julio. *Feudalismo y Consolidación de los Pueblos Hispánicos (Siglos XI-XV).* Barcelona: Editorial Labor, 1984.

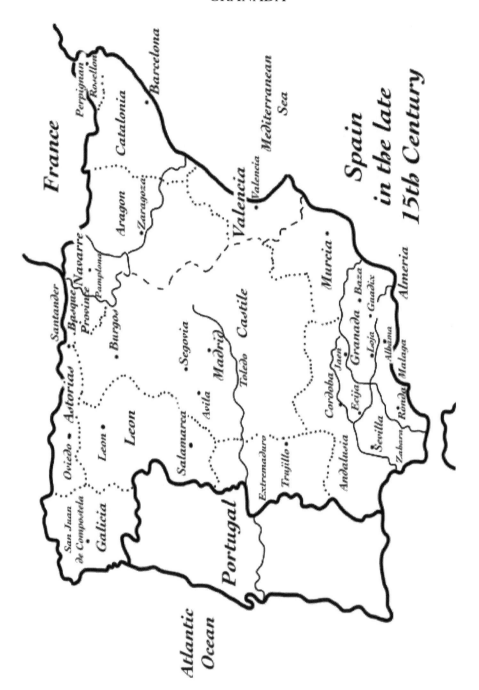

Made in the USA
San Bernardino, CA
06 September 2016